"Her best to date, an enjoyable read, and a portent of even better things to come." —*The Grand Rapids Press*

"A complex cerebral puzzle that will keep readers on the edge until all the answers are revealed."
—*The Midwest Book Review*

"To say that Tami Hoag is the absolute best at what she does is a bit easy since she is really the only person who does what she does. . . . It is testament to Hoag's skill that she is able to go beyond being skillful and find the battered hearts in her characters, and capture their beating on the page. . . . A superb read." —*Detroit News & Free Press*

DUST TO DUST

"Compelling and expertly told. Plot lines smolder and ignite as the suspense builds. The result leaves . . . the reader scorched." —*USA Today*

"[This] wintry tale of crime and punishment packs a powerful thrill. Bottom line: Good cops + bad cops = killer suspense."
—*People* (Page-turner of the week, starred review)

"*Dust to Dust* breathes new life into the old good cop vs. bad cop genre. . . . A roller-coaster ride of a thriller that will leave fans awaiting the next installment." —*New York Post*

"Sharp dialogue and an unusual plot make this a highly engaging outing for Hoag." —*Chicago Tribune*

A THIN DARK LINE

"*A Thin Dark Line* is chilling, it's atmospheric, it's even romantic; but the novel's best achievement is its making readers constantly interrogate their ideas about justice and revenge, their own presumptions of guilt and innocence."
—*US* magazine

"This mystery defies you to put it down, and when you're done you're damn glad you didn't."
—*Detroit News & Free Press*

"Hoag deftly demonstrates that the search for truth is rarely straightforward. Important clues are cunningly buried, and the book's tension is as sustained as it is palpable."
—*Chicago Tribune*

"With a flair for dialect and regional atmosphere, Hoag captures the essence of the Cajun family and working relationships while injecting suspense and heart-pounding terror into a violent tangle of justice, innocence, treachery, and public opinion. A thoroughly engrossing read."
—*Booklist*

"Hoag has evolved into a fine thriller writer. [She] displays a firm grasp on locale [and] there's plenty of suspense in waiting to see how it will all resolve. Psychopathic villains are common enough, but Hoag has managed to endow hers with a scarred entourage that provides a tragic note."
—*Publishers Weekly*

"Hoag is always a good gritty read." —*Kirkus Reviews*

"Hoag writes big, full stories with complex characters and situations. She doesn't shrink from the raw side of crime and the dark side of human nature." —*The Cincinnati Post*

BANTAM TITLES
BY TAMI HOAG

GUILTY
AS SIN

A NOVEL

TAMI
HOAG

BANTAM
NEW YORK

2020 Bantam Books Mass Market Edition

Copyright © 1996 by Tami Hoag

All rights reserved.

Published in the United States by Bantam Books,
an imprint of Random House, a division of
Penguin Random House LLC, New York.

BANTAM BOOKS and the HOUSE colophon are registered trademarks of
Penguin Random House LLC.

Originally published in hardcover in the United States
by Bantam Books, an imprint of Random House, a division of
Penguin Random House LLC, in 1996.

ISBN 978-0-593-15901-9
Ebook ISBN 978-0-553-89845-3

Cover image: Lee Avison/Arcangel Images

Printed in the United States of America

randomhousebooks.com

2 4 6 8 9 7 5 3 1

Bantam Books mass market edition: May 2020

To the Divas,
for support in times of crisis and madness

ACKNOWLEDGMENTS

My heartfelt thanks first and foremost to legal assistant, sister writer, and friend Nancy Koester for acting as my guide into the court system. Your generosity in sharing your expertise and answering my myriad questions was greatly appreciated. Thanks also to attorney Charles Lee, assistant county attorney Steve Betcher, Judge Robert King, and everyone in the Goodhue County Attorney's office for allowing me a glimpse into your world and for answering my questions. My hand to God, the people in the Park County courthouse are pure figments of my imagination, but feel free to fantasize.

Justice has but one form, evil has many.
Moses Ben Jacob Meir Ibn Ezra

GUILTY AS SIN

PROLOGUE

"Time to die, birthday bitch."

Birthday. Thirty-six. The birthday Ellen had been dreading. Suddenly thirty-six seemed far too young.

She flung herself up the stairs, stumbling as one heel caught an edge. She grabbed for the handrail, her fingers scraping the rough plaster of the wall, breaking a nail, skinning her knuckles.

The stairwell was barely lit, drawing in the ragged edges of illumination that fell from the lights in the halls above and below. Security lights. They offered nothing in the way of security. In the back of her mind she heard a low, smoky voice, *"Your boss needs to have a word with someone about security. This is a highly volatile case. Anything might happen."*

She reached the third floor and turned down the hall, heading east. If she could make it down the east stairs—If she could make it to the walkway between the buildings—He wouldn't dare try to take her in the walkway with the sheriff's department mere feet away.

"We've got you now, bitch!"

There were telephones in the offices she ran past. The offices were locked. Her self-appointed assassin was jogging behind her, laughing. The sound went through her like a spear, like the sure knowledge that he would kill her.

Pursuit may not have been his plan, but it had become a part of the game.

The game. The insanity of it was as terrifying as the prospect of death. Beat the system. Wreck lives. End lives. Nothing personal. Just a game.

She ran past Judge Grabko's courtroom and ducked around the corner that led back toward the southeast stairwell. Scaffolding filled the stairwell, cutting off her escape route. The scaffolding for the renovators. Christ, she was going to die because of the stupid plaster frieze.

"Checkmate, clever bitch."

The northeast stairs looked a mile away. Midway stood the iron gates that blocked the skyway between the courthouse and the jail. She lunged for the fire alarm on the wall, grabbing the glass tube that would break and summon help.

The tube snapped. Nothing. No sound. No alarm.

"Oh, God, no!" She clawed at the useless panel. The goddamn renovations. New alarms going in. State of the art.

"Come along, Ellen. Be a good bitch and let me kill you."

She grabbed the handle of the door to the fire hose and yanked.

"You have to die, bitch. We have to win the game."

His hand closed on her arm.

Her fingers closed on the handle of the ax.

JOURNAL ENTRY

They think they've beaten us at our own game.
Poor simple minds.
Every chess master knows in the quest for victory
he will concede minor defeats.

They may have won the round, but
the game is far from over.

They think they've beaten us.
We smile and say,
Welcome to the Next Level.

CHAPTER 1

"He said it was a game," she murmured, her voice whisper-soft, and tight with pain.

She lay in a hospital bed, the deep purple bruises on her face a stark contrast to the bleached white of the sheets and the ash white of her skin. Her right eye was nearly swollen shut, the flesh the color of an overripe plum. Bruises circled her throat like a purple satin band where she had been choked. A fine line of stitches mended a split in her lip.

The pain triggered flashes of memory—sudden, violent, blaring. A memory of pain so sharp, so intense, it took on qualities of sound and taste, the smell of fear, the presence of evil.

"Clever girl. You think we're going to kill you? Perhaps."

Her throat being closed by hands she couldn't see. The instinct to survive surging. Fear of death riding the crest of the wave.

"We could kill you." The voice a silky murmur. "You wouldn't be the first. . . ."

The air caught like a pair of fists in her lungs, then slowly seeped out between her teeth.

Assistant County Attorney Ellen North waited for the moment to pass. She sat on a high stool beside the bed, a legal pad and small cassette recorder on the bedside tray to her right. She had met Megan O'Malley only days before. Her impression of the field agent for the Minnesota Bureau of Criminal Apprehension had consisted of a handful of adjectives: tough, gutsy, capable, determined, a small woman with fierce green eyes and a big chip on her shoulder. The first woman to break the male ranks of BCA field agents. Her first day on the job in the Deer Lake regional office had been day one of the Kirkwood kidnapping. Twelve days ago. Twelve days that had taken the previously innocent, quiet, rural college town into the depths of a nightmare.

In her efforts to crack the case, the chip had been effectively knocked off Megan's shoulder and smashed, and Megan along with it. She had come too close to unraveling the puzzle. Beneath the covers, her damaged right knee was elevated. Her right hand was encased in a cast. According to her doctor, the hand was badly smashed, and he despaired of the "poor darling little bones" recovering, even with the meticulous attention of a specialist.

Megan's transfer from Deer Lake Community Hospital to the Hennepin County Medical Center in Minneapolis was scheduled for Tuesday, weather permitting. She would have been transported the night of her ordeal, but Minnesota had been clutched in the grip of a January storm. Two days later Deer Lake was just beginning to dig out from under ten inches of new snow.

"He said it was a game," Megan started again. "Taking Josh. Taking me. Fooling everyone. *We* fooled you all along, he said . . . *We*, always *we* . . ."

"Did you at any time hear another person in the room?"

"No." She tried to swallow and her face tightened against a new wave of pain.

"We've calculated all the moves, all the options, all the possibilities. . . . We can't lose. Do you understand me? You can't defeat us. We're very good at this game. . . . brilliant and invincible."

Eight-year-old Josh Kirkwood had disappeared from outside the Gordie Knutson Memorial Ice Arena after hockey practice on an otherwise normal Wednesday night. No useful physical evidence left behind. The only witness a woman casually glancing out her window half a block away and seeing nothing to cause alarm: a little boy being picked up from hockey practice; no sign of fear or force. The only trace of him left behind had been his duffel bag with a note tucked inside.

a child has vanished
ignorance is not innocence but SIN

A game. And she had been used as a pawn. The idea brought Megan a rush of useless emotions—anger, outrage, a hated sense of vulnerability. The only satisfaction was in the fact that they had spoiled his little coup de grâce and now Garrett Wright was sitting in a cell in the Deer Lake city jail.

Garrett Wright. Professor of psychology at Harris College. The man the media had pulled in as an "expert witness" to attempt to explain the twisted workings of the mind that had perpetrated this crime. The Kirkwoods' neighbor. A respected member of the community. A volunteer counselor of juvenile offenders. A man above reproach.

But though Wright had been apprehended, there was still no sign or word of Josh.

"You were blindfolded?"

"Yes."

"You didn't actually see Garrett Wright."

"I saw his feet. He has this habit of rocking back on his heels. I noticed it the first time I met him. He was doing it that night. I could see his boots when he stood close enough."

"That's not exactly a fingerprint."

Megan scowled at the assistant county attorney, her temper cutting through the haze of drugs and pain. Goddamn lawyers. Garrett Wright had drugged her, terrorized her, abused her, humiliated her. He may well have ended the career that was everything to her. A decade in law enforcement, a degree in criminology, a certificate from the FBI academy—she was a damn good cop, yet Ellen North could sit here, every blond hair in place, and calmly question her as if she were just another civilian as blind as Lady Justice herself.

"It was him, the son of a bitch. He knew where I was going. He knew I was that close to finding him out. He caught me, beat the shit out of me, wrapped me in a sheet of evidence proving he stole Josh—"

"We don't know yet what the bedsheet will prove," Ellen interjected. "We don't know whose blood is on it. The lab has a rush on it, but DNA tests take weeks. The blood could be Josh's or not. We have the blood samples from his parents. If the DNA analysis shows the blood on the sheet could be from a child of Paul Kirkwood and Dr. Hannah Garrison, we've got something we can use. We might just as easily have a red herring. It would make more sense for the kidnapper to try to throw us *off* his trail—"

"It makes *his* kind of sense," Megan argued. "He believes he can get away with anything, but he underestimated us. We got him dead to fucking rights. Whose side are you on?"

"You know what side I'm on, Megan. I want to see Wright punished as much as you—"

"You can't even come close."

She couldn't argue the point. The bitter hate that laced Megan's tone was indisputable. The emotion Wright had forged and hammered within her with every blow was something deeper than Ellen could even imagine. It was a victim's private rage compounded by the humiliation of a proud cop. Ellen knew that her own personal, moral hunger for justice was a pale appetite in comparison.

"I want him convicted," she clarified. "But the case against him has to be airtight. I don't want his attorney to see even a hairline crack. The stronger our case, the better our chances of squeezing the truth out of him. It could mean getting Josh back."

Or finding out the whereabouts of his body.

She left that line unspoken. Everyone involved in the case knew the chances of finding Josh Kirkwood alive. Wright and his accomplice, whoever that accomplice might be, could not afford to let go the one person who could identify them absolutely as the kidnappers.

"If we can present Wright and his attorney with a strong enough case. If we can threaten them with a murder charge and make them believe we can make it stick even though we have no body, then Wright might give us Josh. We can force his hand if we're careful and clever enough."

"We thought you were a clever girl, but you're just another stupid bitch!" A disembodied voice. Never rising above a whisper, but taut and humming with fury.

She trembled. Blind. Powerless. Vulnerable. Waiting. Then the pain struck from one direction, then another, then another.

A cry of pain, of weakness, of fear started in the heart of her, and Megan struggled to choke it off in her throat.

"Are you all right?" Ellen asked with quiet concern. "Should I call for a nurse?"

"No."

"Maybe we should quit for now. I could come back in half an hour—"

"No."

Ellen said nothing, giving her a chance to change her mind, though she didn't expect that to happen. Megan O'Malley hadn't got where she was in the bureau by backing off. The BCA was the top law-enforcement agency in the upper Midwest. One of the best in the country. And Megan was one of the best of the best. A good cop with the tenacity and fire of a pit bull.

Ellen was counting on that fire. She had a meeting with the county attorney in an hour. She needed Megan's statement and time to fit it into the game plan she was formulating in her head.

She wanted her ducks in a row when she sat down across the table from her boss. Rudy Stovich could be unpredictable, but he could also be herded. In her two years in Park County, Ellen had honed her shepherding skills to the point that they had become instinctive, reflexive. She didn't know that she even *wanted* the Wright case, and still she was aligning her strategy.

"Will you be handling the prosecution?" Megan asked, working hard to even out her breathing. A fine sheen of sweet glazed her forehead.

"I'll certainly be a part of it. The county attorney hasn't made his final decision yet."

"Well, hell, why rush? It's only been two days since we made the collar. Initial appearance is what—all of hours away?"

"The bond hearing is tomorrow morning."

"Will he charge it out or wimp out and go for a grand jury?"

"That remains to be seen."

The media loved to make much of grand jury proceedings. As if the word "grand" somehow implied "better" or "more important." A grand jury hearing was a prosecutor's showcase—they got to present their evidence with no interference from the defense, no cross-examination of their witnesses. There was no need to prove anything beyond a reasonable doubt; all they had to show was probable cause that the defendant committed the crime. The grand jury had its uses. In the state of Minnesota only a grand jury could hand down first-degree-murder indictments. But, as yet, they weren't dealing with murder, and the thought of handing the fate of this indictment into the hands of two dozen citizens made Ellen's palms sweat.

The members of a grand jury could do whatever they wanted. They didn't have to listen to the prosecutor's argument. If they didn't want to believe Garrett Wright was capable of evil, he would walk. She could only hope that the ego appeal of doing a solo act in front of a grand jury didn't override Rudy's common sense.

Stovich had survived more than a decade as Park County attorney not so much by his legal wits as by his political wiles. More comfortable with civil law than with criminal law, he handpicked the few felony trials he prosecuted, choosing them for their political value. His courtroom style was dated and clumsy, with all the finesse of a vaudeville player. But Rudy's constituents seldom saw him in a courtroom, and as a glad-handing, ass-kissing backwoods politician he was without peer.

"Is Wright talking?" Megan asked quietly.

"He isn't saying anything we want to hear. He insists his arrest was a mistake."

"Yeah, right. *His* mistake. Who's his lawyer?"

"Dennis Enberg, a local attorney."

"Is he just a lawyer or is he an asshole lawyer?"

"Denny's okay," Ellen said, flicking off the tape recorder. She'd been in the system too long to take affront. The distinction was one she had made herself from time to time. And, having come from a family of attorneys, she was long since immune to lawyer jokes and slurs.

She slid down off the stool and reached for her briefcase. Megan was slipping away from consciousness. Exhaustion and medication were going to end the interview whether she was finished asking questions or not.

"He's your basic ham-and-egger," Ellen continued. "He does the misdemeanor prosecutions for the city of Tatonka, gets pressed into service as a public defender here from time to time, has a decent practice of his own. You know how the system works in these rural counties."

"Yeah. *Mayberry RFD.* So what're you doing here, counselor?"

She shrugged into her heavy wool coat and worked the thick leather buttons into their moorings. "Me? I'm just here to do justice."

"Amen to that."

Ellen had spent her entire twelve-year career in the service of one county or another. Much to the consternation of her parents, who had wanted her to follow their footsteps into the lucrative life of tax law. Hennepin County, which encompassed the city of Minneapolis and its wealthy western suburbs where she had grown up, had swallowed up the first decade of her life after Mitchell Law in St. Paul. She had immersed herself in the hectic pace, eager to put away as many bad guys as she could. Veterans of the overloaded Hennepin County court system had taken in her enthusiasm with the knowing skepticism of the war weary and speculated on her burnout date.

In ten years her tenacity had only toughened, but her enthusiasm had tarnished badly, coated with the verdigris of cynicism. She still remembered clearly the day she had stopped herself in the hall of the Hennepin County court-house, chilled to the bone by the realization that she had become so inured to all of it that she was beginning to grow numb to the sight of victims and corpses and perpe-trators. Not a pleasant epiphany. She hadn't become a prosecutor to foster an immunity to human suffering. She hadn't stayed in the system because she wanted to reach a point where cases were little more than docket numbers and sentencing guidelines. She had become an attorney out of genetic predisposition, environmental condition-ing, and a genuine desire to fight for justice.

The solution seemed to be to get away from the city, go somewhere more sane, where gangs and major crime were an aberration. A place where she could feel she was making a difference and not just trying to stick her thumb in a badly leaking dam.

Deer Lake had fit the bill perfectly. A town of fifteen thousand, it was near enough to Minneapolis to be convenient, and just far enough away for the town to maintain its rural character. Harris College provided an influx of youth and the sophistication of an academic community. A growing segment of white-collar Twin Cities commuters provided a healthy tax base. Crime, while on the increase, was generally petty. Burglaries, minor drug deals, workers from the BuckLand Cheese factory beating each other senseless after too many beers at the American Legion hall. People here were still shockable. And they had been shocked to the core by the abduction of Josh Kirkwood.

Briefcase clutched in one gloved hand, the low heels of her leather boots clicking against the hard polished floor, Ellen walked down the corridor of Deer Lake Community Hospital. Most of the activity in the hundred-bed facility seemed to center on the combination nurses' station / reception desk in the main lobby, where people with appointments were complaining about the long wait and people without appointments tried to appear sicker than they really were in hopes of getting worked in faster.

A clutch of reporters loitering at the periphery of the sick zone perked up at the sight of Ellen and scooted toward her, pencils and pads at the ready. Two women and four men, an assortment of expensive wool topcoats and scruffy ski jackets, spray-starched coifs and greased-back ponytails. A photographer angled a camera at her, and she turned her head as the flash went off.

"Ms. North, do you have any comment on the condition of Agent O'Malley?"

"Ms. North, is there any truth to the rumor Garrett Wright sexually assaulted Agent O'Malley?"

The second question drew a peeved look from Ellen. "I've heard no such rumor," she said crisply, not even breaking stride.

The key to handling the media in full frenzy: keep moving. If you stopped, they would swarm and devour you and you would be regurgitated as a headline or a sound bite with film at ten. Ellen knew better than to allow herself to be trapped. She had learned those lessons the hard way, having been thrown to the hyenas on occasion as the sacrificial junior assistant on a case.

The lack of a juicy answer seemed only to sharpen the reporters' hunger. Two cut around to her left. Two scuttled backward in front of her. The one on her right hopped along sideways, the end of a dirty untied shoelace clacking against the floor with every stride.

"What kind of bail will the county attorney request?"

"Can you give us a rundown of the charges being filed?"

"The county attorney will be giving a press conference at the courthouse later this afternoon," Ellen said. "I suggest you save your questions until then."

She pushed through the hospital's front door, bracing herself automatically for the cold. A pale wash of sunlight filtered weakly down on the pristine snow. On the far side of the parking lot a tractor rumbled along, plowing the stuff into a minor mountain range.

She headed across the lot for her Bonneville, well aware that hers were not the only pair of shoes squeaking over the packed snow. Looking down from the corner of her eye, she saw the loose lace flapping alongside a battered Nike running shoe.

"I meant it," she said, fishing her keys out of her coat pocket. "I don't have anything for you."

" 'No comment' don't feed the bulldog."

She cut him a glance. He had to be fresh out of high school, so wet behind the ears he shouldn't have been allowed to go out in the cold without a snowsuit. His face was finely sculpted. Black hair with a suspicious red cast swung down across his narrow brown eyes. He swept it back impatiently. *Young Keanu Reeves. God spare me.* Not much taller than her own five feet seven inches, he had the build of an alley cat, lean, agile, with the restless energy to match. It seemed to vibrate in the air around him as if someone had plugged him into a high-voltage generator.

"Then I'm afraid your dog will go hungry, Mr.—?"

"Slater. Adam Slater. *Grand Forks Herald.*"

Ellen pulled open the car door and hefted her briefcase across into the passenger's seat. "The Grand Forks paper sent their own reporter all the way down here?"

"I'm ambitious," he proclaimed, bouncing up and down on the balls of his feet as if he had to keep himself ready to bolt and run at a second's notice. Cub reporter trying to race ahead of the ravenous pack.

"Are you old enough to have a job?" Ellen asked, cranky with his enthusiasm.

"You used to be ambitious, too," he said as she climbed behind the wheel of the car.

She looked up at him, suspicious that he might know anything at all about her.

"I have some contacts in Hennepin County."

Contacts. He looked as if his contacts would have been the guys who stole the midterm from the algebra teacher's desk.

"They say you used to be good when you were there." *Way back when.*

"I'm still good, Mr. Slater," Ellen declared, twisting the key in the ignition. "I'm good in any zip code."

"Yes, ma'am," he chirped, saluting her with his reporter's notebook.

"*Ma'am,*" she grumbled as she put the car in gear and

headed out of the lot. Her gaze strayed to the rearview mirror as she broke for traffic on the street. Mr. Ambition from Grand Forks was bouncing his way back to the hospital entrance. "See if you ever have an affair with an older woman, you little twerp. *Used to be good*. I haven't lost it yet."

She wasn't entirely sure whether she meant her skills in the courtroom or her allure as a woman. As the reporter loped out of view, her gaze refocused on her reflection. Her face was more interesting than beautiful. Oval with a graceful forehead. Gray eyes—a little narrow. Nose—a little plain. Mouth—nothing to inspire erotic fantasies, but it was okay. She scrutinized for any sign of age, not liking the depth of the laugh lines that fanned out beside her eyes when she squinted. How long before she had to stop calling them laugh lines and start calling them crow's-feet?

A birthday was looming large on the horizon like a big black cloud, like the *Hindenburg*. Thirty-six. A shudder went down her back. She pretended it was from the cold and goosed the Bonneville's heater a notch. Thirty-six was just a number. A number closer to forty than thirty, but just a number, an arbitrary marking of the passing of time. She had more important things to worry about—like a lost boy and bringing his kidnapper to justice.

CHAPTER 2

The Park County courthouse was a small monument in native limestone with Doric columns and Greek pediments out front. It dated to the late 1800s, when labor was cheap and time of little consequence. The interior boasted soaring ceilings that most likely raised heating bills, and ornate plaster moldings and medallions that undoubtedly required endowments from historical preservationists to maintain. A restoration was under way on the third floor, scaffolding set against the northeast wall like giant Tinkertoys.

The courtrooms on the third floor were the kind of rooms that called to mind Henry Clay and Clarence Darrow. Between the judges' benches, the jury boxes, and the pews for spectators, a sizable forest of oak trees had fallen for the cause. The wooden floors were worn pale in spots from the pacing of generations of lawyers.

He was well familiar with courthouses like this one, though he had never been anywhere near Deer Lake, Minnesota. Nor would he ever care to venture back here once his mission was accomplished. Damned cold place.

It was a safe bet the Park County courthouse was seldom as busy as it was today. The halls were bustling, not with staff, but with reporters and cameramen and newspaper photographers jockeying for position in front of a podium bristling with microphones. He leaned over the second-floor railing and looked down through the dark lenses of a pair of mirrored military-issue sunglasses.

The kidnapping of Josh Kirkwood had garnered national attention. The arrest of Dr. Garrett Wright had only turned up the fever pitch another hundred degrees. All the major networks were represented, their correspondents instantly recognizable. The syndicated tabloid news shows were here in force, as well, their people skirting the periphery like hyenas looking to snatch a juicy tidbit from the big network lions. Forced to scramble for camera angles were the local newspeople. They had been thrown into the big pond and clearly didn't care to swim with the big fish, but there it was. The story was bigger than small-town sensibilities and small-town manners. It was as big as America and as intimate as family.

Good juxtaposition of images. He committed the line to memory.

The scene below was not unlike a movie set waiting for the arrival of the stars. Lights, cameras, grips, technicians, makeup people dabbing the shine off foreheads and noses.

" 'All the world's a stage,' " he mumbled with cynical humor, his voice raspy from too many cigars and too little sleep the night before. The price of schmoozing. You oiled the wheels with good whiskey and smooth talk, easy smiles and expensive cigars—all to be chased the following morning with a handful of aspirin and a gallon of strong coffee.

He turned slowly for a casual glance at the reporters waiting outside the door to the county attorney's offices thirty feet down the hall. No one paid him any mind. He wore no press pass, had not been asked for any ID. He could have been anyone. He could have been a sniper; there were no metal detectors at the doors of the Park County courthouse. Another detail to file away for future reference. The case was the focus of everyone here to the exclusion of all else. Elvis could have been sweeping the floors and no one would have so much as glanced twice.

He counted this tunnel vision as being both potentially useful and a blessing to him personally. He could live without the interference as he got himself in where he wanted to be. Inside. The bird's-eye view. The catbird seat. Into the inner workings of the small-town justice system taking on a big-time case.

The door to the county attorney's offices opened and the reporters started shouting questions, sending up a racket like a pack of baying foxhounds. He straightened from the railing and propped himself up against a marble pillar, careful to remain in its shadow, his hands stuffed into the pockets of the black parka he had bought after getting off the plane in Minneapolis.

A uniformed sheriff's deputy cleared a path, leading the way for the man he recognized as Rudy Stovich. Tall, rawboned, with a face like Mr. Potato Head and kinky wire-gray hair that was slicked down into a marcel look with a quart of something greasy. Stovich had been featured in one of many news clippings about the case, scowling at the camera, piously promising to prosecute the villains to the fullest extent of the law. It would be interesting to hear what he had to say now that it appeared the villain was not some slimy ex-con from the wrong side of town and the lower end of the evolutionary ladder, but a psychology professor from their own exclusive college.

Garrett Wright was the twist that made the story unique, the hook that made it bankable instead of clichéd.

Stovich stepped into the hall, waving off the shouted questions, mugging an expression of exaggerated impatience. A woman fell into step beside him. Cool, composed, blond hair the shade of polished gold, features that were more interesting than striking. Ellen North, rumored to have her ambitious eye on the county attorney's corner office. She walked past the reporters without mak-

ing eye contact, a queen oblivious to the presence of the
unwashed masses. Classy, self-possessed, not rattled by the
attention of the press. Intriguing.

He stayed where he was as the mob passed by and
headed down the steps for the first floor. Show time.

No director could have choreographed the scene more
perfectly. Just as Stovich and his entourage reached the
first floor, the main doors of the courthouse swung open
and State Attorney General William Glendenning and his
cadre made their grand entrance. They came into the
building on a gust of cold air, stamping the snow from
their shoes, their cheeks and noses polished cherry-red
with cold. Stovich and Glendenning shook hands as flashes
went off in blinding starbursts.

Glendenning opened the proceedings. A seasoned politician, he looked good before the lights—solid, conservative, trustworthy. A pair of rimless spectacles gave him a
certain resemblance to Franklin Roosevelt—more em-
phasis on trust and old-fashioned values. He spoke with a
strong, confident voice. Platitudes and promises of justice,
assurances of his trust in the system and his trust in Rudy
Stovich and his staff. He sounded impressive while he actually said very little; a handy trick in an election year.

Stovich followed, stony-faced and serious, his old
photo-gray glasses cockeyed, his suit looking like something he had pulled out of a laundry basket. His necktie
was too short. He told everyone he was deeply troubled
by the events that had rocked his community. He was just
a country lawyer who had never imagined he would have
to deal with a case of this nature—which was why he was
passing the buck to Assistant County Attorney Ellen
North. She had the kind of courtroom experience it
would take. She was young and sharp and relentless in her
pursuit of justice.

"Slick move, Rudy," he mumbled, leaning once again
on the railing. "Slick as snot, you old country fox."

Dumping the case on her was calculated damage control. He painted himself as a man concerned for justice above all else, willing to admit there was someone better suited to achieve that end—and a woman, no less, scoring a point for him with the growing faction of enlightened young professionals in his constituency. At the same time, he distanced himself from the prosecution, deflected the blows of public criticism, and kept his bulbous nose clean. If Ellen North won, Rudy would look like a wise and humble genius. If she lost, it would be entirely her fault.

Whether Stovich had a genuine respect for his assistant or was in fact throwing her to the wolves was another twist with possibilities. One thing was perfectly clear as Ellen North stepped up to the podium: she wasn't afraid of the job or the press.

Her statement was brief and to the point: she intended to prosecute this case aggressively and win justice for the victims. She would do all that was in her power to try to find the answer to the ultimate question in this situation: the whereabouts of Josh Kirkwood. She refused to take questions from the press, deftly maneuvering her boss back into the spotlight. Ever grateful for a press opportunity in an election year, Stovich grabbed the chance, pulling Glendenning into the limelight with him. Photos with the head honcho of the state's justice system always made for nice campaign posters.

Ellen North snagged a deputy for protection and made her break for the stairs. He watched as several reporters broke away from the pack to pursue her. She stopped them with a look and a sharp "No comment," never slowing her step.

"Mmm—mmm, Ms. North," he growled under his breath as she mounted the steps, the hem of her deep-green skirt swirling around her calves. "I do believe I am in lust."

She came down the hall, the low heels of her boots

smacking sharply against the polished floor, all business and no distractions; her mind occupied by things other than the notion that someone might be watching her from the shadows.

He didn't look like the kind of man who could steal a child and plunge a community into a vortex of fear. Ellen had met Garrett Wright at a number of civic functions over the past two years. He had seemed pleasant enough, not the type to draw attention to himself. He would have melted into a crowd if not for the almost pretty quality of his face—a fine, alabaster oval with a slim nose and a prim mouth.

He took his seat with as much dignity as he could, considering the rattling of the hardware the police had used to accessorize the blaze-orange city-jail jumpsuit. "Ms. North," he said with a spare smile. "I would say it's a pleasure to see you again, but considering the circumstances . . ."

He shrugged, lifting his shackled hands by way of further explanation, then settled them gently on the tabletop. Smooth, pale hands with no scrapes, no contusions, no obvious signs of having struck a woman repeatedly. Ellen wondered if he had put his hands before her knowing she would look. She raised her gaze to his. His eyes were a deep, fathomless brown, large, almost drowsy looking behind lashes most women would have killed for.

"This isn't a social call, Dr. Wright," she said crisply. "Pleasure doesn't enter into it."

"Ms. North will be handling the prosecution," Dennis Enberg explained. He turned to Ellen. "I hear Rudy put on a good show at the press conference."

"I'm surprised you weren't there."

The attorney shrugged it off. "Not my style. It was Rudy's circus. No place for a pissing contest."

In her two-year acquaintance with Dennis Enberg, she would have said it was exactly his style to crash the county attorney's party if he thought it would do him good. She had certainly never known him to demur for the sake of manners. It struck Ellen as a tactical error. Had she been Wright's attorney, she would certainly have done her best to steal Rudy's thunder, if only to make the obvious perfunctory statement of her client's innocence.

"Denny, you know Cameron Reed," she said, nodding to the young man sitting to her left at the fake wood-grain table.

The men half rose from their chairs to shake hands—Enberg, thirty-seven and pudgy with brown hair in serious retreat from his forehead, and Cameron Reed, twenty-eight and fit beyond reason, his hair a shock of rich copper that came with a full accompaniment of freckles. Two years out of Mitchell Law, he was sharp and eager, a true anomaly in the Park County office. How he had ended up in Park County was beyond Ellen—though that thought always brought her up short. No one would have expected *her* to be here, either.

"Dr. Wright, your bond hearing is set for ten o'clock tomorrow morning," she began. "I want you to be aware of the fact that the State intends to serve you at that time with a complaint charging you with a long list of felonies regarding the kidnapping of Josh Kirkwood and the kidnapping and assault of BCA agent Megan O'Malley."

She glanced up at Wright over the rims of a pair of reading glasses that were more prop than prescription. He seemed almost impassive, returning her gaze with his steady dark eyes. No one spoke, and for a few seconds Ellen had the strange sensation that Cameron and Enberg had somehow been frozen out of the moment.

"Is that supposed to induce me to confess to crimes I didn't commit?" he asked quietly.

"It's a statement of fact, Dr. Wright. I want you to be fully aware of my intent to prosecute."

Enberg's brows drew together. "I heard rumors of a grand jury."

"I don't need a grand jury. Of course, if Josh Kirkwood isn't returned, I may well convene a grand jury to consider murder charges based on the evidence we have."

"Murder!" The exclamation propelled Enberg half a foot off the seat of his chair. "Jesus, Ellen! Isn't that a little premature?"

"Even as we speak, the state crime lab is conducting tests on the bloody sheet your client wrapped around Agent O'Malley. Evidence—he said so himself."

"So says a woman who was, by her own admission, drugged and beaten senseless—"

"The lab has confirmed that in addition to Agent O'Malley's blood, there is blood on the sheet type AB negative. Josh Kirkwood's blood type."

"And a billion other people's!"

"Clear evidence of grievous bodily harm," she continued. "From this evidence we might deduce that the reason the police aren't finding Josh is that Josh is dead."

"Oh, for—" Enberg sputtered, at a loss for a suitable diatribe. The red in his face pushed out to the rims of his ears. Seemingly unable to contain his temper to the confines of a chair, he rose and began to pace along the end of the table.

Ellen had seen this act before and, frankly, he had been more convincing. It seemed forced this time, as if he was having trouble working up outrage. He paced along the end of the table, behind an empty chair rather than behind Garrett Wright, which would have been symbolic of his support for his client.

"I didn't kill Josh Kirkwood," Garrett Wright said softly.

Ellen found herself holding her breath, waiting, expectation building inside her. The weight of his silence hinted at an announcement. God, was he going to confess after all? For a heartbeat she had the insane thought he was going to smile; then in a blink the expression was gone and she thought she must have imagined it.

"I'm an innocent man, Ms. North," he said. "I keep telling you that. What would possibly motivate me to kidnap a neighbor's child? I admire Hannah Garrison tremendously. My wife and I consider Hannah and Paul friends. And as for kidnapping Megan O'Malley, that seems more like the work of a madman. Do I strike you as being insane?"

"That's not for me to determine."

"I don't believe this," he muttered. "I'm a professor at one of the most highly respected small colleges in the country. For anyone to believe I could have done any of these things . . . It doesn't make sense."

"*It makes his kind of sense.*" In her mind's eye Ellen could see Megan's face, bruised and battered, the fire of hatred burning in her eyes. "*It was him, the son of a bitch . . . We got him dead to fucking rights.*"

"My job is applying the law to what you did, Dr. Wright, not making sense of it. I leave that unenviable and unproductive task to sociologists."

"I did nothing."

"How strange, then, that Chief Holt apprehended you fleeing the scene."

Wright tipped his head back and blew a sigh at the acoustic tile in the ceiling. "I keep telling you, it was a mistake. I had just got home. I parked my car in the garage and started for the house. I heard what I thought might be gunshots and stepped out the back door to see. I saw a man running toward me from the neighbor's yard. Understandably frightened, I stepped back into the garage with the intent of going into the house to call the police. Then the door flew open and Mitch Holt tackled me."

Cameron leaned forward, his forearms braced on the table, his blue eyes bright. "You thought you heard gunshots in your backyard, so you stepped outside? That seems odd, Dr. Wright. I think that would be the last thing I'd do. Weren't you afraid of being shot?"

"People don't get shot in Deer Lake," Wright scoffed. "I thought it was probably some kids fooling around in Quarry Hills Park, shooting at rabbits or something."

"At night, during a blizzard?"

The muscles around his mouth tightened ever so slightly as he regarded Cameron Reed.

"The man Mitch Holt chased through the woods was dressed in black," Ellen said. "When apprehended, you were dressed in black, breathing hard, perspiring even."

"If Mitch Holt burst into your garage and tackled you, you'd be breathing hard and sweating, too," Dennis said, jumping back into the fray with halfhearted sarcasm. He dropped back down into his chair and crossed his arms. "Mitch Holt never saw the face of the man he was chasing. Agent O'Malley never saw the face of the man who tortured her. I'm told the suspect was wearing a ski mask. My client was not wearing a ski mask when he was tackled."

"But a ski mask was found in the woods along the trail," Ellen reminded him.

"What about the gun?" Enberg challenged. "The paraffin test taken Saturday night revealed no traces of gunpowder on my client's hands."

"People generally wear gloves in the winter," Cameron offered with his own twist of sarcasm.

Denny shrugged dramatically. "So where are they?"

"Disposed of during the chase, like the hat," Ellen said. "They'll be found."

"Until they are, and until you can prove they were on my client's hands, they don't exist."

"You can pretend they don't exist, Dennis," she said. "The same way you can pretend your client is innocent.

Your denial won't change the fact that he's as Guilty as Sin and, barring new developments, will be going away for the rest of his life with no hope of ever setting foot outside the walls of a prison."

She turned her attention back to Garrett Wright as she gathered her notes. "As for your story, Doctor, I've seen sieves with fewer holes. I suggest you do some hard thinking tonight. Though I won't make promises, I think it's safe to say the county attorney's office would view this situation in a kinder light if you were to tell the truth."

"Is it really the truth you want, Ms. North?" he asked quietly. "Or is it another conviction for your record? It's no secret you're a very ambitious lady."

"It's always news to me." Ellen snapped her briefcase shut and rose, giving him a look as cold as steel. "What I want, Dr. Wright, is justice. And make no mistake—I'll get it."

Denny Enberg watched the pair of prosecutors leave, a sick heaviness resting like a stone in the pit of his stomach. Whether it was the prospect of losing the forthcoming battle or the idea of fighting this fight at all that made him nauseous, he didn't know. He wasn't sure he *wanted* to know.

He could feel the weight of his client's gaze on him and felt compelled to dredge up some scrap of wit.

"You always know where Ellen stands on a case," he said, busying himself scooping his notes together. "Just to the right of your jugular."

"Do *you* think I'm guilty, Dennis?" Wright asked.

Color touched Enberg's cheekbones. "I'm your attorney, Garrett. I told you up front, the only thing I ask is that you don't lie to me. You agreed. If you tell me you're innocent, you're innocent. I'll do everything I can to make the court believe it, too."

The jailer came in then, granite-faced, and led Garrett Wright through the door to the cell block. Denny watched him go, listened to the rattle of the leg irons, that weight in his gut growing heavier and heavier.

He always stated his Big Rule to his clients with a bluff sense of worldly wisdom, as if to tell them they might as well not even try to keep the truth from him because he could smell a lie like stink on shit. Most of them fell for it. Most of them were doofus losers who wouldn't have needed his help if they'd had two brain cells to rub together. But the Big Rule had a big catch-22, and he knew it.

If Garrett Wright was guilty, then he was guilty of horrible things, and lying would surely be the least of them.

"That's a pretty lame story," Cameron said as he and Ellen walked toward the security door at the end of the hall. "You might think a professor could come up with something more compelling."

"Maybe that's his angle. It's so weak we're supposed to believe it couldn't be anything but the truth."

The door swung open. Nodding to the officer, they took a right and started down the stairs. Cameron glanced at his watch and grimaced.

"Oh, man, I'm late. I've got to run," he said. "I told Fred Nelson I'd meet with him at four-thirty. He wants to talk dispo on that trucker from Canada. Will you need me later?"

"I don't think so. Phoebe is typing up the complaint even as we speak."

Ellen watched him bolt down the stairs two at a time with the grace of Baryshnikov. She followed, all but dragging her feet, the weight of the day bearing down on her.

Rudy had handed the case to her—or dumped it on her. She still wasn't sure which, still wasn't sure who had manipulated whom in that meeting. The self-preservationist in her told her she didn't want within five miles of this case. It had the smell of bad meat, looked to be rife with booby traps, and the media would scrutinize her every move. Harris College students with picket signs had already begun protesting Wright's arrest on the sidewalk in front of the courthouse. But her sense of justice told her that if Josh Kirkwood and his parents and Megan O'Malley were to get any justice at all, she would have to be the one to prosecute the case. That was a fact that had nothing to do with ego. She was, flat out, the best of the five prosecutors in the Park County attorney's office.

And so, she would clean up the tag-end stuff she had on her schedule, shift newer cases to Quentin Adler, and hope he could bungle his way through them without completely screwing up. And she would concentrate on putting Dr. Garrett Wright in prison.

No reporters were waiting to ambush her in the lobby of the law-enforcement center. Mitch Holt had banished them from his wing of Deer Lake's City Center. The lovely new brick building housed the city jail and police department in one-half of its two-story V-shape and the city government offices in the other.

The atrium at the apex of the V would be lousy with reporters. That was the scene of their last great spectacle related to the case: a live interview with an outraged Paul Kirkwood. Josh's father had been livid at Mitch's request that he come in to be fingerprinted, even though the request had been more than reasonable. It would have been within Mitch's power to haul Kirkwood in as a suspect at that point. Paul had failed to inform the police that he had once owned the van belonging to suspect and convicted pedophile Olie Swain, had in fact denied knowledge of any such van after a witness had come forward to say she may have seen Josh getting into a vehicle of that description on the night of his disappearance.

That still bothered Ellen, like a sliver she couldn't quite get at just beneath her skin. Why lie about the van? Why deny he had sold it to Olie Swain when the proof was right there in the DMV records?

Unfortunately, Olie wasn't around to help solve the mystery. Facing certain prison time on parole violations, to say nothing of the possible charges regarding Josh's disappearance, Swain had committed suicide while in custody. The BCA had gone over his van with every tool they had and had found nothing. Not a hair, not a thread from a mitten, not a thing belonging to Josh. Olie had sworn his innocence to the very end, scrawling it on the wall of his cell in blood.

Cutting through the squad room of the police department, where desks were piled with paperwork and phones rang without cease, Ellen headed for Holt's office. The door to his outer office stood open, but Ellen still paused in the hall and rapped her knuckles on the door frame before sticking her head in. Mitch's administrative assistant, Natalie Bryant, swung around from her filing cabinets with a scowl on her round mahogany face and thunder in the dark eyes behind her red-framed glasses, ready to take a bite out of the interloper. The look relaxed upon recognition to show the same kind of weariness Ellen was feeling.

"Girl, tell me you're going to crack that man like the cockroach he is. I'd pay money to see it," she said, propping a fist on one well-rounded hip.

"I'll do my best," Ellen promised.

"I'd like to do my best all over his head."

"Is Mitch in?"

"He figured you'd drop by. Go on in."

"Thanks."

Deer Lake's police chief sat behind his desk looking the way Ellen imagined Harrison Ford would look after a week-long bender: brown eyes bloodshot and underlined with dark circles, lean cheeks shadowed with stubble. He had jerked loose the knot in his tie and combed his hair with his fingers, leaving tufts standing up here and there.

"Well, it's official," she said. "I have been duly appointed to slay the dragon."

"Good."

His response held more confidence than she could muster at the moment. Ellen glanced around the office. There was no ego wall laden with the plaques and commendations he had garnered in his years as a cop, though she knew there were many. He had been a top detective with the Miami force for a dozen years, coming to Deer Lake after the death of his wife and young son in a convenience-store holdup. He had chosen Deer Lake as a sanctuary in a truer sense than she had.

"I've had my little tête-à-tête with Wright and his lawyer. Basically told him to confess or else. For all the good that will do."

"Oh, for the days of rubber truncheons . . ."

"Yeah," she drawled. "Human rights can be such a drag."

"He doesn't qualify as human in my book." He brightened with sarcastic false hope. "Hey, a loophole! That might be all the defense I'd need."

"I'm going to try to talk to Wright's wife tonight," Ellen said. "She's still at the Fontaine?"

"Yeah. The BCA guys were still going over the house today. We've got Karen under twenty-four-hour surveillance, in case she was involved. I don't think she had a clue what her husband was doing. She's not the brightest bulb in the chandelier, to begin with. Now she's so distraught, she can barely function. I didn't get anywhere with her, but you might have better luck woman-to-woman."

"Let's hope."

She could hear the phone ringing in the outer office, but no calls were being put through to Mitch. Natalie was running interference for him. The last two weeks had been hell on him. As Deer Lake's chief and the only detective on the thirty-man force, he had shouldered the burden of the search for Josh and an investigation that ran virtually around the clock. His professional and personal lives had been under constant scrutiny by the press.

"I spoke with Megan this afternoon," she said as he rose and came around the end of the desk to see her to the door. "She's got a rough road ahead of her."

"Yeah." He tried to put on a game expression, but it hung a little crooked, letting the worry peek through. "But she's a tough cookie. She'll gut it out."

"And you'll be there to help her."

"If I have anything to say about it."

"She's lucky to have you. You're a good guy, Mitch."

"Yeah, that's me. Last of the good guys."

"Don't say that. I'd like to think there's a couple left out there for us single women. It's that hope that keeps us shaving our legs, you know."

The press had either lost her or given up on her for the afternoon. Deadlines beckoned them if Ellen North did not. He had no deadlines except the statute of limitations on his anonymity.

He stood just outside a back door to Deer Lake's City Center, freezing his ass and cursing Minnesota's stringent antismoking laws. In the time it took to smoke a cigarette, he had already lost the feeling in his smaller toes.

She came out of the building through a side door, muttering to herself, head bent as she pulled her keys out of her handbag. He tossed his cigarette butt at a snowbank.

"Ms. North? May I have a word?"

Ellen jerked her head up at the sound of the voice— a honey-and-smoke drawl from the Deep South. Damned reporters. Lurking everywhere but under the bushes—

and they would have been there, too, if the bushes hadn't been buried under three feet of snow. This one came toward her with a long, purposeful stride, the collar of his black coat turned up high, hands jammed into his pockets.

"No—that's your word," she snapped. "I said all I have to say at the press conference. If you didn't get your sound bite then, that's too bad."

She kept walking, frowning as he stayed just in front of her, walking backward. "You're lucky I believe in handgun control," she said. "Don't you know any better than to sneak up on a woman in a dark parking lot?"

He grinned at her, a wicked pirate's grin that flashed white in an angular face shadowed by a day's growth of beard. "Don't you know any better than to assume a stranger coming at you in a dark parking lot is a reporter?"

The question cut through Ellen like a knife. What sun there had been earlier in the day was gone, swept away by a bank of clouds and the onset of evening. Though there was a police force inside the building she had just left, there wasn't another soul in the parking lot. She thought of Josh Kirkwood, his parents, everyone in Deer Lake who had made the assumption they were safe here. Even after everything that had happened in the last two weeks, she still felt personally immune. How stupid. How naive.

An image of Megan flashed through her mind. Megan, her face a palette of bruises and stitches. Megan hadn't seen her attacker. *"We fooled you all along, he said . . . We, always we . . ."*

Even in the faint wash of light from the streetlamps he had to see the color drain from her face. Her gaze darted toward her car, then back to the building, judging distances as her step slowed to a standstill.

"I'm no rapist," he assured her with a certain amount of amusement.

"I'd be a fool to take your word for that, wouldn't I?"

"Yes, ma'am," he conceded with a tip of his head.

"Ma'am," Ellen snarled under her breath, trying to muster up some anger to counteract the sudden burst of fear. She took a slow step back toward the building. "Now I *do* wish I had a gun."

"If I were after you for nefarious purposes," he said as he advanced on her, "would I be so careless as to approach you here?"

He pulled a gloved hand from his pocket and gestured gracefully to the parking lot, like a magician drawing attention to his stage.

"If I wanted to harm you," he said, stepping closer, "I would be smart enough to follow you home, find a way to slip into your house or garage, catch you where there would be little chance of witnesses or interference." He let those images take firm root in her mind. "That's what I would do if I were the sort of rascal who preys on women." He smiled again. "Which I am not."

"Who *are* you and what *do* you want?" Ellen demanded, unnerved by the fact that a part of her brain catalogued his manner as charming. No, not charming. Seductive. Disturbing.

"Jay Butler Brooks. I'm a writer—true crime. I can show you my driver's license if you'd like," he offered, but made no move to reach for it, only took another step toward her, never letting her get enough distance between them to diffuse the electric quality of the tension.

"I'd like for you to back off," Ellen said. She started to hold up a hand, a gesture meant to stop him in his tracks—or a foolish invitation for him to grab hold of her arm. Pulling the gesture back, she hefted her briefcase in her right hand, weighing its potential as a weapon or a shield. "If you think I'm getting close enough to you to look at a DMV photo, you must be out of your mind."

"Well, I have been so accused once or twice, but it never did stick. Now my Uncle Hooter, he's a different story. I could tell you some tales about him. Over dinner, perhaps?"

"Perhaps not."

He gave her a crestfallen look that was ruined by the sense that he was more amused than affronted. "After I waited for you out here in the cold?"

"After you stalked me and skulked around in the shadows?" she corrected him, moving another step backward. "After you've done your best to frighten me?"

"I frighten you, Ms. North? You don't strike me as the sort of woman who would be easily frightened. That's certainly not the impression you gave at the press conference."

"I thought you said you aren't a reporter."

"No one at the courthouse ever asked," he confessed. "They assumed the same way you assumed. Forgive my pointing it out at this particular moment, but assumptions can be very dangerous things. Your boss needs to have a word with someone about security. This is a highly volatile case you've got here. Anything might happen. The possibilities are virtually endless. I'd be happy to discuss them with you. Over drinks," he suggested. "You look like you could do with one."

"If you want to see me, call my office."

"Oh, I want to see you, Ms. North," he murmured, his voice an almost tangible caress. "I'm not big on appointments, though. Preparation time eliminates spontaneity."

"That's the whole point."

"I prefer to catch people . . . off balance," he admitted. "They reveal more of their true selves."

"I have no intention of revealing anything to you." She stopped her retreat as a group of people emerged from the main doors of City Center. "I should have you arrested."

He arched a brow. "On what charge, Ms. North? Attempting to hold a conversation? Surely y'all are not so inhospitable as your weather here in Minnesota, are you?"

She gave him no answer. The voices of the people who had come out of the building rose and fell, only the odd word breaking clear as they made their way down the sidewalk. She turned and fell into step with the others as they passed.

Jay watched her walk away, head up, chin out, once again projecting an image of cool control. She didn't like being caught off guard. He would have bet money she was a list maker, a rule follower, the kind of woman who dotted all her *i*'s and crossed all her *t*'s, then double-checked them for good measure. She liked boundaries. She liked control. She had no intention of revealing anything to him.

"But you already have, Ms. Ellen North," he said, hunching up his shoulders as the wind bit a little harder and spit a sweep of fine white snow across the parking lot. "You already have."

CHAPTER 3

The Fontaine Hotel sat kitty-corner from the City Center, on the opposite side of the park that made up the old-fashioned town square. In ordinary times Ellen would have enjoyed a brisk walk around the park ending in the warmth of the Fontaine's beautiful restored Victorian lobby. But these were not ordinary times. She parked her car in the lot beside the hotel and sat with the heater and fan running full blast, as if the trembling in her arms and legs had anything to do with the cold.

She liked to think of herself as strong, smart, savvy, able to handle herself in any situation. In a matter of moments, in the course of a few sentences, a lone man had managed to summarily unnerve her. Without ever laying a hand on her, without ever making a verbal threat, he had shown her just how vulnerable she really was.

Jay Butler Brooks. She had seen his face on the cover of *People* as she'd stood in the checkout line at the supermarket. She had seen his name on book covers, remembered glancing through an article about him in a recent issue of *Newsweek*.

He was one of the current pack of lawyers-turned-authors. But instead of making his fame with courtroom fiction, Brooks had chosen to capitalize on actual crime. His books sold millions, and Hollywood snapped them up like Godiva chocolates.

The story had left a bad taste in Ellen's mouth. She looked at the business of turning true crimes into entertainment as twisted and sleazy, vulgar voyeurism that only helped blur the lines between reality and fantasy, and further inured Americans to violence. But money talked, and it talked big. Jay Butler Brooks was worth more than most third-world countries.

"I prefer to catch people . . . off balance . . ."

The remembered timbre of his voice rippled through her. Dark, warm, husky. *Seductive.* The word whispered through her mind against her will, against logic. He had said nothing seductive. There had been nothing sexual about the encounter. Still, the word hung in her mind like a shadow. *Seductive. Dangerous.*

"If I wanted to harm you, I would be smart enough to follow you home. . . ."

Reporters came out of the mahogany woodwork the instant she set foot in the Fontaine's elegant lobby. Ellen shouldered her way past them without comment and breathed a sigh of relief at the sight of a uniformed police officer guarding the doors to the elevator. He nodded to her as she stepped into the car and halted those who would have followed her, demanding that they produce room keys. As a number of them scrambled to reach into their pockets, the doors closed.

Wright's wife had been given a room on the second floor to discourage any notions of flinging herself out a window. The woman who answered the door to room 214 was not Karen Wright. Teresa McGuire's pixie face peeked out from behind the safety chain, eyes narrowed with suspicion, mouth tightened into a knot. The victim-witness coordinator for Park County, she had drawn baby-sitting detail because there were no women on either the Deer Lake or Park County forces.

"Ellen! Thank God," she whispered, closing the door enough to slide the chain free. "I thought you were Paige

Price. Would you believe yesterday she actually thought she could talk her way past me just because she once interviewed a friend of mine for a story on victims' rights? That bitch. I wouldn't watch channel seven if you held a gun to my head."

"I hear she's been reassigned to cover that sewage-plant disaster in Minot, North Dakota," Ellen said softly, setting her briefcase on a side table. "She blew it big time getting into bed with the sheriff for her inside information."

A shudder of revulsion jiggled through Teresa's small, plump body. "That is so gross! Paige Price and Russ Steiger. *Anybody* and Russ Steiger. Do you think he ever changes the oil in that hair?"

"I try not to wonder. How's Mrs. Wright holding up?"

Teresa shot a look toward the bedroom that was separated from the entrance by a partial wall. "She's not, poor thing. She keeps saying it has to be a mistake. She's been sedated. I don't know how much good she'll be to you."

Ellen shrugged out of her coat and hung it in the closet. "We have to keep trying to get through to her. She could be the key to this whole thing."

Karen Wright sat in a flowered chintz chair, staring at the print that hung in an ornate gilt frame above the bed: a mother cat watching her plump, fluffy kittens cavort with a ball of yarn. She had curled herself into the chair, pulling her feet up onto the seat and wrapping her arms around her knees. A variation on the fetal position. She was a lovely woman with delicate features and ashblond hair that hung like silk in a classic bob. The only sign that she had spent the past several days in tears was the red that rimmed her big doe eyes and tinted the end of her upturned nose. Somehow the color managed to coordinate with the rose-colored leggings and soft gray sweater she wore.

"Karen? I'm Ellen North with the county attorney's

office." Ellen pulled out the chair from the writing desk and sat. "I'd like to talk with you for a few minutes if that's all right."

"It was a mistake," Karen said without looking away from the print. "Garrett's never even had a parking ticket."

"We have a good deal of evidence against him, Karen," Ellen said gently. "By law you can't be compelled to testify against your husband, but if you know anything at all that could be helpful in finding Josh, you would tell us, wouldn't you?"

Karen nibbled at a cuticle and dodged Ellen's gaze.

"Do you know any reason he would single out the Kirkwoods, any reason he would take Josh?"

The silence stretched into a moment, two.

"This must be especially hard for you. You must feel betrayed, maybe even guilty in a way."

The feelings had to be there somewhere, deep inside. She had been stuffing missing-child fliers into envelopes at the Josh Kirkwood Volunteer Center, had gone to the Kirkwoods' house to baby-sit Josh's little sister, while her husband had been holding them all in the grip of fear. Had he fooled her that completely or had she known all along?

"Karen, you have to be aware that you could be considered an accessory," Ellen said. "People are having a hard time believing you didn't know what Garrett was doing."

Not a flicker of response. Karen combed a strand of hair behind her ear. Slowly, a smile spread across her mouth. "Lily's so sweet," she murmured. "I don't mind watching her. Garrett and I don't have any children." Tears glittered in her big dark eyes. "I suppose Hannah won't let me watch her anymore."

She put her head down on her knees and sobbed softly, as if the prospect of not being able to baby-sit was too much for her but the idea that her husband was some kind of sociopathic monster made no impact on her whatsoever. Ellen didn't know whether to feel sympathy or horror. Frustration took up the slack.

"Karen, you have to listen to me." Leaning forward, she reached out and took a firm hold of the woman's wrist. "Josh is still out there somewhere. If you have any idea where Garrett may have taken him, you have to tell us. Think of Hannah and Lily. Think how much they must miss Josh."

"And Paul . . . ," Karen murmured, lifting her head a fraction. Her gaze fixed on the fringed lamp that sat on the night table. "He has such a nice family," she said wistfully.

"Yes, Josh has a very nice family and they miss him very much. You have to help them if you can, Karen. Please."

Ellen held her breath as she watched the play of emotions in Karen Wright's eyes. Confusion, pain, fear. Was she afraid of her husband? Had he somehow brainwashed her? He was a professor of psychology; he had to know how to manipulate minds.

"He can't hurt you, Karen. It can only help everyone for you to tell us what you know."

Karen slowly pulled her arm from Ellen's grasp and unfolded herself from the chintz chair. Hugging herself, she wandered the room, ending up in front of the antique ash dresser, staring at her own reflection in the oval mirror above it. Slowly, she picked up a brush and started in on her hair with gentle strokes.

"A terrible mistake," she whispered. "Garrett would never . . . He wouldn't do that to me."

Ellen pushed herself to her feet and headed for the door.

"I'll leave you my card, Karen," she said, placing it on the dresser as she passed. "You can call any time of the day or night. Any time you think of something that might be helpful or if you just want to talk."

"No. It's just a mistake," Karen mumbled to herself, stroking the brush through her hair.

He watched Ellen North emerge from the Fontaine Hotel, wondered what she'd got. Karen was there, being watched by a hundred eyes. He wanted to go to her, talk to her, but that wasn't possible. She would never betray him. He consoled himself with that thought even as fear rose inside him like a tide of acid.

Life had betrayed him again and again, tricked him into thinking he wanted one thing when he needed something else. The job, the house, the car, the trophy bride. Every time he grabbed a prize, he found he wanted something else. The hunger never abated, it simply changed its guise.

He wanted someone to blame for that, but he could never see where the blame should lie. When he was younger, he had blamed his parents. His father, a man who settled for less than his family deserved, and his mother, a woman who stood in her husband's shadow. Lately, he had thrown the blame at Hannah's feet. Her career came first, before her family, before him. She had never been any man's shadow. Her shadow fell across him. And he hated her for it.

Ironically, no one else blamed Hannah for anything. Throughout this ordeal they had painted her as a victim, as a valiant figure struggling to cope. Poor Hannah, the mother whose child had been taken. Poor Hannah, she helped so many people, she didn't deserve all this pain.

Poor Hannah, who had left their son standing outside the skating rink while she'd tended someone else's needs at the hospital. Poor Hannah, who'd sat at home waiting for the phone to ring while he had gone out and beat the bushes with the search teams and made pleas on television.

No one ever said "poor Paul." Thanks to that BCA bitch O'Malley, they had turned to him with suspicious

GUILTY AS SIN 43

eyes because of that damned van. They had tried to tie
him to Olie Swain, had tried to blame everything on him
when he had done everything he could to play the hero.

A victim, that was what he really was. A victim of circumstance. A victim of fate. He didn't even have a home
to go to tonight.

"... I don't know who you are anymore, but I know I'm sick
of your lies and your accusations. I'm sick of you blaming me for
losing Josh, when all you seem to want to do is bury him and hope
the cameras get your good side at the funeral!"

"I don't have to listen to this." He looked away from her, away
from the contempt in her eyes.

"No," Hannah said, picking up his coat off the back of the
sofa. She flung it at him, her mouth trembling with fury and with
the effort to hold the tears at bay. "You don't have to listen to me
anymore. And I don't have to put up with your moods and your
wounded male ego and your stupid petty jealousy. I'm through
with it! I'm through with you. . . . You don't live here anymore,
Paul."

The scene played through his mind. Saturday night.
Mitch Holt had come to give them the news of Garrett
Wright's arrest.

Hannah would divorce him. And everyone would
look at her and say, "Poor Hannah." No one would look
at what had been taken from him. No one would say,
"Poor Paul" . . . except Karen. No one understood him
except Karen.

A yawn pulled at Ellen's mouth and she gave in to it,
stretching, rustling the thick down comforter that covered her legs and drawing a one-eyed look from the big
golden retriever sprawled across the foot of her bed.

"I know it's late, Harry," Ellen said, shoving her reading glasses up on her nose. She resettled herself against the
mountain of pillows and among the piles of law books

and fought off another yawn. The cube-shaped clock radio on the cherry bedside stand pronounced it to be 12:25 A.M. "I'm working to put away the guy who took Josh."

The dog whined a little, as if he, too, had absorbed the hours of news coverage about the abduction.

Ellen let *Minnesota Rules of Court—State and Federal* fall shut in her lap as an image of Garrett Wright rose in her mind. The image he had given her in the interview room—pale, drawn, delicate: a victim, not a monster.

Although there were people ready to pin the blame for these crimes on anyone, there were a great many people in Deer Lake who would *not* want to pin the blame on Garrett Wright. People who had trusted him, respected him, looked up to him. The students from Harris. The people who backed the juvenile offenders' program he had helped establish. There would be people who wouldn't want to believe, because, if a man like Garrett Wright could be guilty of something so ugly, then who could they trust?

Who can you trust? The question brought a chill with it. A memory of old cynicism and hard-won wisdom. *Trust no one.*

She didn't want to believe that anymore. She had done her time on cases of smoke and mirrors, where nothing was as it seemed, where enemies came with smiles and stroked with one hand while the other plunged the knife in deep.

"Long ago and far away," she murmured, magic words to ward off the memories.

She could see Wright against a dark background. Staring at her with eyes that were bottomless black holes, soulless, staring into her, through her. The corners of his mouth turned up in a smile that made her blood run cold. He knew something she didn't. The game plan. The big picture. He looked inside her and laughed at something she couldn't see.

Then his image blurred into another. *"I frighten you, Ms. North? You don't strike me as the sort of woman who would be easily frightened."* He stepped closer, leaned closer. She tried to back away and found herself held to the spot, unable to move. She could feel the energy around him. *Seductive.* The word wrapped itself around her like curling fingers of smoke. *". . . assumptions can be very dangerous things . . ."*

Ellen jerked awake with a cry that brought Harry's head up. Her heart was pounding, her glasses askew. She pulled them off and set them aside with a trembling hand as she tried to jump-start her brain. A sound. A sound had snapped her to consciousness. A bang or a thump, she wasn't sure.

Holding her breath, she strained to listen. Nothing. But in the back of her mind that dark voice whispered. *"If I were after you . . . I would . . . follow you home, find a way to slip into your house or garage . . . catch you where there would be little chance of witnesses or interference."*

The killer-blue eyes stared up at her from the pages of the *Newsweek* she had dug out of the recycling bin. She picked up the magazine and glared at his image. It was an artsy shot full of shadows. He stared at the camera, looking tough, his hands curled around the bars of a wrought-iron fence. His hair was brown, cropped short with a hint of a cowlick in front. His face was masculine, angular, with a slim, straight nose and a stubborn chin. In contrast his mouth was full, sculpted, almost feminine, far too sexy. The kind of mouth that hinted at dark, sensual, secret talents.

The headline read "Crime Boss" in bold black letters. The caption—"Crime pays big time for Jay Butler Brooks."

Ellen scowled at the photograph. "I should have had you arrested."

Disgusted with herself, she tossed the magazine aside

and crawled out from under the covers and the books. Trying to ignore the uneasiness that curled through her midsection, she picked up the half-empty glass of white wine from the table and padded barefoot across the plush ivory carpet. Her doors were locked. Her alarm system was on the bed, watching her.

Sipping absently at the wine, she pulled aside the thick swag of ivory lace at the window and looked out at the night. The new snow sparkled like a carpet of white diamonds beneath the light of a crescent moon. Beautiful. Peaceful. No hint of the storm that had slapped Minnesota over the weekend. No evidence of the violence that had put Megan O'Malley in the hospital. No sign of Josh Kirkwood. Just another quiet night in the Lakeside subdivision. The Kirkwoods' neighborhood. Garrett Wright's neighborhood.

Her house was less than two blocks away from theirs. She could see a wedge of lake from her living room, was within walking distance of Quarry Hills Park, where Mitch and Megan and Garrett Wright had played out a life-and-death drama Saturday night. Ellen had been sitting in front of her fireplace sharing cappuccino and conversation with a friend, oblivious to what was happening a stone's throw from her own home.

Harry raised his head abruptly, a growl rumbling low in his throat. The dog jumped down off the bed and stood at attention at the door that led into the darkened hall. Ellen stood in the center of the room, pulse rate jumping, trying to recall in detail the actual act of locking the doors. She had come in from the garage into the kitchen. She always locked the dead bolt as she came in for the night. It was habit. She had gone out the front door for the mail, come back in, turned that dead bolt as her gaze scanned the words YOU MAY HAVE ALREADY WON TEN MILLION DOLLARS.

The doors were locked. There were no odd sounds

emanating from the nether regions of the living room. With that knowledge bolstering her courage, she stepped past the dog and into the hall. Harry gave a little whine of embarrassment and trailed after her, bumping up against her legs as she paused on the short flight of steps that led down to the living room.

Faint silver light filtered in around the edges of the blinds. The comfortable sofas and chairs were indistinct hulks in the dark. Nothing moved. No one spoke. Beneath the warm flannel of her pajamas Ellen's skin pebbled with goose bumps. The fine hairs on the back of her neck rose as another low growl rumbled in Harry's throat.

The telephone trilled its high-pitched birdcall. The sound ripped through the room like a shotgun blast. Harry gallumphed in a clumsy circle, his booming bark all but rattling the framed photographs on the walls. The phone rang again.

The last call she had got in the middle of the night had been Mitch telling her Olie Swain was dead. Maybe Wright had been struck down with remorse and killed himself, too, but she doubted it. She had told Karen Wright to call any time of day or night. Maybe Wright's wife had found her way out of the fog of denial.

"Ellen North," she answered, her voice automatically taking on the same tone she used at the office.

Silence.

"Hello?"

The silence seemed to grow thicker, heavier with expectation.

"Karen? Is that you?"

No response. The caller remained on the line, silent, waiting. Another minute ticked past on the nightstand clock.

"Karen, if it's you, don't be afraid to talk to me. I'm here to listen."

Still nothing except the creepy certainty that someone

was on the other end of the line. The hope that that someone was Karen Wright evaporated. Ellen waited as another
minute slipped past.

"Look," she said crisply, "if you're not even going to
bother to talk dirty to me, hang up and free the line for
someone who knows how to make an obscene phone
call."

Not a sound.

Ellen slammed the receiver down, telling herself it was
a tactical move rather than nerves, a lie that was made
painfully clear by the way she jumped as the phone rang
again. She stared at it as it rang a second and third time,
then gave herself a mental kick and picked it up.

"Ellen North."

"Ellen, it's Mitch. Josh is home."

JOURNAL ENTRY
JANUARY 25, 1994

They think they have us
Guilty as Sin
Caught in the act
Dead to rights

Dead wrong.

CHAPTER 4

"Josh, did the man hurt you?"

Josh didn't answer. He looked away at the poster on the wall instead. The poster was of a man on a gray horse jumping a fence. It was bright and colorful. Josh thought he might like to ride a horse like that someday. He closed his eyes and pretended to dream he was riding the gray horse on the moon.

Dr. Robert Ulrich bit back a sigh, flicked a glance at Mitch, then turned to Hannah. "I can't find any signs that he's been sexually abused."

Hannah stood beside the examination table where Josh sat wearing a thin blue-print cotton gown. He looked so small, so defenseless. The harsh fluorescent lighting gave his skin a ghostly pallor. She kept one hand on his arm to reassure him—and herself. A doctor herself, she knew better than to interfere with the proceedings, but she couldn't bring herself to sit in the chair three feet away. She hadn't broken contact with him since she had opened the front door of the house and found him standing on the step two hours ago.

She had been trying to sleep—something she didn't do very well anymore. The bed seemed too big, the house too quiet, too empty. She had told Paul to leave Saturday night, but he had been lost to her long before that. The happy partnership they had once shared seemed a distant memory. Lately all they had between them was tension and bitterness. The man she had married ten years ago had been sweet and gentle, full of hope and enthusiasm. The man she had faced two nights ago was angry and petty and jealous, discontented and emotionally abusive. She didn't know him anymore. She didn't want to.

And so she had lain alone in their big bed, staring up at the skylight and the black swatch of January night, wondering what she would do. How would she cope, who would she be. That was a big question: who would she be? She certainly wasn't the same woman she had been two weeks before. She felt like a stranger to herself. The only thing clear was that she *would* cope, somehow. She had to for herself and for Lily . . . and for Josh, for the day he came home.

Then there he was, standing on the front step.

Afraid the spell might break, she hadn't let go of him since that moment. Her fingers stroked the soft skin of her son's forearm, assuring her he was real and alive.

"Hannah? Are you listening to me?"

She blinked and focused on Bob Ulrich's square face. He was closer to fifty than forty. He had been a friend to her from the day she had come to interview for a staff position at Deer Lake Community Hospital. He had been influential in the board's recent decision to name her head of the ER. He had delivered Lily and removed Josh's tonsils. He had come to the hospital tonight at her request to examine Josh. He looked at her now with concern.

"Yes," Hannah said. "I'm sorry, Bob."

"Do you want to sit? You look a little woozy."

"No."

Mitch contradicted her without saying a word, sliding a stool up behind her and pressing her onto it with a hand on her shoulder. Her blue eyes were glassy, her hair a mass of golden waves hastily tied back. The past weeks had taken a toll on her physically. Naturally slender, she now looked thin to the point of anorexia. She had stood beside the table for the entire exam, holding Josh's hand, staring at his face, leaning over to kiss his forehead. She didn't seem to be aware of the tears streaming down her cheeks. Mitch pulled a clean handkerchief out of his hip pocket, pressed it into her free hand, and wondered where the hell Paul was.

He should have been here for this, for Josh, for Hannah. Hannah had tried to call him at his office, which was where he had been spending his nights, and had got his machine. Mitch had sent a squad car to the office complex. Nearly two hours later there was still no sign of Paul. And God knew, tomorrow, when Paul would be the center of attention for the press, he would blame the police department for not rushing him to his son's side.

Josh had been absolutely silent throughout the whole ordeal, not uttering a sound of fear or discomfort. He answered no questions.

Mitch hoped the last would be a temporary condition. This was already a case with too many questions and not enough answers. While Josh's reappearance was cause for celebration, it added to the Q column. With Garrett Wright sitting in a jail cell, who had brought Josh home? Did Wright have an accomplice? What few clues they had pointed to Olie Swain. Olie had audited some of Wright's classes at Harris. Olie had the van that fit the witness description. But the van had yielded them nothing, and Olie Swain was dead.

"There's no sign of penetration," Dr. Ulrich said quietly, keeping one eye on Josh, who seemed to be asleep sitting up. "No redness, no tearing."

"We'll see what the slides show," Mitch said.

"I'm guessing they'll be clean."

The doctor had conducted the standard rape kit, searching Josh literally from head to toe for any sign of a sexual assault. Oral and rectal swabs taken would be tested for seminal fluid. Mitch had overseen the exam as a matter of duty, watching like a hawk to be certain Ulrich didn't skip anything, well aware the doctor had little in the way of practical experience with this kind of procedure. Just another of the challenges of law enforcement outside the realm of a city, where rape was not an uncommon crime. Deer Lake Community Hospital didn't even own a Wood's lamp—a fluorescent lamp used to scan the skin surface for signs of seminal fluid. Not that a Wood's lamp would have done them much good in Josh's case. The boy appeared scrubbed clean, and the scent of soap and shampoo clung to him. Any evidence they may have got had literally gone down a drain.

"What about his arm? You think they drugged him?"

"There's certainly been a needle in that vein," Ulrich said, gently pulling Josh's left arm toward him for a second look at the fine marks and faint bruising on the skin of his inner elbow. "We'll have to wait for the lab results on the blood tests."

"They took blood," Hannah murmured, stroking a hand over her son's tousled sandy-brown curls. "I told you, Mitch. I saw it."

He gave her a poker face that told her he was politely refraining from comment. He probably thought she'd finally cracked. She couldn't blame him. She had never put much stock in the ravings of people who claimed they saw things in dreams. If she had been asked to diagnose a woman in her own situation, she would have probably said the stress was too much, that her mind was trying to compensate. But she knew in her heart what she had seen in that dream Friday night: Josh standing alone, thinking of her, wearing a pair of striped pajamas she had never seen before. The same striped pajamas he had been wearing tonight, which Mitch Holt had bagged to send to the BCA lab.

Mitch leaned down to Josh's eye level. "Josh, can you tell me if someone took blood from your arm?"

Eyes closed, Josh turned to his mother, reaching for her. Hannah slid off the stool and gathered him close. "He's exhausted," she said impatiently. "And cold. Why is it so damn cold in this hospital?"

"You're right, Hannah," Ulrich said calmly. "It's after two. We've done all we need to for tonight. Let's get you and Josh settled into a room."

Hannah's head came up as alarm flooded through her. "You're keeping him here?"

"I think it's wisest, considering the circumstances. For observation," he added, trying to take the edge off her panic. "Someone is watching Lily, right?"

"Well, yes, but—"

"Josh has been through a lot. Let's just keep an eye on him for a day or so. All right, Dr. Garrison?"

He added the last bit to remind her who she was, Hannah thought. Dr. Hannah Garrison knew how things were done. She knew what logic dictated. She knew how to keep her composure and her objectivity. She was strong and levelheaded, cool under fire. But she had ceased to be Dr. Hannah Garrison. Now she was Josh's mom, terrified of what her child must have gone through, sick at heart, racked by guilt.

"How's that sound, Josh?" Ulrich asked. "You get to sleep in one of those cool electric hospital beds with the remote controls, and your mom will be right there in the room with you. What do you think about that?"

Josh pushed his face into his mother's shoulder and hugged her tighter. He didn't want to think at all.

Ellen paced the confines of the waiting room like an expectant aunt.

Marty Wilhelm, the agent the BCA had sent down

from St. Paul to replace Megan, sat on the couch, flicking through cable channels with the remote, seemingly mesmerized by the changing colors and images. He looked young and stupid. Tom Hanks without the brain. Too cute, with a short nose and a mop of curly brown hair.

Ellen had taken an instant dislike to him, then chastised herself for it. It wasn't Wilhelm's fault that Paige Price had decided to play dirty and turn the media's attentions on Megan and Mitch's budding relationship. Nor was it Marty's fault Megan had a hot Irish temper and a tongue that was too sharp and too quick for prudence. That Megan had become a public-relations problem which had outweighed her value as a cop had nothing to do with Marty.

All those issues considered, she still disliked him.

He glanced up at her with eyes as brown and vacuous as a spaniel's and said for the ninth time, "It's taking them long enough."

She gave him the same look she had given thick-headed boys in high school and kept on pacing.

The only other person in the waiting area, Father Tom McCoy, rose from a square armchair that was too low for him and stretched a kink out of his back. Having grown up Episcopalian, Ellen knew him only in passing and by reputation. Barry Fitzgerald he was not. Tom McCoy was tall and handsome with an athlete's build and kind blue eyes behind a pair of gold-rimmed glasses. He had come to the hospital wearing faded blue jeans and a flannel shirt that gave him more resemblance to a lumberjack than a priest.

He gave Ellen a questioning look as he fished some change out of his pocket. "Coffee?"

"No, thanks, Father. I've had too much already."

"Me, too," he admitted. "What I really need is a drink, but I don't think the cafeteria has a machine that dispenses good Irish whiskey."

As McCoy walked away, Wilhelm cocked his head. "He's not like any priest I ever knew. Where's his collar?"

Ellen gave him The Look again. "Father Tom is a nonconformist."

"So I gathered. What did you think of his deacon—Albert Fletcher?"

"I didn't know Albert Fletcher. Obviously, he was a very disturbed individual."

Fletcher had fallen under suspicion regarding the kidnapping because of his ties to Josh through the Church as Josh's instructor for religion class and as an altar boy. Obsessed with the Church, Fletcher had crossed the line from zealot to madman, unnoticed until he'd attacked Father Tom and Hannah early Friday morning as they'd sat talking in St. Elysius Catholic Church. He had given Father Tom a concussion with a brass candlestick. Later that morning the mummified remains of Fletcher's long-dead wife had been discovered in his garage. The incident had sparked a manhunt that had ended in tragedy during Saturday evening Mass, where Fletcher, ranting and wild-eyed, had fallen to his death from the balcony railing. Whether or not there would be further investigation into Doris Fletcher's demise had yet to be determined.

So much that was bad had happened in so little time. Kidnapping, suicide, madness, scandal. It seemed as if a hidden seam in the fabric of life had given way, allowing evil to pour into Deer Lake from some dark underworld. And if they didn't figure out how to close it up, it would continue on, poisoning everything and everyone it touched. The thought gave Ellen a chill.

The hospital was quiet, the halls dimly lit. Word of Josh's return had gone out on a need-to-know basis. What staff was on duty at this time of night hovered around the main desk, talking in low tones and casting worried glances down the hall toward the examination room Hannah and Josh had disappeared into with Mitch and Dr. Ul-rich.

Reaching for the can of warm soda she had set on an end table, Ellen froze midgesture as the examination-room door swung open and Mitch emerged. She hustled to meet him.

"Did he name Wright?" she asked.

Crossing his arms over his chest, Mitch propped a shoulder against the wall. "He didn't name anybody. He isn't talking."

"At all?"

"Not a word."

Ellen's sinking feeling was the sure-thing conviction sliding away. An instinctive response that had nothing to do with her sense of compassion. They were separate entities—the lawyer in her and the woman. The lawyer thought in terms of evidence; the woman thought about a small boy who had been through God-only-knew what hell in the past two weeks.

"How is he?"

"Physically, he seems pretty good. No signs of sexual abuse."

"Thank God."

"He may have been drugged or had blood taken from him. His blood had to get on that sheet some way, and he had no injuries to speak of. We'll know more when the lab results are in."

"We'll know what?" Wilhelm demanded, rushing up, his proper paisley necktie flipped over his shoulder.

Mitch frowned at him. "We'll meet in my office at seven and I'll go over it all with both of you."

"What about questioning the boy?" Wilhelm blurted, looking as if he had come all the way to the North Pole only to find out Santa wouldn't grant him an audience.

"It'll wait."

"But the mother—"

"Is an emotional wreck," Mitch snapped. "She didn't see anyone, didn't see a car. All she knows is she has her little boy back. You can talk to her in the morning."

Wilhelm's dark eyes shone bright with temper even though his trademark boyish grin still stretched across his face. "Now look, Chief, you can't shut me out of this. I have the power——"

"You don't have jack shit here, Marty," Mitch said. "Do you understand me? I don't care if the BCA sent you down here with a golden crown and scepter. You try to push me on this and I'll squash you like a bug. Nobody sees Hannah or Josh until they've had some rest."

"But——"

Marty's protest was cut off as the emergency-room doors to the street swept back and Paul Kirkwood stormed into the lobby with a pair of uniformed officers at his heels. His brown hair was windblown back from his lean, angular face. Cold and excitement rouged his cheeks. His deep-set eyes fixed on Mitch as he strode down the hallway.

"I want to see my son."

"Hannah and Josh are being settled in a room."

"Hannah?" he said peevishly. "What's wrong with her?"

"Nothing having Josh back won't cure. She's just a little rattled, that's all."

"And what about me? You think I'm not rattled?"

"I don't know what you are, Paul," Mitch said wearily. "Other than late, that is. Where the hell have you been?" His gaze strayed to the officers who stood behind Josh's father.

"We caught him coming back to his office, Chief."

"Caught me? Am I under arrest here?" Paul's voice was sharp with indignation. "Should I be calling my attorney?"

"Of course not, Mr. Kirkwood," Ellen intervened,

trying to break the mounting tension between the men. "We wanted to make you aware Josh had been returned, that's all. We also thought you might want to be with your son during the physical examination."

"I was out driving around." Paul's mouth turned in a petulant curve. "I haven't been having a lot of success sleeping lately. How is Josh? What did that animal do to him?"

"He's fine," Mitch said, then amended the overstatement for the sake of his conscience. "He seems fine, physically. I'll walk with you to his room, fill you in."

As they started down the hall, Wilhelm started after them. Ellen snagged him by the shirtsleeve and held him back. The BCA agent wheeled on her.

"I'd like to hear a better explanation of where he was tonight."

"So would I. We'll hear it in the morning."

"What if he's involved? What if he's the one who took Josh home? He could skip."

"Don't be stupid," Ellen said impatiently. "If he wanted to skip, do you think he would drop off the son he kidnapped, then drive around town for two hours, then go back to his office, *then* run?"

Wilhelm wagged a finger in her face. "He owned that van."

"That van that yielded us nothing."

"I think we should take Mr. Kirkwood downtown and discuss his whereabouts tonight."

"Then you feel free to express that opinion to Chief Holt. Push him far enough, and you'll be able to question Dr. Ulrich while he tries to set the broken bones in your face. Personally, I've seen enough of this hospital for one night."

Wright's bond hearing was less than eight hours away. Garrett Wright, who would be charged with the abduction of Josh Kirkwood. Josh Kirkwood, who had been returned home safe while Garrett Wright sat in a cell in the city jail.

Hannah refused the offer of a patient's gown to sleep in. She ignored the cot that had been set up for her next to Josh's bed. She pulled her boots off and climbed onto the bed with her son.

Josh played with the control switch, slowly raising and lowering the head of the bed, the foot of the bed, bending it in two in the middle. The ride was not unlike the one Hannah's emotions had been on for the past two weeks. The ride they were still on now. The idea that Josh was back safe was a giddy high. The fear of what had been done to him mentally was a crashing, black low. The feelings chased each other inside her, around and around, up and down as the bed went up and down.

She slipped her arm around Josh and settled her hand over the control. "That's enough, sweetheart. You're making me seasick," she murmured. She smiled softly as one of his sandy-brown curls tickled her nose. "Remember the time we went out on Grandpa's boat and Uncle Tim got seasick after he teased us about being landlubbers?"

She waited for him to roll over and grin at her, eyes bright, giggles bubbling just behind his smile. He would laugh and tell her the whole story, complete with sound effects, and she would feel the most incredible swelling, brilliant, warm rush of love and relief and joy. But he didn't roll over and he didn't laugh. He didn't move. He didn't speak. He just went still. The rush of love was an ache. The joy was tangled in anguish.

The door swung open and Paul stepped into the room looking anxious and hesitant at once. Hannah bit down on the questions she wanted to snap at him. Where had he been? Why hadn't he been here for Josh? How like him to leave the worst moments for her to deal with, then walk in after the fact. And what a sad commentary on their relationship that in this moment that should have been so happy for them both, the first thing she wanted to do was attack him.

He rushed into the room, his gaze fixed on their son.

"Oh, God," he whispered, struggling visibly with a knot of emotions—disbelief, joy, uncertainty. "Josh."

Josh sat up and stared at him, unsmiling.

"I tried to call you," Hannah said softly. "I tried your office—"

"I was out," Paul said shortly, not taking his eyes off his son. He mustered a smile, reaching out slowly. "Josh, son—"

Josh hurled the bed control at him and flung himself at Hannah.

"Josh!" Hannah cried. Her expression of surprise was directed at Paul.

"Josh, it's me, Dad," Paul said, confusion furrowing his brow.

He sat on the edge of the bed, reaching out again to touch his son's shoulder. The gesture was batted away. Josh's legs kicked out as if he were trying to run.

"I don't understand this," Paul said. "Josh, what's the matter? Don't you know me?"

His only answer was a frightened squeal as Paul tried once more to turn Josh toward him. The boy surged against Hannah, pushing her backward.

"Paul, don't try to touch him!" she snapped. "Can't you see you're only making it worse?"

"But I haven't done anything!" Paul stepped back from the bed just the same. "He's my son, for God's sake! I want to see him!"

"No!" Josh's shout was muffled against his mother's body. "No! No! No!"

"Hush, sweetheart," Hannah murmured against the top of his head. Panic rose inside her.

"What's going on in here?" Dr. Ulrich demanded as he strode in from the hall.

"I wish I knew," Paul muttered.

"What did you do that upset him?"

"Nothing! He's my son!"

Ulrich raised a hand. "Just calm down, Paul. I'm not accusing you of anything," he said quietly, turning his back to Josh and Hannah, working his way between them and Paul. "But I think it would be a good idea if you go now and come back in the morning, after Josh has had some time to rest and get his bearings."

"You're throwing me out?" Paul yelled, incredulous. "I don't believe this! After everything I've done to try to get my son back. After everything I've gone through—"

"This isn't about you, Paul," Ulrich said, his voice low. "I'm sure this is upsetting to you, but you know we have to put Josh first. We have to realize it's going to take some time to sort out what happened to him and how he feels about it. Let's you and I go down to the cafeteria and have a talk."

Paul knew a brush-off when he heard one. Ulrich was slowly backing him toward the door, away from Josh and Hannah. Shutting him out. Wasn't that the story of his life? Everything went to Hannah—the glory, the pity . . . their son.

"Jesus, Hannah," he said, "you could help a little here."

"What am I supposed to do?" She looked at him as if he were a stranger, someone to be wary of, someone to keep at bay. Anger burned inside him.

"Some support would be nice!"

"No! No!" Josh mumbled, kicking at the covers.

Dr. Ulrich took another step. "Come on, Paul. Why don't you go down to the cafeteria and get a cup of coffee?

I'll join you in a few minutes and fill you in on the examination."

"He doesn't have any reason to be afraid of me!"

"Paul, for God's sake, *please*," Hannah pleaded.

"Fine," he muttered. "Hell of a homecoming."

Tom McCoy watched from down the hall as Paul Kirkwood stormed into and out of his son's hospital room. His training dictated he try to intervene and smooth things over between family members. His training didn't apply anymore. Not here. Not between Hannah and Paul.

He had tried. Paul resented his attempts, considered it interference rather than help. In the process, Tom's feelings toward Paul had become something less than Christian. It was difficult for him to find understanding in his heart for a man who had married a jewel and treated her like dirt. Paul Kirkwood had so much and was so blind to it—two beautiful children, a comfortable home, a stable career. Hannah.

Therein lay the heart of the problem. Hannah.

Glad for the shadows in the hall, Tom leaned back against the wall and stared up at heaven. He couldn't see it, of course. There was too much in the way—physically and metaphorically.

Hannah had turned to him, the one person she thought she could trust absolutely—her priest. And her priest had committed a cardinal sin. He couldn't for the life of him admit that what he had done was wrong. He hadn't broken any vows. He had kept silent. Locked tight in his heart was the fact that he had fallen in love with Hannah Garrison.

"I could use a little help here, Lord," he murmured. But as he looked up, all he could see was a faint brown stain in the ceiling where a water pipe had once sprung a leak.

With a weary sigh he walked down the hall to Josh's room and cracked the door open a few inches. A lamp on the far side of the bed washed the room in soft topaz. Josh lay curled on his side with his thumb in his mouth, asleep. Hannah lay behind him, his small body tucked back against hers, her arm around him. She looked like an angel who had tumbled to earth, tendrils of wavy golden hair escaping their band to fall against her cheek.

The picture brought a bittersweet ache. He started to turn away from it, then Hannah opened her eyes and looked right at him. And he could no more walk away than he could stop his heart from beating.

"I just wanted to check on you two before I left," he whispered, slipping into the room. "It looks like Josh is out cold."

"The wonders of modern sedatives," Hannah murmured, raising herself on her elbow.

"How are you doing?"

"I've got Josh back. That's all that matters."

"Paul didn't stay."

Careful not to disturb Josh, she sat up and tucked her legs beneath her. "Josh didn't want him here. He acted as if . . . as if he were afraid."

The words had the bitter taste of blasphemy, as if she were somehow betraying Paul by speaking them, even though they were nothing less than the truth.

"God, I hate Garrett Wright for what he's done to us," she admitted. "He did more than take our child. Whatever problems Paul and I had before all this, at least we trusted each other. When Josh reacted to him tonight, I looked at Paul like I'd never seen him before, like I actually believed he could have . . . I don't," she whispered, even as the doubts scrolled through her mind—the lies about the van, the times he had been gone, his answering machine at the office picking up when he should have been there.

Father Tom sat on the edge of the bed, reaching out to

take her hand. She grabbed hold and hung on tighter than she meant to, wishing with all her heart he would put his arms around her and just hold her for a while. The longing that rose in her soul was for comfort and friendship and compassion. Things Tom McCoy would offer freely with no strings attached. He would never suspect her feelings had grown deeper; she would never tell him. She wouldn't risk losing what they had by asking for more than he could give her.

"Don't add more guilt to the burden, Hannah," he said softly.

She jerked her head up and looked at him, her pulse quickening at the absurd idea that he had somehow read her thoughts.

"You can't control a reaction like that. Who knows why Josh reacted badly to his father? He's frightened and confused. We don't know what he's been through. We don't know what Wright might have planted in his mind. Josh responded and you reacted to that. You're allowed; you're his mother."

"And Paul is his father. He would no more hurt Josh than he would—" *Hurt me.* Which he had done again and again; hurt her in ways that didn't leave obvious bruises or scars. "He wouldn't hurt Josh."

"I'm sure he wouldn't."

Tom raised his other hand and brushed a stray tear from beneath her eye. His fingertips threaded into the golden silk of her hair, and she turned her face to rest her cheek against the cool of his palm for just a moment. She held her breath, as if she could hold the moment within it.

"Get some sleep," he whispered, fighting the urge to lean down and press a kiss to her forehead or her lips. Her hand was still in his. He gave it a squeeze. She answered it back. "We'll talk tomorrow."

"Thanks for coming tonight. You've gone above and beyond the call through all of this."

"No," he said. "You deserve a lot more than what you've been given." And he wished like hell he could have been the man to give it to her, but he couldn't be—or so he was told. And so he turned and walked away.

And Hannah lay back down beside her child, listening to the rhythm of his breathing and wishing for things that could never be.

CHAPTER 5

There was no way of containing the news that Josh Kirkwood had been returned. The hospital staff told friends, who told other friends who worked nights and stopped into the Big Steer truck stop out on the interstate for coffee and pie. The Big Steer served as restaurant to the Super 8 motel, where four out of five rooms were occupied by reporters.

They were lying in wait like a pack of wolves when Ellen pulled into the City Center lot at five to seven. She promised to give them something later and hurried into the building, hanging a left into the law-enforcement center.

They met in a conference room that had been dubbed The War Room in the first hours of the investigation into Josh's kidnapping. A time line was taped to one long wall to keep track of everything that had happened pertaining to the case. From a fat red main artery, numerous tributaries branched out in various colors of ink. The notes that had been left by the kidnapper to taunt them were emblazoned across a white melamine message board in Mitch Holt's bold, slanted handwriting. A large cork bulletin board was covered with a map of Minnesota and one of the five-county area. The maps were bristling with pins that marked search areas.

Ellen poured herself a cup of coffee and took a seat at

the table next to Cameron. Wilhelm sat across from her, nursing the same lack-of-sleep hangover she was fighting. Sheriff Steiger had claimed the chair at the head of the table, a minor power play in an ongoing pissing contest with Mitch. Steiger was fifty, lean and tough with a narrow face and a complexion like old leather. Adhesive tape across his nose suggested he had lost a battle in the war for supremacy. The looks the two traded were stony.

As much as she disliked Steiger for the sexist jerk he was, Ellen took no pleasure in the seething enmity between the two men. A successful investigation, an investigation that would lead to a conviction, required teamwork and open lines of communication between all team members.

Mitch paced along the time line as he filled them in on Josh's exam and what had transpired later in Josh's room.

"So Paul Kirkwood is still a suspect," Wilhelm declared.

"Suspect is too strong a word," Mitch said. "Josh's reaction could have been caused by any number of reasons other than guilt on Paul's part. It could have been that Paul shares some physical characteristics with Wright. Or maybe it was the way Paul approached him or something in the tone of his voice."

"We have to tread lightly here," Ellen cautioned. "Mr. Kirkwood is already hypersensitive to the attention he's gotten. He feels victimized by the crime and by the police. If we mishandle this and he's completely innocent, we're going to be looking at lawsuits."

"I'm seeing him this morning," Mitch said. "I'll be the soul of diplomacy."

"I want in on that," Wilhelm said.

"Any progress on finding the location Wright held Megan?" Ellen asked.

"We know it wasn't his own house," Wilhelm said, trying unsuccessfully to stifle a yawn. "We know it wasn't

Christopher Priest's house, even though the initial attack took place in Priest's yard. Wright drove her somewhere."

"We're doing a records search in a fifty-mile radius," Steiger interjected. "Trying to find out if Wright owns any other property in the area."

"He could own it under another name or under a dummy business name," Cameron suggested bleakly. "Or the house could belong to his accomplice, whoever that might be."

"Well, we know now it couldn't have been Olie Swain," Mitch said. "And Karen Wright was locked up tight in the Fontaine last night."

Wilhelm raised his eyebrows. "But Paul Kirkwood, was out driving around town in the middle of the night."

"Maybe we should be looking for connections between Kirkwood and Wright," Cameron said, uncapping a fountain pen and jotting a note on his legal pad.

Mitch looked unhappy at the suggestion. "What motive could cause Paul to conspire with Garrett Wright to steal his own son? That's just fucking bizarre."

"World's full of perverts and kooks, Holt," Steiger commented, chewing on a toothpick. "You ought to know that."

The tension in the room thickened like the air before a lightning strike.

"What about that student of Wright's?" Ellen prompted, steering the conversation back on track. "Todd Childs?"

"We're checking him out, too," Steiger grumbled. "Goddamn pothead."

"And Priest?"

"Him, too."

"Priest passed a polygraph," Mitch reminded them. "He was in St. Peter Saturday. We've confirmed he spent the night in a motel because of the storm. It looks like Wright sent Megan to Priest's place knowing the professor wouldn't be home. The isolated location made it the perfect spot for an attack."

"What about the third professor involved with the Sci-Fi Cowboys?" Cameron asked.

"Phil Pickard," Mitch said. "He's on a year-long sabbatical in France."

"Wright claims he was working in the Cray building at Harris at the time Josh was abducted," Ellen said. "If we could find someone who saw him leave the building before Josh was taken—"

"Trouble is, there was hardly anyone on campus because of winter break," Mitch said. "And there's the possibility that the accomplice picked Josh up. Wright may well have been right where he says he was."

"Agent Wilhelm, I'm assuming you've got someone digging into Wright's past?" Ellen said.

He nodded and rubbed his eyes like a sleepy child.

"And we can hope to hear from the evidence techs as soon as they find anything in the stuff they confiscated from Wright's home?"

"Yes."

Ellen checked her watch and rose, fighting off a yawn herself. "I want to be the first to know."

"What about Stovich?" Steiger scowled at the prospect of having to report to a mere woman or a second-in-command or both.

She looked him square in the eye. "This is my case, Sheriff. Report to me," she said, snapping the latches on her briefcase. "Thanks, gentlemen. We're out of here. We've got a bond hearing to prepare for."

The pack had grown to a mob. Ellen made them follow her all the way to the courthouse and gave them their sound bite on the front steps with the grand facade of justice looming up behind her.

"We're overjoyed at Josh's return. This is the conclusion everyone was praying for."

"How will this affect the prosecution's case against Garrett Wright?"

"Not at all. The evidence against Dr. Wright is more than sufficient. All this shows us is that he wasn't acting alone, a suspicion we harbored all along."

"Is Josh talking?"

"Did he identify Wright?"

Ellen gave them a ghost of a smile. "We're very confident about our case."

She turned and walked away from them with Cameron falling in step beside her. They pushed through the main doors and turned up the steps to the second floor. The reporters didn't hesitate to follow, storming into the building like a human tornado, all noise and motion. Ellen couldn't help but think about what Brooks had said to her about the lack of security. *"This is a highly volatile case you've got here. Anything might happen. . . ."* She made a mental note to talk to Rudy about it. There was no sense taking unnecessary risks.

She kept her poise as the reporters' questions filled up the cavernous hallway and resounded off the high ceiling, drowning out the noise of the third-floor renovations. She let them draw their own conclusions from her cool silence, let them think she had this case in her pocket, when those same questions rattled around inside her like a pair of dice. Would Josh pick Wright out of a photo lineup? Would they get him to talk about what had happened? Or had he been so traumatized he would lock the secrets inside his mind forever?

"You're a cool one, Ms. North," Cameron said with a smile as they entered the sanctuary of the outer office.

Ellen gave him a wry look. "Never let 'em see you sweat, Mr. Reed."

She breathed a sigh of relief. This was her turf, her second home, this warren of scarred wooden desks and ancient filing cabinets that smelled of 3-In-One Oil. Portraits of county attorneys past hung high on the dingy beige walls that were waiting for the renovators. Bulletin boards sported notices and dictates from higher offices and court-related cartoons. Telephones rang ceaselessly, ignored by the people arriving for work in favor of unwrapping the layers of outerwear from their bodies. Someone had started the first pot of coffee—Phoebe, by the exotic scent of it.

The secretary who served as Ellen's assistant shunned the ordinary in most respects, a tendency immediately obvious in her choice of clothes. The standard office look for Phoebe was Holly Hobby meets Buddy Holly—cotton peasant dresses with Doc Marten shoes and black-rimmed nerd glasses. Somehow Phoebe managed to make the look work. Rudy had raised his eyebrows at her more than once, but her work was exemplary, and Ellen was her staunchest advocate.

"What's our treat this morning?" she asked, grabbing her mug off the shelf above the pot.

"Cinnamon Praline," Phoebe said, her voice muffled by the thick llama-wool poncho she was struggling out from under. She emerged with her long kinky hair a wild black cloud around her head. A tiny, breastless thing, she had dressed in filmy layers today—a tunic the color of eggplant over a skirt the color of dirt over a pair of black tights with army boots. She tossed the poncho over her chair, her brown eyes bright with excitement and fixed on Ellen. "Is it true? Is Josh back?"

"He showed up at home around midnight."

"That's so great!" she said, tears of joy welling up. Her emotions never ran far from the surface; only the sheer weight of the boots kept her feet on the floor. "Is he all right?"

Ellen weighed her words as she warmed her hands

with her coffee mug and let the scent of cinnamon tease her nose. " 'All right' might be a stretch, but he seems in good shape physically."

"Poor little kid." Phoebe dug a tissue from somewhere among the layers of her outfit and rubbed it under her reddening nose. "Imagine how scared he must have been."

"It could have been worse," Ellen said.

It could have been unspeakable. Other cases from other places went through her mind as she let herself into her office. Horrible tales of bodies found in pieces cast into drainage ditches or discarded in the woods like so much garbage for scavengers to feed on. They were so very lucky to have Josh back, talking or not. Not even the lingering feeling that it was all part of Wright's twisted game could dampen Ellen's sense of relief.

She tried to hit her office light switch with an elbow, missed, and moved on. Setting her briefcase on the floor beside her desk, she took a sip from her coffee and reached to set the mug on the cork coaster beside her blotter. The mug hit a neat stack of reports instead. Surprised, she pulled back.

She was fanatic about her desk. Her first year in Deer Lake, Phoebe had given her a plaque for Christmas that read *Persons Moving Objects On This Desk Will Be Prosecuted To The Full Extent Of The Law*. It resided in its usual spot at the front edge of the blotter. The stacks of papers and files were neat, but not quite where she had left them. All pens were in their tooled leather cup, but the cup was six inches out of place.

Must have been someone new on the cleaning staff, she rationalized as she moved the reports and unearthed the coaster. But as she shrugged out of her coat and hung it on the rack in the corner, that smoky drawl whispered in the back of her mind—*"assumptions can be very dangerous things. Your boss needs to have a word with someone about security . . ."*

A shiver skittered like a bony fingertip down the back of her neck.

"Things have taken quite an interesting turn, haven't they, Ms. North?"

Ellen wheeled around. He stood just inside the door. The light coming through the window was gray and grainy. It suited him, playing on the angles of his face. He hadn't bothered to shave, looked, in fact, as if he had yet to go to bed.

"How did you get in here?"

A smile quirked one corner of a mouth that would have looked perfect on a high-priced hooker and was somehow sexier on him. "The door was open."

Ellen went on the offensive.

"See this?" she asked, curling her hand into a fist and raising it. "Around here it's customary to make one of these and strike it against a door or door frame prior to entering another person's home or office. We call it *knocking*."

"I'll try to remember that," Brooks commented, strolling away from her.

He started on a slow circuit of the cramped room, absorbing the details of it—the framed diplomas, the well-tended plant on the credenza, the small CD player and neat rack of CDs nestled in among the law tomes in the bookcase. Everything neat and tidy, like Ellen North herself. Not a hair out of place, literally. Her hair was swept back flawlessly into a slick, no-nonsense twist his fingers itched to pull loose.

"Can I help you, Mr. Brooks?" Her tone was acid with sarcasm.

"I came to make an appointment."

"I have an assistant for that. And before you bypassed her desk, you walked past our receptionist, who could also have taken care of you. You actually could have saved yourself a trip—we do have telephones."

"They're ringing off their hooks today." He watched her from the corner of his eye as he circled around behind her desk.

She clearly didn't like him trespassing. She stood with her arms crossed over the front of her smart charcoal suit, her lips pressed into a thin line, her gray eyes narrowed slightly. He could tell she was building up a fine head of steam, and yet she kept it contained inside the pretty, polished exterior.

"I understand the boy showed up last night."

"His name is Josh."

"Reappeared like magic, I'm told."

"Told by whom?"

He chose not to answer. Looking away from her, he noticed the crystal candy dish on the upper right-hand corner of the desk, filled with polite little after-dinner mints in pastel colors. He fished out a green one and met her eyes again as he placed it on his tongue.

"The bond hearing is this morning?"

Ellen had to force her gaze away from his mouth, but jerking it upward was a mistake, because there were his eyes—watchful, unblinking . . . amused.

Picking up her briefcase, she skirted around him. "Yes, the bond hearing is this morning. I'm very busy. If you'd care to make an appointment, stop and do so on your way out."

Jay ignored the dismissal. He surrendered the space behind the desk and sauntered back to the bookcase, scanning the titles of her CD collection. Quiet, orderly music: Mozart, Vivaldi. New Age artists: Philip Aaberg, William Ackerman. Background music. Nothing that could distract her from her work. Nothing that could hint at the woman behind that cool control. The lack of clues only served to intrigue him further.

"You can call me Jay," he offered.

"I can also call security and have you thrown out."

The threat bounced off. "Think he'll make bail?"

"Not if I have anything to say about it."

She settled herself in her chair and slipped on a pair of scholarly-looking reading glasses. If her intent was to hide or tone down her femininity, she failed miserably. The spectacles were more a counterpoint to her looks than a cover. He could imagine leaning across that neat desk and sliding them off her face or kissing her and watching her surprise as they fogged up.

He had the most devilish urge to rattle her, but he would keep it in check. At least for the moment. He was already pushing his luck with her, though he could have argued that was a vital part of the process. He wanted to know more about her; she wasn't the kind of woman who offered those insights freely. On the other hand, it would be essential for him to have her cooperation if he decided to make this case his next best-seller.

It had all the ingredients—a fascinating criminal, sympathetic victims, a setting that would draw readers in; a crime with complications, twists, the extras, the side stories that elevated it above the level of news story. Most of all, it had captured his attention as nothing had in a long time. He didn't know yet what approach he would take or even if he would do it. All he really knew at this point was that he wanted to know more, that he needed the distraction—badly.

He eased himself down into the visitor's chair. "He stays in the can, it shortens your prep time for the probable-cause hearing."

"I'm not concerned."

Picking up a purple glass paperweight from atop a stack of reports, he curled his hand around it as if it were a baseball and he was fixing to throw a slider. The slider was a great pitch. His personal favorite. It looked as if it were going one way, then exploded in another.

"You could set a reachable bail," he suggested. "Buy yourself a little time."

Her eyebrows rose above the rims of her glasses. "And release a kidnapper, a man who brutally assaulted a police officer? You must be insane."

"He *allegedly* committed those crimes. What happened to the presumption of innocence?"

"It's for jurors and fools. And if you quote me on that, I'll sue your ass eight ways from Sunday. I'm not about to let Garrett Wright out of jail."

"What's he gonna do if he gets out?" Jay needled. "Steal another kid? I don't think so. He's smarter than that . . . if he's your man at all."

"He's our man."

"So who brought Josh home?"

Ellen bit down on her reply. He was baiting her and she was sitting here and taking it. Here, in her own office. What the hell was he doing here, anyway? Pumping her for information as if he had a personal stake in the case, as if *he* were Wright's attorney. Denny Enberg should have been sitting in that chair making that same argument. She glanced at the message slips to see if any of them bore the name of Wright's attorney. None did.

"Other than dispensing unsolicited advice, do you have a purpose for bothering me, Mr. Brooks?"

The pirate grin stretched across his mouth. "I bother you, Ms. North? Why is that?"

"It could have something to do with the fact that you're an extremely annoying person."

He splayed a hand across his chest. "Who, me? *Time* magazine said I'm loved by millions."

"So is McDonald's, but you won't find me eating there. I'm a woman of discriminating taste."

The grin curled into a smile that was nothing short of feral. He came out of the chair and leaned across the desk, planting his hands on her blotter.

"I can see that you are, Ms. North," he said in a voice like black velvet. "A woman of incomparable style and taste. Sharp-tongued. Sharp-witted. Makes me wonder what you're doing in a nowhere place, in a nothing job like this."

Ellen resisted the urge to grab her letter opener and stab him with it. For all the satisfaction it would have brought, she had to prepare for court and didn't have time to deal with the mess. She met his gaze with a cool look as she rose slowly from her chair to take away his dramatic height advantage.

"I don't have to justify my life to you. Nor do I have to put up with you, Mr. Brooks. If you're here because you want to do a book about this case, I have no intention of cooperating. I'm asking you to leave. I suggest you do so, or I *will* call security, and won't that do wonders for your image as a beloved personality—front-page photos of you being physically removed from these offices."

Instead of the expected show of bad temper, he stood back and regarded her with a look that suggested he was proud of her. Ellen wanted to throw something at him.

"I look forward to watching you in court, Ms. North. I'll make that appointment on my way out."

As he strolled out, it seemed as if all the energy in the room went with him. Feeling limp, Ellen sank back down onto her chair.

Phoebe burst into the office, eyes as big as saucers, her cheeks glowing. She shut the door and pressed back against it.

"Ohmygod!" she gasped. "I'm in *love*!"

"Again?"

She swept into a chair, perching on the edge of it. "Do you know who was just in here?"

"Jay Butler Brooks."

"Jay Butler Brooks! He is *such* a babe! He was number seventeen on *People* magazine's list of the twenty most intriguing people of the year." She brought herself up short, out of breath, her brows drawing together as the obvious dawned on her belatedly. "What was he doing in here?"

"Annoying me," Ellen groused, digging through her briefcase for the complaint forms against Wright. "You forgot 'pain in the butt' in your tribute."

"I'm not even going to try to turn that into a sexual reference," Phoebe said. "Suffice it to say, I would sit still and let him annoy me all day long if I could just look at him."

"Phoebe, you amaze me," Ellen complained, scanning the pages of the document. "You're an intelligent, articulate, educated woman panting after a man who—"

"—is a total hot babe. Intelligence and hormones are not mutually exclusive, Ellen. You should remember that."

"What's that supposed to mean?"

Phoebe refrained from comment, trooping to the door in her clunky boots. "He made an appointment to see you later. Is he interested in the case? Is he going to write a book?"

"I don't know and I don't want to know," Ellen said stubbornly. "Cancel the appointment. I'm sure I have something more important to do at that time."

"I don't think you'll want to cancel," her secretary warned.

"And why is that?"

"He's bringing the state attorney general with him."

Surely, no bond hearing in the history of Park County, Minnesota, had ever attracted so much attention. The courtroom was full, observers packed on the benches like sardines in a tin. Jay stayed at the back of the mob, timing his entrance so attention would be focused away from him. Wearing a baseball cap pulled low over his shades, he slipped in and took a spot on the aisle. The reporters leaped to their feet, craning their necks for a better look at Garrett Wright as he made his entrance with his attorney.

Wright and his lawyer were flanked by a deputy and the Park County sheriff himself—Russ Steiger.

Another politician in search of a photo op. No sheriff would ever have lowered himself to escorting prisoners, unless he hoped to gain something from the visibility of the case. Wright wasn't even Steiger's bust. According to the *Minneapolis Star Tribune*, Steiger's bust was a 36C who went by the name of Paige Price and didn't mind playing a little horizontal hokeypokey to get her story for the channel-seven news.

Ellen North and her associate Reed had already taken their seats at the prosecution's table. She didn't look up as Wright entered the courtroom, as if she couldn't be bothered to give him the least consideration. She kept her attention on the papers she was idly reviewing, glancing up only when the judge emerged from his chambers.

Everyone in the room rose on command as the Honorable Victor Franken took the bench. Franken was small and bald and misshapen, with an unhealthy yellow cast to his skin. He looked like a hundred-year-old hand puppet in his long black robe, like Yoda from *Star Wars*. He banged his gavel and banged it again, looking secretly pleased at the way people jumped reflexively at the sound.

"This is *The State versus Dr. Garrett Wright*," he croaked, his voice rusted by age. "Who am I dealing with here?" He squinted at the defense as if he hadn't just spent half an hour in chambers with the lawyers involved and grumbled, "Dennis Enberg," then turned his wizened countenance on the prosecution. "Ellen North. Who's that with you?" he barked, and pulled his pince-nez off the withered red nub of his nose, then rubbed them against his robe.

"Assistant County Attorney Cameron Reed, Your Honor," Reed said loudly, rising halfway from his chair.

Franken waved Ellen's associate back to his seat. "Let's have it, Miss North."

Wright and his lawyer were officially served with the complaint. Jay smiled to himself. *Good move, Ms. North*. Having the complaint presented now meant it had to be read aloud into the record. The clerk of the court, a matronly sort who likely had a brood of children of her own, read the charges, one after another after another. Kidnapping, denying parental rights, kidnapping a police officer and causing great bodily harm, attempted homicide, assault, assault, assault—enough counts and variations of assault to sound as if Wright had attacked half the town.

While she did her best to keep the emotion from her voice, the clerk couldn't seem to keep her throat from tightening or her eyes from shooting daggers at the defendant as she read the bit about the bloodstained sheet that had been wrapped around Megan O'Malley—bloodstains that matched Josh Kirkwood's blood type.

Round one went to the prosecution. The members of the media soaked it all in—the allegations stacked one on top of another, Mitch Holt's report of the events that had taken place Saturday night, up to and including the chase and Wright's apprehension.

The defense was allowed to make no rebuttal. Enberg sat scratching the arm of his wool jacket, looking as if he were fighting a losing battle with acid indigestion.

When the clerk finished reading, Franken fixed the accused with a baleful glare. "Dr. Wright, do you understand the charges being made against you?"

"Yes," Wright said softly.

"Don't mumble!"

"Yes, Your Honor!"

"I want you to know that, in the eyes of the court, you are innocent until the State proves your guilt beyond a reasonable doubt." The glare seemed to suggest otherwise, but, then, it could have been cataracts or constipation causing the judge's sour expression. "You will have the opportunity to plead guilty or not guilty. You'll have the right to a trial. If there's a trial, you will have the right to hear the State's evidence, to cross-examine the State's witnesses, and to present witnesses of your own. You may testify on your own behalf or remain silent. You already have a lawyer, so we don't need to talk about that.

"Did you get all that?" Franken shouted.

"Yes, Your Honor."

Ellen rose. Jay leaned to the right for a better look down the aisle. Even through the bars of the gate that kept the spectators at bay, he caught a nice glimpse of leg. She never cast a glance at the gallery, giving the impression that they meant nothing to her. Her only interest was her job—to bring the hobnailed boot of justice down squarely on Garrett Wright's head.

"Based on the complaint and the statements of the officers involved, Your Honor, the State requests the defendant be booked and a date set for the omnibus hearing."

"The purpose of the omnibus hearing, Dr. Wright," Franken explained, "is to hear all issues that can be determined before trial—evidentiary issues, pretrial motions— and determine whether or not there is probable cause to bind you over for trial."

Franken drew a wheezing breath to replenish his withered lungs and fell into a coughing fit, nearly disappearing behind the bench as he hunched over. Everyone in the room seemed to hold a breath, waiting for his tuft of cotton-white hair to vanish as he crumpled to the floor in a small, dead heap. The bailiff peered around the edge of the massive bench. Franken popped up again, like a moldy jack-in-the-box, and made an impatient gesture at his clerk.

"Omnibus hearing on Tuesday, February first?" she suggested.

"Let's see about the bail."

"Your Honor, in view of the seriousness of the charges," Ellen said, "the State requests bail in the amount of one million dollars."

A gasp went up from the gallery. Pens scrambled frantically across paper. The murmur of voices into mini-cassette recorders was like the low hum of an engine. Franken banged his gavel.

Enberg hopped up from his chair. "Your Honor, that's outrageous! My client is a professor at one of the top private colleges in the country. He works with juvenile offenders. He is a well-respected member of this community—"

"Who happens to be charged with heinous crimes," Franken said.

"He has ties to the community, and the charges are ludicrous—"

"And he was apprehended after a lengthy chase. Save it for the hearing, Dennis," Franken ordered. "He's a flight risk. I'm setting bail in the amount of five hundred thousand dollars, cash. Omnibus hearing on the—the—" He shook a crooked finger at his clerk. "Whatever Renee said."

"Tuesday, February first."

"The defendant shall be booked, photographed, and finger-printed," Franken stated. "And he shall undergo a physical exam for scratches, bruises, et cetera, and surrender samples of blood and hair for analysis and comparison with evidence."

He cracked the gavel again, signaling the end of the proceedings. The reporters jumped up and scrambled over one another to get to the door or to get to the lawyers or Paul Kirkwood, who had positioned himself directly behind the prosecutors. Jay eased out of his seat and took a position at the back of the pack.

"He should rot in jail," Kirkwood said. "After what he put my son through. After what he put us all through."

"If Garrett Wright is guilty, then who returned Josh?"

"Has your son identified Garrett Wright as his kidnapper?"

"Is there any truth to the rumor the police are still considering you a suspect?"

Kirkwood's face flushed. His eyes were bright with temper. "I had *nothing* to do with my son's disappearance. I am one hundred percent innocent. Any accusation to the contrary is just another example of the incompetence of the Deer Lake police department."

"Let's break it up, folks!" the white-haired bailiff called. "We've got business to conduct in this courtroom!"

As the circus moved out into the hall, Jay took a seat, keeping his head down as he jotted notes and avoided recognition. As much as he enjoyed his fame and fortune, there was something to be said for anonymity. Particularly now.

The case had drawn him here. He wanted to be able to take it all in without the interference discovery would bring. Unfortunately, he wasn't going to be able to get the kind of access he wanted without using his name like a pry bar.

He took one last look at Ellen North, who sat in conference with her associate at the prosecution's table. He speculated as to what he might get there besides a hot tongue and a cold shoulder. A challenge, some insight, a kick in the ego.

He knew what he wanted. And he could guaran-goddamn-tee it she wouldn't give it to him without a fight.

CHAPTER 6

"The goddamn lawyers strike again."

"I can't believe that bitch asked for a million dollars' bail. A million dollars! Shit!"

"*Ms. North* was only doing her job," Christopher Priest said. He stood at the front of the classroom, a small man with big glasses and bad taste in clothes. His students sometimes teased him about perpetuating the stereotypical image of computer people as nerds, but their comments and suggestions went unheeded. There were certain advantages to the image. Unfounded assumptions could be useful things.

"*Her job*," Tyrell Mann jeered. Even his posture was disrespectful. He sprawled back in his chair with his long arms crossed over the front of his Chicago Bulls starter jacket. "Her job is to fuckin' pin this on somebody. Fuckin' cops would'a nailed a brother for it, but there ain't hardly no niggers in this fuckin' hick town."

"That's not logical, Tyrell," Priest said, unaffected by the bravado or the language.

He had helped found the Sci-Fi Cowboys. Even though there had been encouragement to expand the program, they kept it at a manageable level—ten young men from Minneapolis inner-city schools, teenagers whose brushes with the law ran the gamut from gang activity to grand-theft auto. The point of the program was to bring the

boys' positive qualities of intelligence to the surface, to
interest them in science and engineering through innova-
tive projects with computers and robotics.

The boys had requested this emergency meeting—
a logistical headache that required a dozen phone calls to
schools to get permission for the boys to leave in the middle of the day, and to probation officers to find one willing
to drive them down to Deer Lake. At least the van simpli-
fied matters somewhat. Fund-raising and contributions
had helped pay for a used Ford van four years ago.

"Think," Priest said. "If the authorities were looking
for a scapegoat, would they choose a man like Dr. Wright?"

"Hell no, but that loser they dragged in from the
hockey rink offed himself—"

J. R. Andersen leaned forward in his seat. His rap sheet
included charges for raiding bank accounts electronically.
"Professor, are you saying it *is* logical to believe Dr.
Wright did it?"

The others in the group reacted in an explosion of
sound. Priest waited for the fury to die down.

"Of course not. I'm asking you to look at the system
without emotion coloring your perceptions. The police
apprehended someone they believe to be involved in the
crime." He held up a finger to ward off the automatic pro-
tests. "You are all well aware that the next step in the process belongs to the county attorney's office. It's Ms.
North's job—"

"Fuckin' bitch."

"Tyrell . . ."

Tyrell unfolded his long arms and spread them wide.
"A *million*?"

"A lesson in bargaining. Always ask for more than you
think you can get. The judge cut that number in half."

"Five hundred large. Where we supposed to raise that
kind of green?"

"I'm sure Dr. Wright will appreciate your intentions,"

Priest said. "But no one expects you guys to raise that kind of money."

"I could get it," J.R. offered with a twisted grin, cracking his knuckles with dramatic flair.

The professor ignored the inference. Crime was never rewarded within the group in any way, not even as a joke. "If you want to show your support, there are things you can do. You've got brains. Use them."

"Our name," J.R. said, his gaze sharp on the professor. "We're a media draw."

"Very good, J.R."

"We could start a defense fund for the Doc."

"And the news crews will hear about it and make a big deal about us—"

"And the money will come rolling in."

A knock at the door drew Priest's attention away from the conversation.

"Professor?" Ellen North inched the door open. "I'm sorry to disturb you. I was told you didn't have a class this hour."

"I don't." He stepped into the hall and closed the door behind him. "The Cowboys called an emergency meeting. They were understandably upset over Dr. Wright's arrest, then they heard the news reports of this morning's bail hearing . . ."

He offered a little shrug that sent his shrunken wool sweater crawling up his midriff. "You have to understand, they're not very trusting of the system."

Ellen reserved comment. From her perspective the system wasn't the problem with juvenile offenders, but she hadn't come to Harris College for a philosophical argument.

She wanted to meet and speak with Wright's friends and colleagues herself, face-to-face to look for some hint of doubt or unease in them. It seemed impossible that

Wright could be so twisted without giving someone close to him a clue.

But wasn't that what everyone in Deer Lake wanted to think? That a monster had to look like a monster and walk like a monster and talk like a monster so they could see the monster coming? If evil came in plain clothes and a pretty face, then evil could be anyone anywhere.

"I wanted to ask you a couple of questions about the night Josh Kirkwood disappeared," she said. "It won't take long, but if you'd rather I come back—"

"I heard he's been returned unharmed." Priest raised a bony hand to rub his chin. "A fascinating turn of events. Obviously, Dr. Wright didn't return the child—not that I believe Garrett took Josh in the first place."

"We believe otherwise, Professor."

He put his head a little on one side and looked at her as if he were an android attempting to decipher the illogical workings of the human mind. "Do you truly believe, or are you following a path of least resistance?"

"Believe me, prosecuting a well-respected member of the community is hardly a path of least resistance."

"However, he *is* the bird in the hand, so to speak."

"Just because there's still one in the bush doesn't mean this one isn't guilty," Ellen pointed out. Priest just blinked at her, frowning the way he probably frowned at students who couldn't grasp the latest computer language.

"I want to clarify a couple of points about that night," she said. "You told the police you were here working."

"In the computer center, yes. Garrett and I have a group of students working together on a project involving learning and perception. One of those students was here with me."

"Mike Chamberlain," Ellen said. "Whom you sent on an errand around five o'clock—an errand he never accomplished because he was involved in a car accident."

"That's correct."

"The accident that kept Hannah Garrison at the hospital when she would have been picking Josh up from the hockey rink."

Priest looked down at his loafers. "Yes," he said softly. "If I hadn't sent Mike out at that precise moment, perhaps none of this would have happened. You can't imagine how that makes me feel. I think the world of Hannah. It was such a relief to hear she'd got Josh back—unharmed."

The professor's cheeks colored as he spoke of Hannah Garrison. Interesting. And a little odd. He didn't seem the sort for romantic crushes. Or perhaps the shy glance at his shoes was something else altogether.

Megan O'Malley didn't believe that car accident had been an accident at all, but rather the first move in the kidnappers' game. Was the involvement of Priest's student in that car wreck accidental, or was that all part of the plan as well? If one professor could be involved, why not two?

"After Mike Chamberlain left, you were here alone?"

Priest's eyes narrowed a fraction. His skinny shoulders pulled back. "I thought I was past needing an alibi, Ms. North. I voluntarily took a lie detector test on Sunday."

"I'm aware of that, Professor," Ellen said without apology. "Did you see Dr. Wright here that evening?"

"No. I wish I could say I did, but I was in the machine room in the computer center, and Garrett was in his office."

"So he claims."

"Only the guilty live their lives with alibis in mind."

"You and Dr. Wright are friends. You work together, founded the Sci-Fi Cowboys together. You don't happen to jointly own any property, do you? A cabin, maybe?"

"We're friends and colleagues, Ms. North, not husband and wife."

The door behind him opened, and a tall youth with angry dark eyes glared out over the professor's head. "You got a problem here, Professor?"

"No, Tyrell. There's no problem," Priest said evenly.

Tyrell kept his gaze fixed hard on Ellen. "Hey, you that bitch lawyer."

"Tyrell . . ."

Priest turned and attempted to contain the trouble to the classroom, an effort as futile as trying to shove the cork back in a champagne bottle. The door swung wide and two more members of the Sci-Fi Cowboys stared out, arrogant and indignant and big enough to pick their mentor up and set him aside like a child.

"Dr. Wright is innocent!"

"He's gonna kick your ass in court!"

"Guys! Please go back to your seats!" Priest ordered. They stared past him as if he were invisible, their attention on the woman who was, in their minds, an enemy.

Ellen held her ground. She had tried enough hardened criminals of sixteen and seventeen to know the rules. Show no fear. Show no emotion. With hormones at high tide, the kids had enough emotion for everyone—all of it negative, ready to boil up into violence.

"Dr. Wright will have his chance to prove his innocence in court."

"Yeah, right."

"Court didn't give me a chance. Court screwed my ass."

Priest frowned at her.

"You've got your hands full, Professor," Ellen said. "I'll let you go. If anything occurs to you that may be of help to the case, please call me or Chief Holt."

"When hell freezes over, bitch!" the one called Tyrell shouted as she turned and walked away.

The neighborhood to the south of the Harris College campus had once been a town in its own right. Harrisburg had competed with Deer Lake for commerce and popula-

tion during the latter part of the nineteenth century. But
Deer Lake had won the railroad and the title of county
seat, and Harrisburg had lost its identity. At some point,
what was left of it had been annexed by the Deer Lake
municipality, and someone had slapped it with the nick-
name Dinkytown.

The old buildings on the main drag housed businesses
that targeted the college crowd. The buildings were
shabby, but the signs were trendy and artsy. The Clip
Joint Hair and Tanning salon, the Tome Bookstore, the
Leaning Tower of Pizza, Green World—a nature and
New Age shop—the Leaf and Bean Coffee House, a mix
of bars, restaurants, and tiny art galleries.

Ellen headed for an old creamery building on the north
end. The Pack Rat was a secondhand shop crammed with
a boggling array of junk. Racks of "vintage" clothes from
the sixties and seventies crowded the front of the room. A
hand-lettered sign above them read *Blast From the Past!*
Ellen scowled at the thought that anything she might have
worn in high school was now considered nostalgic.

She worked her way back through the haphazard displays of outdated textbooks and Harris mementos that
alumni had undoubtedly trucked out of their basements
and attics to make room for more timely junk. The clerk
behind the counter was a large girl with a shock of purple
hair, black eye shadow, and a ruby stud in the side of her
nose. She was engaged in animated conversation with a
tall young man as slender as a rope, stoop-shouldered and
rusty-haired. He wore the scraggly chin whiskers that
passed for a beard with the grunge crowd and sucked on a
cigarette with serious purpose. The pair of them caught
sight of Ellen simultaneously and gave her the kind of
look that suggested they were more interested in making
small talk than money.

"I'm looking for Todd Childs," Ellen said.

"I'm Todd." He tapped the ash off his cigarette into a tin ashtray with a plastic hula dancer perched on the rim.

"Ellen North. I'm with the county attorney's office. I'd like to have a few minutes of your time if I could."

He took a last deep drag, crushed the cigarette out, and blew the smoke out his nostrils on a sigh of disgust. "I was just leaving. I've got a class in half an hour."

"It won't take long."

She watched his face as he weighed the merits of denying her. He exchanged a look with Vampira behind the counter. Behind his round-rimmed glasses his pupils were dilated, large ink-black spots rimmed by thin lines of color. Steiger called him a pothead. The scent that underscored the cigarette smoke on him was unmistakable. But smoking a little grass was a long way from being an accessory to the kind of crimes Garrett Wright had committed.

"Clock's ticking," she said with a phony smile.

Todd heaved another sigh. "All right, fine. Let's go back in the office."

He led the way through the maze to a room the size of a broom closet, where he took a seat between piles of junk on the desk. The only chair was a dirty green beanbag. Ellen gave it a dubious glance and leaned a shoulder against the door frame.

Wright's student jumped on the offensive. "The charges against Dr. Wright are so bogus."

"The police caught him fleeing the scene."

He shook his head, fishing in the pocket of his flannel shirt for another Marlboro. "No way. It was some kind of frame job or something."

"You know Dr. Wright that well?"

"I'm a psych major," he said, cigarette bobbing on his lip. "I've spent the last two years of my life immersed in the workings of the human mind."

"So are you the next Sigmund Freud or the next Carl Jung?"

He kept his eyes on her as he lit up and took the first drag. "Freud was a pervert. Garrett Wright is not."

"I admire your loyalty, Todd, but I'm afraid it's misplaced."

He shook his head, his stubbornness manifesting itself in the set of his mouth, a tight hyphen encircled by the ratty goatee. "He would have to be a total sociopath to do what you say he did. No way. We would have known."

"Isn't that part of sociopathic behavior? The ability to fool the people around you into thinking you're perfectly normal?"

The cigarette came up in a hand that wasn't quite steady. He took another puff and looked away.

"You realize there's a strong possibility you'll be called to testify at the hearing next week," Ellen said.

"Oh, man . . ."

"You were with Dr. Wright Saturday morning when Agent O'Malley came to his office. You were a part of the conversation when Dr. Wright and Agent O'Malley were discussing her driving out to Christopher Priest's home. You told the police you left Dr. Wright's office around one-fifteen and didn't see Dr. Wright again that day. You'll have to say that in court."

He banded one arm around his skinny midsection as if he had suddenly developed a stomachache. "Fuck."

"The truth is the truth, Todd," Ellen murmured, caught between sympathy and suspicion. Was he reluctant because Wright was his mentor or because Wright was his partner in crime and he now saw the whole thing unraveling around them? "Think of it this way—you won't actually be testifying *against* Dr. Wright. It's not as if you saw him commit a crime . . . is it, Todd?"

His answer was a long time coming. He stared at the wall, at a Magic Eye calendar that looked as if someone had squirted out ketchup and mustard in no discernible pattern. Ellen wondered if he saw the hidden picture. She didn't. Only the guilty knew the secret. Only the guilty could see the pattern through the chaos.

"No," he said at last.

"I'll let you get to that class." She straightened from the door and started to turn, then looked back at him. "Can you tell me where you were last night around midnight?"

"In bed. Alone." He tossed his half-finished cigarette into an abandoned coffee cup. "Where were you?"

She faked a smile. "One of the perks of the job—I get to ask all the questions."

The scent of smoke lingered on her coat. Ellen sniffed at a lapel and frowned as she wound her way through the outer office to Phoebe's desk.

"Shouldn't your generation be smart enough not to smoke cigarettes?" she complained.

"Yes, but we're largely without focus and grounded in the disillusionment of the times, so . . ." She shrugged, screwing her pixie face into a look of apology.

"Be sure Todd Childs gets a subpoena. And please call Mitch and tell him if he brings Childs in for questioning again, I want to watch."

"Gotcha." Like a kaleidoscope image, Phoebe's features rearranged themselves again, blooming into a look of excitement. "You've got a full house," she said, hooking a thumb in the direction of Ellen's office.

Realization dawned with a sick thud in her stomach. Appointment time. "Oh, God," she groaned. "I must have led a very wicked past life."

"I'd like to lead a wicked present life," Phoebe said. "You could pass that information along to Mr. Gorgeous Blue Eyes if you'd like."

Ellen shook her head and let herself into her office. The room seemed much too small for the size of the egos present. She had the wild feeling that if she opened the window to alleviate the pressure, she would be sucked out and dumped in the snow two stories down.

"Sorry I'm late," she said, setting her briefcase down and shrugging out of her coat. "I've got a lot of legwork to do before the hearing next week."

"You couldn't make Reed do it?" Rudy groused.

"I'm lead prosecutor. I'd damn well better know who I'm dealing with."

Brooks smiled at her, the kind of secret, knowing smile lovers share. Ellen scowled at him and took her seat behind the desk.

"We understand perfectly, Ellen," Bill Glendenning said magnanimously.

The state attorney general sat in one visitor's chair. The eyes behind the spectacles could easily have been mistaken for kind, but she knew better. Bill Glendenning was a shrewd man with a taste for power. She admired and respected him but was careful to temper that admiration with common sense. He was at the top of the food chain; he hadn't got there by being benevolent.

Rudy hovered behind him, too wired to sit down even if there had been a chair available for him. Unable to contain his excitement at having Glendenning in the offices two days running, he paced, his face glowing with zeal or a fever. He pulled a rumpled handkerchief out of his pants pocket and dabbed at his forehead.

"I'm sure I don't need to tell you, Ellen, we have a very unusual situation in this case," Glendenning said in a fatherly voice.

"No, you don't need to tell me." She resented the Ward Cleaver act, but she was careful to keep that resentment out of her reply. Instead, she rose from her chair to counteract the idea that she was a child to be lectured. Keeping every move casual, she stepped around the end of her desk and leaned a hip against it, standing with her arms crossed loosely.

"The abduction itself was an aberration," Glendenning went on. "Things like that don't happen in Deer Lake—or so we all like to think. The fact that it *did* happen here has drawn the focus of the nation. They see it as a metaphor for our times. Isn't that so, Jay?"

Jay blinked at the sound of his name, breaking the trance he had fallen into staring at Ellen North's legs. The lady had a fine set of pegs on her—infinitely more worthy of his attention than Bill Glendenning's pointless pontificating. The attorney general was in this for himself, pure and simple. He was well aware that Jay's name was currently white-hot, and like any politician, Bill Glendenning would gladly bask in the warmth if he could. He wanted a piece of the action, all of the credit, and as much publicity as he could grab. *A metaphor for our times.*

"That's a fact, sir." Jay nodded.

"It's a story bigger than Deer Lake, bigger than all of us," Glendenning went on, shamelessly plagiarizing the words Jay had dazzled him with two nights ago over whiskey and cigars. "Ellen, you understand that, which is part of the reason Rudy entrusted you with this case."

Rudy beamed at the mention of his name, an expression that crashed in the next instant.

"I was taught to put cases on even ground," Ellen said. "I won't approach this case any differently because of the circumstances or because the man who stands accused is someone no one would have suspected."

Impatience flashed behind Glendenning's Roosevelt glasses.

"I'm doing my job," Ellen went on calmly. "My job is to put away Garrett Wright. I can't afford to lose my focus on that end or be distracted by a bigger picture. I can't stop people from taking an interest in this case or dissecting it as a 'metaphor for our times,' but I can't let that become a part of my agenda."

Rudy was turning burgundy from his throat up. He stood behind Glendenning, his eyes bugging out as if he were being choked. "But, Ellen—"

"Is absolutely right," Jay drawled, smiling inwardly at the reactions. Ellen's look was wary. Glendenning scrambled to regroup. Behind him, Rudy Stovich pretended a coughing fit. "Lady Justice is blind, not looking to get her good side in front of the camera."

"My point exactly," Glendenning said, leaning over toward Jay like a buddy on a bar stool. "This is precisely why Ellen is the one to try this case."

"That's why I chose her," Rudy interjected, hooking a finger inside his collar and tugging at the figurative noose around his neck. "I knew from the start she was the one for the job."

Ellen checked her watch instead of rolling her eyes. "Forgive my bluntness, but I have to be in court soon. What does any of this have to do with Mr. Brooks?"

His blue eyes twinkled with suppressed amusement. One corner of his mouth kicked up. He sat with his legs stretched out in front of him and crossed at the ankles. He had made concessions for this meeting. The jeans and denim shirt had been traded in for a button-down blue oxford and khakis. The parka had been replaced by a navy blazer tailored to emphasize the set of his shoulders. But he still hadn't shaved, and his silk tie was loose at the throat. All in all, he looked as if he had been rolled by thugs on his way home from a Chi-O mixer.

"As I'm sure you are well aware, Ellen," Glendenning said, "Mr. Brooks is a fixture in the ranks of true crime best-sellers. His abilities as an author speak for themselves."

"I'm sure they do," Ellen said dryly.

"Justifiable Homicide," Rudy spouted, trying to wedge

himself back into the conversation. "That's a personal favorite of mine."

Glendenning shot him a quelling look over his shoulder. "We're all familiar with Mr. Brooks's work—"

"Actually, I'm not," Ellen lied. "As a prosecutor, I find the growing mania for true crime disturbing and tawdry." She offered a smile of false apology to Jay. "No offense intended, Mr. Brooks."

He rubbed a hand across his mouth to hide his grin. "None taken, Ms. North."

Bill Glendenning's jaw tightened to the quality of granite. Behind him, Rudy looked horrified.

"Jay has taken an interest in this case," Glendenning said. "As a story that will touch the hearts and minds of people everywhere. He has expressed a particular interest in presenting it from our point of view."

Ellen stared at Jay Butler Brooks, disgust twisting inside her. He was sitting beside the state attorney general. Bill and Jay, best pals. Jay Butler Brooks, current darling of the media, a man with money, a man with clout in the publishing world and in Hollywood; a man people would trust just because they had read about him in *People* and *Vanity Fair* and had come to the ridiculous conclusion that they knew him. Bill Glendenning, who would gladly use the publicity such an association would bring to help catapult himself into the governor's office.

Slowly, she retreated back behind the desk on the excuse of sticking papers into her briefcase. "*'Our point of view.'* What exactly is that supposed to mean?"

Brooks pushed himself up in his chair and leaned forward, his forearms on his thighs. Ellen could feel his gaze sharpen on her, but she refused to raise her eyes to meet his.

"A small-town justice system takes on a big-time case," he said. "The last bastion of decency in America assaulted by the poisonous evil of our modern society. This case has captured the attention and imagination of millions. I know it certainly intrigues me."

Ellen bit back a dozen scathing remarks. The case intrigued him, and if it intrigued him enough, he would capitalize on it. Suddenly the reporters who had been feeding off this tragedy seemed like small fish. The shark had just come into the waters.

News was one thing. That Jay Butler Brooks would twist this into entertainment and make a fortune off it was reprehensible beyond words. She wanted to tell him so, but there he sat with his good friend the attorney general and her immediate boss hovering behind them—the nerd boy allowed to tag along with the cool guys because of his potential usefulness.

"What does this have to do with me?" she asked tightly.

"Oh, I am particularly intrigued by your role in all this, Ms. North," he said. "Prosecuting attorney Ellen North leading the charge for justice."

She jerked her head up and stared at him while every internal alarm system she had went off. His slow smile should have come complete with canary feathers sticking out the corners of his mouth.

"I'm just doing my job, Mr. Brooks. I'm not Joan of Arc."

"That's all a matter of perspective."

"Nevertheless, I'm not comfortable with the analogy."

"Ellen, you're too modest," Glendenning said.

She was tempted to remind him that Joan had been burned at the stake, but there was the chance he already knew it. The implications of that made her vaguely queasy.

"Jay has expressed an interest in following the case from the perspective of the prosecution," Glendenning said again. "I've assured him you'll be accommodating."

"Excuse me?" Ellen gaped at Bill Glendenning. "I'll be accommodating in what way?"

"Now, Ellen," he said, returning to that patronizing tone that set her teeth on edge, "we're not suggesting anything unethical. Jay won't be privy to anything sensitive. He simply wants a chance to watch you work. He doesn't need our blessing to do that, but he asked for it anyway, as a courtesy."

As a courtesy that would get him into the good graces of the state attorney general, which would damn well guarantee him access. No, he didn't need permission to watch the case from afar, but stroking Glendenning would grease wheels no reporter could even venture near, and it put Ellen in the untenable position of having to act the gracious hostess or run the risk of angering the powers that held the strings on her job.

The complexity and diabolical qualities of this move hit a nerve inside her and ground on it like a stiletto heel. Her temper flared and she clenched her jaw against the need to let it go. She shut her briefcase slowly, deliberately, the click of each lock as loud as a gunshot in the silence of the room.

She leveled a gaze on Jay Butler Brooks that had turned better men to ashes. "No, you obviously don't need my permission, Mr. Brooks. And it's a good thing because I'd throw you out of here in a heartbeat.

"I'm due in court," she announced with a cursory nod to Glendenning and Stovich. "If you gentlemen will excuse me."

She expected a reprimand, but none came as she walked out of the office. Or perhaps it was that she simply couldn't hear above the roar of her blood pressure in her ears.

Phoebe jumped up from her desk, wide-eyed, abandoning Quentin Adler in midcomplaint.

"Phoebe!" he wailed.

She made a face at the grating sound but ignored him, her attention on Ellen. "What did they want?"

"To make my life a living hell," Ellen snarled.

The phrase attracted Quentin like a bell for Pavlov's dogs. A career grunt in the Park County system, Quentin was a man whose ambition overreached his abilities—a truth that left him with a perpetually bitter taste in his mouth. Fifty-something, he held himself stiffly erect, discouraged from relaxation and respiration by a super-control girdle that seemed to push all his fat up into his florid face. His latest affectation to battle the aging process was a dye job and permanent that left him looking as if he had a head covered with pubic hair—a transformation that coincided with rumors of a fling between Quentin and Janis Nerhaugen, a secretary in the county assessor's office.

"Ellen, I have to speak with you about these cases you've dumped on me," he said.

"I can't talk, Quentin. I've got to be in court. If you don't want them, talk to Rudy."

"But, Ellen—"

Phoebe butted in front of him, pulling a handful of pink message slips out of a patch pocket on her tunic. "I've got messages for you. Every reporter in the western hemisphere wants an interview, and Garrett Wright has fired his attorney."

"There's a big surprise," Ellen muttered. Denny Enberg's heart hadn't been in the case from the start. She wondered if Wright had truly fired him or if he had withdrawn and allowed Wright to call it what he wanted so as not to prejudice his case in the eyes of the press. She would call on Denny later to find out what she could, although she didn't expect to learn much. What went on between a client and his attorney was privileged; a severed relationship didn't change that. "Any word on who's taking his place?"

"Not yet." Phoebe lowered her voice conspiratorially. "He has a really volatile aura."

"Who? Denny?"

"Jay Butler Brooks. It suggests inner turbulence and raw sexuality."

"Ellen, this is important," Quentin wailed.

"Tell that to Judge Franken when he cites me for contempt," Ellen said, handing the slips back to Phoebe. "His aura suggests intolerance. I'm out of here."

CHAPTER 7

"Miss Bottoms," Judge Franken wheezed. "Do you understand the charges against you?"

Ellen had a suspicion much of life was a mystery to Loretta Bottoms. The woman stood gaping at the judge like a beached bass. An exotic dancer whose stage name was Lotta Bottom, Loretta had been working the circuit of strip clubs along the interstate between Des Moines and Minneapolis. She claimed to have been "working her way back home" when she was arrested for soliciting at the Big Steer truck stop on the outskirts of Deer Lake.

She stood before the court in a zebra-stripe knit dress that redefined the limitations of spandex. Built like an hourglass, tilting over on four-inch heels, breasts heaved up into her décolletage like a pair of huge cling peaches. Franken was mesmerized by the sight. When he spoke, he addressed her breasts. Ellen figured he had as much chance of getting an intelligent answer from them as from any other part of Loretta.

"Miss Bottoms, have you discussed the charges with your attorney?" the judge asked.

"Yeah."

"And?"

"And what?" Loretta sank a long red fingernail into her mare's nest of bleached hair to scratch her head. "I don't get it."

Beside her, her attorney, Fred Nelson, rolled his eyes and banged a fist against the side of his head as if trying to dislodge the rocks that would explain his having taken on Loretta as a client.

"Loretta"—he spoke to her as if she were a thick-headed child who had asked "why" ten times too many—"we've heard the police report. The officer tells us he caught you in the men's room of the Big Steer truck stop performing a sex act with a twenty-dollar bill in your hand."

Loretta jammed her hands on ample hips. "I wasn't performing a sex act with a twenty-dollar bill. His name was Tater."

The spectators burst out laughing. Ellen bit the inside of her lip.

Judge Franken banged his gavel. His whole misshapen little head turned maroon—a sign that his temper had been worn down to the nub and his blood pressure was soaring in direct proportion.

"How do you plead, Miss Bottoms?" the judge demanded.

"Well, Freddy here tells me I gotta plead guilty, but I don't see why. It's nobody's business whose dick I had in my mouth."

Franken smashed his gavel down to quell the new wave of mirth. "We've been through this three times, Miss Bottoms," he croaked, trembling with frustration. "You don't have to plead guilty if you don't want to. You can plead not guilty, but then you'll have to come back from Des Moines to stand trial. Do you want to stand trial?"

"Well, I don't really, but—"

"Then do you want to plead guilty?"

"No."

Fred Nelson squeezed his eyes shut. "Your Honor, I have been over this with my client. We discussed the possibility of Ms. Bottoms entering a plea of not guilty, the court setting a date for trial and bail in the victinity of two hundred fifty dollars cash. Then Miss Bottoms can go home and give this matter some more thought."

Two hundred fifty dollars was a usual fine for soliciting, and no one had any hope of or interest in Loretta Bottoms returning to Park County to stand trial. Ellen and Fred had hashed out the agreement in the judge's chambers. The county would get its money out of Loretta in the form of the forfeited cash bail when she failed to appear, and Loretta would be out of everyone's hair. It seemed a sweet deal to everyone but Loretta. The proceedings had already dragged on half an hour longer than they should have because they couldn't state the deal outright in front of God and the court reporter, and the need for discretion had confused Loretta. Franken was sinking down farther behind the bench. In another minute only his wrinkled forehead would be visible.

"Is that what you want to do, Miss Bottoms?" he asked through his teeth.

Loretta batted her false eyelashes. "What?"

No one held back their groans, including Franken. His was the loudest. His head popped up, and he groaned again, louder, a look of surprise widening his tiny eyes. Then he disappeared from view altogether, a dull thump the only clue he was behind the bench.

For a moment no one moved or spoke as everybody waited for the judge to pop back up like a puppet. But the moment stretched into another. Ellen looked to the bailiff, who started for the bench. Renee, the clerk, beat him to it, disappearing behind the bench herself. In the next second her scream split the air like an ax blade.

"He's dead!"

Ellen bolted from her chair and around the bench, where the clerk was on her knees, sobbing hysterically and pulling at Franken's robes.

"He's dead! Oh, my God, he's dead!"

"Call an ambulance!" Ellen shouted, and the bailiff dashed into the judge's chambers. As Ellen called out for someone to help with CPR, she was already tipping the judge's head back and feeling for a pulse.

"Has he got a pulse?" someone asked.

"No."

"Then let's have at it, Ms. North."

The voice registered with a jolt. She jerked her head up, and saw Brooks positioning his hands over the judge's sternum.

"As much as I'd rather have you putting those lovely lips against mine," Brooks murmured, "I think the judge here has a more urgent need."

"He was a good judge," Ellen murmured as she stared out the window of Franken's chambers.

The view overlooked the park and a sidewalk crowded with protesting college students. The imitation gas streetlamps were winking on. Life was continuing. The world was still turning.

The last hour was a blur of paramedics and people rushing in and out of the courtroom. Reporters loitering in the rotunda had stormed the courtroom for this latest twist in the tale, and a near riot had ensued when someone had recognized Brooks. The bedlam had culminated with a deputy clearing the room and the ears of the sound technicians with a shrieking bullhorn. The silence now seemed both welcome and odd.

"He was tough and fair," Ellen said, her thoughts returning to Victor Franken. She wanted to remember him as she had known him for the past two years, not as a crumpled husk on the floor of his courtroom, the black robes he had prized so highly torn open to reveal the thin, sunken chest of a very old man. "He had common sense and a sense of humor."

"Did you know him well?" Jay asked softly.

He watched her from his seat on the end of Franken's massive oak desk. They were the only people left in the room that had been the judge's office and sanctuary. Bookcases towered on all sides of the room, the shelves filled to capacity. The furniture looked so old it might have set roots into the floor. The ferns that sat in massive pots all around the room were the size of bushel baskets. With the green-shaded desk lamp the only light on, the atmosphere was almost forestlike.

Ellen lifted a shoulder. "I know he lost his wife years ago. He lived alone. He liked to garden." She fingered the frond of a fern that filled the window ledge. "The bench was his life. And now he's gone. Just like that."

She brushed a tear from her cheek, not embarrassed to have shed it in front of a stranger. A good man had just vanished from existence. There was no shame in mourning that. Still, she drew in a deep breath and composed herself, turning to Jay with a dignified facade.

"Thank you for helping."

He shook it off, frowning. "I don't need thanks. Jesus, my being there turned the whole thing into a damn circus. I'm sorry that happened."

"So am I," Ellen said. "He deserved a more dignified passing, although I heard him say it more than once—he wanted to die on the bench." She shrugged again and reached for some cynicism to insulate herself. "He got his wish and you got some publicity. Not a bad deal if you look at it that way."

"I didn't come here for publicity."

"No. You came here for a story."

He pushed himself away from the desk and crossed the room slowly, his gaze assessing, scrutinizing. The sensation it evoked was disturbing, but Ellen refused to let herself move away from it, from him. The rule she had applied with the Sci-Fi Cowboys came back to her—show no fear. Jay Butler Brooks posed no physical threat to her, but he was a threat in other ways, a clear and present danger on other levels—professional, ideological . . .

She knew she was leaving one out as he stopped just a hair's breadth too close. His eyes were silver in the colorless light from the narrow window.

"Are you all right?" he asked softly.

Her hair had come loose from its twist as she'd worked to revive the judge. Strands fell along her cheeks, making him wonder how she would look with it all down. Younger, softer, vulnerable—traits that didn't complement her professional image. But the image was slipping now. Her studious glasses were gone, along with the jacket of her charcoal suit. The top button of her proper white blouse was open, giving him a glimpse of the tender hollow where throat met collarbone. The armor was coming undone. She couldn't seem to decide who she should be in this moment—Ellen North the consummate professional, or Ellen North the woman.

An opportune chance for him. The reason he had hung around as the paramedics packed their things and zipped the black bag on old Franken, he told himself. So he could take advantage of her when she was off balance. So he might be able to catch a glimpse of something she never would have shown him otherwise.

What a guy you are, Brooks. Prince of the jerks.

"I'm fine," she announced, though she clearly was not. The hand she raised to comb the loose strands behind her left ear was trembling.

"Looks to me like you could use a drink. I know I could," he admitted. "I never had a judge drop dead on me before—though I admit I wished it a few times."

"That's right. You used to practice before fame and fortune came calling."

He shrugged, ignoring the sting of her words. "I did my time as a lowly associate, chased an ambulance or two, tried a little of this, a little of that. 'Little' being the operative word, according to my ex-wife. She had to be the first lawyer's wife in history who actually wanted her husband to put in eighty-hour weeks."

Even now he could hear Christine's criticism. It had worn a trench into the back of his mind like water running over stone; the years only made it deeper. *"Why can't you work harder? Why haven't you made junior partner? Why won't you join the family firm? You'll never amount to anything the way you bounce around."*

"Well, you got her in the end," Ellen said. *"Justifiable Homicide*—an overworked young attorney is framed for the brutal murder of his scheming ex-wife. The book's dedication: 'To Christine, who, I am pleased to say, will never get a dime of the royalties.' A charming sentiment."

"And well deserved, I assure you." A wry smile twisted across his mouth. "I thought you were unfamiliar with my work, Ms. North."

"I lied," Ellen said without remorse. "I read the article in *Newsweek*."

"And what did you think?"

"I think I made my opinion clear earlier. I don't like what you do."

"I present actual, terrifying events to my readers in a way that can bring them to a deeper understanding of what happened, why it happened, how the justice system worked—or failed to work in some cases," he said. "I give them insight. I give them closure. What's wrong with that?"

"You're a mercenary profiteer who's no better than a vampire. A hack looking to steal the lives and pain of victims to compensate for a lack of any real imagination. You feed off people's fears and morbid curiosities and contribute to the nation's unhealthy obsession with sensationalism," Ellen countered. "Don't try to put a noble face on it.

You're in the entertainment business—those were your own words."

"Everything I say can and will be used against me," he said dryly.

"Do you deny it?"

"No. I'm not a journalist. People get their news from a paper or on TV. They don't fork over twenty bucks in the bookstore for a hardback version of *Time*. People read true crime to escape—same reason people read anything."

"And you don't find that just the least bit twisted? Escaping into someone else's real-life tragedy?"

"No more so than picking up a Stephen King novel or an Agatha Christie mystery. To that reader my book is just a story, something to get lost in and ponder; all the more interesting because it really happened."

Ellen moved away from him then, shaking her head in disgust. "Fine. You go talk to Hannah Garrison about what she's been through and what she's going through, and be sure to tell her it's just a story. That'll be such a comfort to her."

Jay pursued her across the dusky room to the desk, automatically reacting to her righteous indignation. He was contrary by nature, born to take the opposite side just for the sake of a good argument. It wasn't anger that rushed to the fore—it was excitement, adrenaline.

"Hey, I can't change what's happened to make a story a story. It's there, it's happened, it's history."

"So you might as well make a buck off it?" She pulled her jacket off the back of Franken's chair and slipped it on.

"If I don't, someone else will."

"Oh, well, that makes it all right."

"I didn't invent the game, counselor—"

"No, but you're hell-bent on winning it, aren't you? Going straight to the top, dragging Glendenning into it. Of all the dirty—"

"Not dirty," Jay clarified, wagging a finger in her face.

"That's hardball and it's the way I play this game. I go after what I want and I get it."

The declaration hung in the air between them, a challenge that took on deeper nuances as Ellen stared up at him. He was standing too close again. She was leaning toward him. The scant few inches of air between them seemed to thicken, and a dormant sixth sense came to life inside her, rising to the surface like air bubbles in water. Awareness, not of an adversary in a duel of wits, but of something much more fundamental.

"I go after what I want, Ellen North," he whispered again, sliding a hand beneath her chin. His thumb brushed across the bow of her lower lip. "And I get it," he breathed. "Remember that."

"That you're ruthless?" Ellen murmured, telling herself to brand it into her mind.

"Determined."

"Dangerous" was the word she settled on. Dangerous to her in ways she had never anticipated a man could be.

"Damn, I like the way you fight, counselor," he said softly. "How about that drink?"

The invitation in his expression was far more intimate than an offered glass of brandy. That he could slide so easily from contention to seduction, as if it didn't matter what she thought of him, disturbed her.

"Just because we disagree doesn't mean we can't be civil," he said. "I like you, Ellen. You're smart, sharp, not afraid to say what you mean." He chuckled. "I thought ol' Rudy was gonna have a stroke in your office. And you just stood there, cool as well water. What do you say we go find a nice quiet bar with a fireplace and argue the evening away?" He served the suggestion with the kind of smile that could have charmed nuns from their habits.

This was why he was a celebrity, Ellen decided, instead of just a name on a dust jacket. The very air around him vibrated with sex appeal.

"I don't think so, Mr. Brooks. It would be too much like fraternizing with the enemy," she said, stepping away from him, slipping her glasses on—shielding herself against his charm.

"I'm not the enemy. I'm just an observer."

"You may not be *the* enemy, but you're an enemy just the same. I can't differentiate between who you are and what you are, Mr. Brooks." She stared him straight in the face. "Maybe your conscience will let you exploit what's happened in this town—or maybe you don't have a conscience. Either way, I won't condone it and I don't want to be a part of it."

With that she walked out on him for the second time that day.

Jay sat back against the judge's desk and gave a low whistle. He had had doors slammed in his face before. That was nothing new. It went with the territory. Sometimes people were willing to work on a story with him and sometimes they weren't. If he wanted the story badly enough and the front door closed, he went to the back. If the back door closed, he went in a window. If he couldn't get in through a window, he went in through the basement. If he wanted the story bad enough, he would get it. He didn't need Ellen North's cooperation. He could write this story from a dozen different angles.

But he wanted Ellen North's cooperation. Hell, he wanted Ellen North.

He knew better than to get involved with a source. Crossing that line was like walking into a nest of vipers—an invitation for disaster. He would compromise his credibility, color his perception of the story.

As tough as he played this game, he played it by rules. He had already broken one—getting involved with a live case. That was just asking for trouble. Of course, as Uncle Hooter always said, he may not have looked for trouble, but when it came calling, he was never out of earshot.

This case had grabbed him and hung on. He wanted inside of it, wanted to know why it had happened and what it had done to the people whose lives it had touched. He wanted to watch it all unfold—the trial, the strategy behind prosecution and defense, the reactions of the public as sides were taken. Something important was happening here. This wasn't just another crime; it was a crossroads, a crisis point for small-town America. He felt a need to capture that.

And to distance himself from another crisis, he admitted in a shadowed corner of his mind—one he had turned away from before it could suck him in. *This* case was his focus. The trick was to get inside and yet maintain emotional distance. A tough call when a part of him wanted no distance at all between himself and the prosecuting attorney.

But then, it appeared Ellen North would maintain that distance for him. She was as unimpressed with his bag of tricks as a skeptic who had caught sight of the mirrors in a magic show. She didn't give a damn about the bankability of his name, would not have cared a lick that his latest work had been at the top of every best-seller list in the country for three solid months or that Tom Cruise had signed on for the lead in the movie version of *Justice for None*. She didn't care who he was, she cared *what* he was, and she had made up her mind on that score right out of the box.

The hell of it was, she was probably right.

The hell of it was, he wanted her anyway.

CHAPTER 8

Mitch slid in behind the wheel of his Explorer, bone-weary. The better part of the day had been spent overseeing the search for the missing gloves Garrett Wright had cast off during the chase the night of his arrest. Mitch's men and the evidence techs from the BCA had spent two days combing the ground the chase had covered through the woods of Quarry Hills Park, along the cross-country ski trail that ran the rim of the park behind the Lakeside neighborhood, and into the yards of the homes that backed onto the park.

Seven inches of fresh snow had fallen to cover the tracks from the chase, and every step taken by an officer or agent had the potential to further bury evidence that would not be seen again until April. They had gone over the ground with shovels and rakes, dug with garden tools in the areas too small for anything else. And still, in the end, it was dumb luck that did the trick. Lonnie Dietz had plunked down on a fallen log, tired and frustrated, and while he'd stared down at a crevice in the dead tree, something had caught his eye. A small slip of white—the size tag sewn inside the cuff of a black leather glove.

The gloves had been sent to the BCA lab in St. Paul. Then there had been the ever-present press to deal with, the mob of reporters already in a frenzy from the bond hearing. And constantly in the back of Mitch's mind were thoughts of Megan.

She had been transferred to Hennepin County Medical Center in Minneapolis that morning and had gone into surgery for her hand at three. He wanted to be there with her, but the case took precedence. Megan knew that. She had been the first to say it. She was a cop, she understood the priorities. She was a victim as well, which gave her an added motivation to want to see the investigation completed.

She was also alone and afraid. The prognosis for her regaining full use of her hand was not good. If she couldn't use her right hand, she couldn't handle a gun, she couldn't defend herself, she couldn't return to the kind of duty that had been her whole life. All she had ever wanted was to be a good cop.

And all Mitch wanted at the moment was to be able to hold her. He didn't relish the thought of an hour's drive to the Cities, and guilt nipped him at the thought of leaving his daughter with her grandparents for yet another evening, but he started the engine and focused on Megan. The last thing he had expected to find in this nightmare of Josh Kirkwood's abduction was love, and he would never have expected love to come packaged in a tough Irish cop with a chip on her shoulder the size of Gibraltar, but there it was.

He eased the truck out of his parking spot, fighting the urge to gun the engine and send the reporters who had followed him out scrambling for their lives. He waved them off when he would rather have given them the finger, and pulled out onto Oslo Street. He was half a block from the interstate when his cellular phone trilled in his coat pocket.

"Jesus, now what?" he muttered, pulling up to the curb.

Leaving the engine running, he dug the phone out and

unfolded it, telling himself it might be Megan or it might be Jessie calling to see where her daddy was.

"Mitch Holt."

The silence made him think the caller had given up while he had fumbled with his gloves and the pocket flap trying to get to the damn phone, but he hung on, an eerie sensation scratching through him.

"Hello? Who's there?"

The truck engine grumbled to itself. Outside, the shabby little neighborhood that backed onto the interstate was quiet in the twilight. People were in their homes having supper and watching the news as night began to settle down around them. It was the time of night Josh had disappeared.

As the thought shot a chill through him, the voice came over the phone. A whisper.

"Ignorance is not innocence but sin. Ignorance is not innocence but sin. Ignorance is not innocence but sin."

The line went dead.

Mitch sat perfectly still, his heart banging like a fist against his ribs. *Ignorance is not innocence but sin.* The message in the note that had been left behind at the scene of Josh's abduction. Common knowledge, he told himself. The press had splashed it all over. And yet he couldn't shake the sick sensation of dread. His muscles quivered with it. It steamed from his pores even though the temperature in the cab of the truck was below freezing. The number of his cellular phone was *not* common knowledge.

A minute passed. Then five. The phone rang again and the uneasiness pressed down on him like an anvil.

"Mitch Holt."

"Chief, it's Natalie. We just got a call from the sheriff. He's in Campion. They've got a child missing . . . and a note."

Josh sat on the family-room floor, cross-legged, staring at the flames in the fireplace. A giant sketch pad and a new box of markers lay on the floor beside him, untouched. *Aladdin* was running in the VCR, but the cartoon didn't interest him. His baby sister, Lily, however, was delighted and toddled around the room, singing along, dancing with a stuffed Barney the Dinosaur.

Josh didn't care about cartoons anymore. He didn't want to play. He didn't want to talk. He stared at the fire and imagined he was a fireman on Mars, where it was hot all the time and there were no kids.

Hannah stepped down into the family room from the kitchen, rubbing lotion into her hands. The supper dishes were done, such as they were—glasses for soda and plates for pizza from the Leaning Tower of Pizza. Josh's favorite. Nutrition be damned tonight. She had called out for a medium pepperoni and mushroom and offered brownies for dessert. She hadn't made them, either, selecting instead the best from the pans friends and neighbors and absolute strangers had sent over during the course of Josh's absence.

She had brought her son home today. Against Bob Ulrich's wishes. Against the advice of the advocate from Park County Social Services. They had wanted to continue observation, as if Josh were a freak in a sideshow. But he had checked out all right physically, and Hannah had argued that his unwillingness to talk to anyone was no reason to keep him in a hospital bed. It was time to go home, where things were familiar and safe. She was a doctor herself; if Josh exhibited signs of physical problems, she would be the first to notice.

And so they had come home, where reporters blocked the driveway and well-meaning friends crowded the house. Home, where everything looked familiar but nothing would ever be the same again.

Hannah put the thought out of her head. She had sent the friends home, and the police had chased the reporters off the lawn. She had ordered pizza and built a fire and put one of Josh's favorite movies in the VCR. She had made things as normal as she could, considering the circumstances.

Lily danced up to her, all smiles and rosy cheeks, and offered her Barney. Hannah scooped up her daughter instead and hugged her close.

"Mama, Josh!" Lily announced, pointing at her brother.

"Yep, Josh is home. We missed him, didn't we, Lilybug?"

"Josh! Josh! Josh!" Lily sang, euphoric over her brother's return. At eighteen months, she worshiped Josh. He had always been wonderful with her, sweet, gentle, loving. He read her bedtime stories and played with her.

He hadn't spoken a word to her since coming home. He ignored her efforts to engage him in play. He looked through her as if she weren't there. Fortunately, Lily was too excited to notice her brother wasn't returning her affections. It would have broken Hannah's heart if there had been any pieces left intact.

She settled on the couch with the baby in her lap as the movie rolled to a close. Lily twisted around, blond curls bouncing. "More!"

"Let's ask Josh," Hannah said, her eyes on her son. "Josh, honey, do you want to run the movie again?"

He didn't answer, didn't look at her. He sat as he had for the last hour, staring into the fire. He hadn't touched the sketch pad or markers.

The advocate had said to keep them handy, to encourage Josh to draw in the hopes that he would vent his experiences with his kidnappers through his artwork. So far, the only mark on the pad was the one the advocate herself had made, trying to draw Josh into a game of tic-tac-toe.

Josh was keeping his experiences locked up tight, and his emotions along with them. Aside from his violent reaction to his father, he had reacted to nothing and no one.

"More, more, Mama!" Lily insisted.

"Not tonight, sweetheart," Hannah murmured. "It's time to watch something quiet so we can all settle down for bedtime."

Lily protested by taking Barney and moving to the love seat. "Where Daddy?"

"Daddy's staying somewhere else tonight," Hannah answered, watching Josh for a reaction at mention of his father. There was none.

She was angry with Paul for not being there, even though she really didn't want him. He had upset Josh before; she didn't want a repeat performance. Nor did she want the tensions between her and Paul to be telegraphed to the children.

Still, a foolish part of her wanted Paul to assert his rights as a father, to make some kind of stand to keep their marriage from disintegrating. She wanted to see the man she had married, the man she had loved, but he was lost. It seemed he had been an aberration, that for the first part of their marriage Paul had been at his peak and for reasons she couldn't understand had slowly fallen backward until she could no longer reach him, could hardly recognize who he was. It frightened her that she had thought she had known him so well, but now she didn't seem to know him at all.

Sighing, she flipped through the television channels, looking for something without sex, violence, or reality involved, settling on an independent station out of Minneapolis that was running *The Parent Trap* for the millionth time. Hayley Mills in a madcap adventure as twin sisters. Classic fluff from the sixties, when the world had still clung to its last shreds of innocence.

The nineties intruded immediately in the form of a

news bulletin. A grim-faced anchorwoman with a helmet of spray-starched red hair filled half the screen while the photograph of a little boy popped up in one corner under a red banner that proclaimed him missing.

"Oh, my God," Hannah murmured.

"Authorities in the small Park County town of Campion tonight are launching a massive search for eight-year-old Dustin Holloman, abducted from a city park where he was playing with friends after school this afternoon. The abduction bears marked similarities to the case of Josh Kirkwood of Deer Lake, also in Park County. Josh, abducted January twelfth, was returned to his family unharmed late last night. The family of Dustin Holloman can only hope for a similar outcome.

"Dustin is eight years old with blond hair and blue eyes. He was last seen wearing blue jeans and a black-and-yellow ski jacket with an orange stocking cap. Anyone who thinks they may have information about Dustin is asked to immediately call the Park County sheriff's office."

Josh turned slowly and looked at the television screen as it filled with the smiling, slightly blurry image of Dustin Holloman and the hot-line phone numbers. He rose and moved to stand directly in front of the set in the cherry entertainment center, staring without expression at the boy who had been proclaimed missing.

"Josh," Hannah murmured, coming out of her seat, reaching for him. She dropped to her knees on the floor beside him.

He stared at the little boy's photograph and lifted a finger to point at him.

"Uh-oh," he said softly. "He's a Goner."

CHAPTER 9

"Will you disclose the contents of the note?"

"How does this affect the case against Dr. Wright?"

"Do you believe this is the work of the same kidnapper?"

"Do you still believe Wright had an accomplice, or do you think you've got the wrong man sitting in jail?"

"When will you release the contents of the note?"

"How does this change your strategy?"

The questions echoed through Ellen's head, swam through it, whirled around it. The faces of the reporters did the same. Some were familiar, some famous, many obscure. All of them wanted the same thing. The scoop, the hot quote, the exclusive tidbit. After two weeks of covering Josh Kirkwood's abduction, they came to Dustin Holloman's as ravenous as ever, driven by ambition to grab whatever details they could.

"I'm ambitious," Adam Slater had proclaimed yesterday outside the hospital. She had spotted him in the sea of faces, out on the edge, on the fringe of the mob, his young eyes bright as he soaked it all in.

Ambitious. Or maybe "desperate" was the word. Desperate for answers. Desperate for some clue as to why the fabric of this quiet rural county was unraveling. That was what Ellen felt—a sharp, choking sense of desperation, the kind of panic that threatened to swell up and swallow her whole. It was just as strong now, as she pulled into her driveway, as it had been when she had driven away from the reporters in Campion.

Campion was a farming community of two thousand. A simple, quiet place that made Deer Lake, a half-hour drive away, seem like a teeming metropolis. A town too small and too dull to need its own police department, it contracted with the county for the use of deputies to keep things in order. The people of Campion had watched the evening news when Josh Kirkwood had been taken and reflected that the world beyond them was an increasingly dangerous place. Thank God they lived in Campion, where everyone was safe. Until tonight.

News that a child had been taken had the town reeling, stunned and confused. It was déjà vu for the volunteers who flocked over from Deer Lake. Having been through it all before, they organized search teams quickly and set up a command post in the Sons of Norway hall because it was the only place in town big enough. But, as had been the case two weeks before, there was little for the investigation to go on.

"Witnesses?" Ellen hurried toward Mitch, turning her coat collar up against the bite of the wind.

"None," he answered, half shouting to be heard above the pounding of helicopter blades.

State patrol choppers had already begun their search, sweeping back and forth over the town in an ever-widening grid while helicopters from the Twin Cities television stations hovered over the crime scene like vultures. Campion Civic Park had been turned into a surrealistic circus ground, the barren trees and deep snow cover illuminated by portable floodlights and the colored beacons of police vehicles. Yellow crime-scene tape had been wound around saplings and fluttered in the sharp wind like banners around a used-car lot.

"The boy's older brother was supposed to be watching

him," Mitch said as Ellen fell in step beside him. "They were all skating on the outdoor rink over there. The older boys got a hockey game going and the younger kids got pushed out. Apparently Dustin wandered away."

He pulled a gloved hand out of his parka pocket and pushed back a lacework of small branches for Ellen to pass. "Don't worry about where you're stepping," he said bitterly. "The trail the boy took has already been tramped over by sixty or seventy sets of boots."

They skidded down a short slope Ellen could easily envision as a favorite sledding spot for smaller kids. At the bottom, the woods of the park thinned out to brush. Beyond the brush, cop cars sat, strobes twirling, tossing disks of colored light across a winding back street where the nearest house was three hundred yards away. Directly across the street from the park, the tumbledown remnants of what had once been farm buildings crouched, gray and bleak, open doorways and empty windows gaping like wounds black with rot.

Ellen's stomach clenched at the thought of being eight years old, standing in this forlorn spot, knowing you were about to be taken by a stranger.

If the kidnapper had been a stranger. They would have to question the Hollomans and the Kirkwoods, looking for any mutual acquaintances. Josh had not been taken by a stranger. Provided Garrett Wright was the man who had taken him.

She blew out a steamy breath as the doubts surfaced. She believed Wright was guilty, and even she was having second thoughts now. The press would have a field day casting doubt and muddying the waters of the potential jury pool.

"He said it was a game." Megan's words came back to her, bringing a chill that had nothing to do with the falling temperature. If this was all a game to him, then taking Dustin Holloman was a brilliant and ruthless move. In ad-

dition to raising questions in the press, the search for the second missing child would take priority and consume hours of manpower from two law-enforcement agencies already investigating the Kirkwood kidnapping—the BCA and the Park County sheriff's department. The Deer Lake police would be involved because of the possible connection to their own case. They would be forced to widen the investigation because of the involvement of a whole new group of people—the Hollomans and their friends and associates and enemies. In one move their adversary had taken their team and scattered it all over the board.

"This is where they took off," Mitch said, flashing his badge at the deputies who stood wary watch around a naked sapling on the boulevard.

Ellen let him herd her through the group to the center, foreboding pressing down on her like a great weight.

Tied around a branch of the tree was a bright-purple scarf. Crocheted by someone who loved Dustin. He had probably got it for Christmas and had probably wished it were a Power Ranger toy instead. It fluttered on the branch, an oversize ribbon marking a terrible trail. And pinned to the scarf was the note.

> *but sad as angels for the good man's SIN,*
> *weep to record and blush to give it in.*

Ellen shuddered. She couldn't get the sight of that scarf out of her mind. A small symbol of a small child snatched into a madman's game for a purpose known only to him.

He said it was a game.

But with what rules and what goal and what motivation? And what players? Virtually everyone in Deer Lake who had ever had a conversation with Garrett Wright had been questioned. His acquaintances were well-respected professional people, baffled by the turn of events that had landed him in jail. His students had rallied to support him. The faculty at Harris had nothing but respect for him. No one had uncovered or hinted at Garrett Wright being anything other than what he appeared. No secret taste for child pornography. No ties to the criminal underworld. No hidden life of satanic worship.

As his wife had said, Garrett Wright didn't so much as speed in his perfectly sensible Saab, let alone hang out with criminal types. There were precious few people on the list of Wright's known associates who looked even remotely like an accessory to kidnapping and assault.

But someone had brought Josh Kirkwood home and someone had taken Dustin Holloman away.

And she was too damn tired to try to figure it out tonight.

As Ellen reached toward the remote control for the garage door, something hit the driver's-side window with all the force of a rock. Bolting sideways, a little shriek of surprise ripping up her throat, she twisted around wide-eyed to see Jay Butler Brooks looking in at her.

"You gonna sit here all night or put the car away and invite me in for coffee? I'm freezing my ass out here."

Ellen answered him with a scathing look. It was late, she was tired, and she still had work to do before she could lapse into unconsciousness for a few hours. But as she drove the Bonneville into her garage, he sauntered in beside her as if he had every right to be there.

"Glendenning can't force me to be 'accommodating' in my own home," Ellen said, hefting her briefcase out of the car. "As much as I may feel like one from time to time, I'm not a slave."

"I'll take that for you," Jay offered, reaching for the attaché. It was old leather that had taken a beating no live cow could have endured. The size of a small building, it looked as if she had packed it with granite blocks.

"No, you won't," she said, and headed for the door that led directly into the house.

Jay hopped up on the stoop beside her and held the storm door while she dug for her keys. "Ellen, I'd like to talk to you."

"And I'd like to go to bed."

He leaned ahead, into her line of vision, and gave her a slow, sexy smile, glittering with humor. "Can we talk afterward?"

Ellen told herself disgust was what made her fumble with her keys and drop them, not the mental image of Jay Butler Brooks in her bed wearing nothing but a sheet and that smile.

"I'm in no mood for sophomoric humor, and I've had my quota of arguments for the day," she said, letting herself into the mudroom, where Harry lay curled up on his cedar-stuffed cushion. He boomed a bark of greeting and hopped to attention, his toenails tapping out Morse code on the vinyl flooring. Ellen gave the dog an absent pat, still scowling at the man who seemed bent on invading her life. "Why don't you go back to wherever you came from?"

"I came from Campion," Jay said, smoothly stepping inside before she could close the door on him.

"You'd make a great Fuller Brush salesman," Ellen muttered, toeing off her boots and setting them on the mat beside the door.

"Been there. Done that." He pulled off his gloves and stuffed them into his coat pockets. "My respectable old southern family ran out of respectable old southern money long before I went to college."

He offered his hand to Harry. The golden retriever sniffed him, then slurped his big pink dog tongue along the back of Jay's knuckles. Ellen gave her pet a look that branded him a traitor and headed for the kitchen.

"So your morbid curiosity drove you to Campion,"

she said to Jay. "I'm not surprised. The plot grows thicker for you. Did you get a good, close look at the boy's mother? I would suggest Kathy Bates to play her in the movie. I thought there was a strong resemblance—but, then, she was bawling her eyes out, so it's hard to say."

"I didn't go near the woman." Jay stopped in the doorway between the kitchen and dining room. "It makes me sick to think another child is going to suffer. I'm not a ghoul, Ellen, and I resent the insinuation."

She hefted her briefcase onto a cherrywood table with graceful Queen Anne legs, setting it down with a solid thud. "Tough. I didn't ask you to come here. I didn't ask you into my home. And, frankly, I'm in no mood to play hostess."

"I came to see how you were doing," he said. "You've had a hell of a day."

He took in the dining room in a single look—mottled soft gold walls decorated with brass sconces and primitive portraits of eighteenth-century people. Tasteful, simple, classy. The back wall was taken up by a bay window, the center section of which was a door that probably opened onto a deck or patio. Opposite the window, a railing ran some eight or ten feet, providing a graceful spot to look down on the living room below.

"See how you've misjudged me?" He shuffled down the carpeted steps to the living room. With a flick of a switch the brass table lamps filled the room with muted light. "I came here out of concern for you. I mean, we shared a bonding experience of sorts this afternoon, you and I. Trying to raise someone from the dead is a pretty intimate experience."

"Yeah, we're practically blood brother and sister," Ellen said dryly. She slipped her coat off and hung it on the back of a chair, her wary attention on the man who was intruding not only in her house but in her case. He prowled her living room like a restless cat, running a hand over the furniture as if marking the territory.

"And aside from your great concern for me," she said, descending the stairs, "you had no intention of coming here to try for a little inside information on the kidnapping of Dustin Holloman?"

"I can get that information from other sources. Better sources, if you want the truth." He flipped a brass-framed switch beside the fireplace, and flames instantly leaped to life around a stack of fake logs. Neat, clean, no muss, no fuss. He turned his back to the fire, pressing his hands against the screen to absorb the warmth that was real even if the logs were not.

Ellen stood across the room from him, beside a sturdy overstuffed chair. She obviously hadn't made it home before being called to the crisis in Campion. She was still in the charcoal suit she had worn at Wright's bond hearing and Judge Franken's demise. Her hair had come down, pure, straight silk that fell artlessly to brush the tops of her shoulders. Her veneer of makeup and manners had long since worn off. She looked exhausted and short-tempered and utterly unapproachable.

But even as he saw this, he could remember the way she had looked going into the command post in the Campion Sons of Norway hall—shaken, afraid. Their bad guy had thrown them a wicked curveball, and no one had been ready for it.

"The judge on your case dies on you, another child is kidnapped while your bad guy sits in jail," he said, coming toward her slowly. "That's a lot to deal with."

"Yes, and now I have to deal with you," Ellen said, crossing her arms. "Wondering if you're committing my every word to memory or if you've got a tape recorder in your pocket."

"You're damned suspicious."

"I wouldn't trust you any farther than I could throw you."

"After I came to check up on you and convince myself of your well-being?"

"Uh-huh," she said with no conviction.

"You can frisk me if you'd like," he offered in that dark, sexy tone. "But I'll warn you right now—that's *not* a tape recorder in my pocket."

"I'll take your word for it. So now you've seen that I'm still in one piece." She held her arms out from her sides to display the fact. "You've done your Good Samaritan deed for the decade. You're dismissed."

Ignoring the suggestion that he had worn out his welcome, Jay sat down on the fat arm of the overstuffed chair. He could be as deliberately obtuse as a post. It was a skill that had served him well as an attorney and more so as a writer. Persistence was the name of the game when it came to getting information.

"Do you think it's part of Wright's plan?" he asked. "A diversionary tactic? I should have thought bringing back the Kirkwood kid accomplished that."

"But it didn't spread out the defense," Ellen mumbled more to herself than to Jay.

"I don't follow."

"A football analogy. I had a law professor who used to play for the Vikings."

"Ah. I'm a baseball man myself."

"The offensive team shows a formation that causes the defensive team to spread themselves all over the field, inevitably creating holes for the offense to slip through."

"Involving a whole new set of victims in another town forces the investigation to broaden instead of focusing tightly on Wright and Wright's secret pal," Jay deduced. He gave Ellen a nod. "Sharp thinking, counselor."

"It's conjecture and speculation," she said as she went to the door. "For all I know, the kidnapping of Dustin

Holloman is unrelated to the kidnapping of Josh Kirkwood."

He thought of what he'd seen and felt in Campion tonight. The sharp metallic taste of fear, the sense that the
place had somehow slipped into an alternate universe.
Evil. It had been as much a presence as the police and the
press. It seemed to permeate the night, dyeing it blacker,
giving the wind a razor's edge. And fluttering brightly
against it was a little boy's bright-purple scarf tied to the
naked branch of a winter-dead tree.

He remembered thinking, *Jesus, Brooks, what have you
walked into here?*

More than he had bargained for.

"I think we both know better," he said to Ellen, slowly
pushing himself away from the chair. "The question is,
how will it affect the prosecution of Wright?"

Ellen took a deep breath and let it out in a gust, leaning
back against the wall, too worn-out to keep herself upright. "Look, you're right, it's been a long day and I still
have work to do, and there's no point in your staying because I'm not going to share anything with you—"

"Regarding the case or you?"

"Either."

"I just can't win with you, can I?" He pretended frustration, his brows tugging together. But, as always, the
wry amusement was there in his eyes.

Ellen steeled herself against the effect. "Not on your
best day."

Jay weighed the wisdom of trying to press for something more but decided not to push his luck. He needed to
win her over, not piss her off. He was already digging
himself out of a hole after the Glendenning debacle,
which he had to admit had been a major blunder on his
part. Instead of smoothing the track for him, bringing in
Glendenning had had the effect of throwing down a
gauntlet. That's what he got for rushing into this thing,

but he was in it now, a part of it. That had been the goal—to get inside.

"Good night, Mr. Brooks," she said, pulling the door open.

He shoved his hands into his coat pockets and hunched his shoulders against the mere idea of cold, casting a longing look back toward the fire. The retriever lumbered down the stairs and sauntered past him, wagging his tail but not pausing on his way to a warm spot in front of the hearth. The homeyness of the scene gave him a little unexpected kick in a spot he would have sworn was tougher.

"Well," he drawled, moving toward the open door, "at least the dog likes me."

"Don't make too much of it," Ellen advised. "He drinks out of the toilet, too."

He stopped in front of her. Close enough that when she looked into his eyes, she thought she saw something old and sad, like regret. *Foolish*, she told herself. He wasn't the kind of man to have regrets. He went after what he wanted and he got it, and she doubted he ever looked back.

"Good night, Ellen," he murmured, his tone as intimate as if they had known each other for a lifetime. "Get some rest. You've earned it."

With his eyes on hers, he leaned down and kissed her cheek. Not a quick, impersonal peck, but a soft, warm, intimate pressing of his lips against her skin, seducing her to turn toward him and invite the kiss to her lips. The idea sent quicksilver tremors through her and triggered a flood of forbidden questions. What would it be like to feel that incredible mouth of his—

She slammed the mental door on the vision, bringing herself back to the moment, embarrassed that a simple kiss on the cheek could quicken her pulse and send her common sense spinning off its axis. The knowing look on

Brooks's face was enough to make her want to slam the door on him.

"Sweet dreams, Ellen," he whispered, and sauntered out into the night.

Ellen stood in the open doorway, hugging herself against the cold as she watched him cross the street and climb into a dark Jeep Cherokee. The engine roared to life and he was gone, though the uneasy restlessness he had awakened in her lingered.

He kept her off balance—charming one minute, concerned the next, then seductive, then mercenary. Even the article she had read about him had alluded to "contradictions within him that were not easily reconciled." She thought of Phoebe's assessment of his turbulent aura hinting at inner turmoil and raw sexuality. She wondered who he really was, and told herself she didn't need to know. All she needed to know was not to trust him.

Who can you trust?
Trust no one.

Trust no one. The idea made her feel hollow and ill. By nature she wanted to trust. She wanted to feel safe. She wanted to believe those things were still possible, but the evidence didn't back her up. Another child was missing, and she was suddenly surrounded by people she didn't dare turn her back on—Brooks, Rudy, Glendenning, Garrett Wright.

Judge Franken's death suddenly took on symbolic proportions. He was the last honorable man. He was justice, and his death was the death of an era.

"Good Lord, Ellen." She chastised herself for being melodramatic, but the fear remained within her that her world had changed and there would be no going back.

To distract herself, she stepped out onto the porch in her stocking feet to dig her mail out of the box that hung beside the door. Bills, sweepstakes, a month-late Christmas card from her sister, Jill, more sweepstakes. Junk.

She reached in once more, her fingertips brushing something that had got jammed down into the bottom of the box. Making a face, she twisted her hand in the narrow confines, just catching hold of the corner of the paper. She pulled it out, expecting yet another sale flyer. What she got stopped her heart cold.

A crumpled slip of white paper with bold black print.

it ain't over till it's over

CHAPTER 10

"He quotes Oliver Wendell Holmes, Robert Browning, William Blake, Thomas Campbell, and *Yogi Berra*?" Cameron said, settling into a chair at the long table with a raisin bagel in one hand and a cup of Phoebe's Kona blend in the other. "It doesn't follow. Has to be a copycat."

At eight in the morning the conference room was as cold as a meat locker. In a move of fiscal responsibility, the county commissioners had determined it unnecessary to keep the heat in the courthouse above fifty degrees at night. It took the building half the day to warm up. Everyone in the room had hands wrapped around a coffee mug.

"Or one of Wright's supporters," Rudy offered. He had claimed the head of the table for his own. After spending two days in the wake of Bill Glendenning's powerful aura, he felt a rise in his own sense of power. He was in Glendenning's good graces, relatively safe on the sidelines of this case, and Victor Franken had finally croaked, obligingly vacating his seat on the bench. All may not have been right with the world, but Rudy Stovich didn't personally have a lot to complain about.

"It could have been one of Wright's students," Mitch said, his lack of inflection subtly giving away his doubts. He had declined the offer of a chair, opting instead to slowly pace the length of the table. Operating on too little sleep and too much stress, he was fueling his system with high-test caffeine and sugar doughnuts. "Ellen, you said you had a run-in yesterday with the Sci-Fi Cowboys. What's your feeling?"

"I don't know," she said, picking at a blueberry muffin. She was exhausted. Two nights with a total of eight hours' sleep left her feeling heavy and slow, as if the air around her was as dense as water. "Yesterday's mail was on top of it in the box, so I'd say the note had to be there before two o'clock yesterday afternoon." She was repeating the theory she had told last night to one cop and then another and another. "If it was one of the Cowboys, they had to have run straight to my house after I saw them."

"My guys will be canvassing your neighbors this morning asking if they saw anyone around your house yesterday."

And they would probably learn nothing. Her neighbors were professional people, with daytime jobs downtown or at Harris or in Minneapolis. There was always the chance someone had been home with the flu that was going around and had glanced out the window at the right moment, but she felt no hope for that. What she felt was a sense of disquiet that had been lingering since Monday.

Monday night kept coming back to her—waking suddenly, Harry growling, the silent phone call, then the call that Josh was home.

She recited it all for Mitch, step by step, half-embarrassed to be saying it at all. From an objective, rational perspective, nothing had happened. There had been no intruder in her home. The call had probably been a wrong number. But the timing of all that "nothing" made her uneasy.

Mitch stopped his pacing and faced her, pressing his palms flat on the table. "Is your home number listed?"

"Under my initials—E. E. North."

"I got a call myself last night," he confessed. "On my

cellular phone—a number only a few people have access to. The caller whispered, 'Ignorance is not innocence, but sin.' Right after he hung up, I got the word about the abduction in Campion."

Rudy looked alarmed. "Are you saying this lunatic is someone you know?"

"No." Mitch shook his head, his mouth twisting. "Our boy had the balls to call my mother-in-law and weasel the number out of her. I was just thinking, if he had to finagle Ellen's number out of someone, we'd have two people who might possibly be able to identify his voice."

Cameron looked at Ellen with concern. "Why didn't you say anything about this call yesterday?"

"I dismissed it as nerves. Josh came home. I've been busy with the case; I didn't think about it again—until I found the note. Even now I'm not sure it was anything. I mean, you're probably right—Yogi Berra is hardly Wright's style."

"But it might be his partner's style," Mitch argued. "Or it might be his idea of a joke. I'm no expert, but that note sure looked like the others."

"But the press made public the fact that the kidnapper's notes were on common twenty-pound bond and came out of a laser printer," Cameron said, automatically playing devil's advocate. "Any nut with access to a laser printer could have done it."

"True, but the press didn't actually see the notes, the type font, the preference for lower-case letters." He straightened away from the table, pulling his parka off the back of the chair where he had abandoned it earlier. "We'll see what the lab boys have to say. In the meantime, we'll check with your neighbors," he said to Ellen. "One of them might have seen a kidnapper."

He didn't look as if he believed that any more than she did, Ellen thought. Hope had become a scarce commodity. "What's the latest word from Campion?"

"'Help,'" he answered, shrugging into his coat. "They don't have a damn thing to go on. We've set up a multi-jurisdictional team of my people, guys from Steiger's office, and the BCA to work on connections. So far, there aren't any. The Hollomans don't know the Kirkwoods, Hannah isn't their doctor, Paul isn't their accountant, the boys have never met. Dustin and Josh share some physical traits—light hair, blue eyes, same age. That would be more significant if this were a sexual-predator thing, but it doesn't appear to be. It's some kind of goddamn chess game."

Rudy pushed his chair back and rose, hiking up his baggy suit pants by the belt. "Be sure to keep us abreast of the developments, Mitch," he said importantly.

"Yeah, I'll do that. If there are any. Ellen, I want you to call the department if you have any more odd happenings. It may be our boy or not. Wright has a lot of supporters. They may not all confine their anger to the picket line in front of the courthouse. You're a likely target."

"Thanks for reminding me," Ellen said sardonically, then remembered Megan. Megan, who was lying in a hospital bed because of this case. She could have as easily been dead. If the note had come from Wright's accomplice, then that could mean she had been singled out for inclusion in the game, as Megan had been singled out.

"Did anyone tell you Karen Wright went home yesterday?" Mitch asked, backing toward the door.

"Home—as in down the block from the Kirkwoods'?" Cameron said, appalled.

"It's the only home she's got," Mitch said. "The BCA was through with the place, and the city council was making noise about the cost of putting her up at the Fontaine, so we took her home."

"What about the accomplice?" Cameron asked. "If Karen knows something, she could be in danger."

"The BCA has a man on her. We should be so lucky that this creep is stupid enough to come calling."

"I'm concerned with her mental health," Ellen said. "Is she staying alone?"

"She has friends looking in on her, and Teresa McGuire, the victim-witness coordinator, is checking on her and reporting back to my office. Still hoping she'll turn on Wright?"

"She might have an attack of conscience."

"I wouldn't count on it, counselor. Denial is pretty tough armor."

Cameron turned to Rudy as Mitch made his exit and Ellen stuck her head out the door to call for more coffee. "Any word on who'll get the case with Franken gone?"

"None yet. They may delay the whole thing until a replacement is named," Rudy said, then frowned, worrying suddenly that his connection to this case, as much as he had tried to minimize it, would somehow jeopardize his chances for appointment to Franken's seat.

"If that happens, we can count on Wright's lawyer raising a stink," Ellen said.

She walked back along the length of the table slowly, her eyes scanning the mountains of paperwork the case had already generated—piles of statements, search warrants, arrest warrants, police reports. She and Cameron had commandeered this conference room for their own war room, where they could lay everything out and study it. A replica of the time line in the law-enforcement center was taped to one peeling dark-salmon wall.

Lying across a stack of news clippings was the morning *Star Tribune* opened to a photo of Jay Butler Brooks scowling at the camera. The headline read " *'Crime Boss' Fights to Save Judge.* " Ellen tossed it onto the credenza. Behind it dusty, hot air from the vents blew straight up along the old window, where eighty percent of the heat escaped through the glass.

"By law Wright is entitled to that hearing without delay," she said. "I bet they'll divvy up Judge Franken's caseload between Witt and Grabko and float another judge in here to catch the overflow until the governor names a replacement."

Rudy breathed a sigh of relief. "Who *is* Wright's attorney now?"

Cameron shrugged.

Ellen shook her head. "I'm going to see Dennis later. Maybe he'll know something we don't."

"You can bet he knows something we don't," Cameron said darkly. "Rumor has it he had a long talk with his client after the bond hearing yesterday and that he left the jail looking sick."

"He'd just lost a client and a chance for a lot of publicity," Rudy pointed out.

Cameron reserved comment, his gaze steady on Ellen.

"I'll find out what I can," she said. "But how much can he tell me without committing a breach of ethics?"

"How much can he keep to himself without committing a breach of decency?"

"Let me know what you find out," Rudy instructed. "Where do we stand as far as ammunition for this hearing?"

"We've got the statements from Mitch and from Megan O'Malley regarding her abduction and that whole drama," Cameron said. "We won't have the DNA results back on the bloody sheet Wright wrapped around her that night, but we've already got the blood types—one of which is the same as O'Malley's and one of which is the same as Josh's."

"Regarding O'Malley's situation," Ellen said, "as you know, Wright was apprehended fleeing the scene. To paraphrase Megan, we've got him dead to rights."

"But what about the boy's case? So far, we've got a victim who's not talking."

"We've got Ruth Cooper, the witness who identified Wright in the lineup as being the man she saw on Ryan's Bay the day Josh Kirkwood's jacket was found," Cameron said.

Rudy made a rumbling sound in his throat that might have been discontent or phlegm. "I was there. The lineup was wearing parkas and sunglasses. A good defense attorney is going to take it apart like Tinkertoys."

"The visual may be iffy," Ellen conceded, "but you'll remember, Mrs. Cooper also made a voice ID. The two together will be hard to discount."

"We've also got Agent O'Malley's testimony as to what Wright confessed to her regarding Josh," Cameron pointed out.

"He said, she said," Rudy grumbled.

"She's a police officer."

"She's a victim. Hardly an impartial hearsay witness."

Ellen tipped her head. "Maybe, maybe not. I think her credentials will carry her through."

"Wright knows the Kirkwood family," Cameron went on. "And he has a flimsy alibi for the time Josh disappeared. He claims he was at his office working that night, but so far that's just his say-so."

"So what's his motive?" Rudy asked.

"We don't have one, other than that he's playing some kind of sick game," Ellen said. "All we have to do for the moment is get him bound over. We don't need a motive until trial. We have to bear in mind that Wright wasn't even a suspect until Saturday night. The investigation is really just beginning."

Rudy ambled to the window and looked down on the early shift of protestors gathering on the sidewalk.

"It sounds like you've got everything under control, Ellen," he said, glancing at her from the corner of his eye.

Rumors had been churning for months that the yuppies of Park County were looking to root him out of office and replace him with Ellen North. When he moved into Franken's seat, the path would be clear for her. She and her backers likely saw this case as her chance to step into the limelight, but limelight wouldn't be the only thing she would step in. He pulled in a deep, cleansing breath and envisioned his judgeship, so close, he could feel his new black robes draping over him.

"You know, I'm just an old country lawyer at heart," he said. "When I came on this job, there was no such thing as a high-profile case. Folks around here didn't lock their doors. They let their kids run all over town without worrying about them. Deer Lake was the kind of town America is supposed to be all about."

Ellen recognized the speech immediately. He had used it as his closing statement in a drug dealer's trial eighteen months ago. He heaved an exaggerated sigh and twisted his features into the expression of a sad clown.

"Do your best, Ellen," he instructed. "Always let your constituents know you did your best."

"Rudy, I've told you a hundred times, I have no intention of running for your office."

And for the hundred and first time he didn't listen. The irony was too much. Her ambition topped out right where she was. She had no political aspirations, had thought leaving Hennepin County had been a clear statement to that effect. Yet, in the place she had come to settle herself into a comfortable niche, she was constantly viewed with suspicious eyes as being an ambitious woman with her sights on bigger things.

"Yes, well . . . ," he said, sauntering away.

As he opened the door, Phoebe popped in, coffeepot in hand.

"Garrett Wright has a new attorney." Her face glowed with the excitement of it all. She set the coffeepot on the table, unable to give the announcement adequate fanfare without using her hands. "A *big* big shot," she said, bracelets rattling. "Anthony Costello."

Cameron gave a low whistle. "Wow. Where'd Wright get that kind of money? Costello's retainer is more than a professor at Harris makes in a year."

"That was my question, too," Phoebe said, sliding into the chair next to him, settling in for a round of juicy speculation.

"It doesn't matter who his lawyer is." Rudy spouted false confidence like a fountain, the promise of his judgeship making him magnanimous. "We've got the team to beat him. Isn't that right, Ellen? Ellen?"

Ellen jerked her head in Rudy's direction, feeling faint. "Yes, of course."

Her voice sounded far away to her, as if it had come from someone out in the hall. Her hands were curled over the back of a chair, fingertips digging into the upholstery.

"Wright can bring in his big-shot lawyer from the Cities. We've got Ellen," Rudy declared as he marched off down the hall, thanking God he had dropped this hot potato in Ellen North's lap.

"Did you ever come up against Costello when you were with Hennepin County?" Cameron asked.

"A few times."

She imagined if she was to look in a mirror, her reflection would be pale and wide-eyed, but neither Phoebe nor Cameron seemed to notice anything odd about her appearance or her manner. She pulled out the chair and slid into it. Her body seemed to be working independently of her mind, and thank God for that. In her mind she was floundering, scrambling, knocked off balance by a blindside shot.

Tony Costello's was not a name she had ever expected to hear in these offices. He was big money, style and flash, one of the top defense attorneys in the Twin Cities and rapidly making a name for himself on a larger scale. Which was, of course, what he would be doing with Garrett Wright—soaking up publicity like a sponge, posing for the cameras and preaching his propaganda of justice for the common man.

That was why he had taken Garrett Wright's case, Ellen told herself. It had nothing to do with the fact that she was the prosecutor, and it certainly had nothing to do with the fact that they had once been lovers.

Garrett Wright couldn't have known anything about her past with Tony Costello. It was just a coincidence that he had chosen the one defense attorney in the state who knew her better than any other, the one who had slipped under her guard and stabbed her in the back.

Even as she tried to placate herself, the tide of the uneasiness that had been with her since Monday night rose a little higher inside her.

"We've calculated all the moves, all the options, all the possibilities," Garrett Wright had whispered to Megan. *"We can't lose."*

"We can't lose," Anthony Costello said, his voice clear and strong, his eyes on the network cameras. "Dr. Wright is an innocent man, wrongfully accused and wrongfully imprisoned."

Shutters clicked. Motor drives whirred. Cameras loved his face—square, rugged, utterly masculine, perpetually tanned. His eyes were the color of espresso, set deep beneath the ledge of his brow. He had long ago perfected a piercing stare that could make witnesses crumble and jurors sway.

He stood on the front steps of the Campion Sons of Norway hall, the wind ruffling his jet-black hair. The cameras had to shoot up to get him, an angle that made him look taller than five feet ten and emphasized the solid squareness of his build and the excellent hand-tailored cut of his black wool topcoat. He would have preferred to make his first statements to the press regarding his new client in front of the Park County courthouse because he liked the symbolism of storming the halls of justice, but the press was in Campion covering the second child abduction, so he had gone with Plan B. It was the mark of a good defense attorney to be flexible, to be adaptable. He had to be able to shift on the run, think on his feet.

He had begun to formulate a strategy for the defense the moment he had accepted Garrett Wright as a client. He wanted to strike hard and fast at the media, grab their attention and keep it on him. The kidnapping of Dustin Holloman was a terrible tragedy, but Costello had also seen it immediately as the opportunity it was. Naturally, he felt sympathy for the family—in the way one might feel sympathy for fictional characters in a movie. He couldn't allow the feeling to become more personal than that. It was essential for him to put their tragedy in a perspective that would potentially be of some benefit to his client.

"My client sits in jail, his reputation suffering more with every passing hour, while a madman stalks the children of Park County," he said. "The investigation of the kidnapping in Deer Lake was mishandled from the start. As a result, there have been needless deaths, an innocent man has been incarcerated, and now another family has been torn apart."

The reporters clamored for his attention, barking out questions, thrusting microphones up at him. He gave the answer he wanted to give, not caring whether the question had been asked.

"I'm here in Park County to see that justice will be done." Sound bite extraordinaire. "I'm here in Campion as an emissary for my client, to offer his deepest concern to the family of little Dustin Holloman. I know Dr.

Wright would want me to extend a personal plea to the kidnappers to return Dustin unharmed."

He knew no such thing, of course. He had yet to speak directly to Garrett Wright. It was unlikely Wright had even heard about the kidnapping. For all Costello knew, Wright was a coldhearted son of a bitch who wouldn't have felt a second's pity if all the children in Campion were torn from their families and carted off to concentration camps. It didn't matter. As of this moment the press would look upon his client as a compassionate man with a deep, abiding respect for families, for the law, for America.

"Who do you blame for botching the Kirkwood investigation?"

He frowned in the general direction of the reporter who had shouted the question. "I think there's blame enough to go around, don't you?"

Not having paid close attention to the case from the outset, he had spent six hours last night going over news clippings from both major dailies in Minneapolis and St. Paul. He had watched videos of newscasts and interviews, absorbing as much as he could about the principal players, though he wasn't ready yet to single any one out for public castigation.

The female BCA agent was sleeping with the chief of police. A convicted pedophile had been working at the ice arena, then killed himself while in custody. A mummified cadaver had been found in the garage of a church deacon who had eluded capture for two days, then fell to his death before he could be apprehended. There were enough plot twists for a soap opera—which was exactly what had caught the attention of the networks and the tabloids. Immune to everyday crime, they sought the sensational, the kind of stuff writers were paid for in Hollywood. It was so much cheaper to get it from real life.

"But though there has been a gross miscarriage of justice," Costello went on, "I want it made clear that Dr. Wright himself bears no grudges. He still has trust in our justice system and faith that the truth will out and he will be exonerated—just as we all must have faith that the kidnapper of Dustin Holloman and Josh Kirkwood will be found and punished; that justice will be swift and sure."

On that glorious note, Costello stepped down from his impromptu podium and moved quickly through the crowd toward his waiting black Lincoln Town Car, his staff clearing the path for him. He had brought with him an associate, a legal assistant, and a personal assistant who was also his driver. Another of his associates had been sent ahead to Deer Lake for the purpose of leasing an office suite. It would be far inferior to his offices in the IDS tower in downtown Minneapolis, but it would serve the purpose. He believed it was important to establish a presence, like a show of muscle before a fight. It would also be easier to have a base of operations in the town rather than try to do everything long-distance. By the end of the day, the Deer Lake office would have a full complement of business machines and one of his secretaries would be hard at work.

"Excellent presentation, Mr. Costello," Dorman said. A fellow Purdue alumnus, Dorman was twenty-seven, sharp but not ambitious, more interested in being secure than in being famous; comfortable to learn at Costello's elbow, work like a dog, and take none of the credit—all of which made him ideal for his job.

Costello chose his people carefully, with just such things in mind. He accepted no associates with Ivy League educations because he had not been able to afford one himself, and he did not want any snotty, silver-spoon rich kids who felt they were socially superior to him. Nor did he want his office projecting an image of elitism. He was himself the product of a middle-class, blue-collar upbringing, and proud of it.

In choosing associates, he hired primarily family men, none of them taller than he was. Sensitive to society's current mania for political correctness, he had peppered his staff with an assortment of women and minorities. Levine, the legal assistant who sat in the front seat ahead of him, was an equal-opportunity triple score—a black, Jewish woman. He was careful to select female staff members who were neither unattractive nor beautiful.

Everything in the offices of Anthony Costello—from plants to personnel—had been selected by Costello to showcase Costello. That was the way image was made, and in today's world image was everything. Image was perceived as success. Success bred greater success. Success opened the doors of opportunity that led to fame. Opportunity had to be seized and wrung out for all it was worth.

Levine turned sideways in her seat and handed a neatly folded copy of the *St. Paul Pioneer Press* back to him. "Here's the article on the death of Judge Franken, Mr. Costello."

The story was situated directly below the continuation of the front-page piece concerning Garrett Wright's bond hearing, as if one event had led to the other. A photograph the size of a postage stamp portrayed Franken in his robes. He looked like an apple-head doll that had begun to rot. A second, much larger photo depicted the chaos in the courtroom where Franken had died—a group of people huddled over an indistinct form on the floor. The focus of the picture was on one familiar face that had turned to glare at the cameras. Jay Butler Brooks.

Costello hummed a note to himself. A Cheshire-cat smile creased the corners of his mouth.

"I've got a call in to the district assignments clerk," Dorman said, "to find out what kind of delay we can expect."

"Don't be passive, Dorman," Costello said. "We won't *expect* a delay. We'll demand there be none."

His associate's brows rose, a pair of beige hyphens barely discernible from his skin tone. "We could use the extra time to prepare."

"The prosecution would use the extra time to prepare," Costello clarified. "Wright was arrested Saturday night. Prior to his arrest, he had not been a suspect. I can guarantee you the county attorney's office is scrambling to put their case together. Should we allow them extra time to do that, Mr. Dorman?"

"No, sir."

"No, sir," he echoed, his gaze drifting out the window, his memory drifting back in time. "Hit 'em hard, hit 'em fast," he murmured. "We'll have this case dismissed before Ellen North can turn around."

CHAPTER 11

"But though there has been a gross miscarriage of justice, I want it made clear that Dr. Wright himself bears no grudges. He still has trust in our justice system, and faith that the truth will out and he will be exonerated—just as we all must have faith that the kidnapper of Dustin Holloman and Josh Kirkwood will be found and punished; that justice will be swift and sure."

Jay clicked off the nineteen-inch color television that sat on the carton it had come in. Costello vanished, but the smell of his game lingered like bad gas. Jay knew the game plan well enough. He had employed it himself in his brief life as a defense attorney. Costello would attack where and when he could, create opportunities if he had to. He would paint a glowing portrait of his client that would bear only a passing resemblance to the man and slam the opposition with every kind of accusation he could think of. It was a game of diversion that tied in quite neatly with the kidnappers', as it happened. Nice coincidence that they were all on the same team.

He took a last deep drag off his cigarette and threw the butt into the fireplace that was gray with the dust of ashes long since swept away.

His sudden pilgrimage to Deer Lake had left him without many options in the way of accommodations. There wasn't a hotel room to be had for miles; all of them were filled with reporters. Furnished apartments were the domain of Harris College students, who were just returning to classes after their winter break. Impatient and unconcerned with the cost, he had taken this house.

He needed to work, to immerse himself in a world that had no connection with the life he had so abruptly left in Alabama. It didn't matter what it cost him in terms of cash. He would have paid anything to make the fresh memories fade into oblivion. Lobotomy and alcoholism, while they would certainly have dulled the pain, were not viable alternatives. Work was the best thing he could find. Why he had chosen this particular case in which to lose himself was a question he chose to ignore.

"And you don't find that just the least bit twisted? Escaping into someone else's real-life tragedy?"

It's just a story. He repeated to himself the pat answer he had given Ellen, knowing there was more. Still, he clung to the lie for his own sanity's sake.

The case was timely and fascinating. Writing about it was his job, and he was damn good at it. And so he had come to Deer Lake . . .

With such blind, desperate haste that he hadn't packed much more than a change of underwear.

Dismissing the temptation to self-analyze, he turned his attention to his surroundings. Overpriced by Deer Lake standards, the house had been on the market long enough that the owners had gratefully accepted three months' exorbitant rent and turned over the keys and the burden of heating the place.

As yet, he had been unsuccessful in warming it up. Even with the thermostat cranked into the seventies, the rooms seemed cold, as if furniture and family were required for the warmth to stay instead of sailing up through the roof to be swallowed greedily by the cold. He had set himself up entirely in the living room, because the huge stone fireplace at least *suggested* warmth. Unfortunately, the owners had seen fit to take all fireplace tools and accoutrements with them, including the grate. There wasn't so much as a stick of kindling or a kitchen match, let alone a neat stack of fake logs ready to glow with the flick of a switch.

He stood and tried to stretch the kinks out of his back that had set in from sleeping in a sleeping bag on the floor. His gaze did a slow scan of the room, automatically comparing it to Ellen's cozy living room. Here there was only emptiness and impermanence. Instead of overstuffed armchairs, he had badly strung lawn chairs that had been left in the garage. Instead of a cherrywood coffee table, he had a pair of eight-foot fold-down rent-all tables with fake wood-grain tops. Instead of folk art and potted plants, he had leased office equipment—a laser printer, copier, fax-and-answering machine. The tables were strewn with file folders and news clippings. His laptop computer sat open and ready, its screen blank, waiting for him to fill it with the words that would bring this story to life for the hundreds of thousands of people who read his books.

He turned away from it and went to the kitchen for a fresh cup of coffee—from the coffeemaker that sat beside the box it had come in. He had stocked the cupboards with paper plates and cups, the refrigerator with beer, the freezer with pizzas and frozen entrées. Since his divorce five years previous, he had left cuisine to restaurant chefs. Cooking a meal for himself only reminded him he had no one to share it with.

Not that he missed Christine. He occasionally mourned the loss of the girl she had once been—pretty, sweet, undemanding. The wife who had left him was another matter. In retrospect they had been mismatched from the first. Christine had a deep-seated need for stability; he was impetuous and reckless. The bright, hot love that had sprung up between them had quickly cooled and soured to frustration. Frustration fostered resentment. Resentment bred pain. With pain came disillusionment.

And hate. She must have hated me. She must still.

The thoughts he had been trying to hold at bay for the last week crept in. They were never far from the surface when he was tired. He cursed his ex-wife for coming back into his life for those few days last week, however accidental their meeting might have been. He had long been over Christine, but he didn't know that he would ever get over what she had done to him without his consent or knowledge.

In his mind's eye he saw the boy standing beside her with his thick shock of brown hair and sky-blue eyes.

She must have hated me. She must still.

Sipping at the coffee that was strong enough to take the finish off the kitchen cabinets, he wandered through the empty dining room and back to his base of operations.

With four bedrooms, three baths, and a living room with a two-story cathedral ceiling, the house was certainly more than he needed, but not more than he was accustomed to. His home on the outskirts of Eudora was twice this size, a reproduction plantation-era mansion that made the Brookses' ancestral home look like a tacky bungalow. He had built it to impress and to inspire jealousy and to flaunt his success in the faces of the people who had always pegged him as his generation's Bad Brooks, destined to dereliction and drunkenness. He lived in a fraction of it, and the ostentation of the place meant nothing to him on a personal level. He would have been just as satisfied living in a two-bedroom apartment.

He wasn't sure what that meant, considering he had never in his life felt satisfied. There had been a restlessness within him since boyhood and before. All his life his mother had taken great delight in complaining about what a restless baby he had been, so impatient to be born he had come two weeks early and hadn't bothered to wait for the doctor.

"You hit the ground running, boy," Uncle Hooter had often said.

Unfortunately, in all his Johnnie Walker wisdom, Uncle Hooter had never given any indication of where or what he was supposed to be running to. *Trouble* had been the general consensus, and Jay had borne that out well enough. He had been a burden and a blight on the Brooks family name more times than he could count, and yet he always managed to come out smelling like a rose in the end, always twisting disaster into irony.

He was the Brooks who had broken windows and minor laws and major traditions. The one who had forsaken Auburn—the Brooks-family alma mater since Christ was an undergraduate—for a baseball scholarship at Purdue. He was the one who had turned his nose up at the venerable old Brooks-family law practice, the one whose wife had left him. But he was also the Brooks who had made a fortune and a name for himself, the Brooks who was courted by New York and Hollywood and had his face either on the cover or the inside of every known magazine in America. He was the black sheep whose exploits the family had criticized with relish, whose fame they accepted grudgingly, whose money they took without qualm.

There was a book in there somewhere, but he had no desire to write it. He preferred digging for skeletons in the closets of perfect strangers, trying to make some sense of the twists and snags in their lives. And so he had come to Deer Lake.

. . . you're a mercenary profiteer no better than a vampire . . . a hack looking to steal the lives and pain of real people to compensate for your own lack of a real imagination.

Ellen's words echoed sharply in his mind. He told himself they didn't matter, that what she thought couldn't matter to him because he couldn't allow himself to get involved with her. He was here for a purpose, and it wasn't having sex with Ellen North.

He stood at the big windows that rose to a peak in the main wall of the living room and stared out at the harsh white landscape. Ryan's Bay, the realtor had called it, though it wasn't a bay at all but an area of sloughs out on the edge of nothing, west of the part of Deer Lake known to locals as Dinkytown. Whatever water the "bay" held lay secret beneath the dunes of snow, a frozen desert, bleak and uninviting. Blond weeds and cattail stalks rose through the drifts to flutter in the bitter wind.

The nearest house was a quarter mile off to the north, hidden by a thick stand of pine trees. To the east he could see the last Deer Lake neighborhood that straggled out to the edge of the marsh and farm fields, small square houses with smoke curling up from their chimneys into the winter-white sky. The spires of St. Elysius Catholic Church rose above the rooftops, a pair of lances thrusting toward heaven. They seemed a long way from where he stood, though he reckoned it wasn't more than three quarters of a mile. There was a sense of isolation here that had little to do with distance.

Josh Kirkwood's jacket had been found out here, tucked in the weeds just off a trail used for snowmobiling and cross-country skiing. An older woman named Ruth Cooper had gone out with her dog to let him run, even though the windchill factor that day had clocked in at fifty degrees below zero. The Labrador had dragged the jacket up from the weeds, and Ryan's Bay had become the focus of the search and the media.

Jay could very clearly remember the news footage of Paul Kirkwood falling to his knees in the snow, his son's coat clutched in his hands while he sobbed. *"Oh my God, Josh! Josh! Oh God! No!"*

He could still hear the anguish, could feel it run

GUILTY AS SIN 155

through him like a pike. For a fleeting second he put himself in Paul Kirkwood's place and imagined the kind of wild, hot panic that would tear through him if all he had left of his own son was a jacket and a madman's twisted message.

The emotion hit him with physical force, punishing, crushing. Nine times sharper than the pain he had brought here with him. He pushed it away, cursing himself for a masochist. He didn't need to feel what these people felt, he only needed to capture it on paper.

With that squarely at the forefront of his mind, he abandoned his coffee, grabbed his coat, and headed for the door.

The accounting firm of Christianson and Kirkwood was housed in a new two-story square brick building that bore the grandiose name of The Omni Complex. According to the list of tenants in the foyer, the building also housed a real-estate agency, an insurance agency, and a pair of small law firms. Christianson and Kirkwood was located on the second floor.

Jay walked up, found the oak door with the appropriate stenciling job, and let himself into the outer office, which looked like a thousand other outer offices he had been in—white walls hung with pseudo-southwestern artwork, the requisite potted palm, nondescript furnishings of oak and oatmeal-colored upholstery. A secretary with flame-red hair looked up questioningly from her computer terminal and gave a little jolt of recognition.

"Is Mr. Kirkwood in?" Jay asked, flashing a smile. "Name's Jay Butler Brooks. I'd take a minute or two of his time if he's free."

The secretary sucked in a little gasp of breath, her blue eyes round as silver dollars in her freckled face. Apparently rendered speechless, she popped up from her chair and disappeared into Paul Kirkwood's office. Jay eyed the small sofa that had likely been picked more for the decor than comfort, and stayed on his feet. His own face stared up at him from the cover of an outdated *People* magazine on the oak coffee table. *Crime Czar: Jay Butler Brooks Pens Arresting True Crime And Makes A Killing In The Process.* *People*'s penchant for puns never failed to make him cringe.

"Mr. Brooks." A handsome smile turned Paul Kirkwood's mouth as he strode out of his office. "It's a pleasure to meet you."

Jay closed the distance between them. "I have a regrettable habit of dropping in on people. I hope this isn't an inconvenient time."

"No, not at all." Kirkwood met Jay's handshake automatically, but his grip was uncertain. "Come on into my office. Would you like coffee, Mr. Brooks?"

"No thanks." Jay said.

While Paul gave instructions for privacy to his secretary, Jay took a moment to survey the room, looking for clues about Josh's father. As in the outer office, the furnishings were oak with smooth, rounded modern lines. A framed print of wood ducks hung on one dark-green wall. Another displayed diplomas and certificates. The office was neat and tidy—compulsively so. If not for the open file on the desk, he would have thought he had walked into a display in a furniture store. The only sign of Paul Kirkwood living here was the neatly folded green-plaid blanket on the sofa.

"I read in the paper about your performing CPR on Judge Franken," Paul said as he entered the office and closed the door behind him. He was clean-shaven, his pinstriped white shirt neatly pressed, the crease in his brown trousers sharp. "What a strange and unpleasant happening that must have been."

"Imagine how the judge must have felt about it," Jay said dryly. A framed photograph in the bookcase caught his eye: Josh in a too-big baseball uniform, Paul kneeling beside him with a proud and silly grin on his lean, handsome face. The image caught Jay unaware.

"Josh is quite the little athlete, huh?" he asked, nodding to the photo. "Baseball, hockey. He was at hockey the night he was abducted, right?"

"Yes. He plays wing on his Squirts team. Hannah was supposed to pick him up that night, but she got hung up at the hospital. . . ."

He spoke carefully, trying to keep the accusation out of his voice, but a hint of it remained like a phantom coffee stain that wouldn't come out of a shirt. The feeling had become dyed into the fabric of the answer.

"I'm sorry for your pain," Jay said. "I can only imagine the toll this all has taken on you and your wife. And then to have the perpetrator turn out to be someone you knew and trusted . . . Must have been one hell of a shock."

"You don't know the half of it," Paul muttered.

"Let me tell you what I'm doing here, Mr. Kirkwood."

Jay walked around behind the desk and glanced out the narrow window that overlooked the parking lot full of cars crusted in winter grime.

"What's gone on here, what's going to go on here in bringing this case to trial, has caught the interest of the nation," he said, turning around. "A crime like this one in a small town touches a lot of nerves. If a crime like this can happen here in Deer Lake, Minnesota, then it can happen anywhere. People want to feel they have some understanding of why that is and what they might do to prevent it."

"You want to do a book about Josh's kidnapping."

"Possibly. Probably. It's an intriguing story. Complicated. Compelling. I imagine it will prove to be only more so as the trial unfolds."

"And you'd like to make some kind of deal?"

Jay looked up from his examination of the items meticulously arranged on the desk. There were dollar signs in Paul Kirkwood's deep-set hazel eyes.

"Deal?" Jay said, playing dumb.

Kirkwood shrugged. "*Inside Edition* offered me a hundred thousand."

And you're waiting for me to up the ante, Jay thought. He had been through it all before. Sometimes victims threw him out of their houses, outraged at the very idea of a book about their ordeal, and sometimes they wanted him to compensate them for their suffering as if he had perpetrated the crime himself for the sole purpose of setting the scene for a book. And then there were the Paul Kirkwoods of the world. Paul Kirkwood had greed oozing out of his pores like sweat. *And Ellen thinks* I'm *the profiteer.* . . .

"I don't do deals, Mr. Kirkwood. What I write is not a biography. This story will involve many people. If I grant any one of them a portion of the book, then I run the risk of having the story slanted to reflect their view of things. Contrary to what some might believe, I have ethics and I do apply them."

"And your 'ethics' don't include sharing the millions you'll make on a book?" Paul scowled at him, a look that was more petulance than menace. "I fail to see how you can publish a book about events in someone's life without compensating them."

"It's like this, Mr. Kirkwood: the crime, the trial, that's all a matter of public record. If you choose to talk to me, then I may include your point of view. If you choose not to, then I'm forced to form opinions based on the testimony of others and the records of the events that have taken place. It's your call."

"It's *my* life," Paul snapped. "I deserve—"

Jay narrowed his eyes.

"Josh is my son," he said, scrambling to cover his mistake. "He deserves something from this."

Jay had made up his mind on that issue before he'd even

climbed onto the plane to come to Minnesota. He would set up a trust for Josh, as he had for other victims whose stories he had told. A sizable chunk of the book advance and royalties would go into it. This was his standard procedure, a practice he kept absolutely out of the press, for the obvious reasons.

He chose to withhold this information from Paul Kirkwood as well. Paul had failed the test. *It's my life . . . I deserve . . .* Inside Edition *offered me . . .*

"Well, I'll tell you what, Mr. Kirkwood," he drawled, "Josh sure as hell deserves better than what he's got."

Letting that hang in the air, he crossed the room slowly and rested a hand on the doorknob.

"I'll leave my number with your secretary. You can think on it some and call me if you'd like—if you can find time between *Hard Copy* and *Oprah*."

Paul watched him walk out, rage curling inside him. Bastard. He could pay lip service to ethics and the integrity of his story, but he wouldn't pay cash. He would rake in five million and still had the gall to sneer at the man whose suffering would be an integral part of what would make him that fortune.

I deserve . . . Paul refused to feel guilty for thinking it. He *did* deserve something. He was a victim, too.

Even as a part of him insisted on his entitlement, another part of him thought of Josh in the hospital, while another filled with images of that night two weeks ago. All of it twisted inside of him until he felt as if he were caught in a whirlpool sucking him down to drown in panic and remorse.

Josh's frantic cries of "No!" echoed in his ears. He pressed his hands over them. Even with his eyes squeezed tight against the images, he could see his son kicking against the hospital bed, felt as if each kick were landing squarely in his belly.

A thin cry slipping between his lips, he sank down in

the chair behind his desk and doubled over. Shudders racked his body. His mouth twisted open; the chaos in his brain thinned to a single thought—*my son, my son, my son, my son* . . .

Then came the guilt. A wall of it. It was the guilt that made him open the bottom drawer of his desk. It was the guilt that had made him keep the answering-machine tape from that fateful night. He kept the tape in a microcassette recorder he had bought for dictating letters but never used.

He placed the small black rectangle on the desk, pressed the play button. And Josh's voice spoke to him from the crossroads that had turned all their lives onto a dark path.

CHAPTER 12

"*I'm here in Park County to see that justice will be done.*"

Ellen chewed on Tony Costello's words as she drove all the way across town.

"As if the state outside the metro area is a lawless frontier," Cameron complained. "And he's Wyatt Earp, come to bring us justice."

"It's all part of the show," Ellen murmured, turning onto Lakeshore Drive.

"It doesn't bother you?"

"Of course it does. Using the Holloman kidnapping in a naked grab for publicity—it's too sleazy for words. But you can't let Tony Costello get to you any more than you let Denny Enberg or Fred Nelson get to you, Cameron. He's just another hired gun."

"A hired gun in an Armani suit."

"That's what success will buy you in the big city, Cam. If you're willing to pay the price."

"I'm not interested in becoming the next Anthony Costello."

"Glad to hear it. The world has more Tony Costellos than it needs."

"He doesn't impress me."

"Well, he should," Ellen said, turning in at the Kirkwoods' drive. "He's extremely good at what he does.

Don't underestimate him and don't let him get under your skin."

She turned the Bonneville off and sat for a moment, looking at the Kirkwoods' home, a cedar-sided multilevel that fit in gracefully with its wooded surroundings. Built on the last oversize lot on the street, it had an unrestricted view of the lake to the west. On the north and east the thick woods of Quarry Hills Park wrapped the property in a feeling of seclusion that must have cost a pretty penny. On the front yard a half-finished snow fort gave testimony to the normalcy of life in this home before a kidnapper destroyed it.

Her eyes lingered on the Wrights' house two doors down.

Ellen heaved a sigh. "Okay, let's get it over with."

Hannah answered the door, looking pale and thin. The smile she gave as she invited them in was brittle and quick.

"Hannah, this is my associate, Cameron Reed." Ellen pulled her gloves off and stuffed them into her coat pockets.

"Yes, I believe we met last summer over a soccer injury," Hannah said, shaking hands with Cameron.

He smiled warmly. "I recovered fully, and you were right—the scar is a definite icebreaker at the gym." The smile faded. "I can't tell you how sorry I am for all you and your family have gone through, Dr. Garrison."

"Thank you," Hannah replied automatically. "Let me take your coats."

"How's Josh doing?" Ellen asked.

The brittle smile came and went. "It's good to have him home."

"Has he said anything? Given any indication of who took him or where they took him?"

Hannah glanced into the family room. Ellen's gaze followed, searching. Josh was nowhere to be seen.

"No," Hannah answered at last. "He hasn't said a word about it. Come in. I've got coffee if you'd like."

They followed her through the comfortable family room with its sturdy country-colonial furnishings and scattering of toddler's toys, and up the three steps into the spacious kitchen.

"I heard about that boy in Campion," Hannah said as she went through the ritual of setting out mugs and pouring the coffee. "I wouldn't have wished that hell on anyone. My heart goes out to the family."

"It's all the more incentive for us to build a strong case," Cameron explained. "The more pressure we can bring to bear against our man, the more likely he may be willing to give us his accomplice."

Hannah's eyes widened. Her hands were trembling as she set their coffee mugs down. "You're not going to make a deal with him? After everything he's done?"

"No," Ellen assured. "No deals. He's going down for all of it. We're hoping Josh will be able to help us nail him. As I explained to you over the phone, Hannah, we want to have Josh take a look at what we call a photo lineup. If he picks our man out of that, we'll want to proceed with an actual lineup at the police station. We felt it would be less traumatic for him to start with the photographs. We don't want to upset Josh, but his ability to identify his abductor would certainly be key to our prosecution."

"Will he have to testify in court?"

"That will depend on how much he remembers or is willing to tell," Cameron said.

"If Josh is able to testify, we'll do everything we can to prepare him so he won't be frightened," Ellen explained.

Hannah reached up to toy nervously with an earring. "Couldn't he testify on videotape? I've seen that on television."

"Possibly," Ellen said. "There is precedent. I'll talk with the judge when the time comes, but for now all we want is to have Josh look at photographs. Could you bring him in?"

As Hannah left the kitchen, Cameron opened his briefcase, pulled out a sheet of plastic pockets from a photo album, and placed it on the table.

"She's not holding up well," he murmured.

"I'm sure we can't even imagine what it's been like," Ellen said, keeping an eye peeled for Hannah's return. "I heard their marriage is all but over."

"Garrett Wright has a lot to answer for."

Hannah herded Josh into the kitchen. Josh eyed them warily. He seemed like an impostor of the boy in the "missing" posters, with his gap-toothed smile and Cub Scout uniform. The physical resemblance to that boy was there, but none of the sparkle, none of the joy. His eyes looked a hundred years old.

"Hi, Josh, my name is Ellen." She leaned down to eye level with him. "And this is my friend, Cameron. He likes to play soccer in the summer. Do you go out for soccer?"

Josh stared at her, silent. His mother ruffled his curly hair. "Josh plays baseball in the summer. Don't you, honey?"

He looked from Ellen to Cameron, then turned and faced the refrigerator, losing himself in the photographs and school artwork stuck to it with magnets. Hannah knelt down beside him.

"Josh, Ellen and Cameron want you to take a look at some pictures they brought with them. They want to see if the man who took you away from us is one of the men in the photographs. Can you do that?"

He gave no answer, no reaction of any kind. She turned him gently by the shoulders toward the table.

"Just take a look at these, Josh," Ellen instructed, sliding the sheet of photos toward him. "Take your time and look at all the men. If you see the man who took you, all you have to do is point at him."

Ellen held her breath as he bent his head over the pictures, looking at one face, then another. All were mug shots, some of criminals, some of Deer Lake police officers. Garrett Wright's occupied the upper right-hand pocket. Josh looked at them all, his gaze lingering on Wright's face, then moving on.

"All you have to do is point at him, Josh," Ellen murmured. "He's not going to hurt you. We'll make sure he'll never hurt you or any other kids ever again."

His gaze slowly skated back up across the faces; then he turned away and went to the refrigerator to stare at a construction-paper snowman.

"Josh, are you sure you didn't see the man?" Hannah asked, a desperate edge to her voice. "Maybe you should come back and look again. Come on—"

Ellen rose and gently caught hold of her arm before she could drag Josh back to the table.

"It's okay, Hannah. Maybe he just isn't ready to look yet. We'll try it again another day."

"But—" Hannah's gaze darted from her son to the mug shot of Wright.

"It's all right," Ellen said, wishing she felt as nonchalant as she sounded. "When he's ready, he'll talk about it. He's just not ready yet."

"What if he's never ready?" she whispered.

"We'll make the case," Ellen promised. But as they drove away from the Kirkwood house, she wondered if it was a promise she would be able to keep.

Josh was the only witness who could identify Wright and his accomplice. Josh had seen the person who'd picked him up at the hockey rink. The witness, Helen Black, had glanced out her window that night and seen a boy who could only have been Josh willingly climbing into a van. He had to have seen who was driving it.

"Maybe the accomplice picked him up," Cameron offered. "Maybe he never saw Wright."

"Maybe."

He was silent for half a block as they drove past a Kwik Trip and a Vietnamese grocery. "And if we don't have Josh take the stand, Costello will say he couldn't identify Wright because Wright didn't do it."

"Then we jump all over Costello for being a heartless bastard," Ellen countered. "We say we're not putting Josh on the stand, because he's been traumatized and victimized enough. We don't want to put him through the ordeal of cross-examination, to say nothing of having to face Wright in the courtroom."

He nodded as they turned onto Oslo and headed up the hill toward the courthouse. They passed the knot of protestors on the sidewalk and turned in at the entrance to the sheriff's-department lot, swinging around behind the building.

"Poor kid," Cameron said. "It's up to us to get him some justice."

Ellen found a ghost of a smile for him as she palmed her keys. "That's why they pay us the big bucks, Mr. Reed."

"Judge Rudy Stovich." Rudy spoke the title aloud to test the sound of it. Sounded good.

He had occupied this corner office on the second floor of the Park County courthouse for a dozen years. The oak credenza was piled with file folders and law books he never consulted. His desk was awash with debris, the decorative scales of justice that sat on one corner tipped heavily with golf tees. A set of Ping clubs leaned into one dark corner of the room, resting up for the annual February trip to Phoenix. A trip he would gladly postpone in order to move himself into old Franken's chambers.

"Judge Rudy Stovich," Manley Vanloon echoed. He plucked a filbert from the nut dish on the desk and cracked it with a tool disguised to look like an angry mallard. Fine slivers of shell rained down like flecks of tobacco onto the front of his tan wool sweater. He was built like a Buddha, all belly and a round, smiling face. His eyebrows tilted up above his tiny eyes. "Maybe you should go by Rudolph. Sounds more dignified."

Rudy swiveled his chair back and forth as if the motion would act as a centrifuge and separate the good decisions from the bad. "Sounds pretentious. Folks like my country-lawyer image."

"Good point." Manley nibbled his filbert, his gaze speculative as he imagined his pal in judge's robes. He and Rudy had been buddies since snow was cold, backing each other in business ventures and political campaigns. "How long before the governor makes up his mind?"

"Oh, he'll have to wait a decent interval after they bury old Franken. A week or so, I should think. By the way, the viewing is tomorrow at Oglethorpe's. Funeral Friday, three-thirty at Grace Lutheran."

"Grace Lutheran? All this time I thought he was Methodist. He struck me as a Methodist." He dusted the filbert-shell shrapnel off his cardigan and reached for a pecan. "Dinner after the funeral? Friday's all-you-can-eat fish at the Scandia House."

"Yeah, sure," Rudy mumbled dreamily, imagining himself delivering a stirring eulogy before a congregation that would include judges and lawyers and politicians from all over the state. Franken had lived a long time, accumulating a long list of powerful friends and colleagues. The funeral seemed a fitting time for Rudy to impress them all with his eloquence and sincerity.

The intercom buzzed, and Alice Zymanski's voice snapped out of it like a bolt of lightning. "Ellen is here to see you. I'm leaving."

"Send her in." Rudy forced himself to his feet, though it seemed too late in the day for manners. Once he was firmly ensconced in his judgeship, he was going to give up manners.

Ellen let herself in, manufacturing a smile for Manley Vanloon. Manley had amassed a small fortune in real estate during the agriculture depression of the seventies, buying out farms on the fringe of Deer Lake and developing the land into pricey subdivisions for the influx of yuppies from the Cities. He had then bought a trio of car dealerships and had made himself another fortune luring car buyers out of the Cities with his hayseed image, then cleaning their pockets for them.

"Hey, there, Ellen." Manley lifted himself out of his chair no more than he would to fart and settled back down to the business of digging his pecan out of the shell. "How's that Bonneville running? Heck of a nice car."

"Just fine, Manley." She turned her attention to her boss. "I just got a call from the assignments clerk. They're giving Garrett Wright to Judge Grabko. I thought you'd want to know."

"Are you all right with that choice?"

She shrugged. "We could do worse."

"Will you recuse?"

And let Tony Costello throw a public fit about the prosecution delaying his client's right to a speedy trial, to say nothing of alluding to the maneuver as the tactics of someone with a weak case? He had already made noises on both those points at his four o'clock press conference in the courthouse rotunda.

Ellen had sent Phoebe to the press conference as her spy, refusing to show up herself and give Tony the golden opportunity of engaging her in some impromptu sparring. When he marched upstairs to the county attorney's offices afterward, with reporters in tow, she made the receptionist lie and tell him she was out, for the sole purpose of spoiling his big moment of confrontation.

That small victory had been sweet, but the fact that she

was letting Costello affect her decision making irritated her in the extreme. *Strategy*, she told herself. She had to think in terms of strategy rather than in terms of being manipulated. Always put a positive spin on a negative possibility. Control was the name of the game.

"No, I won't recuse Grabko. He knows his stuff. He's fair. I've never had any big complaints about him other than that he tends toward pretension."

Rudy shot an I-told-you-so look at Manley, who pursed his lips as if holding back a belch.

"I'm still amazed Wright got Costello to represent him," Rudy said.

"I'd like to know how that happened," Ellen said. "Who called him in? Wright isn't allowed to make long-distance calls from jail. I doubt Denny Enberg would have been so gracious as to contact his own successor. Who does that leave?"

"Wright's wife."

"Who is barely functioning. I saw her myself the other night. Unless that's all been an act, she could no more have had a coherent conversation with Tony Costello than my golden retriever. That leaves Wright's accomplice."

"Which could mean Costello has been in contact with the kidnapper of that Campion boy," Rudy surmised.

"And fat chance we'll get him to tell us anything."

Rudy made a serious, contemplative sound, arranging his features in an expression he thought would look judicial. "Yes, well, do what you can, Ellen. I'm confident you can handle Costello."

Ellen took the platitude for what it was worth, which was nothing. She left Rudy to his scheming for Franken's seat on the bench and headed back to her own office. The staff was clearing out for the day. Sig Iverson and Quentin Adler were headed out the door, heads bent toward each other as they discussed some point of law or gossip. Phoebe was pulling on her llama poncho over her daisy-print dress and thermal leggings. Her head popped up through the opening and she pulled her mass of kinky hair free.

"I put a stack of messages on your desk," she said, straightening her glasses. "Mr. Costello called again. Mitch called to say no news is bad news and that he's going to Minneapolis tonight."

To check on Megan. The thought warmed Ellen and left her feeling a little empty at once. She leaned a shoulder against her office door and rested her hand on the knob. "Thanks, Phoebe. See you tomorrow."

The secretary frowned at her. "Don't stay too late. You look tired."

"I'm fine."

Phoebe didn't buy it, but she let it drop. Ellen let herself into her office and picked up the stack of pink slips. She noted the fact that there wasn't one from Jay Butler Brooks and told herself she was glad. Still, she caught herself thinking of the moment just before he had left her house last night, when he had stood a little too close to her and held her gaze with his a little too long.

"You can't avoid me forever."

She wheeled around, half expecting to see Brooks standing there, but the timbre of the voice registered a split second before her eyes focused on the man standing inside the door. The light from the outer office cast him in relief, giving him a menacing darkness that seemed fitting. Tony Costello was a shadow from her past coming back to haunt her. She reached around and flicked on the desk lamp to break the spell.

"Avoiding you, Tony? As usual, your ego is working overtime. It never occurred to you that I'm a busy woman with more important things on my agenda than playing an obliging role in your media drama."

"Contrary as ever, aren't you?" he said pleasantly, closing the door behind him. "I was afraid living in the boondocks might have mellowed you."

Ellen settled into her chair, slipping her glasses on and pretending attention to the message slips she had yet to set down. "It has." She glanced up at him over the rims of the glasses. "If you had sneaked up on me like that when I was working in Hennepin County, I would have broken your nose. I've let my self-defense skills slide completely."

"Lucky for me."

He smiled what she knew he considered to be the most charming smile in his arsenal. She remembered it well—square, white against his dark complexion. A smile he had splurged on to the tune of fifteen thousand dollars, mortgaging the house his parents had left him to pay for porcelain caps. He considered it a business investment.

He looked as fit and perfectly groomed as a show horse. The suit today was just a shade bluer than navy, tailored to show off the build he honed in a private gym with a personal trainer. He casually undid the buttons of the double-breasted coat and settled himself easily into her visitor's chair.

"What can I do for you, Tony?" she asked with just enough indifference to irritate him.

He ignored the bait, his gaze steady on hers. "It's been a long time."

"Not long enough."

The hurt appeared genuine but, then, so had his feelings for her, once upon a time.

"You still blame me for what happened with Fitzpatrick," he said. "I was hoping time might have given you some perspective."

"My perspective on criminal tampering with a case isn't liable to change in this lifetime."

He shook his head, frowning. "How could you believe I would do that, Ellen? Ethics aside, how could you believe I would turn on you that way after everything we'd been to each other?"

"Ethics aside." She gave a harsh laugh and rose again, anger humming in her muscles as she paced the small confines behind her desk. "Someone feeds Fitzpatrick's side information, virtually off my desk. The case blows up, and the next thing I see is you and Fitzpatrick's attorney palling around—"

"We were having dinner. That's not against the law."

"It's certainly not against *your* law."

"Oh, Jesus, Ellen," he growled, pushing to his feet. "It was a business dinner—"

"I'm sure it was." Ellen advanced toward him. "Did he slide your thirty pieces of silver to you under the table, or did he have the waiter bring it on a platter?"

"There were plenty of people in your own office who had access to that information. Fitzpatrick could have paid off any one of them."

"Yeah, but you know, Tony, none of them was suddenly driving a Porsche or hanging out at Goodfellows with Gregory Eagleton—"

"And, of course, it never occurred to you that your case blew up because Fitzpatrick was innocent," he shot back. "It never occurred to you that the girl was lying, pressing criminal charges after Fitzpatrick refused to meet her blackmail demands."

The argument touched a nerve that sent a red mist across Ellen's vision. He didn't deny her charges; he diverted attention, tried to shed the blame onto someone else. Pointing the spotlight on the victim crossed the line. She stepped toe to toe with him and thrust a righteous finger at him. "Art Fitzpatrick raped that girl because he believed his money and his position entitled him to do as he damn well pleased. And the thing that makes me sickest is that he was right. He bought his way out of a conviction, and you sold yourself into his good graces."

"Then prove it!" he shouted.

He didn't deny it. He never had.

They had been over this ground so many times, they had worn it to dust. Ellen knew she couldn't prove a thing against him. All she'd had were puzzle pieces and a gut feeling that drilled into the core of her. No hard evidence. Nothing she could take to the county attorney or to the bar association. At the time she had racked her brain trying to come up with a way to punish him, to publicly burn him at the stake, to get him disbarred, to send him to jail. But in the end there had been only the realization that any such effort would blow up in her face. She would be the one publicly humiliated, scorned, and professionally ruined. She was the prosecutor who had been foolish enough to get involved with an ambitious defense attorney.

She had gone into the affair cautious, convinced she was smart enough to handle it. She had come away from it with her self-esteem battered. He had drawn her in, charmed her into believing he had integrity. And just as soon as all her shields were down, he had betrayed her.

Nearly three years had passed and she still wanted to cut his heart out. Not because she had loved him, but because he had used her, made a fool of her, mocked the system she prized so highly.

She turned away from him and rubbed her hands over her face, trying to clear away the lingering haze of emotion. She didn't want to feel any of it. She especially didn't want to feel it in front of him. Control. Hadn't she just been preaching that word? Hadn't she told Cameron not to let Costello get under his skin? And here she was, going off like a bomb the first time he set foot in her office.

"I cared about you, Ellen," he murmured.

"Well, it's all in the past tense, isn't it?" she said, sliding down onto her chair. "Ancient history."

Tony took his seat in the visitor's chair. Like boxers

retiring to their respective corners, she thought. The tension dissipated to a tolerable level.

"I certainly never meant to drive you from the city," he said.

"Don't flatter yourself, Tony," she returned. "You were just a symptom of a much bigger problem. I left Hennepin County because I was fed up to my eyeteeth with all the bullshit game playing. Obviously, you're not content to contaminate just the metropolitan judicial districts. You've decided to take your show on the road."

"I'm representing Garrett Wright."

"So I heard." Ellen fixed her gaze hard on his face. "And how did that happen?"

"It's a fascinating case."

"High profile, you mean. What I want to know is *how* you came to be Garrett Wright's attorney. Who contacted you? Or did you come sniffing?"

"Are you accusing me of soliciting a client?" he asked with a healthy show of affront.

"No, you would never be that crass. So who called you? I know it wasn't Wright himself or Dennis Enberg."

"You also know I won't discuss this with you," he said, poker-faced. "It's privileged."

Ellen leaned toward him, her arms braced on the desktop. "You think so? If Garrett Wright's accomplice contacted you—if you can reveal to us the identity of the kidnapper of the Holloman boy and do not—I will sink my teeth into charges of obstruction and shake you like a dead rat."

Costello smiled like a lover, his dark eyes glowing. "Ah, you're still my Ellen at heart—or should I say at my throat?"

"I never belonged to you, Tony," she said coldly. "I just slept with you. Trust me, it wasn't that big a deal."

"Ouch." He winced. "Hitting below the belt. How unlike you."

"What can I say? You bring out the mean in me. You'll find out the hard way if you're aiding and abetting a kidnapper."

"You're going on the assumption my client is guilty," he said soberly. "I presume him to be innocent, therefore can have no knowledge of an accomplice. I certainly have no knowledge of the Holloman kidnapping."

"God help you if you're lying to me, Tony," Ellen said tightly. "A child's life could be at stake."

"I know what's at stake, Ellen. I *always* know what's at stake."

He opened his Louis Vuitton calfskin briefcase on the chair beside him and withdrew a sheaf of documents. "Demand for Discovery. Since you have virtually nothing on which to base your case, I expect disclosure to happen quickly."

"We've got more than enough for the hearing," she said. "Your little 'rush to justice' ploy is only going to cramp your efforts, Tony, not mine. Send one of your minions around tomorrow afternoon for the papers."

"I'll stop by myself," he said, slipping into his topcoat. "Judge Grabko will be hearing my motion to reduce bail. Admirable the way the district is striving to keep the wheels of justice turning, isn't it?"

"I suppose you're trying to take credit for the work of our assignments clerk." Ellen strove to sound bored. "As if anyone in this district could care less who you are."

Costello narrowed his eyes. He looked cruel, and she knew he had the potential for it.

"I think you could care less, Ellen," he said in a low voice. "Let's hope for the sake of the case you don't let your vindictiveness cloud your judgment. I don't want anyone saying it wasn't a fair fight."

She wanted to pick up her paperweight and hurl it at him, but it was out of reach, and restraint dictated a cooler response. "Why don't you take your ego out for a nice big

dinner, Tony? The energy it consumes must be tremendous."

His mouth twisted into a thin smile. "As a matter of
fact, I am on my way to dinner. I'd ask you to join us,
but . . ."

"I have other plans."

He tipped his head. "Until tomorrow . . ."

He stepped into the dim light of the hall, turning back
to look at her. "You know, Ellen," he said softly, "aside
from the circumstances, it really is good to see you again."

Ellen said nothing. When he was gone, she raked her
hands back through her hair and blew out a sigh as tension
rushed out of her muscles. A logical assessment of their
conversation told her it hadn't been a total bust. She had
scored some points, held her own. Beyond logic, she felt
naked and vulnerable.

He had found a way to hurt her before, when she had
thought she was invulnerable. She had chosen to walk
away, but here he was again, invading her life. No logical
argument could take the edge off her uneasiness.

And at the heart of that disquiet was not Tony Costello,
but Garrett Wright.

Why had he chosen Costello? How could he have
known the one man she would least want to face in court
or out? Who had contacted Costello for him?

Who was the other part of *us*?

*"As a matter of fact, I am on my way to dinner. I'd ask you to
join us . . ."*

Possibilities sprang up like mushrooms in her head. He
could have been talking about members of his staff, but he
might have been referring to the person who had contacted him on Garrett Wright's behalf.

Grabbing her coat and briefcase, she hustled out of her
office. The purveyors of justice had closed shop for the
night, and the dimly lit halls echoed with the hollow,
lonely sound of a single pair of heels. She hurried down

the stairs, cut across the rotunda, and made for the side door closest to the parking lot. She braced herself for the cold as she pushed through the door, then stood on the step.

She scanned the parking lot, looking for Costello, hoping to catch a glimpse of him driving away. But she didn't see anyone. Mumbling a curse under her breath, she started toward her car. She hoped he had gone back to his office first. If she could pick him up there and follow him to the restaurant—

"Ms. North?"

The dark form seemed to fly out of the shadows like a wraith. Ellen bolted sideways, broke a heel, turned her ankle. Stumbling, she dropped her briefcase. Adam Slater stood stock-still, wide-eyed, watching her flounder. The wind blew his hair into his eyes and he swept it back impatiently.

"Jeez, Ms. North, I didn't mean to scare you. I'm really sorry."

Ellen scowled at him. She picked up the amputated heel of her shoe and stuffed it into her coat pocket.

"Mr. Slater," she said, trying to hold her patience. "There really isn't a need to rush at a subject when you are the only reporter in the vicinity."

His lean face contorted into a variety of sheepish looks. "I'm really sorry. It's just that I wanted to catch you before you—well—got away."

"Why aren't you in Campion with the rest of the horde?"

"There's nothing much going on there. I mean, the search, but they haven't found the kid or anything. A bunch of people came back here for Anthony Costello's press conference, but then they went back to Campion for the prayer vigil. I thought I'd hang around, see if I could get a comment from you."

"It's better than nothing, huh?"

"Yeah—I mean—it's something. I mean, what's your take on Dr. Wright bringing in a hired gun like Costello?" He pulled his notebook out of his coat pocket and stood with pen poised.

Ellen's breath rolled out in a transparent cloud and billowed up into the darkness. The sodium-vapor lights around the parking lot were on. One shone down on her Bonneville, spotlighting it as the only car for twenty yards in any direction. The sense of urgency deflated inside her.

"Garrett Wright is entitled to counsel," she answered by rote. "Mr. Costello is very good at what he does."

"Do you think it means Wright's guilty? That he feels like he's going to need a better lawyer than he could find in Deer Lake to get him off?"

"I'm not privy to his thoughts. I wish I were. That would make my job easier." She bent and hefted her briefcase, balancing herself on her right toe to compensate for the missing heel. "I believe Garrett Wright is guilty. I will do everything in my power to prove that and to convict him. It makes no difference to me who his lawyer is."

"Costello doesn't intimidate you?"

"Not in the least."

"Even though he beat you about every two out of three times when you went up against him as a prosecutor in Hennepin County?"

"Where did you hear that?"

He shrugged. "My source in the system."

"Cases are individual," Ellen said, hobbling toward her car. "I'm confident in our case against Garrett Wright. I will also do everything I can to aid in the capture and prosecution of his accomplice."

"Got any clues as to who that might be?" Adam Slater asked, shuffling beside her. "Got any clues about motive?"

"I'm not at liberty to comment."

"I won't use your name," he promised. "I'll call you 'a highly placed source in the county attorney's office.'"

"There are only five attorneys on staff, Mr. Slater. That wouldn't exactly ensure my anonymity."

He rebounded with the undaunted resilience of youth and bounced on to the next question. "There's been no word on motive. What do you think this is all about? Crime is always about something—sex, power, money, drugs. Or in the existential, cosmic view, is it really just about good and evil?"

Ellen looked at him, at the avid light in his eyes as he waited for her answer, for a juicy, sensational tidbit his readers back in Grand Forks could scarf up with their breakfast cereal. She had seen degrees of good and evil all around throughout this ordeal: shades and shadows of darkness, small bright spots of hope for humankind. If Brooks was right about nothing else, he was right about one thing—that the drama being played out around them was, in many ways, a metaphor for the times. But Ellen had no desire to wax philosophical with a reporter who grew up on *Brady Bunch* reruns and was too young to remember the Beatles.

"I'm not an existentialist, Mr. Slater," she said. "I'm a realist. I realistically believe I can win this case. I won't be spooked by an attorney who spends more on suits than I make in a year or by the preposterous notion that we're up against a malevolent entity whose evil genius is larger than all of us struggling against it. When you come right down to it, Garrett Wright is just another criminal. I won't give him any more credit than he deserves."

It made for a good sound bite, she thought as she drove out of the parking lot. Too bad she didn't quite believe it.

CHAPTER 13

Hannah prowled the quiet house alone, soft music from the stereo her only company. Lily was asleep in her crib. Josh had fallen asleep on the couch watching *Back to the Future*.

Hannah had kept the VCR loaded since the night before. She didn't want Josh watching the news. She told herself she was afraid it might upset him, but the truth was that his reaction to the news bulletin about the Holloman kidnapping had upset *her*. She had tried to talk about it with him, but after his initial chilling comment he'd had nothing more to say.

"Josh, do you know who might have taken that boy away from his family?"

He shrugged, indifferent, and turned his attention to his box of markers, taking out each one and subjecting it to intense scrutiny.

"Honey, that little boy's family will be worried sick about him, just like we were worried about you. And he's probably scared, too, the way you must have been. If you could help find him, you would, wouldn't you?"

He pulled a purple marker from the box and held it at arm's length, slowly swooping it through the air as if he were pretending it was an airplane.

He had retreated once more into his imagination. Hannah was at a loss as to how to draw him out or even if she should try. Perhaps it was better to let him come to terms with it on his own, to simply offer him love and support and patience. Then she would think of Dustin Holloman's mother, knowing every fear the woman was experiencing, and she would think she should force the issue, that she should call Mitch and tell him what Josh had said, that she should have told Ellen North, that she should immediately drag Josh back to the child psychiatrist he had seen earlier in the day and relinquish her responsibility.

The arguments tumbled around and around in her mind, in her conscience. Ultimately, she felt she would do nothing, and she felt selfish and weak and wrong because of it. But in her heart she wanted first and foremost to protect Josh, to keep him safe with her, hoping all the ugliness would just go away.

She looked down at him, sleeping soundly, and every molecule of her being hurt. She had failed to protect him once. She didn't want to fail him again, but she was flying blind and she felt so alone. She felt as if she had been taken from the world she knew, where she was certain of her role and her skills, and thrust into an alien world, where she didn't understand the language or the customs.

Until Josh's abduction, she had never faced real adversity in her personal life. She had never acquired the skills necessary to cope. Even now, as she acquired them unwillingly, she wielded them clumsily, uncertainly. She felt out of balance and knew what was missing was her husband's support. She and Paul had been a team for a long time before that balance had begun to shift. To be without him was to suddenly become an amputee.

Beyond the kitchen the door from the garage to the mudroom opened and closed. Hannah whirled around, automatically putting herself between the unseen intruder and her son. Then the kitchen door swung open and Paul stepped in.

"You could have called first," Hannah said angrily as she stepped up into the kitchen.

"It's still my house," Paul answered defensively.

Hannah drew breath for another attack, then stopped herself short. It had become habit—the thrust and parry of verbal warfare. They didn't even bother with greetings anymore. They had shared a decade of their lives, brought two children into the world, and had reduced themselves to this.

"You frightened me," she admitted.

"I'm sorry." He offered the apology grudgingly. "I guess I should have known better. I didn't think you'd get used to having me gone so quickly."

"It isn't that."

He arched a sardonic brow. "Oh, so you've decided maybe there's some reason to be afraid of me after all?"

"Oh, Christ." She pressed the heels of her hands against her closed eyes. "I'm trying to be civil, Paul. Can't you at least meet me halfway?"

"You're the one who threw me out."

"You deserved it. There. Are you happy now? Have we been ugly enough to each other?"

He looked away, staring at the refrigerator and the notes and photos and drawings that cluttered the front of it. Evidence of their life as a family.

"I came to see Josh," he said quietly.

"He's asleep."

"I can't frighten him then, can I?"

Hannah bit her lip on a retort. She wasn't sure what he wanted her to make of it or what she *should* make of it. She didn't want to think Josh had any reason to be afraid of his father. Logic told her there was no reason, that Garrett Wright was the man to blame. Garrett Wright was in jail.

And another child had been taken.

And it was Paul who had caused Josh to react so violently.

"He fell asleep on the couch," she said, and turned and walked down into the family room.

Paul followed her, hands in his pockets, feet seeming to drag across the Berber rug. He looked down at their son over the back of the sofa, some nameless emotion tightening his features.

"How's he doing?"

"I don't know."

"Is he talking?"

She hesitated for a split second, wanting to confide, but realizing she didn't want to confide in Paul. "No. Not really."

"When will he see the psychiatrist again?"

"Tomorrow. Ellen North and Cameron Reed from the county attorney's office came by today with a photo lineup for him to look at to see if he would pick out Garrett Wright."

Anticipation sharpened his expression. "And?"

"And nothing. He looked at it and walked away. He seems to be blocking the whole thing out. Dr. Freeman says it could be a long time before he faces it. The trauma was too much for him. He was probably told not to talk about it. Threatened. God only knows."

"God and Garrett Wright."

Paul bent down and touched Josh's hair. One stray lock curled around his forefinger, and his eyes filled with tears. Hannah stood where she was, knowing that not long ago she would have gone to him and put her arms around him and shared his pain. That she would no longer do so brought a profound sadness. How could their love have gone so completely? What could they have done to stop it from leaving?

"I wish we could go back," Paul whispered. "I wish . . . I wish . . ."

The chant was as familiar as her own heartbeat. Hannah couldn't count the empty wishes, the unanswered prayers. The most important one had come true—to get Josh back—but it had brought on a whole new set of needs and longings and questions she wasn't sure she wanted answers for.

"I wish we could go back . . ." to the time in their lives that seemed like a distant fairy tale. Once upon a time they had been so happy. Now there was only bitterness and pain. Happily ever after was as far beyond their reach as the stars.

"I'll carry him to bed," Paul murmured.

Hannah started to say no, worried that Josh might awaken at the movement and panic at the sight of his father. But she held her breath instead and asked God for this one small favor. Whatever had gone wrong between the two of them, she didn't want to see Paul hurt that way. She didn't want to believe he deserved it.

She followed them up the short flight of stairs and stood in the doorway to Josh's room as Paul settled him into the lower bunk and tucked the covers around him. He kissed his fingertips and pressed them softly against Josh's cheek, then went across the hall and looked in on Lily.

"She asks about you," Hannah admitted.

"What do you tell her?"

"That you're staying somewhere else for a while."

"But it isn't just for a while, is it, Hannah?" he said with more accusation than hope. "You don't need me."

"I don't need *this*," she said sharply as they stepped down into the family room. "The constant sniping, the snide remarks, the feeling that I have to walk on eggshells around your ego. I would give anything for us to be able to set all that aside for Josh's sake, but you can't seem to manage that—"

"Me?" Paul thumped a fist against his chest. "Yeah, *I'm* to blame. Bullshit. *You're* the one who—"

"Stop right there!" Hannah demanded. "I will not listen to this again. Do you understand me, Paul? I'm tired of you blaming me. I blame myself enough for both of us.

I'm doing the best I can. I can't speak for you; I don't know what you're doing. I don't even know who you are anymore. You're not the man I married. You're no one I want to be with."

"Well, that's fine," he sneered. "I'm out of here."

And so the vicious circle completed itself again, Hannah thought as the doors slammed. They had danced the dance so many times, just the thought of it made her dizzy. Exhausted, she sank down onto a wing chair and reached for the portable phone on the end table. She needed an anchor, a friend, someone she could feel safe loving even if he could never love her back.

The phone on the other end rang once, twice.

"God Squad. Free deliverance."

A smile trembled across Hannah's mouth.

"We've got a special on penance tonight—three rosaries for the price of two."

"What about shoulders to cry on?" she asked.

The silence was warm and full. "Buy one, get one free," Father Tom said softly.

"Can I put it on my tab?"

"Anytime, Hannah," he whispered. "Anytime."

Paul picked his way along the edge of the woods that bordered Quarry Hills Park. The moonlight was intermittent, blinking on and off as dark clouds scraped across its path like chunks of soot in the night sky. He knew the way well enough. The path meant for cross-country skiers had been trampled by countless boots in the last few days as the police had combed the hillside for evidence. Tattered ribbons of yellow plastic crime-scene tape clung to tree trunks like synthetic kudzu.

He tried to ignore it and not think about the reason it was there. He needed a break from the nightmare. He needed comfort. He needed love. He deserved something better than Hannah's running him down. She should have been able to see the strain he was under. If she had been a true wife to him, he would have been sleeping in his own bed tonight. Instead, he wanted to seek out another man's wife.

That the man was sitting in jail tonight, accused of stealing Josh, brought on a complex matrix of emotions. None of them made him turn back.

The kitchen light was on in the Wrights' house. From the woods his views of the interior were abstract—a rectangle of kitchen, a square of bathroom wall and ceiling, a triangle of bedroom through the inverted V created between the tied-back curtains.

Karen was home. He had called her from a pay phone and hung up when she'd answered, afraid that her telephone might be bugged. There were no cars in her driveway, no evidence of visitors.

Caution and cowardice and guilt held him there at the edge of the woods. Need finally drove him forward.

He tracked across the backyard to the door that led into the garage and let himself in as he had many times before. Garrett's Saab had been impounded by the police and taken away, leaving Karen's Honda to take up only a fraction of the floor space. This was where Mitch Holt had arrested Garrett Wright. For a second Paul could almost hear the sounds of the scuffle, the low pitch of Holt's voice as he recited the Miranda warning.

Paul barely knew Garrett Wright. They were neighbors, but not the sort who shared summer evenings and backyard barbecues. Wright held himself apart, superior. He gave his life to his work at the college and regarded the people around him as if they were specimens to be studied and picked apart. It brought a certain bitter pleasure to think of him sitting in jail. How superior was he now?

"Paul?"

Karen stood behind the storm door looking fragile and

startled. Her fine ash-blond hair framed her face. A pink rose bloomed across the front of her oversize ivory sweater. Feminine. Delicate. Everything he wanted in a woman.

"Paul, what are you doing here?"

"I needed to see you," he said, pulling the door open. "Can I come in?"

"You shouldn't." But she stepped back into the laundry room anyway.

"I had to see how you're doing. I haven't seen you since Garrett—"

"That was a mistake." She shook her head, not quite looking at him. "Garrett should never have been arrested. He's never been arrested."

"He took Josh, Karen."

"That's a mistake," she mumbled, twisting a finger into her hair. "He would never . . . hurt me like that."

"He doesn't love you, Karen. Garrett doesn't love you. I love you. Remember that."

"I don't like what's happening." The words came on a trembling whine. "I think you should leave, Paul."

"But I need to see you," he said urgently. "You can't imagine what I've been going through, wondering about you—wondering if you're all right, wondering if the police have been interrogating you. I've been worried sick."

He lifted a hand to touch her cheek. "I've missed you," he whispered. Soft. She was so soft. Need ached through him. He needed comfort. He deserved comfort. "Every night I lay awake, wishing you were with me. I think about us being together—really together. It can happen now. Hannah and I are finished. Garrett will go to jail."

"I don't think so," she murmured.

"Yes. You don't love him, anyway, Karen. He can't give you what you need. You love me. Say you love me, Karen."

She hitched a breath, tears spilling over her lashes. "I love you, Paul."

He lowered his mouth to kiss her, but she turned her face away. She pushed at him, her small hands spread across the front of his coat.

"Karen?" he whispered, confused, crushed. "I *need* you."

She shook her head, tears tumbling down her cheeks, her lower lip trembling. "I'm so sorry. It was all a mistake." She slowly sank down along the front of the dryer to sit on the floor. She wrapped her arms around her legs, rested her cheek on her knees and cried softly. ". . . A terrible mistake."

I made a mistake. The line blinked on and off in Denny Enberg's head like a neon sign. On and off, on and off, the relentless beat like Chinese water torture.

"You should be happy, Denny," he mumbled, pouring himself another shot of Cuervo. "You're out of it. You're off the hook."

He had never expected to be put on the hook in the first place. Deer Lake was not a place of intrigue. His clients were generally ordinary, their cases unremarkable. He lived a quiet, decent life, dull by many standards. There was his law practice, his hunting and fishing, his wife Vicki. She worked nights as an LPN at the rest home and was taking classes at Harris to become an elementary-school teacher. They talked about adopting a baby but had decided to wait until Vicki finished school.

The Cuervo went down like liquid smoke. Edges were beginning to blur and soften as he looked around his office. The Manly Man Cave, Vicki called it. The place where he was allowed to hang his hunting trophies and keep his guns and play poker with his buddies once a month. The walls were knotty pine, the floor covered in flat, hard carpet the color of dirt. His inner sanctum. He allowed no clients back here. His secretary left the vacuum cleaner at the door every Friday. He used it once a month.

The building that housed his modest practice sat on the edge of a strip-mall parking lot and had once been a laundromat and dry cleaner's. Now the other half was occupied by a dentist who gave him a deal for referring clients who had ruined their teeth in car accidents and barroom brawls. The kind of clients he handled best—uncomplicated.

I made a mistake.

"Let it go, Denny," he croaked, staring across the room at the ten-point buck that hung above his gun rack. "You can't win 'em all."

That was what he had told Ellen North when she had stopped by trolling for information. *"I wasn't aggressive enough. I let my client down. He fired me. It happens."*

The case could have made him some money, made him a name, but it was gone now, and good riddance. He didn't need the pressure, didn't want the secrets.

"You seem distracted, Denny," Ellen said.

"Yeah, well, it was a big case. I could have used the business it would have brought me. But what the hell. Who needs the headache?"

"Your heart didn't seem to be in it."

"No? Yeah, well . . . Vicki didn't like the idea of my defending Wright."

"She thinks he's guilty?"

"Trick question."

"Withdrawn," she said with a nod.

"Anyway, the crank calls were getting annoying."

"What calls?"

He shrugged. *"The usual 'You scum lawyer' variety. Some people believe he's guilty. Now Costello can worry about it. I'm out."*

She started to leave, turning back toward him at the door, her expression pensive. *"You know I would never ask you to compromise your ethics, Denny. But I trust you to do what's right. If*

Garrett Wright is the monster we think he is, he has to be stopped. His accomplice has to be stopped. If you could do something to stop them, I know you would. You would do the right thing. Wouldn't you, Denny?"

Do the right thing.

I made a mistake.

He tipped the Cuervo over his glass and drained the bottle.

Josh sat up in his bed and looked at the glowing dial of the clock on his nightstand. Twelve A.M. His mom had left a night-light on for him even though he was much too grown-up to have one. He was old now in ways Mom would never understand, in ways he could never explain.

He crawled out from under the covers and went to the window that looked out on the lake. In the moonlight it looked as if it could have been a white desert or the surface of a faraway planet. The ice-fishing huts clustered in an area down the shoreline could have been a village of alien life-forms.

He left his room and went down the hall to check on his mother. The door to her room stood open. She was asleep in bed, though he knew from experience the slightest sound might wake her. He wouldn't make a sound. He could be like a ghost, could move all around, be anywhere and no one would see him or hear. The quiet was in his mind, and he could make it as big as he was and put it all around him like a giant bubble.

He backed away from the door, went down the hall to the bathroom, where a window looked out on the backyard. He climbed up on the clothes hamper and parted the curtains. The snow was silver, the woods beyond like black lace with the here-and-gone moon shining between the bare branches of the winter-dead trees. There was a mystical, magical quality to the scene that called to him.

The feeling frightened him a little, but pulled at him like a pair of big invisible hands. He wanted to be out there, alone, where no one would watch him as if they expected him to explode, and no one would ask him questions he wasn't supposed to answer.

In the mudroom he pulled on his snow boots and put on, over the new purple Vikings sweat suit Natalie Bryant had bought him, the new winter jacket his mom had bought him. People had bought him a lot of presents, like it was Christmas or something. Only when his mom gave them to him, she seemed sad and anxious instead of happy.

Josh knew he was the cause of those feelings. He wished he could fix her broken heart. He wished he could make the world right again, but he couldn't.

What's done is done, but it isn't over.

He didn't like to think about that, but it was in his head, put there by someone he didn't dare go against. The Taker. The Taker said he wasn't supposed to tell, or bad things would happen, and so he didn't talk, even though bad things seemed to be happening anyway. Josh stayed inside his mind, even though it was a lonely place. It was the safest place to be.

As quiet as a mouse, he let himself outside.

The call came at 2:02 A.M., jolting Ellen from a restless sleep. She sat bolt upright in bed, scattering the files and documents she had fallen asleep reading. The fat three-ring binder that was her bible for the Wright case tumbled to the floor with a thud. She stared at the phone, her mind rationalizing as it had Monday night. The call was probably work related. A cop in need of a warrant. There were other cases ongoing in Park County besides the Holloman kidnapping. Or maybe it was about the Holloman case. Maybe it was Karen Wright, calling to confess her husband's sins.

Still, she couldn't bring herself to pick up the receiver. Harry raised his massive head from the mattress and made a disgruntled sound at having his sleep disturbed.

"Ellen North," she answered. Silence hung heavy on the end of the line. "Hello?"

When the voice came, it was whisper soft, androgynous, a disembodied spirit that sent chills rushing over her skin like ice water.

" 'The first thing we do, let's kill all the lawyers.' "

The phone went dead, but the words floated and echoed and wrapped bony fingers around her throat. Ellen pulled the covers up high and sat shivering, wondering, waiting, while the night held its breath around her.

They're running in circles, chasing their tails.
We play the shell game with lightning-quick minds.
Where is Dustin? Where is Evil?
Who is evil?
Who is not?

CHAPTER 14

"Denny Enberg is dead."

"Wh-what?" Ellen had been literally on her way out the door. Her coat was half-buttoned. Her gloves dropped out of her hand.

". . . looks like suicide," Mitch said. ". . . In his office . . . sometime last night . . ."

The sentences came to her fragmented, as if the phone connection were bad.

The first thing we do, let's kill all the lawyers. . . .

"Oh, my God," she whispered, nausea rolling like a ball in her stomach, stirring her meager breakfast of toast and tea.

Even after reporting her crank call and being assured the night commander would send a patrol car past her house, she had slept poorly. Dreams of evil and fear had chased her up from the depths of unconsciousness and trapped her in an exhausting limbo.

"Hell of a way to start the day," Mitch growled. "Denny was a decent guy for a lawyer."

Ellen tried to gulp a breath, dimly aware that she was hyperventilating. Clammy sweat slicked a film over her skin. "Preserve the scene," she said desperately.

"What?"

"Preserve the scene. I'll be right there. I think he may have been murdered."

A steady stream of foot traffic flowed between the Donut Hut on the corner and Denny Enberg's office on the fringe of the Southtown Shopping Center. The press, swarming like flies, drifted back and forth, impatient for the news being denied them by closed doors and burly cops. Several recognized Ellen's car and rushed toward her as she turned into the parking lot. She pretended not to see them, letting them fend for life and limb as she roared past them and into the inner circle of green-and-white police vehicles. She flung her door open as she slammed the transmission into park and hurried toward the building as if she might still be able to prevent what had already happened.

The outer office was crowded. Denny's wife Vicki and his secretary huddled together on the small sofa, holding each other and sobbing, their grief intertwining in a wrenching duet. The air was thick with cigarette smoke and the sour tang of sweat from overdressed bodies and overstressed nerves.

Ellen grabbed hold of a dark-green parka sleeve, not bothering to focus on the face above it. "Where's Mitch?"

"In the back. You don't want to go there."

"It's my job," she snapped, walking away. But it was something else that sent her down the short hall toward Denny's private office. *The first thing we do, let's kill all the lawyers. . . .*

The smell hit her like a rolling wave a dozen feet from the open door. Violent death. A putrid miasma of blood, bladder and bowel content. Thick, choking, cloying, underscored by the sharp, acidic scent of vomit. Ellen tried to breathe through her mouth. Fighting the urge to gag, she stepped into the office and looked for Mitch.

The room was hot and too crowded. Dead animals stared down from the paneled walls with unblinking glass eyes—a deer, a gigantic walleye with nasty teeth sporting the lure that had been his undoing in some northern lake, an assortment of game birds frozen in midflight for all eternity. A radio was playing country music while portable cop radios crackled with static and mumbled messages. The voices of the men present to investigate and gawk ran together in an indecipherable murmur.

Marty Wilhelm's mouth was drawn into a knot, his pallor a sickly pearl-gray. A uniformed officer sat on the low black vinyl sofa with his head down between his knees and a puddle of puke between his boots. Ellen wheeled away from the sight, bile rising in her throat. Mitch caught sight of her.

"Here," he said, thrusting a small jar of Mentholatum at her. "Are you sure you want in on this, Ellen? He used a shotgun. It's pretty gruesome."

"I've seen it before," she said gamely, smearing menthol beneath her nostrils.

"Yeah, but it probably wasn't someone you saw at the courthouse every day."

"I'll be fine."

"You'll be on the floor," he muttered. "You're as white as chalk."

"Who found him?"

"His wife. She got home from work about seven-fifteen this morning. No sign of Denny, no sign that he'd ever come home last night. She tried to call him here and got no answer. It worried her, so she came on down."

"Chief Holt says you have reason to believe Enberg may have been murdered." Wilhelm leaned into the conversation, close enough to let everyone know he was one of the spectators who had lost his breakfast at the sight. Ellen swallowed hard and scooped out another finger of Mentholatum.

"I got a call last night," she said, focusing on Mitch. "A voice I couldn't recognize."

"Male or female?"

"I'm not sure. Male, I think."

"What did he say?"

"He quoted Shakespeare. 'The first thing we do, let's kill all the lawyers.'"

It echoed inside her head, the disembodied voice, the eerie silkiness of the delivery.

"What time was this?" Mitch asked.

"A little after two. I called it in, but what could anyone do?" she said. "I thought it might be a threat directed at me. Your watch commander sent a patrol around. I never imagined—It never occurred to me—"

"You couldn't possibly have known, Ellen," Mitch reassured her. "You still can't know."

"It has all the earmarks of a suicide," Wilhelm said. "There are no signs of forced entry, no signs of a struggle. The gun came from his own rack. He rigged the trigger with string."

"I saw him just last night," Ellen said. "He was distracted, a little down, maybe, not suicidal."

"He had just lost a client in a high-profile case," Wilhelm said.

"But his heart was never in the case," she insisted. "I think he was as relieved as he was disappointed. He told me he'd been getting crank calls."

"Threatening?" Wilhelm asked.

"He described them as the 'You scum lawyer' variety."

"People pissed off because he was defending Wright," Mitch said. "So why would any of them kill him after he'd been booted off the case?"

Wilhelm shook his head. "They wouldn't. What would be the point?"

"You're right," Ellen said, "but he could have misinterpreted. For all we know, he got the same call I got."

"I can't base an investigation on something that vague, Ms. North."

Mitch ignored the agent's play at power. "So you think

what? That Wright canned him for doing a half-assed job and the accomplice whacked him to keep him from talking about things that might have been attorney-client related?"

"An attorney can't reveal that kind of information," Wilhelm argued. "It's unethical. He'd get his ass disbarred."

Mitch shot him an impatient look. "You've never heard of anonymous tips? Jesus, Wilhelm, what were you—hatched yesterday?"

The BCA agent turned pink with temper. "Wright fired Enberg Tuesday. Why wait a full twenty-four hours to off him? It doesn't follow, and the evidence doesn't bear it out."

"Because it's a game to them," Mitch growled. "Wright and his pal like to fuck with people's minds. Wright might have confessed anything to Enberg before he fired him, just for the pleasure of knowing the man would wear a hole in his conscience trying to decide what to do about it. Like pulling the wings off flies, the sick son of a bitch."

The idea shot ice through Ellen's veins. But she did her best to pull together the remnants of the tough shell she had developed working in the city, and shed there two years ago.

"Let's get this over with," she muttered.

Mitch tipped his head in deference. "If you say so."

He steered her in the direction of Denny Enberg's desk. *Be calm, be detached*, she recited, calling up old skills that were rusty with disuse. That was the key, not to think of the body as a human being who had a wife sitting out in the reception area. It was just a body, evidence in a crime, not a man she had spoken with just last night in this very room.

"You know I would never ask you to compromise your ethics, Denny. But I trust you to do what's right. If Garrett Wright is the monster we think he is, he has to be stopped. His accomplice has to

*be stopped. If you could do something to stop them, I know you
would. You would do the right thing. Wouldn't you, Denny?"*

They would never know. Denny Enberg's conscience
was gone, along with most of his head. His body was
sprawled in his desk chair, the shotgun used to kill him
resting between his spread legs, barrel up. Brain matter,
bone fragments, and blood had exploded up and back
from the body, sticking to the knotty-pine paneling and
acoustic ceiling tile in a grisly spray.

Stuart Oglethorpe, Park County coroner and director
of the Oglethorpe Funeral Home, stared at what remained
of Denny Enberg.

"Well, he killed himself," he announced with disgust.

"Maybe."

Oglethorpe glared up at Mitch through his thick black
horn-rimmed glasses. "What? It's plain and simple!"

"Nothing is simple."

Wilhelm blew out a breath. "Look, Chief, he's sitting
in his desk chair, there's no sign of a struggle. Do you
think he just watched the killer walk in and obligingly
opened his mouth for the gun barrel?"

Mitch turned away from him, only half listening.
"There's no suicide note," he mumbled. He pulled a pencil out of the crowded cup beside the bloodstained blotter
and tapped it against the empty bottle of Cuervo. "He'd
been drinking," he muttered. "We don't know how
much."

"That bottle was half-full when I was here," Ellen said.

"What time was that?"

"Seven, seven-thirty."

"And there's only one glass sitting here," Mitch said.
"That's a lot of tequila. The toxicologist can tell us how
much. If he drank enough to pass out, that would explain
the lack of a struggle."

"What about the string on the trigger?" Wilhelm
countered. "The gun was rigged—"

Mitch scowled at him. "For Christ's sake, Wilhelm, if you wanted a murder to look like a suicide, wouldn't you be smart enough to trick out the goddamn gun?" He held up a hand and rolled his eyes. "Don't answer that." Turning to Oglethorpe, he said, "As soon as the scene has been processed, we'll get him bagged and you can transport him up to HCMC. The sooner they get tissue samples to the lab, the better."

"An autopsy?" The coroner groaned. Once a body was transported to the Hennepin County Medical Center, there was no guarantee of its coming back to the Oglethorpe Funeral Home for preparation for the world beyond, and therefore no guarantee of profit.

"I'll call for the mobile lab." Wilhelm's tone indicated that he considered it too much trouble.

"Call for a new attitude while you're at it," Mitch ordered. "If you think crimes should be committed in an orderly fashion, one at a fucking time to fit into your schedule, you're in the wrong job, *Agent* Wilhelm."

The exchange barely registered in Ellen's mind. Her attention was drawn by Denny Enberg's hand, frozen by rigor mortis on the arm of his chair. Broad across the palm, with short, blunt-tipped fingers. The plain gold band on his ring finger gleamed.

Just an ordinary man with a decent law practice and a wife who worked nights. A nice, quiet, ordinary life that had been taken from him by force. If what she suspected was true, he had been used as a pawn, toyed with and destroyed as if he were nothing more than a playing piece in the game.

"I'll talk with his secretary myself," Mitch said, steering her toward the door. "See if he had any late-night appointments scheduled. I wouldn't expect a killer to leave his name, but we might be able to narrow down the time frame. We could even get lucky and find ourselves a witness. He didn't mention anyone to you, did he, Ellen?"

"No. I didn't see anything out of the ordinary, either. My mind was on the case. But humor me and check to see what Todd Childs and Christopher Priest were doing last night, will you?"

"They're on my list."

"And Paul Kirkwood," Wilhelm said.

Mitch's jaw tightened.

"We can't ignore him, Mitch," Ellen murmured with apology in her eyes.

"Yeah, I know," he said with crackling sarcasm. "He *is* from the BCA."

"She meant Kirkwood," Marty grumbled.

Ellen checked her watch as she stepped into the hall. "I've got to get out of here. I've got a meeting at ten, and if I don't shower and change out of these clothes, Judge Grabko is liable to hold me in contempt."

She looked up at Mitch with gratitude. "Thanks for listening to me, Chief. I'm afraid if it had been left up to Agent Wilhelm and our esteemed coroner, Denny would be on an embalming table this afternoon."

"I think Wilhelm got a little more than he bargained for with this field post. He comes here in the middle of a kidnapping. Before his first week is up there's another, and now a potential homicide. Before this thing is over, he's going to wish he could give the job back to Megan."

"How's she doing?"

He glanced away, his jaw tightening. "As well as can be expected. Unfortunately, no one is expecting much—except Megan herself. She's too damn stubborn for her own good."

"She's a fighter."

"Yeah. I'm just worried about what happens if she can't win this fight."

The cruelty of Wright's game just kept spreading out-ward like an ink stain, blacking out Megan's career, Josh's innocence, Dustin Holloman's future, Denny Enberg's life. It had touched Ellen's own life as simply and easily as a phone call.

The first thing we do, let's kill all the lawyers. . . .

"We'll get a trace on your home phone," Mitch said, backing down the hall as someone called to him from Denny's office. "I'll talk to you later."

Ellen nodded and waved him off. For a moment she was all alone, halfway between the death scene and the mourners. She would have to stop on her way out and offer her condolences to Denny's wife, then fight her way through the media mob to get to her car.

All she wanted was a nice, quiet, well-ordered life . . . like Dennis Enberg . . . like the Kirkwoods and the Hollomans.

Suddenly she needed to breathe air that didn't stink of death, to let the cold air clear her head. She turned right, went down the short hall, and let herself out on the back side of the building.

A stiff wind slapped her face. She opened her mouth and gulped it in. Leaning back against the building, she let herself mourn for the loss of a life and the loss of something less tangible—peace and safety, the sense of immunity people here had wrapped around themselves like a warm woolen blanket.

She had left Minneapolis, but she hadn't run from it, no matter what Tony Costello believed. She had chosen to go, had chosen this town and the life she led here. If she had to fight for it, she would fight with everything she had.

Ellen took a final deep breath and walked back inside to face a colleague's widow and the voyeurs who would report this latest tragedy to the world.

CHAPTER 15

Gorman Grabko had an extensive collection of bow ties. As a second-year law student he had been impressed with the idea that every memorable man created his own image. That year he had begun wearing bow ties. He had been wearing them for thirty-three years. Always discreet and tasteful. Never the clip-on variety.

Today he had chosen a dignified gray-on-gray stripe that complemented the steel color in the close-cropped salt-and-pepper beard he wore to hide the ancient craters of rampant teenage acne. The hair on the sides of his square head was darker, with flags of silver at the temples. There was no hair on top of his head. Baldness had been a distinguishing trait of the Grabko men for centuries. He wore it as proudly as his judge's robes and the dark Brooks Brothers suit beneath them.

Grabko was well aware there were judges in the rural districts who paid little attention to style. He had accepted it as his mission to uphold standards. He had degrees from Northwestern, had taught at Drake Law, was a patron of the arts, and aspired to someday sit on the state supreme court.

He hoped that day would not be too far in the future, though it was difficult for a judge to distinguish himself in a place like Park County. For the most part, crimes here were petty, trials simple, the attorneys uninspired. The chance to hear a case the likes of *The State versus Dr. Garrett Wright* was a rare occasion. Gorman Grabko had prepared himself accordingly.

He sat behind his immaculate desk with the air of a benevolent monarch, smiling warmly at Anthony Costello.

"Mr. Costello, it's a pleasure and an honor," he said. "It isn't every day we get an attorney of your reputation in the Park County courthouse—is it, Ellen?"

Ellen made a small motion with her lips. No one could have called it a smile. She wanted to tell Grabko he should be thankful—but, then, that wasn't the comment he wanted to hear. The question was rhetorical, at any rate. The judge continued without waiting for her opinion, essentially shutting her out of their little male-bonding ritual. Or maybe it was less a guy thing than it was a celebrity thing. She could have got a better handle on it if Cameron had been there, but he had a competency hearing in Judge Witt's courtroom that morning, and so she was on her own.

"You're a Purdue man, I'm told," Grabko said.

Costello grinned. "I hope as a Northwestern alumnus, you won't hold that against me."

Grabko beamed, obviously flattered that Costello knew anything about him. "Both fine Big Ten schools. You've certainly done yours proud. You've made quite a name for yourself. I keep abreast of the goings-on in the metropolitan courts," Grabko said importantly, as if he had been appointed to do so by some higher power and wasn't motivated by simple envy.

"I keep busy."

Ellen struggled not to gag on Costello's false modesty. "Dr. Wright was lucky you could squeeze him in between murder trials."

"Yes, things do get hectic in the Cities." Costello cut her a look. "But, then, you knew all about that once upon a time, didn't you, Ellen? It's understandable it could become overwhelming for some people."

He made it sound as if she had cracked under the pressure and been shuttled out to the country to live in shame and secret. Grabko put his head a little on one side and looked at her with a glimmer of suspicion. Ellen narrowed her eyes at Costello.

"'Sickening' is a better word, though some people don't seem to mind wading through sewage. But we shouldn't take up Judge Grabko's time reminiscing," she said with a saccharine smile. "He has a very full schedule."

"I'm concerned about the timetable with your just arriving on the case, Mr. Costello," Grabko said. "Can I assume you'll want the omnibus hearing postponed?"

"No, Your Honor. The defense will be fully ready to proceed. Eager to proceed, in fact. Every day these charges hang over Dr. Wright's head is another day his character is unnecessarily blackened."

Costello hit Grabko full-beam with his game face—tough, direct, intense. "Your Honor, my first duty to my client is to rectify the injustice done him earlier in the week when the late Judge Franken set bail well beyond his reach."

"The man was apprehended running from the scene of a crime," Ellen jumped in.

"Allegedly."

"He brutally beat an agent of the BCA—"

"Allegedly."

"And did his best to escape. He's an obvious flight risk—"

Costello stood abruptly, taking Grabko's gaze with him. He walked toward the windows where milky light drained in through fat venetian blinds.

"Dr. Wright is entitled to the presumption of innocence," he said. "He is, in fact, an innocent man. Under the statutes of this state he is entitled to a reasonable bail. Half a million dollars in cash is hardly reasonable."

Grabko stroked his beard.

"Neither is kidnapping an eight-year-old child or torturing a woman—"

Costello wheeled around. "Oh, come on, Ellen. You can't possibly believe Garrett Wright did any of that. He's a respected professor—"

"I know *exactly* what Garrett Wright is, *Mr.* Costello." Ellen came to her feet, advancing toward him with her hands planted on the hips of her narrow tobacco-brown skirt. "He is a man who stands accused of multiple felonies and did his best to elude capture."

"I don't argue that the *assailant* fled the scene. I argue that my client was not the assailant."

"Funny, then, how he was the one taken into custody."

"He was, obviously, the man captured, but he was not the perpetrator of the crimes."

"The evidence suggests otherwise."

"We'll see about that, counselor," Costello said calmly. "If it goes that far."

Ellen crossed her arms and stood there as Tony slid back into his chair and crossed his legs, carefully straightening the jacket of his pin-striped suit to avoid wrinkles. He looked too cool, like a cardsharp with an ace up his sleeve. She weighed the idea of calling his bluff. Her silence lasted long enough to force his hand.

He looked at Grabko. "Your Honor, I'm going to state right up front, we plan to file a motion to dismiss on the grounds of unlawful arrest. The Fourth Amendment prohibits police, absent exigent circumstances or consent, from making a warrantless entry into a suspect's home in order to make a felony arrest—Payton versus New York."

"Oh, please," Ellen sneered, positioning herself at the side of Grabko's desk. "The man was fleeing arrest, armed and dangerous—you don't consider those exigent circumstances? The situation meets all criteria." She ticked them off one by one on her fingers. "A grave offense was involved, the suspect was believed to be armed, there was obvious likelihood of escape; not only was there reason to believe he was on the premises, Mitch Holt virtually followed him through the door!"

"Virtually, but not actually." Costello directed his attention to the judge, choosing not to waste his energy or his argument on Ellen. It was Grabko he needed to sway. "The truth of the situation is that the suspect Chief Holt was pursuing was wearing a ski mask. He never saw the man's face, had no reason to assume the man he was chasing was Dr. Wright. By his own admission, Chief Holt lost sight of his suspect numerous times during the chase, including just before he burst into Dr. Wright's garage.

"It is our contention that Chief Holt in fact lost sight of his suspect for too long a period of time to continue pursuit into Dr. Wright's garage without benefit of a warrant."

Ellen made no effort to contain the sarcastic laugh. "That is the most preposterous load of—"

"Ellen, that's enough," Judge Grabko said firmly.

She pressed her lips together and took her seat.

"The decision will be mine to make," Grabko said. "File your paperwork, Mr. Costello. Your argument has merit. It's worth consideration."

"But, Your Honor—"

"You'll get your chance, Ms. North," Grabko said, jotting a note to himself. "It sounds to me as if the arrest skirts some boundaries. Convince me otherwise. At any rate, it's an issue for the omnibus hearing, and I believe we're here to discuss the matter of bail."

With one point scored, Costello drew in a refreshing breath and leaned forward, his you're-my-pal look firmly in place. "Your Honor, considering Dr. Wright's ties to the community, his lack of a record, and what can only be

called flimsy evidence against him, we request bail be reduced."

Grabko turned to Ellen, eyebrows raised.

"I believe Judge Franken was more than fair and reasonable, considering the weight of the charges."

The judge sat back and swiveled in his chair, tugging at
a white spot in his beard. "Wouldn't you say, Ellen," he
began in his law-professor voice, "that bail in the amount
of half a million dollars, cash, is, for all intents and purposes, denial of bail?"

Ellen said nothing. Of course it was denial of bail. She
thought of Josh Kirkwood, who had barely spoken a word
since his return. She thought of Megan, battered, broken,
haunted, her career likely ended by Garrett Wright's vicious brutality. She thought of Dennis, the smell of his
death sneaking down the back of her throat. She thought
of Wright himself, imagined she could feel his gaze probing into her as she had that day in the interview room.

"It seems extreme to me," the judge went on. "I'm familiar with Dr. Wright's reputation and with his juvenile-
offenders program, and from what I know of the man, I
have difficulty seeing him as a flight risk at this point."

"But, Your Honor, that's just the point, don't you
see?" she pleaded. "The college professor isn't the man
we're dealing with here. We're dealing with a side of Garrett Wright that might be capable of anything. The man is
evil."

Costello rolled his eyes. "Isn't that a little melodramatic, Ellen?"

"You wouldn't think so if you'd been in your predecessor's office this morning."

He had the gall to let amusement tint his surprise.
"You're blaming my client for Enberg's death? That would
be quite a trick, considering he was in jail at the time."

Grabko frowned at her and brushed a thumb along his
jaw. "One hundred thousand dollars, cash or bond."

"Mr. Brooks, what angle are you planning to take on this story?"

Jay frowned at the reporters that had clustered around him. They had gathered in the courtroom to catch the latest twist of the case. Anthony Costello was going to ask for bail to be reduced. But the stars of the show had yet to come onstage, and the press had grown as restless as toddlers in church. One group was circled around Paul Kirkwood, who had positioned himself in the first row behind the prosecution bench. With a writer's ability to eavesdrop and carry on a conversation at the same time, Jay picked up the gist of Paul's statement—justice, victim's rights, the American way.

"I don't know that there'll be a book," Jay said, shaking his head. "I'm just here as an observer. Y'all are the ones working this case."

He might as well have told them he had come to declare himself dictator and absolute ruler of the state of Minnesota. They heard what they wanted to hear and ignored the rest.

"Will you be working with the family, or are you interested in Dr. Wright's story?"

"No comment, fellas." He flashed them a grin. "Now, listen, y'all got me talking like a lawyer. That's more work than I want to do."

Their eyes lit up like Christmas bulbs, and he knew he had made a grave mistake. A blond with a microphone leaned toward him.

"As a former defense attorney, Mr. Brooks, what is your opinion of the firing of Dennis Enberg, who allegedly committed suicide early this morning, and the arrival of his replacement, Anthony Costello?"

A man had blown his head clean off, and Blondie slid it into the scheme of things as if it were just another point of minor interest in her story. The idea disgusted him. The disgust amused him in a twisted sort of way. Ellen would have said he was no better than this woman, with her hunger for a story. He had come here for what was, on the surface, the same reason. In truth, he had deeper reasons, but they may in fact have been worse.

Self-loathing twisted his mouth into a bitter smile. "Ma'am, I haven't been an attorney in a very long time," he said. "And, hell, if I'd been any good at it, I'd probably still be doing it, wouldn't I? I can't see where my opinion on any of this is worth a hill of beans."

"And yet you don't hesitate to take sides in your books." She refused to be brushed off with "Aw, shucks" and a famous grin. "Your critics—prominent defense attorneys among them—say you have a sharp eye for the law and that your analysis of trials is akin to laser surgery."

At the front of the courtroom the door to the judge's chambers swung open, and instantly the attention of everyone in the room swung forward. Ellen emerged first, looking furious. Jay could tell she was fighting to keep her expression blank, but her whole body looked as tight as a clenched fist, and her eyes glittered with the same kind of fire she had directed at him a time or two.

Costello strolled out behind her, relaxed, confident. He looked directly at the members of the press. The conquering hero. The champion for the common man—provided the common man could come up with the bucks.

The judge, the Honorable Gorman Grabko, climbed to his perch and seated himself. Prim was the first adjective that came to mind. He looked like the kind of man who would use shoe trees and wax his bald spot. Hallway scuttlebutt indicated he was a stickler for form and that he tended to lean toward the defense, holding the prosecution to a higher standard. By the look of things, Ellen had fallen short.

A side door opened and Garrett Wright was led in by a pair of deputies and seated at the defense table.

It was over in a matter of minutes. The skirmish had been fought in chambers, as most of them were. This show was for the record and for the spectators who had gathered to watch the drama unfold.

Costello formally stated his request. Ellen argued against it. Grabko's mind was made up.

"Bail is set in the amount of one hundred thousand dollars, cash or bond," the judge announced.

"This is an outrage!" Paul Kirkwood shouted, leaping up from his seat. His face flushed the color of dried blood, and a vein stood out prominently in the side of his neck. "That animal stole my son and you're letting him out!"

A beefy deputy rushed up the aisle and grabbed hold of him. Paul put a shoulder into him and staggered him back a step toward the defense side of the room.

"You ruined our lives!" he screamed, thrusting an angry fist in Wright's direction.

Grabko smashed his gavel down. He had risen to his feet and called for more deputies. The courtroom rang with shouts and shrieks and the scuffling sounds of physical struggle. More deputies rushed in. Three of them grabbed hold of Paul Kirkwood and herded him toward the nearest exit.

He twisted around as they dragged him. "I want justice! I want justice!"

The reporters rushed after him in a flock. The remaining deputies hustled Wright and Costello out a side door. Grabko shook his head, banged his gavel, and declared court adjourned for the morning. The room was empty in a matter of seconds, everyone running into the hall to catch the continuation of Paul's show. Everyone except Ellen.

She sat at the table with one arm banded across her middle and the other hand raised as a prop for her chin.

She stared up at the empty bench as if she were trying to will the blindfold off the figure of Lady Justice. Jay hung back, his eyes on Ellen. He should have been out in the hall. Paul Kirkwood's penchant for theatrics intrigued him. There was something slightly off about those performances, something that struck Jay as calculated, disingenuous. But he couldn't seem to make himself turn away and walk out.

Instead, he opened the gate and let himself onto the business side of the bar. Because he wanted to hear Ellen's take on things, he told himself. That was all. Not because she looked small and forlorn, sitting there all alone. Not because it touched him in any way that she was taking the loss hard.

"It's only bail," he said.

"Tell that to Paul Kirkwood," Ellen murmured. "Drive out to Lakeside and break that news to Josh's mother. Or maybe you want to call Megan O'Malley in the hospital and tell her?

"It's only bail." She faked a nonchalant shrug as she turned in her chair to face him. "Why shouldn't Garrett Wright be free to walk the streets, free to communicate with his accomplice, who may have committed murder last night? Who is, as we speak, doing God-knows-what to Dustin Holloman."

He moved closer, his hands stuffed into the pockets of his rumpled slate-colored Dockers. He had shed his coat somewhere. A bright silk tie hung like a strip of modern art down the front of his worn denim shirt. The knot was jerked loose and the top button undone as if he just couldn't bear the symbolism of a noose around his neck and yet felt compelled to make a token show of formality.

"You lost the round, not the game," he said, settling a hip on the corner of the heavy oak table. His thigh brushed against the back of her hand.

The contact had the quality of an electric shock. Ellen

tried to cover the involuntary reaction by shifting positions, reaching up to brush at a stray hair that had come loose from her twist. "It's not a game."

"Of course it is. You've played it a thousand times. You know the rules. You know the strategies. You gave up some points. It's not the end of the world."

Ellen glared at him, anger burning through the haze of defeat. "A man gave up his life last night. How many points is that worth?" she asked bitterly, pushing to her feet. "What's that worth to you? Another chapter? A page? A paragraph?"

"I didn't kill him and I can't bring him back. I can only try to put it in context. Isn't that what you want to do? Make sense of it, understand it?"

"Oh, I understand it. Now let *me* put it in a context *you* can understand. It's a game, all right, Mr. Brooks. Dennis Enberg was a piece they didn't need anymore, and now he's dead and his replacement just drew the Get Out Of Jail card for his twisted bastard of a client, and I couldn't manage to stop any of that from happening!"

The rage and the pain boiled up inside her, boiled over the rim of her control. She turned her back to him and pressed her hands over her face, furious with herself. She had thought she had control of her emotions if nothing else in all this madness. She had vowed to fight this battle, but somehow she hadn't seen the possibility for this early defeat. She thought of Costello's threat to get the arrest thrown out and felt sick at the possibility. If she could lose this battle, she could lose that one. That vulnerability was terrifying and raw.

Jay watched her struggle to rein in her feelings. Her back was ramrod straight, her shoulders straining against the need to shake. Despite all the time she had spent working in the system, she had managed to hang on to a sense of right and a sense of honor. She fought hard and took her losses harder. Cynicism hadn't dulled the lance of jus-

tice for her as it had for so many. As it had for him. It
seemed only to have made her more keenly aware of her
place in the scheme of things.

"You didn't think it could happen here, did you?" he
murmured, stepping behind her.

"It shouldn't be happening here," she whispered.
"Children should be safe. Dennis Enberg should be alive.
Garrett Wright and whatever other madman is playing
this game with him should be stopped forever."

"Is that why you left the city?" He was close enough
that the scent of her perfume caught his nose and drew his
head down. The nape of her neck was no more than a
breath away—tempting, too tempting.

He wanted her and knew better than to give in to that
seductive need. She was part of the story. The story was
what he had come here for—to bury himself in it, to lose
himself in it, to run away from his own pain and dissect
someone else's.

The reminder brought a bitter taste of self-loathing.
The anger made him cruel.

"Is that why you left, Ellen? Because you didn't want
to fight this kind of fight? Is that what you ran from?"

She wheeled on him and he caught hold of her arms
before she could slap him.

"I didn't run from anything."

"You were on the short list of up-and-comers in Minneapolis," he said, deliberately goading her. "Then suddenly you're riding roughshod over drunks and losers in
Mayberry."

"I *walked* away. I wanted a saner life. I made a choice,
and I certainly don't have to justify it to you."

"There's sure as hell nothing sane about what's going
on here now," he growled.

Ellen didn't know if he meant the case or the heat
building between them at that moment. He was too close,

his hands too tight on her upper arms, his mouth just inches from hers.

"Let go of me," she ordered, jerking out of his grasp.

The hall door swung open, and Henry Forster, a long-time reporter for the *Minneapolis Star Tribune,* stepped in. Through the perpetually smudged lenses of his thick bifocals, his gaze hit Ellen with full magnified force.

"Ellen, are we going to get a comment from you?" he barked. "Or are we just supposed to draw our own conclusions?"

"I'm coming right now," she said.

Not sparing Jay so much as a glance, she picked up her briefcase and walked out.

He followed at a distance, waiting for her to capture the full attention of the reporters before he slipped into the hall. The wait also gave him a moment to clear his brain. Damn, but he had got his balls in a vise this time.

This was what he got for sniffing around a live case. Ordinarily, he had sense enough to come in after the fact, after the strongest of the immediate emotions had faded away and the parties involved had gained perspective on the crime that had touched their lives. There was no perspective here. This case was as hot as a live wire . . . and just as dangerous.

Scuttlebutt had the body of Dennis Enberg being hauled away for a look-see by a medical examiner. Ellen had as much as said she believed the lawyer had been murdered, even though the official rumor was suicide.

Jay had heard the calls on the police scanner, had found his way to the Southtown Shopping Center and bided his time in the relative warmth of his vehicle until the reporters lost interest in the scene and split in search of quotable sources. A single uniformed cop had been left to guard duty in front of the building.

Jay had wandered up, bummed a cigarette, stayed to chat as if he had nothing better to do with his time. The cop, young and unaccustomed to the sight of gruesome death, had eventually let the details of the scene come rolling out. His hands shook so violently, he could barely bring his cigarette to his lips.

"Man, I mean, you see things like that in the movies, but this was *real*," the kid mumbled. Far across the way, half a dozen cars were parked in front of Snyder's Drug. People came to buy cold tablets and headache remedies, ignorant of the fact that a hundred yards from them a man had had his brain splattered all over the wall of his office.

"It's a tough sight to stomach," Jay said. "Truth to tell, I've seen many a strong man toss his cookies right there and then. And there's no shame in it, if you ask me. Sight like that oughta make any decent person sick."

"Well . . . it did me," the kid admitted. He looked at Jay out the corner of his eye. "I suppose you've seen a lot. I read *Twist of Fate*. That was grisly."

"True enough. Never ceases to amaze me the violence people will do to one another."

"Yeah . . ." He sucked his Winston down to the filter, the ash glowing red as he tossed the butt. The look in his eyes was faraway, deep inside, where people keep their darkest fears and seldom look at them. "I can't imagine sticking a shotgun in somebody's mouth and pulling the trigger."

Murder. As if this case hadn't been sinister enough to begin with.

Jay now shot a sweeping glance across the crowd gathered for Ellen's impromptu press conference. The old warhorse with the beetle brows and bad comb-over who had walked in on them shouted down his colleagues.

"Ms. North, what is your reaction to Garrett Wright's release pending payment of bond?"

"It goes without saying, I'm extremely disappointed." She was all cool control once again, as if those moments of discomposure in the courtroom had never happened.

"However, Judge Grabko listened to both sides and made his decision, and we'll live with it. That's the way our system works."

Which was essentially saying it hadn't worked this time.

"Will Dr. Wright return to his home in the Lakeside neighborhood—virtually yards away from the Kirkwood home?"

"I don't know," Ellen said. "I hope not, for the family's sake."

"What about rumors that Dennis Enberg's body was transported to the Hennepin County Medical Center for an autopsy?"

"Mr. Enberg died a violent and unexpected death. The city and county agencies are obligated to investigate that death to determine beyond question whether or not it was self-inflicted."

"Was there a suicide note?"

"No comment."

"With Garrett Wright in jail at the time, you can't possibly suspect involvement on his part in either Mr. Enberg's death or the kidnapping of Dustin Holloman, can you?"

"I have no comment regarding ongoing investigations."

The stone wall had gone up. She had made her point about Wright's release; the rest would be for show. The tough lady prosecutor showing the world this small defeat didn't faze her. None of these reporters had seen her tears or heard the self-castigation in her voice.

Jay had. And that mattered to him in a way that was patently unwise.

He pulled his gaze off her and continued to scan the crowd. Courthouse personnel hung around the fringes of the media group, curious to see their allegedly ambitious assistant county attorney in action. Until the first kidnapping, press conferences had likely been a rarity here.

A flash of rusty-red hair caught his eye. He moved slowly down the hall, skirting the crowd, like a hunter easing up on wary prey.

Todd Childs had focused his attention on Ellen, his gaze flat and cold behind retro-look glasses. He stood half-hidden by a marble column, wearing a long olive-drab wool coat that looked as if it had been fending off moths in someone's attic for years. A student of Wright's at Harris, Childs had been mentioned in the news reports following the O'Malley incident on Saturday. One of the local TV stations had included a shot of him and a comment as to Dr. Wright's innocence in their follow-up story on Sunday.

Jay eased up beside him, tipping his head conspiratorially. "She's a cool one, isn't she?" he murmured.

"She's a bitch," Childs said between clenched teeth. He jerked his gaze away from Ellen, looking at Jay as if he felt he had been tricked into responding. "You a reporter?"

"Me? Naw. Just interested. How about you?"

He scratched his scruffy goatee and sniffed. "Yeah . . . I'm interested. Dr. Wright is sort of a mentor of mine. The man is fucking brilliant."

"Yeah, but is he guilty?"

Childs glared down at him, pale skin tightening over his bony face. Even though the light in this part of the hall was poor, his pupils were black pinpoints, suggesting he had indulged in some substance other than the dope he smoked, the smell of which had become as ingrained in his ratty coat as the scent of mothballs.

"The man is fucking brilliant," he said again, enunciating each word crisply. "The case against him is bullshit." He cut a nasty glance toward Ellen. "She'll wish she'd never started this."

He backed away from the pillar and turned toward the

steps at the far end of the hall. The sudden mix of voices talking all at once told Jay the press conference was over. He didn't look for Ellen but fell in step behind Todd Childs. Keeping his head down, he hustled down the first set of stairs, coming even with Childs on the second-floor landing.

"So are you involved with the protest out front?" he asked as they made their way toward the ground floor.

"Yeah." Childs shot him a sideways look. "You ask a lot of questions. Who are you?"

"James Butler," he lied without hesitation. "I'm doing some independent consulting work with the county auditor's office. You might have guessed, I'm not from around here. I just sort of dropped in on all of this—like tuning into the middle of a movie, you know?"

"Yeah, well, you know what they say, man," Childs muttered as he flipped down his clip-on shades. "Truth is stranger than fiction."

He pushed through one of the heavy main doors and cut diagonally down the steps, his bushy hair bouncing like a foxtail down the center of his back. Jay watched from the door, his sixth sense stirring restlessly.

"Hey!" a voice sounded beside him. "You're Jay Butler Brooks! Adam Slater, *Grand Forks Herald*. Could I ask you a couple of questions?"

"Yeah, sure," Jay mumbled resignedly. His eyes remained on Todd Childs, who approached the small crowd of student protestors now celebrating his mentor's release . . . and walked right past them as if they weren't there.

CHAPTER 16

The news of Garrett Wright's release on bond swept through Deer Lake and on to Campion like a blizzard wind. Telephones at the courthouse and law-enforcement center were jammed with irate calls from the faction of the population who believed Wright was guilty. In Campion the search for Dustin Holloman went on unrewarded, and the reporters lost interest in shooting still more footage of grim-faced volunteers trudging through the snow. Word that Anthony Costello would be giving a formal statement in front of the Park County courthouse about Wright's release sent them packing.

The sidewalk in front of the courthouse took on the carnival atmosphere of a political campaign riding the tide of victory. The Harris College students who had been protesting Dr. Wright's incarceration took up new celebratory chants. The Sci-Fi Cowboys, freed by a teacher in-service day in the metropolitan school system, had set up a vendor's cart on the sidewalk and were selling T-shirts to raise money for Wright's defense fund. A boom box blasted out rap music with strong themes of injustice and oppression. Deer Lake natives watched the festivities with wary eyes from the front window of the Scandia House Cafe. In typical rural Minnesota fashion, all overt displays of emotion were considered suspicious.

Ellen looked down on the goings-on from the window

of the conference room. Momentum was swinging Wright's way. Just days ago she had held the control. Now her handhold was being pried away one finger at a time.

"Do you think they have a permit to sell those T-shirts?" Cameron asked.

"They do," Phoebe said, holding her glasses on her button nose as she looked down. "I checked. And we can't stop Mr. Costello from speaking on the steps of the courthouse, either."

"He would only use it against us if we tried," Ellen muttered.

She turned away from the window and faced her team. Mitch had seated himself at one end of the table. Steiger positioned himself at the opposite end, standing with one dirty boot planted on the seat of the chair. Wilhelm sat halfway between them, looking shell-shocked, glassy-eyed. The idiot grin he had worn to Deer Lake a week ago had slipped badly in the last few days. Between developments in the Kirkwood case, the Holloman kidnapping, and Denny Enberg's death, the hours had been hellish, the pressure immense, the leads nonexistent.

"I'm familiar with Costello's tactics," Ellen said. "He believes the best defense is a good offense. He'll do everything he can to make us look bad."

"You mean he'll throw as much shit as he can at the wall and hope some of it sticks," the sheriff said bluntly.

"I'm sure he wouldn't put it quite that way, but that's the gist of it. He plays big-league hardball."

"He's an out-of-town stiff," Steiger snorted. "Just because he's from the Cities, we're all supposed to crap our pants at the sight of him. He's just another shyster lawyer."

Cameron rolled his eyes. Phoebe gave the sheriff a look that suggested he smelled as if he had already seen Costello and fulfilled his statement.

"This shyster is like having a great white shark land in our lake, Sheriff," Ellen said. "Do *not* underestimate him."

"He's got his own private investigator," Mitch interjected. "Raymond York. The guy was sniffing around St. Elysius today. Father Tom called to complain."

Steiger scowled at him. "So?"

"So this PI will be working full-time to find anything that might get Wright off the hook, while the rest of us are trying to work this case, find Dustin Holloman, figure out whether or not Denny Enberg killed himself, and deal with our everybody, garden-variety mopes."

"The Holloman case and Denny's death complicate our situation," Ellen admitted. "But if we go on the assumption they're tied to Josh Kirkwood's case, that it's Wright's accomplice carrying on the game, then we're still focused on nailing Wright."

"That could be a dangerous assumption if it's wrong," Wilhelm stated.

"But it's not wrong," Mitch said. "We know the kidnappings are related. The thing we can't be sure of is Enberg. The autopsy is scheduled for Monday. If we're lucky, we'll get the word on fingerprints Monday, as well."

"Did Denny's secretary know anything about any late-night appointments?" Ellen asked.

He shook his head. "She said it was a light day. Three appointments with clients and a couple of reporters dropping by for comments. He didn't have anything scheduled after five, told her he was going to stay late and do some paperwork. I've got guys talking to the clients, trying to get a handle on his state of mind. Barb, the secretary, said he was down about the Wright case, but that he didn't want to talk to her about it."

"No witnesses from around the shopping center?" Cameron asked, tapping the end of his fountain pen against his legal pad, impatient for a break.

"None yet, but we haven't been able to track down the night staff from the Donut Hut. They're gone to Mankato for the day—skiing."

"Well, we know one thing," Wilhelm said. "Wright didn't kill him. He was still sitting in jail at the time."

"Grabko remedied that situation," Mitch muttered.

"It may actually work to our advantage to have Wright out on bail," Cameron offered. "If we can put him under surveillance, he could lead us to the accomplice, to Dustin Holloman, tie the whole mess up in a nice, neat bow."

"Somehow I don't think he'll be that obliging," Mitch said. "But I've already assigned a plainclothes detail to him, in case there's a God after all."

"I've assigned an agent to the surveillance team, too," Marty Wilhelm said without enthusiasm.

"I'm assuming nothing has turned up from the search of Wright's home?" Ellen asked.

He shook his head. "Nothing at all out of the ordinary. You might think he's an innocent man."

Mitch gave him a look that could have frozen fire. "I *don't* think he's an innocent man, Agent Wilhelm. Neither does your predecessor. And you had damn well better not think he's innocent either."

"Hey, I've got an ongoing situation in Campion—"

"Garrett Wright is an ongoing situation," Ellen stated sharply, pulling Wilhelm's attention back to her. "We've got a probable-cause hearing in less than a week and a judge who has 'Innocent Until Proven Guilty' embroidered on his underwear. I need every scrap of ammunition I can get to nail Wright. Costello fired his first shot today—he's going to try to get the arrest thrown out."

"Fuck him!" Mitch jumped to his feet. "That was a righteous bust!"

Ellen held up a hand. "I said he would try. He won't succeed if we have anything to say about it. I don't believe he'll convince Grabko, but in the meantime he'll be feeding his theories to the press, tainting the jury pool."

"Goddamn weasel," Steiger muttered.

Ellen turned to Wilhelm again. "Tell me you've got someone working with the computer equipment you confiscated from Wright's home."

"Yes, but they're not going to find anything. We all know that."

"The notes from Josh's and Dustin Holloman's kidnappings were computer generated and printed on a laser printer. Garrett Wright owns a laser printer."

"But the thing doesn't have a memory. There's no way to tell if the notes came from *that* printer," Wilhelm argued. "And so far we haven't found a computer diskette labeled 'Terroristic Threats and Creepy Poetry.' Wright isn't stupid enough to have hung on to anything incriminating."

Mitch glared at him. "Well, you would know more about stupidity than the rest of us, Wilhelm, but I know this—guys like Wright get cocky. And when they get cocky, they get careless."

"He told Megan they had done this sort of thing before," Ellen said. "He told her they had committed murder. If that's true, then he has to have left a trail somewhere. And if he's proud of his accomplishments, I can't believe he hasn't kept some sort of souvenirs. No luck on the search for another property in the area?"

Steiger shook his head. "Not in Wright's name. Not in his wife's name. Nothing for Priest or Childs."

She looked to Wilhelm. "You haven't found anything in his background?"

Wilhelm dug through a messy file folder on the table in front of him and tugged out a typed report. "He was a Boy Scout."

Cameron took the papers. "Any merit badges for cruel and unusual behavior?"

"I've read the report," Wilhelm said. "There's nothing out of the ordinary. His parents split up when he was a kid. He was raised by his mother, an office manager for a shoe factory in Mishawaka, Indiana. National Honor Society in high school, graduated with honors from Ball State, went on for his master's and doctorate at Ohio State," he recited the history in a bored monotone, surreptitiously checking his watch. "He came here from the University of Virginia and before that Penn State."

"He gets around for someone in a profession where tenure is the big brass ring," Cameron said.

"Have you checked with NCIC?" Ellen asked. "They can scan their database for similar crimes in other parts of the country."

"The man has no record, Ms. North."

"All that means is he's never been caught," Mitch said. He began to pace. "Jesus Christ, Wilhelm, if you don't want to do the job, fucking delegate. I'll call NCIC myself."

Wilhelm scowled at the table, color splashing across his cheekbones. "I'm doing my job, Chief Holt. I can't do everything at once."

"I'm beginning to wonder if you can manage to walk and chew gum at the same time—"

"Time out!" Ellen shouted, rising from her chair. The men looked at her with surprise and annoyance for interrupting their argument. "We've got a case to make. You guys tear each other's throats out on your own time."

"This is pointless," Steiger grumbled, waving a hand at them.

Before he could take his foot off the chair, a beeper went off. Everyone but Phoebe reached for a pager.

"It's mine," Steiger said, reaching for the phone on the table.

Tension crackled like static in the air as he punched in the number and waited. No one spoke. Ellen knew that they were all thinking the same thing, that they were all thinking the worst and hoping for the best.

"Steiger," the sheriff barked. A muscle ticked in his cheek, marking time as he took in the news. Four seconds . . . five seconds . . . Air hissed out between his teeth, taking his color with it. "Shit. Keep it quiet. Don't do anything. I'll be right there."

He slammed the receiver down. "That was Campion. They found the boy's boot with a note inside. 'Evil comes to him who searches for it.'"

The three cops grabbed their coats and headed for the door, grim-faced and silent.

"I'll be there as soon as I can," Ellen promised.

Cameron closed the door behind them and clamped his hands on top of his head. "Shit. Shit, shit, shit."

Phoebe shoved her glasses up into her hair and covered her eyes with her fingers.

Ellen sank back down on her chair. "Look at the timing," she said, her gaze catching Cameron's. "Just as Costello is about to start his press conference with Garrett Wright standing beside him, a clue is found in an identical case twenty miles away."

"You think Costello knows?"

Tony had shown his colors before, but could he be that cold, that ruthless? Could he know the name of the person who held the fate of Dustin Holloman and not tell them?

"I don't know," she whispered.

"That poor little boy," Phoebe squeaked behind her hands.

"The best thing we can do for him is our jobs," Ellen said, fighting to push away the mental fatigue and uncertainty. "Cameron, I want you to write the best damn brief in history on exigent circumstances and probable cause regarding the Fourth Amendment. We're not letting Wright weasel out of this on a technicality."

"You got it."

"I also want you to ride herd on Agent Wilhelm. Keep after him about digging into Wright's background. He should have a man on it full-time. If they can't catch Wright's accomplice, then his past is our way in."

"I'll make some phone calls." He slid into his chair and started making notes.

"Phoebe, it's your job to run interference." Ellen caught one of the girl's wrists and gently pulled her hand away from her damp face. "Are you listening to me?"

"Y-yes."

"I know you're used to giving the defense attorneys free access to files and information. We've always had an open-door policy. You're going to slam that door shut in Tony Costello's face. If he wants something from this of-fice, he has to request it in writing. Make this as inconve-nient for him as possible. I'm never in when he calls. He never gets in to see me without an appointment. Under-stand?"

Phoebe nodded, bouncing her glasses down out of her hair. She shoved them into place, sniffed, and sat up straighter, putting on her bravest face to accept her duty.

"Now, turn that television up," Ellen ordered, nod-ding to the portable set they had perched on a file cabinet. The channel-eleven news camera was homing in on Costello's handsome face. "In the words of Sheriff Stei-ger, let's see what shit he's throwing at the wall now."

"An innocent man is free," Costello began. A cheer went up from the students gathered on the sidewalk behind the press. "Upon reviewing the circumstances and the facts of this case, Judge Grabko has seen fit to grant Dr. Wright bail and reverse the earlier injustice imposed by the pros-ecution and the late Judge Franken."

The afternoon was growing dark with the promise of

night and more snow. Portable lights had been set on the steps of the courthouse to illuminate the players in this melodrama. The cameraman was positioned down the steps, shooting up. The effect was dramatic, with the pillars of the courthouse as a backdrop. Costello looked powerful, his shoulders filling the screen in close-ups, his face as masculine and classic as a Roman sculpture. Garrett Wright stood beside him like a pale shadow, the contrast in their builds and coloring giving him an image of delicacy and refinement.

Hannah stared at him as the camera pulled in close on his face. She watched the press conference on the kitchen television that sat tucked back into a corner on the counter. The ingredients for lasagna were scattered around it. In the family room Lily was dancing to a tune from the talking candlestick in *Beauty and the Beast*.

Josh ignored the video, sitting on a stool in front of the picture window, staring out at the lake. He had taken to carrying his backpack around the house with him, as if he felt a need to keep essential items with him in case he was taken away again. The backpack sat on the floor beside his stool, purple and teal and plump with who-knew-what.

"Dr. Garrett Wright is an innocent man," Costello said. "The presumption of innocence is his constitutional right."

"And what about *our* rights?" Hannah murmured, glaring at the television.

Ellen North had called to break the news about the reduced bail. Not only had the new judge reduced the amount of the bail, he had given Wright the option of securing a bond, which meant he had to come up with only ten percent of the actual amount. For ten thousand dollars Garrett Wright could walk out of jail. No amount of money could free Josh from the prison in which Wright had locked his mind.

"The investigation of Josh Kirkwood's kidnapping

was mishandled from the first," Costello went on, "and right up to the arrest of Dr. Wright—who had never been considered a suspect. He had never been questioned. He had, in fact, offered assistance and had been consulted for his expertise. He was *never* a suspect."

"How do you explain Dr. Wright's capture?" shouted a reporter offscreen.

Costello fixed him with an eagle eye. "Dr. Wright was not *captured*. He was *attacked*. In his own garage, on his own property. That's the truth of this situation. The Deer Lake police department was desperate to make an arrest. Chief Holt lost sight of his suspect during the chase Saturday night, and he grabbed the first person he could. He couldn't let that opportunity slip by when he had already had one suspect die in custody. He needed to arrest somebody and Dr. Wright was handy. But the fact of the matter is, there is a more viable suspect who remains at large. The kidnapping of Dustin Holloman has proved that."

"What about the theory of an accomplice?"

Costello looked disgusted. "Dr. Wright doesn't have *accomplices*. Dr. Wright has colleagues and students and friends."

Another cheer went up from the assembled fans.

Fury boiled up inside Hannah, and she stabbed the power button on the set. Costello froze midword; then the tube seemed to suck his image inside it, leaving only blankness.

She knew the attorney was only doing his job. She knew it was up to the prosecution to prove Garrett Wright's guilt. But it made her sick and angry to see Wright portrayed as a victim. Josh was the victim. Their family had been victimized, their lives torn apart.

She didn't for a second believe Costello's contention that Garrett Wright had simply been in the wrong place at the wrong time. Costello was paid to make his client look innocent. Hannah had known Mitch Holt since the day he and his daughter had moved to Deer Lake, two years before. Mitch couldn't be bought. If Mitch said Garrett Wright was the man, Garrett Wright was the man. On the night of the arrest Mitch had come to the house, wounded and exhausted, and explained every detail of the chase and capture.

She replayed the scene in her mind as she went through the motions of preparing supper for her children, her hands shaking so badly she spilled tomato sauce on the counter. It splashed across the tile like blood, the color of violence and rage. For a long moment she just stood there staring at it. She thought of Megan O'Malley, beaten, the lifeblood of her career rushing out of her. She thought of that night Mitch had come, the night she'd told Paul it was over between them. The last lifeblood of their marriage had been drained from them. She thought of Josh and the blood that had been drawn from his arm.

Hannah didn't know if any of them could ever get back what they had lost. And yet Garrett Wright could make a down payment and buy back his freedom. If he wanted, he could come home to the house down the block. He could resume his residence in Lakeside with no regard for the lives he had wrecked at the end of the street. It seemed he could wipe the slate of his conscience clean as easily as she wiped away the spilled sauce on the counter. No consequences. Clean up the mess and forget about it.

He won't get away with it.

Ellen had assured her the county attorney's office was working diligently to bring the case to trial and to convict Garrett Wright. Mitch had told her all the law enforcement agencies involved in the Dustin Holloman case were focused on capturing Wright's accomplice. She had to trust the system. She believed in it, believed it worked more often than not. She had to believe in justice.

He won't get away with it.

She slid the lasagna into the oven, wiped her hands on

a dish towel, and walked down into the family room. The movie was still rolling, but no one seemed to be watching it. Lily was singing a tune of her own composition and her own language, and wiggling around the cherry trunk that served as coffee table. She had pulled a pair of huge pink play sunglasses out of the toy box and wore them at a jaunty angle. Hannah grabbed a discarded baseball cap and plunked it sideways on her daughter's head, finding a smile that had become too rare in the last weeks.

"Hey, Lily-bug, are you doing the diaper dance?" she asked, squatting down and wiggling her own behind, sending Lily into a giggling frenzy.

Hannah laughed, amazed at how good that felt. Then her gaze strayed to Josh and the laughter died. He hadn't moved from the window, his expression hadn't changed. He didn't seem to be with them. His emotional isolation took on magical physical properties—an invisible force field around him that didn't allow him to see or hear or reach out to the people who loved him.

The idea came with a swift needle stab of pain. A force field was something Josh would have created a story around . . . before. He was fascinated by science fiction, loved to make up his own tales after watching *Star Trek: The Next Generation*. Since fall he had carried a notebook with him everywhere—his "Think Pad" he called it—to draw pictures of rocket ships and race cars. He had filled the pages with his thoughts and ideas.

The notebook was gone now, given over to the state crime lab. The kidnapper had used it as one of his taunts, placing it on the hood of Mitch Holt's truck. Another piece of Josh's childhood gone.

Even as she thought it, Hannah's gaze caught on the sketch pad the county child advocate had given Josh. It lay on the floor, pushed aside, unused, blank. She shivered at the thought that Josh's mind might be that blank. There was no way of knowing as long as he chose not to share his feelings. He had spent another fifty minutes with the psychiatrist that afternoon staring at the woman's aquarium, watching the fish swim back and forth. His only comment had come at the end of the session. He had turned to Dr. Freeman and said, "They're trapped, aren't they? They can see out, but they can never get out."

As he sat staring out the window, Hannah couldn't help but wonder if he felt the same way.

On impulse, she turned away from him and went back through the kitchen to Paul's immaculate home office. He had yet to clean out the room, though she supposed that day would come when he would box up his half of their marriage and take it all away.

Hannah found what she was looking for on a shelf in the closet, where Paul kept supplies—a brand-new blue spiral notebook. From the organizer on the desk she chose the most exotic-looking pen she could find—a fat red one with a fancy blue clip and a removable cap. She left the office and went into the laundry room, where one cupboard drawer held gift wrap, tape and string and sheets of stickers. Digging through the mess, she found an assortment of stickers she knew would appeal to Josh and used them to decorate the cover of the notebook. With a laundry marker she carefully wrote *Josh's New Think Pad* across the center of the cover, then at the very bottom printed *To Josh From Mom*, and finished the line with a heart.

He was still sitting by the window when she returned to the living room. Lily had lost all interest in the movie and was busy dragging toys out of the toy box.

"Josh, honey," Hannah said, laying a hand on his shoulder, "I've got something for you. Will you come sit with me on the couch so I can give it to you?"

He looked up at her, away from the window and the dark view of the lake, then gathered up his backpack and went to the couch. He sat back in a corner, the pack on his lap, his arms around it as if it were a favorite old teddy bear. Hannah took the opportunity to close the drapes, though she left the stool he had been using. Sitting next to him, she resisted the urge to pull him close. Dr. Freeman had impressed upon her the need to give Josh a little breathing room, even though what she wanted most to do was hold him twenty-four hours a day.

"Remember your Think Pad and how it got lost?" she asked.

Josh nodded, though his attention seemed to be caught on the baseball cap Lily had discarded on the floor.

"I remember how you used to draw and write in it all the time. All the neat pictures you used to do with space-ships and everything. And I got to thinking you probably still miss it. I mean, that sketch pad you got is pretty cool, but it's sort of big, isn't it? You can't really carry it around. It won't fit in your backpack. And so . . . ta-da!" She held out the new notebook in front of him. "Josh's New Think Pad."

Hannah held her breath as he looked at it. He made no move to take it at first, but his gaze traveled the cover from top to bottom, taking in the stickers of the starship *Enterprise* and football helmets and Batman. Slowly he uncurled one arm from around his backpack and reached out with his forefinger. He touched one sticker and then the next. He traced beneath the title, then dragged his fingertip down to the bottom of the page. *To Josh From Mom.* He opened his hand and stroked the line, his expression wistful and sad.

"Go ahead, honey," Hannah whispered around the lump in her throat. "It's yours. Just for you. You can write down whatever you want in it—stories or secrets or dreams. You don't ever have to share it with anyone if you don't want to. But if you want to share it with me, you know I'll listen. Anything you want to tell me, you can, and it'll be all right. We can work out anything because we love each other. Right?"

His eyes filled with tears as he looked at the notebook, and he nodded slowly, reluctantly. Hannah wished she could have known what part of her statement made him hesitate. Was it that he didn't believe he could tell her or that he didn't believe they could work it out? She had no way of knowing. All she could do was offer him support and reassurance, and hope to God the promises she made him weren't empty.

As he took the notebook from her, she pulled him close and kissed the top of his head.

"We *will* work it out, Josh. However long it takes. It doesn't matter," she whispered. "I'm just so happy to have you home, to be able to tell you how much I love you." She pulled back from him a little and made a goofy face at him. "And get mushy all over you."

A tiny smile of embarrassment hooked one corner of his mouth and he rolled his eyes. Like the old Josh. Like the boy who loved to kid with her and laugh. "It's okay, Mom," he said in a small voice.

"It better be," Hannah joked. "'Cause, you know, even when you're a grown-up and the star quarterback in the Super Bowl, I'll still be your mom and I'll still get mushy."

Josh wrinkled his nose and turned his attention back to the notebook. He ran his finger over the stickers one by one, naming each one in his head. He recognized them all from Before, when he had been a regular kid, when life had been simple and his biggest secret had been kissing Molly Higgins on the cheek. He wished he could go back to Before. He didn't like secrets, didn't like the way they made him feel inside. But he had to keep them now. There could be no telling. He had been warned.

So he chose not to think about the secrets at all. He would think about other things, like his new pen and how it looked like something astronauts might use, and his new Think Pad. Blank pages just for him, not for sharing with strangers or anyone. Blank pages that were like part of his imagination—space for thinking and storing thoughts away. He liked that idea—taking thoughts out of his head and storing them away where he didn't have to think them anymore.

He slipped the notebook into his backpack and carried it to his room.

CHAPTER 17

Ellen pulled her glasses off and rubbed her hands over her face, unconcerned about her makeup. Her makeup was long gone. There was no one around the office to see her anyway. Even the cleaning people had come and gone. Ellen had done the reverse—she had gone to Campion and come back.

At Campion she had run the gauntlet of reporters and stood in the windswept parking lot of the Grain and Ag Services on the edge of town, where Dustin Holloman's boot had been found in the cab of an employee's pickup.

"Doesn't this confirm Dr. Wright's innocence?"

"Will you try to delay next week's hearing?"

"Is it true Garrett Wright was never a suspect before his arrest?"

"Is it true Wright plans to sue for malicious prosecution?"

"Is the owner of the pickup being questioned? Is he a suspect?"

The questions came at her like lances. The reporters swarmed around her, their eyes bright and feral.

The parking lot was a rough sea of ice, rutted and polished by truck tires. Under the sodium-vapor security lights it took on a pearly glow. The buildings and huge metal bins of the grain elevator made an austere backdrop, Shaker-plain and simply functional, unlit, unwelcoming.

Clouds had taken the daylight early and snow had begun to fall. Small, sharp flakes hurled down from heaven on a frigid, unforgiving wind.

The BCA mobile crime lab was parked at a cock-eyed angle twenty feet away from the lone pickup truck. Evidence technicians swarmed around the truck, working in the brilliant light of portable halogen lamps.

"They're taking their time," Mitch said. "They don't want to miss so much as a hair—which is all well and good, but the guy who owns the truck raises cattle and his dog rides around with him in the cab. They'll be here all night getting hair off the goddamn seat cover."

Ellen squinted against the pelting snow and the glare of the lights. "Who owns the truck?"

"Kent Hofschulte. He works in the office here."

"Any connection to the Hollomans?"

"Casual acquaintance, I hear. You want details, you'll have to talk to Steiger."

She stepped a little closer to the truck just as an evidence tech moved aside from the open driver's door. Dustin Holloman's boot sat on the bench seat of the truck, center stage under the halogen spotlight. A single winter boot, the purple-and-yellow nylon of the upper portion too bright in this bleak setting.

She had returned to the office because she had more cases than Garrett Wright's on her schedule. There were loose ends that needed tying, and then there were Quentin Adler's endless questions about the two cases she had handed over to him. But she had appetite for neither the work she needed to accomplish nor the turkey sandwich she had picked up at Subway for her supper. All systems were crashing due to lack of fuel, but the thought of food turned her stomach.

Out of practice. When she had worked in Minneapolis, she had got to the point where she could go from a murder scene to dinner and not think twice about it. The mind was an amazing machine, able to develop what defenses it needed. But it had been a long time since she had needed defenses.

"Call it a night," she murmured, checking the clock. Nine-fifteen. Poor Harry wasn't seeing much of his mistress these days. At least he had Otto. Otto Norvold, her neighbor and fellow dog lover, who didn't mind seeing to Harry when Ellen had to put in a late night.

She sorted through the stack of files in front of her, taking those pertinent to Wright and two other cases she would have to deal with the next day—a burglary for which she expected the defendant to cop a plea, and a DUI she fully intended to put in jail for as long as she could. The files went into her briefcase; then she set about her daily ritual of arranging everything left on her desk in precise order. She had learned long ago that her office was the one place in her professional life where she could always be guaranteed order and control. She exercised the ritual with religious dedication and found it much more calming than the pointless raking of a Zen garden.

Satisfied with the task, she pushed her chair into its cubbyhole, dug in her coat pockets for her gloves. Her mind was already halfway out the building, wondering how much snow had fallen in the two hours since she had come back. Four to six inches was predicted. The road back from Campion had already begun to drift over in spots.

She dug her keys out of her purse, slung the bag over her shoulder, and started for the door just as the telephone rang.

"What now?" she muttered on a groan, fearing the worst behind the screen of annoyance.

"Ellen North," she said into the receiver.

Nothing.

"Hello?"

It was Monday night all over again—the heavy sense

of a presence on the other end of the line, a silence that seemed ominous. Her stomach churned as the line from last night's call played through the back of her mind. *"The first thing we do, let's kill all the lawyers."*

"If you've got something to say, then say it," she snapped. "I've got better things to do with my time."

A breath. Soft and long. It seemed to come out of the receiver and curl around her throat like a snake. "Ellen . . ."

The whisper was little more than thought. Androgynous. As thin as gauze.

"Who is this?"

"Working late, Ellen?"

She slammed the receiver down. Mitch had set up a caller-ID tracer on her home telephone, but there was nothing on the office phones, and she questioned the legality of installing anything.

The call had come in on her direct line, a number that was not listed in any public directory. Did that mean the caller was someone she knew or someone who had been in her office without her knowledge? Business hours were long over. Had the caller caught her here by chance or was he aware hers was the only office light on in the building?

"The first thing we do, let's kill all the lawyers. . . ."

"Working late, Ellen?"

She cast a glance at her window. Even with the blinds drawn, the light would be visible from outside. Lifting the blinds away from the glass at one side, she tried to peer out, but there was nothing to see except the weird mix of night and swirling snow.

"Your boss needs to have a word with someone about security. This is a highly volatile case you've got here. Anything might happen. . . ."

"Ellen . . . you're a likely target. . . ."

"The first thing we do, let's kill all the lawyers. . . ."

The blinds clattered back against the window glass. Ellen grabbed up the receiver and punched the number for the sheriff's department in the adjacent building. For two years she had worked in this building without fear. She had never felt a need for a security guard, had never turned a hair walking the halls alone at night. That sense of calm was one of the things she had come here looking for. In Deer Lake she could walk her dog along the lake at night, she could leave her bedroom window open and go to sleep with a cool fall breeze caressing her face. Now she was calling for a sheriff's deputy to escort her to her car.

The deputy who appeared at the office door five minutes later was Ed Qualey. Pushing sixty, he was lean and sinewy with a pewter-gray flattop and piercing blue eyes. He had testified in court for Ellen from time to time. A good, solid cop.

"I hope I didn't pull you away from anything too important," she said as they headed together down the dimly lit hall.

Qualey shook his head. "Naw, accident reports is all. Nothing much more than fender benders going on around here tonight. I'm on light duty, anyway. Banged up a knee playing hockey. I guess all the action tonight was over in Campion, huh?"

"Mmm."

"Well, I don't blame you for wanting a walk to your car. Everyone's a little edgy these days. A person just don't know what to expect anymore."

"I used to have a motto," Ellen said. " 'Expect the worst, hope for the best.' "

Qualey frowned as they started down the stairs. "We're sure getting more of the one than the other lately. You parked on the side?"

"Yes."

They cut across the rotunda, the sound of their footfalls soaring up three stories. A sharp crack rang down one of the dark corridors, and Ellen flinched, then scolded herself. The building had a century's worth of creaks and groans.

"Too bad about Denny Enberg," Qualey said. "He was a decent sort for a defense attorney. Everyone says it looked like suicide."

"Looked like. We'll see what the ME has to say."

Qualey hummed a noncommittal note. It struck Ellen that people would have much preferred Dennis to have stuck a gun in his mouth and ended his own life, as terrible as that would have been. They would rather he had been so crushed by the weight of his problems that he saw no other way out, because then the madness was contained to one man. Something to lament, but not contagious. The alternative was vulnerability, and no one wanted any part of that.

Ellen's Bonneville was the only car in the courthouse lot. Sixty yards in the other direction, adjacent to the sheriff's department and county jail, a dozen or so vehicles were clustered together like a herd of horses, snow mounting on their backs.

The wind swept in from the northwest, wrapping itself around the contours of the buildings, creating small powdery-white cyclones that skittered across the unplowed parking lot. The sidewalk had disappeared. Streetlights took on the hazy glow of tiny moons. The streets themselves were all but deserted. Residents had chosen to hole up for the evening, to wait for the ten o'clock news and the predictions for the morning commute to work and school.

"Thanks, Ed," Ellen said, waving him off as they neared the car.

"No problem. Stay warm." Hunching his shoulders, he started up the slight grade toward the sheriff's-department entrance.

Ellen hit the button on her remote that unlocked her car doors and brought the interior lights on. Her gaze swept the area, seeing it in a far more critical light than she had when she had parked here in Rudy's personal spot two hours ago. The spot that was close to the building, that had looked so handy, that shortened her walk through the weather, now struck her as a stupid choice. Better to have parked in the second row, away from the building—where shadows and shrubbery could offer cover—and under a security light.

Still, no deadly figure darted out of the darkness along the building. She had almost begun to relax as she rounded the trunk and came up along the driver's side of the Bonneville.

The momentary letdown made the instant burst of fear seem all the more extreme. A gasp caught in her throat as she jumped back, the deep, new snow grabbing at her boots like chilled quicksand.

Scratched into the paint of the driver's-side door in large, irregular letters, was a single ugly word—*BITCH*.

CHAPTER 18

The weapon of choice was a switchblade knife, conveniently left behind—plunged to its hilt in the left front tire.

"There won't be no patching that," Officer Dietz said. Lonnie Dietz was fifty, a decent officer with a bad Moe Howard toupee, which was covered tonight by a towering fake fur hat that made him look as if he had a pack of weasels nesting on his head. "You got a spare?"

"Just that little doughnut thing," Ellen said, hugging herself, her eyes on the knife.

The first thing we do, let's kill all the lawyers. . . .

"You have any ideas who might have done this, Ms. North?" Officer Noga asked. Noogie Noga was roughly the size of a grizzly bear. A native of Samoa, he had come to Minnesota on a football scholarship and stayed even after a bum knee had ended his NFL hopes.

Ellen shrugged. "Specifically? No. But I've been getting some odd phone calls."

"Related to the Wright case?"

She nodded. "I just got another one before I came down. That's why I had Ed here walk me down."

"What did the caller say?" Noga asked, pencil poised against his notepad.

"For a long time there was nothing, then he said my name, asked if I was working late."

The three cops looked at one another blankly, and frustration knotted in Ellen's chest. She couldn't blame them for thinking she was overreacting. Stated flatly, the call lost all its darker, disturbing qualities.

"The call that came last night after two in the morning said, 'Let's kill all the lawyers,'" she added, hugging herself a little tighter. She felt as if she were being split in two, half of her the cool professional, the other half a panicking creature.

"Shi—oot," Noga muttered as the import hit. Everyone on the job had heard the gruesome details of Dennis Enberg's death.

"But you don't have any idea who's making these calls?" Dietz asked.

"I can't recognize the voice. It's too soft, indistinct. I'm not even sure if it's a man or a woman."

"And no one's threatened you outright?" Qualey asked.

"There are plenty of people unhappy with me for prosecuting Garrett Wright, but none of them have made an overt threat to my face."

She listed the names for Noga, the faces floating through her head like puzzle pieces. Wright was out on bail, but he would never risk such a foolish gesture himself, and she doubted Costello had let him out of his sight. Then there was Todd Childs, and Christopher Priest. Karen Wright. Paul Kirkwood, who blamed her for Grabko's decision on bail. The students who had taken up Wright's cause on the picket line in front of the courthouse.

Her confrontation with the Sci-Fi Cowboys came most vividly to mind. *"Hey, you that bitch lawyer . . ."* *Bitch lawyer . . . BITCH.* She could see Tyrell's angry face, eyes seething with hate.

She didn't want to blame the Cowboys out of hand. The whole point of the program was to show that these young men had the potential to be productive citizens. But she had worked in the system and knew too well the destruction and violence these kids were capable of. She had seen too many with no conscience and no respect for anyone or anything.

"The program has sure got a lot of press," Qualey said.

Dietz sniffed and spit a gob into the snow. "I don't care what anyone says. They're a bunch of city punks. Did you see them out here today with that damn rap music cranked up? We don't need their kind of trouble. If I want to fear for my life walking around town, I'll go up to Minneapolis and take a stroll down Lake Street after dark."

"We'll check it out, Ms. North," Noga said. "See what we can come up with on any of those people."

He crouched down and snapped a couple of Polaroids of the damage, slipping the undeveloped photographs inside his parka.

Ellen stared at the word gouged on her car door. An angry scrawl written with a blade deadly enough to kill. The knife handle thrusting up from the tire was like a misplaced exclamation point. She shivered at the thought of what might have happened had she come out of the building alone and surprised the vandal at work.

"You'll have to have someone take care of that tire," Dietz said. "Won't happen tonight. You want a ride home?"

"I'll take her, officer."

Ellen jerked around at the sound of the voice. Brooks stood behind her, his shoulders hunched, coat collar pulled up high. He squinted against the wind and the cold and her scrutiny.

"What are you doing here?"

The annoyance in her tone didn't stop Jay from asking himself the same question. He had notes to go over and sort, and phone calls to make to pry into the past lives of Garrett Wright and his disciple Todd Childs, and he sure as hell would rather have been in his rented house making use of the fireplace tools he had picked up that afternoon than standing out in a snowstorm. But here he was.

"I heard the call on the scanner," he said. And a chill had gone through him. He tried to tell himself it was adrenaline, the excitement of a new lead, a fresh angle. Then he tried to put it off to the fact that he hadn't got warm since he'd stepped off the plane into the great white North. Then he thought of Ellen, fighting a battle because she believed in the cause, standing up beneath the burden of it with grace and courage. Ellen, alone, victimized for doing her job.

Not that she wanted him there.

She looked at him askance. "And you didn't have anything better to do than check out a simple vandalism?"

He cast a pointed look at the knife handle jutting up from her tire. "Doesn't look so simple to me, counselor."

Her pique couldn't quite hide the glimmer of fear in her eyes as her glance stayed on the knife. Her lack of a snappy comeback told the rest of the truth. She was scared, plain and simple. She could more than hold her own in a verbal sword fight, but when the hardware was the real deal, that was a whole different ball game.

Noga looked from Ellen to Jay and back. "Ms. North?"

Ellen's knees had gone wobbly as she stared at the knife. "*The first thing we do, let's kill all the lawyers. . . .*" Dennis Enberg's body, his head shattered like a rotten melon . . . "*The first thing we do, let's kill all the lawyers. . . .*" Garrett Wright walking free . . . Dustin Holloman's little boot left to taunt them . . . *BITCH . . . BITCH . . . "The first thing we do, let's kill all the lawyers. . . ."*

"Come on," Brooks said, stepping close enough to slide an arm around her shoulders buddy-style. "Let's go get some hot coffee in you."

"That sounds good," Ellen heard herself say, the professional still attempting to function, still pretending she could handle all of this madness at once.

"We'll finish up here, Ms. North," Noga said. "We'll call you as soon as we have anything." He turned to Jay with a shy smile and stuck out his hand. "It's a pleasure, Mr. Brooks. I really enjoy your work."

"Well, thank you, Officer Noga. I'll tell you what, it's always gratifying to hear that from people in law enforcement."

What Ellen thought of as his public face beamed with a big old country-boy grin. She imagined she could actually feel the level of energy in and around him increase by a thousand volts. It was a wonder the snow didn't melt beneath his feet. Amazing.

Dietz jumped in, thrusting out his report notebook. "Would you mind an autograph? *Twist of Fate* was my favorite."

"Thank you. Hear that, Ellen?" he said as he scribbled his name across the paper. "These gentlemen actually enjoy what I do."

"There's no accounting for tastes," she grumbled.

"Come along, Ms. North," Brooks said, resting a big gloved hand on her shoulder. "I know just the place to warm you up." He gave her a roguish look as they waded through the snow toward his Cherokee. "Note what a gentleman I'm being. I could have said I'm just the man for the job."

"You just did."

"And, true as it might be, I am much too well brought up to take advantage of a vulnerable woman."

"Yeah, right." Ellen stiffened against another attack of shakes. She needed to focus. She focused on Brooks, tried to stir up irritation to warm her and center her thoughts. "I'd bet my last dime you would take advantage of your own mother if it meant getting the story you want."

"That wounds me, Ellen. Here I am, rescuing you in your hour of need and you impugn my motives."

"You've made your motives very clear," she said as he handed her up into the passenger side of the truck. "And I quote, 'I'm here for a story. I go after what I want and I get it.'"

"Excellent memory. People must have hated you in law school." He stamped back around the hood of the truck and climbed in on the driver's side. "You know, where I come from, folks at least pretend gratitude, even if they are truly unappreciative."

"I didn't need rescuing," Ellen said. "I'm perfectly capable of taking care of myself."

"Oh, you fend off knife-wielding maniacs every day, do you?"

"I didn't have to fend off anyone."

"Yeah, well, the night is young," he growled.

He put the Cherokee in gear and did a slow U-turn to get out of the lot. The truck's heater was on full blast. The wipers beat furiously at the snow hurtling down. The street was a broad ribbon of white corrugated with tire tracks.

A nice night to curl up by the fire with a good book and a cup of hot chocolate, Ellen thought as she looked out the window, wishing she could do just that, knowing that she would have been doing just that if not for Garrett Wright and his faceless partner. Instead, she would have another night of preparation for the battle with Costello. Another night of trying to piece together the facts to come up with some kind of theory as to why a man like Garrett Wright would steal a child and hold a community in the grip of fear. Another night of sifting through the growing haystack of information, searching for a clue as to who Wright's accomplice might be . . . as to who her tormentor might be.

Were they one and the same? Had they killed Denny Enberg? Would they try to kill her?

BITCH.

"The first thing we do, let's kill all the lawyers."

She felt as if she were fighting battles on all fronts at once, as if she were surrounded. She put her back to the door and faced her unlikely rescuer.

"Where are we going?"

"Someplace quiet, out of the way, homey. Your place, actually." He glanced at her, studying her in the gloom of the instrument panel. "I'd take you to my place, but guests tend to be put off by a total lack of furniture."

"Where are you staying?"

"I rented a house out on Ryan's Bay."

"Ryan's Bay? That's where Josh's jacket was found."

"A macabre coincidence," he assured her. "Honest."

"I'm sure you're probably guilty of many things, Mr. Brooks. But I think we're safe in eliminating you from the list of possible accomplices."

"You have a list?"

"Figure of speech."

"Mmmm. You have theories," he murmured. "I have a couple of my own."

He gunned the engine, plowing up the incline of her driveway.

"Thank you for the ride," Ellen said politely, her gaze fixed on the dark house, fear swelling inside her at the thought of going in alone. But she let herself out of the truck before Brooks made it around the hood.

"I'm not helpless," she insisted as he pulled her keys out of her hand. She twisted away from him when he would have taken her briefcase from her.

"No, you're not helpless. You're a damn target," he grumbled, stomping through the snow to the front door. "Your buddy Enberg is lying on a slab tonight, shorter by a head; somebody uses your car for an Etch-A-Sketch and leaves you a switchblade. If you think I'm letting you walk into this house alone, you are dead wrong—pardon the expression."

"And who appointed you to the role of guardian?" Ellen demanded, walking into the foyer and toeing off her boots.

"Nobody. I do as I please."

"Well, it doesn't please me."

"Nothing much about this case pleases me." He stepped out of his boots and took off his parka.

Ellen stood off to the side, watching as he turned on lights and lit the fireplace.

"Lucky you," she said, "you can walk away from it. It's just another story. The world's full of them, I'm sad to say."

"I'm not going anywhere."

"Why not?"

"Because what doesn't please me personally makes for a hell of a book."

"Why this case of all cases?"

He stared into the fire, his face an inscrutable mask, no hint of the engaging rascal who charmed his way past barriers with a wink and a grin.

"I have my reasons," he said darkly.

"Which are—?"

"None of your business."

"Oh, fine. You can butt into other people's lives, novelize their suffering, sell it for a profit, but your life is off-limits?"

"That's right," he said, coming toward her. "Though I may indeed be guilty of many things, none of them is criminal. Therefore, my private life remains just that—private."

"What a convenient double standard."

He ignored the gibe and curled a hand around her arm.

"Come over here by the fire. You need to warm up. Christ, you're shaking like a hairless dog in a meat freezer."

He led her across the room, hooked a footstool with one stockinged foot, and dragged it into place in front of the fire.

"Sit." He pressed her down with a hand on her shoulder. "Do you have any liquor?"

"In the hutch in the dining room. I'll get it."

"You'll sit," he barked, his expression promising dire consequences.

Ellen shrugged off his hand. "You know, I really don't need you barging into my house, bossing me around, Brooks. This day has been rotten enough as it is. I didn't ask to have you—"

The telephone on the table behind her rang. She wheeled around to stare at it, and what little bravado she had left vaporized, leaving cold, hard fear behind. She hated it. The sanctity of her home had been violated, by such a simple act as a phone call.

"Reach out and touch someone."

"The first thing we do, let's kill all the lawyers. . . ."

"Ellen?" Jay stepped into her line of vision, bending down a little to look into her eyes. "Ellen," he asked gently, "aren't you going to get that?"

The machine clicked on before she could answer. A woman's voice, pleasant but concerned.

"Ellen, honey, it's Mom. We just wanted to see how you're doing. We heard about the reduced bail. Daddy says not to take it too hard; the game isn't over yet. Call when you get in, sweetheart. We want to get together with you for your birthday."

Her parents wanted to know how she was. She was tired and heartbroken and too damn scared to answer her own phone.

"It's s-so wrong!" she whispered. She closed her eyes

and fought against tears. She couldn't afford to cry. The game wasn't over.

He said it was a game.

A game—with lives and minds and futures and careers at stake. A game with no rules and no boundaries, faceless players and hidden agendas.

Jay watched her struggle. She cared too much, fought too hard, took it all to heart. While he had stopped believing in anything, walked away from fights, let nothing touch his heart . . . except the sight of this woman crying.

If you had any sense, you'd walk away from this, Brooks.

Instead, he reached for her, gathered her close, guided her head to his shoulder. She resisted each movement, holding herself as stiff as a board. He dropped his head down, let his cheek brush her temple.

"It's okay," he whispered. "Any port in a storm, counselor. You just go on and cry. I promise, it's off the record."

The tears came in a hard torrent, soaking into his shirt. She curled her fists against his chest but didn't try to push him away. Jay wrapped his arms around her slender shoulders, feeling for the first time in forever an urge to protect, as ironic as that was. He wanted to protect her while she was doing her best to protect herself from him. She didn't trust him, had every reason *not* to trust him.

You're a damn fool, Brooks.

He was an observer, just passing through her life. That was how he liked it—sliding like a shadow from one vignette to another, watching, absorbing, interpreting, moving on, never letting it touch him too deeply, never letting his heart get involved. That was smartest, safest, easiest. That was why he shied away from live cases, preferring to trail in after the physical and emotional firestorms had passed. Like a scavenger.

Yet here he was, with his arms around the prosecuting

attorney, a part of his mind gravitating down the hall where there had to be a bedroom.

A fool and a scoundrel.

But the recriminations didn't make him let go. They didn't stop him from breathing in the soft scent of her or turning his head and touching the tender skin of her temple with his lips. The warmth that swelled within, the hunger for this contact, were only partly sexual, making him wonder dimly who was finding more comfort in the embrace. He felt as if he'd been starved of human contact and knew that the abstinence was an act of both self-denial and self-preservation.

Ah, what a sorry soul you are, Brooks. . . .

Sorry and alone.

The need overtook the inner voice. He kissed her cheek, damp with tears. He kissed her mouth, soft and trembling. His lips moved slowly, sensuously, over hers. Gentle, hesitant, needing more than he dared take. Needing the fresh taste of her like air, like water. Her mouth opened beneath his and he caught her breath and gave it back. Slowly he skimmed the soft inner swell of her lower lip with the tip of his tongue, then ventured deeper into the satin warmth of her mouth. With one hand he cradled her head, his fingers threading through the silk of her hair. He framed her face with the other, fingertips skimming the line of her cheek, the pad of his thumb probing the very corner of her mouth. A soft sound of desire escaped her and the need leaped inside him like a flame.

Need. Hot, bright need. It took Ellen by surprise, but she grabbed it with desperation and hung on. The alternative was fear and weakness. This was a surging sense of life; vital, fragile and strong at once. She felt as if she were absorbing everything about the moment—the feel of his mouth, full against hers, hot and wet; the taste of him dark and erotic; the feel of his tongue against hers, searching, stroking, imitating the rhythm of sex. He pulled her close, closer, his hand sliding down the small of her back, pressing her hips forward into his, letting her feel his arousal, *his* heat, *his* need.

The insanity of what she was doing struck her and she turned her face away.

"I can't do this," she said, breathless. "I can't get involved with you. My God . . ." She shook her head, stunned that she had let him kiss her, touch her. Stunned at what the kiss had made her feel. "This is a really bad idea. I think—"

"That's your problem, sugar," he said in a low, dangerous tone. "You think too damn much."

Cupping her chin in his hand, he turned her back toward him and lowered his mouth to hers again. But the moment was gone, the kiss still and passionless. He opened his eyes and found Ellen's wary gray ones staring up at him.

Her breath caught in her throat at the emotion in his face. Just a fleeting glimpse, there and gone. Pain and longing. Every time she thought she had him pegged, he turned colors on her. It was easiest and best to think of him as a mercenary, but he had layers and shadows, dimensions that tempted her to look deeper. She couldn't afford to get pulled into something. She was already up to her neck in one mire.

"I'll get us that drink," he muttered, his voice lower, rougher than it had been.

He turned away, walked up the steps to the dining room, and pulled a full bottle of Glenlivet from the liquor cabinet. She watched his movements, studied the dark look on his face, wondering what it was about, what *he* was about. Which Jay Butler Brooks was the real man? The charmer? The mercenary? The man with the haunted face?

Don't go down that road, Ellen. . . .

The warning came as she mounted the steps. He splashed the Scotch into a pair of short, thick tumblers.

"I—I have to check on Harry," she said awkwardly, stepping past him.

She hurried through the kitchen to the laundry room, where she was greeted enthusiastically by the big retriever. She let him out into the fenced backyard where he spent most of his days and stood for a moment in the open doorway, breathing in the crisp night air to clear her head. The snow was still coming down.

Harry did his business, then made a mad dash around the yard, excited by the fresh powder. Ellen left him to play, knowing they would both regret it later when he came in wet and aromatic and would have to be banished from his usual spot on the bed.

When she came back to the living room, she took her coat off and hung it in the closet. Jay stood with his back to the fire, watching her, tumbler of Scotch in one hand, the other stuffed into his pants pocket. Too aware of his gaze, Ellen picked up her glass from the coffee table and sipped at it. The liquor seared a smooth path to her stomach.

"It's been quite a day," she said, settling herself into the corner of the couch. She pulled her legs beneath her, careful to keep her skirt around her knees.

"Why didn't you take that call?" he asked. Though the tone was casual, those cool blue eyes focused on her like a pair of lasers.

She weighed her answer. Her impulse was to keep the calls a secret, to protect herself from yet another avalanche of publicity. Of course, Brooks would have no desire to inform the press. He was here for his own purposes. She had to think he would guard the confidence jealously. And if she didn't give it to him, he would dig for it.

"Cranks," she said with an air of dismissal. "I've had a

couple of calls. My nerves are just a little too frayed right now to take another one."

A half truth, Jay decided. Better than a lie. Less than trust. He couldn't have expected more.

"Enberg's secretary told me he'd got some nasty calls," he said. "Think they're related?"

"It wouldn't follow. We were on opposite sides."

"That all depends on your point of view. From where I stand, ol' Denny looked like he'd just as soon throw the game."

"The first thing we do, let's kill all the lawyers. . . ."

Ellen looked away from him, into the fire, curling her fingers tighter around her glass. Dennis had got calls, and now Dennis was dead. She was getting calls and . . . In the flames of the fire she could see the switchblade protruding from the tire of her car and the word scratched into the paint. *Bitch.*

"Rumor has it you think Enberg had some help with that shotgun," Brooks said, his eyes narrowed as he watched her for a reaction.

"Where did you hear that?"

"Around."

"If there's a leak on this case—"

"No one fed it to me," he said. "I don't have a mole in your office, if that's what you're worried about. This is a small town, Ellen. People like to talk. I know how to listen."

"I'm not paranoid," she said defensively. "Corruption makes no geographical distinctions. A week ago Sheriff Steiger was trading information for sex."

The pirate's grin made a return even as he feigned shock. "Are you suggesting something tawdry, Ms. North?"

"In your dreams."

"Mmm . . . I should say so," he drawled, his gaze caressing her bare calf.

He moved away from the fire, prowling, his eyes locked on her. Once again playing the rogue, the sexual tomcat, master at seduction.

"The point is," she began.

"The point is, I don't pay for information—cash or favors," he said, easing himself down beside her. His hard, muscular thigh brushed her bare foot. "And so far, the only one who's made any noise about it is Paul Kirkwood."

"Paul asked you for money?" Ellen said, surprised. "Well—for Josh, I suppose," she rationalized.

He shook his head. "I get the impression Paul thinks about Paul first and the rest of the world can queue up behind him, including his son."

"He's under a lot of pressure," she said with forced neutrality.

He made a dubious sound and pulled a cigarette out of the pack in his shirt pocket. Ellen took it from his fingers and, ignoring his frown, set it out of his reach on the end table.

"He was a suspect for a while, you know," she pointed out.

"But he isn't anymore."

"There's no evidence against him." Even as she said it, she was recalling the night Josh had been returned. Paul nowhere to be found for hours, showing up at the hospital in a snit. The story Mitch later relayed of Josh reacting violently to his father's appearance in his room.

"There was that bit about the van," Brooks offered.

"That went nowhere."

Wilhelm was supposed to be looking for connections between Paul and Wright. He had turned his suspicion on Kirkwood days ago but hadn't said a word about it since. Ellen had to wonder if he had followed up or if the other cases had taken all his attention.

"What about Todd Childs?" Jay asked carefully, watching her through his lashes.

Ellen gave a little shrug. "What about him? We'll be serving him with a subpoena calling him to testify at the hearing. He isn't happy about it, but life is hard."

"Maybe he decided to take it out on you."

"It's hard to imagine his getting up the energy for that kind of rage."

"*She's a bitch.*" Jay could hear Todd Childs's voice, see the venom in his eyes as he watched Ellen talk to the press. "Rage can be chemically induced. I'd hazard a guess he'd know all about that. I had me a little chat with Todd this morning." He took another sip of his drink and looked at her sideways. "Just long enough to give me the willies."

"Oh, great," she groaned. "That's what I need—you tampering with my witnesses."

She swung her feet down off the couch and sat with her elbows planted on her thighs and her face in her hands.

"I wasn't tampering," he said. "I can have a conversation with anyone I choose. I'm a private citizen."

"With an in to the state attorney general and a truck parked in my driveway."

She had to fight the urge to get up and peek out her front window for signs of reporters staking out her house. The unwanted, unwarranted publicity that Mitch and Megan's relationship had drawn was fresh in her mind. It had indirectly cost Megan her field post, and she and Mitch were on the same side. Ellen shuddered to think what the ramifications of having Jay Butler Brooks in her home might be. He was looking for inside information. She was the lead prosecutor on the case.

She turned and looked at him. "I don't need any more complications in my life."

Complications. The case. His involvement in it. The attraction that sparked between them whether she liked it or not. It struck him as funny, in a bitter, twisted sort of way, that he had come here to escape the complications of his own life and had become a complication in someone else's. And Ellen had come to Deer Lake to escape the complications of her life in Minneapolis and now found herself in the center of a madman's web.

He stared at Ellen. Backlit by the fire, her hair was burnished gold. The barriers were down. He could have turned the moment to his advantage. Instead, he tossed back the last of his Scotch and set the glass aside.

"No," he said. "You need a break. In the case and *from* the case. So tell me about your mother."

"My mother?"

"You know, the woman who gave you birth. The woman who called to see how you're doing."

Suspicion lowered her brows. "Why?"

He dropped his head back against the couch and rolled his eyes. "I reckon she called because she loves you, but that's just speculation on my part. If you're asking why I asked, it's called making conversation. Or if you're intent on casting me as a bastard, call it looking for background."

That was the problem with him, Ellen thought—there was no telling which definition suited.

"My mother is an attorney," she said. "My father, too. And my sister, Jill. Tax law."

"Ah, a nest of lawyers," he said with a warm, teasing smile. "And you're the white sheep."

The term brought pleasant surprise. Her father called her the white sheep, always with a gleam of pride in his eyes.

"My father says I inherited the recessive North gene for justice. His grandfather was a circuit court judge back in frontier times. They called him Noose North."

Jay laughed. Ellen let herself relax marginally, glad for the diversion. Whatever his motive, she had to be grateful. She needed the downtime, a chance to lower her shields for a moment or two. She turned toward him, once more tucking herself into the corner of the couch.

"Anyway, they have a nice practice in Edina—the suburb where I grew up."

"And you're close."

"Yeah," she said, smiling to herself.

Glancing up, she caught a glimpse of something sad in Brooks's eyes. He covered it in a blink.

"You come from a family of lawyers, too," she said.

He leaned toward her in confession. "I'm the black sheep."

"Big surprise. You were an attorney, though," she pointed out. "Why not with the family firm?"

"I go my own way. Make my own rules. I was too much of a rebel for an old southern law firm, as contradictory as that may sound to a Yankee."

"Your opinion or theirs?"

He narrowed his eyes at her, not liking the probing quality of her gaze. "We were talking about you."

"And now we're talking about you. Do you have a problem with that, Mr. Brooks?"

"Oooh, trick question." He grinned and tipped his head. "I can't wait to see you handle a cross-examination. You know what I thought when I first laid eyes on you? I said to myself, *Jay, that little gal looks sharp as a tack and cool as tungsten steel. What the hell do you think she's doing here?*"

"Asked and answered."

"You seemed evasive."

"Not so. There simply isn't anything more to tell."

"Then your leaving Minneapolis had nothing to do with the rape trial of Art Fitzpatrick?"

The shields came up again. "What would make you ask that?"

"It was the last trial of any real consequence you were involved with up there."

"A number of victims of other crimes might beg to

differ with you. I tried any number of cases after Fitzpatrick."

"But none so high profile. A prominent businessman accused of an ugly crime. It was common knowledge you took the loss hard."

"A rapist went free. Of course I was unhappy. And, in point of fact, I was not the lead prosecutor on Fitzpatrick. That was Steve Larsen's case. I was his second. May I ask why and how you've been digging up this information?" Just what did he know about the Fitzpatrick case? Did he know about her relationship with Costello? About Costello's link to Fitzpatrick?

"It's part of my job," he explained. "I know you think I'm just as lazy as a poor boy's sigh, too unimaginative and slothful to create plots of my own; that I just waltz into the middle of a story and save up the news clippings. But the fact is, I do my homework, Ellen, same as any good journalist."

"Then why aren't you doing homework on Wright? Why dig into my boring past when you could be revealing this man for the monster he is? You could actually be doing someone some good."

"You don't want me tampering with the case—unless it's on behalf of the prosecution. Is that it?"

"Associate you with my office and run the risk of having my conviction thrown out on appeal? No, thanks. I would just like to think that maybe you wanted something more out of this than money."

"Such as?"

"Justice."

"That's your quest, counselor. I'm just an observer."

"And that excuse is supposed to absolve you of all responsibility, humanity, compassion, emotion? How can you look at Josh, at his parents, and not feel something?"

He felt plenty. Pity, compassion, sympathy . . . lucky, confused. He had come here to escape his own tearing sense of loss. Had come deliberately to study people who had lost more, thereby consoling and punishing himself at once.

"You don't know what I feel," he said quietly.

"And you won't tell me."

"Not tonight." He drew in a deep breath, mustered a weary smile, and pushed himself to his feet. "I think you've had enough intrigue and twisted drama to last you. What you need is a good night's sleep."

He offered her a hand up from the couch. She gave it a dubious look.

"Is that an overture, Mr. Brooks?" she asked dryly, accepting the gesture just the same.

"Hell, no." He pulled her close, bending his head down so that his gaze met hers full force. "I'm being damned gallant. When you go to bed with me, sweetheart, the last thing you'll be getting is sleep."

Remarkably, Ellen caught herself smiling at his audacity.

"You're incorrigible, Mr. Brooks," she murmured. "Among other things."

She walked with him to the door, where he dealt with laces on his boots and zippers on his parka.

"I don't see how people live in this state," he complained. "It's too damn much work."

"Winter is nature's way of weeding out the faint of heart," Ellen said. "Thanks again for driving me home."

"You ought to have a cop sitting out front," he cautioned.

She shook her head. "With all that's been going on, there's no manpower for baby-sitting detail. There's a patrol car prowling the neighborhood, and I've got a trace on my phone. And I've got Harry. If someone tries to break in, he'll knock them down and lick their face until help arrives."

"I could stay all night," he offered with a leer.

"I don't think so."

"Like I said before," he murmured, hooking a finger under her chin, "you think too much."

Ellen caught her breath, expecting him to kiss her. Half hoping he would. But he turned and walked out. And she was left alone to call herself a fool.

CHAPTER 19

By Friday morning Mother Nature had dumped six inches of new snow on southern Minnesota, and a blast of air had come sweeping down from Saskatchewan to stir it into a ground-scudding cloud that limited visibility to a fraction of a mile. The temperature, which had been teetering on the brink of tolerance, went over the edge and into a long, hard fall, taking spirits with it. School was canceled. Roads outside of Deer Lake were closed. In Campion the search for Dustin Holloman had to be called off because of the danger to the volunteers. No one spoke of the danger to Dustin.

The hope was that his kidnapper was keeping him safe and warm, that he would eventually be found or returned unharmed, as Josh had been. The hope was that they would get lucky. The idea that they were all relying on the kindness and benevolence of a psychopath sat like a mace in the center of Mitch's chest. There was no way of knowing what the next move in the game would be. No way of knowing when their luck would run out.

The pressure had snipped his temper down to the short hairs, so that even at nine o'clock in the morning his daily quota of patience was nearly spent.

Ignoring the proffered chair, he paced the width of Christopher Priest's small office, a room crowded with file cabinets and bookcases. Short towers of text and reference books and stacks of student papers were neatly aligned across the surface of the scarred old desk. A personal computer sat whirring softly to itself, green cursor blinking impatiently beside a prompt sign on the screen.

"So the Sci-Fi Cowboys spent the night in Deer Lake?" he asked.

Priest watched him with owl eyes and an impassive expression. "Yes. The Minneapolis schools were off yesterday and today for in-service. We had arranged for the boys to spend the weekend in Deer Lake doing fund-raising activities for Garrett's defense."

"And they stayed where?"

"At the youth hostel here on campus."

"Supervised?"

"I was with them most of the evening. We had a celebratory dinner with Garrett and his attorney," he said with just a hint of smugness, his gaze sliding toward Ellen.

"What time did you finish?" she asked.

"Things started breaking up around eight."

"And what about the rest of the evening? Can you account for the whereabouts of all the boys?"

A hint of angry color stained his cheeks. He tugged at the too-short sleeves of his black turtleneck. "They're not prisoners, Ms. North. A bond of trust is essential to the success of our program."

"Yeah, well, maybe that trust isn't always deserved," Mitch grumbled.

Priest gave a little sniff of affront. "Just what is this about, Chief?"

"Last night someone defaced Ms. North's car with a switchblade."

"And you automatically assume that *someone* is one of the Cowboys? That's patently unfair and discriminatory."

"Not at all, Professor," Mitch said, bracing his hands on the back of the chair he had declined. "With all due respect to your program—and you know I've been a fan in the past—your kids are A-students in this kind of shit. They have records. They have motive. They are, therefore, *logical* suspects. You, of all people, should be able to grasp that."

"The Cowboys aren't the only people in town unhappy with Ms. North," Priest pointed out.

"No, they're not," Mitch conceded. "And my office will follow all possible avenues. Which brings me to my next question—where were you last night around nine?"

Priest's jaw dropped, a show of spontaneous emotion that looked genuine. "You can't possibly think I would be involved in something so—so—"

"Juvenile?"

His face flushed and he shot up from his chair. "After all the hours my students and I put in at the volunteer center— After I've bent over backward to help with the investigation— I took a polygraph, for heaven's sake! I can't tell you how angry this makes me."

Mitch straightened, shoving the chair into the front of Priest's old oak desk with a rattle and a thump. "Welcome to the club, Professor. I've been working this case around the clock from day one and it just keeps getting worse. I can no longer afford to be polite. I can't afford to worry about whether or not it offends people to be questioned. I don't have time to step around egos. Here's the bottom line: Garrett Wright stands accused. You are a friend and colleague of Garrett Wright. That makes you fair game."

"Chief Holt is simply doing his job, Professor," Ellen said, working to show a little diplomacy, though her own temper was slipping. She'd had to begin the day arranging to have her car towed from the courthouse lot to Manley Vanloon's garage for repairs and repainting. Stooping to what she felt was an abuse of her position, she had called Manley himself and asked him to have one of his service mechanics deliver a loaner to her house before answering all of the calls from the hardworking people who needed jump-starts for frozen batteries.

"I understand your protective attitude toward the Sci-Fi Cowboys," she said. "But the fact remains, their very existence makes them logical suspects in the vandalism."

Priest regarded her with the thinnest hint of a frown touching his wide, lipless mouth. "Is it standard procedure for victims to attend police interrogations of suspects?"

"This isn't an interrogation, Professor," she said, "although Mitch or one of his men will need to talk with all the boys, just as they will be talking with other possible suspects. What I've come for is to request that you turn over to my office a list of names and addresses for all the Sci-Fi Cowboys past and present."

"For what purpose?" he asked tightly. "So the police can harass everyone who ever knew Garrett? This is an outrage!"

"As part of the ongoing background check," Ellen answered, rising. "We need to speak with as many people who have worked closely with Dr. Wright as we can. It's nothing extraordinary, Professor. I was surprised Agent Wilhelm hadn't already made the request."

"It's an invasion of privacy."

"No, it's not."

She leveled a steely look at the little man with his shrunken sweater and oversize eyeglasses and moral outrage cracking his usual emotionless facade. Two weeks ago she had thought he was a generous, compassionate man of foresight; a helpful citizen who had thrown himself into the efforts at the Josh Kirkwood volunteer center and volunteered to aid the police with his computer skills. Today she harbored suspicions that he might be protecting a criminal or worse—that he was himself a player in Garrett Wright's twisted game.

Megan had suspected Priest. Olie Swain, the convicted

pedophile who had committed suicide in jail, had audited Priest's computer courses. Their association may have gone deeper. Megan had been investigating the possibility when she was attacked—in the front yard of Priest's secluded country home. There may well have been more to that than mere coincidence. Every way Ellen turned, reality was mutating into something ugly.

"It's called doing a thorough job," she said. "And if it weren't for the fact that it's touching you directly, you'd be glad for it."

She picked up her briefcase and nodded to him. "Thank you for your time, Professor. If you could put that list together today and fax it to my office, I would appreciate it. If you choose to be stubborn, I can get a warrant, but I really don't think you want to play that game. The publicity could only hurt the Cowboys. I know you don't want that."

"No, I don't," he said, blowing out a breath. His arms fell to his sides, bony shoulders slumping in defeat. He looked from Ellen to Mitch, the uncharacteristic emotions draining from his face, leaving the slate blank. "I don't want that at all. I'm sorry if I overreacted, but this program means a great deal to me. And having tried to help with the investigation into Josh's disappearance, then having this kind of scrutiny turned on me and the Cowboys . . . I don't know," he muttered, shaking his head. "I feel a certain sense of betrayal."

"I understand, Professor," Ellen said. "I think we both do."

The closest Mitch came to acknowledgment or apology was a twist of his mouth. As he turned toward the door, a pair of lanky teenagers stepped in.

"Hey, it's Lady Justice!" Tyrell Mann said with a big grin splitting his face. He strutted past Ellen. "Our man Costello kicked your pretty behind yesterday, Lady Justice."

Ellen borrowed an attitude from Brooks. "It's only bail."

"Give it up, Goldie," Tyrell sneered, leaning over her. "You haven't got a prayer."

She held her ground, staring him square in the face, meeting the belligerence burning in his eyes full on. "We'll see. You know what they say—it ain't over till it's over."

She watched for a flicker of recognition or wariness, but there was nothing. His lip curled derisively. "You ain't got shit on the Doc."

Mitch stepped in, planting a hand on Tyrell's chest and moving him back. "You'll show the lady respect."

Tyrell glared at him. "Who the fuck are you?"

"Tyrell," Priest said, stepping between them, "this is Chief of Police Holt."

"A cop." Contempt twisted Tyrell's features. "I should'a guessed."

The other boy stepped forward with the plastic smile of a salesman, sticking his hand out. "J.R. Andersen, Chief. Tyrell's cranky. You'll have to excuse him."

"No, I won't," Mitch said flatly. "But I don't have time for this now. We'll have a little chat later today, Tyrell."

"The hell—"

"We *will*." He turned to Priest. "I'll set something up for this afternoon. Someone will call you."

Priest looked resigned and unhappy. "Can we at least do it here in my office?"

"Do what?" Andersen asked.

Mitch nodded and ushered Ellen out into the hall, closing the door behind them.

"I hate to come down on them," he said as they made their way toward the stairs. "It *is* a good program, but the potential for trouble is there, too. I mean, if you think about it, what's worse—below-average kids with no consciences or smart kids with no consciences? And don't try to tell me Tyrell there has a conscience lurking under all that hostility. He's a stick of dynamite with a short fuse."

The question was, Had Garrett Wright provided the spark that had ignited an act of violence against her? Ellen turned the possibilities over in her mind as they walked. Priest's office was located on the fourth floor of Cray Hall, a dank old mausoleum of a building, each level a maze of narrow hallways and cracker-box offices. Not even the mustard-colored walls could save the place from cheerlessness.

"There's no denying Tyrell blames me for Garrett Wright's predicament," Ellen said. "But the professor had a point—the Cowboys aren't the only ones in Wright's corner."

"We know Wright himself has an alibi for last night," Mitch said. "After dinner he was with Costello in Costello's office until nearly ten-thirty. Then Costello drove him home."

"Home—to Lakeside?"

Mitch answered her look of shock with one of sympathy. "It's part of the show, I suppose. If he's an innocent man, why shouldn't he feel free to live in his own home?"

"Because it shows a callous disregard for the feelings of the Kirkwoods," she said angrily. "But, hey, who cares about them? Not Tony Costello, I can guarantee you that."

Not only was Wright's return to his home an affront to the Kirkwoods, it completely screwed any chance they might have had to turn Karen Wright.

"Wright isn't paying him a five-figure fee to be sensitive," Mitch said.

"If Wright *is* paying him that kind of money, I'd like to know where it's coming from. Pity we don't have just cause to seize his bank records." She stopped on the landing, her eyes brightening as the proverbial lightbulb flashed on above her head. "But we *should* be able to seize his current month's records from the phone company. If we can get our hands on those, we'll be able to see if any of the strange calls that happened during Josh's abduction came from Wright's house—which, of course, they won't have because he would never be that careless—but we may be able to find out whether or not Karen Wright was the one who called in Costello. If she didn't, that strengthens my suspicion that Costello was contacted by the accomplice. If I can find a way around Costello's argument of privilege and nail his ass with charges of complicity . . . Oooh, that would be *sooo* sweet."

Mitch arched a brow as they started down the last flight of steps. "Remind me never to get on your bad side.

"We haven't been able to locate Todd Childs," he said. "He isn't answering his phone, doesn't appear to be home, and he isn't scheduled to work at the Pack Rat until Monday. No one seems to know where the hell he might have gone in weather like this, but no one's seen him since yesterday afternoon."

And since then, Dustin Holloman's boot had been discovered and someone had carved up her car.

On the first floor they crossed another empty hall and went into the foyer, where double doors flanked with sidelights afforded a view of the horrendous weather. Snow blew across the campus like bleached-white sheets torn free from a clothesline. Even through the doors the sound of the wind was an ominous roar. Small trees bent away from it like cowering stick figures. Across the street someone in a cardinal-red parka rushed along, being blown south like a scrap of bright wrapping paper.

"Goddamn this weather," Mitch grumbled. "I don't mind winter, but this is ridiculous."

"It certainly doesn't seem to be playing on our side."

Ellen set her briefcase at her feet and set about the task of wrapping her thick wool scarf around her head and neck. "Let me know as soon as you've talked to Childs," she said. "We've got him on the list to testify at the omni-bus hearing. We'll look like idiots if it turns out he's in-volved."

"I've got someone on it."

"What about the employees from the Donut Hut? Any word on what they might have seen the night Denny died?"

"They're stuck in Mankato, but we're not sure where they're staying." He clamped a pair of earmuffs on his head and flipped up the thick hood of his parka. "I spoke with Vicki Enberg. She says Dennis told her he wished he'd never got involved with the case, but he wouldn't say whether or not Wright had confessed anything to him. She doesn't believe he killed himself, but we have to con-sider the source there."

"Do *you* believe he killed himself?" Ellen asked.

Mitch looked out at the desolate snowscape. "To tell you the truth, counselor, I don't know what the hell to believe anymore."

"I don't believe it's necessary, Ellen," Rudy said, moving restlessly behind his desk. He shoved aside a stack of pa-perwork and rummaged through a pile of newspaper clippings—all identical, featuring a photograph of him angrily pledging to pursue justice in the case he had dumped on Ellen. "The sheriff's department is right next door."

"Which does no good if the trouble is *in* the court-house," Ellen insisted. "This is a highly volatile situation, Rudy, and it's getting personal. We're going to be putting in a lot of hours on this in the next few days before the pretrial. I don't want to have to fear for my life while I'm at it. I mean, my car can be repainted, but next time this jerk might decide to carve *me* up."

Scowling, he pulled a scrap of a page from under a yellow legal pad and discovered a long-forgotten grocery list. "No one can get in the building at night without a key."

"Big deal. So they come in during the day and hide in a broom closet until night. Or they jimmy a lock or they get in through a window. Then what?"

He crumpled the grocery list, tossed it at the waste basket, and missed. Grumbling, he bent to retrieve it, and his eyes widened as his gaze caught on something he had discarded earlier. "Ha!" he huffed, unwadding the ball of paper.

Ellen watched him with a mix of disgust and disbelief. "You know, I'm sorry to trouble your mind with this, Rudy, but I would prefer not to end up like Dennis Enberg."

"He committed suicide."

"I don't think so, and if you would pay attention to something other than taking Judge Franken's seat on the bench before it even has a chance to cool, you wouldn't think so either."

"Ellen! I don't know what you're talking about. How could you suggest such a thing? Judge Franken isn't even in the ground yet. The funeral is today. This is part of his eulogy I'm holding."

Meaning tomorrow, after the eulogy had been delivered in front of a crowd of court cronies and minor muck-a-mucks, and the judge was put in permanent cold storage, it would be all right to angle openly for the appointment.

"Fine," she said. "You're a choirboy, Rudy. Now can I have my security guard?"

"It's not that simple. I can't just hire someone. I'll have to talk to the county commissioners."

"Oh, great. Maybe they'll approve the funding sometime before the year of the flood. Can't you just arrange something with Steiger?"

"Maybe, but they've got their hands full, you know. I don't know that Russ has a man to spare."

Ellen blew out a breath. "All right. I can't wait to hear what the press has to say about this. Park County can't protect its children, can't even protect its own attorneys. . . . I suppose you'll want me to make a statement. Tell the press it's out of your hands. Make the usual 'If it were up to me' noises."

Behind the lenses of his crooked glasses, Rudy's eyes sharpened and narrowed. "They know about your car?" he asked.

"The phones are ringing off their hooks," she said, poker-faced. She had yet to check her own messages, had no idea how many calls might have come in from the press. Rudy didn't seem to notice that she hadn't answered his question. The prospect of bad publicity had snagged his full attention.

"What about these weird calls you've had? Do they know about that?"

"We've managed to keep that quiet so far, but you know how it is. This is a small town."

Rudy pursed his lips and ran a broad hand over his slicked-down hair, his hand coming away from the gesture as greasy as if he had palmed a bucket of fried chicken wings. Without thinking, he used the leg of his suit for a napkin. He strolled back and forth in front of the window. Outside, the weather and the release of Garrett Wright on bail had combined to keep the protestors off the streets.

"You think it's one of those science-fiction kids?" he asked.

"I have no idea. It could be."

"Could be. But you think it is, don't you?"

"I don't know."

He frowned a little, wondering what good it would do him if he did get that kind of admission from her. The program was popular and politically correct and had brought Deer Lake a lot of good publicity. Sig Iverson, whom Rudy had chosen to succeed him as county attorney, had already associated himself with Christopher Priest the past fall, acting as chaperon on a couple of Sci-Fi Cowboy trips to science fairs and competitions. If Ellen took a stand against the group and they in fact turned out to be rotten troublemakers, she would get an edge on Sig. In the meantime, if Rudy took no action and she ended up getting attacked, it would definitely reflect badly on him.

"I'll see what I can do," he said at last. "Twist Russ's arm a little. I'll take care of it. We don't want you getting hurt, Ellen. You know I think of the people in this office as family. I certainly don't want any harm to come to one of my office daughters."

Ellen forced a smile, thinking he probably would have sold his "daughter" to gypsies by now if not for the bad press. "Thanks, Rudy."

"Are you going to the funeral?" His attention had already returned to his eulogy notes.

"Of course." She didn't have the time to spare, but she felt a certain obligation, having been one of the people who had worked to revive the judge. She wondered if Brooks would feel any obligation or if he would attend in search of color commentary for his book.

"Where are we at with the case?" Rudy asked.

"Nothing new. We're at the mercy of the crime lab waiting for any info on evidence. The DNA testing of the bloody sheet won't be completed for another month."

"But it matched Josh Kirkwood for type."

"Yes. And since we have only to show cause, I think we're safe. Figuratively speaking, Costello would shred that sheet to rags in front of a jury, but by the time we get that far, he'll have to fight the DNA experts."

If we get that far.

"We have plenty to get him bound over for trial," she

stated, as much to counteract her own insidious doubts as to convince her boss.

She would have liked to talk through the problems with him, as she had with her old boss in Hennepin County; to strategize, theorize, play devil's advocate. But Rudy had never been a confidant. The best she could do was find a sounding board in Cameron and trust her own instincts.

She pushed the sleeve of her blazer up with one finger and checked her watch. "I've got to get upstairs. Good luck with the eulogy."

Ellen headed to her office, where the phones were still ringing almost without cease. Word would have spread by now about the vandalism of her car. She had officially become a target.

Phoebe stood up from her desk, her fresh-scrubbed face bright with panic.

"I'm sorry, Ellen," she said, clutching her hands against the bodice of her prison-gray jumper.

"Sorry?"

Quentin Adler butted into the conversation from the side. "Ellen, I need to talk to you about this burglary case."

"In a minute, Quentin."

"I tried to stop him, but he frightens me," Phoebe squeaked. "He's a Leo, you know. I can't relate to Leos."

"What?"

"You know," Quentin complained, color mottling his fleshy face. "That burglary you dumped on me—Herman Horstman. I can't find the deposition you took from his girlfriend, and now she's suddenly gone to Mexico and—"

"Mr. Costello," Phoebe admitted, squeezing her eyes shut as if bracing herself for a blow. "He's in your office. I'm *really* sorry!"

"—and I'd like to know how a little tramp like that

gets the money to fly to Cancún, but that's neither here nor there. I need that deposition, Ellen."

"Quentin," Ellen said sharply. "Take a number and wait."

She reached around him and plucked Phoebe by a sleeve.

"Tony Costello is in my office? Alone?"

"I'm *really* sorry!" Phoebe mewed. "I *tried*. It's just that the phone won't stop ringing and—and—I heard you were a-a-t-t-acked a-a-and he fr-frightens me!"

"Oh, Phoebe, don't cry!" Ellen pleaded.

Phoebe sat back against the edge of her desk and covered her face with her hands. "I-I-I-I'm t-t-ry-y-ying!"

"Ellen, I have to say I resent your attitude," Quentin pouted. "You dumped this case on me—"

Ellen wheeled on him, barely resisting the urge to grab hold of his lapels. "Quentin, I am not your mother, I am not your secretary. I gave you my files on the case. If you can't find something, deal with it. Now, please excuse me while I go eviscerate Mr. Costello."

She stormed into the room and slammed the door.

"How dare you!" she snapped. "How dare you come here and bully my secretary and walk into my private office without an invitation! I ought to call security and have you thrown out of the building!"

"You do that, Ellen," he said. "That will only add credence to my story when I relate to the press how you've attempted to shut me out. How you don't answer my phone calls and refuse to schedule me for appointments. I've left no fewer than five messages this morning alone."

"Oh, pardon me that my life doesn't revolve around you, Tony. You think I should just drop everything and answer to you because I was once foolish enough to become involved with you?"

He stepped closer, but she refused to back away.

"No," he said quietly. "I think you're shutting me out

to punish me, and if that's true, then maybe you should remove yourself from this case and give it to someone with no emotional baggage."

"You'd like that, wouldn't you?" Ellen said with a humorless laugh. "I'm far and away the best prosecutor in this office and you know it. You think I'll hand this case over so you can maul a lesser attorney in court? Get real."

On that shot she walked away from him, taking her place behind her desk. She did a quick scan of the room, looking for anything out of place, any indication that he had taken advantage of his time alone.

"You realize you're laying the groundwork for an appeal." He sat once again, control firmly in hand. He seemed almost casual, though she knew he was equally dangerous in this mood as when he was in full fury—if not more so.

Ellen arched a brow. "Already planning the appeal? That bodes ill for your client. I'm not concerned, at any rate. I haven't done anything unethical. If you try to drag the past into it, the spotlight will end up on you, Tony. I don't think you'd like to be the star of that particular show."

He leaned back, a smile cutting across his handsome mouth. "You've still got it, Ellen. Hard as nails and twice as sharp when you have to be. I used to love debating with you. Passion at the touch of a button."

That many of their debates had taken place in bed or ended up in bed was a point he undoubtedly wanted to make. But she wouldn't give him the satisfaction.

"Let's stick to the subject," she said, resting her arms on her blotter. "You, of all people, have no business coming into my office without my permission."

"You don't really think I came here to steal something, do you?" He had the gall to look amused. *Poor, paranoid Ellen.* "In the first place, I know you would never leave anything of real value to a case lying around. I know how you operate—you've got every scrap of pertinent information tucked away in your neat little three-ring binder in your briefcase, which you never let out of your sight. Secondly, I don't need to steal from you to make my case. My client is innocent."

"Save it for the judge."

"With whom we have an appointment in five minutes," he said, consulting his platinum Rolex.

"What?"

He tipped his head. "I *tried* to call you, Ellen. I need to see Grabko, and I certainly don't want to be accused of trying to have an ex parte conversation with him."

"I have a meeting with someone else in five minutes."

"Not anymore," he said. "Rule number one in the laws of courtroom survival: don't piss off the judge."

"And what's so pressing that we have to attend to it right now?"

"I'm going to petition the court for the release of Josh Kirkwood's medical records," he said smoothly.

"What? Why?"

"Because I have reason to believe the child has been physically abused—by his father."

CHAPTER 20

"Of all the dirty, sleazy, underhanded, back-alley tricks, this absolutely takes the prize!" Ellen ranted, too furious for circumspection. She paced a track behind Judge Grabko's visitors' chairs, her red wool blazer open, hands jammed on her hips.

Costello sat with his legs crossed, a long-suffering expression directed at the judge. "It's a legitimate request, Your Honor. My client is entitled to present facts that exonerate him, including evidence pointing to other suspects."

"Legitimate?" Ellen repeated. "It's utter bull!" She turned toward Grabko. "Your Honor, Mr. Costello isn't preparing a defense here. He's preparing to mount a smear campaign against Josh Kirkwood's parents in order to divert attention away from his client and the hard evidence against him. An act so low I can't believe even Mr. Costello isn't disgusted by the mere concept."

Judge Grabko fingered his plaid bow tie, a frown bending the line on his forehead. "Have a seat, Ellen. We'll discuss the issue like rational adults."

She forced herself to comply, bristling inwardly at Grabko's patronizing attitude. He seemed bent on treating her like a second-year law student, and she knew the show was for Costello's benefit. But she also knew she had to rein in her temper. She couldn't let Tony get her back up.

She settled in the chair, straightened her jacket, crossed her legs, and picked a fleck of lint off the leg of her black slacks, flicking it subtly in Tony's direction.

"Your Honor," she said with forced calm. "Josh Kirkwood's medical records have no bearing on his abduction."

"They do if Paul Kirkwood is guilty of the crime," Costello said. "In that event, they go to motive. During their investigation and questioning of potential defense witnesses, my associates have had several incidents mentioned to them. Seeing the child with bruises, injuries, a broken arm at one point—"

"He's an eight-year-old boy," Ellen interjected. "They fall off bikes and out of trees. They play rough sports—"

"They fall victim to abusive parents. Paul Kirkwood is known to have a volatile temper, to be subject to mood swings—"

"Paul Kirkwood isn't on trial here—"

"Perhaps he should be."

"Perhaps he would be if he had been the one chased down and apprehended by the police," Ellen said derisively. "What possible motive could Paul have for stealing his own child, then playing twisted mind games with the police? But let's say for argument's sake Paul kidnapped his own child and led police on a bizarre hunt—why would he then turn around and bring Josh home? None of this follows any known form of logic, and you know it."

Costello arched a thick brow. "The infamous accomplice was *your* theory," he said. "But we're getting off the point, here, Your Honor." He dismissed Ellen, giving Grabko his full attention. "The boy's medical records—"

"Fall under doctor-patient privilege," Ellen argued. "They are private and beyond the scope of this hearing."

"That will be for me to determine, Ms. North," Grabko chastened.

Elbows on the arms of his chair, he steepled his long

fingers in front of him and looked from one attorney to the other. A Vivaldi concerto played softly in the background. The judge shut his eyes for a moment and breathed deeply, letting the purity of the music cleanse his mind.

"Ellen," he said in his law-professor voice, "would you deny a defendant the right to present a defense on the grounds that that defense implicated another suspect?"

The letter of the law. All emotion pared away. No bias.

"No, Your Honor, of course not. It's part of the adversarial system."

"You simply object to having Paul Kirkwood singled out as that other suspect?"

Justice was supposed to be blind, impartial, unsentimental.

"The police investigated the possibility of Mr. Kirkwood's involvement and dismissed it," she said. "There was no real evidence against him—"

"If we could get those records—" Costello began.

"The family has been through hell as it is, Your Honor."

Costello cut her a look from the corner of his eye. "We can subpoena the records."

"It is within your rights to try, Mr. Costello," Grabko said. "However, the family also has the right to seek a protective order to prevent you from doing so."

He pursed his lips and let his eyes drift shut once again as the second movement of the concerto built to a finish. Ellen held her breath, waiting, muscles tensed. It hadn't occurred to her that Grabko's tendency toward pretension included a tendency toward theatrics. This was his big case, his time to shine, to get his name in the papers. *The distinguished Judge Gorman Grabko.*

Vivaldi soared from a shelf loaded with scholarly treatments of the gentlemanly art of fly-fishing.

"The court will request the records," Grabko said at

last. "I will review them privately to determine relevance to the case, and we'll go from there."

Costello smiled. "Thank you, Your Honor."

They emerged from Grabko's chambers half an hour later, walking into the empty courtroom, where Ellen had a DUI sentencing scheduled for two o'clock. The buzz of conversation from the hall penetrated in a dim way. Lawyers hanging around, chewing the fat with county welfare advocates, cutting deals with prosecutors while they waited for their cases to be called in Judge Witt's court.

Intermingled with the usual crowd were reporters, lying in wait like cheetahs ready to jump up and run down their prey. There had been more than a few in the hall when she and Costello had come up. By now they would be thick all down the corridor. Between her own headline potential as a victim of vandalism, and Costello's sensational bomb, they had to be drooling in anticipation.

In no hurry to throw herself into the fray, she paused in front of the bench and leaned back against it, crossing her arms over her chest. "Your media puppets await."

Costello looked amused. "What makes you think I asked them here?"

"I haven't been innocent in a very long time, Tony. Whenever two or more reporters are gathered, you'll give them a show. And they'll eat this up—your casting the blame on the family. The stuff tabloids are made of. It's disgusting."

"It's a valid argument," he said, bracing a hand beside her shoulder. "You know as well as I do Kirkwood has inconsistencies in his story."

"It's a big leap from 'Can you prove you were getting a burger at the Hardee's drive-through while your son was being abducted?' to 'Isn't it true you abducted your own son?' " Ellen pointed out. At the same time she dismissed the little voice of truth that reminded her she had never been very comfortable with Paul's excuses herself. "Your client was caught red-handed."

"He has an alibi for the night Josh Kirkwood was abducted."

"Which is about as phony as your tan. He has no witnesses to corroborate—"

"I'll have to correct you there, Ellen." A nasty, anticipatory gleam in his dark eyes, he took his briefcase to a counsel table, popped it open, and extracted a sheaf of documents. "Disclosure pursuant to rule 9.02. Happy reading."

Ellen scanned the first page, where one of Tony's assistants had typed an elaborate explanation of the fact that they as yet had no written or recorded statements from witnesses. What a joke. Tony would never take a written statement prior to trail for the express reason that he would be compelled by law to turn it over to the prosecution. The second page stated Wright's alibi for the time of Josh's abduction. As he had stated repeatedly, it said he was in his office in the Cray building, at Harris. What he had never said before was that he was working in the company of a student—Todd Childs.

Ellen's heart picked up a beat. She turned the pages to the witness list, and a chill of apprehension pebbled the skin of her arms and ran down her back. At the top of the list was Todd Childs, 966 Tenth Street NW, Apartment B.

"When did you speak with Todd Childs?" she asked carefully.

"Does it matter?"

"It matters that he has already stated to the police he wasn't with Dr. Wright that evening."

"He'll swear under oath that he was."

"He's lying."

"Prove it."

"I intend to," she said, anger shuddering through her.

"You might have taken notice of his name on *my* witness list."

He raised his brows in mock innocence. "Was it? Things have been so hectic this week. . . . Has he been served?"

"I'm sure you'll be stunned to hear we've been unable to locate him. You wouldn't happen to know where he's staying, would you?"

Costello deflected the pointed question with a humorless laugh.

"Ellen, your paranoia is reaching new heights if you believe I'm hiding a witness from you."

She took the verbal shot and pressed on, immune to his attempts to hurt her. "How is it you've spoken to him while the cops can't even find him?"

"That might have something to do with the caliber of cops you're working with."

"You underestimate them, Tony. And I think you underestimate me, which is fine. It'll be all the more gratifying when I kick your ass next week."

"You're overestimating your case, Ellen," he said. "And you're grasping at straws going after Wright's phone records. You can't believe you'll find anything linking Dr. Wright to the kidnapping, which means you're really looking for something else. I'm surprised Judge Grabko didn't call you on it."

"Actually, I don't expect to find anything at all," she admitted coolly. "I don't expect to find your phone number listed under calls placed on the twenty-fifth, for instance. Which will mean that Karen Wright didn't call you on behalf of her husband. And if Karen Wright didn't call you, then who did?"

"So we're back to *that* conspiracy theory. You know, maybe you need help for this, Ellen. Although I'm sure our mutual friend Mr. Brooks will find your psychological quirks an interesting added facet for his book."

"Mutual friend?" she asked, the cool disinterest in her tone completely at odds with what she was feeling. "I've barely met the man," she lied. "How do you know him?"

What did he know? Did he know about Jay's connection to the attorney general? He had a private investigator working the case. Did he know Brooks had taken her home last night? Would he try to make an issue of it?

"I met him years ago, actually," he answered casually. "We were both at Purdue, though we were several years apart. Small world, isn't it?"

Ellen felt the floor dip beneath her feet. Brooks knew Costello. They had gone to the same college. He had never said one word.

"Ellen? Are you all right?" Costello asked. "You look a little pale."

"Don't worry about it, Tony." She spurred herself to move, to turn away, to duck her head. "It's nothing the truth won't cure."

She hefted her briefcase onto the other counsel table and stuffed the disclosure into the appropriate file folder. "You don't have to concern yourself about my mental state—unless, of course, I'm right and your client's accomplice called you in on this case, thereby making you an accessory in the Holloman kidnapping."

She clicked the locks closed and gave her adversary a final, challenging stare. "As an officer of the court, I'm sure I don't have to remind you of your obligation to report Todd Childs's whereabouts to the police—should you *happen* to see him. Who knows? Maybe we can kill two birds with one stone—serve our witness and nail an accomplice all in one shot. Wouldn't that be nice and neat?"

"Only two birds?" he questioned. "I thought you were after my head, too."

"Oh, I am, Tony," she said with a nasty smile. "You'll be my bonus dead duck."

He stepped close enough that she could smell the expensive aftershave he wore and lowered his head as if to share a secret.

"It's so nice to know you still think of me as special," he murmured.

God, she hated that he thought he could manipulate her with memories and sex appeal. "*Special* isn't how I think of you, Tony. You're at the wrong end of the adjective spectrum altogether."

"Does that mean you won't have dinner with me for old time's sake after all this is said and done?" he asked, his tone still intimate, his expression hungry and amused.

"I'd rather have my limbs gnawed off."

He had the nerve to laugh and the gall to hold the door for her as they left the courtroom.

They were mobbed as soon as they stepped into the hall, a dozen voices shouting questions at once. Bodies pressed in on them, hands thrusting forward with microphones and tape recorders. Ellen found herself trapped at Costello's side, her shoulder brushing against his arm. As she was jostled, she had to steady herself with a hand against the small of his back. She hated to touch him.

"*Our mutual friend Mr. Brooks . . .*"

"Ms. North, is it true you've been threatened?"

"*We were both at Purdue . . .*"

"Ms. North, are there any suspects in the vandalism?"

"*Small world, isn't it?*"

"Mr. Costello, does Dr. Wright have any comment on possible involvement of the Sci-Fi Cowboys in the attack on Ms. North?"

"Mr. Costello, is it true you're pushing for the investigation to turn toward Paul Kirkwood?"

"My client is innocent," Costello shouted, fixing his eagle glare just to the left of a portable sun gun. "The police have been negligent in pursuing leads that might take their investigation in a direction they don't want to consider. My investigators have pursued *all* leads. I can guarantee you that when the hearing begins next week, Dr. Garrett Wright will not be the only one on trial."

The statement had the effect of pouring gasoline on a fire. The noise level rose to a deafening din. Wanting nothing more than to escape, Ellen positioned her briefcase to use as shield and battering ram and started against the current of the crowd.

"Ms. North, do you have any comment?"

"Ms. North, can we get a statement?"

She lowered her head and pushed forward, slamming the briefcase into someone's knees. Down the hall the door to Judge Witt's courtroom opened, and the old bailiff, Randolph Grimm, barged into the hall, shouting for quiet, his face as red as a cherry tomato.

"Keep it down out here! Court is in session! Don't you people have any respect?"

Without waiting for an answer, he raised his cane and smacked it against the wall, the sound ringing out like a gunshot. People ducked and gasped and swung toward him. Cameramen wheeled with tape running.

Ellen took advantage of the diversion to make her escape, rounding a jungle gym of scaffolding and riding a service elevator down to the second floor.

Costello was going to turn the spotlight on Paul. Theoretically, the ploy would have no bearing on the probable-cause hearing. Grabko had to base his decision whether or not to bind Wright over for trial on the evidence presented, and Tony had no real evidence against Paul Kirkwood. But there wouldn't be a potential juror in the district who wouldn't have picked up on a story as sensational as this.

"You have to get it to a jury first, Ellen," she muttered as the elevator landed and the doors pulled open.

Phoebe stood outside the county clerk's office with a ream of paperwork clutched to her meager bosom and a shy smile on her face, absorbed in conversation with the boy wonder of the *Grand Forks Herald*. Adam Slater's eyes widened as he caught sight of Ellen. He swung away from Phoebe, digging a notepad out of the hip pocket of his baggy jeans.

"Hey, Ms. North, can I ask you a couple of questions about last night?"

"I'm surprised you aren't upstairs with the rest of the pack."

Slater shook his head. "Can't get anywhere that way. Everyone will have the same story. If I want to make my mark, I've got to get something fresh. You know, like they say in baseball—hit 'em where they ain't.'"

"Charming analogy," Ellen said, "but I don't want you swinging your bat around my secretary. Is that understood, Mr. Slater?"

His smile went flat. Beside him, Phoebe stood with her jaw dropped and her cheeks tinting.

"I have no comment for your story," Ellen went on. "You'll have to use someone else to make your mark. Phoebe, let's go. We've got work to do."

She started toward the office but turned back when Phoebe didn't fall in step behind her.

The girl had ducked her head in abject embarrassment. "God, I'm really sorry, Adam. I didn't—"

"Phoebe," Ellen said sharply.

"Man, this sucks," Slater complained, flopping his arms at his sides. "We were just talking."

Phoebe kept her head down as she walked beside Ellen. Neither spoke. In the outer offices phones rang, and Kevin O'Neal, the county SWAT commander, stood talking and laughing with Sig Iverson and Quentin Adler.

"Hey, Ellen," O'Neal called as he caught sight of her. "The ATF caught your pals the Berger boys down in Tennessee."

"Was there gunplay?" she asked with sadistic hope.

"Gave up without a fight and with a van full of stolen cigarettes. ATF wants to keep them on the federal beef. What do you want to do about extradition?"

Ellen shook her head. "Good riddance. Save the county some money."

She turned around just as Phoebe was slinking behind her desk.

"I'd like to speak with you in my office."

The girl didn't answer but followed Ellen as if going to her death.

"How do you know Adam Slater?" Ellen asked as soon as they were in the office.

"I met him at the Leaf and Bean last night," she said quietly, still hugging her papers. "We drank coffee and listened to music. Thursday is open-mike night."

"Did you know he was a reporter?"

"Yes. He said so. We didn't talk about the case, Ellen. I know better."

"I know you wouldn't mean to say anything, Phoebe, but he's a reporter. They have ways of wheedling information out of people. Believe me, I know."

"Our mutual friend Mr. Brooks . . ."

"I was very up-front with him about it," Phoebe said. "I told him right off I couldn't say anything about the case, and he was fine with that. Maybe he just wanted to have coffee with me. Maybe he just likes me as a human being. Our psyches are very in tune."

Ellen rolled her eyes. "Oh, please, Phoebe. He's a reporter looking to make a name for himself. He'll do anything to get what he wants. That's what reporters do—they screw people over for their own glorification."

"I'm here for a story . . . I go after what I want and I get it."

"Well, I'm sorry I'm not as cynical and paranoid as you are." Tears beaded on Phoebe's lashes. "And I'm sorry you don't trust me, Ellen."

"It's not you I don't trust," Ellen said softly. She let out a pent-up breath, trying without success to force the tension out of her shoulders. "It's the rest of the world I don't trust—Adam Slater included."

God, what a tangled mess. She took her secretary to task for talking to a cub reporter from a nothing newspaper in nowhere, North Dakota, while Jay Butler Brooks, renowned rogue and writer, old college buddy of her archnemesis, had been making himself at home in *her* home, drinking her liquor . . . kissing her, touching her, reaching past her barriers.

Who do you trust?

Phoebe? Adam Slater? Costello? Brooks?

Trust no one.

"Rumor has it you think Enberg had some help with that shotgun."

"Where did you hear that?"

"Around."

"If there's a leak on this case—"

"No one fed it to me. I don't have a mole in your office, if that's what you're worried about. . . ."

"I'm not paranoid."

If she *was* paranoid, it didn't mean they *weren't* out to get her.

She stood at her window and looked out. Deer Lake was a ghost town, windswept and deserted; a place from a science-fiction movie, where all had been abandoned in an unknown moment for unknown reasons. "Abandoned"— it was a good word for what she was feeling. Abandoned by the security and trust and safety she had embraced here.

"We can't take chances," she said, turning back toward Phoebe. "Look what happened with Paige Price and Steiger, and that whole mess. This case is too important. We can't risk a mistake. Josh and Megan are counting on us."

"And Dustin Holloman," Phoebe added in a small voice. She gnawed her lower lip for a moment, a moment of silence for the victims, then swiped a tear from her cheek. "I'm s-sorry. I-I w-w-w-ouldn't—"

Ellen held up a hand. "I know you wouldn't, Phoebe. Just be careful. Please."

She nodded and sniffled and pushed her glasses up on her nose. "Cameron and Mitch and Agent Wilhelm are waiting for you in the conference room."

Ellen briefed them on the meeting in Grabko's chambers. Mitch reacted with anger, Cameron with disgust. Marty Wilhelm looked troubled and confused.

"Is abuse a possibility?" he asked.

"Absolutely not," Mitch said. "I've known Hannah and Paul since I moved here. There's no way."

"But Costello is right," Wilhelm argued. "Paul Kirkwood has a temper. We've seen it."

"Hannah would never allow him to hurt Josh. She wouldn't put up with that kind of shit for a minute."

"Then what's she doing married to the jerk? She doesn't strike me as the kind of woman who would put up with any of Paul Kirkwood's lesser qualities, but there she is. There might be a lot we don't know about their marriage."

"He's changed," Mitch said. "People do."

Cameron arched a brow. "The question may be— How much? Has he gone off the deep end? We know the marriage is all but over. Paul isn't living at the house. We know Josh reacted very badly when Paul showed up to see him in the hospital."

"And you think it's because he's a child abuser and Hannah knows it but has failed to report it," Mitch stated flatly.

"Stranger things have been proved true."

His face set in stubborn lines, Mitch turned his scowl from Cameron to Wilhelm and back. "Use your heads.

We're saying Wright's accomplice nabbed Dustin Holloman. Nothing in that case points to Paul."

"Maybe there are three of them," Wilhelm suggested.

"Yeah," Mitch said. "Maybe Deer Lake has a whole underground community of psychotic child abusers and they're all trying to draw suspicion off their pal Wright."

"There's no point in fighting about this among ourselves," Ellen said. "Costello is forcing the issue. If he's looking at Paul, then we'd better make at least a token show of looking at Paul or we'll end up with egg on our faces."

"There was the van—" Wilhelm started.

"All together now." Mitch raised his arms like a symphony conductor. "The van that yielded us nothing."

"Mitch is right," Ellen said. "Don't waste time on the van. Talk to people around Paul. Talk to his secretary. Talk to his partner."

"He won't be any help pinning down Paul's movements in any way," Cameron said. "I know Dave Christianson from my health club. He's been working strictly from home for the past three months. His wife is having a difficult pregnancy with twins."

"Okay, so we talk again with the secretary," Wilhelm said. "And the security guard at his office complex. Neighbors. See what we can tie him to. Maybe he's not in with Wright. Maybe he's trying to frame Wright."

Mitch slapped his hands down on the table. "Jesus Christ, Costello would love this. We're here to discuss new evidence against his client and instead we're tripping over conspiracy theories. This isn't a case we're on, it's a fucking Oliver Stone movie."

"Evidence?" Ellen asked, sitting up straighter. "What evidence?"

Wilhelm pushed a curled tube of fax paper across the table to her. "I pulled some strings and got a friend in the lab to release a preliminary report on some more of our physical evidence—the gloves, the ski mask, and the sheet that was wrapped around Agent O'Malley the night she was attacked."

"And?"

"The glove has bloodstains that look to match Agent O'Malley for type. We already know about the blood types on the sheet. Now we're looking at hairs recovered from the sheet. Four distinct types. One unidentified. One consistent with Agent O'Malley. One consistent with Josh. And one consistent with Garrett Wright."

"We finally catch a break," Ellen said, a sense of relief seeping through her.

"Regarding the stocking cap," Wilhelm went on, "they found two distinct types of hair—one consistent with Wright, and one matching the unidentified hair found on the sheet.

"The question now," he said, "is, Who does that other hair belong to? And if we got a sample from Paul Kirkwood, would we get a match?"

CHAPTER 21

Father Tom sat in a pew toward the back of the church. On the left-hand side of the aisle—opposite where his one-time deacon, Albert Fletcher, had fallen to his death six days ago. Albert, devout servant of the Lord, his faith turning into fanaticism into madness; his madness leading him to his death, here, in this place he had loved. Tom couldn't decide if it was poetic or ironic. It was sad, he knew that. And it struck him as cruel, as many things did these days.

He sat alone. The weather had kept the faithful few away from morning Mass. He had gone through the motions for his own sake, hoping he would feel something, some kind of deep, binding affirmation that he still belonged in the vestments. But all he felt was hollow desperation, as if he were truly, totally, spiritually alone, abandoned by the same God who had allowed Josh to be taken and Hannah to suffer and Albert to die.

He had considered confessing his feelings, but he already knew the empty platitudes that would be handed him in response. He was being tested. He needed to reflect, to pray. He needed to keep his faith. A pat on the head and a hundred Hail Marys. At most, they would send him on retreat for a week or a month to one of the secluded spots where the Church tucked away its embarrassments—the alcoholic priests, the burnouts, the mentally fragile, the sexually suspect. Time to reflect among the casualties, but not too long, because the archdiocese was woefully short of priests and better to have one in place who had lost his faith than not to have one at all. At least he could go through the motions.

The politics of the Church disgusted him, and always had. He had come to the priesthood for better reasons, nobler reasons. Reasons that were drifting away from him.

He tipped his head back and looked up at the soaring ceiling with its delicate gilt arches and ethereal frescoes. St. E's had been built in the era when minicathedrals were still affordable and parishioners tithed to the Church instead of to their IRAs. The exterior was of native limestone. Twin spires thrust heavenward like lances of the soldiers of God. The windows were stained-glass works of art, jewel-tone mosaics depicting the life of Christ. Inside, the walls were painted slate blue and trimmed with lacework stencils in gilt and white and rose. The pews were oak, the kneelers padded with worn velvet. It was the kind of place meant to inspire awe and offer comfort. A place of ritual and wonderful mysteries. Miracles.

He could have used one about now.

Along the south wall a rack of cobalt-glass votives cradled the flames of three dozen prayers, filling the air with the buttery scent of melting wax. On the wall beside the tiers of candles, the handmade posters put up by the catechism classes praying for Josh's safety had been replaced with prayers for Dustin Holloman. Prayers children should never have to make, fears their lives should never have known.

In the silence he could hear the memory of his father's voice as he read the Billings newspaper three days after the fact, because that was as fast as the mail could get it to them on their small ranch near Red Lodge, Montana.

Every morning Bob McCoy would come in from chores and read the paper while he had his breakfast, and shake his head and say, "The world's going to hell on a sled."

Tom thought he could hear the runners screeching. But the thump that resounded in the church brought him back to reality, such as it was. Someone had come in the main doors at the back, the main doors that needed oil in their hinges. He turned in the pew, squinting to recognize the man walking toward him from the dark shadows beneath the balcony.

"I'm looking for Father Tom McCoy."

"I'm Father Tom," he said, rising.

"Jay Butler Brooks."

"Ah, the crime writer," he said, offering his hand.

Jay clasped the priest's hand in his and gave it a pump. "You're familiar with my work, Father?"

"Only by reputation. My reading taste runs more toward fiction. I get enough reality on a daily basis. What can I do for you, Mr. Brooks?"

"I'd like a moment of your time, if I might. I wasn't interrupting anything, was I?"

Tom McCoy cast an ironic glance around the deserted church, but the emotion that twitched the corners of his mouth seemed self-deprecating. He looked nothing like any priest Jay had ever seen or imagined. He was too young, too handsome, built like an athlete, and dressed like a slacker in creased black jeans and a faded green sweatshirt from the University of Notre Dame. The clerical collar seemed at odds with the cowboy boots. A man of contradictions. A kindred spirit.

"We're not exactly having a rush on salvation today," he said.

"With weather like this I reckon folks figure they'll take their chances," Jay reasoned. "What's another day or two in purgatory, give or take?"

"You know about purgatory, Mr. Brooks? Are you Catholic?"

"No, sir. I was born a Baptist and later converted to cynicism, but I do know all about purgatory." Weariness crept into his voice against his will. "Y'all haven't cornered the market on hell or its suburbs."

Father Tom tipped his head in concession. "No, I suppose not. Did you want to go into my office?"

Jay shook his head. His gaze scanned the grand interior of the church, taking in the windows, the statuary, the cast bas-relief plaques that hung at regular intervals along the wall. "This is fine. Quite a place you've got here."

The altar was traditional, draped in linen, set with brass candelabra, a gleaming chalice, a huge old book with marker ribbons trailing from between its pages. According to the newspaper articles from one week ago, the demented deacon had given Father McCoy a concussion with one of the brass candlesticks from that altar. Jay wondered if it was sitting up there now, absolved of guilt, or if the police had taken it away as evidence.

From the huge crucifix that hung behind the altar, the delicately carved face of Christ glowered down at him as if in disapproval of his thoughts.

Father Tom moved farther down the pew. Jay sat beside him, his parka rustling like newspaper. He had unzipped it as a concession to being indoors, but the cold seemed to have sunk into him bone-deep in the ten minutes it had taken him to get there, navigating the Cherokee along unplowed roads and through three-foot drifts. At any rate, the church didn't seem as warm as the interior of the truck. The thermostat probably went up only for parishioners. No sense heating the barn when the flock was gone.

"You're here to do a book," Father Tom said flatly.

"You disapprove."

"It's not my place to approve or disapprove."

A smile cracked Jay's face. "Well, I've never known that to stop anybody."

"Hannah and Josh have been through enough," McCoy said without apology. "I don't want to see them hurt any more than they already have been."

Jay arched a brow at the omission. "And Paul?"

The priest glanced away. "Paul has made it clear he doesn't want anything from me or the Church."

"Can you blame him?"

"Not for that."

His candor was surprising, but, then, nothing much about Tom McCoy seemed ordinary. Depending on who you asked around town, Father McCoy was a rebel, refreshing, an affront to the traditions of the Church. He did not define himself by uniform or convention. His parishioners either loved him or tolerated him. Behind the lenses of his gold-rimmed glasses, his blue eyes were honest.

"I'm not interested in exploiting victims, Father."

"You'll record their suffering, dissect their lives, package their story as entertainment, and make a whole lot of money. What do you call that?"

"The way of the world. Stuff happens. People want to know about it. Their knowing doesn't change what happened. Nothing can. What I'm after is the truth. Reasons. Motives. I want to know where ordinary people find the strength to deal with extraordinary tragedy. I want to know what the rest of us can learn from them."

"And make a lot of money."

"And make a lot of money," he admitted. "The poor might be rich in the kingdom of God, but I'll take mine now, thanks."

"Hannah isn't ordinary," Father Tom said. His expression softened slightly, tellingly. "Ask anyone. She's stronger than she knows. Kind. Good. I can't begin to tell you what she's meant to this community as a doctor, as a role model."

"It must have been difficult to see her go through this," Jay offered, watching closely for the true reaction. Anger. There and gone. Quickly veiled by something more acceptable. But there was no priestly wisdom forthcoming, no magic motto meant as a blanket banality for all-purpose suffering.

"It's been hell," McCoy said frankly. "I've been a priest for more than a decade, Mr. Brooks. I have yet to understand why bad things happen to good people."

"God's will?" Jay ventured.

"I certainly hope not. What purpose is served punishing the faithful and the innocent? I'd call that sadism, wouldn't you?"

Jay leaned back and crossed his arms, regarding Tom McCoy with a quizzical scrutiny. "Are you sure you're a priest?"

He gave a humorless laugh and looked away. The word "no" reverberated in the air around him. "After the last couple of weeks, I don't think any of us can be sure of anything."

The answer struck a chord. Truth. The kind nobody really wanted to hear.

"But you must see this all the time," McCoy said. "It's your job—going from one set of victims to another. Does it get to you, or are you immune?"

"Not immune; careful. I keep my distance. Don't let it get personal. I'm there to ask questions, look for answers, patch it all together and move on." Even as he rattled off his stock answer, he could see Ellen in his mind's eye. He could feel her in his arms, feel her fear, her tears soaking into his shirt. Some distance.

"It's not about me," he said. That was a lie, too.

He might have called coming to Deer Lake running

away, but he couldn't escape the fact that immersing himself in this particular case was certainly about him, about his own sense of loss. It was about punishing and comforting himself with perspective, which made him both selfish and opportunistic. Why couldn't he have just jumped on a plane to Barbados after seeing Christine? He could have been soaking up sun and rum instead of freezing his ass and digging up unwanted emotions out of the deepest corners of his soul.

"I'm just recording the story," he stated, as if that could make it so.

"Nothing personal," Father Tom said. His gaze had narrowed, focusing deeper than the surface excuses and public facade. "Do you have children?"

Depends on who you ask, he thought, but he kept that answer to himself. Confession was for the regulars of St. Elysius, not smart-mouth mercenary hacks from out of town.

McCoy interpreted the silence as a no. "Have you met Hannah and Josh?"

"Not yet."

"Why is that? The story is about their lives."

"There are other people involved. I've been busy getting background, getting to know the players."

"Really?"

"If you're waiting for me to say it didn't seem right to approach her, you'll be waiting a long time, Father," he said, wondering just how many strikes God would list against him for lying to a priest.

He had been avoiding Hannah Garrison on the excuse that the story was about more than her son. It was about the court system and the cops and Garrett Wright and Dennis Enberg. But at its heart it was about a little boy. An eight-year-old boy who had had his whole life pulled up by the roots.

He had chosen this story specifically for the parallels, to force himself to examine the pain and to probe the questions while maintaining his usual safe distance . . . and he had shied away from the heart of it. Josh. Josh, who was eight years old, freckle-faced, gap-toothed. Who liked to play hockey and Little League. He remembered the picture in Paul's office—Josh in his baseball uniform with Paul, the proud father, beside him. The fist of longing tightened.

What the hell are you doing here, Brooks?

Father Tom rose to his feet. "Let's take a ride, Mr. Brooks. There's someone I think you should meet."

They drove down Lakeshore, past Garrett Wright's home with a few intrepid reporters parked out front, on to the Kirkwood house, and turned in the driveway. Jay had parked in front of this house once before only to back off and drive away. Nothing had changed in the few days in between. The snow fort in the front yard was still half-finished. He wondered if Josh would ever finish it or if what he had gone through had so changed him that something as simple and childish as a snow fort would forever-more seem unimportant.

Father Tom stepped out of the Cherokee. Jay gave a cursory glance at his minicassette recorder lying on the console between the seats and left it.

They walked up the driveway together, Jay quietly absorbing the feel of the place, the detail. The house was the last one on the block. It looked comfortable, the kind of place to raise a family. From the front step the view of the street and the rest of the neighborhood was limited, cut off by the attached garage that jutted out in front of the house itself. The view was of the lake and the trees that lined the banks. Through the lacework of leafless branches and across the frozen expanse, the buildings of Harris College were just visible.

It was on this step that Josh Kirkwood had been left four nights ago. Alone. Dressed in a pair of striped pajamas. His mother had seen no one, no car. Garrett Wright's house was just down the block, but as yet no evidence had been found to suggest Josh had ever been inside it. Karen Wright had been under guard that night at the Fontaine Hotel.

Who had brought him back? Todd Childs? Christopher Priest? Or was Wright's accomplice someone so anonymous he or she was able to move around town freely, unknown, unseen, unsuspected? And what was the connection to Wright? Or was the connection to the people who lived in this house?

Hannah Garrison opened the door, a smile lighting her face when she saw Father Tom.

"You forgot your gloves again," she chided. "If you don't end up with frostbite, it'll be a miracle."

"Well, that would certainly improve my stock with the bishop."

Hannah had been the less visible one during the ordeal, staying in the background while her husband joined the search teams and played to the press. But Jay had watched her one television interview enough times that he had already memorized the sound of her voice, the cadence of her speech, the cornflower-blue of her eyes. He knew she blamed herself because she hadn't been there to pick Josh up that night. He had seen the pain in her face, heard the confusion in her voice. She'd had the perfect life and suddenly it was broken all around her.

And he wanted to write a book about it.

"Jay Butler Brooks, ma'am," he said, offering his hand.

The pretty, fragile smile went brittle, and her gaze cut to her friend, Father Tom.

"I thought it was important" was all he said.

"I'm not a reporter, ma'am," Jay said.

Hannah lifted her chin, her gaze cool. "I know what you are, Mr. Brooks. Come in," she said. She directed them, not into the family room where the television was on and toys were scattered across the floor, but into a formal dining room with furniture that likely hadn't been used since Christmas. She was distancing him from her real home, from her children. Jay accepted the subtle slight as part of the big picture, part of the whole story, part of who Hannah Garrison was.

She took the seat at the head of the table. Even though she looked as if she had been ill—thin, pale, with dark circles beneath her eyes—her bearing was regal. Her wavy golden hair was pulled back from her face, accenting the kind of bone structure that made fashion models wealthy, but she wore no makeup, no jewelry. Her sweatshirt was a well-worn relic from her alma mater, Duke University. She could have made a gunnysack look chic.

"My husband told me he'd spoken with you," she said.

"Why does that make me think I've already got a strike against me?"

"Certainly you have in Paul's eyes. I make my own judgments."

Jay nodded. "That's fair. I've been told you're a remarkable woman, Dr. Garrison."

She moved one long, elegant hand in a dismissive gesture. "By circumstance, that's all. Which is why you're here, isn't it?"

"I won't lie to you about that, Dr. Garrison. I'm a writer. You've got a hell of a story here. I'd like the chance to tell it."

"And if I decline, you'll tell it anyway?"

"Probably. I'd like to be able to include your perspective, but it's up to you whether or not you want to participate."

"Well, that was simple. My answer is no. Living this nightmare once is quite enough. I don't have any desire to go through it again in retelling the tale to you or in thinking thousands of people will live it vicariously reading your book."

"Not even if it might help someone to understand—"

"Understand what? No part of this is understandable. I know. I've spent every night, every day, trying to understand. All I've got for the effort is more questions."

"There will be a considerable amount of money for Josh," Jay said. He found it very telling that Hannah herself hadn't spoken a word about payment when it had been virtually the first thought in her husband's head.

She gave him a frosty look. "I won't prostitute my son or myself, Mr. Brooks. We don't need your money. All I want is to get away from this nightmare, for us to distance ourselves from it emotionally and get on with our lives. Any money associated with what happened would only be like dragging the experience with us. It would be like blood money."

She stood and smoothed her hands along the baggy hem of her sweatshirt. "No. That's my answer. Would you like coffee?"

Subject dismissed, on to obligatory hostess duties. Jay had the feeling that if he had come here a month ago, Hannah would have been softer, gentler, less blunt, more elaborate in her guise of good manners. The ordeal had pared away the unnecessary in her, cut away the crap of social ceremony, leaving only the honest, the essential. Like many people he had interviewed, people who had gone through harrowing experiences, Hannah had seen how much of life is just bullshit, just meaningless ritual made important to give humankind some pretense of being better than the rest of the animals on the planet.

In another part of the house a telephone rang. She excused herself to answer it.

"The trust fund will be set up," he said to Father Tom. "They can do what they want with the money. Give it away for all I care."

The priest gave a lazy shrug. "It doesn't matter to you. You've absolved yourself, done your part, paid your fee."

"I can't win for losing around here," Jay grumbled. "If I kept every nickel for myself, I'd be a greedy son of a bitch. If I give it away, I'm trying to buy a conscience."

"Are you?"

He barked a laugh and looked away. What the hell would he want with a conscience? It was just excess baggage, another rock around his neck to drag him down. If he had a conscience, he would have to believe that it was all his own fault that Christine had kept his son from him all these years, that it wasn't just virulent spite on her part. He hurt enough as it was. To think it was his own doing that had taken eight years of his son's life away from him, denied him even knowledge of the boy, would be too much.

A mop of sandy-brown hair and a pair of big blue eyes suddenly appeared in the doorway to the family room. The eyes were somber with a steady stare.

"Hi, Josh," Father Tom said in a casual voice. "Would you like to join us?"

The boy eased the rest of his body into view but kept one hand on the doorjamb. The other clutched the handle of a bulging nylon backpack. He was dressed in baggy blue jeans and a Blackhawks hockey jersey several sizes too big. He made no move to come forward.

Jay turned sideways on his chair and rested his forearms on his thighs. "Hey, there, Josh," he said quietly. "My name's Jay. Your dad tells me you're quite the baseball player."

Josh's expression didn't flicker. There was no relaxation at the mention of his father, no response at all. He had a face made for a mischievous grin. Jay remembered the smile from the photograph in Paul's office—shining eyes and shy pride—and the photograph from the "missing" posters—a gap-toothed grin and a Cub Scout uniform.

Slowly Josh crossed the hall and came into the dining room, skirting all the way around the room, his eyes on Jay. When he was even with Father Tom, he stopped and dug a spiral notebook out of the backpack, opened it, and tore out a page.

"I guess hockey is the sport now," Jay went on, making conversation to break the tension that filled the room, hoping he might strike the right chord and draw the boy out. "We don't play much hockey where I come from. We don't have any winter to speak of."

Josh paid no attention to him as he knelt on the floor and carefully folded the sheet of paper in half and in half again. When he was finished, he stood, hooked his backpack over one shoulder, and walked a straight line across the area rug, as if he were on a tightrope. When he reached the table, he held the paper out for Father Tom.

"For me?" he asked, accepting the gift.

Josh nodded. "But don't open it now."

"All right." He slid the note into an inner pocket. "I'll save it for later."

The boy nodded again, scooted behind Father Tom, and scurried along the edge of the room again to the doorway, watching Jay with those big, somber eyes.

Hannah came back, pausing to touch her son's head. Josh ducked out from under the caress and disappeared into the family room.

"I'm sorry for the interruption," she said. "Did you decide about the coffee?"

Jay rose. "No, thank you, ma'am. I've got to be going." He dug a card out of one of the many pockets on his parka and handed it to her. "In case you change your mind."

"I won't," she said firmly, but tempered it with an apologetic look.

She was a far cry from her husband. Their marriage would be a story in itself, he supposed. Which of them had changed for better or worse? How long would they have hung on if Josh's abduction hadn't pulled them apart?

"It was a pleasure meeting you, Hannah," he said. "Father Tom is right. You're an extraordinary person. Whether you care to think it or not."

A deep sadness darkened her eyes. "But that's just my point, Mr. Brooks—I don't want to be a heroine. I just want our lives back."

It didn't look as if she would get that any time soon, he thought with pity when he stepped out through the front door and a photographer shot his picture from the window of a Toyota parked on the street.

"She doesn't deserve what's happened to her," Father Tom said once inside the Cherokee.

Wasn't it the role of priests to listen to their faithful ponder the cruelties of the world? Jay thought. Tom McCoy seemed to have more questions than answers, a burden that appeared to be weighing on him heavily.

"In my experience, Father," Jay said, "life is scattershot with random acts of cruelty. Trying to make sense of it either keeps us human or makes us crazy."

Father Tom said nothing but slipped Josh's note out of his coat pocket and unfolded it.

The drawing was simple: a sad face with blank dark eyes, set in the center of an inked-in black square. The caption broke his heart. *When I was lost.*

Josh wasn't the only one who had been lost in this ordeal. Lost lives, lost love, lost trust . . . lost faith. Tom had tried to make sense of it, had prayed for some comfort, but all he felt was fear as the faith that had anchored his life slipped farther and farther away, and all he wanted to hold on to was another man's wife.

When I was lost . . .

He folded the page and tucked it back into his coat pocket.

The funeral dragged on interminably. Victor Franken had accumulated scores of acquaintances in his seventy-nine years, none of whom was shy about using his death as an excuse to show off their skills as orators. The weather had prevented those from any distance outstate from coming, which the locals interpreted as meaning more time on the pulpit for themselves.

Ellen sat toward the back of Grace Lutheran, fanning herself with her program, wondering if all the hot air was coming from the furnace or if it was simply a by-product of this many lawyers in one place.

The narthex was crowded with reporters, lying in wait to jump people for comments on their way out. Franken's relatives sat in the front pews, including the great-grandson from LA, who had opened the ceremonies with an interpretive liturgical dance that made the locals squirm in their seats. Minnesotans rarely interpreted anything with their bodies, and never clad in a black unitard.

Life in Deer Lake had taken on all the weirder qualities of a Fellini film, with Rudy Stovich as the sad clown. He stood at the pulpit, his voice rising and falling as dramatically as his expressions.

Mike Lumkin, an attorney from Tatonka, leaned into Ellen and whispered, "If he's like this on the bench, I'm going into real estate."

"Cross your fingers," she whispered back. "Maybe he'll be discovered by television. He could be the next Wapner."

"Who'll play Rusty?"

"Manley Vanloon."

"Sounds like an episode of *Hee-Haw*," he said with a

grimace. "Hey, we need to talk dispo on Tilman. What do you think about time served?"

"I think you're dreaming. Time served and eighty hours of community service."

His eyes bugged out. "Eighty?"

"Ninety?"

"Sixty."

"A hundred."

"Eighty sounds good," he said reasonably, and sat back as Rudy launched into the last leg of his tribute.

Ellen stifled a sigh. She tried to block everything around her from her mind in order to give Judge Franken her own personal tribute. Brief and to the point. He was a good man, a good judge, he would be missed.

The burial had to be postponed until a good thaw. After the final prayer, and three verses of "Abide with Me," everyone trooped to the church basement for cake and Jell-O from the Lutheran ladies' auxiliary and conversation that centered not on Judge Franken but on Garrett Wright and the kidnappings. Ellen made one obligatory round of the room and escaped through a little-used side door that let out onto the parking lot.

By the time she made it back to the courthouse, those who had remained behind to conduct business were closing down for the night and for the weekend. Coats were going on, computers and typewriters turning off, pumps going into tote bags while feet were sliding into snow boots.

Quentin Adler stood with briefcase in hand, talking at Martha, their receptionist. "I would have gone to pay my respects, but I'm up to my ears in work," he stated importantly. "You know, Rudy asked me to take on some of Ellen's cases."

Ellen rolled her eyes and ducked behind him, heading to Phoebe's desk. Her secretary sat with her woolly poncho across her lap, her expression that of a third-grader who was being made to stay late after school.

"Do I have any messages?" Ellen asked, pretending not to notice the pout.

"Your mail is on your desk. Someone sent you roses. Pete Ecklund wants to cut a deal on Zimmerman. A gazillion reporters called. Agent Wilhelm says toxicology shows traces of Triazolam in Josh Kirkwood's bloodstream," she recited, thrusting the slips up at Ellen. "Do I have to stay?"

"Got a hot date?" Ellen raised her brows, trying for girlish camaraderie.

"Not anymore."

"No, you don't have to stay." Ellen dropped her gaze to the note from Wilhelm and tried not to feel like an evil stepmother. "But we could use your help tomorrow afternoon."

Ignoring the hefty sigh, she went into her office. *Triazolam.* She went directly to the bookcase and pulled a reference book that listed virtually every drug, legal and otherwise, known to mankind. Triazolam, better known as Halcion. A central nervous system depressant once commonly prescribed as a sleeping pill, also commonly used in psych wards. She scanned the list of side effects that included memory loss and hallucinations. *When withdrawn suddenly, there may be bizarre personality changes (psychosis) and paranoia.*

That might have been one explanation for Josh's behavior, she thought. A strong enough dose could have kept Josh in a hypnotic state during his captivity, during which time Wright could have planted anything in his mind—including threats. Taking him abruptly off the drug might have set off a mild psychosis.

She dialed Wilhelm's number and noticed for the first time the bouquet of red roses in an all-purpose green office vase. Brooks was her first thought. The bastard

thought he could ease past her guard with flowers and that
damned smile. He and Costello had probably had a good
chuckle, strategizing about her over drinks. Sandwiching
the receiver between her shoulder and ear, she plucked the
note card out from between the thorny stems and tore it
open.

"Agent Wilhelm."

"Ellen North here. Thanks for calling about the tox
report," she said. "It might answer some questions for us."

"I've got people looking into prescriptions for Halcion
filled locally," he said. "We might get lucky. Then again,
it might have been filled in Minneapolis where there must
be a couple hundred pharmacies."

"Gotta start somewhere," Ellen said. "Have you got a
report on O'Malley's blood tests? She believed Wright in-
jected her with something while she was unconscious. If
we could get a line on both drugs . . ."

The rustle of paper sounded like static over the phone.
"Hang on."

Ellen opened the note card. A folded piece of paper
dropped out. The card itself was blank. Odd. Ellen set the
card aside and opened the folded paper.

evil comes to SHE who searches for it
search S for SIN
see where we've been

Ellen dropped the note and shot up out of her chair,
jumping back from the desk. The telephone receiver clattered down over the drawer fronts and dangled.

"Ms. North? Are you there? Ms. North? Hello?"
search S for Sin . . . see where we've been . . .

"Oh, God," she whispered, looking wildly around her
office. Her sanctuary. The one place in her professional
life she felt she had absolute control. Her gaze landed on
the filing cabinets.

search S for Sin . . .

Shaking, she jerked the drawer open and flipped through the files. One stood out—cleaner, stiffer, unworn. The word "sin" in bold caps on the tab.

He'd been in her office. The son of a bitch had been in her office.

She lay the file atop the others in the open cabinet and turned the cover back. Staring up at her from the small square of a Polaroid snapshot, blank-eyed and expressionless, was Josh Kirkwood.

CHAPTER 22

The day had seemed to last forever, and yet night fell too soon. The contradiction, Hannah thought, was just a reflection of her own inner turmoil. She had been gone from the hospital longer than two weeks. She couldn't imagine leaving Josh and Lily, and yet she missed her work terribly. She missed the place and the people, her patients, her co-workers, her friends, the normalcy of routine, the drudgery of paperwork. Most of all, she missed who she was at work. The strength of mind and will she wore in that role seemed to have come off with the white lab coat and the fake brass name tag.

She would never have said she defined herself by her job. It wasn't who she was, it was what she did. But without the frame of reference it provided, she felt lost. And with the feeling of loss came guilt. She wasn't only a doctor; she was a mother. Her children needed her. Why could she not define herself in those terms?

The curse of the nineties woman, she thought, struggling for a sense of humor. A futile struggle. The day had held little to laugh about and was only going to get worse.

The weather had forced her to cancel Josh's appointment with Dr. Freeman. A friend from the hospital had called and told her Dr. Lomax was beginning to make noises to the administration about officially naming him temporary director of the ER—a condition he would then fight to make permanent. Director of the ER—the promotion that had passed over his head and landed squarely on Hannah's shoulders just a month ago. She worried that they might actually listen to him, then raked herself over the mental coals for letting anything but Josh's situation take precedence in her mind.

Ellen North had called to tell her they had another piece of physical evidence against Wright, but that Garrett Wright's attorney wanted access to Josh's medical records, a ploy meant to divert attention away from Wright and onto Paul.

And Jay Butler Brooks wanted to write a book about it all.

Hell of a day.

Costello's charge occupied her mind like a big black rat chewing at her nerves. The implication was that Paul had abused Josh—a charge that she had rejected out of hand. Paul would never intentionally hurt his children. He didn't even believe in spanking. And yet how many times lately had she been struck by the horrible sensation that he had become a stranger? He had lied to her, lied to the police, evaded questions and twisted nonanswers into self-righteous outrage.

She remembered too well how Megan O'Malley had questioned her about Paul after Josh's jacket had been found on Ryan's Bay.

"When did you start to notice a change in him? . . . He's been withdrawing more recently? . . . Does he normally ignore his answering machine when you call him at the office at night?"

"Why are you asking me these questions? You can't possibly think Paul had something to do with this."

"It's just routine. . . . Mother Teresa would need an alibi if she were here. When we catch this guy, his lawyer will probably try to pin it on someone else . . . If he's sleazy enough, he'll ask where you were . . . and where Paul was."

"I don't know where Paul was. He was gone when I woke up.

He said he went out on his own, just driving around town, look-ing . . ."

She didn't know where he had been that morning or why he hadn't called her back the night Josh went missing or why he had lied to police about once owning a light-colored van. She didn't know why Josh had recoiled from him that night in the hospital.

Another tide of guilt rose into her throat. It wasn't that she believed Paul was capable of any of it, it was that she couldn't be sure he wasn't.

She knew that he was coming to dinner. That he would be there in a matter of minutes.

She had managed to prepare the meal, even though her attention had been fractured. The salad had been tossed. The scent of rosemary chicken and roasting potatoes filled the air.

In the family room Lily was stacking blocks in a pre-carious tower. Josh had built himself a fort with chairs and footstools and couch cushions, creating a space he could go into and shut everyone else out. Hannah had herded him out of his bedroom every day to prevent him from doing just that—shutting her out, shutting himself in with the memories he refused to share. The fort reminded her he could keep the rest of the world out without walls, with only his silence.

He had spent the better part of the day in his new bur-row, with his backpack and his new Think Pad. Hannah had been relieved to see him making use of the notebook. Perhaps memories and feelings would start flowing onto the pages, then spill over and out of him, and he would begin to talk about what he had been through.

Ellen had asked about him, whether or not he seemed to be opening up. Hannah knew it would help the case against Garrett Wright, but there was no pushing Josh, as tempting as it might have been. Dr. Freeman said Josh had to come to it in his own time, that trying to force him to talk about what had happened could trigger a trauma from which he might not recover for months or years. He needed time.

The probable-cause hearing began on Tuesday.

She stepped down from the kitchen into the family room. "Josh, time to get cleaned up for supper. Dad will be here any minute."

Josh peered up at her from under the couch-cushion roof of his little hut. He had said nothing one way or the other about Paul's intended visit.

Paul had called midmorning. He wanted to see the children, especially Josh. He had always been so proud of Josh, so pleased to have a son. His own father had never taken much interest in his bookish younger son, preferring the company of Paul's older brothers. To have Josh reject him had to hurt unbearably.

"Come on," she said, lifting the cushion.

Josh slapped his Think Pad shut and clutched it to his chest. Hannah leaned down, brushing a hand over his sandy curls.

"Dad's really looking forward to seeing you," she said. "He misses you and Lily."

Josh said nothing. He had yet even to ask why his father was no longer living in the house. His lack of curiosity unnerved her.

Beyond the kitchen a door opened and closed. Paul coming in from the garage. Josh's eyes widened and he bolted like a deer, jumping out of his fort and running for the hall that led to the bathroom and bedrooms. Lily smashed her blocks down and dashed in a mad circle around the living room, squealing, "Daddy! Daddy!"

"I forgot the ice cream," Paul announced as he stepped into the kitchen. The tone was challenging, defensive. In truth, he hadn't forgotten at all. After Costello's announcement had been splashed all over the news, he hadn't been able to bring himself to go into a store. People would stare at him, think God-knew-what. They would forget all about him putting in hours on the search, making pleas on television. They would think back to the day Mitch Holt had told him to come in to be fingerprinted. They would remember O'Malley ragging about that goddamn van.

Lily scrambled up the steps into the kitchen, her little face wreathed in smiles. "Daddy! Daddy!"

She flung herself at his legs and Paul scooped her up, perching her in the crook of his arm. "Well, at least someone is glad to see me."

"Don't worry about dessert," Hannah said. "People are still bringing food to the house. We've got enough brownies to last into the next millennium."

Lily looped her arms around his neck and lay her head down on his shoulder. "Daddy home. Home, home. *My* Daddy!"

Paul brushed an absent kiss across her forehead and set her down on the kitchen floor.

"Where's Josh?" He unbuttoned his long wool topcoat and went to hang it in his office.

"He's getting washed up," she answered, carrying the salad bowl to the table, stepping around Lily, who had seated herself in the middle of the floor, lower lip trembling threateningly.

"Has he said anything?"

"No."

"What the hell is that psychiatrist doing? Besides charging us a hundred fifty bucks an hour."

Hannah's eyes flashed impatience as she turned toward the stove. "She's a psychiatrist, not a plumber. She can't just Roto-Rooter out his memory. It's going to take time."

She bent down to reach for Lily. The baby twisted away from her and began to sob.

"Da-a-d-dy!"

"Meanwhile, Anthony Costello is going to make me out to be some kind of child abuser. Did you hear about that?"

Hannah bit back the remark that burned on the tip of her tongue. Once again Paul had managed to make this about him. What would people think of *him*? How would this inconvenient delay in Josh's recovery affect *him*?

"Yes, I heard. Ellen North called."

"Sure," Paul sneered. "She can't manage to stop it from happening, but she can handle calling around to dispense the bad news. You know, it really pisses me off that the county attorney isn't handling this himself. What is it with him? We're not important enough for him to bother with? Have we finally stumbled onto someone who doesn't worship the great Dr. Garrison as a goddess?"

"Stop right there, Paul. Just drop it," she said sharply. "You're here to see the children. We're going to be a family tonight. I don't care what it takes, we're going to at least pretend we haven't grown to hate each other. No sniping. No snide remarks. No poor put-upon Paul.

"Do you understand me? Have I made that clear enough? We're going to be a family tonight," she declared. "Now, pick up your daughter and pay some attention to her while I go get Josh."

She turned away from him and her heart stopped. Josh stood at the foot of the steps. Face scrubbed, hair damp, blue eyes wide and somber, backpack clutched to his chest.

Lily let out another wail. Paul abandoned her, turning toward his son instead, a brittle grin stretching across his face like a crack in a plaster wall.

"Hey, Josh. How ya doin', slugger?"

As Paul descended the steps, Josh backpedaled. Hannah watched them, frozen at the kitchen counter. Lily's plaintive squalling stabbed into her brain like an ice pick, but she couldn't bring herself to tend to her daughter. Her gaze was riveted on the scene before her.

"I've missed you, son," Paul said in a wheedling voice. "Won't you let your ol' dad give you a hug?"

Josh shook his head, taking another step back, his arms tightening around his backpack.

"Paul, don't push it," Hannah said with gentle desperation. For all the good it would do. Already she knew he wouldn't listen, that he would try too hard and ruin his chance and whatever fragile hope she had held for a normal family evening.

He moved toward Josh, bending over, reaching out. "Josh, come here."

"No."

"Josh, please—"

"No."

"Dammit, Josh, I'm your father! Come here!"

He lunged for Josh's arm. Josh twisted out of reach, dropped to the floor, and scooted inside his furniture fort, dragging his backpack with him. Hannah launched herself into the family room, grabbing Paul's arm, holding him back from pursuit. He looked at her, his face a contorted mask of hurt and disbelief.

"He's my son," he said in a tortured whisper. "Why is he doing this to me?"

Hannah closed her eyes and put her head on his shoulder, hugging him because it had once been a natural thing to do, apologizing for reasons she didn't fully understand. In the background Lily cried as if her world had come to an end, and Hannah wondered in that moment if it hadn't.

But the moment passed and the doorbell rang, and she pulled herself away from the man who had been her husband. She felt Josh's eyes on her as she crossed the family room, watching her from under the cover of his couch-cushion roof.

Mitch stood on the front step looking tired and apologetic. His brows drew together as he met her gaze, and Hannah could only assume that she looked like hell.

"Hannah? Honey, what's wrong? Has something happened?"

She forced what would have to pass for a smile. "Oh, it's just another fun-filled evening at the Kirkwood house. What can I do for you, Mitch?"

"I'm looking for Paul. Is he around?"

"What now?" Paul loomed up behind Hannah, bracing a hand against the door frame, silently barring Mitch's entry. "Have you decided to take up Costello's cause?"

Mitch let the shot bounce off. "We need to have a little talk. Would you mind coming down to my office?"

"Now? Yes, I'd mind that very much. If you have something to say to me, say it here."

Mitch looked from Paul to Hannah and back. "All right. It's about Dennis Enberg. I need to know what you were doing in his office Wednesday night and whether he was dead or alive when you got there."

"The clerk at the Blooming Bud says it was a mail order," Wilhelm said, flipping through his pocket notepad. "No name, no return address, just an order for a dozen red roses, instructions for the note card to be included, and cash—including a tip for the delivery person."

"And the clerk didn't think that was strange?" Cameron asked.

"She thought it was romantic. A secret admirer."

"So did I," Phoebe admitted in a tiny voice. She gave Ellen a guilty glance. "I thought they were from—Well, you know Jay Butler Brooks sends out very strong sexual vibes, and your horoscope is predicting a magnetism thing, and . . ."

She trailed off, Wilhelm looking at her as if she had just hopped off the spaceship.

"It's not your fault, Phoebe," Ellen said. "You didn't

do anything wrong. What I want to know is when that son of a bitch was in my office."

No stranger could have wandered in during the day without drawing notice, which meant he had somehow managed to slip in during the night. So much for Rudy's argument that they didn't need better security. The idea that it might have been days ago somehow disturbed her. It added to the sense of vulnerability, suggested a certain omnipotence in their adversary. He could reach out and touch whoever he wanted, whenever he wanted, wherever they were.

"Have you noticed anything missing?" Wilhelm asked.

"No."

"He could have been looking for files about the case."

"I keep my notes with me. Obviously, we don't keep any physical evidence here. Anything left in these offices regarding the case, Wright's attorney has legal access to. What would be the point in stealing it?"

She shook her head. "It's just another part of the game. Another taunt."

Wilhelm slipped his notepad into his shirt pocket and zipped his parka. "We'll see what we can find. We've bagged the card and the note. The fingerprint guys should be done in an hour or so."

Leaving their grimy black dust behind, marking every surface, making sure Ellen wouldn't forget anytime soon that her sanctuary had been invaded.

"So now you're going to try to blame me for Enberg's killing himself?" Paul ranted in the dining room. "Or do you think maybe *I* killed him for no earthly reason?"

Mitch jammed his hands at the waist of his trousers. "I'm not saying either of those things, Paul. If you'd spare the histrionics for five minutes, we could get this over with."

"You come into my house, accuse me of God-knows-what— I think I have a right to be upset!"

"Fine, but you know your children are in the next room, Paul. Do you have the right to upset and frighten them, too? Is that what you want? Haven't they been through enough?"

"Haven't we all?"

"Two clerks at the Donut Hut both say they saw a Celica that matches yours to a T."

Paul looked dumbstruck. "Doughnut helpers. Doughnut people come forward days after the fact and you beat a path to my door."

"They've been out of town." Mitch advanced, forefinger drawn to thrust at Paul. "We just located them this afternoon. They saw what they saw. I don't care if they sell doughnuts or donkey dicks. They both saw a car at the side lot of Enberg's office that sounds remarkably like yours. Now, I'm asking you nice here, Paul. I'm giving you a chance to tell me your side. Quit jerking me around before you piss me off and I haul your ass down to the station.

"Start talking, Paul," Mitch ordered. "And don't try to tell me you weren't there if you were. The fingerprints will be back Monday."

Paul slumped down onto the chair at the head of the table. "I went to see him . . . on a personal matter. He was drunk. I left."

"You went to consult the lawyer who had once represented the man who stole your son. Interesting choice of attorneys."

"He was my attorney first."

And now that attorney was dead.

Hannah heard it all as she stood in the hallway, and hours later, with the clock ticking off the minutes to midnight, she still felt wrung out. She wished there was something mundane to occupy her, but the ruined dinner had been disposed of, the remnants of the frozen pizza thrown out. Lily's toys were in the trunk, Josh's videos neatly stacked.

The children were tucked in bed. Lily had gone down with a fight, overtired and out of sorts. Hannah tiptoed into her room. The night-light cast a soft pink glow that just touched her daughter's face. She was sleeping hard, sweat dampening her golden curls, a frown furrowing her little brow.

What impact would all this have on her? Hannah wondered. She was just a baby. Would she remember any of it? Would all of it linger in the dim reaches of her memory, haunting her forever?

Josh was out, too, sleeping flat on his back, utterly still. He had always been as active in his sleep as he was awake, kicking off his covers, sleeping in all known positions all over the bed, dragging stuffed animals with him, dropping them off the top bunk to the floor between bedtime and morning. Since his return he had slept only on the lower bunk with just a favorite old stuffed monkey snuggled next to him.

Hannah slipped into his room and sat down on the floor at the foot of the bed, where she could watch him sleep, where she could be near him physically if in no other way. She had spent so much time in this room when he had been gone because it helped her feel spiritually closer to him, and now that he was home, she felt a distance between them that couldn't be bridged.

She wanted to gather him close and by the will of her love alone drive out the darkness that had settled over him like soot. But she only sat there, feeling helpless and alone. For someone who had always taken charge of her life, it was like being cast adrift in the ocean.

She thought of all the other times she had done this— sat with him in the dark, watching over him, dreaming for him. Before he was born, when the discomfort of pregnancy had kept her awake, she had spent long quiet hours in the night sitting, her hand on her belly, thinking of the future. How she would love him, teach him, protect him. What a sweet young man he would grow to be, with her sense of duty and Paul's sensitivity, and a solid foundation of love and stability.

She looked around the room, cataloguing the familiar. A friend had painted murals depicting different sports on each wall. The small desk between the windows was stacked with books and action figures and the photo albums she had brought in here when Josh was missing, as if concentrating on the memories of the happy times might conjure him up like a spirit from another dimension.

His backpack leaned against the nightstand, flap rolled back so it could accommodate his new Think Pad along with everything else he had packed inside. Hannah inched toward it, one eye on Josh. She wouldn't touch it, wouldn't give in to the overwhelming desire to see what he had put into the notebook she had given him. She had promised it was his, that he wouldn't have to share it with anyone until he was ready. All she wanted was to peek into the bag, to see if she could get some idea of what he had been carrying with him. Maybe if she knew what he carried with him to feel secure, she could do something to give him that security, give him some kind of assurance.

The illumination from the night-light was too faint to see well. She shifted onto her knees and tilted her head to a better angle, but all she could make out was the Think Pad and pen, one of the walkie-talkies he had got for Christmas, and a scrap of bright knit fabric tucked behind it. A stocking cap or mitten the blaze-orange of a hunter's garb.

Odd. There hadn't been any gear like that in the house since Paul had come out of his manly-hunter phase two years ago. They had got rid of all the equipment and clothing at a rummage sale to benefit the conservation club. But Josh was carrying a piece around with him. Carrying it as if it were a long-treasured possession he couldn't bear to do without.

The peculiarity of it jarred her. She had taken pains to make everything in the house seem as normal, as familiar, to Josh as possible. Then to find something out of time, out of place . . . She sneaked another peek at Josh. He sighed in his sleep and turned his face away from her.

Ignoring her conscience, she reached for the backpack. It could be important that she know . . . It could break Josh's trust in her if he woke up and saw her.

If she could just tip it, get a better look . . .

The walkie-talkie shifted. Josh stirred, mumbled, turned onto his side, curling into a fetal position beneath the covers. Hannah held her breath and counted to ten, then pulled the bag a little closer to the night-light.

The rib pattern of the knit came into focus, and a wedge of a patch that had been sewn in place—an insignia of some sort, a brand name or a club name arching over the silhouette of a deer. She could make out only some of the letters: P I O N.

Campion.

Fear snaked through her, coiling in her throat, squeezing her heart. *Campion.*

"Oh, my God."

Her mind formed the words, but she didn't know if she spoke them aloud. With a shaking hand, she reached into the pack and caught hold of the fabric between her fingers. A stocking cap. Small and nubby with wear. She pulled it from the bag while revulsion roiled inside of her. The shaking traveled up her arms, into her chest, until her whole body was jerking, as if giant unseen hands had her by the shoulders. She wanted to drop the cap, to throw it out of the house as if it were a carcass crawling with maggots. Instead, she held it to the light and read the patch.

Campion Sportsmen.

She twisted the cap inside out.

Printed in block letters on the laundry tag was a single name.

DUSTIN.

JOURNAL ENTRY
FRIDAY, JANUARY 28, 1994

We have thought out a cunningly conceived plot.
Deep and dark.
Black and brilliant.
They cannot outmaneuver us.
Because their minds are so small.
We despise them.

CHAPTER 23

Josh sat, body drawn into a tight ball, arms wrapped tight around his knees, back pressed up against a corner post of his bed. He kept his head down, peeking up only occasionally. There were too many people in his room. He didn't want any of them to be there. His room was *his* space, not theirs. His things were *his* things; he didn't want them touched by outsiders.

His mom stood near the door, crying. Josh hated that. He hated hearing her cry and he hated knowing that it was all his fault. He had hardly ever seen his mom cry or get hysterical like other kids' moms sometimes did—until lately. Since Dad had started getting more angry and they fought all the time. But she cried only in private then. This was different. This was because of him.

She never should have gone into his backpack. He never thought she would. Mom was big on respecting people's privacy. It hurt him that she had looked. It hurt him more that he couldn't answer her questions. He couldn't tell her about the Taker, or bad things would happen. Worse things than what were already happening. The idea scared him so much he wanted to cry himself, but he didn't dare do that either.

"Josh? Can you tell us anything at all about how that stocking cap got into your backpack?"

Chief Holt sat on the edge of the bed, looking at him

with a really serious face. Josh glanced up at him; then his gaze darted to the humongous police officer standing by the dresser. Handcuffs glinted on his thick black belt. Maybe the cops would arrest him and throw him in jail. Maybe they thought that other kid was a Goner because of him. Fear lumped in his throat and he tried to swallow it down.

"Have you ever seen this boy, Josh?" The other cop in regular clothes held out a flyer with a picture of the Goner. Josh put his hands over his face and peeked out through the narrow cracks between his fingers. This cop looked kind of like Tom Hanks, only he didn't seem like he would be funny at all. He looked impatient.

"Did someone give you the hat, Josh?"

"Did you find it someplace?"

"It's really important for you to tell us."

"You could save that little boy's life."

They didn't understand. They didn't know about the Taker or what it was like to be a Goner. There were so many things they didn't know about at all. Josh squeezed his eyes shut tight. In his mind he opened the door to his secret place and went inside, where no one could touch him or frighten him or ask him questions he had been told not to answer.

Wilhelm turned away from the bed, flapping his arms at his sides in frustration. Mitch rose slowly, as worn out as an old, old man.

"Isn't there *something* we can do?" Wilhelm whispered urgently. "Hypnosis? Sodium pentothal?"

"Yeah, Marty," Mitch muttered. "I'm certain it's okay to drug small children in order to coerce answers out of them."

He turned to Hannah. She was shaking, and her eyes were red-rimmed and wild. It would not have surprised him at all to have her fall apart, but she held herself together, toughing it out when she had to have precious little strength left. She pushed past him and went to Josh, pulling him into her arms and rocking him, probably as much to comfort herself as to comfort her son.

At least they had managed to keep the press away, Mitch thought. For now. Because Hannah had called him at home, he had been able to order radio silence and gather his people through less trackable means. It wouldn't last, of course. By the time they left the house, there would probably be reporters camped on the lawn. But for the moment that burden was off.

Another burden absent was Paul. No one had called him. He would have argued that he had a right to be there, and he probably did, but he was a complication no one needed. Especially not Hannah, and especially not after his performance earlier in the evening. She needed an emotional anchor, someone to calm her, and to that end they had called Father Tom. He stood in the bedroom doorway looking like a vagrant—unshaven, his brown hair sticking up in spots.

"If you've got any clout with the Man Upstairs, Father, we could use a break here," Mitch said.

"If I had any clout, we wouldn't be here." His gaze on Hannah and Josh, he crossed the small bedroom and bent down to touch Hannah's shoulder and murmur something in her ear.

"What do you think?" Ellen North asked, backing into the hall.

Mitch followed her. He could feel Wilhelm at his heels and wished Megan were here instead.

"Hannah says Josh hasn't been out of her sight any waking moment since he came back. No one could have given the thing to him without her seeing. And Josh hasn't let the backpack out of *his* sight, so . . ."

"Someone came into the house in the dead of night and planted it in Josh's backpack? Without Hannah's knowing?" she said. "That seems pretty far-fetched."

"If you've got another explanation, let's hear it."

"Wright is back home just down the block," Wilhelm said.

"He'd never risk coming near this house," Mitch insisted. "But we'll need a list of everyone else who has been here in the last few days."

"The key is the boy," Wilhelm said. "He's got the answers to all our questions locked up in his head. I say we try hypnosis."

Mitch looked to Ellen. "Would anything he revealed under hypnosis be admissible in court?"

"It would be a fight. Even if we got it in, the defense would tear into it big-time. In general, the testimony of small children isn't considered very reliable. Children are highly suggestible, susceptible to having ideas planted in their minds—conscious and subconscious. But if Josh could reveal something that would put you on track to finding Dustin Holloman, or tell us who the accomplice is, or point us toward more solid evidence, that would certainly be worthwhile, whether it was admissible or not."

Mitch weighed the pros and cons. "I'll talk to Hannah about it."

"Did you find anything else in the backpack?" Ellen asked.

"It's in the dining room."

The pack lay open, the items pulled from it strewn across the cherry table like the entrails of a gutted animal. Sadness settled in Ellen's chest as she looked at the things Josh had packed, as if he were afraid he might be taken again and this time wanted pieces of his life with him. There were several small, obviously cherished toys, and a Cub Scout pocket knife. A flashlight to ward off darkness. A walkie-talkie to call home. A child-size travel toothbrush with a Teenage Mutant Ninja Turtle on the handle. A snapshot of him with his mother and baby sister at the baby's baptism—Josh in a miniature blue suit, his hair slicked into place, a proud grin on his face as he held the baby.

"Poor kid," Wilhelm mumbled, running a finger along the seam of an old grass-stained baseball.

"Like his life isn't bad enough right now," Mitch growled, "we have to come into his house and violate what little privacy he has."

Ellen stared down at a spiral notebook. *Josh's New Think Pad. To Josh From Mom.* A carefully drawn heart punctuated the sentiment. Mitch was right. It felt as if they were reaching dirty hands into Josh's childhood and soiling it forever. These things were his private possessions, pieces of his boyhood. And they would rub the glow of innocence from them and call them evidence.

She pulled a slim Cross pen from her purse and used it to lift the cover of the notebook. The action was old habit, meant to keep her fingerprints off potential evidence, but in her mind she also thought of it as prevention against tainting the book in a more intimate way. This had been a special gift from a mother to her son. No one else should have touched it, ever.

She knew what she wanted to find: the names of Josh's abductors, drawings of the place they had held him. What she found were small, strange pictures of black squares and sad faces and thin, wavy lines. On one page he had written *When I was a Goner*, and beneath the words the tiniest pinpoints of ink made eyes and a mouth. There were no admissions, no revelations, just the fractured thoughts of a damaged child.

"I don't see any point in holding this stuff," she said. "Dust what you can for prints, for all the good that'll do us."

The front door opened and closed, bringing in a gust of cold air and animosity. Sheriff Steiger's voice grated like sandpaper over asphalt.

"Where the fuck is Holt?"

"Chief's in the dining room, Sheriff."

Mitch made a sound between his teeth.

Ellen drew her coat around her. "I'm gone. Call me if you need me."

Steiger nearly bowled her over on his way into the room, his craggy face set in furious lines. Ellen dodged him, wanting no part of the jurisdictional skirmish that was about to take place. The Holloman case belonged to Park County, not City of Deer Lake. Mitch had pulled an end-around on Steiger, calling Wilhelm instead on the argument that the BCA was overseeing all the investigations. Russ Steiger wouldn't see it that way.

"Heading out, Ms. North?" Noga asked, reaching to open the door for her. The big man winced as voices barked in the dining room like the report of machine-gun fire.

Ellen shook her head. "Yep, the testosterone level in there is getting a little deep for me. Good night, Noogie."

She stepped out into the cold, digging the keys to her loaner out of her coat pocket. The Manley Vanloon Pace Car, she called it. Never one to miss an opportunity to capitalize, Manley had given her a great, big rolling advertisement: an enormous white Cadillac with painted flames arching back from the tires. The front doors were emblazoned with the slogan "Vanloon Motors: Steal a Hot Deal from 'Crazy' Vanloon." The embarrassment was almost enough to turn her into a pedestrian.

In her peripheral vision she could see someone had blocked the Cadillac in the driveway. She stopped in her tracks when she saw who it was.

"Another long night, counselor," Brooks said, easing out of the Cherokee. "Another long *cold* night. I'll say this for your weather—it's sure as hell conducive to long nights warming the sheets with a partner. Never thought I'd look at sex as a survivalist tactic. Does that take the fun out of it?"

"I wouldn't know." Ellen marched to the Cadillac.

"We could find out," he drawled. The hood of his parka framed his face, giving Ellen the impression of a wolf staring at her from inside its lair. His interest in her was self-serving, an idea that was degrading enough when applied to her professional capacity. That he would use her sexually as well touched every red button she had.

"I'd sooner die of hypothermia, but I'd rather not do it here, so will you kindly get your truck the hell out of my way?"

He leaned back in surprise, as if her verbal punch had hit him squarely in the mouth.

"What are you doing here, anyway?" she demanded. "You didn't pick this up on any scanner."

"I followed Steiger. We were having a drink down at the Blue Goose."

"How cozy. If you want to get into bed with somebody, I hear he's not averse to getting screwed for a little information."

"He's not my type, thanks."

"Well, I've got news for you, Brooks. Neither am I. Did your friend Costello tell you differently?"

"Costello? What the hell does he have to do with us?"

"You tell me. No." She held up a hand to forestall the answer. "I've been lied to and manipulated enough lately."

"I haven't lied to you."

"Semantics. You haven't told me the truth, not that I give a damn what you do. Move the truck. I'm going home."

She slid behind the wheel of the Cadillac and slammed the door shut, hoping she would catch some of his fingers. But he went back to his truck unmaimed and backed it out into the street. Headlights coming from the south heralded the arrival of the first media scavengers. In a matter of moments the street would be clogged with them. The noise would wake the neighbors. They would come out on their steps to investigate and watch for glimpses of themselves on the morning television news.

The windows in the Wright house were dark. Was he sleeping, oblivious to the latest turmoil, or was he sitting in the dark, smiling?

"You'll make a mistake eventually," Ellen murmured. "All I have to do is get you to trial."

As she turned the corner onto her street, the headlights behind her followed. Brooks. Visions of vehicular homicide flashed through her head. She could nail Brooks and destroy this god-awful car in one stroke. She was tired, depressed, disillusioned—the perfect time for a confrontation.

Get it over and done with. Get him out of your life before you can screw up again.

She said nothing as she let him in. Harry trotted into the kitchen to greet them, took one look at her face, and beat it back to the bedroom.

"Don't take your coat off, you won't be staying," Ellen said, shrugging out of hers.

"Do I get to hear the charges against me, or are we skipping straight to sentencing?"

He leaned back against the wall, at ease, as if it would make no difference what she accused him of. He likely didn't care, she thought. He'd made his purpose clear up front. It wasn't as if he hadn't warned her. She was the one who had fooled herself, fooled herself into thinking she wouldn't make the same mistake twice, fooled herself into believing she was too smart, too savvy—the same way she had with Costello.

"You went to Purdue on a baseball scholarship," she began, reciting the information she had confirmed in the *Newsweek* article.

"That's not considered a crime in most states, even if I couldn't hit a high inside fastball."

Ellen ignored his attempt at humor. "You stayed on at Purdue Law."

"Much to the dismay of my family. They could hardly show their faces at the Auburn alumni functions."

"Tony Costello went to school at Purdue."

He didn't so much as blink. "Small world, isn't it?"

"You show up in town with an interest in this case. Then suddenly Wright fires his attorney and brings in Costello, an attorney he can't possibly afford on a professor's salary."

His eyes widened then, the amusement in them stoking the fires of Ellen's temper.

"Are you implying *I* brought Costello in?" he asked. "To what end?"

"You came here for a story. Maybe you had a particular ending in mind. Maybe you get off on manipulating people. Maybe you're no better than Wright, and it's all a game to you."

"Well, aren't I the criminal mastermind!"

Ellen glared at him, advancing on him, her body rigid with rage. "Don't you dare be amused at me. I don't give a shit what your game is. All you need to know is I'm not playing anymore. No more view inside the prosecutor's office. Take that to Bill Glendenning if you want, but I don't think he'll be quite so starstruck after he considers the ramifications of involving you in this. He wants to run for governor. People in Minnesota won't take kindly to the idea that he traded a child's justice to bask in the glow of a dubious celebrity."

Brooks winced. "Ouch. That's a mean tongue you got there, sugar. You ought to have it registered as a dangerous weapon."

His gaze drifted to her mouth, and she realized that this time *she* was the one who had stepped too close. If he straightened away from the wall, they would be touching. But she refused to back away.

"What would you say if I told you I don't know Costello from a sack of pig feed?" he asked.

"I'd say I have no reason to believe anything you tell me."

"Hmm . . . We're having a little problem with trust here, Ellen."

"You can't have trouble with something that doesn't exist," she said. "I don't trust you, and I sure as hell don't trust Costello."

Curiosity sharpened his gaze. "And why is that? What'd he ever do to win your animosity?"

"He's a shark. He'll do whatever he has to do to win a case or anything else he happens to want."

"And did he want you?" he asked. "Is that what this is really all about, Ellen? Costello fucked you over figuratively *and* literally—"

"Get out of my house," she ordered. "I've said what I had to say. You know where the door is. Find it. Use it."

He caught her by the arm as she started to turn away. In one dizzying move Ellen found her back to the wall and Brooks leaning in on her, his face inches from hers.

"I don't think so, counselor," he said. "Not until I've had a chance to defend myself."

"This isn't a trial. You don't have any rights here. I don't have to listen to you. I don't have to deal with you."

"You damn well *will* listen to me," he growled. "I've been accused of a lot of things in my life. Hell, I've been guilty of most of them. But I don't know Costello more than to nod and say hello. I met him once at an alumni dinner. He tried to sell me on doing a book about a case he was involved with. I declined. I have no interest in making Anthony Costello's career for him. I didn't come here looking to renew the acquaintance, and I sure as hell didn't bring him in."

"And you want me to believe it's just a coincidence you're both here?"

"Believe what you want. I've had my say. I came here to watch this thing unfold; to get a story, not make one."

"Well, you're getting your money's worth, aren't you?" Ellen whispered bitterly.

"And then some."

He held her gaze with his, his expression taut, intense. *Dangerous*. The word came back to her again and again when she thought of him. He was a threat. Professionally. Sexually.

"You're a story all by yourself, Ellen." He brought one hand down from the wall beside her head and traced his thumb across her chin and down the column of her throat. "I want to know more about you. I want to know everything. Hell, I just plain want you."

The admission triggered an automatic quickening in her body, one that brought a flash of embarrassment and shame. Nothing had changed. She still didn't trust him. He had nothing to gain by admitting collusion with Costello, plenty to lose. He had everything to gain by seducing her.

"I'd take you right here, right now," he whispered, settling his thumb in the V of her collarbone, his fingertips subtly kneading the tender area just above her breast. "If you'd let me."

She found her voice with great difficulty. The words came out thready. "I won't."

"No." The look that came into his eyes was weary. "No. You're too smart, too careful, too neat and tidy. No room on the agenda for a wild card like me. I'm not some instant fire you can turn on and off with a switch. You get too close to me, you might end up getting burned. God forbid you should take a chance, make a mistake."

"This isn't about just me."

"Isn't it? If it weren't for this case, would we be in your bed right now?" he asked, his mouth too close to hers, his eyes too blue. "Would I be inside you right now, Ellen?"

Her mouth had gone dry. "If it weren't for this case, you wouldn't be here."

That was the bottom line. She drew it unerringly. He couldn't argue. The truthfulness of it did nothing to assuage the ache of desire inside him. The foolishness of wanting this particular woman did nothing to change the fact that he did. It wasn't just sex; sex could be easily had. Women had always come willingly to his bed. But that wasn't his need. His need was for *this* woman, who was all the things he had never been—dedicated, good, the champion for justice sacrificing her own needs in her duty to others. He had spent his whole life shrugging off obligation, pursuing his own ends, justifying all means. He could put whatever face on it he liked, but in the end he was exactly what she had called him from the start—a mercenary, and a damn good one, worth millions. That it had ultimately cost him his family, his soul, was not self-sacrifice, but irony.

"No," he said at last. "But I'm here now. Will you try to redeem me, Ellen?"

Would there be any point in trying? She didn't ask, afraid of what his answer might be. The look that had come into his face was a little stark, a little haunted, as if he were afraid of the answer himself. The look touched her in a way she couldn't afford to allow. Not now. Not when so much was riding on her shoulders. And after the trial was over, he would be gone, mission accomplished, on to someone else's tragedy.

"If you want redemption, talk to a priest," she said quietly. "You're not my responsibility, and I'm not fool enough to think you should be."

"No. You're nobody's fool." He backed away from her and turned to the cherry hutch where she kept her meager supply of liquor. He helped himself to two fingers of Scotch, tossing it back in a single shot. "And I'm nobody's front man. I came here for my own reasons. I came here looking for answers."

She had the distinct feeling that the questions had little to do with Josh Kirkwood or Garrett Wright. That perhaps they were far more personal than professional. "And are you finding them?"

He smiled sadly as he twisted the cap back onto the bottle of Glenlivet. "No. The questions only get harder. Joke's on me."

She followed him to the door, wrestling with the need to ask for the truth and the wisdom of letting it go. In the end she said nothing, and he seemed to know why better than she did.

"You're right. Stick to the straight and narrow, counselor," he said. "You're better off. I'm no good for anybody. That's a known fact."

He leaned down and kissed her good night, a tender kiss that tasted of longing and Scotch, and walked out into the night.

The streets of Deer Lake were absent of life. Even stray dogs had more sense than to be out roaming in the middle of the night when the temperature was dipping to minus twenty and the windchill factor was doubly cold. A night for fools and cops. The patrols stayed on the roads to rescue the idiots who ran into ditches. The detectives came out for the latest clue in the ever-twisting case.

Jay sat at the corner of Lakeshore Drive with the motor running, debating a return to the Kirkwood house. But the press had descended, and he knew that any opportunity he might have had to catch a fresh insight was gone. He found he had no hunger for it now, at any rate. The adrenaline rush that had come with the call to Steiger at the Blue Goose was spent. All he felt now was a restlessness and an emptiness that would make him avoid going to the house on Ryan's Bay.

He drove away from Lakeside, took a right on Oslo, and headed to Dinkytown, where the businesses looked abandoned, the buildings decayed. A night clerk stared out the window of a garishly lit convenience store, an oasis beckoning no one.

Lights still glowed in a few dorm windows on the Harris campus, but the class buildings stood dark. Even in the dead of night, Harris College gave the impression of tradition and money. The buildings were solid, substantial, erected in an era when college meant more than a means to higher earning. The grounds were parklike, studded with tall hardwood and pine trees.

Garrett Wright claimed he had been working here in Cray Hall the night Josh had been taken, as did Christopher Priest. If they were partners in this madness, then why would they not have given each other alibis? It could have been part of the game, Jay supposed. It could have been a small bit of truth to help Priest fool the polygraph.

Curiouser and curiouser, this case, he thought as he left the campus the back way, driving slowly south on Old Cedar Road. The secrets and sins that lay beneath the surface of seemingly ordinary lives had always fascinated him. The things no one suspected were going on behind facades of normalcy in picture-book settings like Deer Lake.

Jay let the Cherokee roll to a stop in the middle of the deserted road, lit his last cigarette, and sat staring out the passenger window. A chunk of moon glowed down on the winterscape, giving the snow a silver cast, turning the bare trees to silhouettes of black against a starry sky of midnight blue. The land that ran west of the college was farmland and woodland, rolling hills and fields where stubbled cornstalks poked up through occasional thin spots in the snow. A setting of apparent peace.

Running south, the road eventually skirted the eastern edge of Ryan's Bay, where Josh's jacket had been found nine days ago. According to Agent O'Malley's theory, this was where the game had been put in motion, along this strip of lonely county road. It was here that the car accident had taken place, the accident that had kept Hannah Garrison late at the hospital. Christopher Priest had sent a student on an errand. The student had taken the back way off campus, as students often did. His car had hit an unexpected—and, O'Malley speculated, a *manufactured*—patch of ice that sent him into the path of an oncoming vehicle. The elderly female driver of the other car had been killed instantly; a passenger in her car had died of a heart attack upon arrival at Deer Lake Community Hospital. Two other passengers had been transported by helicopter to Hennepin County Medical Center in Minneapolis, where the student now lay in critical condition, having developed a bacterial infection that was threatening to take his life.

So many lives touched or taken by this game. And if O'Malley was right, it had started here, in this quiet, pretty spot on the far edge of town. Like a stone dropped into the lake, the effects had rippled outward in ever-widening circles.

Cause and effect. The chain reaction of events. He wondered how much the master of this game had foreseen, how much he had known going in and how much had been twisted serendipity. He couldn't have known that Ellen North would get the case, or that the story would have been seized on by a writer from Eudora, Alabama, as an escape and an act of self-examination. Yet he had chosen an attorney who had ties, however oblique, to them both—Anthony Costello.

The sense of being watched by brilliant dark eyes from a darker dimension sent a current of uneasiness down his spine.

He was no longer an observer, but a player. Another one caught in the web of this crime.

"It's your job—going from one set of victims to another. Does it get to you, or are you immune?"

"Not immune; careful. I keep my distance. Don't let it get personal."

Liar.

A chill tightened his shoulders, and he reached to turn up the heater only to find it cranked to high already. Damn cold place. And here he sat like a damn fool in a truck in the middle of nowhere. He would sure as hell rather have been in bed . . . with Ellen, who thought he was not only involved in this case, but playing some sinister role. Ellen, who didn't trust or respect him. Who shouldered the weight of winning justice for a child, for a family, for a cop, for a town.

"You're just a regular damn prince, Brooks," he muttered.

He reached for another cigarette, finding the pack empty. Putting off the inevitable reality of a sleepless night and more introspection, he swung the Cherokee around and headed back through the Harris campus, taking the shortest route to the Tom Thumb. The clerk, a thick-bodied kid with volcanic patches of acne pebbling his red face, sold him a carton of Marlboros and made the usual tired, obligatory comment about the cold. Fresh out of small talk, Jay grunted an answer and pushed out the door.

A lone car rolling south held him up at the edge of the Tom Thumb lot. Directly across the street squatted the Pack Rat secondhand shop where Todd Childs worked part-time when he wasn't concocting alibis for his mentor. No one had seen him since before Ellen's car had been vandalized. Rumor had him stashed in a Twin Cities hotel courtesy of the Costello team, who had leaked the information about his pending testimony. But it seemed just as possible that Childs was tucked away in a farmhouse somewhere, guarding Dustin Holloman and carrying out the legwork of Wright's demented scheme while Wright himself sat at home playing innocent.

Jay eased the truck out into the street, angling across the northbound lane, something about the Pack Rat holding his attention. A reflection in the window. An odd glow coming from within. Light. A faint glow, like the beam of a flashlight.

Odd time of day to be browsing for bargains in a junk shop.

He turned the corner and doubled back down the alley, cutting the engine and the headlights on the truck as he rolled up behind the store. The security light was out, if there had ever been one, but enough illumination leached over the roof from the streetlight on the corner to set the scene. A set of crumbling concrete steps with a bent pipe railing led to the only back door. A Dumpster sat to one side of the steps. At the foot of the steps waited a dirty gray Crown Victoria from the late eighties. It sat, engine running, exhaust billowing from the tailpipe—ready for an escape that was now blocked by the Cherokee.

Who the hell robbed a secondhand shop? What was there to steal? There probably wasn't anything in the store worth more than ten bucks, and Jay couldn't imagine that there would be a lot of money in the till. Maybe the place had a safe. Employees would know. Like Todd Childs. Or maybe Childs had left something crucial in the building, something he couldn't risk coming back for in the light of day.

Jay called 911 on his cellular phone and reported a break-in in progress, then let himself out of the truck, pocketing the keys, careful not to let the door slam. Precious minutes would tick by before a patrol car could arrive. The perpetrator wouldn't escape by car, but if he

could get out of the building, he could still run. If it was
Childs, and if Childs was Wright's accomplice, this was
the chance to nail him and possibly bring the case to a
close.

*And if you catch yourself a suspect, just think of the publicity
angle*, he thought sarcastically. That would be Ellen's first
reaction—not that he had found some scrap of nobility
within and helped them catch the bad guy, but that he
wanted to help himself. Not that it should have mattered
to him what she thought.

He made his way toward the building, the snow
squeaking beneath his feet. He hoped that the rumble of
the car's engine masked it, or that the midnight visitor was
too intent on his task to hear. His lungs holding on to his
breath, he eased up one step and then another.

The door burst open as Jay reached for it, hitting him
hard, knocking him back and off balance. A black-clad figure followed, rushing him, swinging something short and
black. It caught Jay on the side of the head and shorted out
all thought. He felt himself falling backward, off the steps,
arms flailing, colors bursting and swirling inside his head.
He hit the rutted ice pack of the parking area hard.

He fought for orientation, struggled to discern up
from down. A car door thumped shut and an engine
roared. He managed to turn himself onto his hands and
knees as the Crown Vic's headlights blazed on, blinding
him. The car roared, tires whining on the ice as it rocketed
backward. The sickening crunch of metal on metal told
Jay the Cherokee wouldn't be spared any more than he had
been. Then there was no time to think of anything as the
car lurched forward, charging him.

He lunged sideways, his feet slipping out from under
him, his left elbow cracking hard on the cement steps. He
caught hold of the steel-pipe post that thrust up crookedly
from the top step and heaved himself up. The bumper of

the Crown Victoria followed just behind, the metal grating over the concrete of the second step.

Engine and tires screaming, the car rocked backward once again, once again smashing into the Cherokee, pushing its nose sideways and opening enough space in the alley for the car to turn north.

The son of a bitch was going to run. If the cops didn't show in the next ten seconds, he would be gone.

Rage pushed Jay off the steps. He staggered drunkenly toward the mangled Cherokee, trying to run and struggling to keep himself upright. The passenger door was jammed shut, punched in like a second-rate boxer's face. He lost seconds as he stumbled around to the driver's side. The Crown Vic inched forward, toward the street and freedom, its back end sliding sideways as the tires spun to gain purchase on the slick surface.

Spewing curses, Jay stabbed the key at the ignition again and again, his vision blurred and swirling, doubling, tripling. Hit the bull's-eye. Cranked it over. The engine roared to life, a belt inside it screaming like a banshee at the wounds that had been inflicted. He threw the transmission in gear and stepped on the gas. The four-wheel drive grabbed hold and the truck shot forward, rearending the car but at the same time giving it the push it needed to reach the plowed street.

The car lunged west down the residential side street. Jay turned the Cherokee out of the alley, the wheel seeming to spin too far, too easily. The truck rocked sideways, then straightened, and he stomped on the gas. The brake lights of the Crown Vic flashed two blocks down as it turned south. Taking the same turn, the Cherokee sideswiped a station wagon, careened across the street, and nicked the front end of a Honda, the sound of glass shattering a high-pitched accompaniment to the crash of steel.

They made a right onto Mill Road. Jay spun the Cherokee's wheel hard, swinging the nose of the truck around just as the front wheels jumped the curb. The truck plowed through the deep snow on the boulevard, narrowly missed a tree, and bucked back down onto the road.

The paved road gave way to gravel. The streetlights ended, and the velvet-black of the country night enveloped them, only a wedge of moon and headlights brightening the dark. The road split between farm fields, rose and fell with the hills, then plunged down, curving into a valley dark with the winter skeletons of a thick hardwood forest.

With every turn the Cherokee's steering loosened more. With every curve and dip, Jay's battered brain swam wilder and wilder. Too fast, he thought. Out of control. The pop of gravel beneath the tires was like firecrackers snapping. The road was icy in patches, rutted and rough. He didn't know shit about driving in these conditions. The Crown Victoria was running away from him, putting more ground between them with every jog in the road.

It disappeared over a crest. Jay followed, foot too heavy on the gas. The Cherokee left the ground as the road dropped sharply down. There was no way to pull the truck down, to rein it in, to make the hard right-angle turn.

I'm fucked, he thought, gripping the steering wheel, bracing his body as best he could.

The truck plunged nose-first into a thicket, bounced up hard, throwing Jay around the cab like a rag doll. The headlights flashed at crazy angles as the Cherokee bucked and skidded down the slope, spraying up snow in blinding plumes, coming to a violent stop when it slammed sideways into a tree trunk.

Jay landed against the mangled passenger door, his head smacking hard against the cracked window. His mind drifted ever farther from his body, the connection between the two pulling as thin as hair. The truck's radiator hissed. The lights on the police scanner glowed red in the gloom of the cab. The radio crackled, picking up the transmission of the patrol car that had finally arrived on the scene at the Pack Rat.

The last conscious thought Jay had was *You blew it, hotshot.*

CHAPTER 24

"Tell me what you remember."

Jay closed his eyes and winced. Pain ran down his right side like a mallet playing xylophone on his ribs. Dr. Baskir, a small man with an enormous nose and a lilting Indian accent, had examined him thoroughly upon his delivery to the Deer Lake Community Hospital, addressing his various bruised and battered body parts as if each possessed self-awareness. He told the ribs they were not broken and tried to verbally placate his muscles, announcing to Jay in a whispered aside that they were likely to be "angry" for days to come. He had deftly stitched two gashes in the side of Jay's head, picking broken glass out of his hair with tweezers and muttering to the hard plates of bone in his skull.

The upshot was that he would live to tell about his adventure. The downside was that the cops would make him tell it over and over. Already he had related the details to the sheriff's deputy who had picked up the chase down Mill Road and arrived on the scene just moments after the crash. The patrolman who had taken the call to the Pack Rat had been next and another patrol officer who had been called in by the owner of one of the smashed cars on the route of the chase.

Now the unholy trinity of Steiger, Wilhelm, and Holt stood in a semicircle around the end of the emergency-room examining table. All of them looked grim and surly, adjectives that likely applied to himself as well. He sat on the table in his bloodstained, rumpled khakis, his shirt gone, cut to shreds by overzealous volunteer ambulance people. Dr. Baskir had swathed his ribs in a tight, unyielding bandage that kept him from inhaling more than a teaspoon of air at a time. His chin was split, his head felt as if someone had taken a ten-pound hammer to it, and he was fucking cold.

"I've told you twice," he said through his teeth.

"You didn't recognize the guy coming out of the store?" Holt asked.

"He was wearing a ski mask. He hit me fast and kept on running. I don't know how tall he was. I don't know what he looked like."

"You don't know shit, do you, hotshot?" Steiger snarled. The overtures to buddyhood they had made in the Blue Goose Saloon earlier in the evening were forgotten now that he had been deprived of sleep and glory.

"What did he hit you with?" Wilhelm asked.

"Some kind of club. Short. Black. Hurt like fucking hell."

Holt traded looks with the BCA man. "Sounds like what Wright used to work Megan over."

"Sounds like. But it could have been just a flashlight."

"Or some piece of junk from that rat hole," Steiger groused. "Who the fuck robs a place like that? What's the point?"

"Good question," Mitch said. "The owner says he never keeps more than fifty bucks in the place, and that goes home with him Friday nights. All his help knows that."

"Maybe they weren't after money," Ellen suggested.

She stood just inside the door, leaning against the jamb, hoping she looked relaxed instead of dead on her feet. The men made a little break in their circle, looking at her with a certain amount of annoyance. She returned the favor, in no mood for niceties. Her gaze landed on Brooks, and a sharp sliver of alarm wedged into her at the sight of him. She forced her attention to Mitch.

"If it was Childs, maybe he had something stashed there," she said. "If he's tangled up with Wright, it might be evidence."

Wilhelm yawned hugely. "We're tearing the place apart right now. There had better be something there. It's going to take forever to go through it all."

"There's no guarantee he didn't take it with him," Mitch said. "And there's a good chance 'it' doesn't have anything to do with this case."

"Any word on the car?" Ellen asked.

"Childs drives an old Peugeot," Mitch said. "We got nothing on this Crown Vic—"

"Including the tag number," Steiger complained.

"It was dirty," Jay said. "It was dark."

"Yeah, yeah . . . Why should we assume it was Childs or that this break-in has one goddamn thing to do with the kidnappings? If you ask me, it's just another big huge waste of time, taking our attention off what we ought to be doing just because Truman Capote here decided to play Dirty Harry."

Jay cocked a brow. "There's an image for you."

The sheriff gave him a look. "My men have a description of the car. If they see it, they'll stop it. That's as far as we're taking it. I'm going home."

Jay tried to sit up a little straighter, immediately regretting it. "But shouldn't you do a house-to-house or garage-to-garage or whatever you want to call it? What if this *is* your guy? What if he's the one who took the Holloman kid?"

"Do we have any reason to think it is? Do we have any reason to think it isn't just some doped-up kid looking to score a few bucks?"

"But if it was Childs—"

Steiger turned his back and headed for the door. "I'm going to bed. Nobody call me unless there's a major felony involved."

"Man," Wilhelm said to no one in particular. "When the bean counters get a load of the overtime on this gig, they're going to eat me alive."

Mitch glared at him. "Tell them to sell tickets. They'll be back in the black in no time."

"Very funny."

As the agent disappeared into the hall, Mitch looked to Ellen. "He thought I was joking?"

Shaking his head, he turned back to Jay. "Bottom line here, Mr. Brooks. You should have let us handle it. We're the cops, you're the writer," he said in an exaggerated, patronizing tone. "Remember that from here on out. We've got enough trouble without having civilians kill themselves trying to do our jobs for us. If that deputy hadn't caught sight of you, you'd be a Popsicle by now. And if there'd been anybody in those cars you hit, I'd be hauling your ass downtown. I don't give a damn who you are. As it stands, you'll be getting a hefty citation."

"I'll pay the damages," Jay muttered. Working to dredge up some humor, he cast a hopeful look at Ellen. "Maybe I can sweet-talk my way out of that ticket."

Mitch barked a laugh. "Yeah, when pigs fly. Try it here, where there's a full medical staff to put the pieces back together." He turned to Ellen. "I'm out of here. There's nothing more we can do tonight. Wait and see what Wilhelm's guys come up with—but, you know, Steiger might be right for once in his miserable, brain-atrophied life—it could be nothing. I've got to get some sleep. I'm picking Megan up from HCMC at noon."

Ellen nodded. When Mitch exited the room, she suddenly realized the folly of coming down here. What had she been thinking? She could have sent Cameron as her backup; she had already taken one call for the night. Or she could have waited until morning. Brooks hadn't offered them any revelation, no evidence, nothing but a writer's hunch that the man he had pursued had been their man.

"What do you have to say for yourself?" she demanded.

"I wish I'd taken the insurance on the rent-a-Jeep?"

She just stared at him.

"So," he said, "is this where you tell me you think I staged it all to boost interest in my book?"

"I don't think you'd go so far as to risk killing yourself. That would rather defeat the purpose, wouldn't it? Then again, the waiting room is SRO with reporters ready to tout you as a would-be hero."

Jay gave a harsh laugh that ended in a hiss of pain and eased himself down off the table, gritting his teeth. It wasn't that she didn't think him capable of concocting the whole thing as a publicity stunt, or calculating enough to capitalize on a real brush with death. But had he ever given her reason to believe otherwise? Had he ever given himself reason to believe, for that matter?

"Believe me, counselor. I'm nobody's hero. I had no intention of trying to catch the son of a bitch until he tried to kill me. *That* pissed me off."

"What were you doing there in the first place?"

"I was just riding around, contemplating the meaning of life. Ironic that I ended up damn near getting my ticket punched, isn't it?"

"Don't be a smart-ass."

"Oooh, that's a tall order, sugar. Might as well ask a cat to change his stripes."

Ellen refused to be amused. How could he make wisecracks? He could as easily have been in a body bag right now, could have been killed in any number of ways, according to his story. And the evidence bore his story out.

"Do you have any idea how long it takes to freeze to death on a night like this?" she asked.

"No, but I'd say I'm well on my way there." He opened and closed drawers in the table base in search of something to use as a shirt. "Christ, don't they have heat in this place? What do y'all do up here—freeze the germs to death?"

"Make all the jokes you want, but I personally feel that enough people have been broken or killed in this god-damn game! There's nothing funny about it!"

She turned her back to him, cursing herself mentally for letting her control slip. This wasn't the time or the place. He wasn't the man to lose it for.

She needed to hang on, tough it out. The hearing would begin Tuesday. She couldn't afford to let the pressure get to her now.

"I have to go," she whispered.

Jay watched her move toward the door, telling himself to let her go. Leave awkward enough alone. Then he reached out anyway and caught hold of her shoulder.

"Ellen, wait."

She stopped but didn't turn. Over her shoulder he could see she had closed her eyes.

"You didn't have to come down here," he said. He was glad she had; it had to be a sign of a crack in her armor, one that he might charm open to let himself in. "You were worried about me?"

"It must be the sleep deprivation."

"Must be."

He stepped around in front of her, hooked a knuckle under her chin, and lifted her face. Her skin looked too pale, accented by harsh shadows of exhaustion and etched with fine lines of strain.

"Thanks anyway," he whispered.

She let him settle his mouth against hers. It was just a kiss. Something both of them could easily walk away from, and would.

"Get some sleep," he murmured. The pirate's smile showed. "Will you dream about me?"

"Not if I have any sense left at all," she said sadly, and walked out.

Paul sat in his borrowed car at the end of Lakeshore Drive. He wouldn't dare stay long for fear some cop car would come rolling up and hassle him, and then the press would descend again. Two weeks ago he had sought out the media. Now he found himself sneaking around, driving someone else's car so he wouldn't be recognized. He was being made to feel like a criminal.

There was no one he could turn to for support. His family in St. Paul had never been anything but a burden and an embarrassment to him. He wasn't one of them—blue-collar, beer-drinking dullards. Collectively, they had the intellectual depth of a mud puddle. He had no real friends, he was finding out. The people who had called to offer their sympathy at the start of this ordeal now looked at him with a subtle reserve in their eyes. He saw it, sensed the emotional barriers they were erecting.

None of them had offered him the use of their car. None of them would have understood his sudden need for anonymity. A reporter had bartered with him for the use of this one—exclusive comments for occasional use of the dirty, nondescript sedan.

Karen was the person he wanted to go to. He had tried to call her tonight just to hear her voice as she answered the phone, but the number had been changed and the new one was unlisted. He couldn't go to the house because Garrett was there. Karen wouldn't come to him because she was frightened.

It wasn't that she didn't love him. He knew she did. He thought back to the last time they had made love, a week into the search for Josh. The day they found Josh's jacket out on Ryan's Bay. He had fought with Hannah that night. He had fought with Mitch Holt. Holt thought he should be more supportive of Hannah, that he shouldn't blame Hannah. Hannah, Hannah, Hannah. He had retaliated in his own way by going to Karen. Karen understood him. Karen loved him. Karen didn't blame him for anything.

They seldom met at her house, because the risk was too great. But he had gone there that night. She had taken him into the guest bedroom and they had made love on clean peach sheets. She did all the work of arousing him, teasing him, caressing him, riding him until he grabbed her and rolled her beneath him and fucked her until he couldn't see. She took everything he gave her and clung to him afterward.

"I wish you could stay."

"I can't."

"I know. But I wish you could." She raised her head and gazed at him. *"I wish I could give you all the love and support you need. I wish I could give you a son. . . . I'd have your baby, Paul. I think about it all the time. I think about it when I'm in your house, when I'm holding Lily. I pretend she's mine—ours. I think about it every time we're together, every time you climax inside me. I'd have your baby, Paul. I'd do anything for you."*

Of course, she couldn't do for him the thing he needed most now. She couldn't be with him, couldn't support him, couldn't take his mind off his worries—because of Garrett. It was the fault of that North bitch that Garrett Wright was out on bail. He should have stayed in jail until the trial. After the trial he would be out of the way permanently.

That part wouldn't change. It couldn't. It all had to work out for him, Paul thought. He deserved it.

CHAPTER 25

The courthouse was officially closed Saturdays, which meant that not only would they have the office to themselves, but the press would be locked out of the building. Thank heaven for small favors, Ellen thought. They had been rabid last night, descending first on the Lakeside neighborhood after the discovery of Dustin Holloman's stocking cap, and then on the hospital after Brooks's wild chase. She hadn't thought they would let her out of the hospital intact, tearing at her verbally, sending up a racket more suited for a soccer stadium than for a hospital waiting room. And waiting for her out in the cold of the parking lot like a junkyard dog was Adam Slater.

"Willing to freeze my *cojones* for a comment," he said with a grin, dancing from one battered Nike to the other.

"I have no comment." Ellen barely broke stride as she stepped around him.

"Aw, come on, Ellen," he whined. "Just a sound bite for the folks back in Grand Forks. Just a quick line about the deviant brilliance of evil."

"How about the twisted deviance of the media masquerading in the guise of public service?" she said. "I have a job to do, Mr. Slater, and I'm sick to death of having to trip over you people every time I turn around. I don't owe you a comment, and you may *not* call me Ellen."

He hadn't liked that. No comment *and* she had chased

him away from her secretary. He would no doubt make her look like the Bitch Queen of the North in the *Grand Forks Herald*. Big deal. She had been called worse things and survived. The personal opinions of reporters were the least of her worries.

She went into her office and spent an hour cleaning, wiping the fingerprint grime away and setting things back the way she wanted them, trying without success to erase the feeling of having been invaded.

How the hell had he got in here without her knowing it?

How could Dustin Holloman's stocking cap have ended up in Josh Kirkwood's backpack?

Phoebe arrived, her natural ebullience apparently still weighted down by Friday's incidents. Dark circles ringed her eyes. Even her springy mane seemed to be drooping, hanging down her back like a limp rope, bound midway by a strip of black ribbon. She dropped her black leather backpack into her chair and made a beeline to the coffee-maker.

Cameron showed last, bearing a container of chocolate-chip cookies in apology for being late.

"I swung by the law-enforcement center," he said, depositing his briefcase on the conference table and shrugging out of his ski jacket. "The stocking cap definitely belongs to Dustin Holloman. His parents identified it."

"I know. I've already spoken with Steiger."

Phoebe frowned down into her steaming mug of Irish-cream blend. "It's just too creepy that Josh had it."

"The cops are fuming," Cameron said. "They're going to look like total stooges in the press. The bad guy waltzed right past them into the Kirkwood house and planted that thing. Unbelievable."

"We're not going to look so brilliant ourselves," Ellen reminded him. "Unless he has a tunnel running beneath the Lakeside neighborhood, Garrett Wright can't be the one who planted it."

"The shell game continues." He pulled three files out of his briefcase and laid them on the table. Pointing to each, he said, "Wright's house phone, office phone, cellular phone. Let's see if we can find a winner in one of these."

None of the records showed the strange, taunting calls that had been made to Hannah, to Mitch, to Ellen. There was no unusual recurring number. They found nothing, which, to Ellen's way of thinking, was *something*. None of the records showed a call to Tony Costello's office, which meant Karen Wright hadn't called him in. And if Karen Wright hadn't called him in, then that left one obvious choice.

Ellen knew Costello was capable of ruthless selfishness. What he had done on the Fitzpatrick case had proved the point well enough. But this was a step beyond. A child was still missing. It sickened her to think he might have knowledge of the crime and the criminal and not do anything about it.

Beyond appealing to him as a human being, she had no recourse. He had technically done nothing illegal. He would make the blanket of confidentiality stretch to cover his ass. Charges of aiding and abetting would be turned inside out and jumped through like circus hoops. If she brought the issue to the attention of the press, she had no doubt he would fight dirty to discredit her.

"But what if someone else brought it up?" she mused aloud, tapping her pen against her lower lip. "What if we could get Wilhelm to turn the heat up on Costello?"

Cameron snickered, a nasty gleam coming into his eyes at the idea of duping Wilhelm into something. "Yeah, ask Marty. He'll say anything—as long as he thinks it's his idea."

"All he has to do is make some noise, talk about trying

to get a warrant for Costello's phone records. It's about time Costello had the press snapping at his heels instead of wrapped around his little finger." She turned to Phoebe. "See if you can get hold of Agent Wilhelm. Ask him to stop in later."

Phoebe nodded and slipped out of the room, a silent wraith in coffeehouse black.

Cameron arched a brow. "Is she in mourning or something?"

"Death of a budding romance. One of the lesser vultures had her in his sights. I cut him off at the knees and sent him crawling."

"Wow. What a mom you'd make, Ellen."

Ellen gave him a wry look. "Is that a proposal?"

"Observation. You're lovely, but you frighten me."

She managed a chuckle at his teasing. "Thank you, Cameron. You're the little brother I never wanted."

"Hey, my sisters all say the same thing!"

"Go figure."

He sobered then, looking at her with concern. "How are you doing after last night? Jeez, Ellen, you could have called me to go to the Kirkwoods'. After what happened here—"

"I wasn't sleeping anyway," she said. "Every time I closed my eyes, I saw that photograph of Josh."

"Maybe the lab wizards will be able to pick something up from it. Find something in the background that might give us a clue to where he was held."

The image was too clear in Ellen's mind. Josh in striped pajamas, his face as blank as the background. His skin color washed sickly white by the flash; a stark contrast to the darkness behind him. He appeared to be standing in a black void.

"Maybe," she murmured without hope.

"So is Grabko going to find anything in those medical records?"

Ellen shook her head, grateful for the change in subject. They had business to do. Better to focus on what they had to do rather than on what they couldn't change or had no control over.

"Costello's blowing smoke," she said, "hoping the press will yell fire."

"But he's planting doubt in Grabko's mind while he's at it."

"Grabko has to rule on the evidence. This ought to tip the scales in our favor." She tapped the copy of the fax with the preliminary lab analysis. "Josh's blood was on that sheet. Josh's hair was on that sheet. Garrett Wright's hair was on that sheet. That's our first concrete piece of physical evidence that ties Wright to Josh."

"Makes you wonder what the hell Wright was thinking, wrapping that sheet around O'Malley that night."

"He was thinking he would escape. He was thinking he was invincible, that even if he gave us that evidence, it wouldn't make any difference because we wouldn't have him."

It was a taunt, the same as that photograph of Josh. Had that file been in her cabinet a day or a week? When had she last opened that particular drawer?

She slid her reading glasses down her nose and peered at her colleague over the rims. "How's that brief coming? We *will* have Garrett Wright, won't we?"

He shot her a cocky grin as he pulled a document from his open briefcase. "Anthony Costello should wish his high-priced associates could write a brief this good. He doesn't have a leg to stand on when it comes to arguing this arrest away on the basis of Fourth Amendment rights."

Ellen plucked the brief from his fingers and looked it over. She felt as much confidence as she could that Grabko would rule in their favor. Cameron's arguments were dead-on, but beyond that the case was too big to throw out the arrest on a dubious technicality.

Costello had to know that as well. This was just another example of what Ellen called a "kitchen sink" defense, where the lawyer threw in everything he could find—including the proverbial kitchen sink—in the attempt to muddy the waters and cloud the issues. And to divert the energies of the prosecution. Cameron had spent hours on this brief, constructing an argument against what was essentially a bluff on Costello's part. He could have been using that precious time helping to strengthen the case against Wright.

"Did you hear the toxicology reports came back on Josh's blood?" she asked. "Traces of Triazolam, aka Halcion."

"If we can put Wright at a pharmacy filling that prescription . . ."

"We'll be too lucky for words," Ellen finished.

"Bet Todd Childs could get us some Halcion if we asked nice."

"If we could find him."

"Or someone who buys pharmaceutical goodies from him."

"We need more manpower. Our resources are spread too thin as it is without sending guys out hunting for Childs's buyers. We don't even know that he deals drugs, just that he indulges. Have you got anything from Wilhelm's guy regarding Wright's background?"

Cameron rolled his eyes. "Yeah, a lot of lame excuses. They faxed me the same information two days in a row."

"Oh, great."

"Mitch put in a request to NCIC for cases with a similar MO perpetrated in any of the areas Wright has lived since 1979, but nothing has come back yet. He requested info on unsolved murders in the same geographical areas as well."

364   TAMI HOAG

"Building a haystack to find our needle," Ellen grumbled, thumbing through the thin file folder Cameron handed across to her.

"And the thing is, of course, we don't have time for it. Even if NCIC gets back to us before the hearing, all we'd have is conjecture and supposition. There won't be any time to investigate. We won't have anything admissible."

"No, but we have to think beyond the hearing. Have you found anything on your own?"

"It's all in there, such as it is. I started at Harris and worked backward. Before coming here Wright taught briefly at the University of Virginia; before that, Penn State—where Christopher Priest also taught during the same period." He bobbed his eyebrows. "Neat coincidence, huh?"

Nerves prickled along Ellen's spine. "I don't believe in coincidence. Where did you get that information?"

He looked sheepish. "I read it in the *Pioneer Press.*"

"God," she groaned, "the press has better access to information on our suspect than we do."

"They had a head start. A lot of what they've written on Wright is coming out of old pieces they did on the Sci-Fi Cowboys a couple of years ago. I looked them all up at the library and made copies. They're in there, too."

Ellen flipped through the pages of typed notes to the clippings. One featured a photo of Christopher Priest and one of the Cowboys bent over a small robot that was supposed to scoop up balls and deposit them in a basket. Wright and three more boys stood in the background, their faces distorted by the poor quality of the copy.

"Priest sent over his list of Sci-Fi Cowboys past and present," she said. "Grudgingly, I might add."

"You think there might be something there?"

"I don't know. I think he doesn't want the scrutiny. He may talk those kids up like they're National Honor Society material, but he knows darn well any one of them could have taken a knife to my car." She stared at the article titled "Juvenile Hall Meets Hallowed Halls." "Anyway, I called a couple of people I know in the Hennepin County system to see if they might be able to help us track down some of the former members to get their take on Wright. And I got my hands on rap sheets on the present members. I want to know who we're dealing with."

"Priest could make some big noise if he thinks we're stepping over right-to-privacy boundaries," Cameron warned. "He's connected, you know. The Sci-Fi Cowboys is a popular tax-deductible contribution with some major political players."

"He's an inch away from being considered an accessory. I don't care if he's connected to the pope."

"He passed a polygraph," Cameron reminded her.

"Big deal. All that means is he's devoid of emotion when he has to be. It's not a stretch to imagine that. He could pass for an android most of the time."

She turned back to the initial typed report listing Wright's former teaching positions, tapping a finger under "Penn State." "Wright and Priest were at Penn State during the same time period. It makes sense to request the NCIC reports on unsolved kidnappings and murders in that geographical area first."

"Done."

"Good."

"But if Wright's done this kind of thing in the past," Cameron said, "he's done a bang-up job covering his tracks. I haven't found a hint of trouble in his background. He grew up in Mishawaka, Indiana. His parents split when he was eleven. Father remarried and moved to Muncie. Wright and his sister stayed with the mother, who died of a brain embolism a few years ago."

"Sister?" Ellen perked up. "Where's the sister? Have you talked to her?"

"I've got nothing on her. She's probably married

somewhere. Wright himself would be the only one to ask, and I can't see him giving us that information out of the goodness of his heart. I'd say the sister's a dead end, though she may come out of the woodwork now to star on *The Ricki Lake Show*—the siblings-of-evil-serial-criminals segment.

"Slight change of topic," Cameron said, waving a photocopy of Wright's official written alibi. "Wright states he came home for a late lunch Saturday, the twenty-second, then returned to Harris around two-thirty. They have a witness who claims to have seen Wright's Saab headed south on Lakeshore at that time.

"Now, we, of course, don't believe Wright was driving the car, because that was about the time O'Malley was attacked. But we also know Christopher Priest was in St. Peter. So who do we think was driving the Saab? Childs? The wife?"

Ellen pulled her glasses off, pushed her chair back, and stood slowly, grimacing at the tension that had settled in her back.

"We know Priest stayed in St. Peter Saturday night," she said. "Does he have anyone who can verify he was there Saturday afternoon?"

Cameron checked his notes. "He had lunch with a professor friend from Gustavus Adolphus. Time unspecified. I'll double-check."

"God, what a Gordian knot," she murmured, turning toward the window. The park across the street was empty. Downtown looked windswept and deserted. Yellow ribbons that had been tied to every light pole as a symbol of hope for the return of Josh Kirkwood now fluttered for Dustin Holloman. The posters and pleas that had been plastered to the windows of stores and restaurants had been replaced with a fresh set.

"We have only to put doubt in Grabko's mind that it was Wright behind the wheel." Cameron walked around the end of the table and settled a hip on the credenza. "All we have to do is get him bound over for trial. It's up to the cops to catch the accomplice."

"I know. I just can't shake the feeling that Costello's got a big fat rabbit to pull out of his hat."

"Childs."

A scowl knitted Ellen's brow. "Grungy weasel. I can't wait to get him on cross and nail him for the lying little shit he is. Although I have to say, I'm hoping the police find him first—up to his ears in incriminating evidence.

"No," she said. "It's not just Childs. I know Costello. He's always cocky, but there's a certain quality to this. . . . I've been over his disclosure until I've got it memorized, and I don't see any red flags, but there's still . . . something."

"You're working too hard," Cameron pointed out. "And they're working hard to make you crazy. Between vandalizing your car and that business last night, you've got good call to be jumpy. But we've got enough to hang Wright at the hearing. Costello can't change the evidence we've got." He gave her a smile. "Aren't you the one who said 'Don't let him get to you'?"

"Was that me?" She forced a laugh. "What was I thinking?"

That she knew Tony Costello, knew all his tricks, all his secrets. But now the ground had shifted beneath her feet—or Costello had pulled the rug out from under her. Again. *"Our mutual friend Mr. Brooks . . . Small world, isn't it?"* In her mind's eye his image faded into Jay's, dark eyes turning translucent blue. *"Then your leaving Minneapolis had nothing to do with the rape trial of Art Fitzpatrick? . . . I do my homework, Ellen. . . ."*

Or he had it handed to him.

She told herself it shouldn't have mattered. She knew better than to trust either of them. She knew better than to let her guard down.

Then why did you go to the hospital last night, Ellen?

She raised a hand and brushed her fingers across her lips, the memory of his kiss stirring, warm and restless inside her.

"Let's get to work," she said. "I want plenty of rope in that figurative noose."

They settled back into their chairs. Cameron pulled a cookie out of the tub and munched on it as he looked over their list of evidence.

"So, aside from the arrest itself, do you have any idea what Costello is going to challenge?"

"No," Ellen admitted. "And he'll wait till the eleventh hour to tell us, you can bet on that. Speculate, though. What do you think he'll try to get rid of?"

"The gloves. They weren't discovered for days. He'll argue they could have been planted. He'll argue they could belong to anybody, that we don't have proof they're Wright's."

"Good points. So we don't enter the gloves as evidence at the hearing. We hang on to them for trial. By that time we should be able to prove they *are* his. If we're extra lucky, the snow will be gone by then and we'll find the gun to go with the gloves. Has anything turned up as to Wright having registered a handgun in this state?"

"Nada. Big surprise. I'm checking with Virginia, Pennsylvania, Ohio, and Indiana, but maniacal serial criminals tend to think themselves above such mundane formalities."

Ellen conceded the futility of it. "He'd never be so careless as to leave a paper trail. What else?"

He shrugged. "We've got the ski mask, the bloody sheet, Mitch's testimony, Megan's testimony, Ruth Cooper's lineup ID—"

"Which happened B.C.—Before Costello."

"So? Wright had an attorney. It went down by the book. No problem. We've got a hell of a lot more than

Costello. His witness list consists of Childs, who we can turn inside out, the neighbor who saw Wright's Saab on Saturday, and Karen Wright. What's she going to say? All anyone's been able to get out of her so far is that her husband's arrest is just a big misunderstanding."

"Good question. No one has ever claimed she's an alibi witness. If Wright was at work at the times the crimes were committed, as he claims, what *can* she say?"

"That he called her on the telephone!" they said in unison.

They both grabbed the phone records again.

The door swung open and Ellen glanced up, expecting to see Phoebe, her eyes widening instead on Megan O'Malley with Mitch standing right behind her.

"Megan!" she said with genuine surprise. "It's good to see you up and around!"

"And more or less in one piece," Megan said dryly.

She looked like hell. The bruises on her face had reached the putrid-fruit stage. The crescents beneath her vibrant green eyes were the color of eggplant. She limped in, leaning heavily on one crutch. Her right hand was encased in a rigid cast that extended to the very tips of her fingers.

Cameron moved to pull a chair out for her, but she waved it off. Mitch cut her an impatient look that she completely ignored.

"Finding any goodies?" she asked, scanning the papers strewn over the table.

Ellen closed the folder and rose, blocking her view. "Just hunting for tidbits," she said casually. "You know, phone records, that kind of thing. Dry stuff. Are you all set to testify?"

Megan's mouth curved in a nearly feral smile. "I can't wait."

"We're not staying," Mitch said, catching Ellen's body language. "I just wanted to let you know I talked to Hannah about trying hypnosis with Josh. We talked to the psychiatrist and she's reluctant, but she agreed to try it."

"When?"

"Tomorrow. Four o'clock. Her office in Edina. We'll videotape the session, just in case."

"I want to be there."

"I knew you would."

"Have you found anything in Wright's background?" Megan asked. "Any connection to Priest or Childs?"

"We're looking," Ellen said. "Priest and Wright taught at Penn State during the same period. We're checking into it. As far as Childs goes, nothing. We know he went to high school in Oconomowoc, Wisconsin, and that he's willing to perjure himself. We know he's nowhere to be found at the moment. We know someone broke into the Pack Rat last night—might have been Todd, might have been anybody. Wilhelm is supposed to be there right now. The evidence techs are going over the place. Of course, we don't know what they should be looking for, so how can we expect them to find it?"

Megan scowled. "I wouldn't expect Wilhelm to find Waldo."

"The thing is," Cameron said, "it could be just another diversion. One more stunt to make Wright look innocent."

"But why target a place where Wright's phony alibi works?" Megan's gaze sharpened as the wheels of her mind began to spin. "And why pull this stunt that late at night when it was just a fluke that anyone would happen by and see?"

"So," Ellen speculated, "maybe it *was* Childs and he sneaked in because he had something stashed there—drugs, for instance—which he grabbed and ran with. In which case your BCA pals are spending a lot of manpower on nothing."

"That's the way it goes," Megan said. "Though I

wouldn't want to be in young Marty's shoes when he has to explain that to headquarters."

Phoebe came slinking back into the room. "Agent Wilhelm is on his way over."

"My cue to leave," Megan said. "If Wilhelm catches me here, he'll pop a cork and I'll end up hitting him with my crutch."

Ellen walked her and Mitch to the door of the outer office, sympathy welling inside her at Megan's hobbling gait, and at the proud tilt of her chin.

"You know about the benefit for Wright tonight?" she asked Mitch.

He nodded. "Got it covered. We'll keep an eye on Wright, see who approaches him. If Childs is there, we'll grab him."

"Good. Thanks for stopping in. Mitch, I'll see you tomorrow. Let's keep our fingers crossed that Josh can clear everything up for us. In the meantime, we keep digging."

"The key is Wright's past," Megan insisted. "I wish I could help with that hunt."

Ellen gave her an apologetic look. "You know I can't involve you, Megan. You're not the agent in charge anymore, you're a victim."

Megan's eyes blazed with a hatred Ellen could only guess at. "I know exactly what I am. And I have Garrett Wright to thank for it."

"Ellen's hands are tied, Megan. You know that," Mitch said.

He had stopped by her apartment that morning, fed her two cats, and turned the thermostat up so the place would feel more like a home than like a cold, drafty converted attic—which was essentially what it was. The third floor of a big old Victorian house on Ivy Street, it was probably the least accessible apartment in town. Two flights of stairs to climb with a bum knee and a crutch. He had to clench his jaw to keep from commenting yet again on her stubbornness.

Megan stood by the window in her pink living room, stroking the head of her little gray cat with her good hand, cradling the bad one against her. The set of her mouth was stubbornness personified.

"You're off the case, Megan," he reminded her. He stepped around a pair of boxes she had yet to unpack. Josh had been kidnapped her first day on the job here.

"Officially," she said grudgingly. "But that doesn't mean I couldn't do a little background work off the record—"

"And risk getting the case turned on appeal? You're not thinking straight. Come here," he said, turning her gently toward the old camelback sofa. "You need to sit down or that knee is going to swell up like a water balloon."

That she didn't put up a fight told him she was as near exhaustion as she looked. She eased herself down on the couch and sat quietly while he pulled a box of books over to prop up her leg.

"I just feel so damn helpless, Mitch," she admitted as he carefully tucked a pillow beneath her damaged knee. She heard the little tremor in her voice and knew he had, as well.

"I know you do, honey. I know exactly."

He had been in the same boat, hadn't he? she thought. On rougher seas than this. He had been a detective on the Miami force at the time his wife and son had been gunned down. She knew damn well he wouldn't have been allowed within a hundred yards of the investigation. And the guilt still weighed on him.

"It's so hard," she whispered, sliding her good hand over his. "We're cops. We're trained to think a certain way, to act, to go after the bad guys. To have that taken away when we need it most . . . It's hard."

Mitch settled himself on the couch beside her, draping

his right arm behind her shoulders. Friday, the black cat, hopped onto a stereo speaker box, curled his paws beneath him, and watched them across the gathering gloom of late afternoon.

"You still haven't told me what your surgeon had to say yesterday."

Megan looked away. If she stared at her cat instead of at Mitch, it would be easier to lie, and that was what she wanted to do—lie, to Mitch, to herself.

"What does he know?" she muttered.

Mitch held back a sigh. Bad news. News that hurt her and frightened her, not that she would want to admit to either, or to concede defeat.

"Yeah." He drew her over to lean against him. "It's too soon for them to know anything for sure."

"It is," she said, her voice tightening. She settled her cheek into the hollow of his shoulder, and he could feel her chin quivering. "They can't know yet."

She didn't want to hear it yet. She wasn't ready to accept it, wouldn't go down without a fight. As much as Mitch admired her courage, he knew it would only make it harder for her in the end. He already knew the prognosis. He had called her doctor, lied and told him he was Megan's brother Mick. The hospital would release information only to family, and Megan's family didn't give a rat's ass what happened to her.

The best thing the orthopedic surgeon had to say was that they hadn't had to amputate her hand. There would be more surgery and months of physical therapy, but it was unlikely she would ever regain full mobility.

Mitch would have sent Garrett Wright to the blackest pit of hell for what he'd done to Megan, to Josh, to Hannah, to Deer Lake. If he was lucky, he would get to help send him to prison. Justice and the law were seldom one and the same. He had learned that lesson the hard way a long time ago.

"We have to get him, Mitch," Megan mumbled against his chest, where her tears soaked into his flannel shirt. "He has to pay."

"He'll pay, sweetheart." Mitch wrapped his arms around her, hoping to God the promise didn't sound as hollow to Megan's ears as it did to his own.

She sniffed and raised her head, fighting to force one corner of her mouth up. "Don't call me sweetheart."

"I will if I want to," Mitch growled, gladly falling into what had already become an old joke between them. "What are you gonna do about it, O'Malley? Beat me up?"

"Yeah. With one hand in a cast."

The smile sobered. Her gaze remained locked on his. "What am I going to do, Mitch? Being a cop is all I've ever wanted."

He brushed a tear from her cheek. "But it's not all you've got, Megan. You've got me. You'll find a way around the obstacles. And I'll be there, hanging on to your good hand."

"Jeez, Holt," she whispered, leaning up to kiss him. "You ought to write that down for Hallmark."

CHAPTER 26

The music wasn't half-bad—a fusion of blues and rock with lyrics by an English major. The band was a campus group that called themselves HarriSons. The lead singer was a rangy, raw-boned kid in ripped blue jeans and a sweaty T-shirt. He hugged an old red Stratocaster guitar and squeezed his eyes shut tight beneath the brim of a dirty baseball cap as he coaxed the music out of his soul.

Jay took a long pull on his three-dollar beer and did a slow scan of the place. Wright's followers had taken over the Pla-Mor Ballroom, a dance hall located just off campus. The Pla-Mor had apparently hit its peak in the forties and had not been changed a lick since. The dance floor had been sanded dull by decades of scuffing feet. The lights were kept low to serve the dual purpose of setting a mood and hiding the fact that huge scabs of plaster had flaked off the walls.

The place was likely cheap, and it was handy and served its purpose well enough. There were enough tables and chairs for 250—all of them full. The place was SRO. It looked as if everyone in Deer Lake who believed in Wright's innocence had felt compelled to trudge out into the cold night to show their support. At five bucks a head admission, and with the jacked-up prices on the beer and setups and the Sci-Fi Cowboys' fifteen-dollar T-shirts, Wright's supporters would probably raise enough tonight to pay for a couple days' worth of Anthony Costello's time.

The man himself sat at the table of honor, his client beside him, the pair of them holding court like monarchs. Wright's wife and Costello's lackeys filled the rest of the chairs. A steady stream of students and what were probably faculty members offered words of friendship and support. Wright's expression was serene. Not the cocky, bullshit arrogance of his attorney, but a glassy calm, as if he knew something the rest of them didn't.

I want inside his mind, Jay thought, but knew he would have to wait. If Costello allowed the good doctor to say anything at all before the hearing, it would only be more propaganda. Still, the experience of an introduction was in itself useful, and so, as the band announced its break, he pushed himself out of the dark corner he had taken as his watch post and sauntered toward the table.

He spotted no fewer than three plainclothes cops. A squad car sat in the parking lot. If the accomplice showed with Dustin Holloman in tow, they'd be on him like flies on roadkill. But if he showed up the same way everyone else showed up, looking ordinary, unassuming, offering Dr. Wright nothing more than a handshake and a smile, would anyone be the wiser?

There was nothing to make Wright himself stand out in a crowd, no glowing eyes, no sign of the devil branded into his forehead. That was what frightened and fascinated people most—that monsters moved among them, unknown, unsuspected. They stood behind them in the line at the bank, bumped carts with them at the Piggly Wiggly. It was just that factor that kept readers returning to his work, Jay knew—the need to pull cases apart in the attempt to see the signs that should have been obvious to those involved. Too many times there was nothing there to see.

Costello spotted him before he reached the table, and a

big, hungry smile stretched across the lawyer's face. He rose to offer the kind of hand-pumping, back-thumping greeting that struck Jay as too familiar. He endured it with a pained smile.

"Jay, I'm glad you could make it to our little soiree!" Costello said, the benevolent host although he'd had nothing to do with setting up the party. "We heard you had a little adventure last night."

"That's one word for it." Jay discreetly rotated the sore right shoulder Costello had slapped. He had crawled out of the sack after noon feeling as if he had been trampled by a herd of Clydesdales. Only steady, lowdose self-medication of the Jack Daniel's variety had taken the edge off the aches.

"And of course the cops are trying to somehow associate that break-in with Dr. Wright." Costello made a grave face at the injustice. "The level of incompetence here is unbelievable."

The usual defense attorney shuck-and-jive. The cops are screwups, the prosecutors thickheaded plodders with no view of the big picture. Jay knew the drill. He had spouted the same trash talk himself once upon a time. He let it go in one ear and out the other as he turned to look at Garrett Wright—who was watching him with steady dark eyes and a placid half smile.

"Mr. Brooks," he said, rising, offering a hand that seemed nearly delicate. "Anthony tells me you've taken an interest in the case with an eye toward doing a book."

"Possibly. Depends on how it all shakes out in the end."

The smile took on amusement. "You mean it depends on my guilt? Quite a commentary on our society, isn't it? People don't want to read about innocence. They want twists, betrayal, blood."

"That's nothing new, Dr. Wright. People used to pay money to go to hangings—and they took their kids."

"So they did," he conceded with a tip of his head. "Perhaps what mankind has been evolving toward all these centuries is simply a more streamlined, brilliant savagery."

"That would certainly explain serial criminals, wouldn't it?" Jay said. "You might just have a topic there for your next academic publish-or-perish project, Dr. Wright."

"No, no. Learning and perception are my areas of expertise. I don't pretend to be an expert on criminal behavior."

Then again, maybe he didn't have to pretend. Jay reserved the comment, filing it away for future use in print. He let his gaze slide to Wright's wife, who sat beside him, pale almost to the point of appearing translucent. She flicked a nervous glance up at him, and a fleeting smile trembled across her mouth as she looked away. She looked distinctly unhappy when Christopher Priest slid into the chair beside her.

In an effort to look hip, the professor had dressed himself up in a black turtleneck a size too small. It clung to his bony shoulders like a diver's wet suit, the effect making his head look gigantic. He leaned ahead of Karen Wright to snag Garrett's attention.

"We've sold out of T-shirts. The boys are ecstatic."

"They should be proud," Costello interjected. He turned a shrewd eye back to Jay, shifting his position subtly to block Wright and the professor from view. "You know, Jay, this story could be told from a number of perspectives. Dr. Wright's innocence—the rallying of his friends, colleagues, students—"

"The brilliance of his attorney." Jay forced a grin. "Damned if this isn't sounding like a sales pitch, Tony."

Costello didn't bother to feign contrition. "I would be remiss if I failed to cultivate all possible venues to express my client's innocence."

"Yeah, and we've all heard what happens to attorneys who don't defend their clients with vigor," Jay said dryly, making a gun out of his thumb and forefinger and holding it to his temple.

Costello's face reddened. "Dr. Wright was still in jail at the time of Enberg's death. He would have to be something other than human to have been involved."

Jay arched his brows, just for the pleasure of seeing Costello's blood pressure jump a notch. To his credit the attorney reined in his temper before it could do more than tighten his smile.

"Jay," he said, slapping the sore shoulder again. "You're wasting your talents. You'd give Lee Bailey a run for his money in cross-examination."

"Yeah, but then that'd be work," Jay drawled. "I'd sooner watch. Leave the tough stuff to you and *Lee*."

Ellen watched the exchange of grins and handshakes from just inside the door.

"What would you say if I told you I don't know Costello from a sack of pig feed?"

That you're a liar, Mr. Brooks.

She had wanted to believe him and he had betrayed her. A sense of loss accompanied the anger as she watched them together.

It certainly had the look of best pals. A laugh, a grin, a slap on the back. Brooks and Costello, the law-school alums. A complementing pair of sharks—Costello the formal predator in a steel-gray Versace suit, Brooks the yuppie-turned-street person in creased Dockers and battered, unshaven face. And beside Costello, Garrett Wright, who turned and looked straight at her across the room. He smiled slowly, knowingly.

Ellen moved, seeking out the cover of a gaggle of tall

college boys, cursing herself for giving in to the urge to come here. She and Cameron had worked until nine—Phoebe had begged off at eight, urgently needed in places unknown—then gone for a late dinner at Grandma's Attic. She should have gone home after Grandma's hot apple crisp. She should have, at this very minute, been deeply unconscious in her bed.

But the temptation had been too great—just to slip in for a few moments, to see for herself the kind of turnout, the mood and look of the crowd. The event had started at seven. The press would be long gone by nine, sound bites recorded, photos shot. She would be able to slip in, stay in the shadows, observe. By the time the money takers at the door spread the word of her presence, she would have seen enough and slipped back out. It seemed worth five dollars, even if that money was going to Wright's defense fund.

Now, in retrospect, it was a stupid idea. Wright himself had spotted her. She felt as if everyone in the room were turning to look at her. The tide of the crowd seemed to be running against her, taking her deeper into the midst of the enemy when she wanted nothing more than to make her way to the exit.

"Hey, what's *she* doing here?"

"Isn't that Ellen North?"

"She's got a lot of nerve."

The comments came with barbed looks and pointed fingers. Ellen answered none of them, feigning calm as her heartbeat raced. She moved against the grain, her focus on the exit sign at the back of the room. She could have sent Cameron as her spy. She could have relied on the reports of Mitch's men. But no. She had to see for herself. She couldn't trust anyone else's perceptions. She had to sink herself into this thing up to her chin. Now she felt as if she were drowning in it.

A hand closed on her elbow. She tried to jerk free but the hold only tightened.

"What the hell are you doing here?" Brooks asked, his voice a low growl.

"I'd ask you the same question, but it was fairly self-evident."

She tried once again to jerk herself free, but he was too close, moving with her—no—herding her. The course had changed without her consent. The exit was drifting off to the right. They were moving, instead, toward the dark hall where the coat check was located.

"You're drawing conclusions without facts, counselor," he said as they passed the small oasis of light that was the coat check and moved to the edge of darkness.

Ellen put her back to the wall beside the emergency exit and gave him a furious look. "And I'd be an idiot to accept your version of facts, Mr. Brooks. Besides, I thought you didn't care what I believed or didn't believe."

"And I thought you didn't care what I did or didn't do," he shot back.

"I care that you lied to me. Beyond that, you can go to hell."

"I didn't lie to you."

"Ha! You tell me you don't know Tony Costello, that you don't have anything to do with his being on this case. Then I walk in and hail, hail, the gang's all here, the whole team rallied round the table, smiling, joking, slapping backs. Forgive me if I have a hard time believing a word that comes out of your handsome mouth, Brooks, but I wasn't born yesterday. Now, if you'll excuse me, I'd like to go. I've seen all I need to see."

Ellen could see curious glances being directed at them, and she hoped she had been right in assuming the reporters had all come and gone. What a hell of a photo op this would be—the prosecuting attorney having a tête-à-tête with Jay Butler Brooks at a rally for the defendant.

One of Mitch's plainclothes guys stepped past the gawkers, his right hand inching discreetly beneath the tweed sport coat he wore.

"Is everything all right, Ms. North?"

Brooks released her arm and stepped back into the shadows.

"Yes, thanks, Pat," Ellen said, smoothing her coat sleeve. "I was just leaving."

"Would you like an escort out?"

"No, don't bother. I'm parked close by. I'll be fine. You've got better things to do here."

She stepped past him and found a clear path to the front hall. The band had come back onstage from their break. The attention of the crowd turned toward them as the lead guitar took off on a wild, wailing riff.

Ellen berated herself mentally all the way to the main doors. *It doesn't matter what he does, what he says, what he thinks. You know better than to trust anyone. You don't have time to care.*

The people coming in from their cigarette breaks gave her a wide berth and sidelong glances.

Let them think what they want. What difference does it make if they believe in Wright? You know the truth.

Of course, she didn't. None of them knew the truth—except Josh, and he was keeping it locked tight within his mind. What part of the truth she did know she would wield like a club come Tuesday, and if Wright's believers came away with their illusions bruised and broken, it was nothing to her.

Ducking around a pair of incoming Harris students, she stepped outside into the cold night. The parking lot in front of the dance hall was full. A green-and-white Deer Lake cruiser sat in the far corner, waiting for action that wasn't likely to happen. Ellen made her way to the east side of the old clapboard building. She had been lucky to get the spot on a residential street, pulling into the slot just as a Lincoln Town Car pulled out.

"Hey, lookee here, boys. It's Ms. Bitch Lawyer."

The voice brought her up short. A crucial mistake on her part, Ellen realized, as Tyrell Mann and his cohorts took advantage, moving away from the deeper shadows along the side of the building to step in front of her. A quick assessment of the situation told her she could be in trouble. They were out of view of the parking lot. To the east, a cedar privacy fence blocked the view into the neighboring house. The nearest house across the street was dark. The Manley Vanloon Pace Car sat at the near curb a dozen feet ahead. So close and so far. The music from the dance hall penetrated to the outside world, loud enough to mask the sounds of a struggle.

Tyrell's smile flashed bright in his dark face as he flicked away his cigarette. "You got a fuckin' nerve coming here, lady."

"I paid for the privilege," Ellen said. "That's all you should care about."

"We care about the Doc. He's our man," J. R. Andersen said.

"Yeah," Speed Dawkins chimed in. "He's our man. He's *the* man—"

"And you tryin' to throw his ass in jail," Tyrell said, the smile gone.

The image of the switchblade that had been left in her tire came sharply into focus in Ellen's memory. She had spent part of the evening going over the file on the Sci-Fi Cowboys, with an eye to possible suspects in her vandalism. Andersen was a white-collar criminal, stealing money electronically. Dawkins had been in and out of drug-related trouble. Tyrell was a fairly recent addition to the group, a bright kid with a rap sheet that skirted the edges of some serious stuff—assault charges that had been bartered down, robbery charges that had been reduced because he wasn't the principal player and the county juvenile facility was bursting at its seams, a rape charge that had been dismissed.

At seventeen Tyrell was already a hard case. Vandalism wouldn't have been anything to him. Where he would draw the line was questionable. Ellen had seen too many kids just like him who made no distinctions at all, kids who wouldn't hesitate to pull a gun and shoot someone for their starter jacket or kick their head in for pocket money.

"I don't have to tell you how the system works, Tyrell," she said. "And I shouldn't have to tell you that your hassling me won't help Dr. Wright's cause."

"I don't want you tellin' me nothin', bitch."

"I'm sure you don't, but you'd better listen." In her coat pocket she singled out the biggest key on her ring to use as a defense weapon and curled her fist around the rest. "You and your buddies fuck up here and you go to jail, and the Sci-Fi Cowboys will be no more. How do you think Dr. Wright and Professor Priest and the rest of your backers would feel about that?"

She wanted him to see reason. He heard only challenge.

He took half a step closer. "Is that a threat, Ms. Bitch Lawyer?"

"It's a fact. You and I both know the only reason your ass isn't sitting on a Hennepin County cot right now is the Sci-Fi Cowboys. You want to trash that, Tyrell?"

"Naw. That's not what I fuckin' wanna trash."

Ellen chanced a quick glance at the other two. Dawkins was watching Tyrell, ready to take his cue. Andersen stood back a little, his expression blank, his thoughts unreadable. In some ways he was more a wild card than Tyrell. His IQ was in the genius range, his probation officer's comments laced with hints of well-camouflaged sociopathic tendencies. He could intervene with charm or just as easily be the mastermind who came up with the foolproof way to dispose of her body.

"The dance is *inside* the building, boys."

Ellen did her best to swallow her sigh of relief at the sound of Brooks's voice.

Impatience flashed in Tyrell's eyes. "Who the fuck are you? The Lone Fuckin' Ranger?"

"More like the Lone Fuckin' Witness." Jay stepped in front of Ellen, then backed her up to put some space between them and the angry-looking kid in the Bulls jacket. "With the lone fuckin' cellular phone and my finger on the lone fuckin' speed-dial button for the cops. Do you understand what I'm fuckin' tellin' you, you fuckin' little shit?"

His voice rose with each angry word. He had come out here to confront Ellen. Now he found himself in the unlikely role of rescuer, holding his pocket cellular phone up as if it were a live grenade.

"Come on, Tyrell," Andersen said, cuffing his buddy's shoulder. "I'm freezing my dick off. Let's go in."

He started toward the building. Dawkins hesitated. Tyrell stood his ground.

"Come on," Andersen said impatiently. "Before the professor blows a circuit."

Tyrell thrust his chin out at Jay. "Fuck you, man. We was just talkin' to the lady."

The trio swaggered off together toward the yellow light of the parking lot. Ellen watched them go, slowly letting the air out of her lungs.

"Thanks," she said to Brooks. "He's a loose cannon in Wright's arsenal. I wasn't sure what he might do."

"Yeah, well, I'd'a looked pretty damned stupid if he would have pulled a gun and gone off on me. The worst damage this phone can do is leak battery acid." He held it out to her. "You want to call this little encounter in?"

"They didn't break any laws. I just want to go home." And double-bolt the doors, and sink into a hot bath and a big glass of brandy. "Good night, Mr. Brooks," she said, starting for the Cadillac.

"Not so far, it isn't." His footsteps crunched over the snow behind her. "I came here for the same reason you did—to observe."

"I think, then, that maybe you should look the word up in the dictionary. You seem to have observation confused with participation."

"Costello is as much a part of this story as you are, Ellen. Of course I'm going to speak with him."

"I don't want to hear about it."

Ellen let herself in the car. She hit the power locks, even though Brooks had pulled up on the curb. She turned the key in the ignition, but the big engine made no sound at all, made no effort to start, made not even a grumbled refusal to start. The Manley Vanloon Pace Car had died.

"Hell and damnation!" Ellen swore, smacking her gloved fist on the steering wheel.

Fuming, she popped the hood, dug the pocket flashlight out of her purse, and climbed out of the car. The Cadillac's engine was the size of a small country, but parts were parts—or, in this case, parts were nowhere to be seen. The distributor was gone.

"Shit!"

"Ms. North . . ." Jay clucked his tongue. "Such language."

Ellen shot him a scathing glare.

He held up his phone like a prize. "Want to call a cab?"

"Don't be an ass."

"Want to call a cop?"

What would be the point? The Pla-Mor was packed to the rafters with suspects. The possibility of anyone's coming forward as a witness was laughable. Although Tyrell and Andersen and Dawkins had been in the immediate vicinity, they wouldn't have been foolish enough to hang on to the distributor. The offense was too petty for the amount of time and energy it would consume.

"Come on." Brooks pocketed the phone and pulled out his keys. "I'll give you a ride."

"I think you've already taken me for a ride," she said dryly.

"I'll take you straight home. Scout's honor."

He took her straight to *his* home.

Ellen gave him a speculative look across the cab of the GMC Jimmy he had talked Manley into renting him. "You were never a Boy Scout, were you?"

He grinned. "No, ma'am, I never was."

"I could use that phone now," she grumbled, "to report my own kidnapping."

"Or you could relax and enjoy my famous southern hospitality."

"So far, 'enjoyable' is not the word I would use regarding our association."

"What word would you use?"

Unsettling. It came to her instantly, but she kept it to herself. She knew instinctively it would please him. He enjoyed knocking her off balance, used it to his own advantage—like now.

"It's time we had a talk," he said. "I figured it was best held in a place you can't have me thrown out of or walk away from."

They turned off Old Cedar Road and drove into the development area around Ryan's Bay. The moon was waxing toward fullness, its light casting the bay in otherworldly shades of silver and white. Ellen had biked the trails out here many times in warm weather, had always felt a certain parklike comfort about the area. Now every time she went by that spot on the trail, she would think about Josh's little ski jacket planted among the reeds, a note tucked into one pocket.

" 'My specter around me night and day like a wild beast guards my way. My emanation far within weeps incessantly for my sin.' " She murmured the lines from William Blake's poem, her gaze on the frozen reeds that thrust up from the drifts of snow. "That was the note left in Josh's coat pocket."

"I know," Jay said softly.

"How? We didn't release that one to the press."

"I'm not the press."

He turned the Jimmy in at a driveway and hit the remote switch to raise one door on a three-car garage. The house was enormous by Deer Lake standards. And outrageously priced by Deer Lake standards—Ellen had seen the ads in the newspaper. She imagined he was paying a hefty price to rent it, but the money probably meant nothing to him. He had made a sizable fortune turning crime into entertainment. He would do so again with this case, and she would be part of the story.

He had the kind of money it would take to hire Tony Costello, the kind of money it had taken to bail Garrett Wright out of jail.

And she had wanted to trust him.

Without a word to Brooks, she left him in the gourmet kitchen and walked through the living room to the wall of glass that looked out on the frozen countryside. She could hear him pouring drinks, then, nearer, starting a fire in the stone fireplace. When he came to stand beside her, he had shed his parka.

"Whiskey and soda," he said, handing her a paper cup.

He set his on the ledge and leaned his shoulder against the window frame. He had turned no lights on in the room, letting the fire and moonlight provide all they needed. Darkness seemed to bring out the moods in him. The Cheshire-cat grin and lazy, good ol' boy manner came off like a mask.

"I have a son," he said without preamble.

He didn't look at Ellen to catch her reaction, concentrating his effort on controlling his own. He took a swallow of his whiskey and dug a cigarette out of his shirt pocket as the liquor slid like molten gold into his belly.

"The punch line is that I didn't know it, and he *doesn't* know it." He lit the cigarette, took a deep pull on it, and blew the smoke up at the moon. "He's eight. Just like Josh. His mother—my ex-wife—took him away from me before I even knew he existed. It's a hell of a strange thing, finding out after the fact that a part of you has been missing for the better part of a decade."

"I take it she was pregnant when she left you," Ellen said quietly.

"I figured that much out during the divorce war, but I never dreamed it was mine." He gave a bitter half laugh. "I was chasing ambulances back then, working like a dog, miserable as hell. Christine and I . . . well, it was pretty much over but the shouting. She found herself a lawyer higher up on the food chain, a drone, the kind of guy who only wants a partnership and a new BMW every year. . . . I just assumed the baby was his. I didn't think she could have hated me so much. I was wrong."

It surprised him, how close to the surface the sadness was. Must have been the whiskey—historically, it brought out the latent despondency in Brooks men. Uncle Hooter came to mind, sitting on the veranda on a warm summer night, sobbing at the memory of a dog he had lost as a boy.

As he let the silence drag on, Ellen watched his face, naked in the moonlight, battered and beard-shadowed, tight with a kind of pain that had nothing to do with his physical wounds.

"How did you find out?"

The tip of his cigarette glowed red as he inhaled. An odd dot of color among the shades of gray. "Her grandfather lived in Eudora. She never came to visit, but they came back when he died. The funeral was ten days ago. I suppose she didn't think I'd be decent enough to pay my respects, but there I was, and there she was with her balding senior-partner husband . . . and my son." He smiled in a way that made her heart ache. "Damned if he isn't the spittin' image . . ."

"Did you ask her?"

"She said to me, 'Carter Talcott is the only father he's ever known. He's a happy little boy. We have a nice life. Don't ruin that for him, Jay.'" His chin quivered a little. He shook his head. "Christ, what did she think I would do? Tell an eight-year-old boy right there the man he's called Daddy his whole life isn't? That I was such a bastard his mama saw fit to keep him a secret from me all these years? God."

He took a last drag on his cigarette and carefully crushed the butt out against the cold windowpane.

"What did you do?"

"I came here," he said simply. "I'd been watching the case on the news, in the papers and all. I flew to Minneapolis that very night. Ran away. Came to see what real suffering was all about. Try to make some kind of sense of it, get some perspective.

"You know, my son is alive and—and he lives with people who love him. And I didn't even know I was missing him, so—" His Adam's apple bobbed in his throat as he broke off and swallowed. "It's not like the Kirkwoods or the Hollomans, not like having him stolen by some maniac and taken to God-knows-what fate. It's not like Mitch Holt, who had his boy gunned down by some junkie. I don't have any call to complain just because I won't be the one taking my son to Little League."

But he did, Ellen thought. He had every reason to hurt. That his tragedy wasn't on the same scale as the Kirkwoods' didn't make it any less a tragedy. And yet she could see him trying to grasp that line of reasoning, trying to minimize the pain. She caught a glimpse of vulnerability she would never have suspected lay beneath the layers of charm and cynicism. And she had a feeling it came as much of a surprise to him. Out of the blue. Blindsiding him. Sending him scrambling for familiar ground.

"You won't try to work something out?" she asked. "Some kind of joint custody? Recognition as the boy's biological father, at the very least?"

He shook his head. "He's happy. He's got a nice, normal life. What kind of son of a bitch would I be to come barging in and turn that all upside down?"

"But if you're his father—"

"Carter Talcott is his father. Me, I just provided the raw materials."

He tossed back the last of his drink, crushed the cup in his hand, and turned to face her, his expression colder, tougher as he wrestled to regain control. "I'm not looking for advice or sympathy," he said tersely. "You wanted to know why I came here, why I picked this story. There it is. It doesn't have a damn thing to do with Anthony Costello. I couldn't give a shit about the money I'll make. I came here to lose myself in someone else's misery.

"If you want to think I'm a bastard, go right ahead, because I surely am. Any number of people will gladly tell you so. I just want you to hate me for the right reasons, that's all. If I'm going to stand accused of something, I'd rather it be a sin I've actually committed."

He walked away from her, across the room, tossed the empty cup into the fireplace and watched the flames swallow it up.

"Finish your drink," he growled without looking up. "I'll take you home."

Ellen left the cup on the window ledge beside his crushed-out cigarette and moved slowly toward him. The house was cold, despite the fire, a kind of cold she associated with emptiness, with loneliness. Leaning back against the stone beside the fireplace, she took in the furnishings of his "home," office machines and lawn chairs, an army cot and a thick down sleeping bag. A transient's home.

"I don't hate you," she whispered. "I hate this case. What it's doing to this town. What it's doing to me. It's reminded me of things I'd rather not believe about human nature—my own included."

"You? But you're the heroine of the story."

"No. I'm just doing my job, a job I walked away from two years ago because I couldn't stand what it was turning me into. Being a cynic wears you down, burns you out. I didn't want to stop caring about the people who needed justice. I thought if I came here, it wouldn't take so much out of me, that there'd be something left over for me. And now . . ."

"And now you have Garrett Wright and Tony Costello and a dead lawyer and a missing boy . . . and me."

From some reserve she didn't know she had, she found a smile to match his. "And you. Well, maybe you're not all bad. You're a diversion, at least," she teased. "Although I can ill afford to be diverted."

"A diversion?" He tried the word on his tongue like a piece of strange fruit. The old devilish sparkle rekindled in his eyes. "Mercy, Ms. North, you make me feel like a gigolo."

"You've been called worse things."

"By you, no doubt."

"No doubt."

She hadn't realized he was so close, close enough to raise his hand and touch her cheek. Close enough to draw her to him with just a look, with just the longing in his pale eyes. He leaned down and kissed her, his lips warm and tasting of whiskey.

"My God, I want you, Ellen," he whispered.

"I can't. The case—"

"This has nothing to do with the case." Sliding a hand into her hair, he undid the clip that held it back. It fell free around her shoulders.

"This is just us," he murmured, pressing a kiss to her temple. "It's just . . . I need . . . to touch you. Let me touch you, Ellen."

His vulnerability touched her. The yearning in his smoky voice touched her. The attraction that had sparked inside her from the first flared up as hot and bright as the flames of the fire. He was nothing she had been looking for. She wasn't a woman given to fits of passion. She didn't lower her guard. But even as his lips brushed her cheek, she could feel logic slipping away.

She made one last, halfhearted reach for it, drawing a breath for the voice of reason. Jay seemed to sense the words before she could form them. He touched a forefinger to her lips.

"Don't think," he whispered. "Not tonight. Please."

Please. They could have this night, cross this line. There would be no going back. There would likely be regrets, but those were in the gray mists of the future, and they didn't outweigh the need to connect, to touch, to shut out the rest of the world for a few hours.

Ellen closed her eyes as he framed her face in his hands and kissed her again, deeper, slower. She let her mouth open beneath the pressure of his, allowed him access, shivered as he took it. He drew her away from the wall. Her coat fell to the floor. She slid her hands up the front of his shirt and brought them back down, parting the buttons from their moorings.

Impatient for the feel of her hands on his skin, he

slipped the shirt off and tossed it aside, pulled his dark T-shirt off over his head and flung it away. The firelight played over the ridges and planes of muscle in his chest. His shoulders were broad, in the way of a man who did physical work.

Ellen touched her fingertips to his belly, felt the muscles quiver beneath the tight bandage that bound his ribs.

"Will this be all right?" she asked. "You won't hurt—?"

"That's not where I hurt," he whispered. Curling his fingers around her wrist, he raised her hand and pressed it over his heart.

The honesty of the gesture surprised her. She spread her fingers and felt his heartbeat. He was just a man and he hurt and he wanted this time with her to escape that pain. She hurt in her own way, for her own reasons. She wanted the same escape. It was as simple and as complicated as that.

Leaning into him, she pressed a kiss where her hand had rested. Then Jay's mouth was on hers again, hotter, hungrier.

They sank to their knees together. His fingers stumbled down the line of buttons on her blouse. He pushed the blouse and her cardigan off her shoulders without completing the task, the need to see her, to taste her, too urgent.

She hadn't bothered with a bra. Her breasts were there for the taking, the color of cream, the texture of silk, a size that filled his palms perfectly. He cupped them together, rubbing his thumbs across the rosy buds at their center, the need snapping inside him like a whip as they hardened beneath his touch. Bending her back over his arm, he lowered his head to take one tightened peak between his lips.

The sensation was electric. A gasp caught in Ellen's throat. She clutched at his shoulders, then his head, raking her fingers through his short hair, pulling him tighter against her. The need for this act, for this man, burned within, wild, hot, too intense. She had never known what it was to let go of her self-control completely, but she felt it sliding away from her now. The feeling was terrifying and exhilarating at once.

He lifted his head and looked at her, his lower lip slick and shining, the pupils of his eyes huge, ringed with neon blue. He looked uncivilized, as if the same fire in her had seared away the thin veneer of manners he wore in public, revealing what she had sensed all along was at the core of him—something dangerous, untamed, raw.

He moved away from her for a moment, and the sudden absence of his body heat left her feeling cold. She pulled her blouse together over her breasts as she watched him snatch the thick down sleeping bag from the cot and spread it open in front of the fireplace. Then he offered her his hand.

She stood, passive, as he undressed her. He freed her arms from the blouse and sweater, caressing her shoulders, her back, her belly. He hooked his thumbs in the waistband of the leggings she wore and drew them slowly down her hips, kneeling at her feet to remove them. All thoughts of being cold vaporized as he reached up and inched her silk panties down, following their descent with his mouth.

He pressed a hot, openmouthed kiss to the soft spot below her navel as he slid his hands around to cup her buttocks, then dragged the kiss lower to the tender area just above the delta of dark-blond curls, then lower.

Ellen gasped at the touch of his lips, at the bold probing of his tongue. She tried to step back, but he held her easily, his fingers stroking, kneading, pulling her closer, tilting her hips into the shocking intimacy of his kiss. The intensity of the pleasure stunned her, scared her, swept her toward a towering precipice—and left her hanging there.

An involuntary whimper of frustration escaped her as Jay pulled her down to the floor with him and pulled her hard against him. He shared the taste of her own desire with her. She ran her hands along the taut muscles of his back, his arms, feeling his strength. His urgency seemed to feed her own.

When he rose on his knees to unfasten his trousers, she rose with him, pushed his hands away from his belt and unbuckled it herself. Her fingers trembled as she unbuttoned his khakis and eased the zipper down. She touched him through the fine silk of his boxers, savored the feel of his hardness beneath the whisper softness of the fabric.

Jay tolerated her delicate teasing with gritted teeth, holding on to his control until he could stand it no longer. He wanted her, needed more than the tentative feather touches she was giving him.

"Jesus, Ellen, touch me," he rasped, closing her hand around his shaft, guiding it slowly up and down the length of him. "Feel what you do to me . . . how much I want you."

A sense of feminine power swelling inside her, Ellen followed his commands, savoring the feel of him in her hand. Hot, hard, thick, pulsing. She traced her fingertips over the tip of him and found a spot that made him suck his breath in through his teeth. With his hand still curved over hers, she reached down and cupped him, and a shudder rippled through his whole body.

He drew away just long enough to shuck his pants and fish a condom out of his wallet. He came back to her ready, eager, the muscles in his arms trembling as he braced himself over her.

She arched up to meet him. Her eyes drifted shut as he entered her. Her body tightened around him like a fist.

"Sweet heaven," he groaned, fighting the instinctive urge to possess, to bury himself in a single stroke. "Relax for me, sweetheart," he whispered, slowly drawing her leg up along his thigh.

He slid a hand beneath her hip and lifted her into him, allowing himself to sink deeper, closer to oblivion. She caught her breath, then let go a sigh of pure sensual pleasure. Slowly, erotically, they moved together, without words, the glow of the fire gilding their bodies.

Ellen let go of the self-restraint that was so much a part of her, shivering inside at the idea of her own vulnerability.

Jay felt as if his soul were just an inch from hers, straining to connect in a way that was primal, more than physical, deeper than anything he'd known in a long time. More than he'd bargained for in coming to this place. He had meant to lose himself, now he wanted nothing more than to hold on to this moment, this night, this woman. The idea scared the hell out of him.

Then they were both beyond thought. There was only need and urgency, a rush to an explosion of bliss.

Ellen cried out as her climax came in wave upon wave. She held Jay tight as he came just after her. Even as the tension began to ease out of his body, she held him, suddenly afraid of what she would feel when she let go— alone.

Odd, when she had always felt comfortable with herself, self-sufficient, self-reliant, capable of sharing a relationship or going her own way. She had never defined herself in relation to her status with a man. It was the case, she supposed. She had been feeling the weight of it pressing down on her like a pile of stones. For just a while she had felt the burden lift. For the time she could lie here next to Brooks with his arms around her, she felt . . . safe.

Safe. With a man she barely knew and barely trusted.

———

At 4:06 A.M. an explosion rocked Dinkytown. The blast shattered windows up and down one block, including all the windows in the Pla-Mor Ballroom. At 4:08 Alvin Underbakke called 911 to report the incident and request the fire department come and put out the blaze that was engulfing a big white Cadillac across the street from his house.

CHAPTER 27

"Where were you at four this morning?" Mitch asked, his hands braced on the back of the chair he should have been sitting in.

Tyrell Mann met his gaze with arrogance. "Gettin' my beauty z's. Where'd you want me to be, Chief? What you tryin' to pin on my black ass?"

"Let's get something straight here, Tyrell," he said. "I don't give a shit what color your ass is, or any other part of you, and, frankly, I'm about ready to take that chip off your shoulder and put it where the sun don't shine. All I care about here is getting a straight answer. Where were you?"

"Like I said—asleep. We went to the party for the Doc, then crashed."

"At the hostel on campus?"

"Whatever."

Mitch straightened away from the chair and advanced toward him.

"Yeah, at the hostel," Tyrell gave in. "Why?"

"Someone blew up Ms. North's car this morning."

A nasty smile split Tyrell's features. "Was the bitch in it?"

Mitch leaned down into his face. "You know, Tyrell, it's that attitude that's going to land your ass in jail for the

rest of your life one of these days. I thought you had to
have some brains to get into the Cowboys."

"I got brains enough to know I can have a lawyer here
if I want one."

"Why would you need a lawyer, Tyrell? You're not
under arrest. Should you be?"

"Fuck you, Holt."

Ellen watched the exchange from the hall, where a
one-way mirror gave a thirty-inch view of the show. The
chances of one Cowboy giving up another were nil. The
chances of their being tripped up in their story was slim.
No one was going to get anything out of Tyrell. Down
the hall Agent Wilhelm and J. R. Andersen were going
through the same song and dance. Andersen played innocent, false concern oozing out of him like sap.

If one of the Cowboys had torched the Cadillac, it was
going to take an eyewitness to finger him, and people in
Deer Lake were in their beds at four o'clock on a Sunday
morning. No one had seen anything. No one had seen
Tyrell Mann or J. R. Andersen or Speed Dawkins or Todd
Childs or anyone else.

They were wasting their time. Again. Ellen wondered
if Garrett Wright was home right now browsing the Sunday *Star Tribune*, smiling to himself.

She checked her watch and shook her head. They were
due at the psychiatrist's at four. She needed to call Cameron to let him know to pick her up at the law-enforcement
center. She wasn't looking forward to the hour-long drive.
Cameron would no doubt have as many questions for her
as the reporters who were stationed outside the building,
waiting.

News of the car fire had come to her at Jay's house via
her beeper. He had driven her to the scene, raising a few
eyebrows among the cops hanging around. Luckily, by
then the reporters had already come and gone. Unluckily,
they had gone in search of her. Rumor that the charred

wreck might have been hers had sent them off in full cry. By the time they found her, they were foaming at the mouth, rabid for answers. She offered them none. Brooks shucked off their interest in him with the explanation that the explosion had damn near rolled him out of bed.

That the only explosion either of them had paid any attention to was of a sexual nature was nobody's damn business, but the reporters would make it their business, and Ellen knew it. She had watched it happen to Mitch and Megan. And if they chose to do so with her and Brooks, how long would it be before they jumped onto the fact that Costello and Brooks were fellow Purdue alums or that Brooks had been seen slapping shoulders with Costello at the benefit? The media had the power to turn a trial into a circus, complete with sideshows. She didn't want to see that happen for the sake of Hannah and Josh. Or for her own sake, for that matter.

She pushed through the door into the squad room and headed for an empty desk. Christopher Priest rose from the chair where he had been left waiting, fury rouging his pale cheeks.

"This is an outrage, Ms. North. How much longer are the boys going to be interrogated without the benefit of counsel?"

"They aren't being interrogated, Professor. They're being questioned."

"I've called an attorney."

"You have that right."

"I've told you the boys didn't have anything to do with this. They were at the hostel. I checked on them."

"So you said. At about four A.M. Quite a coincidence."

His glare took on a sharpness Ellen felt like the blade of a razor, though he didn't raise his voice a decibel. "I resent the implication. First you take me to task for not supervising them closely enough. Now you call me a liar when I *do* check up on them."

"I didn't call you a liar, Professor," she said calmly. "I said it was an extraordinary coincidence. Just like Tyrell and Andersen and Dawkins being seen in the vicinity of my car last night, then the car's being disabled and subsequently blown to kingdom come."

"They're easy scapegoats," Priest began.

"No. Nothing about any of this is easy. I know you've got a vested interest in their innocence, Professor, but somebody has to be guilty, and it just might be your boys." She picked up the telephone receiver but pressed the plunger down with her finger, eyeing Priest curiously. "As long as we're standing here, Professor, can you tell me if you were with anyone last Saturday afternoon, after your lunch with your friend from Gustavus?"

The fury in his eyes was the strongest emotion she'd seen in him, yet he contained it.

"You're making enemies, Ms. North," he said quietly. "You'll wish you hadn't."

The Taker had warned him this would happen. Josh sat in the cushy blue chair in Dr. Freeman's office, staring past her to the fish tank that was stuck into the wall. He had been told someone would try to get inside his mind and open all the doors. He had been told never to let that happen. He knew how to do that. It was stupid simple. He imagined his body as just a shell and drew his Self inward, like a ghost, into his mind, where he shut the doors and windows tight.

It didn't make him happy to do this. At first he had thought of this place in his mind as a special safe place, but he didn't like all the things the Taker had put there. They made him sad. They scared him. They made his tummy feel weird. But he had been warned and he was afraid to disobey. Too many bad things had happened already.

He didn't like the way any of the grown-ups around

him were acting. It had been a relief to come to Dr. Freeman's today. She was a pretty lady with dark-brown skin and a kind smile. She usually just talked to him, real easy-like. She asked him questions, but not the same way the cops had asked him questions. She never got that tone in her voice as if she wanted to shake him, or that tone that made him think she was almost afraid of him. She never seemed to mind when he didn't answer her. But then today she started talking about relaxing and asking him if he had ever played like he was hypnotized.

Bingo.

She wanted to hypnotize him. Just another trick to try to get him to say the things the Taker had warned him not to.

Josh gave Dr. Freeman a look of huge disappointment, got up from the chair, and went to stare at the fish, trapped inside that tank the same way he had to stay trapped inside his mind.

Watching on the other side of a one-way mirror, Hannah pressed ice-cold hands to her cheeks and willed herself not to cry. Mitch gave her shoulder a sympathetic squeeze. Agent Wilhelm blew out a sigh of frustration. Ellen North exchanged looks with Cameron Reed.

"It's too soon, I suppose," Ellen said.

Wilhelm grunted. "It might be too late for Dustin Holloman."

Rage twisted inside Hannah. It wrenched her out of Mitch's grasp and launched her at the BCA agent.

"Don't you dare blame Josh!" she snarled, hitting him before Mitch could pull her back. "He's just a little boy! It's not his fault you can't do your job! It's not his fault the world is crawling with scum like Garrett Wright!"

Hannah clawed Mitch's arm to pry it away from her,

the fury burning inside her. It terrified her, but she couldn't begin to suppress it. It was like acid in her chest, like blood pumping from an artery that had been severed.

"Let me go!" she shouted.

Ellen stepped forward, putting herself in front of Wilhelm. "Hannah, please calm down," she said quietly. "We don't blame Josh—"

"I'm taking him home," Hannah declared.

The decision was made without the usual mental weighing of pros and cons. It blurted out of her, this voice of instinct, now that the layers of education, domestication, socialization, had been slashed and torn apart.

She no longer cared what anyone thought. She knew she no longer bore any resemblance to the Woman of the Year image everyone in town had of her, and she didn't give a damn. All she cared about now was Josh, protecting him, fighting to get him the justice he deserved, fighting to protect him.

"I'm taking my son home," she said again, looking over her shoulder at Mitch, who had brought them up in his Explorer.

"I'm sorry it didn't work out, Hannah, but we had to give it a try—for Josh's sake as well as our own."

"No," she murmured as his hold on her arm relaxed and she stepped away from him. "None of this has been for Josh's benefit. Don't you realize that, Mitch? Nothing that happens now can change what Garrett Wright did to him or to our family. Nothing. Ever. The only thing we can hope for is revenge."

She walked out of the room, heading toward Dr. Freeman's office. At the door, she straightened her burgundy sweater and pushed her hair back over her shoulder. Then she knocked once and let herself in.

"Josh, we're going home," she announced, holding out her hand to him.

Mitch shot a glare at Wilhelm, who stood frowning, rubbing the sore spot in the hollow of his shoulder.

"Are you taking sensitivity training from Steiger in your spare time?"

"We're *all* stressed out," Wilhelm grumbled.

Ellen turned back to their window on the psychiatrist's office and watched through the smoky glass as Hannah knelt down to gather her son in her arms.

"Who can blame her?" she murmured to Cameron. "She's right. We didn't want this for Josh's sake; we wanted it to save our own hides. Sometimes I hate this job."

"For all we know, Wright beat us to this hypnosis thing," he said. "The man's a psychology professor, specializing in learning and perception. He might have wrung this kid's mind out like a sponge and put in whatever he wanted."

"There's a cheery thought," Ellen mumbled. "Think Dr. Freeman would give us a group rate?"

The session over, Dr. Freeman let herself into the room on their side of the glass. She offered no apologies and spared them none of her own feelings. She had felt it was too soon to try to pry into Josh's memories, and she had been right. He didn't trust her yet, and after this it would probably be some time before he would.

Mitch ushered Hannah and Josh out to his truck. Wilhelm climbed into his car alone and headed across town toward St. Paul and a meeting with Bruce DePalma, his special agent in charge. Ellen crossed the parking lot with Cameron.

"Think we should check my car for bombs before we get in?" he asked, only half teasing.

"It wasn't a bomb. It was just a flaming rag stuffed into the gas tank."

"Just."

The end result was the same. The Cadillac was trashed. Poor Manley had been stunned, walking around and around the burned-out hulk—although he had perked up when the press had turned their attention on him, the prospect of more free advertising offsetting his grief. He had even gone so far as to offer Ellen another loaner—on camera. She had declined, saying instead that she would take her own car back as soon as his people could spray some primer over the damage to the driver's door.

The worst thing was not knowing whether she was a target of Wright's supporters or Wright's accomplice. Or both. And aside from scaring the shit out of her, whoever was responsible had managed to further disrupt her life and add to the already overwhelming burden of the case.

She had planned to visit her parents after the session with Dr. Freeman. They lived just blocks away from Freeman's office, had called twice in the past week because they were concerned about her. But she had called them and canceled, not wanting to complicate Cameron's evening, and so he turned south on France Avenue and headed toward the freeway.

Maybe it was just as well, Ellen mused as they passed shopping centers and intersections that gave glimpses of quiet suburban neighborhoods. On the surface, a visit seemed to offer what she needed—support and sympathy. But what she was feeling couldn't be cured by going home. Just as it hadn't been cured by leaving the Cities two years ago—only put off for a time.

She fought it now as it rose to the surface like oil. The fear that what she had walked away from when she had left the Hennepin County system wasn't just politics or disillusionment, but the knowledge of a world and a system in decay, and the knowledge that she was as much a part of the problem as she was disgusted by it.

She thought of the many rape victims whose cases she had prosecuted over the years, the ordeal the system put them through, making them relive the crime over and over during the investigation and trial. It was no different now with Josh. He would be victimized all over again in the name of justice, and again in the name of therapy. His life had been violated, and he and his mother would be put through hell by the people who were supposed to protect them and help them in order to get a conviction. For the first time in two years she felt jaded and old in a way that had nothing to do with her upcoming birthday.

The feeling nagged her as they left the suburbs behind and the view softened to the rumpled white blankets of farm fields and valleys shaded gray with naked woods. And as they neared Deer Lake, another eerie restlessness crept in as she looked off at the countryside—the idea that their nemesis was out there somewhere right now, that if they just turned down the right road, they might drive right past the house where Dustin Holloman was waiting to be rescued.

Cameron took the exit at the Big Steer truck stop and rolled down the frontage road past Dealin' Swede's A-1 Auto and Manley's two biggest dealerships, where yellow ribbons had been tied to every car on the lots and the showroom windows had been painted with the slogan "Bring Dustin Home." Even the giant inflatable blue gorilla that hovered above the roof of the Pontiac place had been adorned with a yellow ribbon, fluttering gaily around its neck.

Driving through the streets of town, Ellen saw the same symbols over and over. The ribbons on the front doors meant to show support and perhaps to ward off the evil. The posters taped to store windows. The new banner the town council had had hoisted across Main Street— "Protect Our Children!"

The plea struck Ellen as personal. The citizenry turned instantly to the police they otherwise seldom thought about, expecting the crime to be solved, regardless of the lack of clues. They turned to the court system they likely knew nothing about, calling for justice at all costs. The pressure of their silent demands settled on her shoulders, turning the muscles to rock.

"Did you want to go back to the office?" Cameron asked. "We could try to contact some more of Wright's old chums."

"I'll pass for once," Ellen said. "I think we've suffered enough for one day. All I want to do is get some sleep."

"Yeah, I don't suppose you got much last night."

You don't know the half of it.

It seemed impossible that she had spent the night with Brooks. It seemed impossible that she had let her guard down that much. And with Jay Butler Brooks, of all men. But they had reached out to each other . . . and it had been incredible.

And it was incredibly complicated.

"Apparently, Manley thinks you're cursed," Cameron said, pulling into Ellen's driveway beside the Bonneville. The driver's door wore a big splotch of gray primer where the word "BITCH" had been.

"Can you blame him? Frankly, *I* was afraid to have my car at his garage. I don't want to be responsible for his business going up in flames."

"*You're* not responsible," Cameron reminded her. "You're the victim."

"Be that as it may, I'm dangerous to know."

"Do you want me to come in with you?"

"No." She nodded toward the gray sedan parked at the curb. "Mitch gave me a guard. I'll be fine. Thanks for the ride."

"Try to stay out of trouble for a few hours," he said, offering her a gentle version of his teasing grin.

"I'm going to bed early. How much trouble could I get into?"

Visions of Jay's pirate smile rose in her memory as she drove the Bonneville into the garage.

"God, Ellen," she mumbled as she hefted her briefcase out of the car. "Of all the lousy times to develop a libido."

"You won't hear me complaining."

She whirled around. Brooks came out of the shadows of the garage. He hadn't bothered to shave, apparently hadn't bothered to run more than his fingers through his hair.

"Dammit!" Ellen complained. "I'm not going to have to worry about Wright's accomplice getting me. You'll give me a heart attack first! What the hell are you doing in here?"

"I had my doubts about your surveillance team. Decided to test them for myself." He reached out and took her briefcase from her. "They failed."

"I can see that. How did you get in? Everything was locked."

He pulled a credit card from his coat pocket and held it up. "Don't leave home without it. I parked on the next block, cut through the alley, hopped your fence—"

"And Harry?"

"Greeted me with tail wagging. He's not exactly Cujo." He nodded toward the door that led directly from the garage to the backyard. "You need a dead bolt there. I jimmied the lock with the credit card. Any two-bit burglar could do it."

"There's a comforting thought."

"Look on the bright side, sugar," he said, following her into the house. "At least I was the one to show you your security shortcomings. The only thing I'm after is some wild, hot sex."

"Oh, is that all?"

"You weren't so blasé last night." Wicked mischief lit his eyes as he planted a hand on either side of her and trapped her with her back against the wall. "As I recall, you said something more along the lines of *all that, Jay?*"

"I was probably referring to the size of your ego."

His grin deepened. "You're blushing, counselor."

"It's the sudden warmth."

"Hear! Hear!"

He brushed his mouth across hers, his lips cold, his tongue warm, his gaze holding hers. Ellen's body responded to his as if they had spent years together instead of just a night. It was a frightening thought—that they could be so in tune, that she could be so easily won over, that her body could so eagerly shut out her mind.

She turned her face away. "I need to let Harry in."

She brought the dog in and gave him his supper. She could feel Jay watching her as she hung up her coat and turned up the thermostat. The quality of his gaze unnerved her—the intensity of it, the sense that he wasn't just watching her but observing her, studying her.

She drew a deep breath as she faced him. He had turned the fireplace on and stood with his back to it. In the deep shadows of the room he looked like the kind of man no sane person would cross paths with. In another time, in another place . . . they would never have met. That was the bottom line.

"I've been thinking," she began, pacing nervously between the coffee table and the wing chair.

"Uh-oh."

"Last night . . . last night was . . . incredible—"

"But . . ."

"It can't happen again."

"Because?"

"Because everything. Because of the case. Because of who I am. Because of who you are."

"Those are all the reasons we're together."

"I know." She shook her head. "It can't work, Jay."

"It worked pretty damn good last night," he said, moving toward her.

Ellen held her ground. "You know what I mean. I've got priorities."

"And I'm not one of them."

"Would you want to be? You've got priorities of your own. I doubt I'm one of them."

"Not so," he said. "I believe I made my interest in you clear from the first."

"Your interest in me as a player," Ellen clarified.

"You still don't trust me," he charged.

"You know the position I'm in," she said, stepping around the heart of the issue. "You were an attorney, you should know better than to take it personally."

"That's a little hard to do, all things considered," he said with a sarcastic laugh. "I thought we were past the cover-your-ass stage. You know, I've already seen yours from some very intimate angles."

"Thank you for pointing that out," Ellen said sharply, her temper fraying down to the nub. "Would you care to see it again so you can describe it accurately in chapter nineteen?"

"Jesus Christ, you are so—" He broke off, clamping his teeth down on his temper, reining back the wrong words before they could make a bad situation worse. "Dammit, Ellen, don't you know I wouldn't do anything to hurt you?"

"No, I don't know!" she shot back. "I know you're the one who keeps warning me away and then pulling me back until I feel like a paddle ball. I know your stated purpose in coming to Deer Lake, and I've made it very clear that I hate it. I know you went to law school with Tony Costello, but you claim you don't know him. You pretend to be my friend, then get pissed off when I don't let you in on what you know damn well has to be confidential. You walk into my life out of the shadows like a stalker, then tell me you want to keep me safe. What the hell am I supposed to think about you?"

The question lay between them like a gauntlet. Ellen waited for him to take it up. Neither of them moved. He stood with his hands jammed at the waist of his jeans, eyes narrowed, mouth set in an uncompromising line.

"I've known you a week," she murmured. "A week. One of the worst damn weeks of my life. What am I supposed to think? That you're a hero? That I should trust you? Do you know what happened the last time I trusted a man who said he was my friend, who said he understood?

"He took that trust and used it, used me to buy himself some power. A rapist walked free."

"Fitzpatrick?" Jay whispered.

"His victim was counting on my team. Art Fitzpatrick had destroyed her life, and he walked away from that like it was nothing, because I was stupid enough to trust the wrong man. Tuesday I get to stand across a courtroom from that man, knowing he'll stop at nothing to get what he wants."

"Costello."

He closed his eyes and muttered the name like a curse. The puzzle pieces he had been playing with for a week fell into place. He had known about the Fitzpatrick debacle, of course, but there had been no direct connection to Costello. Costello hadn't represented Fitzpatrick. But he sure as hell would have courted Fitzpatrick and his counsel for future reference. And he had gone through Ellen to do it. That son of a bitch.

"He'll do whatever he has to do to win a case or anything else he happens to want."

"And did he want you? Is that what this is really all about, Ellen? Costello fucked you over figuratively and literally?"

The words exchanged in anger Friday night came back to him now. Costello had betrayed Ellen, and Costello was here, Wright's attorney of choice—a choice made after Ellen had been given the case, a choice made after Jay himself had come into the picture. Christ almighty, no wonder she was paranoid.

And what do you do, Brooks? Jerk her around like a goddamn rag doll.

He had played on her emotions, purposely kept her off balance in the attempt to get what he wanted—the story, the inside track . . . the woman; this woman who stood before him with her defenses worn thin, her pride held up like a shield.

"How's that for an extra twist to your plot, Mr. Brooks?" she said bitterly. "Maybe you'd rather write that story. Maybe you'd rather exploit those people, though I don't imagine sexually abusive corporate magnates sell as well as stolen children. You'd rather tap into that deeper vein of emotion, hit us where we'll all bleed. Well, congratulations, Jay, you managed to hit a double bull's-eye with me. You should be so proud."

"Ellen—" he began, reaching out toward her.

She stepped back from him, holding her hands up in front of her, warning him away. "I think you should leave. The night is young. You can go home and write this little fight scene down while it's fresh in your mind. You can call Costello up and compare notes about my sexual performance. There's just nothing like firsthand experience when it comes to research, is there?"

"Stop it."

"Don't give me orders in my own home, Brooks. I'll call that officer in here and have him throw your ass in jail."

She *would*, of that Jay had little doubt. Ellen didn't make a bluff she wouldn't back up.

"Ellen, I'm sorry," he offered. "I'm a son of a bitch. I admit it."

"And you think that somehow gives you license to go

on being a son of a bitch," Ellen said, shaking her head in disbelief. "As long as you warn people ahead of time, then they can't very well complain, can they? As long as you tell them up front you came to use them—"

"I didn't come here to use you."

"Didn't you? Do you even know the difference anymore? You tell me last night didn't have anything to do with the case, but you turn around and use it against me in—in thinly veiled threats."

"That's not true. You're twisting this out of proportion."

"Am I? Let's see," she said with cutting sarcasm. "Last night we slept together. Today I go to witness the hypnosis of my victim. And here you are tonight, looking for a little pillow talk and getting ugly when I tell you no. What does that add up to?"

"So much bullshit," he snarled, annoyed with her assessment of his character and angry because in his heart he knew she wasn't far wrong. He *did* want to know what had happened with Josh. He would have tried to get her to talk about it. But he didn't think of going to bed with her as part of the process, a sacrifice in the name of duty.

"God, you're no better than that reporter who was screwing Steiger," she said with disgust.

"I do not prostitute myself for information." Jay took a step toward her and then another, backing her up until a wing chair stopped her. "I've said it before: what happens between us is between us. Maybe we met because of this case, but I sure as hell wasn't thinking about the case last night. I was thinking about how hot you were, how soft, how tight you were around me."

With every word his voice dropped and softened. He leaned closer and closer until they were nearly belly to belly, thigh to thigh.

"What we had last night wasn't about the case," he murmured. "You know damn well it wasn't."

She almost wished it had been. But there was no call for righteous indignation. She was a grown woman who had made a choice. He hadn't seduced her; he had needed her. And she had wanted him. And a part of her wanted him even now.

"You're a woman, Ellen. You're not this case. You can't just let it swallow you whole. Isn't that what you wanted away from?"

Yes. But where did she draw the line . . . and where did he? Where did the case end and their personal lives begin? Could the two even be separated or were they as hopelessly intertwined as everything else in this web?

"The choice doesn't seem to be mine to make this time," she said sadly. "I walked away from it once, but the evil came to me this time, to this place. Costello came here. You. The media. Hannah's turned to me. And Josh. And the people I work with. And the people I work for." She forced half a smile, half a laugh. "I'm surrounded."

"I'm not the enemy, Ellen."

No. He was one of those mythical creatures— sometimes good, sometimes bad, always shadowed and mysterious, his role unclear until the end of the story.

"You know what I'm dealing with," she said. "It's up to me to get justice for these people. This is the toughest case I've faced in my career. And I'm rusty. And it scares the hell out of me that this son of a bitch might just outsmart me and walk. And you—you just show up on my doorstep because you want to have sex."

"I came over here because I was concerned about you, Ellen," Jay said stubbornly. "And I'm not leaving."

The steel in his tone made her eyes widen. "Excuse me?"

"Jesus, Ellen, someone blew up your damn car. You've been threatened. You've been singled out for attention from this lunatic and his pals and you've got Barney Fucking Fife parked in front of your house. If I can get in here without his knowing, your nemesis sure as hell can. I'm not leaving. I don't want to see you get hurt."

He didn't want to see her get hurt, but he would hurt her himself. He would be a villain in one sense or another. He would write about this case, turn it into a diversion to be read and tossed aside and left on airplanes. He would reduce her to a character, and Hannah and Josh, and Mitch and Megan. He would take what he wanted from this and leave. He had given her a part of himself, but he would still leave.

"Point taken," she said. "And I appreciate the thought. I'll have that dead bolt installed first thing tomorrow."

"And tonight?"

"I'll take my chances."

"No," he argued. "A chance is the last thing you're willing to take. It's smarter to walk away, play it safe. You got burned once, why risk it again?"

"I took a big chance last night."

"And now you regret it."

"No," Ellen admitted. "I just see the wisdom in not taking it again."

Jay studied her face for a long moment—the honesty, the resolve, the regret for this moment if not for the night they had spent in each other's arms. He might have tried harder to change her mind. He might have seduced her, but then every rotten thought she had about him would have been true, and for the first time in a long time someone else's opinion mattered to him. For the first time in forever he caught himself wanting to be something he wasn't. Noble.

Life had become too damn complicated.

"Please, Jay," Ellen murmured. "It's not that I don't want to. I just can't. Not now. I'll have the officer come in and spend the night on the couch. Please go."

"You'd rather have some fat ol' cop eating doughnuts on your sofa than have me in your bed? Christ."

"No, but it's for the best." She handed him his coat and started up the steps for the dining room. "I wish things could be different, but the case is the case, and I am who I am, and you are who you are. . . ."

"And I'm no damn good for you," he said. "Well, sugar, that isn't exactly headline news."

"Maybe after this is all over . . . ," Ellen began, but she stopped herself. What was the point in saying it? They had shared a night and made no promises.

"Say good night, Ellen," she ordered herself.

"Good night, Ellen," he echoed, lowering his mouth to hers.

He kissed her slowly, deeply.

"If you decide to take that chance, counselor," he whispered, "you know where to find me."

Then he slipped out the door.

Ellen stood at the storm door until the glass frosted over and the cold chilled the heat of need on her skin. But the heavy sense of yearning, of regret, remained as she took her briefcase to bed.

CHAPTER 28

Monday morning brought an article in the *Pioneer Press* about the harassment of the Sci-Fi Cowboys; phone calls from the mayor, two state senators, and three congressmen; and the threat of a lawsuit. Rudy darkened Ellen's office door before her first cup of coffee could turn cold.

"They have no grounds for a lawsuit," Ellen assured him, rubbing a smudge of fingerprint dust from the gooseneck of her lamp. "Priest has his nose out of joint because his pets might turn out to be bad boys after all. Mitch had good cause to haul those kids in and question them."

Rudy had somehow managed to tie his necktie over the top of one collar point. Green and yellow, it looked like an oversize garter snake trying to choke him.

"Ellen, that program has garnered national attention. Do you have any idea of the people who back it?"

People with money. People with clout on the local and state levels. People Rudy had sucked up to, or would, at some point in his career.

"I endorsed it myself." Stopping by her window, he looked out, as if he expected an angry mob to be clamoring at the steps. He pulled a roll of Tums out of his pants pocket, thumbed off two, and popped them into his mouth.

"It's a fine program," Ellen said. "It wouldn't be your

fault if it turned out to have some rotten apples in the barrel."

"We can't have them suing the county attorney's office, for God's sake."

"They're making noise, that's all."

"Can't you make a statement of some kind? Placate them."

Ellen bit down on a rebuke of his cowardice. "Rudy, I have every reason to believe those kids torched that Cadillac. I will not placate them. And what if it turns out Priest is involved with Wright in the kidnappings?"

"He passed the polygraph. He was in St. Peter when O'Malley was attacked—"

"We know Wright is the one who attacked Megan. That doesn't absolve Priest of guilt. He could be making this stink now for the sole purpose of getting us to back off so he can have room to maneuver."

"Good grief."

Ellen watched him stroke his hand back over his steel-wool hair. She could all but hear the oily wheels of his mind spinning as he tried to sort the dilemma into an order from which he could somehow benefit.

"Relax," she said. "The public will side with Priest. Sig Iverson will side with Priest. You can remain safely neutral. *I'm* the bad guy. You can't lose, Rudy. Unless, of course, Priest turns out to be a kidnapper and the Sci-Fi Cowboys fried that car."

She almost laughed as his face contorted through a full range of expressions from relief to panic. He couldn't seem to decide which one to settle on.

"You can make the statement," she said. Stepping up to him, she reached up and tugged his collar free of his tie. "'No comment regarding ongoing investigations.' You have confidence in my abilities—this said with a grave expression that might leave room for doubt. Same old noncommittal song and dance. Fred Astaire couldn't do it any better than you, Rudy."

He scowled at her askance as he tried to catch his reflection in the glass of a framed certificate hanging on the wall. "You know that smart tongue won't do you any good when you run for office," he said, snugging the knot in his tie.

"For the millionth time, I have no intention of running for office."

He listened as well as he ever did.

"Where is Jay Butler Brooks?" he asked testily. "I thought he'd be in the offices more. I want to sell him on an idea for a book."

"Your life story?"

"Career of country lawyer," he said, dead serious. "I've faced some fascinating cases in my day. Like the time the Warneky brothers tipped a cow onto their hired man. It *seemed* like an accident, but—"

"You know, Rudy," Ellen said, tapping a finger against her watch, "I'm sure it's the stuff of a blockbuster, but I've got to be in Grabko's chambers in five minutes. He's ruling on Josh Kirkwood's medical records. I'll update you later."

She hurried out of the office, pausing by Phoebe's desk only long enough to instruct her to lock up after Rudy. She took a back staircase to avoid reporters and had to squeeze her way around workmen's scaffolding, swearing under her breath as plaster dust rained down on her, dotting her navy-blue blazer like talcum powder. Brushing away the residue, she slipped past the law library and ducked behind a granite column to scope out the situation in the main hall.

Family court was in session. The hall in front of what had been Judge Franken's courtroom was clogged with kids and husbands and wives glaring at one another, county social workers and attorneys, all waiting their turn before the substitute judge the district had sent. Beyond them, milling around Judge Grabko's door and spilling out onto the rotunda balcony, were the esteemed members of the press, waiting to catch first word of Grabko's ruling.

Waiting to catch me, Ellen thought. They were steamed that the *Pioneer Press* had scooped them all on the interview with Christopher Priest, and they would take it out on her.

"I'll run interference if you give me an exclusive."

Ellen jerked around. Adam Slater had slipped up behind her and stood close enough to touch. Dressed in grunge flannel and a letterman's jacket, he could have easily blended into the family-court crowd. His hair swung down into his eyes as he made a show of licking the tip of his pencil and poising it above his reporter's notebook.

"You just don't give up, do you?"

"It's a common misconception that Generation X'ers have no focus. So are you really going after the Sci-Fi Cowboys? They're supposed to be the big success story. Bad boys turned good, snatched from the jaws of sociopathy and trained to use their powers for the good of mankind. That's what everyone believes—notable exception: you."

"It's a wonderful program," Ellen said by rote. "I hope it turns out the boys had nothing to do with the explosion."

"And the kidnappings?"

"No one ever said they were suspects in the kidnappings." She shot a nervous glance toward Grabko's door and the crowd in front of it. The natives seemed to be growing restless, and there was no sign of Costello. He had either sneaked in early or was waiting to make his entrance. She was screwed either way. *Should have brought a deputy with me*.

"Routine background checks are being run on all of Dr. Wright's close friends and associates," she said. "Now,

I've got to be in judge's chambers, Mr. Slater. I held up my end of the bargain. It's your turn."

He scribbled a last line in his notebook, then tucked it into an inside coat pocket and slicked his hair back. "No sweat, Ms. North."

He strutted off toward the family-court crowd, drawing a bead on Quentin Adler. "Hey, Curly!" he bellowed, thrusting an accusatory finger in Quentin's face. "You and me gotta have some words, man. You screwed me over!"

Quentin nearly gave himself a whiplash looking to one side and the other for a more likely target than himself. "Me?" he squeaked, color crawling up his neck.

Slater jabbed him in the sternum with his finger. "Those charges were, like, *so* bogus!"

His voice rang off the walls, drawing the attention of the bored reporters. He backed Quentin toward them as he ranted on, backed him toward the open area around the balcony, giving Ellen a route along the wall. She took it, head down, hustling toward the side door to Grabko's chambers. By the time anyone caught sight of her, she was able to throw out a handful of "no comments" and duck into the outer office.

"It's all in the wrist, Mr. Costello," Grabko said, demonstrating his casting move in slow motion.

Costello stood beside him, looking like an ad for *GQ* in a pearl-gray suit that was worth a month of Ellen's salary. His shirt was as white as an angel's wings, his tie perfectly knotted. It was difficult to imagine he and Rudy Stovich belonged to the same species.

"As in so many aspects of life," Grabko preached, "success in fly-fishing is a matter of concentration, logic, and grace."

"And me without my waders," Ellen muttered, skewering Costello with a look. He gave her a smile that was all too generous.

With great care Grabko set his rod into a carved-walnut wall rack. "Do you fish, Ellen?"

"Only in the metaphorical sense," she said, sliding into a chair. "Catch anything, Tony?" she asked under her breath as he settled into the chair beside her.

"That remains to be seen," he murmured.

The judge sank down into the pillow softness of his leather chair, straightened his red-striped bow tie, and immediately began to pet his beard, stroking it like a cat. His gaze fell on Ellen with fatherly concern.

"I hear we're lucky to have you among the living, Ellen."

"I don't believe it was an attempt on my life, Your Honor. Just a warning."

"Dr. Wright was disturbed to hear about it," Costello said.

"That my car blew up or that I wasn't in it at the time?"

"You'd be surprised at his concern, Ellen."

"Yes, I would be, seeing as how I have every intention of putting him behind bars for the rest of his life."

"He's also concerned about the allegations against the Sci-Fi Cowboys. He doesn't want to see the program suffer because of its ties to him."

"If the program suffers, it's because of the attitudes of the individuals involved," Ellen said. "I think Dr. Wright and his colleagues may have overestimated a couple of their boys."

"Do you have any evidence against the young men?" Grabko asked.

"Nothing solid at this point. The police and the BCA are working on it, but they're being spread thin these days. Thanks to your client and his friends," she said, turning back to Costello.

He shook off the responsibility. "My client is an innocent man. Our case will speak for itself."

"Which brings us to the business of the day," Grabko said. He tapped the cover of a red file folder sitting squarely on his blotter. "Josh Kirkwood's medical records. I spent a good deal of time looking them over."

Ellen pulled in a breath and held it.

"Parental child abuse is a horrible crime. One we seldom suspect in a family like the Kirkwoods'. A dangerous oversight on our part. Abuse knows no socioeconomic barriers."

"Our point, exactly, Your Honor," Costello said, leaning forward in his chair.

"However . . ." He drew the words out, savoring his moment. "I found nothing in Josh Kirkwood's records that could be construed as out of the ordinary or as being relevant to the case."

The breath sighed out of Ellen. "Just as we expected all along."

Costello gave a subtle shrug. You win some, you lose some. He had got what he wanted out of the play—media attention, the opportunity to sow the seeds of doubt.

"I suppose I shouldn't be surprised," Costello said. "Hannah Garrison is head of the ER at the hospital where Josh has been treated. Well respected, well liked, the kind of woman who might be able to persuade a fellow doctor or nurse to see an incident her way."

"And convince them to falsify records?" Ellen said. After everything she had seen Hannah put through, she could have throttled Costello for taking this tack. "Watch where you're stepping, Tony. You're about to put your handmade Italian loafer in a big hot pile."

"I'm not trying to portray the mother as the villain," he defended himself. "The husband is emotionally abusive and manipulative. He coerced her or convinced her."

"And maybe there's life on Uranus, but your speculation on that subject isn't admissible either," Ellen said sharply. "The issue at hand is the medical records. You're dead in the water, Tony. Let's move on."

"Fine." He reached into his briefcase and pulled out a document. "Motion to dismiss."

"And our argument against dismissal," Ellen said, handing over Cameron's brief.

Grabko accepted the paperwork with the satisfied glow of a teacher taking extra-credit projects from his favorite students.

"And," Costello said, pulling another rabbit from his hat, "in the event we do proceed, motion to suppress the lineup ID."

Ellen jerked around in her chair, gaping at him. "What? On what grounds? That was a perfectly good by-the-book lineup!" She turned to Grabko. "Your Honor, great pains were taken to ensure the fairness of that lineup."

"You were there, Ellen?"

"No. Mr. Stovich oversaw the process personally. But I've spoken with all parties involved."

Costello handed the motion to Grabko. "Then you should be aware of the fact that Dr. Wright's attorney was barred from the room where Mrs. Cooper filled out her written report."

"*Barred?*" Ellen said, incredulous. "I hardly think so. Dennis Enberg was present at the lineup. If he wasn't in the room when Mrs. Cooper filled out the paperwork, it was his own choice."

"That's not the way I hear it."

"From who?"

"From my client—"

"Oh, there's a reliable source—a psychopathic child stealer."

"And from Mrs. Cooper herself. Her affidavit is attached, Your Honor."

"I'd like a copy of that, if you don't mind," Ellen snapped.

Costello permitted himself the tiniest of smiles. "Of course, Ellen. You *did* specify your office wanted everything in writing and handled through the proper channels. I've sent your copies over via messenger."

Fury burned in Ellen's cheeks. She glared at him and mouthed *You son of a bitch.* The smugness in his expression made her want to choke, particularly because she knew its origin. He had turned her own trick back on her. In the normal course of events around a rural courthouse, challenges were made over the phone or hashed out in person. Formalities were waived. She had imposed by-the-book standards on Costello to punish him, to slow him down, to irritate him. And here she sat. . . .

"And what kind of messenger did you send? A dog team via Winnipeg?" she said sarcastically. "I should have been notified about this Friday at the latest."

Manufacturing a look of abject innocence, Costello directed his explanation at Grabko. "We weren't able to contact Mrs. Cooper until Friday afternoon, Your Honor. With the time constraints—"

"Cheerfully accepted by you, Mr. Costello," Ellen pointed out.

He ignored her. "We're doing the best we can, Your Honor. And we are thoroughly prepared for the hearing. We hoped you'd be lenient with regards to service of this motion, all things considered."

The judge tugged at the white spot in his beard, looking grave. "I can't disregard the motion, considering its gravity. And I do feel the circumstances can be considered good cause to make an exception to the general rule. Ellen, if you feel this upsets the balance, if you feel you need more time . . ."

"No, Your Honor," she said tightly. "We're ready. I just don't appreciate being ambushed—especially with something as groundless as this."

"Why don't we let the judge decide the merits of the motion, Ellen?" Costello suggested in a patronizing tone.

Grabko perched a pair of reading glasses on his nose and turned to the affidavit. "According to Mrs. Cooper, Mr. Enberg expressed an interest in coming into the room where she was filling out her report, but one of three officers present in the room turned him away, then followed him out."

"I don't believe it," Ellen challenged. "What officer? Let's get him in here."

Costello huffed a laugh. "I'm sure he'll tell us the truth when he sees what's riding on his story. Every cop in town wants to see my client publicly hanged. Mrs. Cooper is the only impartial witness to what happened."

"Dennis Enberg would never have allowed himself to be barred from the room if he had wanted to be present," Ellen argued.

"He's not here to tell us that, though, is he, Ellen?"

"Yeah, what a lucky stroke for you, Tony," she said, her words dripping venom. "Right about now Denny is on a stainless-steel table at Hennepin County Medical Center getting himself sawed in half by a medical examiner."

"Ellen, please," Grabko chastised her. "I'll call the officer in, and I'll speak with Mr. Stovich, but as Mr. Enberg isn't able to speak for himself on the matter, I have to concur with Mr. Costello—Mrs. Cooper is the least biased of all involved parties."

"But, Your Honor, Mrs. Cooper never mentioned this when I spoke with her."

"Did you ask her specifically?"

"I had no reason to ask such a question. We spoke at length about the lineup procedure—"

"And she had no reason to think anything was out of the ordinary," Costello said. "She isn't an attorney. She isn't a police officer. She had no way of knowing proper procedure. She trusted the police to conduct themselves properly, and they betrayed that trust."

"I'm sure that's what you led her to believe," Ellen sneered.

"That's enough, Ellen." Grabko set the affidavit aside. "I'll speak to all parties involved and come to a decision. Is there anything more we need to discuss today?"

Costello lifted his hands. "Nothing further, Your Honor."

"No, sir," Ellen said grudgingly.

"Fine," Grabko said, straightening the stack of documents. "I'll see you both here tomorrow morning."

"You really are a sleaze, Tony," Ellen muttered as they left Grabko's chambers for the outer office. His secretary had vanished, leaving them alone.

"Why?" Costello pulled up short of the hall door and faced her, standing close enough for confidentiality. "Because I'm doing my job? Because I don't believe my client is guilty?"

"You don't give a damn if he is. You play this system like a pickup soccer game. Nothing matters except that you win. You trick my witness into doing your dirty work for you. You call Josh Kirkwood's father a child abuser and impugn the reputation of his mother. If you publicly accuse Hannah Garrison of falsifying those medical records, I hope she sues your ass eight ways from Sunday."

He made a pretense of being hurt. "That's not a very charitable sentiment toward someone who is genuinely concerned for your safety, Ellen. You could have been killed in that car."

"Is that your unbiased opinion, or do you know something the rest of us don't?"

"Yes, Ellen, I am not only trying to acquit a guilty monster, I am also in on the conspiracy to kill you. Christ, can't you take anything I say to you at face value?"

"The fact that you have at least two faces complicates the issue."

He shook his head. "You always took it too personally," he said almost to himself. "The job is the job, Ellen. Just because we stand on opposite sides of the courtroom doesn't mean we can't set it aside when we walk out the door."

"Oh, that's rich coming from you, Tony," she sneered. "You're never off the job. As far as you're concerned, there are twenty-four billable hours to a day. No situation, no relationship, is exempt. Don't even try to argue with me on that score, and don't delude yourself into thinking you can win me over. I know just what lengths you'll go to."

Their past hung between them, dense with complicated facts and feelings and fears that had never been proved true or false.

"Be careful, Ellen," he said at last. "While you're busy watching for me to strike, there's a real snake out there."

"And his name is probably already in your Rolodex."

"Your imagined accomplice?"

"Technically, I believe I would be correct in calling him *your* accomplice."

"In your delusions of vengeance." He buttoned his jacket and tugged it straight, preparing himself for the cameras. "Nice try, siccing the BCA after me, getting Wilhelm to make noise about a warrant for my phone records. Sadly, it's just another example of how this investigation is being botched—which is what I'll have to point out to the press."

"Point away, Tony," Ellen said with a knife-edge smile. "All the press needs is a suspicion of your involvement and they'll be digging like badgers. Who knows what they might turn up? I know I'll be standing right there to see what crawls out of your lair."

She jerked the door open and stepped out into the hall, eager for once to upstage him in front of the cameras.

"I don't know how much help I can be to you, Mr. Brooks," Christopher Priest said without apology. His expression was as neutral as his voice, his face the blank oval of a mannequin's.

His office was exactly what Jay had imagined: a claustrophobic little cube crowded with books and file cabinets. A computer monitor on the desk displayed an endless repetition of starbursts. The room was filled with the stuff of academia—textbooks and reference books and student papers—but with none of the personal bric-a-brac that would have given a flavor of the man whose name was on the small placard outside the door. The desk was too neat, the office as devoid of personality as the professor himself.

"Some of my students and I were involved with the volunteer effort to find Josh," he said, seating himself with prim precision. "We set up computer stations at the volunteer center and went on-line to disperse and receive information through the various networks. That's the extent of my connection."

Jay voiced his skepticism. "That's a bit of an oversimplification, don't you think, Professor? You volunteered to help with the investigation, then one of the cops involved was attacked in your own front yard, then your best friend was arrested. . . . You must be feeling like this whole thing is sucking you in like a tar pit."

"It's been a little overwhelming, yes," he conceded.

"And Dr. Garrison is a friend of yours, right?"

"I know Hannah," he admitted. "I admire her. She's an extraordinary woman."

Jay took in the hint of color that touched the professor's pale cheeks when he spoke of Hannah. "Man, if I had all that buzzing around me, I'd be feeling downright dizzy. Now the cops are looking for that student—Todd

Childs—and looking at the Sci-Fi Cowboys. You must feel almost as if *you're* under attack."

Priest stared at him like an owl from behind his over-size glasses. "I had nothing to do with any crime. Neither did the Cowboys."

"Circumstances suggest otherwise where the boys are concerned."

"Circumstances aren't always what they seem. The Sci-Fi Cowboys are a very select group of young men, Mr. Brooks. Handpicked for their talents and potential."

"Aren't most of their talents against the law?"

"*Academic* talents," Priest specified, unamused. "They are very bright young men who deserve a chance to prove they can be productive members of society."

"And they're no doubt grateful for the opportunity," Jay said. "Giving a kid a gift like that inspires loyalty. Kids with the kind of backgrounds the Cowboys have might express that loyalty in, shall we say, *inappropriate* ways."

"I stand behind the Cowboys," Priest said flatly. "I've said all I'm going to say about the subject to the police and to the press—and to you, Mr. Brooks. If you came here hoping for an admission of guilt, there's no point in continuing this conversation."

"No, no, not at all—"

"I know what you told the police about the encounter with Tyrell and the other two boys Saturday night," he said in a strangely quiet voice, as if it were a lurid secret.

"I simply told them what happened, Professor. I'm not taking sides."

"Aren't you?" His thin lips pressed together. "You're not . . . aligning yourself with Ms. North?"

"What would make you think I was?"

"The two of you had words at the benefit. You followed her out."

And he had been watching from his post beside Garrett

Wright's wife. The idea stirred a strange sense of violation.

"Ms. North has a philosophical objection to my work," Jay said with a well-rehearsed sardonic smile. "She has managed to equate the writing and publishing of true crime with the Romans selling tickets to watch Christians being devoured by lions."

Priest considered the response. "An interesting correlation. The readers of your work are, of course, insulated from the immediate horror of the violence, but perhaps the two *do* share a common attraction."

"Not for me."

"Hmm, well, it's all in our perception, isn't it?" he said. "And perception is dependent upon what? You can present the same set of facts and circumstances to five different people, and they may give you five different interpretations—which is why many seasoned courtroom attorneys will tell you there is nothing so unreliable as an eyewitness. The opinions we form are based on individual perceptions, something science has yet to fully understand.

"Fascinating, isn't it?" He gave his head a slight shake, as if humans were simply too much trouble, and cast an affectionate glance at his computer screen. "The human mind can be infinitely logical and pragmatic, or stubbornly irrational. A hopelessly vacant mind can hold a kernel of brilliance. A brilliant mind can be fatally flawed."

"Which would you say applies to our kidnapper?"

A slight smile touched the corners of his mouth. "I wouldn't say. Human behavior is Dr. Wright's specialty, not mine."

"But you were working on a project together, right?"

"We *are* working on a joint project, dealing with, as it happens, learning and perception."

"You've known each other a long time, you and Dr. Wright?"

"We both taught at Penn State."

"Yeah, but y'all knew each other before that, didn't you?"

"I don't know what you're talking about," Priest said guardedly.

Jay feigned innocence. "Well, gee, you know, I was just doing a little digging. Background work and all. Talking to an old colleague of yours from Penn State who mentioned you all grew up in the same town."

"I grew up in Chicago."

"Huh, well, you know, I'd read that," he said, scratching his head. "Strange thing for a friend to be wrong about, wouldn't you say?"

"Nevertheless," Priest said impatiently, "I might have visited Indiana as a boy, but I didn't grow up there."

"So you *didn't* know Dr. Wright?"

"We became friends at Penn State."

"Good friends. The kind of friends who share things, stick up for each other, help each other out."

"Is there a point to this line of questioning, Mr. Brooks?"

Jay gave a shrug and a smile. "I'm just trolling, Professor. Looking for background. I never know what I might find or where it might lead me. For instance, you might just up and say you'd do anything for Garrett Wright. Who knows where an answer like that might lead?"

"To a dead end." Priest rose. "I'm sorry to cut this short, but I have a class to prepare for, Mr. Brooks."

Jay checked his watch. According to the helpful young lady in the main office, Christopher Priest didn't have another class until evening.

"I guess I'll just have to check that background the hard way," he said, pushing himself to his feet. "Thank you for your time, Professor."

He turned back at the door, catching Priest staring at him with that blank face. "That student who was in the

car accident the night Josh was abducted—was he working on that joint project with you and Dr. Wright?"

"Yes, he was."

"Hmm. I wonder what his perception of that coincidence would be."

"I'm afraid we'll never know," Priest said. "I received
word this morning he passed away."

Jay sensed the news hit him harder than it had the professor. Death—delivered off the cuff, as an after-thought,
with no more remorse than was socially required.

He stepped into the hall, his head buzzing. The car accident had set everything in motion; now the student who
had been running an errand for Priest was dead. Todd
Childs was a student of Wright's and Priest's. Olie Swain,
the prime suspect until his jailhouse suicide, had audited
classes of both men. Megan O'Malley had suspected
Priest. She had been attacked in the yard of Priest's secluded country home.

Christopher Priest seemed as much a part of the story
as Garrett Wright, and yet no one had anything on him.
He was as clean as Teflon, visible in his efforts, first, to
help in the effort to find Josh, and now, in his support of
his colleague.

"*We* are *working on a joint project*. . . ."

He had passed a polygraph.

"*. . . it's all in our perception, isn't it?*"

Priest and Wright went back a long way. It wouldn't
have been a stretch to imagine them as partners in more
than a school project. A pair of sharp, calculating minds.
Wright, handsome and charming; Priest, socially awkward with a crush on Hannah Garrison. Motive had been
an elusive creature in this crime from the first. There had
been no ransom demand. No one seemed to have it in for
Hannah or Paul. The taunting, the planted evidence, suggested it was all about superiority, a game of wits. But
taking Josh Kirkwood had also given Christopher Priest a

chance to be close to Hannah, a chance to offer his help, to call attention to himself.

And damned if it wouldn't sell books, he thought. The twisted tale of the psychopathic professors. Brilliant minds fatally flawed.

But had Priest had opportunity to take Dustin Holloman, to plant those clues? It seemed unlikely he would take that kind of chance, knowing the police had their eyes on him. And then there was Todd Childs to consider. . . .

He turned down another hall. He could take a look at Wright's office as long as he was here, see if it offered any insights. The cops would already have taken the place apart hunting for evidence, but it was still important for him to have a sense of the places the people he wrote about inhabited. To be able to describe Garrett Wright's perfectly normal office would add to the unsettling idea that anyone could be warped beneath their ordinary facades. That kind of chill brought readers back again and again. Like Romans to the Colosseum.

The door to Wright's office stood slightly ajar. Jay brought himself up short at the sight. His escapade at the Pack Rat was still fresh in his mind—in the form of a dull headache that had nagged him since the accident. He moved cautiously along the wall, determined not to be taken by surprise this time.

Sidling up to the door, he gently eased it open another fraction of an inch, expecting to see Todd Childs.

The room was awash in paper. Books had been torn from their shelves and left on the floor. The place looked as if it had been tossed by goons, and in the middle of the mess stood Karen Wright. She looked utterly lost, fragile, overwhelmed by the state of the place. And he would take advantage of that, bastard that he was.

Not giving himself time to turn noble, Jay rapped his knuckles twice on the door frame and let himself into the office.

"Mrs. Wright?"

She jerked around and looked up at him. "I—I can't find anything," she said meekly.

"Well, ma'am, it is a hell of a mess," he said. "What is it you're looking for?"

"Books. Garrett asked me to pick up some of his books. He'll be angry about this. He likes his office neat and orderly."

"Do you have any idea who did this?"

"The police. They said they were looking for evidence."

Looking for evidence and taking a little revenge, Jay reasoned. Garrett Wright stood accused of attacking and savagely beating one of their own. Cops didn't take a thing like that lightly.

"You should have seen our house when they finished," she murmured as she began to set her husband's desk to rights. "They even took up floorboards. All for nothing. I told them they wouldn't find anything, but they wouldn't listen to me."

"They're stubborn that way."

She picked up a coffee mug that had been knocked to the floor and held it to her chest like a treasured doll. "You're that writer, aren't you? Garrett told me you're going to do a book about the case. He shouldn't be going to court. It's all a big mistake."

"Is it?" Jay asked quietly, watching her carefully.

"He wouldn't take Josh."

Her gaze was like a butterfly, lighting and flying away from point to point, all around the room. She might have been lying, or she might have been afraid. Or she might have been as cracked as Grandma's china, as Teresa McGuire, the victim-witness coordinator, had suggested to him over coffee and cinnamon rolls at the Scandia House.

"Garrett wouldn't have," Karen said, shaking her head. "No. He wouldn't have. . . . He wouldn't do that to me."

"Wouldn't do what?" he asked, trying to keep her attention focused on him.

"He doesn't like children," she mumbled. "He didn't like *being* a child."

"Did you know him as a child?"

A thin smile trembled across her mouth, and she wandered off toward one of the gutted bookcases.

Jay moved with her to keep her face in view. "I heard you helped out at the Kirkwoods' while Josh was missing. You helped take care of the baby."

Karen might have been Wright's spy—willing or unwitting—filling him in firsthand about the havoc he was wreaking on the lives of Hannah and Paul.

"Lily," Karen said. This time the smile was fuller, richer. "She's so precious. I'd give anything for a little sweetheart like her."

"You don't have any children of your own?"

The smile fell. "Garrett and I can't have children."

"I'm sorry," he said automatically. "That was good of you to help the Kirkwoods. Was that your idea?"

"Oh, I didn't mind at all. Hannah and Paul are friends."

She used the present tense as if it were still true, as if she had no grasp of the magnitude of the charges against her husband. As if by saying it was all a mistake, everyone would accept her word and they would all continue their lives as if nothing had happened.

She set the coffee mug aside, picked several books up off the floor, and slid them into place in the bookcase.

"Garrett doesn't like messes," she said with an odd light of amusement in her eyes.

"Well, he seems to have got himself smack in the middle of a big one."

Karen Wright shook her head. "Oh, no," she said. "It's all just a big mistake."

CHAPTER 29

"Barred from the room!" Mitch exploded. "Bullshit!"

Cameron winced. Phoebe cowered. Ellen looked him in the eye.

"Were you present in the room when she filled out her statement?"

He raked a hand back through his hair as if trying to scratch loose a memory. "Not right away. Stovich was bending my ear for a couple of minutes. When I did step into the room, no one said a goddamn thing to me. Everything was fine. If someone had tried to stop Dennis from going in, he would have squealed like a stuck pig."

"That's what I said," Ellen complained. "And Grabko should know it, too. Costello has him dazzled. I've never seen so much preening and posturing in my life. While you were at the autopsy, Grabko was calling your officers in this afternoon to get their take on it, but my gut tells me we've already lost the round."

"Fuck me," Mitch grumbled. "After all the trouble we went to, putting that lineup together. Jesus Christ." He pulled in a deep breath and huffed it out. "How bad does this hurt us?"

Ellen considered for a moment, turning her pencil over and over in her hands. "For a hearing in front of a judge, not a lot. But I wanted Ruth Cooper on the stand in front of a jury," she admitted. "Costello would have taken apart the lineup ID because Wright was too bundled up for a dead-on no-doubt *that's him*. But her testimony combined with the voice ID would have made an impact."

"Can you salvage anything?"

"She can testify that she saw a man on Ryan's Bay that morning, that he came to her house, that he spoke to her. Then Costello is going to get up on cross and ask her if that man is in the courtroom, if she can point him out to us, and she's going to have to say no."

"Shit."

They sat in silence for a moment, mourning the loss of their witness.

"So," Ellen said, regrouping. "What's the word from the ME?"

"Preliminary results of the autopsy show nothing to indicate murder," Mitch said. "Unless something strange turns up in the lab, he's going to sign it off as suicide."

In her heart Ellen knew Dennis Enberg had been murdered. The shadowed voice that had haunted her since that night whispered in the back of her mind. *"The first thing we do, let's kill all the lawyers."*

"He had a blood alcohol level of .30, so he was good and drunk."

"Too drunk to rig up the gun?" she asked.

"There are too many factors we don't know. He could have tricked out the gun when he was at .10 then drunk some more to get up his nerve. Or he could have been passed out and been fed that gun by a killer. The killer could have bashed his head in and *then* pulled the trigger to make it look like suicide."

"Any opinions from the BCA?" Cameron asked.

"I haven't heard from them directly. Wilhelm and Steiger are off chasing a lead on the Holloman kidnapping. The mother got a phone call, allegedly from the boy."

A chill crawled down Ellen's spine. "Just like what happened with Josh."

"Apparently so. They traced the call to Rochester. They're down there now checking it out. I don't expect them back tonight."

The inconvenience was too timely. Ellen had asked the three principal law-enforcement officers to meet to go over everything they had one last time before the hearing. She wanted to have the clearest possible picture as to the status of the case, the most up-to-the-minute information from the BCA on the analysis of the evidence. With Wilhelm gone she would have to track down the information by phone. A time-consuming process, and the clock was ticking. Four-forty.

Not for the first time, she felt as if their nemesis had a bird's-eye view of everything going on on their side of the case. He had been three steps ahead of them all the way, playing with them like a cat with a mouse.

"*We can't lose,*" Wright had told Megan. "*You can't defeat us. We're very good at this game. Brilliant and invincible.*"

What if they were?

"The report on the fingerprints in Enberg's office is about what you'd expect," Mitch went on. "The place was a mess. There were prints everywhere. God only knows the last time he cleaned the place."

"Prints on the gun?"

"Denny's only."

"What about time of death?" Cameron asked.

"The ME put it around one A.M., give or take an hour."

"My mystery call came at two," Ellen murmured.

"And the help at the Donut Hut put Paul Kirkwood at Enberg's office around nine-thirty," Cameron said. "That rules him out."

"Unless he came back later," Ellen offered.

Mitch shook his head. "I don't figure Paul for this. What's his motive? Enberg was no longer representing Wright, and he was doing a half-assed job before he got canned. Why should Paul off him?"

"Why should Paul go to see him?" Ellen asked.

"It makes sense if Paul was Wright's accomplice," Cameron suggested.

"We've had this conversation before," Mitch said. "It's too bizarre for words."

"Well, Costello would buy half of it." Ellen tossed her pencil down. "He's already tipped his hand. He's going to do his best to divert attention to Paul. Grabko ruled against him on the medical records, but that isn't stopping him from making his case to the press."

"Asshole lawyers," Mitch muttered. He caught himself too late and gave Ellen a look. "Present company excluded."

She shrugged it off. "What about the Sci-Fi Cowboys? Has anyone confirmed their whereabouts on the night Dennis died?"

"All present and accounted for, provided you can believe the people who gave them alibis. They were in Deer Lake as a group on Tuesday to meet with Priest and returned to the Cities that evening. They didn't come back until Thursday afternoon."

"Any holes in their stories for Saturday night?" Cameron asked.

Mitch shook his head. "Not yet. I'd bet my pension Tyrell Mann torched that Cadillac, but I don't have a witness and I don't have any evidence. In other words, at the moment we don't have shit. It's as simple as that."

Ellen pulled her glasses off and rubbed her hands over her face. "Nothing is simple where this case is concerned."

"That's old news, counselor," Mitch said. "If anything new comes in, I'll call. I'll be at home if you need me. Jessie's making dinner for Megan, and I get to help." A spark of happiness lit his bloodshot eyes. "I'd better stop for antacid on the way. Kindergartners aren't known for their culinary talents."

Ellen followed him to the conference-room door. In

the outer office Quentin was regaling someone with his harrowing tale of being accosted outside family court.

". . . and just as security arrived," he said, gesturing like a maestro, "the guy steps back and says, 'Hey, man, you're not who I thought. Sorry!'"

Ellen pulled her attention back to Mitch. "How's Megan doing?"

"Chomping at the bit to testify. She doesn't like being on the sidelines, you know. She's a cop right down to her toenails." A shadow of doubt crossed his face as he weighed the wisdom of telling her something. Then he set his jaw in a stubborn line and plunged in. "I dumped Wright's background stuff on her to sort through."

"Mitch—"

"I don't want to hear it, Ellen. We're just too short-handed with everything that's been going on. And she's too damn sharp to waste," he argued. "I'll keep the paper trail clean."

His expression softened. "She needs it, Ellen. She needs to know she can still do the job."

"Fine," Ellen surrendered, too tired to fight, and too concerned for Megan's well-being. It wasn't as if Megan were being given access to physical evidence. The information she would be looking over was cut-and-dried, facts that were years in the past. Anything she might find had already become a part of history and couldn't be tampered with. God knew they needed all the help they could get.

"Quentin's still reliving his narrow brush with excitement," she announced back in the conference room.

"Polishing up the performance for his paramour," Cameron suggested with a smirk. "By the time he tells Jan, he'll have it sounding like a fight scene from *Die Hard*."

"Our comic relief," Ellen said, settling back into her chair.

Phoebe fluffed herself up like a little quail, tilting her chin to a proud angle. "Well, I think it was really gallant and original of Adam, the way he helped you."

Cameron pulled a face of mock horror. *"Adam?"*

Ellen frowned at her secretary. "There was nothing noble about it. It was a business deal. And he enjoyed himself. He got to be annoying *and* got rewarded for it. And what's with the first-name basis?"

"Nothing." Phoebe's gaze landed everywhere but Ellen's face. "That's his name, that's all. What am I supposed to call him?"

"A distant memory," Ellen suggested sharply. "We've talked about this, Phoebe. He's a reporter. Being cute doesn't cancel that out."

"You don't know him," Phoebe said stiffly.

"Neither do you."

"I'd never get to know anyone if I was as paranoid as you are. Just because *you* never trust anyone doesn't mean people aren't trustworthy."

"That's an admirable attitude," Ellen said impatiently. "But you know something, Phoebe? This isn't Mister Rogers's neighborhood. This is a big case full of bad people out to get what they can and to hell with everyone else. So maybe you could do us a favor and grow up. You can make nice with anyone you want after it's over."

Phoebe stood abruptly and gathered up her notebook and a messy stack of files. "If you're through lecturing me, I'll go make those phone calls to the BCA now."

Ellen pulled a typed list of names and numbers from one of the files and held it out.

"After you call the BCA, please call these probation officers and see if they've got anything for me."

"You're so insensitive!" Phoebe charged. Dumping the files onto the table, she ran out of the room.

"I'm guessing it was something you said," Cameron offered with a pained look. "Are you going after her?"

"No, dammit. I'm not her mother. I'm her bitch queen boss," Ellen muttered glumly.

She had more important things to expend her energy on than her secretary's love life. What difference did it really make, anyway? Slater's paper didn't mean anything to anyone who didn't live in Grand Forks.

She put her head in her hands and groaned. "Why didn't God make all secretaries postmenopausal?"

"Because then male bosses would never get any exercise chasing them around their desks?" Cameron offered.

A weak chuckle rippled out of her. Sobering, she raised her head and looked at her bright-eyed young associate.

"I've got a bad feeling, Cameron," she confessed. "The day before the hearing, and our boy pulls a stunt like that call to Dustin Holloman's mother. What do you think he might have in store for the main event?"

"I don't know," he admitted quietly.

Ellen stared out the window at the ominous gray of the sky and felt foreboding thicken the air around her. "I don't want to know."

The old habits came back, like ghosts, unwanted, unwelcome, bringing with them an uneasy sense of déjà vu. In her days on the fast track, the night before a major court appearance became a time of ritual, almost superstition. Too wired to relax, too afraid there was something she had overlooked in her preparation, Ellen would spend the evening in her office, poring over and over the evidence, the questions she wanted answered, the strategy she intended to employ against her opponent.

In the two years since she had come to Deer Lake, there had been no nights like that. Until this one. In the usual course of Park County events, an omnibus hearing would last twenty minutes and there would be half a dozen scheduled for a morning—most of which would never take place because the defendant would plead out. Garrett Wright's hearing would be a whole different kind of circus. Because of the charges. Because of the defendant. Because of Costello. This would be a minitrial, complete with all the drama.

She shooed Cameron out the door at eight-thirty but flatly refused to go with him. She both needed and hated the need to fall back into the old rhythms. She both recognized and resented the edgy restlessness that hummed through her like an electric current.

It pushed her out of her chair and walked her up and down the length of the conference table, where she had spread out every document, every note they had. The heat in the building had been turned down into the refrigeration zone again, the county commissioners unwilling to bend the utility budget for the comfort of one attorney. She paced with her coat on, vaguely amazed that she couldn't see her breath.

They had enough. Megan's and Mitch's statements alone should have been enough to get Wright bound over for trial. In addition, they would have the testimony of the BCA criminalist as to the preliminary findings on the ski mask that had yielded Wright's hair, and the sheet Wright had wrapped around Megan, the sheet that had yielded strands of Josh's hair and more of Wright's hair, and bloodstains that were consistent with Josh Kirkwood's blood type. It should have all made for a prosecution slam dunk, but still the doubts crept in, eroded her confidence, choked her. Old, familiar feelings.

As Mitch had predicted, Wilhelm had not yet returned from Rochester. The call to Dustin Holloman's mother had been traced to a pay phone in a mall, where there had to have been a number of witnesses. The BCA and local cops had spent hours canvassing the stores and hallways, showing Dustin's photograph, asking people if they had seen anyone suspicious using the phones, asking if they might have seen anyone using a small tape recorder at the phones.

It would have been lunacy for the kidnapper to drag the boy himself into such a public place. Every newspaper and television station in the state had been flashing Dustin's picture since the night of his disappearance. Most likely the kidnapper had recorded Dustin's message and played the tape over the phone.

Still a risky proposition, Ellen thought as she made another slow circuit around the table. Brazen. Bold. He was feeling cocky, invincible. He had taken a careless chance just for the purpose of tying up the BCA. Or perhaps what he wanted was the public acknowledgment of his brilliance. But all it would take was one witness, one bored store clerk, one man sitting on a bench waiting for his wife, one teenager impatient to use the same phone, and they would have a description.

The prospect brought a small adrenaline rush— another old, familiar feeling. There had always been a high associated with cracking a big case; a tense excitement in watching the cops close in, knowing that the next part was her part.

It stirred within her now at the thought of Wilhelm bringing back a description, an artist's sketch, a videotape from a security camera. Who would they see? Todd Childs? Or someone they had never seen before?

Adam Slater's question about the Sci-Fi Cowboys came back to her as she stopped along the section of table where their file was laid out. None of the boys had been considered suspects in the kidnapping, but she now had firsthand knowledge of the lengths to which they would go to support their mentor. If they would commit vandalism, if they would commit arson, what else might they do? She had a good idea from their rap sheets—they had committed robbery, car theft, assault, drug deals, attempted rape. Would it be a stretch to include kidnapping?

Theoretically, perhaps not. Logistically, it wasn't realistic. The Cowboys were minors, living with parents, with guardians. They attended school, answered to probation officers. Slipping out of a dorm to set a car on fire was one thing, being able to commit to the kind of complicated scenario these kidnappings had followed would require total freedom of movement. Nor was it realistic to think Garrett Wright would put his trust and his future in the hands of someone so young.

Childs was a better bet. Childs, the psych major fascinated with the human mind.

Learning and perception was Wright's specialty.

What had they done to Josh's mind? What had they planted in his young mind to make him close himself off so completely?

As her own mind pondered the questions, Ellen paged slowly through the materials they had gathered on the Cowboys. The list of past members, the photocopies of old newspaper articles. One prominent headline announced the admittance of one of the first Cowboys into the University of Minnesota Medical School. Another had won a scholarship to MIT. Success story after success story.

She went down the list of names, many of which had been checked off or had notations beside them regarding the person's whereabouts. According to Wilhelm, the people he'd had checking into the past Cowboys were turning up nothing but young men who had become productive members of society and thanked Garrett Wright and his colleagues for it. Car thieves, vandals, burglars, gangbangers, all of whom Garrett Wright had helped turn around. Had any one of them ever seen Wright's other side? Had they ever looked into his eyes and had a mo-

ment of terrible revelation? Would they tell anyone if
they had?

So far, the answer to that question was no.

Her gaze settled on an article she had reviewed before.
The photo showed Christopher Priest and one of the boys
in the foreground, the one who had gone on to MIT,
working with a robot. Garrett Wright, with boys named
James Johnston and Erik Evans, stood in the background.
The article was dated May 17, 1990, the second year of
the Cowboys' existence. The murkiness of the copy gave
Wright a sinister look. Or perhaps it was that he hadn't
realized the camera would catch him in its frame, and he
had been showing his true face, the one that hid beneath
the handsome mask.

The idea sent a finger of unease down Ellen's spine.
Public sentiment was running higher and higher in
Wright's favor. With every new exploit of Dustin Hollo-
man's kidnapper, the public grew less patient with the
prosecution—or persecution, as some saw it—of Garrett
Wright, their local hero, their respected teacher.

"I'm beginning to feel like the only person in the
movie who knows the charming count is a vampire," she
muttered.

Pulling the telephone toward her with one hand, she
reached for the list of probation officers Phoebe hadn't
called.

She made contact with two, both of whom had burned
out and left the job within the last year, and scratched the
names of two former Cowboys off her list of possible
character assassins. Montel Jones, Sci-Fi Cowboy turned
engineering student at the University of Minnesota, had
died in a plane crash in 1993. James Johnston had breezed
through his undergraduate work in three years and was
currently going for his master's in counseling. His former
probation officer told Ellen that Garrett Wright's program
was the reason.

Darrell Munson, probation officer to two of the original Cowboys, had left not only the profession but the state, moving to Florida to run a diving school. His answering machine picked up with steel-drum music. Ellen left a message and hung up, feeling no sense of accomplishment at all.

But, then, what had she really expected? That one of Wright's former charges would suddenly blurt out a tale of bizarre abuse after all this time? Contacting the past Cowboys had never been more than an exercise in grasping at straws.

A knock on the outer-office door broke into her concentration. It might have been Wilhelm coming with news, or Deputy Qualey, her guard for the evening, or Cameron coming back because he'd had a brainstorm.

Brooks stood in the hall holding a picnic basket.

"Why am I not surprised?" Ellen muttered. "Why would I actually believe you would stay away merely because I asked you to?"

"Can I assume that's a rhetorical question?" he asked, eyes sparkling with mischief.

"How did you get into the building?" she asked irritably. "How did you get past the guard?"

"I bribed him with a chocolate cupcake and an autographed copy of *Justice for None*. Good thing I'm not a psycho killer, huh?" He stepped past her and set the picnic basket down on the receptionist's counter. "I told him you and I were old friends from law school and I wanted to make sure you got supper—knowing how nervous you are the night before a big case and all."

"He's supposed to call up—"

"I told him it was a surprise. Gave him a little wink, a little nudge. He's a nice fella—Ed. A little too nice." He turned serious. "He didn't check the basket. He didn't frisk me. He figured he knew me—which, of course, he doesn't—so I must be all right."

"I don't know you, either," she said quietly. "Should I be in fear of my life?"

He took in the sight of her standing there swallowed up by her winter coat, her hair back in a haphazard knot that allowed thick strands to escape. Her eyes were bloodshot, the circles beneath them growing darker and deeper every day. This case was dragging on her, but she withstood it because it was her duty. He could have kicked himself for ever insinuating she was a coward, that she had been running away when she'd left Hennepin County.

"Actually, I think you know me pretty well," he admitted. "You sure as hell hit some nails on the head last night. I admit I'm a son of a bitch, but I'm contrite about it. Doesn't that just make you want to marry me?"

"Is that what you came here for?"

"No," he murmured. "I wanted to make sure you got supper. Knowing how nervous you must be the night before a big case and all."

The admission was earnest, the apology sincere. Ellen's wariness melted.

"I'm surprised you wanted to bother," she said.

"Why?" he asked, moving closer with just a shift of his weight. He caught a strand of her hair over his fingers and brushed it back behind her ear, his fingertips skimming the soft skin there. "Because I didn't get what I wanted last night? I don't give up that easily."

"I'm not sure if that's good news or bad news."

"Then maybe I should sweeten the deal. It comes complete with cupcakes, fried chicken, and information."

"Information?"

"Supper? It's a package deal, counselor. You gotta eat the chicken to get the scoop."

Ellen's stomach made the decision for her. The egg-salad sandwich she'd pulled out of the vending machine in the cafeteria for supper had ended up in the trash, and lunch had been a hastily grabbed cup of peach yogurt hours before. The aromas escaping the basket were too much for her.

She led the way to her office, taking her place behind her desk. They spread the containers of food out on the blotter. Crispy fried chicken, cole slaw, french fries, buttery biscuits, the promised cupcakes.

"Are you sure you're not trying to kill me?" she said. "This looks like death by cholesterol."

"It's my Southern-fried Lawyer, Night Before a Big Case special. I'm from Alabama, you know. We have a strong belief in the powers of grease. Chow down."

Ellen stabbed her plastic fork into a chicken breast and tore a succulent piece of white meat free. "So what's this hot information?"

"I heard about the phone call to Dustin Holloman's mother," Jay said, wandering to the bookcase to peruse the compact disks. "I heard it came this afternoon around four-fifteen."

"Yes. The BCA guys traced it to Rochester. Frankly, I'm surprised you didn't beat it down there with the thundering herd."

"It's another snipe hunt."

"Another chapter. 'The Pathetic Desperation of the Futile Search.'"

He ignored the gibe. "I was over at Harris College having a little chat with Professor Priest at about two, two-thirty. He hustled me out, told me he had a class to prepare for."

"He *is* a teacher."

He selected a Philip Aaberg CD and loaded it into the player. New Age piano music with a subtle western edge drifted from the small speakers. "So, according to the main office, he didn't have another class until seven tonight. Now, maybe he just doesn't appreciate my unique brand of southern charm, but that doesn't explain why he was driving out the campus gates when I was coming out of Cray Hall at two-fifty."

"Why were you leaving the building after him if he threw you out of his office?"

"I made a detour past Garrett Wright's office, where the lovely but loony Mrs. Wright was trying to find some books her husband had asked her to stop for."

Ellen stilled. "What books?"

"She didn't say, but I can't imagine there was anything left that might have been incriminating in any way. The cops had tossed that place like a Caesar salad."

"What *did* she have to say?"

"That her husband shouldn't be on trial, that this is all a big mistake. She said Garrett wouldn't steal a child, because he didn't like children, that he hadn't liked *being* a child. I asked her if she had known him as a child, but she didn't answer me that, either. That little gal is one blade shy of a sharp edge, if you ask me."

Her appetite suddenly on hold, Ellen sat back in her chair. "According to what we know, Karen and Wright met in college."

"So he told her he had a rotten childhood. Confession is part of courtship, isn't it?"

"I wonder what else he might have confessed to her."

"You'll never know, counselor. A wife can't be compelled to testify against her husband."

"No. She's on Costello's list to testify on behalf of Wright. Of course, she's hardly a credible witness. Not that that will stop Tony from trying to get some mileage out of her," she grumbled. "So you're leaving Cray Hall and you see Priest driving away. He could have gone anywhere. He could have gone to the dry cleaner's. He could have gone home."

"But he didn't."

"You followed him?"

"All the way to the interstate. He turned south."

Toward Rochester, an hour away. Ellen felt her pulse pick up a beat. If Priest was Wright's accomplice, would he have been so reckless as to leave an interview with a prominent crime writer in order to drive to the site of the next move in his sick game? Did he feel that invulnerable?

"Something else funny about my little visit," he said. "I talked to a professor at Penn State who used to know Priest and Wright, who told me they were all kids in good old Mishawaka. They were different ages, from different parts of town. He didn't know either of them back then, but he thought it was quite a remarkable coincidence that they had all ended up at Penn State. When I mentioned it to Priest, he flat out denied it. Said he grew up in Chicago."

"Why would he lie about that? It's easy enough to check out through school records."

"I don't know. Anyway, when I heard about the call to Mrs. Holloman," he went on, "I got hold of Agent Wilhelm and told him. I figured you'd want to know, too, and I wasn't going to count on his getting back to you tonight."

"Yeah, so what's in it for you?" she asked, her gaze sharp on him.

"Nothing."

Ellen gave him a speculative look as she raised her fork. "You're turning into a regular good guy, Brooks. You'd better look out, you'll ruin your reputation."

She had said it before, Ellen thought, that for someone who claimed to be a mere observer, he had a hard time grasping the concept. More often than not his involvement had struck her as being self-serving, but what she saw in his face now, in the amber glow of her desk lamp, looked an awful lot like honesty. As if he cared. And it hurt him to care.

He had come to Deer Lake to lose himself in someone else's misery, he had said. But the misery of Dustin's parents and Josh's parents was too close a cousin to his own. He had a son. Had lost that son before he'd even known the child existed. Had found him and had him taken away again all in the space of a day. Ellen could feel the tug to reach out to him.

She reached for the telephone instead and punched in Mitch's home number. His machine picked up, but he answered himself as soon as Ellen began to leave her message. She told him everything Brooks had told her and added a couple of her own hunches, all to be relayed to Megan. Diversionary tactics aside, the case was revolving around Wright and his circle of acquaintances; revolving in what seemed to be a spiral into the past. He had done this before. *They* had done this before. Christopher Priest had been heading south at three o'clock. The call had come a little past four o'clock. If Megan could dig up just one key piece . . .

"I thought O'Malley was off the case," Jay said carefully as Ellen hung up the receiver.

Regarding him with a poker face, she said nothing for a moment that stretched into another.

"You wanted me to trust you," she said at last. "I'm trusting you with this: Agent O'Malley is digging into Wright's background because Wilhelm wasn't getting the job done."

Jay gave a low whistle. "She's a little biased, don't you think?"

"I think she's a damn good cop, and there's nothing she can do to change Garrett Wright's past. Anything she comes up with will be established, corroborated fact."

"Still, if Costello catches wind of this—"

"I'll know where he got it, won't I?"

"And you'll cut out my black heart with a grapefruit knife."

"Worse. I'll let you answer to O'Malley. She won't bother with a knife."

Unfamiliar pleasure coursed through Jay. It was about trust. Something Ellen had no reason to offer freely and every reason not to offer at all.

He rose from his chair and rounded her desk to kneel down beside her. Taking her hand, he raised it to his mouth.

"My lips are sealed," he said, each word a caress against her fingertips.

She tried to draw her hand away, but he held it firm, and drew the end of her middle finger between his lips. Her breath shuddered at the subtle abrasion of his teeth along the pad of her fingertip, at the touch of his tongue, at the gentle sucking.

"Jay . . ."

He drew his lips down her palm, lingered at the delicate skin inside her wrist. "You trust me, Ellen?" he whispered, drawing her up from her chair.

Apprehension and desire shivered inside her. "There's so much at stake here, Jay."

"I know," he said, knowing she meant the case, knowing there was more.

"I've never been anyone's hero, Ellen," he said. "I've lived my life for myself and to hell with everyone else. I've never had any trouble justifying or rationalizing or outright lying when it suited my cause. And I look at you and I think: Brooks, you got no business touching her, 'cause she's better than you'll ever be. But I want you anyway."

"And you always get what you want."

"I used to think so," he murmured. "Now I stand back and look at what I've got and none of it means a damn thing to me. The money, the house, the spite I prized so dearly . . . I look at Hannah Garrison, see her fighting for her child . . . I look at you, see you fighting for justice . . . What have I ever fought for besides my own gain? What good have I ever been to anybody?"

He forced a smile that was sad and wry. "Looks like you might redeem me after all."

"No," Ellen whispered. "I don't want that responsibility. That's your choice. It has to be what you want."

"What I want," he echoed, pulling her closer. "I want you."

He kissed her slowly, deeply, and Ellen thought she could taste his yearning and the confusion that shrouded it. She kissed him back, her own emotions kindred spirits of his.

When he lifted his head a fraction, the need in his eyes took her breath away. The need to be touched by something good.

As tempted as she was, Ellen knew she couldn't fight that battle for him. She had her own war to wage, her own enemies all around.

"I need to prepare for tomorrow," she murmured.

He kept his arms around her. "You need a good night's sleep—preferably with me. You can prepare until your eyes bleed, but that won't make you any more ready. You can't give more than all you've got, Ellen. You've done the best you can."

Her best. Her best hadn't measured up so far. She closed her eyes and saw Garrett Wright smile that knowing, omnipotent smile that made her think he already knew the outcome of his game.

"That's what scares me most," she confessed in a whisper. "What if my best isn't good enough?"

She moved away from him, feeling rumpled and wilted, trying in vain to smooth some of the wrinkles out of her blouse. Back in Hennepin County she had kept a change of clothes in her office. But Hennepin County was miles away, literally and figuratively. She didn't have a change of clothes here. She didn't know that she had any of what she really needed. The sharp edge, the bright eye, the quick mind. She didn't know that she hadn't left it all in Minneapolis.

Watching her struggle, Jay remembered the blind panic that struck in the eleventh hour before a case went to court, the naked insecurities. He had never measured up to the standards of his family, and what if they were right? What if, behind all the bluff bravado, the swagger, the smile, there really was nothing of substance to call on when he needed it most?

The anxiety was one of the many things about being a trial lawyer that he never missed. There was no panic associated with what he did now, dealing with cases after the fact. It was safer. It hurt less. *Maybe you're the coward, Brooks. . . .*

Ellen hadn't wanted this case, but she had accepted the challenge—not for personal gain or glory, but because she knew she was the county's best hope for justice.

Too good for you, Brooks . . .

He crossed the room to where she stood, staring out through the barely parted blinds. Slipping his arms around her from behind, he pressed a kiss to her hair and whispered, "You'll win," as if his own conviction was enough to make it so.

"I wish I could be sure of that," Ellen said. But the one thing she knew with any certainty was that in this game, where the stakes were so high, there was no such thing as a sure thing. And she had the sick feeling that the other team was playing with a stacked deck.

At eleven-ten she trudged up the stairs to the third-floor law library. She had the dubious services of Deputy Qualey for another forty minutes. Time enough to pull the books she needed, for all the good they would do her. If Grabko had already made up his mind about the lineup ID, he would have found precedent to back himself. Anal-retentive bugger that he was, he would no doubt have scoured every obscure text of U.S. case law in existence to support his decision. Ellen had assigned Cameron the task of finding rulings to back their position. He had carted a stack of books home with him. But she wanted a solid familiarity with the cases cited in the general rule regarding violation of the right to counsel, and so she found herself in the darkened halls of the third floor.

She had thought of bringing Qualey up with her but had taken pity on him and his bum hockey knee. After Brooks had gone, she'd had her chat with Ed about security, and he had assured her he'd let no one else in. The third floor was vacant, the courtrooms and construction junk waiting out the night.

Logical assurances warred with creepy sensations. Chiding herself for being skittish, Ellen let herself into the library and flipped on the lights.

It was a room designed for function. Industrial-grade carpet the color of pea soup, no-frills oak bookcases varnished dark with age, mission-style library tables and straight chairs that had been in place long before the retro-mission decorating craze.

She prowled the stacks with purpose, pulling the books she needed and carrying them to a table. She had memorized the names of the cases, state and federal— *United States v. Wade, Gilbert v. California*, Minnesota: *State v. Cobb*, and *State v. Guevara*. She forced herself to look them up, to mark the pages. No sense getting all the way home only to discover she'd pulled the wrong book. Be thorough. Stay focused. Fight the nerves.

The first two cases were nearly thirty years old. *State v. Cobb* was dated 1979, not that it mattered if the ruling applied. *State v. Guevara* was the most recent, 1993, and the most pertinent, if memory served. That had been a child-abduction case as well, up in Dakota County on the southeast side of the metro area. A witness had picked Guevara out of a lineup, but Guevara's attorney had gotten the lineup thrown out. Unease crawled along Ellen's nerves as she remembered the trial had ended in an acquittal.

She was trying an entirely different case, the logical side of her brain argued. Guevara had been charged not only with kidnapping, but had been indicted by a grand jury on murder charges. The fact that the little girl had never been found had weighed more heavily with the jury than any other aspect of the case.

But that lineup might have tipped the scales the other way. . . .

Ellen turned the pages. Page after page of case law, stopping cold when she reached *State v. Guevara*.

Someone had been here before her and marked the page with a slip of white paper. She turned the book sideways and, heart pounding, read the message on the note.

it is a SIN to believe evil of others, but it is
seldom a mistake

The clock on Josh's nightstand ticked one minute past midnight. Hannah sat cross-legged on the sleeping bag she had spread out on the floor across the room from Josh's bed. Anticipation wound like a watch spring inside her, tightening with every passing minute, building to she knew not what.

A battle, she thought. A battle for her son. Not simply for justice, but for Josh himself. He had been taken from her. She had played the role of victim, but no more. The longer she thought about it, the more clearly she could see it—the challenge of something evil, the role she needed to play. The struggle in the courtroom would begin in a matter of hours, but the battle would go on beyond the

courthouse, beyond the reach of Ellen North or Anthony
Costello. She could see that now.

Closing her eyes, she summoned the evil, a faceless entity. In her mind's eye she could see herself standing on a
dark plain, the sky low and leaden. She could see Josh
standing off to one side, just beyond her reach, his face
completely without emotion, sightless. And she could feel
the evil, cold and heavy.

"You can't have my son. I'll kill you if I have to."

"I've already taken him. He's already mine."

"I'll kill you."

She raised her hand and a knife appeared in her grasp.
She slashed downward through the oppressive air, slicing
the blackness like a canvas that split open to reveal a wall
of blood. The blood poured over her, knocking her off
her feet, filling her mouth and nose, choking her, drowning her. She fought to come awake, but it dragged her
down like an undertow, and then there was nothing.

Josh dreamed of a sea of blood. He was floating on it, like
floating on an air cushion in the lake. Safe, but not safe.
Safe because the Taker said so, and that scared him because
he didn't want to trust the Taker anymore. He could feel
his mother pulling at him, her hands reaching up from the
sea to grasp at him. He wanted to go with her, but he was
afraid that if he did, the Taker would drown them both.
But if he stayed where he was, the Taker would always be
with him, and the Taker scared him more and more. He
could see the other Goner in his dream, being held above
him by the Taker's hands, the hands tightening and tightening; the boy opening his mouth to scream but no sound
coming out, his eyes going wider and wider with terror, a
terror Josh could feel inside himself. He didn't like the
feeling. It made him want to cry. It made him want to be

sick. It made him want to turn to his mother, but she was beneath the blood sea.

In a panic, he turned within himself, using the Taker's trick to trick the Taker. He opened the door inside his mind, went into the smallest, most secret room, and vowed not to come out ever again.

it is a SIN to believe evil of others, but it is seldom a mistake

Ellen saw the note on the table before her, heard the message—an eerie whisper that seemed to surround her. She could feel his presence, feel his hands close around her throat.

Evil.

The hands tightened. She lunged up out of the chair and across the tabletop, sending books tumbling into the blood that covered the floor. She landed in it herself on her hands and knees and slipped and slid as she struggled to stand. She couldn't breathe, could feel her windpipe collapsing in on itself. Fighting, she staggered up and twisted around. Garrett Wright sat in the chair she had vacated, smiling. The hands around her throat were invisible.

"The first thing we do, let's kill all the lawyers."

The line rang in her ears, louder and louder, until the words were indistinguishable.

Gasping for air, she jerked upright in bed and stared at the phone on the nightstand. Fear rose in her throat until she thought she would gag on it. But she forced herself to reach out and pick up the receiver.

"Ellen North," she said, her mouth as dry as cotton.

The silence was a heartbeat, and then came the voice, gruff and unsteady.

"It's Steiger. We've found the Holloman boy. He's dead."

JOURNAL ENTRY
FEBRUARY 1, 1994

Our litany of sins is an old classic song
We started young and have lasted long
Infused with new blood, our game will go on

CHAPTER 30

"Ms. North, how will this affect the charges against Garrett Wright?"

"Ms. North, are you ready to admit you're prosecuting the wrong man?"

"Ms. North, are you holding to your accomplice theory?"

"Ms. North, is it true your lineup witness recanted her identification of Wright?"

"Ms. North!"

"Ms. North!"

"Ms. North!"

The frantic voices echoed in Ellen's brain, louder and louder and louder, like the voice in her nightmare, until all she heard was noise.

"Stop it!" she shouted, turning her face up into the punishing hot spray of the shower, trying to wash away the images, sharp and painful, in her memory. A child's body, the purple marks of strangulation a circlet of bruises around his small throat. A child's body with a slip of paper pinned to the striped pajamas he wore. A message that cut to the bone: *some rise by SIN, and some by virtue fall.* A child's body discarded like a blown tire along the side of the road, abandoned at the base of the sign that welcomed visitors to Campion, *A friendly place to live.*

The black humor, the twisted psychological intent of

leaving the body when and where it was found, sickened Ellen almost as badly as the murder itself. The message was arrogance, disrespect for the police agencies involved; a callous disrespect for life, for decency, for small-town values. Just as the note in the book had been a nose-thumbing at the court system, a sneering disregard for the sanctity and security of the courthouse.

The total package of crimes that made up The Game was among the worst she had ever dealt with. With the discovery of Dustin Holloman's body, the situation, difficult enough to this point, had reached critical mass.

She could still hear the hysterical sobs of the Holloman family; the shaky voices of the cops. Even the coroner, the irascible Stuart Oglethorpe, had wept as Dustin's lifeless body was zipped into the too-big black bag and loaded into the hearse.

Ellen had held herself together as best she could, struggling to put a brave face over the emotions that ravaged her. She represented justice. If any entity needed to show strength in the face of evil, it was justice. The people looked to her, to the system, to make things right, to avenge the wrongs. She had to stand strong.

A blessed numbness had descended to insulate her. The miraculous self-protective properties of the human psyche at work. She had gone through all the motions, consulted with Steiger and Wilhelm as the evidence techs from the BCA mobile lab processed the scene under the harsh white glare of the portable halogen lights.

Individual faces in the surrounding crowd caught in her peripheral vision. Henry Forster from the *Star Tribune*. A correspondent from *Dateline*. Jay.

He had come there for the story. The cynic in her reminded her of that fact, but it couldn't discount the bleak expression on his face or the sound of his voice when several of the reporters had turned to him for opinions when they could get no answers from anyone else.

"It's a tragedy," he said in a rough, low voice. "There's nothing I can say to make it any less senseless."

His words stayed with her as she prepared herself for the day, slicking her hair back into a twist, selecting her best black suit from the closet. Dustin Holloman's death was a tragedy that should never have happened anywhere, but most of all not here. This was a crime against the community of Park County, the murder of a collective innocence.

Ignorance is not innocence but sin.

Garrett Wright and his shadow may have viewed the innocence of this place as ignorance, but the sin was theirs, and they would be made to pay. They would damn well be made to pay. The vow burned in Ellen's mind, in her heart. *She* would see to it. She hadn't asked for this battle, hadn't wanted it to come here, but she would fight it with everything she had.

Not giving a damn if the reporters followed her, she drove across town to the new office complex on Ramsey Drive, where Costello had rented a suite for his stay here. The extravagance sickened her. This was what Tony Costello was all about—money, power, a staff of drones to do the work, an image polished to a diamond shine.

She marched past the secretary, homing in on Costello, who stood in the hall giving orders to one of his associates. Dorman's eyes widened at the sight of her. Costello's expression was guarded.

"Have you heard?" she demanded.

"About the Holloman boy?"

"He's dead."

Costello reached for her arm. "Let's go in my office."

Ellen jerked away from his touch. "Let's not. I'd rather your staff hear exactly what kind of a bastard they're working for—if they don't already know."

Anger flashed in his dark eyes and he took another step toward her. "Ellen, you're out of line—"

"*I'm* out of line? My God!" She shook her head in disbelief. "You could have saved that child. You could have at least been a coward and called in anonymously. But if Wright's accomplice is nailed, then Wright is nailed, too, and you'll be damned if you'll lose a case over something as trivial as a child's life."

She could see the secretary, wide-eyed and uncertain. Another associate, an African-American woman, stepped into the hall from an office, looking shocked. Costello's face was a stony mask.

"You'll be damned, all right," Ellen snarled. "I'm filing a complaint with the professional-relations board today. If I find one shred of evidence linking you to that boy's murderer, I will ruin you, Tony. You're as guilty of his death as if you put your hands around his throat and choked him yourself!"

She stormed out of the office, half expecting him to follow, but he didn't. She had taken him by surprise, knocked him back on his heels, and she could imagine what he was thinking. No time to appear in front of the press that waited in the hall. Better to say nothing, leave them wondering, leave her to deal with them, the cold-hearted son of a bitch.

She pushed past the reporters, letting them draw their own conclusions as to why she would pay a visit to the opposition less than two hours before they were due in court.

By the time she arrived at the courthouse, the full flock of vultures had descended. The scene in Campion had been processed and abandoned, picked clean of details and metaphors, photographed from every possible angle. They perched themselves on the main steps of the courthouse, hovered around all the entrances. The only way into the building was to run the gauntlet, eyes forward, stride purposeful, mouth closed. They hurled their questions at her like stones and chased her into the building, demanding the answers she had refused them just hours before.

"Ms. North, how will the discovery of Dustin Holloman's body affect the charges against Garrett Wright?"

"Ms. North, are you ready to admit you're prosecuting the wrong man?"

"What were you doing at Anthony Costello's offices? Will there be some kind of deal?"

"Are you dropping the charges?"

"Ms. North, are you holding to your accomplice theory?"

"Will you try to pin this on the Sci-Fi Cowboys?"

"Doesn't the Park County attorney's office have anything to say for itself?"

"Yes." She tossed a glare over her shoulder without breaking stride. "I have a hearing to prepare for and a suspect who's as Guilty as Sin. If you let this latest atrocity sway you from believing that, then you're just buying into his sick game and you're as much accomplices as the person who dumped that child's body."

If she had meant her words to silence or humiliate them, she would have been disappointed. As it was, the rise in volume as they all clamored to speak at once came as no great surprise. *Just like old times*, she thought as she stepped past the deputy who had been stationed outside the office door. *Only worse.*

The office was in a state of stunned chaos. Phones rang incessantly and seemed to go unanswered. One of the secretaries from Campion sat at her desk, weeping. Phoebe knelt on the floor beside the woman's chair, offering Kleenex and sympathy, her own eyes red-rimmed and brimming with tears. Rudy stood in the center of it all, looking like a captain on the deck of a sinking ship.

"This is an absolute nightmare," he said half under his breath, glaring at Ellen as if the idea of dumping Dustin Holloman's body in plain sight mere hours before the

probable-cause hearing had been her idea. "Bill Glendenning called me at home to demand an explanation. He said
from the position of his office, it appears you've lost all
control of the situation, Ellen."

You, not *we*, Ellen noted as she went into her office,
Rudy following. He was ready to cut the ties and blame
her in order to save his ass and his prospective judgeship.
She wheeled on him.

"*I've* lost control? *I* never had control! I had a case to
build and I've built it. I'm not omnipotent. If *I* were in
control, none of this would ever have happened!"

"You know what I mean."

"Yes, I certainly do." She didn't care that Quentin
Adler stood just behind him in the doorway, soaking up
every word to be regurgitated later at the water cooler.
"You've really painted yourself into a corner this time,
haven't you, Rudy? You dumped this case on me because
you didn't have the guts to take it on yourself. Now
what?" she demanded. "God forbid you should look at
the evidence we have against Garrett Wright and back me
up."

"I've backed you in this from the beginning, Ellen," he
said indignantly. "I gave you my full confidence. I gave
you free rein."

He had given her ample rope and half hoped she would
hang herself with it, but not before he could get himself
clear of her kicking feet. He had never in all his scheming
scenarios imagined anything as dire as this latest turn of
events. If he washed his hands of her now, he would appear weak. If he backed her and she failed, she would take
the brunt of the criticism, but the fallout would be on
him. His decision-making abilities would be questioned.
His qualifications as a judge would be questioned. He
could almost feel the robes slipping from his grasp.

"Do I need to remind you Mitch Holt ran down Garrett Wright himself?" Ellen asked. "He's guilty."

"Not of killing that Holloman boy."

"That's not the case we're hearing. But don't worry, Rudy, when that one comes in, I will be first in line. I want to nail that son of a bitch's hide to the wall and pick my teeth with his bones. Now, if you'll excuse me," she said, backing him out into the hall, "I've got a battle to wage."

"All rise! Court is in session. The Honorable Judge Gorman Grabko presiding."

The bailiff smashed the gavel down again as the noisy crowd surged to its feet. Jay watched as Gorman Grabko emerged from his chambers with a theatrical air of dignity, bald head polished to a high sheen, beard neatly trimmed. A gray-striped bow tie perched above the neck of his robes, properly discreet. He climbed up to his aerie on the bench and settled himself with quiet ceremony, arranging his stack of files and books just so before looking out on the assembled mob that filled his courtroom shoulder to shoulder.

Jay followed the judge's eyes, trying to imagine the scene from Grabko's point of view. Looking past the counsel tables into the gallery, he would see Paul Kirkwood sitting in the front row with a sour expression. Rudy Stovich right beside him, his greased gray hair rising off one side of his head like a loose asphalt shingle. He would see Mitch Holt in a suit and tie and Megan O'Malley wearing the ugly badges of her beating—bruises that had reached the pomegranate-and-puce stage, stitches crawling over her lower lip like a centipede.

The Harris College contingent had arrayed themselves on the other side of the aisle, behind the defense table. Christopher Priest and the assistant dean, a cadre of students—Todd Childs noticeably absent. Karen Wright, looking fragile and lovely in rose-petal pink. And the press all around.

From his lofty seat Grabko could literally look down on the lawyers—every judge's secret joy. At the prosecution table Ellen stood, her back rigid, her jaw rigid, her hands curled into fists at her sides. She was furious, almost to the point of shaking, Jay would have bet. And he had a sinking feeling her temper was directly attributable to the discussion that had gone on in chambers moments before, where Grabko would have announced to the lawyers his decisions on motions they had made prior to today.

Costello had filed two of note, had broadcast them to the press with fanfare: a motion to dismiss and a motion to suppress the lineup identification. He stood at the defense table with his associate, smartly decked out in a tailored tobacco-brown suit, black hair gleaming almost blue under the lights, his expression allowing just a hint of overconfidence.

Christ, would Grabko have been so easily led? Would the news of the Holloman boy's death have swayed him as it had many of the reporters who had been on the scene in the pearl-gray hours before dawn? His decision on the dismissal had to be based on the evidence regarding the issue of the constitutionality of the arrest, but that didn't mean other factors couldn't influence him subconsciously or otherwise. If Grabko had been sufficiently starstruck by Costello, if he had already been leaning toward the defense . . .

Anxiety knotted in Jay's gut. He hadn't been able to get the morning's images out of his head. In the usual course of his job, he had seen hundreds of crime-scene photos, some grisly beyond imagining, but he had never actually been to a scene like this one.

He would never forget the sight of that small, lifeless body, would never forget the raw, nameless emotion that had cut through him, or the anguished keening of the boy's mother. There were no words to describe the kind of desperate tension that had thickened the cold air along that stretch of road leading into Campion. Acrid, volatile, like a toxic chemical cloud that could have ignited and exploded at the slightest spark.

And he knew it was all part of the master plan mapped out by Wright and his partner. A move meant to shock, meant to thumb their noses at their opponents in the game. *some rise by SIN, and some by virtue fall.* Who represented virtue more than the police, more than the prosecutor, more than a child? The goal was to get away with murder, to defeat the justice system and destroy the servants of that system in the process; and to destroy two innocent families in the bargain.

The pure evil of it was stunning.

And fewer and fewer people were willing to believe the defendant standing at the table was capable of embodying that evil. Evil was supposed to be ugly, instantly recognizable. Not a respected college professor who rehabilitated delinquents. Not an attractive, quiet man in a conservative blue suit.

"Be seated," Grabko intoned. He perched a pair of half glasses on his nose and consulted a document, as if he had no idea what case was coming up before him. "We are here on the matter of *The State versus Dr. Garrett Wright*. This is the omnibus hearing. For those of you in the gallery unfamiliar with our system, the omnibus hearing is the equivalent of a probable-cause hearing, wherein the State bears the burden of proof to show that the defendant indeed may have committed the crimes of which he stands accused and should be bound over for trial.

"Counsel for the defense," he announced, "please state your names for the record."

Costello and his minion rose in unison. "Anthony Costello, Your Honor. Assisting me will be my associate, Mr. Dorman."

"Counsel for the prosecution."

"Assistant County Attorney Ellen North, Your Honor."

"Assistant County Attorney Cameron Reed, Your Honor."

"Mr. Costello," Grabko said, turning his attention back to the defense. "Regarding your previously filed motion to dismiss on the grounds that in the process of arresting Dr. Wright the Deer Lake police force violated his rights under the Fourth Amendment of the United States Constitution: I have carefully considered your argument and weighed all factors involved, including Chief Holt's statement and the prosecution's argument."

He paused for effect, stroking a hand down his beard, as if he were just now coming to his conclusion. Jay pulled in a breath and held it.

"I find your argument has merit. There was a certain delay between pursuit and apprehension, wherein Chief Holt lost sight of his suspect."

A gasp went up in the gallery. In the front row Paul Kirkwood leaned forward to grasp the railing, as if preparing to vault over it.

"However," Grabko said, "the length of the delay is in dispute, and I am convinced the rule of exigent circumstances applied. Therefore, motion to dismiss is denied."

Another wave of sound rolled through the courtroom. Grabko banged his gavel and frowned at the gallery. "I will have order in this courtroom. This hearing is a legal proceeding, not a play. Those in the gallery will remain silent or be removed."

Threat made, he resettled himself like a tom turkey that had had his feathers ruffled. He carefully set aside the documents concerning the first motion and took up another.

"With regards to the defense motion to suppress the lineup identification. Motion granted."

Ellen rose from her chair as the gallery behind her defied fate and burst into a cacophony of sound. "Your Honor," she shouted over the noise as Grabko cracked his gavel down. "Your Honor, I request the record show——"

"Ms. North," Grabko snapped, scowling at her over the rims of his glasses, "you made your opinion of my ruling abundantly clear in chambers. Unless you would care to be served with a charge of contempt, I suggest you not make it again."

Biting down on her temper, she did a mental count to ten. "Yes, Your Honor."

"You may call your first witness, Ms. North."

"The State calls Agent Megan O'Malley."

Mitch gave Megan's good hand a squeeze. She rose from her seat on the aisle and made her way slowly through the gate and toward the witness stand, trying not to lean too heavily against her crutch, too aware of the eyes that followed her, scrutinizing, speculating. The bailiff hovered at her shoulder, as if he expected her to swoon. She backed him off with an icy glare and took her time climbing into the witness box.

Standing behind the table, Ellen assessed her witness as Megan was sworn in, noting with grim satisfaction that the BCA agent had taken no measures to cover the damage that had been done to her. She wore no makeup and had pulled her dark hair back off her neck, revealing the fading choke marks around her throat.

"Agent O'Malley," Ellen began, "please state for the record your occupation."

"I am—was—the Deer Lake regional field agent for the Minnesota Bureau of Criminal Apprehension."

"You say 'was.' Has your status with the bureau changed recently?"

"Yes," Megan answered grudgingly. "I'm currently on medical leave."

"Due to injuries suffered on January twenty-second, 1994?"

"Yes."

"Agent O'Malley, you were the agent in charge of the investigation of the abduction of Josh Kirkwood, were you not?"

"That's correct."

"And were you investigating that crime on the twenty-second?"

"Yes, I was."

"Would you please tell the court what happened on that morning?"

"Objection," Costello said in a bored tone. "Relevance."

Ellen cut him a look. "Goes to motive, Your Honor. We intend to establish a chronology of events that led to the vicious attack against Agent O'Malley."

Grabko pursed his lips and nodded. "Overruled."

Ellen stepped out from behind the table and walked slowly toward the witness stand, pulling Grabko's attention away from Costello. "Please continue, Agent O'Malley."

"I had stopped my car on the side of Old Cedar Road, got out of the vehicle, and was examining a set of skid marks made on the road during an auto accident that had taken place on the night of Josh Kirkwood's abduction, directly prior to his abduction."

"Why were you interested in the accident site?"

"I was suspicious of the cause and the timing of the accident. The resulting injuries to the drivers and passengers delayed Josh Kirkwood's mother, Dr. Hannah Garrison, in leaving the hospital to pick him up from hockey practice. In the time between the accident and Dr. Garrison's arrival at the ice arena, Josh was abducted."

"And while you were examining these skid marks, were you approached by anyone?"

"Yes. Dr. Garrett Wright stopped and expressed an interest in my purpose for being there. I simply said I was checking something out."

"To the best of your knowledge, was Dr. Wright aware of the accident that had taken place?"

"Yes, he was. The driver of the car that caused the accident was a student at Harris College who was involved in a project Dr. Wright and Professor Christopher Priest were heading."

"Did you see Dr. Wright again later that day?"

"Yes. I went to Harris College looking for Professor Priest. The professor wasn't in his office, but I found Dr. Wright there, along with a student."

"How was Dr. Wright dressed at that time?"

"He was wearing a shirt and tie and dark trousers."

"You spoke to him then?"

"Yes. Dr. Wright informed me that Priest had gone to St. Peter and would likely return to his home around two-thirty P.M."

"Was Dr. Wright aware of your intention to go to his colleague's home?"

"He offered to give me directions."

"Did you inform anyone else of your intention to go to Priest's home?"

"No."

"And where is Professor Priest's home located?"

"10226 Stone Quarry Trail. Outside of town."

"In a wooded, relatively isolated area, correct?"

"Yes."

"When you arrived at that location, was Professor Priest at home?"

"No. The house was locked and dark. There was no car. I proceeded to walk around the property, the south end of which abuts Quarry Hills Park. As I neared the end of a storage shed on the southeast corner of the property, I saw a trail of footprints in the snow leading from the south—the park—into the shed. I found that suspicious, so I drew my weapon, announced myself as a law-enforcement officer, and demanded the person in the shed come out."

"Did the person come out?"

"No."

"What happened then?"

Megan blinked slowly, the scene flashing in broken frames behind her eyelids like a poorly spliced film.

A weird twilight quality to the afternoon. The sky leaden, snow falling thick and heavy. A forest of black, winter-dead trees surrounded the property.

"I decided to go back to my vehicle and radio for backup," she said.

Her heart beat a little harder. She was moving past the shed. Thirty feet and she would be clear of it. She got no farther than fifteen.

"Someone burst out of the shed."

The first blow struck with a power that sent her sprawling headlong. The gun flew out of her hand. She could see it, sailing away, falling, disappearing into the snow. She lunged toward it, kicking, flailing like a beached swimmer.

"I—I tried to get the gun. He came down on top of me."

Black clothing, ski mask, eyes, and a mouth. A short black club swinging down at her.

"He . . . struck me," she said, the tension building in her chest. "With a baton—um—like a nightstick. Hard."

Again and again. Hitting her shoulder. Hitting her a glancing blow off the side of her head. Striking her right hand as she held it up in defense, the blow so vicious that the pain roared up her arm and exploded in her brain.

The memory of the pain brought a wave of nausea. She pulled a slow, unsteady breath deep into her lungs.

"I lost consciousness," she said quietly.

"When you regained consciousness, where were you?"

"Tied to a chair. I don't know the location."

"Can you describe the surroundings?"

"I was blindfolded. I had only a small wedge of vision at the bottom of the blindfold."

Ellen paused, resting a hand on the smooth old wood of the witness stand as gently as if it were Megan's hand. From this close she could see that Megan's ashen pallor had nothing to do with the quality of the lighting, and that despite the coolness of the room, a fine film of perspiration misted her forehead.

"Megan, I realize this is difficult for you," she said, with genuine sympathy. "But will you tell us what happened while you were held captive in this place?"

Megan swallowed hard. Control. She was a cop. She had testified a million times.

She had never been a victim.

She turned a narrow gaze on Garrett Wright, sitting so calm, beaming false innocence, and damned him to the vilest, blackest corner of hell.

"He . . . beat me . . . repeatedly," she said, cursing the tears that filled her eyes. Damned if she would let them fall. "He choked me. He talked about killing me—maybe he would, maybe he wouldn't. He talked about taking Josh. He called it a game."

"And he made you a pawn in his game, didn't he?"

"He told me I would be their next move." And the sense of helplessness and humiliation had nearly been worse than the pain.

"Agent O'Malley, even though you couldn't see your assailant's face, you came to a conclusion about his identity. How did you arrive at this conclusion?"

"Only two people knew I had gone to Priest's home, Garrett Wright being one of them. He had also seen me examining the skid marks at the accident site. If he was involved, he would have known I was onto something.

"I had met and spoken with Dr. Wright on several occasions. I was familiar with his patterns of speech. I knew his height in relation to my own. I had also noticed he had a pronounced habit of rocking back on his heels. I could see a section of floor beside my chair. I saw his boots, saw him rocking back on his heels while he went on and on about how brilliant he was," she said bitterly.

"And did he say anything specific that rang a bell with you?"

"Yes. I asked him why he had singled out Josh, why the Kirkwoods? With great contempt he said, 'Why not? Such a perfect little family.' When I had spoken with Dr. Wright earlier in the day, he used the same phrase to describe the Kirkwoods—'such a perfect family.' "

Ellen walked away from the stand, letting the testimony hang there, not only for Grabko, but for the press as well. Let them look at Megan, bruised and beaten; let them look at the well-dressed, well-groomed man who stood accused and begin to realize what a monster they had in their midst.

Slipping her reading glasses on, Ellen chose a report from the documents Cameron had spread out on the table.

"The injuries you suffered at the hands of this man were severe, weren't they?"

"Yes."

"According to the medical report, marked people's exhibit C, you sustained a concussion, multiple severe contusions, bruised kidneys, cracked ribs, damage to your right knee. Nearly every bone in your right hand sustained multiple fractures—extensive damage that will require a number of operations if you're to have any hope of regaining mobility."

She paused, looking up at Megan with sympathy, with apology. "Agent O'Malley, considering the extent of the damage to your hand, can you realistically hope you'll ever be able to resume your full duties as a field agent for the Bureau of Criminal Apprehension?"

The question hit Megan like a brick to the solar plexus. The answer was one she had evaded and denied and lain awake nights contemplating. It scared the hell out of her. All she had ever wanted in life was to be a good cop. And if she couldn't be a cop, then what was she—*who* was she?

The tears blurred her vision, and she blinked furiously as she lifted her chin to a proud angle. "It's not likely. No."

Ellen glared at Costello. "Your witness."

He rose, his expression cool, unmoved, his brows drawing together as he consulted a newspaper clipping. "I have to confess, I'm a little confused here, Agent O'Malley. You've told the court you were investigating aspects of the Kirkwood abduction on the twenty-second. Is that correct?"

"Yes."

"But according to an article in the *Star Tribune*, dated Saturday, January twenty-second, you had already been officially relieved of your post, temporarily suspended from active duty. According to your special agent in charge, Bruce DePalma, you had been replaced in the Deer Lake region by Agent Martin Wilhelm the day before because of your mishandling of the investigation."

"That's a lie," Megan said sharply.

Costello arched a brow. "You're calling your special agent in charge a liar?"

"No, Mr. Costello," she said plainly. "I'm calling *you* a liar."

Judge Grabko gave a little jolt in his seat, scowling ferociously. "Agent O'Malley, I expect a certain decorum in my courtroom. Especially from those in law enforcement."

Megan made no effort to apologize. If the pompous old fart wanted contrition, he'd damn well have to ask for it.

Costello pressed on, having no desire to break his

rhythm. "You'd been working the case for ten days with no satisfactory result. One suspect had died in custody—"

"Objection," Ellen snapped, rising. "There's no point to this attack. Agent O'Malley isn't on trial."

"Your Honor, we feel Agent O'Malley's status with the BCA, as well as her mental state on the twenty-second, are very much factors here—"

"This is a hearing, Mr. Costello," Ellen said, "not a trial. You have the right to cross-examine the witnesses, not impeach them."

Grabko smacked his gavel down. "This is *my* courtroom, Ms. North. I will oversee the implementation of the rules."

"Yes, Your Honor," she said tightly. "Please do."

"Objection overruled. Please continue, Mr. Costello."

Costello stepped out from behind the table and sauntered into the open area in front of the bench. "Had you been directed by Special Agent in Charge DePalma to appear at BCA headquarters in St. Paul on Saturday the twenty-second?"

"Yes," Megan admitted grudgingly.

"And yet you were wandering around Deer Lake, looking at skid marks, asking questions—by your own admission, continuing an investigation that you no longer had any connection to. Is that correct?"

"No. I still felt a very strong connection to the case. Josh was still missing. I still had questions. I felt obligated to try to get answers. Appearing at headquarters did not outweigh the need to find a child in danger and apprehend the creep responsible."

"So you defied direct orders from your superior?"

"Delayed."

"Because you didn't want to let go of the case?"

"I may not have been agent in charge of the investigation any longer, but I was still a cop," Megan said. "I felt a moral obligation."

"There was quite a lot of hoopla surrounding your assignment to the Deer Lake region, wasn't there?" Costello asked, changing lanes with the skill of a Grand Prix driver.

"I guess."

"You're being modest. You were the first woman in the history of the BCA to hold a field post. Isn't that right?" he said with phony amazement.

"Yes."

"There was a great deal of pressure on you to solve the Kirkwood case? More so than if you had been a man?"

"I wouldn't know," Megan said, deadpan. "I've never been a man."

Snickers rattled through the gallery. Grabko bumped his gavel and glared at them.

"The press was scrutinizing, quite literally, your every move," Costello went on. "Headquarters was breathing down your neck. You were operating under tremendous stress. Is that a fair assessment?"

"Yes."

"And you wanted very badly to solve the case? In fact, your very career was riding on it?"

"I wanted to solve the case. That was my job."

"You were desperate?"

"Determined."

Costello turned his profile to the gallery and smiled the charming, wide, white smile, shaking his head. "You have a stubborn propensity for rationalization, Agent O'Malley."

"Objection!" Ellen snapped.

"Sustained. Please confine yourself to questions, Mr. Costello."

He nodded slightly and moved back to the defense table. Dorman sat at attention like a trick poodle, holding out the proper statement, which Costello accepted and paged through.

"Agent O'Malley, at any time during the course of the

investigation, was Dr. Wright considered a suspect in the disappearance of Josh Kirkwood?"

"No. Not until he abducted and assaulted me and Chief Holt ran him down."

A muscle ticked in Costello's jaw. His dark eyes flashed as he turned toward Grabko. The judge leaned over the witness stand, temper rouging his cheeks above his beard.

"Agent O'Malley, I'm quite certain you know better than to answer in such a manner. Do so again and you may be held in contempt."

"Yes, Your Honor." She tipped her head in a way that would seem deferential to Grabko but kept him from seeing her eyes.

"Isn't it true," Costello went on, "that in fact you had considered a number of other people as suspects, including Paul Kirkwood?"

"As dictated by standard operating procedures involving abductions, the immediate family was considered as part of the dual investigation."

"You were a little more rigorous in your consideration of Paul Kirkwood than someone just going through the motions."

Megan narrowed her eyes at him. "I'm a good cop. I never 'just go through the motions.'"

"That's admirable. So you were dead serious when you brought Mr. Kirkwood in to be fingerprinted?"

"Mr. Kirkwood was fingerprinted for elimination purposes only."

"You spoke with Dr. Wright and his student on the twenty-second," Costello said, switching tacks again. "But you actually went to Harris College in search of Professor Christopher Priest. Is that right?"

"Yes."

"Why?"

"I wanted to ask him some questions."

"Did you consider *him* a suspect?"

"There was that possibility."

"You gave Dr. Wright the impression that you would be going out to Christopher Priest's residence later that day. Can you say whether or not Dr. Wright or Todd Childs might have spoken about that afterward with other people?"

"I couldn't say."

"Is it possible your conversation might have been overheard by someone in the hall outside the office?"

"I couldn't say."

"So you can't conclusively say that Dr. Wright was only one of two people who knew you were going to Professor Priest's home?"

"To my knowledge, he was."

"What time was it when you arrived at Priest's home?"

"Approximately one forty-five P.M."

Costello arched a brow for his audience. "But Dr. Wright had specified Priest wouldn't be back until around two-thirty. Why did you get there so early?"

Megan cocked her head to a belligerent angle. "I wanted to be there to welcome him home."

"Agent O'Malley," Grabko cautioned.

"You considered him a suspect," Costello said.

"Asked and answered," Ellen said wearily, rising. "Your Honor, can we ask Mr. Costello to cut to the chase here? It simply isn't relevant whether there was one suspect or a dozen. Dr. Wright is the man who was apprehended."

Grabko's face tightened as if he wanted to deny her but couldn't. "Let's move on, Mr. Costello."

Costello didn't bat an eye. "Agent O'Malley, did you see the face of the person who attacked you at the Priest residence?"

He hit her from the side, sent her sprawling. The gun flew out of her hand. . . .

"No."

"Did you see the face of the person who assaulted you while you were held at this undisclosed location?"

The pain came from all directions at once, striking her shoulder, her knee, her hand, again and again.

"Agent O'Malley?"

"I saw his feet."

Costello looked indignant. "And on the basis of *that* you would have us try a respected member of the community for heinous crimes?"

"No! I—"

"Did you recognize his voice?"

"You think we'll kill you, clever girl? You wouldn't be the first by a long, long way. . . ." A whisper, soft, disembodied . . .

"No, but—"

Costello wheeled away from her. "You didn't see him, couldn't recognize him, he never spoke his name," he said, his voice growing louder with every syllable. He flung her written statement down onto the table and turned back toward her. "Is there *anything* you can tell us, *former* Agent O'Malley, that should make us believe your conclusion that your assailant was Dr. Garrett Wright is anything more than the desperate grasping of a woman who'd bungled the case and had to do something to keep her career from going down the toilet?"

"Objection!" Ellen shouted.

Grabko pounded for order.

The sounds were blocked in Megan's mind by the white noise of fury. The fine thread on her control snapped, and the rage poured through her and out of her.

"I can tell you he's guilty!" she shouted, coming up out of her seat. "I can tell you he's a sick son of bitch who thinks it's a game to steal children and ruin lives, and he deserves worse than anything this court will do to him!"

"Order!" Grabko screamed, pounding like a carpenter. The head snapped off his gavel and sailed at the defense table. "Order!"

The bailiff started toward the witness stand, but jumped back at the sight of Megan's crutch.

Megan's focus was on Costello, who stood no more than a foot away, his face calm, his dark eyes bright, the barest hint of a smile tightening the corners of his mouth.

Oh, God, O'Malley, you played right into his hands. Way to go.

She had to appear just exactly as he had wanted to paint her—obsessed, biased, out of control. Desperate. The realization made her feel ill, dizzy. She sank weakly back into her chair and closed her eyes.

"No further questions," Costello said, and walked calmly back toward his client.

CHAPTER 31

"The State calls Chief of Police Mitch Holt," Ellen said calmly, as if her first witness hadn't just been hustled out of the courtroom.

She didn't blame Megan for losing her poise. Considering what Wright had put her through, it was a wonder she hadn't pulled a gun and shot him—and Costello, too, while she was at it. The big question in Ellen's mind was what impact Megan's emotional testimony would have. The press might take her side—or not—but Grabko was clearly pissed off. This hearing was his show and Megan had upstaged him. Would he look at her testimony and see anything but red?

With luck Mitch would settle the judge and the gallery. He made an excellent witness—businesslike, his face set in the stony no-nonsense expression of a veteran detective. He took the stand and swore the oath, his gaze fixed on the defense table.

"Chief Holt, will you please tell the court about the events that occurred on the night of January twenty-second?" Ellen prompted.

"At approximately eight forty-five P.M. I received a call from Agent O'Malley," Mitch said. "She was in obvious distress. She wasn't allowed to say much. Then an unidentified male came on the line and instructed me to go alone to the southwest entrance of Quarry Hills Park at nine-fifteen."

"Did he say why?"

"He said they had a present for me, that they wanted to win 'the game.'"

"And you went to the park as instructed?"

"Not as instructed. I immediately sent an unmarked car with two officers to the southeast entrance of the park, another to the southwest, and came into the park myself on foot from the west."

"Where the park adjoins the Lakeside neighborhood?"

"Yes. I waited in the cover of the trees. At nine-oh-five a late-model GMC four-by-four truck entered the park, drove some distance along the road, and stopped. The driver got out, went to the passenger side and let the passenger out, then marched her approximately thirty feet back to the south."

Megan, limping heavily, unquestionably badly injured. The fury he had felt then burned again like a coal.

"A struggle ensued between them," he stated flatly. "I ran out from the woods with my weapon drawn, announced myself as a police officer, and ordered them to freeze."

"At this point, did you recognize either person?"

"Yes. I recognized Agent O'Malley. The assailant was wearing a ski mask."

"Was he armed?"

"Yes. He had a nine-millimeter semiautomatic handgun."

"And was he threatening Agent O'Malley?"

"Yes. At one point he had the gun pressed to her temple." And Mitch had known a wrong move, a wrong decision, and she would be dead right there and then, before his eyes.

"I ordered him to drop the weapon, informed him he was under arrest," he went on. "Agent O'Malley knocked him off balance. He pushed her at me, fired several rounds, and jumped back into the truck, which was still running. I jumped into the back of the truck, fired a shot through the back window in order to break the glass, ordered him to stop the truck."

"Did he?"

"No. He returned fire, then lost control of the vehicle."

The truck roared off the path and into space, landed bucking, skidded sideways, sending up a spray of snow.

"I was thrown clear. The truck slammed into a tree."

"You then pursued the suspect on foot?"

"Yes. He ran west, into the woods and up the hill toward Lakeside, occasionally stopping to fire at me."

"Were you hit?"

"One shot cut through the sleeve of my coat and grazed my arm."

"But you continued pursuit?"

"Yes. At one point he discarded his ski mask. I found it lying on the ground along the trail."

"What did you do with it?"

"Left it where it was. The crime-scene unit later photographed it in place, then bagged it as evidence and sent it to the BCA lab to be processed."

"Your Honor," Ellen addressed Grabko as Cameron rose and presented several photographs to the clerk. "The ski mask itself is still at the BCA lab, but the State would like to introduce the crime-scene photographs in its stead for the purpose of this hearing."

"Mr. Costello?" Grabko asked, arching a brow.

"No objections, Your Honor."

Grabko nodded to his clerk. "Receive the photographs into evidence."

"Where did the suspect appear to be headed?" Ellen asked, turning back to Mitch.

"The Lakeside subdivision," Mitch said. "He ran up through the backyards of the houses on Lakeshore Drive."

Running along the cross-country ski trail, darting in and out between the snow-frosted spruce trees. The cold air like razors in his lungs. Thinking how insane it was to be chasing a college professor who drove a Saab and worked with juvenile offenders.

"I pursued the suspect through the yards, heading north. I saw him let himself into a garage through the back door, followed him in, took him down, and arrested him."

"And is that man sitting in the courtroom?"

"Yes, he is." He glared at the man whose game had shredded the fabric of life in Deer Lake irreparably. "Dr. Garrett Wright, the defendant."

"Thank you, Chief Holt," Ellen said with a nod. "No further questions."

Mitch watched Costello rise, wondering if he would play the same game he had played with Megan—moving closer and closer into her space until she lashed out at him. He would have liked the chance to lash out at Costello, himself. Preferably in a dark alley with no witnesses. It had killed him to sit impassively in the gallery watching Megan unravel. A female bailiff had escorted her from the stand into the jury room after her final outburst. He wanted only one thing more than he wanted to go to her, and that was to nail the lid on Garrett Wright's coffin.

"Chief Holt," Costello began, standing at ease behind the defense table. "You testify the suspect was wearing a ski mask when you first encountered him in the park. You did not see his face at that time?"

"No."

"Did he speak to you?"

"No."

"The truck he was driving was registered to whom?"

"Roy Stranberg, who was in Arizona at the time. The truck was stolen."

"And were Dr. Wright's fingerprints found in this truck?"

"No."

"And when you were pursuing the suspect through the woods, did you see him discard the ski mask? Did you see his face?"

"No."

"That's a fairly dense woods, isn't it, Chief Holt? A lot of trees?"

"That would be the definition of a woods, yes," Mitch said dryly.

"You didn't have a clear and constant view of the suspect, did you?"

"Not constant, no, but the gunfire kept me apprised of his whereabouts."

Another snicker ran through the gallery, but Costello jumped onto the opportunity.

"And when you apprehended Dr. Wright, was he in possession of a weapon?"

"No."

"According to the statements, Dr. Wright's hands were later tested for gunpowder residue and the tests were negative—isn't that right?"

"Yes."

Costello steepled his fingers and arranged his features in a contemplative mien. "So you're running through the woods. It's dark. It's snowing. You're dodging gunfire, dodging trees. You lost sight of your suspect more than once, didn't you?"

"I saw him just fine when he went into that garage."

"But you had lost sight of him prior to that?"

"For no more than seconds."

"How many seconds?"

"I didn't time the instances."

"Five seconds? Ten? Twenty?"

"Less than twenty. Less than fifteen."

"But you have no way of knowing for certain?"

"No."

"So it could be possible that the man you saw going into that garage wasn't your suspect at all, isn't that right?"

"That would be unlikely."

"But possible?"

"Remotely."

"Prior to making the actual arrest, did you have any reason to believe the suspect you were chasing was Dr. Wright?"

"Agent O'Malley had told me it was Dr. Wright."

"I see," Costello said with an exaggerated nod. He turned sideways, cocking a hip against the table, absently twirling a pencil in his hands. "Chief Holt, when you received that phone call from Agent O'Malley and heard that she was in distress, in danger, what did that make you feel?"

Mitch squinted at him, suspicious. "I don't follow."

"Were you in fear for her life?"

"Of course."

"And when you saw her in Quarry Hills Park and she was obviously badly wounded, did that make you angry?"

"Objection," Ellen said, looking askance at Costello. "Is there a point to this?"

"A very sharp one, Your Honor."

Grabko nodded. "Proceed. Answer the question, Chief Holt."

"Yes."

"It made you angry. You were frightened for her. You wanted to get the person responsible. You wanted that badly."

"That's my job."

"But your feelings went beyond a professional concern, didn't they? Isn't it true you and Agent O'Malley are involved—"

"Objection!" Ellen surged to her feet. "This is abso-

lutely outside the scope of this hearing! We're here to review facts and evidence, not the personal lives of police
officers!"

Grabko smacked his new gavel. "I don't want to hear
another lecture from you, Ms. North," he snapped. "Mr.
Costello, perhaps you'd better state your point for the
court."

Ellen tossed her pencil down and crossed her arms.

"Do you have a problem with my suggestion, Ms.
North?" Grabko asked coolly.

"Yes, I do, Your Honor. It gives Mr. Costello the opportunity to present his case to the press, which is very
likely the reason he went down this road in the first place."

Grabko stuck his lower lip out like a pouting child.
"The outcome of this hearing will not be based on the
opinions of the press, Ms. North. The decision is mine
and mine alone, to be made on the basis of the evidence
presented. And so it is for me to decide the relevance of
Mr. Costello's line of questioning. If I feel it bears merit,
I'll allow it. If not, it will be disregarded."

"And will it be disregarded by every potential juror
who reads the *Pioneer Press* or watches *KARE-Eleven
News*?" Ellen argued. "We may not have a jury seated,
Your Honor, but we have a gallery who will act as jury *and*
judge. If Mr. Costello has to make this lame argument,
please let him do it in sidebar."

The judge's eyes scanned the eager faces in the gallery,
every last one of them salivating at the idea of hearing
something someone didn't want them to hear.

"Sidebar," he declared unhappily.

They arrayed themselves at the side of the bench,
Costello and Ellen shoulder to shoulder, flanked by their
associates.

"Now, by all means, Mr. Costello," Ellen said under
her breath with sharp-edged sweetness, "enlighten us as to
your big-city legal brilliance."

Costello smiled. "You'll have to forgive Ms. North, Your Honor. It's understandable she wouldn't want this particular subject raised—the effect of personal relationships on motivation."

The subtext cut to the quick. Ellen was stunned that even he would skate so close to such a dangerous edge. Turning back to the judge, she shifted her body just slightly and planted the heel of her pump on Costello's handmade Italian oxford, grinding down on his little toe.

"Your Honor, Chief Holt and Agent O'Malley were acting in their capacity as law-enforcement officers. They are here today testifying in that capacity," Costello said through his teeth as he tried to surreptitiously wrench his foot out from under hers. "But as Ms. North well knows, Your Honor, emotions spill over from our personal lives into our professional. Particularly in a highly charged situation—which this obviously was. If those emotions affected Chief Holt's judgment, I think the court should know about it."

"Will it make your client any less guilty?" Ellen asked.

"My client is an innocent man, victimized by circumstance and Agent O'Malley's desperate attempt to cling to her own professional life."

Ellen narrowed her eyes at him. "Your Honor, may I suggest the only 'desperate attempts' we're looking at here are Mr. Costello's attempts to introduce a wholly inappropriate line of questioning."

"No, you may not," Grabko said. "You will kindly stop trying to make my decisions for me, Ms. North, and remember your place here in this courtroom."

"My place?"

Cameron nudged her back a step in warning. "Your Honor, I don't have as much experience in this type of proceeding as Ms. North or Mr. Costello," he said, his freckled face shining with humility, "but I thought the defense, if they are to present a case at all, are to bring hard evidence that is clearly exculpatory in nature, rather than speculative theory. Am I wrong about that?"

Grabko's expression softened somewhat at the opportunity to play law professor, and the tension diffused. "You're correct, Mr. Reed. However, statements can be exculpatory, can they not?"

"Uh, yes, Your Honor."

"And, theoretically, even a statement from a prosecution witness can be considered such if given proper weight and light."

And fertilized by the right defense attorney. Cameron's attempt at diplomatic steering had just been bent into a pretzel by Grabko's love of the sound of his own voice.

"Proceed with caution, Mr. Costello," Grabko went on. "I want to hear a definite point made in the questioning, not counsel giving testimony in the guise of cross-examination."

Costello nodded. "Of course, Your Honor. Thank you, Your Honor."

Ellen refused to give him the satisfaction of looking at him. Taking no chances, Cameron physically turned her back toward their table.

"Nice try, Opie," she said under her breath.

He leaned his head toward hers as he took his seat. "You're pissing him off, Ellen."

"He's pissing me off."

"Yeah, but his fate isn't in your hands."

"In my dreams."

Costello resumed his place behind the defense table, maintaining distance from the witness stand.

"Chief Holt, is it true you and Agent O'Malley are involved personally?"

Mitch's jaw hardened. "I don't see how that's any of your damn business, Mr. Costello."

Grabko leaned toward the box. "You'll answer the

question, Chief Holt, and please refrain from using profanity in my courtroom."

"Yes, Your Honor," he responded grudgingly, glaring at Costello. "Yes, we are."

"So when you saw Agent O'Malley in danger, in pain, your reaction went beyond ordinary professional concern."

"Yes."

"You wanted to get the person responsible, and Agent O'Malley told you the person responsible was Dr. Garrett Wright."

"Yes."

"You believed the person you were pursuing was Dr. Wright. Dr. Wright lives on Lakeshore Drive. The chase took you in that direction, and when you saw someone going into Dr. Wright's garage, you pursued, even though you admit you had lost sight of your suspect for an unknown period of time. Isn't that correct?"

"Seconds," Mitch specified. "A heartbeat. What are you getting at, Costello? Spit it out and spare us the theatrics."

He wanted to punch the smug little smile off Costello's face, and he realized that the distance the attorney was keeping between them was aggravating him more than if the son of a bitch had been standing a foot away, as he had done with Megan.

"You wanted to see Agent O'Malley keep her position here as regional agent, didn't you?"

"Agent O'Malley is an excellent cop."

"And your lover. And Agent O'Malley had decided, based on virtually no evidence, that Dr. Wright was guilty. She told you Dr. Wright was the one. You pursued Dr. Wright."

"I pursued the suspect," Mitch corrected him, his blood boiling at the insinuation. "I apprehended the suspect. I didn't give a damn if he was Dr. Wright or Dr. Spock."

"It never occurred to you that the man you ultimately apprehended and the suspect you chased through the woods in the dead of night were not the same person?"

"Never."

"Dr. and Mrs. Wright live at 93 Lakeshore Drive, is that correct?"

"Yes."

"Can you tell me who lives just two houses north, at 97 Lakeshore Drive?"

"The Kirkwoods."

"Paul Kirkwood?"

"Yes."

"No further questions, Chief Holt."

Ellen watched Costello as he settled into his chair.

"He's really going to do it, isn't he?" Cameron whispered. "He's going to try to pin this on Josh's father."

"He'll do whatever he has to," she murmured. "Garrett Wright and his shadow aren't the only ones playing a game here."

She rose again just as Grabko started to dismiss the witness. "Redirect, Your Honor?"

Impatience flashed in Grabko's eyes, but he grumbled a yes and sat back to pet his beard.

"Are the houses on Lakeshore Drive numbered on the back side, Chief?"

"Not that I'm aware of."

"So when you followed the suspect into that garage, you didn't know if you were in 93 Lakeshore Drive or 95 or 91."

"I had no idea. It didn't matter."

"The suspect you chased through the woods was dressed in black, is that correct, Chief?"

"Yes. Black pants, black boots, black jacket."

"And how was Dr. Wright dressed when you apprehended him?"

"He was in black pants, black boots, and a black ski jacket."

"Did he show signs of physical exertion?"

"Yes. He was breathing hard, perspiring."

"And do you have any idea what the temperature was that evening?"

"About twenty degrees with a windchill factor of six degrees."

"Not the kind of night the average person would break a sweat, was it?"

"Objection."

"Withdrawn," Ellen said, biting down on a sly smile. "In regards to the tests for gunpowder performed on Dr. Wright's hands: would the outcome of the tests be affected if he had been wearing gloves at the time he'd used the gun?"

"Yes."

"No further questions, Chief Holt. Thank you."

The final witness for the prosecution was a criminalist from BCA headquarters in St. Paul. Norm Irlbeck had been on the scene the night of O'Malley's abduction, had been the one to collect the bloodstained sheet that had been draped around Megan. Ellen showed him photographs of the sheet taken at the scene and at headquarters.

"Is this the sheet, Mr. Irlbeck?"

"Yes, it is." He nodded a big, square head that sat like a block atop a big, square body. His voice was the deep, sonorous voice of authority that caught Grabko's attention and held it.

Ellen handed the photographs over to the clerk. "The sheet is still undergoing some tests in the lab—is that correct?" she asked, coming back toward her witness.

"Yes. The DNA tests will take another four to five weeks to complete."

"But there have been some conclusive preliminary findings, have there not?"

"Yes, there have been. Two distinct types of blood were found on the sheet. O positive, which is the blood type of Agent O'Malley, and AB negative, which is the blood type of Josh Kirkwood."

"And the extensive DNA tests now being conducted will determine if indeed the AB-negative blood is in fact Josh Kirkwood's—correct?"

"Yes."

"Hairs were also found on the sheet?"

"Yes. Hairs that were tested against samples and were found to be consistent in type with Agent O'Malley, Josh Kirkwood, and the defendant, Dr. Garrett Wright. There were also hairs from an unidentified fourth person."

"What about the ski mask found along the trail of pursuit, Mr. Irlbeck? Were hairs also found on that?"

"Yes. Hairs that were consistent with the defendant and also hairs that matched those unidentified from the sheet."

"Thank you, Mr. Irlbeck. I have no further questions."

"Mr. Irlbeck," Costello said before Ellen was even back to her seat. "Is the analysis of hair an exact, reliable science?"

"No, it is not."

"You can't make an absolutely positive identification as to whether a hair found on a sheet belongs to a particular person based strictly on the study of the hair itself."

"No, sir."

"Do you have any way of determining who last wore that ski mask?"

"No, sir."

"And do you have any way of knowing precisely *how* any of the hairs came to be on that sheet?"

"No, I do not."

"Could they have been deliberately placed on the sheet?"

"Possibly."

"No further questions."

"We have enough," Cameron said, ignoring the chairs and sitting on the credenza. Phoebe handed him a white deli sack and placed Ellen's on the table without looking at her.

Ignoring her secretary's pique and the food, Ellen paced the length of the conference table. She was too nervous to eat. Their part of the hearing had gone well enough, even with Costello scoring a few points, but the afternoon would be Tony's show, and what little control she'd had in the morning would be taken from her.

"We've got more than enough," Mitch said, pacing the lane on the other side of the table. "Even if Grabko is tempted to buy into Costello's bullshit, there's more than enough weighing on Wright to push him into a trial. Grabko would never have the guts to cut him loose."

But how much nerve would it take, Ellen wondered, with the press shouting out all the things Garrett Wright could not have done? He could not have brought Josh home. He couldn't have taken Dustin Holloman or killed Dustin Holloman. That was the public's focus now—the monster at large. Grabko's decision was to be based on law, but he was just a man, as susceptible to rumor and pressure as anyone.

"It's pretty clear which way he's leaning," she said. "I haven't seen a judge give that much leeway in a pretrial since *Perry Mason* went off the air. I'm sorry he let Costello put you through that, Megan."

Megan sat at the end of the table, looking small and battered, as if the ordeal of the morning had caused her to pull in on herself. "I'm the one who should apologize," she mumbled, eyes down. "I know better than to let some asshole lawyer punch my buttons."

The tension in her voice, in the set of her jaw, hinted at a torrent of emotion building up behind the walls Megan erected around herself. Ellen had seen it happen before. Cops made lousy victims. They were, by nature, control freaks; victims were stripped of all control, all pride, all dignity.

"It's not your fault, Megan," she said.

"He made me look like a raving lunatic who'd say anything, do anything, to get that arrest on my record."

"Or like someone who was damn sure of her facts and set on convicting a guilty man," Ellen countered. "It's all in your perception. People see what they want."

"We know what they want to see when they look at Wright," Megan said. Nobody wanted to believe a man like Garrett Wright was capable of evil. And with the death of Dustin Holloman, the people of Park County would be even less willing to accept Wright as their devil.

"So we have to prove them wrong," Ellen said, her gaze direct, her meaning clear.

Megan nodded. "Yes, we do."

CHAPTER 32

"The defense calls Dr. Garrett Wright to the stand," Costello announced, setting the crowd buzzing, a noise that rose up to the high ceiling of the old courtroom like a swarm of yellow jackets.

It appeared to be a bold move, playing his ace first, offering up his client for direct scrutiny and cross-examination. That the defendant himself would be testifying at all was highly unusual for a probable-cause hearing, but, then, nothing about this case was ordinary. Jay sat back with his arms crossed, considering the strategy. If Wright was the sociopath Ellen painted him to be, then he was a consummate liar, an actor with a role he relished—the mild-mannered professor, well deserving of public sympathy.

Jay had to admit, he'd seen it before. A mind as cold as arctic ice; capable of charm, just as capable of murder. He had once sat opposite just such a man in a visitation booth in Angola Penitentiary one hell-hot Louisiana summer. A man who was pleasant, articulate on all the political issues of the day. Well-read, bright, with a sharp, sardonic wit. A man who had held three truck-stop waitresses hostage as sex slaves for three months, tortured them to death, then took up taxidermy and mounted their heads and breasts for his own private trophy room. D. Rodman Madsen, a sales rep for an irrigation-pump company, twice voted salesman of the year, and treasurer of the local Elks lodge. A killer behind the socially acceptable facade. No one who knew him had ever suspected.

Garrett Wright took the stand and quietly recited the oath. In his blue suit and regimental tie, he gave the appearance of the quintessential young professional—attractive, conservative, educated. Jay could all but hear the gears grinding in the minds around him, the sly speculation, the denial, the disbelief. Even the judge looked down on Garrett Wright with barely concealed incredulity, as if astonished to find such a man before him as the focus of a court proceeding.

Costello began by asking for Wright's litany of professional credits, the degrees, the résumé, then segued into his civic achievements before coming to the heart of the matter.

"Dr. Wright, where were you on the evening of Wednesday, January twelfth, between five-thirty and seven-thirty P.M.?"

"I was working," Wright said mildly. "Researching documented case studies I thought might pertain to an ongoing study some of my students are involved in concerning learning and perception."

"And where were you doing this research?"

"In a storeroom in the basement of the Cray building."

"On the campus of Harris College?"

He gave a sheepish little smile. "Yes. I'm afraid I have more books than my office can hold. I've more or less taken over a room in the basement as an auxiliary office."

"Were you alone that evening?"

"No. Todd Childs, a student of mine, was with me until about eight-thirty."

"And when did you first hear about the abduction of Josh Kirkwood?"

"Later that evening. On the ten o'clock news."

"Do you know Josh?"

"As well as I know any of my neighbors' children—enough to recognize him, to say hello."

"You know his parents?"

"Hannah and Paul, yes. They're acquaintances of mine and my wife. Casual friends."

"Has there ever been any trouble between you?"

"No. None."

"In fact, you spoke with Dr. Garrison several times after her son was abducted, didn't you? To offer sympathy, to give advice."

"Yes. In fact, I called her the night of the twenty-first to give her the name of a family therapist I know in Edina. It was clear the ordeal was taking a terrible toll on their marriage."

"And the press called on you several times after Josh went missing, to act as a consultant, is that right?"

"Yes, although I told them repeatedly I have no expertise in the area of criminal behavior."

"Prior to the night you were arrested, were you ever questioned by the police regarding Josh Kirkwood's disappearance?"

"Not as a suspect, no. They asked me some general questions—had I noticed any strangers in the neighborhood, had I noticed anything different about the Kirkwood household lately, that sort of thing."

"And what did you tell them?"

"That I couldn't be of any real help to them. I spend most of my time at the college or in my office at home."

"And where were you the afternoon of Saturday, January twenty-second?"

"Working. The new term began Monday. I was preparing."

"Were you alone?"

"Todd Childs was with me until about one-fifteen. I was alone after that. I went home briefly for a late lunch, around one-thirty, returned to campus about an hour later. Otherwise I spent the afternoon and evening in the Cray building."

"Arriving home at what time?"

"Around nine-fifteen that evening."

"And will you please tell the court in your own words what occurred when you arrived home?"

"I had just parked my car in the garage and started for the door into the house when I heard what I thought might be gunshots behind the house. I stepped out the door, saw a man running toward me. I thought he might be a burglar or something, some kind of criminal. So I jumped back inside with the intention of going into the house to call 911. The door burst open, and the next thing I knew I was being tackled and told that I was under arrest."

"You had no idea what was going on that afternoon and evening with regards to Agent O'Malley being kidnapped and assaulted?"

"Of course not. How could I know anything about that?"

"How, indeed," Costello said, turning toward the gallery. "Dr. Wright, do you own a ski mask like the one we saw earlier in the prosecution photographs?"

"I did at one time. I used to be something of a fanatic about cross-country skiing. I used to ski three times a week, regardless of the cold, but I haven't done that the past couple of winters."

"And do you have any idea what became of your ski mask?"

He shook his head. "I don't know. I think my wife may have gotten rid of it at a garage sale."

"Do you own a handgun?"

"No. I'm a strong proponent of gun control, as a matter of fact. I would never have a gun in my home."

"And finally, for the record, Dr. Wright, did you kidnap Josh Kirkwood?"

"Absolutely not."

"Did you kidnap and assault Agent Megan O'Malley?"

"Absolutely not."

"Thank you, Dr. Wright. No further questions."

Ellen rose before Costello was halfway back to his seat. She marched smartly around the end of the table to take command of the stage. She had watched Wright and Costello weave their web, drawing in Grabko, drawing in the press. They played their roles to the hilt. It was her job to make the audience forget their performances, to make them forget Garrett Wright's history of selfless duty to the community, to stick her fingers through the holes in his story and rip the fabric of his lies to shreds.

"Dr. Wright, this storeroom you use in the basement of the Cray building is in the northwest corner of the building, is it not?"

"Yes, it is."

"The first room at the bottom of the stairs?"

"Yes."

"And just off the first-floor landing of those stairs is an exit that leads past some trash Dumpsters to a small faculty parking lot. Is that correct?"

"Yes, it is."

"A very handy spot to have an auxilary office," she said. "Easy to come and go quickly without being seen."

"Objection."

"I'll rephrase, Your Honor," she offered, glad to make her point a second time. "Did anyone see you exit the Cray building on the night of the twelfth?"

"I didn't see anyone."

"You told us one of your students, Todd Childs, was with you that evening."

"Yes, that's correct."

"Todd Childs and no one else?"

"No one else."

"Dr. Wright, can you explain why, in his initial reports

to the police, Mr. Childs said nothing about being with you that evening?"

"Objection. Calls for speculation."

"Sustained."

"How about on the twenty-second? Can anyone back up your statement that you returned to the Cray building after your late lunch or that you then worked until past nine o'clock that night?"

"I was alone and unaware that I might need an alibi later," he said dryly.

There was the barest hint of amusement in his eyes as he held Ellen's gaze for just a second. The kind of look that suggested he was only letting her play at control. The idea twisted inside her like a worm boring through her confidence. The image of Dustin Holloman flashed behind her eyelids. *some rise by SIN, and some by virtue fall . . .*

"And on the twenty-second," she said, pressing on. "After Todd Childs left your office, you didn't see anyone, not another living soul, all day and half the evening?"

"No, I didn't."

Ellen crossed her arms and arched a brow as she paced slowly in front of the witness box. "Doesn't that seem odd? As you stated, the new term was to begin the following Monday. Do you think you're the only teacher with an office in the Cray building who needed to prepare?"

"I can't speak for my colleagues," Wright said calmly. "Perhaps they were more well prepared than I. Or maybe the weather kept them from coming in to work. We were having a snowstorm."

"Yes, we were," she said, nodding. "The weather was cold, nasty. Yet when Chief Holt arrested you, you were hot, perspiring. You were not wearing gloves. Can you explain that, Dr. Wright?"

"I had just been subjected to a frightening experience, Ms. North. I'd heard gunshots, saw a man rushing toward me, a man who then broke into my garage and attacked me. That seems just cause for a little perspiration."

"And the gloves?"

"I'd forgotten them."

"On such a bitterly cold night?"

"I was tired. It was late."

"The windchill factor was six degrees."

"Yes, I cursed myself all the way home."

He gave her the look again. Intimate. Amused. Unnerving. Drawing her into a strange, shared moment that no one else seemed to see. Ellen turned her back to him and went to the prosecution table on the false pretense of consulting her notes.

"Dr. Wright, Agent O'Malley testified that when she spoke with you in Professor Priest's office earlier in the afternoon, you were dressed in a shirt and tie and dark trousers. At the time Chief Holt arrested you, you were dressed head to toe in black. Why is that?"

"I changed clothes when I came home for lunch," he answered, unperturbed. "It was Saturday. I knew I was going to spend the rest of the day alone. I decided I might as well be comfortable."

"So you dressed up like a ninja warrior?"

"Objection!" Costello shouted.

"Sustained." Grabko frowned at her. "Ms. North, you know better."

"Yes, Your Honor," Ellen said blandly, turning away. "No further questions."

Murmurs raced through the gallery as she took her seat. Ellen knew what they were about. Why hadn't she confronted him? Why hadn't she hammered at him until he confessed—if there was anything for him to confess. The same questions courtroom newcomers always asked. The same ideas law professors beat out of their students early on. Garrett Wright would never confess on the stand. He would never admit to anything in a confrontation. He had his story, he had his act, and he would stick with them. She would end up looking a fool if she pressed him. There was no point asking questions if she knew the answers would be lies she couldn't break.

"The defense calls Annette Fabrino."

The woman who took the stand had a softly rounded body and the face of a Raphael cherub. She looked out on the crowd like a deer caught in headlights, clearly unnerved at the prospect of testifying in front of an audience. Costello stepped close to the witness stand and attempted to put her at ease with a charming smile.

"I have just a couple of questions for you, Annette," he said kindly. "It won't take long at all. First of all, can you state for the record your home address?"

"Ninety-two Lakeshore Drive."

"Just down the block from Dr. Wright's home?"

"Yes."

"On Saturday the twenty-second, did you look out your front window around two-thirty?"

"Yes, I did. My husband was supposed to have been home from a business trip around two, but he was late and he hadn't called. I was worried about his making it back at all because of the weather."

"What did you see when you looked out?"

"I saw Dr. Wright go by in his car, headed south."

"Are you sure of the time?"

"Yes. I was checking my watch every few minutes."

"Thank you, Annette." Costello flashed the smile again and slipped his hands into his trouser pockets. "That's all. Not so bad, was it?"

A rose blush bloomed across Annette Fabrino's round cheeks.

"Mrs. Fabrino," Ellen began as Costello walked away from his witness, "your house is on the west side of the street, isn't it? The Tudor on the corner?"

"Yes."

"And you state you saw Dr. Wright's gray Saab going south. That means the driver was on the far side of the car from you."

"Uh—yes."

"And it was snowing quite heavily that afternoon, wasn't it?"

She nodded. "Oh, yes. It was really coming down. That was why I was nervous. I had heard the roads were getting bad."

"So with the snow coming down and the driver on the opposite side of the car, when you say you saw Dr. Wright drive past, did you actually get a good, clear look at his face?"

"Well . . . ," she faltered. "Well, no. Just a glimpse, I guess."

"You knew it was his car."

"Yes. It's the only one like it in the neighborhood."

"So it seems reasonable that you expected him to be the one driving," Ellen said equably. "But could you say with certainty it was?"

Annette Fabrino looked anything but certain. She glanced left to right across the courtroom, looking for reassurance from someone. She tried to settle her gaze on Costello. Ellen moved into her line of vision, not wanting to allow Costello a second to imply through his body language that his witness was betraying him.

"I thought it was him," she said hesitantly.

"But could you swear it?"

"No."

"No further questions," Ellen said with a pleasant smile. "Thank you for your cooperation, Mrs. Fabrino."

"The defense calls Todd Childs."

The bailiff opened the door to the jury room and Todd Childs emerged. Costello had somehow managed the trick of secreting Childs into the courthouse over the lunch break. And that wasn't the only magic he had performed. He had taken Grunge Man and so transformed him Ellen had to stare for a long moment to be sure this was in fact Todd Childs. The ponytail had been clipped off at the nape, the flannel traded for a button-down oxford with a tie. Clean-shaven and clear-eyed, Todd Childs took the stand and the oath.

He was polite under direct examination. Yes, sir. No, sir. Not a hint of belligerence. Costello painted him as a candidate for the Young Republicans. Trustworthy, reliable, a scholarship student who earned pocket money as a tutor. The profile and the appearance bore no resemblance to the young man Ellen had spoken with at the Pack Rat. Costello had obviously been putting him up somewhere, having him groomed and coached, and was likely paying him for his trouble.

"Todd, were you with Dr. Wright on the evening of the twelfth?"

"Yeah, I was." He glanced down, pretending to pick lint off his new slacks. "Downstairs in the Cray building. We were going through some data we compiled in the study last year, and looking for correlations in past studies."

"In your statement to the police made on January twenty-fourth you said you were at the movies that night."

Childs glanced up at Costello, over at Wright, and down again. "I was mistaken. I went, but it was the late show, not the early one."

"What theater did you go to?"

"The mall in Burnsville."

"Had you heard anything about the abduction of Josh Kirkwood?"

"No."

"On Saturday, the twenty-second, Agent O'Malley

stopped by Professor Priest's office while you were there, didn't she?"

"Yeah."

"After she left, did Dr. Wright seem upset or excited?"

"No."

"Did he talk about going after her or going to Christopher Priest's home?"

"No."

"Did he say anything about Josh Kirkwood's abduction?"

Todd bobbed his head down between his shoulders. "Yeah. He said it was a shame, 'cause they were such a nice family."

Costello turned around with a gracious gesture. "Your witness, Ms. North."

Ellen walked toward the witness stand with her hands clasped in front of her, as if in prayer, her expression pensive. "Todd, you've known Dr. Wright for a long time, haven't you? Ever since you began taking classes at Harris—isn't that right?"

He looked at her out the corner of his eye, suspicious. "Yeah."

"You declared your major early on. You always wanted to go into psychology."

"Yeah."

"And Dr. Wright wasn't just a teacher for you, was he? He was your adviser, your mentor."

"Yes."

"Your friend?"

He gave her a hard look. "I respect him very much."

"That's admirable, Todd."

"He's an admirable man."

Ellen tipped her head. "Very few admirable men stand accused of kidnapping and assault."

"Your Honor!" Costello whined.

"Ms. North, don't make me warn you again," Grabko said coldly.

"I'm sorry, Your Honor," she said, remorseless, her attention never leaving the witness. "You respect and admire Dr. Wright. How much? Enough to lie for him?"

"No!"

"Objection!"

"Sustained."

"Where did you go to the movies that night, Todd?" she asked without slowing a beat.

"I said—Burnsville."

She feigned puzzlement. "Burnsville? You drove all the way to Burnsville to go to a late movie on a Wednesday night and that *slipped your mind* when you were talking to the police?"

"I told them I was at the movies."

"I see. Then it was the fact that you had been with Dr. Wright at the time of the kidnapping that *slipped your mind*? Or was it the fact that you claim to have been at the movies *in Burnsville* that slipped your mind, because there is no mention of Burnsville in your original statement."

"It didn't seem important."

"Until the police tried to check out your story at the Deer Lake theaters," Ellen said sharply. "You've got a 3.85 GPA at Harris, don't you, Todd?"

"Yes."

"Then I should think it's safe to assume you know the meaning and the ramifications of perjury—"

Costello threw up his arms. "Your Honor, this is badgering."

"Change your tone, Ms. North."

"Yes, Your Honor," she said automatically, never looking away from Childs. "Todd, where have you been staying the last few days?"

"Objection."

"Sustained."

"Were you aware the Deer Lake police were looking—"

"Objection. Relevance," Costello argued, getting to his feet.

"It's relevant to the credibility of the witness, Your Honor. If Mr. Childs has been hiding out, avoiding—"

Grabko cracked his gavel, his cheeks tinting pink above his beard. "Ms. North, do not persist in this."

She spread her hands. "I'm sorry, Your Honor, but the witness has given conflicting statements to the police and to this court. He is extremely biased toward the defendant and—"

"You've made your point, Ms. North," Grabko said.

She nodded her understanding and stepped back from the witness stand. "No further questions."

Childs climbed down from the box and was met on the other side of the gallery gate by Mitch Holt and a uniformed officer.

"What the fuck—?" he snapped, jerking his arm back from the officer's grasp.

Costello shot to his feet. "Your Honor, this is an outrage!"

The crowd broke their silence as the scuffle in the aisle continued and reporters jumped up on their chairs for a better view. The bailiff hurried through the gate as Mitch and Officer Stevens took hold of Childs, and herded the lot of them toward the door, with Grabko destroying another gavel behind them.

The judge ordered the attorneys to the bench once again. Ellen took her place beside Costello, feeling the anger roll off him in waves as he accused her of turning the hearing into a circus sideshow.

"Really, Mr. Costello," she said calmly, "don't you think you're being a little paranoid? The police have been looking for Todd Childs for days to question him on that break-in. Since they've had no luck and received no cooperation in finding him, I'm sure they felt they had to grab him when they could."

"In front of the court?" he bellowed, his temper boiling up.

"I don't appreciate the theatrics either, Ms. North," Grabko said sternly. "I'll be speaking with Chief Holt about this."

"He should be taken off the case entirely," Costello fumed. "The conflict of interest is obvious."

"The issue is not germane to this hearing, Mr. Costello," Ellen said.

"For the last time, Ms. North," Grabko said through his teeth, "refrain from doing my job for me. Now, go back to your places and we will resume this hearing in a civilized manner. Call your next witness, Mr. Costello."

As they returned to their tables, the door at the back of the courtroom opened, and a neatly turned-out middle-aged man with slicked-back dark hair strode purposefully down the center aisle with a small manila envelope in one gloved hand. He leaned over the rail and handed the envelope to Dorman. Gravely murmured words were exchanged. Something bright and feral flashed in Costello's eyes as he turned back toward the court.

"The defense calls Karen Wright."

Karen Wright settled herself in the witness chair. Ellen wondered if the thin veil of calm about her was drug induced. Her dark eyes were wide, unblinking. She fixed her gaze on Costello and waited for him to begin. He took his place at the corner of the stand, not wanting to obstruct anyone's view of her—pretty in pink, her ashblond pageboy sleek and silky, her mouth slightly trembling.

"Karen, I want to thank you for testifying here today," he began gently. "I know this is difficult for you. This entire ordeal has been very hard on you, hasn't it?"

"You can't know." She lifted a lace-edged handkerchief to catch a tear that had yet to fall. "It's been terrible.

All of it. I never would have thought—" She cut herself off and closed her eyes for a moment. "It's terrible. I hate it."

"Karen, how long have you and Dr. Wright been married?"

A nostalgic little smile tugged at one corner of her mouth. "It seems like forever. Sixteen years."

"And in all that time, has Garrett ever been in trouble with the law?"

"No." She shook her head, twisting her hankie in her lap. "Garrett has never even had a traffic ticket. He's a very careful man. He shouldn't have been arrested. None of this should ever have happened."

"Has he ever spoken ill of the Kirkwoods?"

"No. Never."

"And you?"

"I considered them friends," she said, dropping her gaze and her volume.

"In fact, you helped them out while Josh was missing, didn't you, Karen?"

"I sat with Lily." A pair of tears skittered down her cheeks. "Such a little sweetheart. I love babies," she admitted. "Garrett and I can't have children," she added, dropping her gaze to her lap again, as if the fact carried shame with it.

"Karen, where were you the evening of the twelfth?" Costello asked abruptly, steering her away from potentially dangerous waters.

"At work. I do secretarial work part-time for Halvorsen's State Farm Insurance in the Omni Complex."

"Do you often work in the evening?"

"I—no." She closed her eyes again and drew in a hitching, shallow breath.

"Karen, *were* you working that night?"

A strange keening sound came up the back of her throat, and she began to rock herself forward and back.

Even with her arms wrapped around herself, she was clearly shaking. The tears spilled over her lashes.

"It's not fair," she whimpered. "It's not fair. . . ."

"Karen," Costello murmured. "Please answer the question. It's very important. You were at the Omni Complex that night. Were you working?"

She looked at him, her pretty face twisting with torment. Her eyes scanned the crowd, resting on someone in the gallery, then moving to her husband, who stared back at her blankly.

"I'm so sorry," she whispered, dropping her gaze to her lap. "I'm so, so sorry. Please don't . . ."

"Karen," Costello prompted. "You have to answer the question."

She dropped her bomb with a voice so soft everyone in the courtroom was straining to hear.

"I stayed late because . . . I was having an affair with Paul Kirkwood."

The admission hit Ellen like a sonic blast. Behind the bar the courtroom erupted, Paul Kirkwood's voice rising above the others.

"That's a lie! Goddamn you, Wright! You put her up to this! You'll pay, you son of a bitch!"

All Ellen could think was that someone had already paid—Josh.

"It is within counsel's rights to attempt to prove someone other than the defendant committed the crime," Dorman recited. He stood at Costello's shoulder like an overeager valet.

Costello had settled himself into one of Grabko's visitor's chairs, legs crossed, suit coat arranged to minimize wrinkles, manila envelope in one hand. Ellen could feel his eyes on her, calm, sharp.

"It's a goddamn smear campaign and it's unconscionable!" she snapped, beyond circumspection, beyond anger. She may have drawn blood from some of his witnesses, but he had nicked a major artery and was waiting to see if Grabko would allow it to bleed out. She was too furious to sit, but she kept herself planted in the chair with Cameron standing guard behind her.

The judge glared at her in affront. "Ms. North, I won't have that kind of language in my chambers, particularly from a lady. This is a place of civil discussion."

"There's nothing civil about what Mr. Costello is attempting to do here, Your Honor. I don't care if he couches it with excerpts from Elizabeth Barrett Browning. It stinks to high heaven!"

Grabko had ordered them into his chambers before all hell could break loose in the courtroom. The dissonant clamor of the gallery as they adjourned from the room had been deafening. Ellen could only imagine what was going on out there now. A feeding frenzy. Paul Kirkwood pinned up against the gallery railing as the rabid mob tore chunks out of him. She wouldn't have minded tearing some chunks out of him herself if what Karen Wright claimed was true, but his infidelity was an issue of its own.

"Paul Kirkwood's sexual exploits are well outside the scope of this hearing," she said, turning toward Costello. "Although, if it's true, it gives your client motive beyond mere evil."

"On the contrary," he said coolly. "It gives Paul Kirkwood motive."

"Which is what?"

"We think the boy might have discovered his father's dirty little secret and Paul saw abducting the child as a way of killing two birds with one stone—shut the boy up and get his rival for Karen's affections out of the way."

"Why stop there?" Ellen said sarcastically. "Don't you think he might have been on the grassy knoll the day Kennedy was shot?"

"Ellen, facetiousness is not called for here," Grabko chastened.

"Not unless it's in the guise of a defense," she muttered, then winced as Cameron surreptitiously pinched her arm.

"Mrs. Wright is prepared to testify she had a tryst with Paul Kirkwood in a vacant office in the Omni Complex the night Josh disappeared," Costello said. "That Paul was to meet her at six forty-five that evening and did not show up until seven. He wouldn't account for the time he had been gone, and he seemed extremely agitated."

"So says the wife of your client," Ellen said. "It's absurd that she's even on the stand."

Costello ignored her. "Her testimony sets the stage, Your Honor. Paul Kirkwood has been under suspicion from the first. He's without an alibi for the time of the abduction, had a connection to the van owned by Olie Swain—who may well have been his accomplice. He repeatedly lied about the van. In her statement to the police the Ryan's Bay witness said the man who came to her house was looking for his son's dog and called it by name. Who's to say it wasn't Kirkwood himself?"

"Anyone with half a brain," Ellen grumbled. "If you'll recall, that witness identified your client in the lineup."

"She identified a man in a parka and sunglasses."

"She singled him out by his voice."

"Paul Kirkwood wasn't in the lineup. She did the best she could. For all we know, Kirkwood disguised his voice. He was trying to pin this thing on Dr. Wright—"

"Then why didn't he introduce himself as Garrett Wright?" Cameron asked. "Why implicate himself in any way? It makes no sense."

"And I say there's room for doubt," Costello declared with an elegant shrug. "The police went so far as to fingerprint him."

"For elimination purposes!" Ellen argued.

He gave her a look. "You know perfectly well the difference between what the police say and what they mean, Ellen."

Ellen sniffed. "Two days ago you thought they were too stupid to tie their own shoes; now you think their every action is fueled by an ulterior motive."

"And there's still the matter of the actual arrest," Cameron began.

"Easily explained if Kirkwood set out to frame Dr. Wright," Costello said. "The hairs on the sheet, the hairs in the stocking cap—evidence easily planted. In fact, the criminalist stated there were unidentified hairs on both items. I suggest Mr. Kirkwood be asked to surrender hair samples." He turned to Ellen with exaggerated seriousness. "For elimination purposes, of course."

She curled her fingers around the arms of her chair and resisted the urge to take samples of Costello's hair with her bare hands. He undoubtedly would have been delighted to have her try. His goal from the first had been to make her look bad in front of Grabko, to get any edge he could any way he could. And she had let herself be drawn into his traps again and again. That truth made her want to tear her own hair out. She was supposed to have got over him, not just away from him and his kind. She was supposed to have changed her life and herself, not simply let the old Ellen go dormant to be reawakened.

"Your Honor," she said with forced calm, "Paul Kirkwood is not on trial here. He was investigated and eliminated as a possible suspect. There appears to be a direct connection between the abduction of Josh Kirkwood and the abduction and murder of Dustin Holloman. In fact, the Holloman case has been used to taunt the authorities in such a way as to make Wright look innocent. If Paul Kirkwood is the villain here, and trying to make Garrett Wright take the fall, it doesn't follow.

"We have to proceed with this case, make our judgments about this case, on the basis of the evidence we have. The evidence we have points clearly to Dr. Wright and an accomplice who has yet to be apprehended."

Grabko pursed his lips and dug a fingertip into his beard as if in pursuit of a tick. "The Holloman case is outside the scope of this hearing," he said. "Paul Kirkwood is directly related to the case before us. Although I don't necessarily care for your method in bringing Mr. Kirkwood's possible involvement to light, Mr. Costello, this is a hearing and not a trial, and I am inclined to allow more leeway. After all, it is the truth we're after."

"Absolutely, Your Honor," Costello said gravely.

"We sometimes lose sight of that ultimate goal in our adversarial system," Grabko pontificated, warming to his topic. "Ambition crowds out purer motives. The rules of court are bent and corrupted. The truth is lost in a scramble to win."

He paused, pleased with the ideals he had just brought out like shining jewels to show off to his small audience. It never occurred to him to look beyond his own brilliance to see which of the factions before him was guilty of the sins he had named.

"We'll hear what Mrs. Wright has to say," he said, snapping out of the afterglow.

Costello waited until everyone else was halfway out of their chairs to speak. "Before we adjourn, Your Honor," he said, lifting the envelope. "My associate, Mr. York, has brought in a piece of evidence I believe will add validity to our defense." As smooth as a magician performing sleight of hand, he opened the envelope and produced a microcassette tape. "This is a tape from Paul Kirkwood's office answering machine with messages from the night his son was abducted."

"And how did you happen to come by that?" Ellen asked sharply.

Costello's expression was carefully blank. "Apparently, someone dropped it through the mail slot at my office suite—anonymously."

"I'll bet."

"You've heard this tape, Mr. Costello?" Grabko asked.

"No, sir. My assistant, Ms. Levine, listened to it and deemed it important enough to send it straight over. I suggest we all listen," he said, placing the cassette on Grabko's desk.

Ellen felt as if she'd been broadsided with a mallet. The hell he hadn't heard it. He would never have wasted a dramatic moment on a pig in a poke. Tony Costello knew exactly what was on that tape, and he was betting it would score him big points.

She shot to the front edge of her chair, bracing one hand against the desk, her fingertips inches from the tape. "I have to object, Your Honor. There was nothing in counsel's disclosure about this tape. We have no idea where it came from or how it was obtained or who *allegedly* left it or what their motives might be."

"Mr. York has already managed to check with two of the parties who have messages on the tape, Your Honor," Costello said. "They confirm having made the calls on the night of the twelfth."

"Let's have a listen," Grabko said, reaching for the cassette. "We can all hear the tape now, and, if there is any question as to its validity or admissibility, we'll deal with those issues later."

Ever efficient, Mr. Dorman produced a microcassette recorder from the pocket of his Brooks Brothers suit, popped his own cassette out of it, and handed the machine to Grabko.

The first thing they heard was background noise, the sound of an engine; then came the voice, and it pierced Ellen's heart like a needle.

"Dad, can you come and get me from hockey? Mom's late and I wanna go home."

CHAPTER 33

"Dad, can you come and get me from hockey? Mom's late and I wanna go home."

His son's voice played through Paul's head over and over, as it had been doing for the last three weeks. An endless loop of innocence and accusation that raked through his brain like talons.

And layered over it, Mitch Holt's voice, low and tight.

"What the hell were you thinking, Paul? Jesus Christ, Josh called you for help! You didn't so much as answer him. You pretend you never heard him. You hold on to the goddamn tape for three weeks and never say one fucking word! How do you explain that, Paul?"

And layered over that, Ellen North's icy tone.

"The defense is building a case against you, Mr. Kirkwood. I'm not so sure that shouldn't be my job. You lied to the police. You withheld information—"

"*You blamed Hannah,*" Holt said. *"All this time you dumped the guilt on her head. You son of a bitch. You never even had the guts to stand up and tell the truth.*"

The truth will set you free.

The truth would ruin him.

He couldn't believe this was happening to him. After all he had been through. After all he had suffered. Now this. Betrayal by the one person he thought had loved him. Karen.

It was incomprehensible to him to think that she could turn on him so completely. She loved him. She wanted to have his children. Her marriage to Wright was a sham—she had said so more than once. Garrett Wright couldn't give her what she needed, what she wanted. Garrett Wright loved his work, not his wife.

Paul shuddered at the memory of that moment in the courtroom. Every eye had turned on him, avid, accusatory. The press he had courted and played to from day one had turned on him. Damn them all. They had wanted Hannah for their heroine from the first. The grieving, guilt-ridden mother. Hannah, with her golden tresses and tragic blue eyes. Hannah, the dedicated doctor, the woman of the year. Hannah, Hannah, Hannah.

They would turn to her now with gushing sympathy, and he would be the sacrificial goat. They would never ask what had driven him from his home. They would never want to hear that Hannah wasn't any kind of wife, that she ignored her children in favor of her precious career, that she had done her best to emasculate him.

He had thought of trying to get to her before they could, but they had been all over him, swarming around him, their questions stinging his ears and stabbing his conscience. They had followed him to his car and followed his car as he tried to escape. He had finally turned out on the interstate and opened up the Celica's engine, leaving them behind as the speedometer swept toward ninety.

It was dark now. The press would have been to the house and gone long ago. Hannah had given them nothing in the past—a single interview, a photo op as the priest helped her into the volunteer center downtown. Paul had to think she would shun them again, even if it meant giving up a chance to publicly humiliate him. And the reporters would call her noble and long-suffering and paint her as the good woman betrayed. The idea turned his stomach.

The anger and anxiety churned inside him like acid, like a virus that raced through his system and pulsed just beneath his skin. It spread over his brain like a fungus and left him feeling feverish and bruised.

He drove down Lakeshore, driving through the neighborhood *he* had chosen for its prestige, toward the home *he* had wanted, with its lakefront view and park out the back door. This was the life he had coveted since his youth. Now it would end up being Hannah's. She would get the sympathy *and* the house. The irony was as bitter as bile.

Passing Wright's home, he fought the urge to drive his car in through their front door. He would have liked to have seen the look on Karen's face when he confronted her.

"I love you, Paul. . . . I'd have your baby, Paul. . . . I'd do anything for you."

Except lie for him in court.

She could have given him an alibi. Instead she brought the whole world down on his head. Some love.

Women. Bitches, every last one of them. The bane of his existence. His mother, Hannah, O'Malley, Ellen North . . . Karen.

"I stayed late because I was having an affair with Paul Kirkwood."

Was. Past tense.

"I love you, Paul. . . . I'd have your baby, Paul. . . . I'd do anything for you. . . . I'm so sorry. . . . It was a mistake. . . ."

A mistake.

God knew he'd made plenty of them, not the least of which had been keeping that damned tape.

"We know the call came before six-fifteen, Paul. Were you there? Did you hear it? Where did you go when you left the office? Why can't we find anyone to corroborate that story? Why didn't you tell us about the call, Paul? How could you let Hannah take the blame?"

Because it was her fault. All of it. If she had done her

duty . . . if she had been there for her son . . . if she had been a decent wife . . .

Guilt was the last emotion Hannah wanted to feel. She had been drowning in it for weeks now. A mother's guilt compounded by a doctor's sense of failure because the patient she had stayed at the hospital for that night had been lost as well. But what came tonight was different, more futile, less deserved.

Could she have been a better wife, a better lover, more supportive, less critical? What had she done to make Paul hate her so? Why had he turned to Karen Wright?

The questions infuriated her. There were more important ones to ask. Had Paul been in his office when Josh had called him that night? Why had he lied and lied and lied—about the van, about so many things? Why was Josh so terrified of him? Why did he seem like such a stranger? Was he involved in all the horror that had taken place over the last three weeks? Perhaps it was because the possible answers to these questions frightened her so badly that she let the others creep into her mind and divert her attention. They made her angry with herself for thinking them, but they didn't make her husband out to be a monster.

"Do you think your husband abducted Josh?"

"Do you think he killed the Holloman boy?"

"He had access to a van—"

"Did you know about the affair?"

"Damn you, Paul," she whispered. Pulling her hands up out of the soapy water, she gathered up the dish towel and pressed her face into it.

She didn't know how much more she could stand. Dawn had brought the news of Dustin Holloman's murder, and with it fear and a terrible relief that it was someone else's child who had died and not hers. Josh seemed more withdrawn than ever, but he was still with her, phys-

ically. And as long as she had him with her, there was
hope. And then had come the news from the courthouse.
Not from Mitch or from Ellen North, but from the reporters who had come to the house demanding answers as
if she owed them something for all the hell they had put
her through.

"*Can we get a reaction from you about your husband's illicit
affair with the wife of the man on trial for abducting your son?*"

If she had been shaky before, that had put her over the
edge. And once again she had turned to Tom McCoy.

God, Hannah, you're not even calling him Father anymore.
She remembered the pretense of title when they were
speaking, because she didn't want to upset him or jeopardize their friendship. But in her heart she had grown beyond thinking of him as her priest. The need she felt for
his company, for his support, for his comfort, was stronger than that.

*And people think Paul is rotten for cheating on me. What
would they think if they knew I'd fallen in love with a priest?*

Of course, no one would ever know, most of all Tom
himself. He was too good a friend to lose. When the news
came from the courthouse, she had called him. He had
come and chased the press away, and forced her to eat
chicken soup, and read stories to the kids. He sat with her
on the sleeping bag in Josh's room, watching Josh drift off
to sleep, then shooed her out of the room because he
knew she needed the break but would never take it.

A deep ache of yearning rolled through her, and she
closed her eyes against it. Hadn't she endured enough
without having to fall in love with a man she could never
have?

The sound of the door opening from the garage into
the laundry room tore her out of her self-pity. A wild,
primal instinct swung her hand to the knife block on the
counter. Dustin Holloman's killer was still at large. Who

was to say he wouldn't come back for Josh? If Josh could identify him . . .

The kitchen door swung open and Paul cast a look at the knife in her hand.

"I suppose I can guess what you'd like to do with that," he said.

The panic bottomed out, leaving a thick, sour anger in its wake. Hannah set the knife aside. "It wouldn't be worth the trouble."

He gave a bitter laugh. "And the press wondered why I would cheat on you."

Somehow the admission of guilt cut more coming from Paul's own mouth. The same mouth that had pledged love and fidelity. She had kissed that mouth in play and in passion, had loved its smile, worried at its frown. It had told her lies and tasted another woman.

She wanted to launch herself at him, to punish him. But when she opened her mouth to speak, the fight went out of her.

"I loved you," she said quietly, knowing immediately that wasn't true. She had loved someone else, not this bitter, angry man. "What happened, Paul? What happened to you?"

"Me?" he said, incredulous. "Maybe if you'd paid attention to something other than your career the last few years, you wouldn't have to ask."

Hannah shook her head. "No, Paul, this isn't about my work. For once, it really is about you. You turned away from me. You turned to another woman. You made that choice. We had something wonderful and you threw it away."

"Yeah, fine, blame me," he said impatiently, starting past her.

"I will blame you," she said sharply. "I just wish I knew how much to blame you for."

He wheeled around, brows lowered. "What the hell is that supposed to mean?"

"It means Josh called you that night and you *did nothing*."

"I wasn't in—"

"But no one can say where you were. Were you with *her*?" She swung an accusatory finger in the direction of the Wrights' house. "When I was frantic, trying to find Josh, trying to call you, were you down the hall screwing Karen Wright? Where were you when Josh needed you?"

"It was your night to—"

"No! Don't you dare blame me. I was trying to save a life. You were fucking yours away—or worse. And you had the gall to dump all that guilt on me, as if you hadn't done anything wrong, as if you hadn't lied to me and to the police and done God knows what else!"

The implication struck Paul hard. "*The defense is building a case against you, Mr. Kirkwood. . . .*"

"I would never hurt Josh," he insisted.

The doubt in her eyes was stark. "Then why won't he let you near him?"

"You can't think I took him," he said, stepping toward her, wanting to shake her. "You can't think that!"

"Why can't I? You've lied about everything else!"

"*The defense is building a case against you, Mr. Kirkwood. . . .*"

The press was on him. The prosecution was eyeing him. Now this. St. Hannah casting judgment. And no one would blame her. She was golden; he was nothing, nobody. In that moment he hated her enough to want her dead.

His control snapped. There was no thought, only action, only fury. "You bitch!"

Hannah saw the blow coming. The back of his hand caught her hard on the jaw, snapping her head to the side. The world blurred and tilted, and she staggered sideways, knocked off balance by the slap and by the idea of it. Never in her life had she been struck by anyone for any reason. As often as she had seen the aftermath of domestic violence in the ER, she had never in her darkest dreams imagined she would become a victim.

Paul advanced toward her, his eyes dark with rage, his mouth twisting.

"Paul, no!" Tom McCoy shouted, lunging up the steps to the kitchen.

Paul wheeled on him, arm drawn back. Tom blocked the punch and caught Paul square in the mouth with a right cross that dropped him to his knees. The action was automatic, instinctive. It stunned him to the core of his soul. He stared down at Paul, who sat back on his heels, his hands covering his mouth, blood leaking between his fingers.

"Why did you come here, Paul?" he asked. "Haven't you done enough damage already?"

Paul glared up at him, wiping his mouth on his coat sleeve as he rose to his feet. "I came to get my stuff."

Tom shook his head. "There's nothing here for you. Get out."

"You can't throw me out of my own home."

"This isn't your home," Hannah said. The ache inside her rivaled the pain in her throbbing jaw. "You just gave up your rights here. Get out before I call the police."

He looked from her to Father Tom, eyeing the priest's sweater and jeans and stocking feet.

"Oh, I get it," he said snidely.

"Don't say it, Paul," Tom warned. "At the moment I can't see that there'd be any sin in my beating the snot out of you."

Silence descended. Paul picked the dish towel off the counter and blotted at his mouth.

"I'll have your things delivered to the office," Hannah said.

She leaned against the refrigerator as he left, refusing to look at him. But in the corner of her eye she could see their Christmas photo, still held to the refrigerator door by magnets shaped like candy canes. The back door closed.

"Are you all right?" Tom asked, stepping closer, reaching out to her.

"No," she whispered.

He took her in his arms as if it were the most natural thing in the world, cradled her head against his broad shoulder and stroked her hair with his hand. The love that welled inside him was the purest, the strongest he'd ever known in his life. He loved her in a way that meant he would do anything for her, be anything for her. He couldn't see how that could be wrong.

"I don't understand," she murmured, her arms tight around him. "We had a nice life. Why did it have to go so wrong?"

He couldn't share the answer that came to him— *So you could love me*. He didn't know if it was God's will or just his own.

He knew what the monsignor would tell him—that this was a test of his faith and his duty to the Church. The idea that God would use people that way, like pawns in a game, only made him want to rebel.

"I'm sorry, Hannah," he murmured. "I'd give anything to change it for you."

"I just want to walk away from it. Take the children and go someplace new and clean and start over."

"I know."

"Would you go with me? I could use a friend when I get there," Hannah said, pretending it was a joke.

But when she looked up at him, what she saw in his earnest blue eyes wasn't humor but truth. A truth that didn't need words. A truth that spoke to her battered heart. A truth he sealed with a kiss. A kiss so tender, so sweet. Full of the kind of promise she wanted to grab with both hands and use as a shield against an uncertain future.

Instead she put her head back on his shoulder, and they stood there for a long while, each wondering where they would go from here.

"So where do we go from here?" Cameron asked.

They had assembled in The War Room at the law-enforcement center, where the time line of all that had taken place in the last three weeks stretched the length of one wall.

"We've got to take a closer look at Kirkwood," Wilhelm said. "See if we can put him in the wrong place at the wrong time. Confiscate his phone records. Check—"

"What about the suspect we've got?" Mitch asked irritably. "Garrett Wright is the man."

"But the tape—"

"Doesn't prove shit."

"How can you say that? The boy called—"

"And Paul was otherwise engaged."

"But his mistress can't account for the time—"

"And why would he keep that tape?" Cameron asked.

"Guilt," Mitch said simply.

"Yeah," Steiger interjected around the toothpick he was chewing. "The kind that comes with a sentence to the state hotel."

"Don't be stupid," Mitch snapped. "If Paul *was* guilty of taking Josh, getting rid of that tape would have been his first priority. If he had taken the boy, he would never have gone up to Ruth Cooper's house and said he was looking for his own damned dog."

"Unless he's nuts."

Wilhelm was like a puppy with a new chew toy. "And there's the connection to the van. And the kid's reaction. And—"

"And I've got a man standing before the court tomorrow," Ellen said sharply. "We've built a case against Garrett Wright. Mitch apprehended Garrett Wright. Agent O'Malley identified Garrett Wright. Our erstwhile witness identified Garrett Wright. What the hell are you doing to help me get Garrett Wright to trial?"

Wilhelm pouted, looked down at his coffee. "Wright couldn't have taken the Holloman kid."

"We're not dealing with Holloman," Ellen reminded him. "I'm sure you'd like to wrap all the crimes up in one neat package with one perp and move on, but that's not the way it works. We've focused on this game being played by Wright and an accomplice. Did you ever stop to think, Agent Wilhelm, that they *want* you to run off half-cocked after Paul Kirkwood?"

"We have to follow *all* leads, Ms. North," he said. "I've asked Mr. Stovich to get search warrants for Paul Kirkwood's home and office, and for a locker he rents at the U-Store-It on the south side of town. We'll execute the warrants tonight if we get them in time. In light of what's on that tape, I'd say we've looked the other way long enough where Paul Kirkwood is concerned."

Ellen couldn't argue. As much as she hated having the investigation pulled in another direction, it seemed they had no real options. Costello had leaked word of the cassette tape to the press. The police had to act on it.

She looked to Cameron. "Will you go with them?"

"Sure."

Turning to Mitch, she asked, "Did you get anywhere with Todd Childs?"

He scowled. "Yeah, I got threatened with a lawsuit for false arrest."

Ellen pretended surprise. "Did Mr. Childs get the impression he was under arrest?"

"A simple misunderstanding," he said, straight-faced. "He calmed down after we gave him a cup of decaf."

"And got his prints off the cup?"

"They're being run in St. Paul even as we speak. If we can put him at Enberg's office, that would give us a nice big lever to crack this thing open."

"How soon will you know?"

"Couple of days."

"The hearing will be over tomorrow morning," Cameron said. "Grabko could rule as soon as tomorrow afternoon."

"We need a break, gentlemen," Ellen said. "And we need it tonight."

Steiger pushed himself to his feet. He had shed the adhesive tape from his nose, but the bruising remained, streaking across his hard cheekbones like war paint. "Grabko dismisses, you can always charge him again later. It's not like double jeopardy."

Ellen stared at the sheriff. "And if he hasn't packed up his little Saab and driven off into the sunset, we might actually get him to trial. I don't want to take that chance. I want him bound over. Tomorrow."

"I've got men double-checking all hot-line tips that came into Campion," Steiger said, moving toward the door, declaring the meeting over for himself. "Don't get your hopes up."

Seeing his chance to escape, Wilhelm hustled after him. "A—yeah—Sheriff, I wanted to talk to you about those hot-line tips."

Ellen watched their defection with a mix of anger and despair. If Wright's plan had been to divide and conquer, he was scoring points tonight. The revelation of Paul Kirkwood's answering-machine tape was acting like a wedge, splitting her team even more decisively than the kidnapping of Dustin Holloman had.

"Cameron, go offer them some suggestions," she said with a meaningful look.

He grabbed his coat and hustled out.

Silence hung in the air for a moment before Ellen turned to Mitch. "Well, do you want to jump on the bandwagon of people who think I should have asked the judge for a postponement right off the bat?"

"The Twenty-Twenty Hindsight Club?" He made a face. "Why would I join them? The membership requirements are too low. Who's on your case?"

"Well, let's see," she mused, tapping her chin with a forefinger. "Not counting you? Everybody. Stovich, the state attorney general, the press, half the population of Deer Lake."

"Pointless bullshit."

"That's easy for you to say."

"Are you forgetting the Olie Swain debacle?"

"Sorry. No."

She blew out a sigh and rose with all the energy of a ninety-year-old arthritic. She stared at the time line, wishing something would jump out at her. Some heretofore overlooked minutia that would spark The Big Revelation and point to Todd Childs or Christopher Priest. Nothing. If anything, the words and lines and arrows became less coherent, a hopeless jumble of scribbling. The only name that leaped out at her was Paul Kirkwood.

Paul had owned Olie Swain's van. Olie Swain, the convicted child molester. The van had yielded them nothing. Paul had excuses instead of alibis. They had no hard evidence against him. Paul had searched tirelessly for his son in brutal subzero temperatures. His son, who wouldn't let him get within an arm's length.

"What do you really think about Paul?" she asked quietly.

Mitch's face was blank as he walked along the time line, his eyes resting on every notation that mentioned Paul. "I've said it before—I think people would like for Paul to be the bad guy in all this. He's not well-known, he's not well liked. They'd rather think someone like him lost his marbles than believe a man like Garrett Wright is an evil genius."

"I could see people thinking that when it was Josh missing," Ellen said. "They wanted to contain the malignancy to one family. But how does he tie in to Holloman? It doesn't make sense."

"Depends on how you want to spin it, counselor. Who's framing who?"

"You're not beginning to have doubts, too, are you?"

He ran a hand back through his hair, leaving it standing up in tufts. The exhaustion dragged on his face, pulling at the lines time and trouble had dug in. "In my gut I don't think Paul did it, but as Megan has pointed out to me more than once, I might be bringing too much of my own personal experience into it. Regardless, Wilhelm was right—we'll have to dig deeper into the possibility. I don't look forward to executing those search warrants, but it's got to be done."

More time spent chasing wild geese, Ellen thought, while Garrett Wright sat back and smiled, and his accomplice slipped in and out of the shadows unseen, unsuspected.

"We need a loose thread we can pull on," she said. "How's Megan coming with Wright's background?"

"Nothing yet. It's slow going. If Wright's never been caught to this point, he probably hasn't left behind many bread crumbs."

"We can't let him get away with this, Mitch." She stopped at the time line entry for January 22. *Agent O'Malley assaulted and kidnapped. Suspect apprehended after foot chase: Garrett Wright.* It was all a game to him. "That's what this is all about for him—beating the system, slipping out of the noose. He even spotted us evidence to make it interesting."

The idea that he might win terrified her.

"On a related topic," Mitch said, "I've a got a witness

who may have seen your mad bomber early Sunday morning."

Ellen brightened. "A witness? Who?"

"Wes Vogler. He's a trucker who lives over in that neighborhood. He was leaving for a run early Sunday morning, saw a black kid cut across the Pla-Mor parking lot. Didn't think much of it because a couple of black families have moved into the neighborhood recently. When he got back home today, heard about the explosion and the timing of it, he got suspicious, decided he should come in."

"You think he saw Tyrell?"

"Maybe. Or he saw an opportunity to get some kid into trouble," he said. "Wes's neck is a little on the red side. He's none too excited about Deer Lake becoming 'ethnically diverse.'"

"Put together a photo lineup. If Vogler picks him out, we'll get Tyrell in for a live performance."

"If we can find him. He seems to have made himself scarce. The Minneapolis cops are watching for him."

Ellen frowned as she gathered up her things. "I don't know if I should be relieved or in fear for my life."

"The kid's a loose cannon, but he's not stupid," Mitch said. "After today he's got to know things are leaning Wright's way. What good would it do him to hurt you?"

"None," Ellen admitted. "But he might think it'd be fun, anyway."

Megan O'Malley's apartment was the only one on the third floor. Jay knocked and waited. On the other side of the door something fell to the floor with a thud. The curse that accompanied it was short and raw.

"Who is it?"

"Jay Butler Brooks, ma'am."

The door swung back as far as the safety chain would allow, and O'Malley glared out at him.

"I'll cut straight to the bottom line here, Brooks," she said shortly. "No comment. No comment. No fucking comment."

"I'm not a reporter."

"I know what you are. What do you want?"

"To make you a proposition."

Her green eyes narrowed with suspicion.

"I know you're looking into Garrett Wright's background. I'd like to help."

"I don't know what you're talking about," she said flatly. "I'm on medical leave."

"Ellen North told me," he confessed. "She also told me you'd rip my heart out of my chest with your bare hands if I betrayed the secret."

She stared at him for a minute, debating. "It'd be hard right now," she said, deadpan. "I'd probably have to use a garden claw."

She fumbled with the chain, then swung the door open, inviting him into the apartment. Packing boxes were stacked all around the main living area that comprised both living and dining room. Soft-pink walls and white woodwork. Antique furnishings and mismatched flea-market finds. The old round oak table was piled and strewn with papers and photocopies of police reports. A black cat with a white bib and paws positioned himself in the center of it all.

"You'll have to forgive the mess," Megan said, hobbling to her chair and easing herself down. Her right hand, in its pristine cast, was cradled gingerly against her midsection. "Getting the shit beat out of me put me behind in my decorating schedule."

"Some things take precedence," Jay remarked, sliding into the chair across from her. The cat lowered its eyelids and ears to half-mast and stared at him.

"I hear you're doing a book." O'Malley's expression was closed, giving away nothing, the eyes sharp with the same watchful caution he'd seen in many a cop over the years. "You should know I have a deeply ingrained aversion to opportunists."

"That's not why I'm here."

She laughed. Fine lines etched by pain dug in at the corners of her mouth. "You want in on the investigation, but it's got nothing to do with the book you'll make a few mil off? Let me save us both some time here, Mr. Brooks. I know how the world works."

"I have no doubt of that, Agent O'Malley. A woman doesn't get where you are in law enforcement on fresh-faced innocence."

"No, most of us make it this far on sex."

"Bullshit, ma'am," he said with a polite smile. "I know your service record. You're damn good at your job."

"Yes, I am. What's that got to do with you—if you're not angling for a story?"

"You want to nail Garrett Wright."

"Upside down to a cross. So?"

"So I can help you. I've got a house full of office machines. Fax, computer with a modem, multiline phone. You're having to waste a lot of time, running things through Holt's office to maintain your cover. I eliminate the middle man. I'm your cover. I'm your legs. I'm your hands. I make a damn good living off my ability to do thorough research. I don't see how this is any different."

"It's different in that you're a civilian and this is a live case," she said. "It's different in that your being in on it could bust the whole thing."

"*Your* being in on it could bust the whole thing," he pointed out. "Costello is already making noises about conflict of interest regarding Mitch Holt. Imagine if he found out the woman hell-bent on sending his client to prison for the rest of his life was in any way still Involved with the investigation. He'd take what's left of your career, cut it up into little bite-sized pieces, and wash it down with champagne."

"Is that a threat, Mr. Brooks?"

"No," he said, never taking his eyes from hers. "I'm merely pointing out that my involvement wouldn't be any more potentially dangerous than yours. Less so. After all, the machines are mine, I have no personal ties to the case. There's no law against my looking into someone's background, provided we're dealing with public record."

She thought on that for a moment, watching him, reading him. "Does Ellen know you're here?"

"No. She's got problems enough tonight," he said, wishing he could solve all those problems for her.

"You never answered my question," Megan said. "If this isn't about your book, then what?"

He rose then, discomfort disguised as restless curiosity. He didn't want her looking too close, which could have been an indication of a lie, or of a truth that lived deeper than he wanted her to see. She suspected the latter. Jay Butler Brooks struck her as the kind of man who would look you straight in the face when he lied to you, his pretty blue eyes shining with sincerity. He had been a lawyer once, after all.

"When did you see your first murdered child?" he asked, glancing at her from the corner of his eye as he leaned a hip against a stack of boxes.

"My second week in a uniform," she said. "A three-year-old killed by her alcoholic mother's alcoholic boyfriend."

"I saw mine today."

Dustin Holloman. He fingered the spines of some of her old textbooks, but she knew he wasn't seeing the titles. He was seeing a child's body, the same way she did whenever that three-year-old girl came to mind with sharp, grim detail, even a decade after the fact.

"I came to Deer Lake for my own reasons, Agent O'Malley. Selfish reasons, I readily admit. I thought I could maintain some emotional distance on this case, but I stood by the side of that road this morning and listened to that boy's mama cry. . . . I don't want to be the kind of man who can keep his distance from something like that."

His voice had tightened, his emotion touching Megan.

"I want to help," he said. "I need to." He looked up at her then with no mask, no pretense. "You know what it is to need to prove yourself, even if you're the only one looking."

"Yes," Megan whispered, her gaze straying to the cast on her hand. "Yeah, I do."

"So what do you say? Am I in?"

It wasn't her natural inclination to trust at all, let alone to trust a man like Brooks. But she wanted Wright behind bars; he could help speed the process. They needed a break and they needed it fast. The key had to be buried somewhere in Garrett Wright's past, but with everything else that had been thrown at them in the last week, none of the agencies involved had been able to devote the time needed to the search. She was the only one really looking, and the injuries Wright had inflicted were holding her back, slowing her down. Brooks could be her legs, her hands, another brain working to decipher the puzzle.

Or he could be weaseling his way into a best-seller.

Garrett Wright stood on the brink of walking away from every evil thing he'd done.

"You're in," she said at last. "Don't make me regret it, Mr. Brooks. I don't want to have to dig out that garden claw."

They began executing the search warrants at nine forty-three, beginning, at Mitch's insistence, at the Kirkwood home. He did his best to smooth the process for Hannah, glad that Father Tom was close at hand to offer her support and comfort while the officers looked for any evidence that her husband was the one who had stolen her son and put her through hell.

As much as he loved what he did, there were times when he hated being a cop.

He expected the search of Paul's office to be punctuated by threats of legal action from Paul, but Paul was not in his current home-away-from-home. The blankets were neatly folded on one end of the couch with the pillow placed on top of them. The desk was immaculate. There was no sign that Paul had been there at all. There was no sign that Costello's PI, York, had let himself in and helped himself to evidence at some point during the last twenty-four hours. Not surprisingly, they found nothing.

By the time they reached the U-Store-It at the edge of the industrial park on the south side of town, it was past midnight. The night watchman, a grizzled old geezer named Davis who had bad teeth and beer breath, had to be roused from a deep, snoring sleep on the cot in the office. Grousing about the cold, he led them down the rows of storage units. Each was about the size of a one-car garage with bright-orange overhead doors and numbers stenciled on the cinder block with black spray paint. They stopped at number thirty-seven. Davis knelt down on the concrete apron, grumbling nonstop as he opened the padlock with the key from the office.

The locker was stacked with the usual castoffs of suburban life. Out-of-season lawn furniture and an old canoe. An outdated bedroom set and boxes of old baby clothes Hannah probably hadn't been able to bring herself to part with. The thing that set Paul Kirkwood's locker apart from most Mitch had seen was the fact that it was perfectly ordered. No teetering towers of haphazardly packed junk. Everything labeled and lined up, the neatness speaking to Paul's compulsive tendencies.

Davis declined the invitation to watch and shuffled back toward the office, lighting a cigarette. Cameron Reed stood at the door, the lone witness, hands in his coat pockets and shoulders hunched as the others went about their business. Mitch purposely avoided the more personal memorabilia and went instead to the dresser of the old bedroom set. So it was he who made the very discovery he had been praying they wouldn't find.

Tucked back into a bottom drawer, neatly folded and stored in a black plastic garbage bag, were a pair of boy's jeans and a blue sweater.

The clothes Josh Kirkwood had been wearing the night he'd disappeared.

CHAPTER 34

As birthdays went, number thirty-six was off to a pisser of a start.

The thought was selfish on the surface, but Ellen knew that wasn't it at all. She had hoped for something better today for Josh, for Hannah, for Megan, for justice. She had hoped for an eleventh-hour gift in the form of evidence. And deep in a small, primitively superstitious part of her brain, she had held out the unspoken hope that they might get that gift because it was her birthday. She felt foolish admitting it even to herself.

The gift they received was from a higher power with an exceedingly black sense of humor. Evidence that clearly implicated Paul Kirkwood. At least in the eyes of the person who mattered most—Gorman Grabko.

"In light of the discoveries we've had since we adjourned yesterday, I don't see that I have a choice, Ellen," the judge said, frowning at her gravely from behind his desk.

She refused to look at Costello, knowing too well what she would see in his face. Victory.

"But, Your Honor," she said, "we don't know how those clothes came to be in the Kirkwoods' storage locker—"

"The door was padlocked, Your Honor," Costello said.

"Locks can be picked. Mr. Costello should consult with his associate Mr. York on that subject," Ellen said bitingly. "What we have here—"

"Is a mess, Ms. North," Grabko declared. "The prosecution clearly was not thoroughly prepared to bring these charges before the court."

"But, Your Honor, Chief Holt *apprehended* Garrett Wright. We have evidence—"

"What the prosecution has," Costello said, going for the kill, "are some half-baked notions unsupported by fact and not fully investigated. Ms. North wanted a slam dunk on this case for reasons of her own and has proceeded in a fashion that skirts the bounds of ethics, persecuting an innocent man."

The verbal knife slipped cleanly between her ribs. Ethics. Ambition. Costello had no respect for the first and lived and breathed the second. She was his mirror opposite in those aspects, and yet he neatly turned it all on her without batting an eye.

Her fingers curled on the arms of her chair, holding her down. "That is a completely unfair, inaccurate assessment, Your Honor. My only interest in this case is justice."

"And to that end, I see only one choice," Grabko said, steepling his fingers before him. "I must grant Mr. Costello's motion to dismiss and hope that the county attorney's office and the law-enforcement agencies involved do a better job of untangling this case before it is brought before the court again."

In her mind Ellen heard a gavel fall. Case dismissed. As simple as that, her nemesis had turned the tables on her. As simple as that, like a trick in a parlor game. And now she would have to walk into that courtroom packed with press and citizens and cops, and stand there while Garrett Wright was declared a free man. She would have to call Hannah Garrison before the press could get to her and tell her the man who had stolen her son would return to the house down the block a free man.

The failure was crushing. She could barely rise beneath the weight of it. But she forced her shoulders back and her chin up and started for the door. Cameron and Dorman went out first. Ellen would go next. Costello would come behind her and relish his own entrance like an overbearing stage actor.

Behind her she could hear the door close on Grabko's private bathroom, where the judge invariably retreated moments before taking the bench. Which left her alone with Costello. She turned toward him with her hand on the doorknob and simply looked at him in his tailored suit and smug satisfaction.

"Don't take it so hard, Ellen," he said. "You just didn't have enough to win the game this time."

"You'll never get it, will you, Tony?" she said, shaking her head. "This should never be about winning or losing. It should be about the truth."

The light in his eyes hardened and glittered. "No, *you'll* never get it, Ellen. It's always about winning. Always."

Ellen singled out faces on her way in. Mitch, drawn and grim. Karen Wright, vacuous. Christopher Priest sitting beside her, expressionless. Noticeably absent was Paul, who had yet to be located after the search of his storage locker. Nor was Brooks among the information-hungry throng. His absence struck her harder than she should have let it. It shouldn't have mattered. She knew better than to allow herself the comfort of relying on someone, especially him.

Dismissing those thoughts, she took her place beside Cameron at the table.

It was over in a matter of moments. More moments than were strictly necessary, simply because Grabko liked to pontificate to a captive audience. Through the entire speech Ellen stood at the table, aware of every eye on her back. Her mind raced ahead, laying out the scenario for what would happen next. The press would champion Costello and she would be crucified. Rudy would lay the blame entirely at her feet in an effort to keep himself from being tainted. Garrett Wright would be painted as a martyr, and the people of Deer Lake would call for the head of Paul Kirkwood.

Worst-case scenario.

The hell of it was, as much as she had professed not to want it, she knew she would have taken the case again if she had it to do over.

Grabko pronounced the case dismissed and rapped his gavel dramatically. Behind the bar the gallery exploded into a deafening cacophony of sound. The doors to the hall burst open, and half the reporters poured out into the hall to array themselves for the inevitable impromptu press conference, while the other half pressed up against the railing in a mob, shouting questions.

"Ms. North, will charges be brought against Paul Kirkwood?"

"Dr. Wright, will you be filing suit against the county attorney's office?"

"Ms. North, is there any truth to the rumors of your dismissal from the county attorney's office?"

Costello flashed them all his legal-eagle look and placated them with promises of answers out in the rotunda. Ellen refused to acknowledge them at all, keeping her back to them as she pretended to arrange the files in her briefcase. She could hear Cameron giving them the party line about an official statement coming from the office later in the day.

"Ms. North?"

The voice was too close, too soft for any reporter. Ellen jerked her head up. Garrett Wright stood no more than a foot from her, his expression calm, almost apologetic. He offered her his hand.

"No hard feelings," he said, the consummate gentleman. "You were only doing your job."

And I beat you. We beat you.

She could hear the words as clearly as if he had spoken them aloud. She could see them, deep in his eyes, in a moment just like the one they had shared in the interview room of the city jail. A moment no one else in the room had experienced. She could feel the reporters staring at them. She could hear the whir of motor drives on cameras, but she knew not one photograph would capture what was passing between them.

She ignored the offered handshake and stood a little straighter. "I'm still doing my job, Dr. Wright," she said softly. "You know what they say—it ain't over till it's over."

"What does this mean?" Hannah asked, stunned, shaking. She sank weakly onto the couch, her knees buckling beneath her. She found herself holding the portable phone to her face with both hands because her fingertips had gone numb and she thought she might drop it.

"It means Wright is a free man—for the moment," Ellen North said. "But it isn't over as far as I'm concerned. I'll do everything in my power to get him to trial, Hannah. I promise you that."

Hannah stared across the room to the corner where Josh had sequestered himself for the morning. He faced the wall with his knees drawn up to his chest and his face hidden. Her son was locked in a mental prison, and the man who had put him there was walking free.

"You did that already, didn't you?" she said, the bitterness thinned by abject disappointment.

"I'm sorry, Hannah. What we had against him should

have been enough, but with his accomplice still at large, and with the evidence that came to light yesterday . . ."

Ellen's voice trailed off. She was trying to be diplomatic, Hannah thought. The news was bad enough without emphasizing the fact that Paul was now wanted for questioning, that Josh's clothes had been found in the storage locker Paul rented because he had never been able to abide a cluttered basement.

Mitch had broken that news to her in the dead of night. *I don't know how to tell you this, Hannah. . . . We're not sure what it means. . . . The clothes could have been planted there for us to find. . . . We need to talk to Paul. . . . You don't know where he is?*

I don't know who *he is,* she thought. *I don't know what he's become. I don't know what he might be capable of. I don't know why Josh is afraid of him. I can't believe he struck me.*

"But Mitch caught Garrett Wright," she said, talking more to herself than to Ellen.

"I know. Mitch knows. Costello blew enough smoke to cloud the issue for the judge. We just need a little more time, another piece of solid evidence against Wright or a break regarding his accomplice. It'll come, Hannah. Hang in there. And please let me know the minute Josh has something to say about what happened."

Hannah held the phone in her lap for a long while after the connection had been broken. Her line to justice, she thought, cut off, and she and her children were left holding the frayed end of what should have been a lifeline to pull them past this ordeal.

Of the things she had to hope for, justice had seemed the most realistic, the most attainable. She could hope for Josh's recovery, but there was no guarantee how long that hope would have to last or that it wouldn't be crushed in the end. She had hoped for a mend in the tear of her relationship with Paul, but that would never happen. Their marriage was over. And so she had hoped for justice.

There was a system in place to mete it out. There were people who cared fighting on her side. But the irony in the fight for justice was that not everyone played fair.

Lily scrambled up onto the couch beside her and reached for the phone. Holding it up with both hands, she began an animated conversation of gibberish punctuated by the word "Daddy."

Hannah thought of calling Tom but denied herself the comfort. On top of everything else, she didn't want the guilt that came with thinking she had corrupted him.

She knew there were people on the outside of her ordeal looking in who didn't believe she felt guilty enough for her initial sin of being late to pick up Josh that night because she hadn't thrown herself prostrate in front of the nation, sobbing and begging forgiveness. They didn't know anything. The pain was hers to bear. She wouldn't allow herself the luxury of begging for the sympathy of strangers. Her punishment was to cope, to care for her children, to deal with every individual rock in the avalanche that was raining down on their lives.

Like Garrett Wright going free.

Leaving Lily to her imaginary telephone conversation, Hannah went to her son and knelt down behind him. She put her arms around him and kissed the top of his head. He didn't move. He didn't speak.

"We won't let him beat us, Josh," she whispered. "I won't let him take you from me. I won't let you down again. I promise."

Even the worst day in the history of mankind had only twenty-four hours. Ellen repeated that mantra all day long. All during her conversation with Hannah. All through Rudy's "damage control" meeting. All through the brief but excruciating official press conference. This day had only twenty-four hours, and she would live through them to fight another day. Costello had roused the tiger within her. She wouldn't be happy until it tore his throat out, eviscerated Garrett Wright and his partner.

Rudy hadn't fired her. Wouldn't fire her. He needed her. He was too wily not to see that. He needed her now for a whipping boy, and he would need her later when this case went to trial. Whether or not he would put her in first chair or hide her as second to Sig Iverson's figurehead prosecutorial post remained to be seen, but he needed her either way. Ellen intended to make the most of that.

Tomorrow they would regroup. She would call her cops together for a strategy session. By tomorrow Todd Childs's prints could have matched up with prints found in Denny Enberg's office, and they would have the lever they needed to crack him open. By tomorrow they might have preliminary reports back from Dustin Holloman's autopsy, which was where Wilhelm and Steiger had spent the afternoon. If the ME came up with a few stray hairs, a skin scraping from under the boy's fingernails, a DNA fingerprint in the form of a drop of blood . . . they'd be back in business. If Megan could dig up just one anomaly in Garrett Wright's perfect past . . .

She grabbed the phone and dialed Megan's number again, getting the answering machine. O'Malley had been out all day. Mitch had said she'd found a better place to work, but he didn't have a number or the time to discuss it. Some of Harris College's rowdier students had used Garrett Wright's release as an excuse to run amok on campus and call it a victory celebration. Their celebration had spilled out into Dinkytown in the form of skirmishes, vandalism, and general mayhem. With an official victory party scheduled for eight o'clock and a promised appearance by the man himself, the police were bracing themselves for a night of trouble.

Ellen checked her watch. Nine-nineteen. The party was already well under way. She had given Phoebe orders to attend but suspected her once-loyal secretary was more likely to spend the evening giving Adam Slater an exclusive than paying attention to what was going on around her.

Their candidates for Accomplice of the Year would be there—Christopher Priest and Todd Childs. The Sci-Fi Cowboys would be there—would Tyrell Mann risk an appearance? Garrett Wright would be center stage with his wife beside him. Karen, drugged and distant, the secrets of her marriage locked inside her seemingly vacant mind.

Ellen would have bet Karen's affair with Paul was what had set the game in motion. It was Wright's motive for choosing Josh, for framing Paul. And Dustin Holloman had been nothing more than a pawn to make Wright look innocent.

But who had orchestrated the second half of the match? And why was Paul Kirkwood suddenly missing if he was guilty of nothing more than adultery?

The questions swarmed around Ellen's brain. She allowed herself a little groan as she rose from her chair and went to the window. Suppertime had come and gone without supper. The lack of fuel was dragging her mood down when she thought it couldn't sink any lower.

She was alone in the office. Beaten, hungry, freezing, old, and alone.

"Don't forget feeling sorry for yourself, Ellen," she muttered as she stretched, then rubbed her hands together to ward off frostbite.

For once she *wished* Brooks would show up uninvited. But for all she knew, he had jumped sides now that Wright was off. The story of a "good" man triumphing over a prosecutor out to get him would make a much better book than the tale of said prosecutor's failure to get a vicious monster to trial.

"I go after what I want, Ellen North. And I get it."

Then in her mind's eye she saw his face the night before the hearing began, right here in her office.

"*I've never been anyone's hero. . . .*" Eyes shadowed with old pain, old uncertainty. "*Will you try to redeem me, Ellen?*"

That look lingered in her mind, until the practical side of her reared up. She was wasting time. She had a whole table of notes and statements to go over. Again. That was what she had wanted this quiet time for. Not for feeling old and alone and sorry for herself. Not for romanticizing about tarnished knights and wounded souls.

The phone rang and she flinched. She let it ring as she ticked off possible callers. It was her mother. It was Megan with the much-needed clue. It was Jay. It was some damned reporter who had wheedled her direct-line number out of Rudy. It was—

"Ellen North," she said, grabbing up the receiver, forcing herself past the apprehension.

"Ellen, Darrell Munson. Sorry it took me so long to get back to you. I just got home from a dive trip off Key West."

Munson. That name clicked slowly into place. Probation officer turned beach bum.

"Thanks for calling back," she said without enthusiasm. The Sci-Fi Cowboys trail had led nowhere but to the Garrett Wright alumni fan club. She couldn't find much hope that this call would be any different from the rest, but she went through the motions, explaining to Munson the situation.

"That's pretty hard to believe," he said, his voice going cold over the line. "I knew Dr. Wright fairly well. Had nothing but respect for the man. I'm not happy to hear you're looking to discredit him."

"I'm doing my job, Mr. Munson," Ellen explained. "The evidence is compelling or we wouldn't be proceeding. If Dr. Wright is innocent, then he has nothing to worry about. He certainly wasn't anyone's first choice as a suspect."

"Yeah, well . . . ," he said grudgingly. "What was it you wanted from me?"

"I wanted to know if you kept track of the kids you had in the Sci-Fi Cowboys program. We're contacting past members as part of Wright's background check."

"I had two the first year the program started; then I got out of Dodge and came down here."

"Tim Dutton and Erik Evans."

"Yeah. Sure, I know where Tim is. He sends me Christmas cards. He's an apprentice electrician up in New Hope. Erik, I lost track of. Last I knew he was at the U studying computers. Really bright kid. Very personable. A minister's son."

"Doesn't sound like your average juvenile offender."

"I don't suppose he was. He had some emotional problems, some problems at home. His mother was in and out of institutions. It all dated back to that business with the neighbor kid when Erik was ten. That kind of trauma would screw up anybody."

"What trauma?"

"He saw a playmate hang himself."

"Oh, no."

"Yeah. It was a bad deal. The kid's mother blamed Erik. She was pretty vocal about it. It was all over the news at the time. I'm surprised you don't remember it. Slater was the kid's name."

Ellen jerked her head up. "Excuse me?"

"Slater. Adam Slater."

A chill washed over her. *Adam Slater. Oh, my God.*

"Uh—uh—could you describe Erik Evans for me?"

"Last time I saw him, he was five four, five five, slim, blond."

Blond. The part of her brain that specialized in denial grabbed hold of the detail.

"Thank you. Thank you, Mr. Munson," she stammered. "You've been very helpful."

She dropped the receiver before she could recradle it. Erik Evans. The kid in the newspaper photo standing beside Wright. Blond, smallish.

Kids grew. People dyed their hair.

She hurried to the conference room and homed in on the file lying among all the others. Her hands were shaking so badly, she could hardly pick through the reports and clippings. She dug front to back, back to front. The article was gone.

Adam Slater.

Reporter for an inconsequential paper. No one had bothered to check press credentials. There were too damned many reporters to sort through. Besides, all they were after was news. They were nuisances, irritations, nothing more.

Perhaps it was just coincidence that Adam Slater the reporter from Grand Forks shared a name with a child dead eleven years. A child who had been playmates with a future Sci-Fi Cowboy.

"You don't believe in coincidence, Ellen," she muttered.

Adam Slater was romancing Phoebe, charming her, winning her over. Ellen had warned her he had an ulterior motive. God, she had never dreamed it could be this.

In her mind's eye she saw the note that marked the very page she needed in the book of Minnesota case law in the third-floor library. *it is a SIN to believe evil of others, but it is seldom a mistake*

Sin. So many of the notes had included references to sin.

Erik Evans was the son of a Methodist minister.

They had been turning over every rock they could find, hunting for Garrett Wright's accomplice, and he had been standing there the whole time, right beside them, taking it all in. He had been along the roadside in the pre-dawn gray the morning Dustin Holloman's body had been found. If she was right, he was the one who had strangled the boy and propped him up against that signpost with a note pinned to his chest. *some rise by SIN, and some by virtue fall*

Erik Evans. Adam Slater. Garrett Wright's protégé.

She had to call Mitch. Slater was likely at the victory celebration, privately gloating. Probably with Phoebe. Oh, God, Phoebe. What if the party was over? What if she was with him? What if Adam Slater decided she wasn't useful anymore?

Dropping the papers she held, Ellen reached for the phone and stopped cold.

Lying across the base of the telephone was a single red rose, its stem entwined with the cord that should have been plugged into the wall jack.

"My sources tell me you've been asking too many questions, Ms. North." He stood in the doorway to the conference room, his dyed hair drooping over one eye. "I think it's time you stopped. Forever."

CHAPTER 35

"Light that and you're a dead man," Megan said.

Jay paused, lighter halfway to the cigarette dangling from his mouth.

"Haven't I been abused enough?" she said. "Did I survive that beating only to die of lung cancer contracted through secondhand smoke while trying to crack the case?"

Jay pulled the cigarette and set it on the table beside the pack. "Do you realize tobacco is a substantial part of the southern economy?"

"Uh-huh," Megan said without sympathy. "*Y'all* might try joining the age of enlightenment sometime in this century. Until that magic moment, you can take your filthy little death stick outside and kill yourself with it."

They had already had this argument three times. Jay had lost each round. He knew he could have pulled rank on her—it *was* his house, after all—but every time he had ended up taking himself out onto the deck in the frigid fucking cold to stand at the front window glaring in at her. He blamed his ingrained southern manners but knew the truth was that he liked Megan, and she sure as hell *had* suffered enough.

"You could let me have my way just once," he pouted.

"Quit your whining. I could hit you in the head with

a hammer just once, too," she said. Her eyes focused on the file spread out before her. "Have you got any answers back yet on that AOL bulletin board?"

He hit a series of keys, calling up the proper screen on the computer. It had been his suggestion to go into America Online and hit the bulletin boards of alumni groups from the colleges where Garrett Wright had taught. They were hoping a former student might come forward with a nasty long-dead rumor or a memory of some peculiar incident that would give them a starting point.

"Only good stuff from UVA," he said, scanning the replies to his innocuous question—*Were you ever a student of Dr. Garrett Wright (psych) and how did you like him?* "Salt of the earth. Prince of a guy."

"He's a fucking madman," Megan snapped, throwing down her highlighter. "Can't *anybody* see that?"

Embarrassed at losing her cool yet again, she glanced at Brooks sideways and tried for humor. "Gee, honey, maybe I need an Excedrin."

He didn't smile. The look in his eyes was too astute for comfort. "Maybe you need a break," he said. "You've been going hard for hours, Megan, and you know you're not up to it."

The tenderness in his voice slipped around her guard. She'd never had any defense against tenderness. Looking away from him, she gathered together the threadbare scraps of her composure.

"I see him slipping away," she said quietly. "He said he would win, and I can't stand the thought of that happening. Don't tell me I need rest. I don't need anything more than I need that bastard's head on a pike."

Jay heaved a sigh and ignored the craving for nicotine. He could see the pressure of this case squeezing Megan like a vise. She was a perfectionist, proud, a control freak like half the cops he'd known. Garrett Wright had broken her physically, and the posttraumatic stress was breaking her mentally.

Garrett Wright, who was a free man tonight.

Ellen was likely taking the news only slightly better than Megan. Ellen, too conscientious, too focused on what she perceived as her responsibility—justice for all. She would take this defeat as a personal affront and dive back into the fight with single-minded determination.

He had wanted to be there for her after the news of the dismissal had come. But it had seemed even more important to stay here with O'Malley, to think harder, dig deeper.

He who skated across the surface of life, never getting involved, always standing back to observe from a distance.

Unbidden, his gaze strayed to the rug in front of the fireplace where he and Ellen had made such sweet, hot love Saturday night.

"I need a drink," he growled, pushing himself up from his lawn chair. "Want one?"

"As well as that would go with the narcotics I'm taking, I'll have to settle for a Coke," Megan said. "With ice, please," she called as he disappeared into the kitchen.

She looked at the sea of paper she had spread out across the long table. Notes, faxes from the colleges Wright had taught for, faxes from half a dozen law-enforcement agencies local to those colleges, faxes from NCIC. And in it all, she had found nothing.

"We can't lose," he whispered. *"You can't defeat us. We're very good at this game."*

An involuntary shiver rattled through her. The will it took to shut that black box of fear left her feeling weak.

Focus. She needed to focus. Concentration kept her on an almost even keel. She dug out her list of calls and ran down the names, awkwardly marking the ones she would call back in the morning. Contacts she'd made at law-enforcement conferences and in the agents' program at

Quantico. Not for the first time since all this had begun, she wondered what kind of life she would be living if she had accepted the FBI field post in Memphis all those years ago. Memphis was a long way from Garrett Wright. But it was also a long way from Mitch and Jessie, and she wouldn't have given them up for anything. Not even for a climate without the word "windchill" in it.

The NCIC request for unsolved child abductions, and abductions/murders, in the geographical areas where Priest had taught had yielded them little. Nothing that matched the macabre game that had played out here. It hadn't struck her until after the bad news of the dismissal had come from the courthouse that they might be looking on the wrong side of the win-lose column altogether. It didn't appear Wright wanted this case to go unsolved. It appeared he had every intention of framing Paul Kirkwood. If he framed Paul, who was to say he hadn't done the same thing before?

Maybe they didn't need information on *unsolved* crimes. Maybe they needed to look at cases that had been closed. Unfortunately, no one in law enforcement was as eager to share information on cases they believed to be tied up, neat and tidy, as they were to share information on cases they wanted to clean up. Megan knew it would take days of hounding to get anything.

Newspapers were the place to go. Newspaper-morgue librarians, and public-library reference-desk librarians. She had started calling immediately, requesting any stories found be faxed to Jay's machine ASAP. She had wheedled and begged, pleaded and lied and tossed around a rank she no longer held, then crossed her fingers and hoped that in the end the story of Josh and Dustin Holloman was enough to compel complete strangers in other states to do work they didn't really have to do.

Several faxes had rolled in late in the day. None of

them were the piece they needed. Jay had put out the same request over a number of computer networks, using his name and his fame as a lure. Nothing had come of any of it yet.

Except to dispel her sense of powerlessness and uselessness. Garrett Wright had taken so much from her, but he hadn't taken the most important things that made her a good cop. Her mind. Her heart. Her determination. She could still do the job. She would just have to go about it differently, that was all.

"Christ," Brooks muttered, staring at the computer screen. "Everybody in the damn country has a story to tell. Here's a woman in Arkansas who claims her Welsh corgi was abducted by space aliens."

"Sounds like a book to me," Megan said, easing herself up out of her chair, moving carefully against the stiffness in her aching muscles. "Have you attracted anyone besides lunatics?"

He scrolled down through the responses, skipping over states outside the regions they were searching and past stories of S-and-M queens and visitations from alternate dimensions. Megan watched over his shoulder, amazed and disappointed at once.

"You're a wacko magnet, Brooks. Is that the price of fame?"

"I don't mind paying the price," he drawled. "Just so long as I get reimbursed."

He blew out a sigh and rubbed his eyes. "I need a break. I gotta get out of here for a while."

"Sure, go ahead," Megan said. "I'll hold the fort."

"You sure you don't want a breather, too?" he asked, shrugging into his parka.

"I'm sure." She gave him a sly smile as she slid down into his chair in front of the computer. "Three's a crowd. Say hi to Ellen for me."

She heard the kitchen door close, listened dimly to the muffled rumble of his truck's engine as she continued to go over the responses. His taillights were still visible heading east on Mill Road when she hit pay dirt.

She read through the scant few paragraphs regarding a crime that had been solved nearly ten years past. Her sixth sense—her cop sense—was humming on high voltage. Logic told her it was a long shot, but it was the first shot they'd had.

Sandwiching the telephone receiver between her shoulder and ear, she punched the number for the Pennsylvania state police. "Mr. Brooks, I think maybe we just caught a break."

"We didn't think you'd dig that deep," Slater said, stepping casually into the room, his hands in the pockets of his black ski jacket. "The investigation isn't your job, after all."

"My job is to prove my case," Ellen said, using her peripheral vision to search out a usable weapon within reach.

He shook his head and smiled slowly. "If you'd left the investigating to the cops, we might not have had to kill you."

"Kill me and you'll be found out anyway." She was amazed that she could sound so calm, so rational, when every alarm inside her was screaming. "It won't take long for the cops to put two and two together. They'll follow the same trail I did."

"I don't think so. They'll be more apt to follow the same trail they followed with Enberg." Feigning sadness, he said, "Poor guy, he just couldn't take the pressure."

The scene from Denny's office flashed through Ellen's mind. The blood, the gore. Brain matter clinging to the wall behind his body. His head mostly gone, blown away. Nausea swirled in her stomach.

"No one will buy that," she challenged, her fingers surreptitiously curling around the shaft of one of Cameron's fountain pens. She slipped her fists into the deep pockets of her heavy wool coat. "I don't own a gun. I wouldn't have one."

Slater took another step forward into the room. "Don't be so literal. There are lots of ways a person can commit suicide. Hanging. Carbon monoxide. Pills. Razor blades."

Ellen stepped back. If she could keep enough distance between them, get on opposite sides of the conference table . . . If she could just get to the outer hall . . .

"All I have to do is scream," she said. "There's a security guard—"

"Nice try, Ms. North, but I happen to know Mr. Stovich no longer saw the need, what with the charges against Dr. Wright being dropped." He flashed a quick grin and chuckled. "According to my good friend Phoebe, ol' Rudy was pretty steamed about the way you blew the case."

"You should be proud of yourself," Ellen said, refusing the bait. "Your efforts paid off. Keeping the cops busy running from one incident to another. Planting that evidence in Paul Kirkwood's storage locker. The credit is yours, not mine."

He grinned again and tossed his hair back out of his eyes. "Yeah. I done good."

"You murdered an innocent child."

"Nice touch, huh?"

"You don't feel anything?"

He shrugged, looking all of sixteen, innocent, oblivious to the consequences of his actions. "Sure. It was a rush choking him."

"Then why didn't you kill Josh?"

"Because that wasn't the plan." He shook his head. "You still don't get it. The game is more fun when you spot the other team points."

"You're not worried about his talking?"

"No," he said flatly, moving forward. "And I'm tired of you talking. Let's get on with it, Ms. North."

Ellen had rounded the end of the table, putting it between them, but Slater was nearer the door. He stood quietly, without the bouncy energy she had come to associate with him. As if he had pulled that energy inward and held it at the core of him, burning hot and intense. His dark eyes were bright with it, watching her with predatory anticipation.

"If you think I'm just going to let you kill me, you're not as smart as I thought," she said. "I have every intention of fighting. Defense wounds will raise eyebrows."

"There won't be any."

She inched along the table, passing the stacks of files, the reports, the notes—none of which would have pointed to Slater. He was right. If it hadn't been for her own digging, if it hadn't been for her calling on old contacts in the world she'd left behind, no one would have looked at him twice. Christ, *she* hadn't looked at him twice. The only reason she had kept searching for information on the past Cowboys was that she had the connection and was desperate enough to play a long shot.

"When did Wright single you out?" she asked. "Did he find out about the Slater boy when you came into the Cowboys?"

Pride and amusement glowed in his too-young face. "He built the Cowboys around me," he bragged. "I'm the reason the Cowboys exist. Ain't that a kick in the head? The program exists because Garrett wanted me."

The irony was as twisted as barbed wire. A program heralded nationally for turning so many young lives around had come into being as a cover for the utter corruption of one.

"Is it just Wright?" Ellen asked, her fingers clenching

and unclenching on the pen in her coat pocket. She stood directly across from him now. Equal distance to the door. He had fifteen years on her, but she would be running for her life. "Or is Priest in on it, too?"

"I won't tell you everything, Ellen."

"Why not? I'll be dead anyway."

"True, but I don't want you to die satisfied. I want you to die wondering. That's just another point for my team."

"What a waste," she said, focusing on her anger instead of her fear. "To take someone as bright and talented as you and turn you into a common criminal."

"There's nothing common about me, Ms. North." His expression turned stony. "Garrett searched a long time to find me—a child who understood the game, someone as superior as he is."

"Superior?" Ellen arched a brow. "He's nothing but a bully and a coward and a murderer."

His eyes narrowed above reddening cheekbones. From his left jacket pocket he pulled a stun gun, a black plastic rectangle that didn't look any more menacing than a television remote control. "No more talk, bitch."

Ellen bolted for the door. Slater caught her at the end of the table, grabbing hold of her left arm and swinging the stun gun to her chest. She twisted away from him, and sixty thousand volts of electricity went dead against the thick wool sleeve of her coat. Screaming, she pulled the fountain pen from her pocket and stabbed with all the wild fury of the survival instinct.

Slater shrieked as the pen sank into his face through the hollow of his cheek and tore downward. The blood came in a gush as the soft tissue ripped open. Ellen wasted no time looking. She pushed off and lunged for the door, shouting for help, knowing the building was empty, knowing the sound would never reach the deputies in the building next door.

She could hear Slater coming behind her as she ran through the outer office. Chancing a glance over her shoulder, she slammed a thigh into the corner of Phoebe's desk. Black stars bursting in her head, she half sprawled across the desk, and her right hand hit the stapler. She closed her fingers around it and ran on.

"You fucking bitch!" Slater sobbed behind her.

He launched himself at her as she flung the door open, tackling her with his arms wrapped around her upper body. They landed on the floor, Ellen taking the brunt of it as she was sandwiched between the floor and her assailant. Her forehead hit hard. Her breath left her in a painful whoosh. But she pulled her feet beneath her and fought to buck Slater's weight off her.

They wrestled across the floor, Slater grabbing at her shoulder, trying to turn her onto her back beneath him. Ellen bit at his fingers, the blood dripping from his face into her eyes, into her hair, running down her cheek. She twisted suddenly beneath him and swung the stapler against his temple and cheekbone, snapping his head to the side, dazing him and giving her just enough opportunity to roll free.

She scrambled to her feet and started to run, realizing too late that she was pointed in the wrong direction—away from the sheriff's department. Now she would have to get to the first floor and double back.

Slater caught her at the stairs, grabbing the collar of her coat and a handful of hair, yanking her almost off her feet. The stun gun came up and Ellen blocked the hit with her shoulder. The gun gave an angry, crackling buzz. No defense wounds, he'd promised. If he'd nailed her the first time, there would have been none. The voltage would have dazed her senseless, and he could have quickly and easily slit her wrists for her.

Her left arm was wedged between their bodies. Ellen

groped, latching on to Slater's testicles, squeezing as hard as she could. A howl pierced her eardrum and he shoved her away, doubling over, clutching himself. Ellen's shins hit the steps, then she fell up on her hands and knees. The stapler clattered free.

Up.

Shit. No options. Run now, figure it out later.

"Time to die, birthday bitch."

Birthday. Thirty-six. The birthday Ellen had been dreading. Suddenly thirty-six seemed far too young.

She flung herself up the stairs, stumbling as one heel caught an edge. She grabbed for the handrail, her fingers scraping the rough plaster of the wall, breaking a nail, skinning her knuckles.

The stairwell was barely lit, drawing in the ragged edges of illumination that fell from the lights in the halls above and below. Security lights. They offered nothing in the way of security. In the back of her mind she heard a low, smoky voice, *"Your boss needs to have a word with some-one about security. This is a highly volatile case. Anything might happen."*

She reached the third floor and turned down the hall, heading east. If she could make it down the east stairs—If she could make it to the walkway between the buildings— He wouldn't dare try to take her in the walkway with the sheriff's department mere feet away.

"We've got you now, bitch!"

There were telephones in the offices she ran past. The offices were locked. Her self-appointed assassin was jog-ging behind her, laughing. The sound went through her like a spear, like the sure knowledge that he would kill her. Pursuit may not have been his plan, but it had become a part of the game.

The game. The insanity of it was as terrifying as the prospect of death. Beat the system. Wreck lives. End lives. Nothing personal. Just a game.

She ran past Judge Grabko's courtroom and ducked around the corner that led back toward the southeast stairwell. Scaffolding filled the stairwell, cutting off her escape route. The scaffolding for the renovators. Christ, she was going to die because of the stupid plaster frieze.

"Checkmate, clever bitch."

The northeast stairs looked a mile away. Midway stood the iron gates that blocked the skyway between the courthouse and the jail. She lunged for the fire alarm on the wall, grabbing the glass tube that would break and summon help.

The tube snapped. Nothing. No sound. No alarm.

"Oh, God, no!" She clawed at the useless panel. The goddamn renovations. New alarms going in. State of the art.

"Come along, Ellen. Be a good bitch and let me kill you."

She grabbed the handle of the door to the fire hose and yanked.

"You have to die, bitch. We have to win the game."

His hand closed on her arm.

Her fingers closed on the handle of the ax.

He threw his body against the door and slammed it, snapping a bone in her wrist. Ellen screamed, the pain dropping her to her knees.

Sobbing, cradling her broken left wrist against her middle, she knelt at the feet of her killer. The workmen's tarps were spread all around, covered with plaster dust as thick and fine as flour, scattered with scabs of old plaster and empty Mountain Dew cans.

"Come along, Ellen," Slater said, squatting down. "Be a good bitch and let me kill you."

He never noticed her right hand until it opened two inches from his face, throwing plaster dust into his eyes and into the gaping wound in his cheek.

Ellen stood and jerked the ax free. She whirled just as

Slater lunged at her, grabbing her ankles, hitting her in the thigh. With the stun gun.

The current seared through her skirt, stormed along her nerve pathways. It hit the brain instantly, leaving behind stunned bewilderment. In a fraction of a second all control of arms and legs was gone. She fell like a stone, the ax sailing five feet away.

She lay on the tarp, eyes open as Slater bent down close.

"Some rise by sin, and some by virtue fall," he murmured, his ravaged face inches from hers. "Some by virtue die."

The dispatcher, a round Nordic-looking girl with flyaway blond hair and an unflattering uniform, led Jay down the walkway between the sheriff's department and the courthouse, batting her lashes and offering her opinion that *he* should have starred in *Justifiable Homicide* instead of Tom Cruise.

He flashed her the smile, an absent, halfhearted gesture. "Thank you, Mindy, but I'm more comfortable being a writer. I really didn't have anything to do with the movie."

In fact, the story had been virtually unrecognizable by the time Hollywood had finished with it. Jay had shrugged off that irksome little detail on the way to the bank. It didn't matter. It was just entertainment. He got paid either way.

A twinge hit his atrophied conscience. The people he wrote about were real, not fictional. They had lives that went on after the crimes that were his focus. They were people like Hannah Garrison and Megan and Ellen.

"Well, you should think about it," Mindy bubbled on, unlocking the door to the courthouse. "You're way better looking. He doesn't really have much of a chin, you know. Not that he isn't cute. He is. But you should have ranked lots higher than him in that *People* list, too. I don't know who makes that thing up. He's a Scientologist, too. Did you know that? That just spooks me. It's like a cult or something." Her small eyes rounded suddenly. "Ooh! You're not a Scientologist, are you?"

"No, ma'am. I belong to a snake-handling religion," he drawled, straight-faced, lifting his hands as if each contained a fistful of writhing copperheads. "Nothing more spiritual than takin' up snakes."

Poor Mindy. The girl backed away, fighting a horrified grimace with her inbred Minnesota manners. Jay thanked her politely as she scooted back toward the sheriff's department.

As he headed through the deep gloom toward the stairs, he kept imagining the expression on Ellen's face as he shared the news that he was helping O'Malley hunt for leads on Wright's past. The image that came to mind was pride, which the cynic in him dismissed. He was a grown man, and he told himself he had long ago burned out his need for approval from "respectable" people like his family, like Ellen.

He climbed the stairs to the second floor, shaking his head a little as he saw the door to the county attorney's offices standing open, light spilling out into the dark hall. He hadn't even bothered going by Ellen's house, despite the hour. She wouldn't go home to lick her wounds. She would go right back to the job and dig in harder than before.

He expected to find her in the conference room, bent over a pile of statements, glasses slipping down her nose. But the room was empty. Jay's nerves tightened as he took in the papers strewn across the floor. Papers painted with bright, thick splotches of blood.

Ellen lay flat on her stomach on the filthy tarp like a broken doll, her arms flung out to the sides at odd angles. She fought to make her brain work, tried in vain to will her arms to move. She had heard footfalls, knew someone else had come into the building. At the sound of Jay's voice calling her name, she tried to scream, but the sound was contained in her mind. Slater, straddling her on his knees, tightened his hand around her throat and squeezed until she couldn't breathe.

He had spent the last few minutes cutting a length of rope free from the scaffolding and fashioning a noose. All the while she lay helpless, unable to move, but able to watch him. At the first sound of another person in the building, he crouched over her and expertly slipped his fingers into position around her larynx.

She closed her twitching eyes and tried to direct her scattered mental powers to Brooks. *Please come looking, Jay. Please come upstairs. Please hurry.*

Footsteps sounded again below them. Hurrying. Breaking into a jog. Again in her mind she screamed, but no sound broke past the hold Slater had on her throat. What if Jay didn't come? What if he left the building, went back to the sheriff's department? Slater would have time to kill her and get away. Even if he had lost his chance to make it look like a suicide and clean up all evidence of himself after, he would still be able to kill her and escape.

She had to do something. Now.

The feeling was coming back into her arms. First, in the form of throbbing pain in her broken left wrist, then in small muscle spasms. If she could reestablish the connection between thought and movement . . .

Slowly her fingers curled into a fist, scraping chips and nuggets and chunks of old plaster into her palm. She would get only one chance. If she failed . . .

With all the concentration she could muster, she ordered her arm to move, to swing, ordered her fingers to open. Some of the debris fell short. Some hit the balusters of the railing and bounced back. The rest sailed into space and fell to the first floor. A meager effort to pin her life on. If Jay wasn't looking . . . Even if he noticed it, he might be too preoccupied to think it significant.

Slater, on the other hand, found it too significant. His hand tightened savagely on her throat. He bent down close and whispered hoarsely in her ear. "You fucking bitch. You are dead. Now."

His mouth closed on her ear, his teeth biting into the cartilage.

Ellen's mouth stretched open as she tried to gasp breath, succeeding only in dragging her tongue through the plaster dust. Her vision blurred with spiderweb lines of blackness. Her lungs burned with the desperate need for oxygen.

The instinct for survival shot adrenaline through her in a burst, jolting her body to action. Kicking, flailing, she swung an arm back, catching a finger in the torn flesh of his face and digging into the wound.

Plaster bits raining down to the floor of the rotunda caught Jay's eye as he hurried toward the stairs. Then came the cry—strangled, masculine. Above him—where the plaster had come from.

"Ellen!"

He shouted her name as he bolted for the stairs. If she was up there and not able to make any sound to call him, there was no time to spare. He didn't have the luxury of calling in cops.

He made the third-floor landing and ran toward the hall with no sense at all of what he might be rushing into—a knife, a bullet, a body. There were no thoughts at all for his own safety. His only thought was Ellen, that she was in danger, that she needed help.

"Ellen!"

Slater punched at her head, batted at her broken wrist, breaking her hold on his torn face. He pushed to his feet just as Jay came into view at the north end of the hall. Snatching up the fire ax, Slater rushed him.

Ellen struggled to her knees, gasping for air. In horror, she watched Slater bring the ax back and swing it like a baseball bat.

Jay dodged sideways, and the blade of the ax sang through the air. Too damned close. Before Slater could pull it back for another swing, before Jay could give any thought to his plan, he stepped in close and landed a left cross on Slater's jaw. Slater staggered sideways and dropped to one knee.

He came up swinging the ax backhanded. Jay ducked low and caught him hard in the ribs, knocking the wind from his lungs. He let his weapon go. The ax clattered to the floor, the handle spinning out of reach. Moving in quickly, Jay aimed a boot at Slater's chin as he doubled over. But Slater caught the kick and jerked Jay off his feet.

Jay landed hard on his back. Before his vision cleared, Slater was over him, the pale beam of the security light glinting off the blade of a hunting knife he had pulled from his coat.

Ellen staggered to her feet as Jay went down, fear and fury and pain coursing through her. Slater was the key to the evil that had contaminated her haven. He had killed

Denny Enberg and Dustin Holloman. He would have killed her if not for Jay. And now he would kill Jay.

Jay managed to twist out of the way of the first knife strike, though the blade sliced the sleeve of his coat, releasing a mass of goose down that puffed up into the air between them. He wasn't as lucky the second time, or the third.

Slater stabbed viciously, his mouth open, the gaping wound sucking in and blowing out with his breath, blood and spittle spraying in a pink foam. The blade of the hunting knife struck Jay's forearm as he tried to defend himself, tearing coat sleeve and muscle, hitting bone. He punched out with his other hand, barely connecting with Slater and leaving himself open to another assault.

The blade sank deep into the hollow of his right shoulder, and a white-hot burst of pain spread through his brain like a dark cloud, dimming his vision. He could feel the blood well up like water from a spring as his arm went dead.

Move, move, move!

Twisting, kicking, he got Slater off him and his feet beneath him. He scooted backward in a frantic retreat, with Slater in aggressive pursuit.

He hit the railing that overlooked the rotunda, saw Slater pulling the knife back, raising it high, the look in his eyes pure animal bloodlust, not human in any respect.

A hundred hard, clear truths cut across Jay's mind at the speed of light. He would never know his son. He had wasted too much time on spite. The only people who would mourn his passing would be the ones who made money off him. And what had begun with Ellen, what she had awakened in him, would die in this moment, unfulfilled.

———

Screaming, Slater pulled the blade another inch higher over his shoulder. Ellen hurled herself at him, hitting him in the side of the neck with the stun gun, shooting sixty thousand volts of electricity directly to his brain.

Eyes wide, he dropped to the floor, his body jerking and convulsing, then going utterly still.

Ellen stared at him, the horror of the last few moments hitting her. The strength that had carried her through vanished, and tremors shook her.

"It's all right," Jay murmured, sliding his left arm around her and gathering her close. He pressed his face against the cool silk of her hair and kissed her. "It's over, baby. It's over."

An insidious numbness was creeping through him, creeping in on the edges of his mind. He felt that the energy that comprised his being was gathering into a softly glowing ball and slowly drifting out of the wounded shell of his body. He fought the sensation, as seductive as it was. All he wanted was to hold Ellen, shelter her.

"Oh, God, you're bleeding!" she whispered. She fumbled to press a hand against the gushing wound in his shoulder. His blood oozed out between her fingers and ran in rivulets down her hand.

"Don't worry," he told her. "I can't die a hero." He gave her a pale shadow of his smile. "It'd be too damned ironic."

CHAPTER 36

In his dream Josh saw blood. Rivers of it. Geysers of it. Smooth, oily pools of it. He was in it up to his chin. The undercurrent pulled at his feet. The hands of the Taker closed around his ankles and tried to pull him down. The Taker had chosen him. The Taker wanted him. It frightened him to disobey. He had gone into the smallest box of his mind to hide, and still the Taker had hold of him, pulling on him.

He had been told to obey. Bad things would happen. Terrible things. They had already started. Josh could see his whole world tearing apart, just the way the Taker had shown him. But still he clung to the sides of his box, holding on to what was left of his world.

If he could just hide long enough . . . If he could make himself even smaller inside the shell of his body. If he could get back inside the box . . .

His hands were slipping. He gulped a breath as the Taker pulled him under, through the blood.

Then, just as quickly, he was free. He broke the surface, soared, as if he had been thrown clear of a slingshot. Into the light. Into the air. He could breathe again. He was flying. And below him the blood drew into a smaller and smaller puddle, and then it was gone.

Josh's eyes snapped open. The room was dark, except for the night-light and the numbers on his clock. He felt as if he had been sleeping for a long, long time. Days instead of hours. His mom was asleep in the sleeping bag on the floor. She looked so tired and worried. Her brow was frowning.

Because of me.

Because of the Taker.

There was so much she would never understand. So much he wished they could both forget and just start over, as if they hadn't even been alive until today.

Maybe they could do that, if he wished it hard enough, if he was good enough . . . if he could only find the courage.

CHAPTER 37

The farmhouse sat on an isolated, wooded acreage just over the county line to the south in rural Tyler County. The nearest neighbors were Amish farmers who had no interest in the comings or goings of the "English." Ellen had to imagine they were taking notice this morning. Cars from the Tyler and Park county sheriff's departments, the Deer Lake PD, and the BCA filled the yard while news vans and reporters' vehicles clogged the road. Uniformed officers kept the press at bay while the detectives and evidence techs went about their work.

Parked in the machine shed was a rusting white 1984 Ford Econoline van. A match in age and condition to the van Paul Kirkwood had once owned and sold to Olie Swain. A match to the van a witness had seen at the hockey rink about the time Josh was abducted. A small toolbox behind the front seat held a roll of duct tape, folded squares of cloth—probably for administering ether— hypodermic needles and syringes for injectable sedatives. A kidnapper's tool kit.

Ellen backed away from the shed, shoulders hunched against the cold, and looked around the neat farmyard with its small buildings and perimeter of pine trees, boughs laden with the fresh snow that had fallen in the night. Great pains had been taken to make everything appear normal. The driveway was neatly plowed. A family of concrete deer stood posing in the yard near the bird feeder. Curtains hung at the windows. Christmas lights still hung from the eaves.

All part of the game.

Slater was under guard at the hospital, where he was being observed for any lingering effects from the electrical shock. He wasn't talking, but his name had provided the key they needed. Ellen, vaguely dopey from the pain medication Dr. Lomax had given her before setting her wrist, had called Cameron from the hospital in the middle of the night and set him to work digging up information in Adam Slater's name. In short order they had a phone number, and from the phone number came an address.

Dawn had just lightened the gray of the eastern horizon. Ellen hadn't slept in any restful way, just in fits and starts in a hospital bed. Nightmares of the ordeal jolted her awake every time she drifted off. The feeling of Slater's hands tightening on her throat.

She had moved to Deer Lake to escape the violence and cynicism of the city, yet it was Deer Lake where she had been attacked, where she had been pushed to violence to save her own life and Jay's. A point for Wright's team. Just another ripple in the pond. Just another ramification of their game, along with broken trusts and a broken marriage, lost innocence and lost lives.

She thanked God Jay was not among the body count. Though he had lost enough blood to require a transfusion, the wounds themselves were not life threatening. Still, every time she closed her eyes, Ellen saw that horrible instant when Slater had pulled that bloody knife back for one final thrust, and everything inside her had clenched like a fist.

"You ready to go in, counselor?" Mitch asked, laying a hand on Ellen's shoulder.

She nodded and they moved toward the house. Cameron had argued that she was in no condition to go to the scene, but she wouldn't back down. She let him take the official role, but she needed to be there. It didn't matter that she hurt all over or that she could barely speak because of the bruising in her throat. She had accepted this case, and it would be her fight until the end.

Wilhelm unlocked the back door with a key from Slater's key ring, and they trooped in, holding their breath in anticipation of what they might find. The house was neat and tidy, with doilies on the end tables and a family photo of strangers hanging on the living-room wall.

Probably the family of one of their victims, Ellen suspected. Maybe even the real Adam Slater's family. She should have appreciated the twisted sense of humor, she supposed. If Slater hadn't taken the name of his first victim, he might never have been found out.

All part of the game.

"The game is more fun when you spot the other team points."

One of the two bedrooms was decorated for a little boy, with shelves lined with an assortment of toys, each tagged with a name and date. Trophies from past games won. The notion sickened her. She stood in the hall, resisting the need to lean against the wall and risk ruining latent fingerprints. Leaning against Cameron, instead. He put a brotherly arm around her shoulders and stood silent, his face pale.

They all wore the same face, Ellen thought dimly. Mitch and Wilhelm and Jantzen, the Tyler County sheriff. Even Steiger wore it. Drawn, pale, grim, eyes hollow. There was a sheen of tears in Mitch's as he came out of the room.

"There's a red sneaker in there," he said tightly. "With the name Milo Wiskow. That's the case Megan dug up in Pennsylvania. All we have to do is find a connection between Wright and this house, and he goes away forever."

End game.

They found what they needed in the basement, where

Megan had been tied to an old wooden straight chair and
tortured. The short black baton Wright had used to beat
her hung on a pegboard above a small corner workbench,
as if it were a common handyman's tool.

The basement was divided into three rooms, one of
which was padlocked from the outside. Again, Wilhelm
provided the key from Slater's ring, and they walked into
the small chamber where the boys had been held.

The only furnishing was a cot. The only light a bulb in
the ceiling with a switch outside the door. A video surveillance camera and stereo speakers hung high on the
walls, their wiring connecting them to a system in the
main workroom. From a pair of stools at the counter,
Slater and Wright could watch their captive, speak to him,
play the cassette tapes that were neatly stacked beside the
tape deck.

Handling it gingerly with latex gloves, Mitch slipped a
tape into the deck and hit the play button. Garrett Wright's
voice came over the speakers, smooth and eerie.

"Hello, Josh. I am the Taker. I know what you think
about. I know what you want. I can make you live or die.
I can make your parents live or die. I can make your sister
live or die. It's all up to you, Josh. You do what I say. You
think what I tell you, remember what I tell you. I control
your mind. I know everything you think."

"Jesus," Mitch muttered as he stopped the tape.

Mind control. Psychological terror of children. Having been in the cell where Wright had kept the boys, Ellen
found it too easy to imagine how frightened they must
have been, how lonely, wondering if anyone would come
to save them, wondering if they would live or die, wondering if they might somehow unwittingly cause the
deaths of the people they loved.

*"I am the Taker. I know what you think about. I know what
you want. . . ."*

She thought of Josh sitting in the psychiatrist's office as

the doctor tried to coax answers from him. No wonder he wouldn't speak. Wright had buried the fear so deep inside his young mind, it could take years to extract it. He might never feel safe again.

"Bastard," Steiger growled.

The shelves above the cassette deck housed a small library of audio- and videotapes. A sight that was horrible and welcome at once. Wright's training as an academician and a psychologist, as well as his own over-confidence, would do him in. He had apparently documented his games, his mind-control experiments . . . his crimes. Not even Tony Costello would be able to explain away videotape.

"He believed he'd never get caught," Ellen said, her voice a whispery rasp. "He thinks he's invincible."

"He's dead fucking wrong," Mitch growled. "Let's go pick him up. We can sort through this stuff later. I want that son of a bitch in a cell."

"Chief?" Wilhelm called from a desk ten feet away. "I think you might want to take a look at this first."

"What is it?"

"See for yourself."

Wilhelm had pulled a three-ring binder from a row of similar binders and placed it on the blotter open to page one. Ellen stepped in beside Mitch and looked down at the childish handwriting.

JOURNAL ENTRY
AUGUST 27, 1968

They found the body today. Not nearly as soon as we expected. Obviously, we gave them too much credit. The police are not as smart as we are. No one is.

We stood on the sidewalk and watched. What a pitiful scene. Grown men in tears throwing up in the bushes. They wandered around and around that corner of the park, trampling the grass and breaking off bits of branches. They called to God, but God didn't answer. Nothing changed. No lightning bolts came down. No one was given knowledge of who or why. Ricky Meyers remained dead, his arms outflung, his sneakers toes up.

We stood on the sidewalk as the ambulance came with its lights flashing, and more police cars came, and the cars of people from around town. We stood in the crowd, but no one saw us, no one looked at us. They thought we were beneath their notice, unimportant, but we are really above them and beyond them and invisible to them. They are blind and stupid and trusting. They would never think to look at us.

We are twelve years old.

We.

"My money is on Priest," Mitch said, hitting the blinker.

His Explorer led the procession of police vehicles turning onto Lakeshore Drive. A mob of press had already arrived and staked out Wright's lawn, making themselves useful for once, virtually trapping him in his own home. "Megan had her eye on him. They may have known each other as boys; they taught together at Penn State. They founded the Cowboys together, and according to Slater, the Cowboys were formed around Wright's plan to develop him as a protégé."

Ellen sat tense in the passenger's seat, anticipation tightening every muscle in her body. "But if they were in on this game together," she croaked, "then why didn't they alibi each other for the night Josh went missing? Why have Todd Childs get up at the hearing and contradict the statement he gave the police?"

"You said he wanted to spot us points. Besides, they alibi each other, and those of us who believe one is guilty automatically believe the other is guilty." He turned in at the Wrights' driveway and cut the engine. Reporters swarmed toward the truck. Ignoring them, he gave Ellen a hard look. His game face. "Let's see if Dr. Wright might be able to help us with the answers to those questions. He can provide the commentary when we play those video-tapes."

A whole other crop of questions assaulted them as they made their way to the front door, hurled by the news-hungry like rice at a wedding. Steiger barked something out, grabbing the opportunity to look important.

Mitch hit the doorbell and waited, hit it again. "Dr. Garrett Wright," he said in a loud voice, "this is the police. Please come to the door. We need to speak with you."

They waited a moment that stretched into another. Mitch lifted his two-way. "Noogie? You got any action back there?"

Noga's deep voice came back. "Nothing, Chief."

Mitch knocked on the door again. "Dr. Wright, this is Chief Holt. We need to speak with you."

"He has to be home," Wilhelm muttered. "He was at the victory celebration last night. We know he came back here."

"But did he stay?" Mitch asked. "If he caught wind of his boy wonder going down last night, he may just have split."

Mitch hit the button on the radio again. "Noogie? Take a peek in the garage. What have we got for vehicles?"

"Got a Saab and a Honda, Chief."

"All present and accounted for," Mitch said. He cast a look at Ellen. "I say we go in. We've got probable cause."

"And an audience," Wilhelm said through his teeth.

"Then get them the hell off the yard, Marty," Mitch ordered. "Make yourself useful for once."

As Wilhelm turned away, Mitch tried the doorknob. "Locked." He raised the radio again. "Noogie? You got any company back there?"

"No, sir."

"Then do your thing."

"Ten-four."

Noga was the force's official battering ram. The house door hadn't been made that Noga couldn't bust off its hinges with a shrug. In a matter of moments the front locks were tumbling and the big officer pulled the door open.

The house was quiet. Tastefully, expensively decorated in neutral tones and sleek, pale oak furnishings. Mitch scanned the rooms visible from the foyer.

"Dr. Wright?" he called, sliding his Smith & Wesson nine-mil from his shoulder holster and holding it nose up. "Police! Come out where we can see you!"

The silence hung around them.

"I guess we get to do this the hard way," he muttered, turning toward Ellen and Cameron. "Wait outside. I don't want any chance of this turning into a hostage situation. Noogie, back me up."

Ellen laid a hand on his forearm. "Be careful, Mitch. He doesn't have anything to lose now."

They moved down the halls of the house, Mitch taking the lead, his back to one wall. Each closed door represented a potential nasty surprise. The tight quarters of an unfamiliar house were always a dangerous setting. They opened doors that led to a bathroom, to a guest room, to Karen Wright's hobby room. Not a sound. Not a thing out of place.

They could have easily left in the night, Mitch thought. With the charges dismissed, he had had no choice but to pull the surveillance team or risk charges of harassment. In the back of his mind he made a note to check with the twenty-four-hour car service that taxied people from Deer Lake to the airport in Bloomington. The Wrights could have been halfway to Rio by now.

He sidled up beside the last door on the upper level, reached over, and knocked. "Wright, come out with your hands up! You're under arrest!"

Nothing. He turned the doorknob and pushed the door open, holding himself against the wall. No shots blasted out at them. And then he slipped inside the master bedroom and found out why Garrett Wright hadn't answered them.

Garrett Wright lay spread-eagled on the king-size bed, naked, his throat cut from ear to ear, a butcher knife buried to the hilt in his chest, his dead eyes gazing up at a heaven he would never know.

"He's not stiff yet," Mitch said. "He hasn't been dead more than a few hours."

Ellen took a long look at the gaping wound that nearly severed Garrett Wright's head from his body, then turned away, taking in the room. "There's no sign of a struggle."

"Too bad. He should have had to look death in the face. He should have had to feel the fear his victims felt."

"The cars are here and Karen Wright is missing," Wilhelm said. "Either she did it and walked away or the killer took her with him."

"Paul Kirkwood publicly vowed revenge," Cameron reminded them. "He was having an affair with Karen."

"Get out APBs on both of them," Ellen said. Her gaze drew back to the man whose life had bled out of him.

A murderer. A man whose mind and heart had been as dark as the blood that soaked the ivory sheets around him. He had tormented, tortured, killed, and called it a game. Heartless and cruel. And even with his death, it continued. He had driven someone else to kill, and that person would touch other lives, and the effects would go on and on like a stream of oil bleeding into the ocean.

———

"I always wanted children," Karen said, rocking the baby in her arms. "Garrett and I couldn't have children. But Paul and I can. We can have Lily."

Hannah stared at the woman who had invaded her home sometime in the hours before dawn. Karen Wright. Vapid, innocuous Karen. Always trying to help. Doe-eyed, pretty Karen. Her husband's mistress. Wife of the man who had kidnapped her son.

Hannah had awakened to the sound of a voice singing softly down the hall. A woman's voice coming from Lily's room. Groggy and confused, she'd crawled out of the sleeping bag in her leggings and baggy sweatshirt, her hair falling out of its loose braid and into her eyes.

She stood now in the hall between the bedrooms, still hoping this was yet another of the strange nightmares that had been plaguing her since the start of the ordeal; knowing it was not. Karen Wright stood in her daughter's room, holding Lily and a gun.

"How did you get in here?" Hannah demanded.

"With a key," Karen said matter-of-factly, never taking her eyes off Lily. "I have copies of all of Paul's keys." She smiled dreamily. "I can have the key to his heart now that Garrett won't come between us."

She rose from the rocking chair, juggling Lily and the nine-millimeter gun, the load seeming too much for her. "You're so sweet, aren't you, Lily?" she cooed. "I've always pretended you were mine. I wanted Garrett to get you for me, but he only takes little boys. That's the way it's always been. He hated children."

"You can't have her," Hannah said flatly.

Karen's eyes narrowed, her mouth twisted on the bitterness. "You don't deserve her. I do. I give and give and never get anything back. It's *my* turn. I told Garrett. He wouldn't listen. I told him I wanted Paul. I *love* Paul. Paul could give me a baby. But no. He had to make Paul look guilty. He had to ruin what *I* wanted. He made a very big mistake."

Her arms tightened on the baby, and Lily squirmed and frowned. "Down!"

"No, no, sweetheart," Karen said with a sudden smile, stroking Lily's cheek with the barrel of the gun. "You're going to be my little girl now. We have to go away and make a new life with your daddy. We'll be a happy family."

"What about Garrett?" Hannah asked, inching forward to block the door. Damned if she was going to let a madwoman walk out of her house with her daughter. She would do whatever she had to do. She had pledged to keep her children safe. She was all through being a victim.

Karen's eyes glazed with tears. "Garrett . . . wouldn't listen. He wouldn't let me be happy." A single tear skimmed her cheek. "I love Paul, and Garrett made me betray him. He shouldn't have done that."

Lily twisted in her grasp, pushing against the arm that was banded around her middle. "Lily down!" she demanded. She looked to Hannah. "Mama, down!"

Anger flashing across her features, Karen gave the baby a shake. "Stop it, Lily!" She turned Lily's head toward her with the barrel of the gun. "*I'm* your mommy now."

Josh watched the scene from behind his mother. No one had noticed him. No one would. He could be like a ghost. The quiet was in his mind, and he could make it as big as he was and put it all around him like a giant bubble. He saw the gun. He heard the words. Karen was going to take Lily. Just as he had been taken. Just as that other boy had been taken. The other Goner was dead now, just as Josh had been warned. Now Lily, just as he had been warned. Bad things would happen if he told anyone the truth. But he hadn't told anyone and bad things were happening anyway.

The fear inside him struggled against the need to be free of it. He wanted to be free. He wanted his family to be free. He thought maybe if he wished hard enough . . . If he was good enough . . . If he could only find the courage . . .

"Does Paul know you're doing this?" Hannah asked, edging into the room. If she could get to the changing table, she could grab the baby powder, throw it in Karen's face, get Lily away from her before she could use the gun.

"Paul loves me," Karen said, hefting Lily on her hip. "I'm what he needs. I'm the kind of woman he deserves."

"You're right about that," Hannah said, laughing bitterly. Paul had brought this nightmare on them with his groundless discontent, with his myopic self-absorption. Karen Wright was exactly what he deserved.

"We'll be a happy family," Karen said, jerking Lily against her as the baby tried to squirm out of her grasp. "Lily, stop it!" she shrieked, raising the gun. "Don't make me hurt you!"

As she brought the butt of the gun down toward Lily's head, Josh burst to life. Hurling himself into the room, flinging his body at Karen Wright's legs.

"Josh, no!" Hannah screamed.

Then everything was a blur of sound and motion as she jumped to grab Karen's gun.

"If it was Paul, Wright would have struggled," Ellen said.

"Unless they drugged him first," Wilhelm offered.

"Paul wouldn't have the guts to kill like that," Mitch said. "With a gun, maybe. With a knife, no way."

"Karen got tired of his trying to control her the way he did his victims," Ellen theorized. "He used her to get to Paul. God only knows how he might have used her before."

"The question is, Where did she go?" Cameron said. "And was she alone?"

"Get on the phone to the cab company," Ellen told him. "I have a hard time believing Paul dropped by and picked her up after she essentially testified against him in court."

"Tracks," Noga said suddenly. He had been leaning against the wall, pale and wobbly. Straightening, he turned toward Mitch. "There were tracks in the backyard."

In the fresh snow.

"Let's go." Mitch started for the door, tossing instructions over his shoulder to Wilhelm. "Secure the scene and keep the press out."

Ellen followed him out the kitchen door, through the garage where Wright had first been arrested, and to the backyard, where reporters were creeping around the perimeter of the property in the attempt to get an angle no one else had.

"Mitch, we'll need to make some kind of statement," Ellen said. "Get a photo of Karen to the TV people. If she's a possible killer, the public needs to know."

"Do what you have to."

He had just turned to follow Noga north along the footprints. North, toward the Kirkwood house, when the sound of gunshots cracked the crisp morning air.

They crashed into the dresser, sending a lamp tumbling; fell against the white wicker rocker and onto the floor, kicking and gouging. The gun flew free, spinning across the carpet. Hannah lunged for it but was pulled up short as Karen grabbed hold of her braid with a savage tug. Fingernails raked down her face. Karen's knee caught her in the stomach as Karen lunged forward. Too late.

Josh raised the black pistol with both hands and

pointed it squarely at Karen Wright's forehead, just inches away, the barrel wobbling gently back and forth.

Karen went still. Lily lay on the floor near the crib, sobbing. Hannah struggled to sit up, to move back from Karen, her eyes on Josh.

"You're bad," Josh said to Karen, his blue eyes flat. "You can't take my sister. I won't let you."

"Bad things will happen, Josh," she said in an eerie tone. "You know and I know. The Taker will punish you."

"The Taker is dead," he said.

Hannah's heart nearly stopped. She moved back from Karen and edged around toward Josh, holding out her hand. "Josh, honey, give me the gun."

"I have to stop them," he said, tears swimming up. "I'm the only one. It's my fault. They'll hurt you and Lily."

"No, sweetheart," she whispered as she crouched down beside him.

His small hands were tight on the stock of the pistol, knuckles white as he aimed the barrel at Karen Wright's face. "She's a Taker, too. They have power. She'll take Lily. She'll hurt her. I have to stop them. It's up to me."

"No, Josh," Hannah said, inching closer. "I won't let her take Lily. Give me the gun."

He made no move to obey. Hannah eased her arms around him, waiting to hear the terrible sound of a shot. If she moved too quickly, if she tried to pull the gun away, it could go off. As much as she wanted justice, she didn't want it like this. She didn't want it weighing on Josh for the rest of his life.

Trying not to shake, she slipped her hands over his on the stock of the pistol. "It's over, honey."

His body was quivering in the circle of her arms. His eyes were locked, wide and staring, on Karen Wright as he struggled within himself.

"Give me the gun, Josh," Hannah whispered. "They don't have any power over us. Not anymore. It's over. They won't hurt anyone ever again. I promise. You're safe. I'll never let anyone hurt you again. I love you so much."

If only love were enough to protect them, she thought. If only love were enough to heal the damage that had been done. She willed her love to be enough in this moment, enough to bring Josh back from the edge. If he crossed this line, even if he crossed it only in his mind, he would be lost.

I lost him once, God. Please don't make me lose him again. Please let us start over. Now.

Josh stared at Karen, felt the trigger in the curve of his finger. He wanted to be free. He wanted things the way they had been before. If he killed all the Takers . . .

"No, Josh, *please*."

His mother's voice seemed to come from within his own mind. There were so many things she couldn't understand.

Please . . .

He wanted to be free.

He stared at Karen and felt . . . nothing.

"He's dead," he whispered as realization dawned inside him. The connection was gone, broken in the night. He was free.

Free . . .

Pulling his hands away from the gun, he turned to his mother, put his head on her shoulder, and started to cry.

Hannah hugged him to her with one arm as she held the pistol trained on Karen. In another part of the house she heard a door open, and Mitch Holt's voice came like the voice of salvation.

CHAPTER 38

"She wanted what she thought I had," Hannah said softly.

She stood in the doorway to Josh's room, watching him sleep. The day had been a marathon. Police trooping through the house, wanting statements, asking questions, taking photographs. The press mounting a fresh full-scale campaign to get her to talk to them. Newspapers, magazines, tabloids. Television newsmagazines, talk shows, agents from Hollywood who wanted to put together movie deals. She had shut them all out and let in only one person—Tom McCoy.

"She wanted a happy family. We had that once," she said wistfully. "Once upon a time . . ."

The story of the Wrights' lives had unfolded throughout the day as the police and prosecutors examined the journals found in the farmhouse. A double life led from childhood on. Garrett—intelligent, sociopathic, controlling, manipulative. His sister, Caroline—a shadow, subservient, introverted. The children of a cold, bitter woman who valued appearances over substance; abandoned by their father, who had remarried and started a new family.

Garrett had taken control of Caroline, absorbed her into his life and into his psyche, until they seemed to become a single entity. She had managed to break free of him when she ran away from home at seventeen, only to have him find her again a year later. And the control, the manipulation, the whole twisted cycle started all over again. They lived as husband and wife, kept up a flawless front as the psychology professor and his demure, quiet spouse, while Garrett masterminded and played out his sick game.

"I keep wondering," Hannah murmured, "if Wright singled us out because he thought we had a perfect family, or because he knew we didn't."

"Have you spoken with Paul?" Tom asked, propping a shoulder against the door frame, watching Hannah. In this light the bruise her husband had left on her jaw looked like a shadow.

"He contacted Mitch after the news broke. He'd checked into a hotel in Burnsville. He said he went there because he wanted time to think." Mixed feelings wrestled within her like a pair of cobras. She didn't want Paul near her or the children, and yet she resented the fact that he had fled and left them to face the consequences of his mistakes. "I didn't call him back. I don't have anything to say to him my lawyer can't say more diplomatically."

This was where he was supposed to counsel her, Tom thought. If he was a good priest, he would tell her there was still hope, that wounds could heal, that what was broken in her marriage could be made whole through prayer and faith. But he didn't believe it was true, and he didn't see himself as a good priest. He didn't really see himself as a priest at all anymore.

"I'm sorry," he said with sincerity.

"So am I," Hannah whispered. Vignettes of her marriage flashed through her mind as she looked at Josh. The good times, when life had held such promise. "It should have been forever."

Instead the promise had been broken, and she was left to rage and mourn the jagged pieces.

Tom's hand closed around hers, offering comfort, offering strength. Bringing a thin veil of guilt to the complex mix of emotions she was already struggling with.

"I could use a glass of wine," she said, turning away.

Evening was closing in outside. It only seemed like midnight. Exhausted from the ordeal of the day, both Josh and Lily had crashed late in the afternoon, but the night still stretched ahead. Long hours of quiet waiting to be filled with introspection and pointless longing.

She filled two glasses with chardonnay and carried them to the family room, where Tom was tending the fire. The light caught on the gold rims of his glasses, warmed the color of his strong, handsome face. He was in jeans and one of his lumberjack shirts. She saw no evidence of his clerical collar.

"What will you do?" he asked, setting the poker back in the stand. "Will you stay?"

"No." She waited for him to admonish her, to tell her she needed time, that she should wait and sort things out when the emotion had passed and she could think more clearly. But he said nothing. "We have a lot of memories here, but even the good ones hurt. I think it's best if we make a break. Go somewhere new. Give Josh a fresh start."

She settled into the corner of the couch nearest the fire and sipped her wine. "You've been such a good friend through all this. I don't know how to thank you."

"I don't need thanks," he said, lowering himself to the edge of a chair that was close enough that their knees nearly touched.

"I know it's your job, but—"

"No. This isn't about my duty as a priest. Or maybe it is." He drew in a deep breath. Anticipation and dread held it in his lungs a moment. "I'm leaving the priesthood, Hannah."

The look on her face was less than he had hoped for, but no different from what he had expected. Shock with an underlayer of fear.

"Oh, Tom, no." She set her glass aside with a hand that trembled. "Not because of— Please don't say I drove you to—" Her blue eyes shimmered like the lake in summer. "I've got more guilt than I need already."

"It's not for you to feel guilty, Hannah," he said, leaning toward her, his forearms resting on his thighs, his face earnest. "There is no guilt. I feel what I feel, and no rule can convince me what I feel is wrong.

"How can it be wrong to love someone? I've chewed on that question until there's nothing left. I don't see how it can ever be reconciled." He smiled, a sad, fond smile. "Monsignor Corelli always said my philosophy degree would get me in trouble. I think too much. You know, I've never been very good at toeing the company line."

"But you're a wonderful priest," Hannah insisted. "You make people think, you make them question, you make them look deeper within. If we don't do those things, what are we?"

"Stagnant. Comfortable. Happy," he conceded. "Growth hurts. Growth precipitates change. Change is frightening. It would be easier for me to stay in the Church," he admitted. "Safer. It's what I know. There are parts of it I love. But if I have to be a hypocrite to do it . . . I can't live like that, Hannah."

Still more of life's endless supply of irony, Hannah thought. He was a good priest, but he was too good a man to stay a priest. He couldn't go against his principles, even if his principles went against the Church.

"I shouldn't be dumping this on you tonight," he said, glancing away. "It's just that . . . I've made the decision, and you've made yours . . . I don't want to add to your burden, Hannah. I just wanted you to know."

He went back to the fire and poked at the logs, kicking up sparks like a swarm of fireflies that shot up the chimney. He loved her. There had been a time, Hannah thought, that she would have said love would be the one thing to get her through an ordeal like the one they had just been through—her husband's love. But Paul didn't love her, and in all the madness the love she had found within her was for this man. This man who was supposed to be beyond her reach.

It seemed they deserved something better than to be pulled apart. But could they have something more? Something that wouldn't wither in the shadow of their past or be crushed by the burden of complicity.

"I need time," she said, going to him. "I think we both do. We've been through so much, so fast. I know I have to get away from it. I have to clear it all out, sort it into some kind of order. Can you understand that?"

"Yes." He looked down at her, his eyes searching hers, his hands reaching up to frame her face, to touch her hair. "As long as you don't clear me out when you're sorting through the rest of it. Don't throw away what we could have together because it would be easier, Hannah."

There was nothing easy about any of it, she thought, closing her eyes against the bittersweet pain. The weight of her choices pressed down on her, a burden she couldn't bear at the moment. Time. They needed time. Sliding her arms around his waist, she hugged him tight and whispered, "I love you."

He bent his head and kissed her cheek. She felt his gentle smile against her skin. "Then I can wait as long as it takes. Just don't let it take forever."

Ellen sat back in her desk chair and allowed herself a long, slow, heartfelt sigh. It felt like the first good breath she'd had all day. It was certainly the first moment's rest. Exhaustion felt like an anchor strapped to her shoulders. Pain throbbed through her body. Neither dimmed the sense of relief. It was over.

Garrett Wright had been passed on to a higher court

for judgment. Karen Wright had been transported to the
state psychiatric hospital for an evaluation she would almost certainly fail. Adam Slater was under twenty-four-
hour watch in the county jail. The BCA and FBI were
working through the journals and contacting law-
enforcement agencies in the other states where Wright
had played his game, wrapping up cases that went back
twenty-six years. Cases that had gone unsolved. Cases
that had ended in convictions of innocent people, convictions that would now be overturned all these years after
the fact.

The ripples were still going out from the rock in the
pond. And they would go on and on and on. The surface
would eventually smooth over, but underneath, the
changes would remain. The people of Deer Lake would
pretend to forget, but they would lock their doors and
watch their children and never quite trust in the way they
had. She would settle back into her old routine, but she
would never feel the same kind of peace. And Brooks . . .

She had to think this had changed him as well. She
didn't want to believe he could involve himself in the lives
of the people who had been violated by these crimes and
not be touched in some fundamental way. He had come
here to stand on the edge of it and look in, but he had been
drawn in time and again. He had saved her life. He couldn't
be the same man who had come to Deer Lake two weeks
ago, the mercenary looking to score off the suffering of
others.

Or maybe he would go back to Alabama and write his
book and make a lot of money and play himself in the
movie version because everyone knew he was better looking than Tom Cruise. *People* would name him the Sexiest
Man Alive, and she would never see him again except on
the dust jackets of the books she wouldn't buy.

The events that had taken place, the revelations that
had been made, were just what he had come looking for

Sensational, twisted, complex. Erik Evans / Adam Slater's story alone was worthy of a book. What went wrong in a child's mind to turn him into a killer? She had to admit she was curious herself. She wanted to be able to comprehend what had happened, make some kind of sense of it.

Maybe she would end up picking up one of Brooks's works after all. Maybe there was some value in standing back from a crime and analyzing the why. Maybe there would be some comfort in isolating the madness of what had gone on. Then again, she'd been in the system too long to be naive. She knew too well there was no isolation of evil. It crept out and spread like a killing vine. Even to places like Deer Lake.

A knock at her door jolted her back to the moment. The excitement of the day had culminated with a press conference at six o'clock. Bill Glendenning had beat a path down from his lofty office in St. Paul to personally commend her in front of the multitude of television cameras— with Rudy right by his side. The air of excitement had lingered, keeping people in the courthouse longer than usual as they hung around to rehash the fantastic details of the day and of Wright's lifetime exploits.

Cameron stuck his head in the door, eyebrows raised. "You need a lift home?"

"No, thanks. I'm fine. I'm just winding down here before I have to fight my way through the media hordes. Did you find anything in Slater's phone records yet?"

He frowned. "Sorry. Costello's number isn't there. Not on the house phone, not on the cellular phone. If we don't make that connection, he's off the hook."

"And Tony Costello slips out of the grip of justice like the slimy eel he is."

"If it's any consolation, I think it'll take him a long time to crawl out of the hole he's in," he said, leaning a shoulder against the doorjamb. "As it turns out, he was representing one of the country's more despicable career criminals."

"And he got him off," Ellen said soberly, knowing that was how Tony would look at it. Not as a shameful humiliation, but as a game won. The only difference between him and his client had been that Costello's games were sanctioned.

"I'll keep digging," Cameron promised. "How about you? Anything on Priest yet?"

"There's no mention of him by name in the journals. He claims the reason he lied about growing up in Mishawaka is that he had some emotional problems at the time and ended up quitting school. He falsified records to get into college, claiming he graduated from a good school in Chicago. He adamantly denies all knowledge of Wright's activities, but it's hard to believe he never suspected anything. At best, he had to have held a suspicion that might have prevented a lot of suffering if he had acted on it.

"The FBI has had him all afternoon. They confiscated all the records on the joint learning-and-perception project Wright's and Priest's students were working on, in case there might be something in that. They'll get the truth out of him eventually. And when they do, there'll be a line of attorneys waiting to prosecute."

"You'll be filing perjury charges against Todd Childs?" he asked.

Ellen nodded. "I'm betting he's the one who broke into the Pack Rat, too, though I don't know that we'll ever prove it. Childs knew we were looking for him, and Costello had told him to drop out of sight. Trouble was, he had product stashed at the store and knew it wouldn't be there long if he didn't get it." She gave a shrug that pulled on muscles better left alone. "That's my theory, anyway. We can worry about proving it another day."

"In the meantime, you should go home and sleep for a day or two," Cameron suggested. "You'll need your res

Rumor has it you'll be first in line for Rudy's job when he takes Franken's seat on the bench."

"That's news to me. As usual."

He laughed, though it didn't make him look quite as young as it had a week ago. "I'll call you tomorrow."

He started to back out the door, then leaned in again. "I thought I'd stop by Phoebe's house and see how she's doing. She's really upset about the Slater thing. She's blaming herself for what happened to you. I'm worried about her. Any wisdom you want me to pass along?"

"Yeah. Tell her it's not a crime to trust someone, even if they don't deserve it," Ellen said. She felt for sweet, gullible Phoebe. It would take her a long time to get over what had happened, even longer to shed the guilt. "I don't blame her for what happened. Slater would have found a way to get what he wanted. I'm just glad he didn't hurt her physically."

"Amen to that."

Another victim in the game, Ellen thought sadly. Phoebe's trust and loyalty. She made a mental note to stop by Phoebe's house herself if she didn't show up for work in the morning.

She was trying to work up the energy to get out of her chair and put her coat on when Megan came to the door.

"I thought you'd be out celebrating," Ellen said, motioning her to a chair.

"I'm waiting for Mitch. He's in with the Feebies and Priest," she said. "We'll celebrate later. What about you? All this wrapped up and the Minneapolis cops picked up your mad-bomber friend, too."

"All I want is a long, hot soak and a bed," Ellen confessed. "It's a relief to have it over. There's a lot of satisfaction in knowing we've put an end to a long line of horrible crimes. But there's something in turning over that big rock and seeing what was under it that puts a damper on my appetite for festivities. The world's full of rocks, you know. I just want to finish the job and move on to the next one."

Megan nodded, reflective. "Well, I just wanted to thank you personally for letting me in on this. I know you took a risk."

"It paid off. You're a good cop, Megan."

She smiled with a kind of shy pride that was touching. "Yeah, I am. And now I see that I can still be a good cop whether I can handle a gun or not. There can still be a place for me on the job. That means a lot to me. Thanks, Ellen. And thanks to your friend Brooks. If he hadn't offered to help, I'd still be on the phone calling directory assistance."

"He did what?" Ellen asked stupidly.

"He offered me a deal. He knew I was looking into Wright's background—"

"And he wanted to use it." Ellen's heart sank as her temper rose from the ashes of exhaustion.

"No," Megan said. "He wanted to help. He offered me the use of his computer, his fax, his phones. We worked together half of Tuesday night and all of yesterday. That was how we found that case in Pennsylvania. He didn't tell you this?"

"We got a little sidetracked with a homicidal maniac," Ellen said, her mind spinning. "Then, at the hospital, it was Mitch who told me about the Wiskow case."

Because Brooks had been busy getting himself stitched back together.

He had offered to help. For the sake of the case, or for the sake of his book?

Megan rose carefully, pulling her crutch up under her left arm. "You know, he's a pretty decent guy for someone who used to be a lawyer. No offense."

"None taken," Ellen murmured.

He had come to Deer Lake to watch, to observe from a distance, to soak it all in and sell it.

He had helped crack the case. He had saved her life . . . and stolen her heart. She hadn't wanted to admit that, but it was true. She hadn't wanted to believe it. Her life had been a whole lot simpler before he'd come into it, with his voice like smoke and eyes that saw through all her barriers. He had reached past those barriers and touched her, awakened something within her she had denied—need, the need to feel, the need to care too much.

He had come here for the case, and the case was over.

"Damn you, Brooks," she whispered to the empty room. "Now what?"

"I suggest a steak dinner and a long, slow night in bed," he drawled, stepping in from the dark hall. "Together. Sleeping."

He looked much the way he had the first night she'd seen him, that wicked pirate's grin cutting across a two-day beard. His coat hung open, giving a glimpse of the sling that held his right arm against him.

Ellen ignored the idea that she had conjured him up out of her imagination and scowled at him instead. "Is there a line out there?"

"No, ma'am. I'm the last."

"What are you doing here?" she asked with concern. "You should be in the hospital."

He shook his head. "Dr. Baskir sent me on my way."

"I have a hard time believing that."

"All right," he admitted with a sheepish look. "Maybe I sorta talked my way out."

"*That* I believe."

He grinned again as he came around the end of the desk, perched a hip on one corner, and grabbed up her paperweight as if it were a baseball. "My Uncle Hooter always said I could charm the skirt off a Sunday-school teacher."

"A useful talent. Who did you charm to get in here?"

"My old friend Deputy Qualey. Did you know he once thwarted a burglar by throwing a live snake on him?"

"What was he doing with a live snake in the first place?"

"Don't know. Don't want to know. Sure as hell don't want to write a book about it."

"No," Ellen said. "You've got enough to write about with this case. Twisted minds, sex, violence, corruption. Everybody's favorite stuff."

"There isn't going to be any book," Jay announced, watching her reaction. She met his gaze with wary surprise. "I kind of lost my objectivity."

And gained things he still wasn't sure he wanted—sympathy, nobility, a conscience. They felt like medals that had been pinned to his chest instead of his shirt.

"Megan told me what you did to help, Jay," Ellen said. "Thank you."

"Yeah, well, don't let it get around. You'll ruin my reputation as a scheming opportunist."

"Some people might catch on when no blockbuster best-seller comes out of this."

"That's a chance I'll have to take. It's not that I think there's no value in telling the tales," he qualified. "It just won't be me telling them."

"So you came all the way to Minnesota, froze your butt off, and nearly got killed all for nothing?"

"I wouldn't say that," he said in a low voice, stepping close. "I wouldn't say that at all. What I'll take from here is more valuable than any story."

"You're leaving?" Ellen blurted, then scrambled to cover. "I mean—well—I guess if there's no book to write . . ."

He had come here for a book. That was all. He had his life in Alabama. She had hers here. Their paths had crossed and now they would move on.

It just seemed so soon.

"I've got a son I'd like to meet," Jay said quietly. "Just meet him, get to know him. I've missed eight years of his life. I'm damned lucky I don't have to miss any more. I'm damned lucky I have a choice."

Ellen found a smile for him. "I'm glad you're making that choice, Jay. I hope it all works out."

"Yeah," he said, fragile hope building in his heart. It had been so long since he had allowed anything in there but cynicism.

"After that," he said, setting the paperweight aside, "I was thinking I might try my hand at fiction."

"Really?"

"I'm thinking about a female protagonist," he said, watching her carefully. "The days and nights of a beautiful assistant county attorney."

He straightened from the desk and stepped closer, his gaze holding hers. Ellen smiled slowly.

"Want to help with the research?" he whispered in a voice like smoke over satin as he leaned down to kiss her. "I suggest we start with the nights. . . ."

EPILOGUE

_____

She sat alone in the small white room, the only light coming from the moon through the barred window high on the wall. Truly alone for the first time in her life. Like a balloon cut free. From other rooms like hers she could hear the eerie keening and crying of faceless people. Night sounds. Sounds that gave her an odd sense of comfort.

Softly humming a lullaby to herself, she rocked her pillow in one arm while she wrote on the wall with a blue crayon.

JOURNAL ENTRY
FEBRUARY 3, 1994

Goodbye to Garrett
Goodbye to we
Hello to me
Who will be my family?

Inside my mind
Inside my heart
Outside these walls
A new game to start

One day . . .